The Adventures of Joseph Rouletabille

The Adventures of Joseph Rouletabille

Gaston Leroux

MINT EDITIONS

The Adventures of Joseph Rouletabille was first published in
contains work that was first published between 1907 and 1913.

This edition published by Mint Editions 2021.

ISBN 9781513282305 | E-ISBN 9781513287324

Published by Mint Editions®

MINT
EDITIONS
minteditionbooks.com

Publishing Director: Jennifer Newens
Design & Production: Rachel Lopez Metzger
Project Manager: Micaela Clark
Typesetting: Westchester Publishing Services

Contents

The Perfume of the Lady In Black

THE SECRET OF THE NIGHT

THE MYSTERY OF THE "YELLOW ROOM"

I

In Which We Begin Not to Understand

It is not without a certain emotion that I begin to recount here the extraordinary adventures of Joseph Rouletabille. Down to the present time he had so firmly opposed my doing it that I had come to despair of ever publishing the most curious of police stories of the past fifteen years. I had even imagined that the public would never know the whole truth of the prodigious case known as that of the "Yellow Room", out of which grew so many mysterious, cruel, and sensational dramas, with which my friend was so closely mixed up, if, propos of a recent nomination of the illustrious Stangerson to the grade of grandcross of the Legion of Honour, an evening journal—in an article, miserable for its ignorance, or audacious for its perfidy—had not resuscitated a terrible adventure of which Joseph Rouletabille had told me he wished to be for ever forgotten.

The "Yellow Room"! Who now remembers this affair which caused so much ink to flow fifteen years ago? Events are so quickly forgotten in Paris. Has not the very name of the Nayves trial and the tragic history of the death of little Menaldo passed out of mind? And yet the public attention was so deeply interested in the details of the trial that the occurrence of a ministerial crisis was completely unnoticed at the time. Now the "Yellow Room" trial, which, preceded that of the Nayves by some years, made far more noise. The entire world hung for months over this obscure problem—the most obscure, it seems to me, that has ever challenged the perspicacity of our police or taxed the conscience of our judges. The solution of the problem baffled everybody who tried to find it. It was like a dramatic rebus with which old Europe and new America alike became fascinated. That is, in truth—I am permitted to say, because there cannot be any author's vanity in all this, since I do nothing more than transcribe facts on which an exceptional documentation enables me to throw a new light—that is because, in truth, I do not know that, in the domain of reality or imagination, one can discover or recall to mind anything comparable, in its mystery, with the natural mystery of the "Yellow Room".

That which nobody could find out, Joseph Rouletabille, aged eighteen, then a reporter engaged on a leading journal, succeeded in discovering. But when, at the Assize Court, he brought in the key to the whole case, he did not tell the whole truth. He only allowed so much of it to appear as sufficed to ensure the acquittal of an innocent man. The reasons which he had for his reticence no longer exist. Better still, the time has come for my friend to speak out fully. You are going to know all; and, without further preamble, I am going to place before your eyes the problem of the "Yellow Room" as it was placed before the eyes of the entire world on the day following the enactment of the drama at the Chateau du Glandier.

On the 25th of October, 1892, the following note appeared in the latest edition of the "Temps":

"A frightful crime has been committed at the Glandier, on the border of the forest of Sainte-Genevieve, above Epinay-sur-Orge, at the house of Professor Stangerson. On that night, while the master was working in his laboratory, an attempt was made to assassinate Mademoiselle Stangerson, who was sleeping in a chamber adjoining this laboratory. The doctors do not answer for the life of Mdlle. Stangerson."

The impression made on Paris by this news may be easily imagined. Already, at that time, the learned world was deeply interested in the labours of Professor Stangerson and his daughter. These labours—the first that were attempted in radiography—served to open the way for Monsieur and Madame Curie to the discovery of radium. It was expected the Professor would shortly read to the Academy of Sciences a sensational paper on his new theory,—the Dissociation of Matter,—a theory destined to overthrow from its base the whole of official science, which based itself on the principle of the Conservation of Energy. On the following day, the newspapers were full of the tragedy. The "Matin," among others, published the following article, entitled: "A Supernatural Crime":

"These are the only details," wrote the anonymous writer in the "Matin"—"we have been able to obtain concerning the crime of the Chateau du Glandier. The state of despair in which Professor Stangerson is plunged, and the impossibility of getting any information from the lips of the victim, have rendered our investigations and those of justice so difficult that, at present, we cannot form the least idea of what has passed in the 'Yellow Room' in which Mdlle. Stangerson, in her night-dress, was found lying on the floor in the agonies of death.

We have, at least, been able to interview Daddy Jacques—as he is called in the country—a old servant in the Stangerson family. Daddy Jacques entered the 'Yellow Room' at the same time as the Professor. This chamber adjoins the laboratory. Laboratory and 'Yellow Room' are in a pavilion at the end of the park, about three hundred metres (a thousand feet) from the chateau.

"'It was half-past twelve at night,' this honest old man told us, 'and I was in the laboratory, where Monsieur Stangerson was still working, when the thing happened. I had been cleaning and putting instruments in order all the evening and was waiting for Monsieur Stangerson to go to bed. Mademoiselle Stangerson had worked with her father up to midnight; when the twelve strokes of midnight had sounded by the cuckoo-clock in the laboratory, she rose, kissed Monsieur Stangerson and bade him good-night. To me she said "bon soir, Daddy Jacques" as she passed into the "Yellow Room". We heard her lock the door and shoot the bolt, so that I could not help laughing, and said to Monsieur: "There's Mademoiselle double-locking herself in,—she must be afraid of the 'Bete du bon Dieu!'" Monsieur did not even hear me, he was so deeply absorbed in what he was doing. Just then we heard the distant miawing of a cat. "Is that going to keep us awake all night?" I said to myself; for I must tell you, Monsieur, that, to the end of October, I live in an attic of the pavilion over the "Yellow Room", so that Mademoiselle should not be left alone through the night in the lonely park. It was the fancy of Mademoiselle to spend the fine weather in the pavilion; no doubt, she found it more cheerful than the chateau and, for the four years it had been built, she had never failed to take up her lodging there in the spring. With the return of winter, Mademoiselle returns to the chateau, for there is no fireplace in the "Yellow Room".

"'We were staying in the pavilion, then—Monsieur Stangerson and me. We made no noise. He was seated at his desk. As for me, I was sitting on a chair, having finished my work and, looking at him, I said to myself: "What a man!—what intelligence!—what knowledge!" I attach importance to the fact that we made no noise; for, because of that, the assassin certainly thought that we had left the place. And, suddenly, while the cuckoo was sounding the half after midnight, a desperate clamour broke out in the "Yellow Room". It was the voice of Mademoiselle, crying "Murder!—murder!—help!" Immediately afterwards revolver shots rang out and there was a great noise of tables and furniture being thrown to the ground, as if in the course of a struggle, and again the voice of Mademoiselle calling, "Murder!—help!—Papa!—Papa!—"

"'You may be sure that we quickly sprang up and that Monsieur Stangerson and I threw ourselves upon the door. But alas! it was locked, fast locked, on the inside, by the care of Mademoiselle, as I have told you, with key and bolt. We tried to force it open, but it remained firm. Monsieur Stangerson was like a madman, and truly, it was enough to make him one, for we heard Mademoiselle still calling "Help!—help!" Monsieur Stangerson showered terrible blows on the door, and wept with rage and sobbed with despair and helplessness.

"'It was then that I had an inspiration. "The assassin must have entered by the window!" I cried;—"I will go to the window!" and I rushed from the pavilion and ran like one out of his mind.

"'The inspiration was that the window of the "Yellow Room" looks out in such a way that the park wall, which abuts on the pavilion, prevented my at once reaching the window. To get up to it one has first to go out of the park. I ran towards the gate and, on my way, met Bernier and his wife, the gate-keepers, who had been attracted by the pistol reports and by our cries. In a few words I told them what had happened, and directed the concierge to join Monsieur Stangerson with all speed, while his wife came with me to open the park gate. Five minutes later she and I were before the window of the "Yellow Room".

"'The moon was shining brightly and I saw clearly that no one had touched the window. Not only were the bars that protect it intact, but the blinds inside of them were drawn, as I had myself drawn them early in the evening, as I did every day, though Mademoiselle, knowing that I was tired from the heavy work I had been doing, had begged me not to trouble myself, but leave her to do it; and they were just as I had left them, fastened with an iron catch on the inside. The assassin, therefore, could not have passed either in or out that way; but neither could I get in.

"'It was unfortunate,—enough to turn one's brain! The door of the room locked on the inside and the blinds on the only window also fastened on the inside; and Mademoiselle still calling for help!—No! she had ceased to call. She was dead, perhaps. But I still heard her father, in the pavilion, trying to break down the door.

"'With the concierge I hurried back to the pavilion. The door, in spite of the furious attempts of Monsieur Stangerson and Bernier to burst it open, was still holding firm; but at length, it gave way before our united efforts,—and then what a sight met our eyes! I should tell you that, behind us, the concierge held the laboratory lamp—a powerful lamp, that lit the whole chamber.

"'I must also tell you, monsieur, that the "Yellow Room" is a very small room. Mademoiselle had furnished it with a fairly large iron bedstead, a small table, a night-commode; a dressing-table, and two chairs. By the light of the big lamp we saw all at a glance. Mademoiselle, in her night-dress, was lying on the floor in the midst of the greatest disorder. Tables and chairs had been overthrown, showing that there had been a violent struggle. Mademoiselle had certainly been dragged from her bed. She was covered with blood and had terrible marks of finger-nails on her throat,—the flesh of her neck having been almost torn by the nails. From a wound on the right temple a stream of blood had run down and made a little pool on the floor. When Monsieur Stangerson saw his daughter in that state, he threw himself on his knees beside her, uttering a cry of despair. He ascertained that she still breathed. As to us, we searched for the wretch who had tried to kill our mistress, and I swear to you, monsieur, that, if we had found him, it would have gone hard with him!

"'But how to explain that he was not there, that he had already escaped? It passes all imagination!—Nobody under the bed, nobody behind the furniture!—All that we discovered were traces, blood-stained marks of a man's large hand on the walls and on the door; a big handkerchief red with blood, without any initials, an old cap, and many fresh footmarks of a man on the floor,—footmarks of a man with large feet whose boot-soles had left a sort of sooty impression. How had this man got away? How had he vanished? Don't forget, monsieur, that there is no chimney in the "Yellow Room". He could not have escaped by the door, which is narrow, and on the threshold of which the concierge stood with the lamp, while her husband and I searched for him in every corner of the little room, where it is impossible for anyone to hide himself. The door, which had been forced open against the wall, could not conceal anything behind it, as we assured ourselves. By the window, still in every way secured, no flight had been possible. What then?—I began to believe in the Devil.

"'But we discovered my revolver on the floor!—Yes, my revolver! Oh! that brought me back to the reality! The Devil would not have needed to steal my revolver to kill Mademoiselle. The man who had been there had first gone up to my attic and taken my revolver from the drawer where I kept it. We then ascertained, by counting the cartridges, that the assassin had fired two shots. Ah! it was fortunate for me that Monsieur Stangerson was in the laboratory when the affair took place and had seen with his own eyes that I was there with him; for otherwise, with this business of my revolver, I don't know where we should have been,—I should now be under lock and bar. Justice wants no more to send a man to the scaffold!'"

The editor of the "Matin" added to this interview the following lines:

"We have, without interrupting him, allowed Daddy Jacques to recount to us roughly all he knows about the crime of the 'Yellow Room'. We have reproduced it in his own words, only sparing the reader the continual lamentations with which he garnished his narrative. It is quite understood, Daddy Jacques, quite understood, that you are very fond of your masters; and you want them to know it, and never cease repeating it—especially since the discovery of your revolver. It is your right, and we see no harm in it. We should have liked to put some further questions to Daddy Jacques—Jacques—Louis Moustier—but the inquiry of the examining magistrate, which is being carried on at the chateau, makes it impossible for us to gain admission at the Glandier; and, as to the oak wood, it is guarded by a wide circle of policemen, who are jealously watching all traces that can lead to the pavilion, and that may perhaps lead to the discovery of the assassin. 'We have also wished to question the concierges, but they are invisible. Finally, we have waited in a roadside inn, not far from the gate of the chateau, for the departure of Monsieur de Marquet, the magistrate of Corbeil. At half-past five we saw him and his clerk and, before he was able to enter his carriage, had an opportunity to ask him the following question:

"'Can you, Monsieur de Marquet, give us any information as to this affair, without inconvenience to the course of your inquiry?'

"'It is impossible for us to do it,' replied Monsieur de Marquet. 'I can only say that it is the strangest affair I have ever known. The more we think we know something, the further we are from knowing anything!'

"We asked Monsieur de Marquet to be good enough to explain his last words; and this is what he said,—the importance of which no one will fail to recognise:

"'If nothing is added to the material facts so far established, I fear that the mystery which surrounds the abominable crime of which Mademoiselle Stangerson has been the victim will never be brought to light; but it is to be hoped, for the sake of our human reason, that the examination of the walls, and of the ceiling of the "Yellow Room"—an examination which I shall tomorrow intrust to the builder who constructed the pavilion four years ago—will afford us the proof that may not discourage us. For the problem is this: we know by what way the assassin gained admission,—he entered by the door and hid himself under the bed, awaiting Mademoiselle Stangerson. But how did he leave? How did he escape? If no trap, no secret door, no hiding place, no opening of any sort is found; if the examination of the walls—even to the demolition of the pavilion—does not reveal any passage practicable—not only for a human being, but for any being whatsoever—if the ceiling shows no crack, if the floor hides no underground passage, one must really believe in the Devil, as Daddy Jacques says!'"

And the anonymous writer in the "Matin" added in this article—which I have selected as the most interesting of all those that were published on the subject of this affair—that the examining magistrate appeared to place a peculiar significance to the last sentence: "One must really believe in the Devil, as Jacques says."

The article concluded with these lines: "We wanted to know what Daddy Jacques meant by the cry of the Bete Du Bon Dieu." The landlord of the Donjon Inn explained to us that it is the particularly sinister cry which is uttered sometimes at night by the cat of an old woman,—Mother Angenoux, as she is called in the country. Mother Angenoux is a sort of saint, who lives in a hut in the heart of the forest, not far from the grotto of Sainte-Genevieve.

"The 'Yellow Room', the Bete Du Bon Dieu, Mother Angenoux, the Devil, Sainte-Genevieve, Daddy Jacques,—here is a well entangled crime which the stroke of a pickaxe in the wall may disentangle for us tomorrow. Let us at least hope that, for the sake of our human reason, as the examining magistrate says. Meanwhile, it is expected that Mademoiselle Stangerson—who has not ceased to be delirious and only pronounces one word distinctly, 'Murderer! Murderer!'—will not live through the night."

In conclusion, and at a late hour, the same journal announced that the Chief of the Surete had telegraphed to the famous detective, Frederic Larsan, who had been sent to London for an affair of stolen securities, to return immediately to Paris.

II

In Which Joseph Rouletabille Appears for the First Time

I remember as well as if it had occurred yesterday, the entry of young Rouletabille into my bedroom that morning. It was about eight o'clock and I was still in bed reading the article in the "Matin" relative to the Glandier crime.

But, before going further, it is time that I present my friend to the reader.

I first knew Joseph Rouletabille when he was a young reporter. At that time I was a beginner at the Bar and often met him in the corridors of examining magistrates, when I had gone to get a "permit to communicate" for the prison of Mazas, or for Saint-Lazare. He had, as they say, "a good nut." He seemed to have taken his head—round as a bullet—out of a box of marbles, and it is from that, I think, that his comrades of the press—all determined billiard-players—had given him that nickname, which was to stick to him and be made illustrious by him. He was always as red as a tomato, now gay as a lark, now grave as a judge. How, while still so young—he was only sixteen and a half years old when I saw him for the first time—had he already won his way on the press? That was what everybody who came into contact with him might have asked, if they had not known his history. At the time of the affair of the woman cut in pieces in the Rue Oberskampf—another forgotten story—he had taken to one of the editors of the "Epoque,"—a paper then rivalling the "Matin" for information,—the left foot, which was missing from the basket in which the gruesome remains were discovered. For this left foot the police had been vainly searching for a week, and young Rouletabille had found it in a drain where nobody had thought of looking for it. To do that he had dressed himself as an extra sewer-man, one of a number engaged by the administration of the city of Paris, owing to an overflow of the Seine.

When the editor-in-chief was in possession of the precious foot and informed as to the train of intelligent deductions the boy had been led to make, he was divided between the admiration he felt for such detective cunning in a brain of a lad of sixteen years, and delight at being able to exhibit, in the "morgue window" of his paper, the left foot of the Rue Oberskampf.

"This foot," he cried, "will make a great headline."

Then, when he had confided the gruesome packet to the medical lawyer attached to the journal, he asked the lad, who was shortly to become famous as Rouletabille, what he would expect to earn as a general reporter on the "Epoque"?

"Two hundred francs a month," the youngster replied modestly, hardly able to breathe from surprise at the proposal.

"You shall have two hundred and fifty," said the editor-in-chief; "only you must tell everybody that you have been engaged on the paper for a month. Let it be quite understood that it was not you but the 'Epoque' that discovered the left foot of the Rue Oberskampf. Here, my young friend, the man is nothing, the paper everything."

Having said this, he begged the new reporter to retire, but before the youth had reached the door he called him back to ask his name. The other replied:

"Joseph Josephine."

"That's not a name," said the editor-in-chief, "but since you will not be required to sign what you write it is of no consequence."

The boy-faced reporter speedily made himself many friends, for he was serviceable and gifted with a good humour that enchanted the most severe-tempered and disarmed the most zealous of his companions. At the Bar cafe, where the reporters assembled before going to any of the courts, or to the Prefecture, in search of their news of crime, he began to win a reputation as an unraveller of intricate and obscure affairs which found its way to the office of the Chief of the Surete. When a case was worth the trouble and Rouletabille—he had already been given his nickname—had been started on the scent by his editor-in-chief, he often got the better of the most famous detective.

It was at the Bar cafe that I became intimately acquainted with him. Criminal lawyers and journalists are not enemies, the former need advertisement, the latter information. We chatted together, and I soon warmed towards him. His intelligence was so keen, and so original!— and he had a quality of thought such as I have never found in any other person.

Some time after this I was put in charge of the law news of the "Cri du Boulevard." My entry into journalism could not but strengthen the ties which united me to Rouletabille. After a while, my new friend being allowed to carry out an idea of a judicial correspondence column, which he was allowed to sign "Business," in the "Epoque," I was often able to furnish him with the legal information of which he stood in need.

Nearly two years passed in this way, and the better I knew him, the more I learned to love him; for, in spite of his careless extravagance, I had discovered in him what was, considering his age, an extraordinary seriousness of mind. Accustomed as I was to seeing him gay and, indeed, often too gay, I would many times find him plunged in the deepest melancholy. I tried then to question him as to the cause of this change of humour, but each time he laughed and made me no answer. One day, having questioned him about his parents, of whom he never spoke, he left me, pretending not to have heard what I said.

While things were in this state between us, the famous case of the "Yellow Room" took place. It was this case which was to rank him as the leading newspaper reporter, and to obtain for him the reputation of being the greatest detective in the world. It should not surprise us to find in the one man the perfection of two such lines of activity if we remember that the daily press was already beginning to transform itself and to become what it is today—the gazette of crime.

Morose-minded people may complain of this; for myself I regard it a matter for congratulation. We can never have too many arms, public or private, against the criminal. To this some people may answer that, by continually publishing the details of crimes, the press ends by encouraging their commission. But then, with some people we can never do right. Rouletabille, as I have said, entered my room that morning of the 26th of October, 1892. He was looking redder than usual, and his eyes were bulging out of his head, as the phrase is, and altogether he appeared to be in a state of extreme excitement. He waved the "Matin" with a trembling hand, and cried:

"Well, my dear Sainclair,—have you read it?"

"The Glandier crime?"

"Yes; The 'Yellow Room'!—What do you think of it?"

"I think that it must have been the Devil or the Bete du Bon Dieu that committed the crime."

"Be serious!"

"Well, I don't much believe in murderers[1] who make their escape through walls of solid brick. I think Daddy Jacques did wrong to leave behind him the weapon with which the crime was committed and, as he occupied the attic immediately above Mademoiselle Stangerson's room, the builder's job ordered by the examining magistrate will give us the key of the enigma and it will not be long before we learn by what natural trap, or by what secret door, the old fellow was able to slip in and out, and return immediately to the laboratory to Monsieur Stangerson, without his absence being noticed. That, of course, is only an hypothesis."

Rouletabille sat down in an armchair, lit his pipe, which he was never without, smoked for a few minutes in silence—no doubt to calm the excitement which, visibly, dominated him—and then replied:

"Young man," he said, in a tone the sad irony of which I will not attempt to render, "young man, you are a lawyer and I doubt not your ability to save the guilty from conviction; but if you were a magistrate on the bench, how easy it would be for you to condemn innocent persons!—You are really gifted, young man!"

He continued to smoke energetically, and then went on:

"No trap will be found, and the mystery of the 'Yellow Room' will become more and more mysterious. That's why it interests me. The examining magistrate is right; nothing stranger than this crime has ever been known."

"Have you any idea of the way by which the murderer escaped?" I asked.

"None," replied Rouletabille—"none, for the present. But I have an idea as to the revolver; the murderer did not use it."

"Good Heavens! By whom, then, was it used?"

"Why—by Mademoiselle Stangerson."

"I don't understand,—or rather, I have never understood," I said.

Rouletabille shrugged his shoulders.

"Is there nothing in this article in the 'Matin' by which you were particularly struck?"

"Nothing,—I have found the whole of the story it tells equally strange."

"Well, but—the locked door—with the key on the inside?"

---

1. Although the original English translation often uses the words "murder" and "murderer," the reader may substitute "attack" and "attacker" since no murder is actually committed.

"That's the only perfectly natural thing in the whole article."

"Really!—And the bolt?"

"The bolt?"

"Yes, the bolt—also inside the room—a still further protection against entry? Mademoiselle Stangerson took quite extraordinary precautions! It is clear to me that she feared someone. That was why she took such precautions—even Daddy Jacques's revolver—without telling him of it. No doubt she didn't wish to alarm anybody, and least of all, her father. What she dreaded took place, and she defended herself. There was a struggle, and she used the revolver skilfully enough to wound the assassin in the hand—which explains the impression on the wall and on the door of the large, blood-stained hand of the man who was searching for a means of exit from the chamber. But she didn't fire soon enough to avoid the terrible blow on the right temple."

"Then the wound on the temple was not done with the revolver?"

"The paper doesn't say it was, and I don't think it was; because logically it appears to me that the revolver was used by Mademoiselle Stangerson against the assassin. Now, what weapon did the murderer use? The blow on the temple seems to show that the murderer wished to stun Mademoiselle Stangerson,—after he had unsuccessfully tried to strangle her. He must have known that the attic was inhabited by Daddy Jacques, and that was one of the reasons, I think, why he must have used a quiet weapon,—a life-preserver, or a hammer."

"All that doesn't explain how the murderer got out of the 'Yellow Room'," I observed.

"Evidently," replied Rouletabille, rising, "and that is what has to be explained. I am going to the Chateau du Glandier, and have come to see whether you will go with me."

"I?—"

"Yes, my boy. I want you. The 'Epoque' has definitely entrusted this case to me, and I must clear it up as quickly as possible."

"But in what way can I be of any use to you?"

"Monsieur Robert Darzac is at the Chateau du Glandier."

"That's true. His despair must be boundless."

"I must have a talk with him."

Rouletabille said it in a tone that surprised me.

"Is it because—you think there is something to be got out of him?" I asked.

"Yes."

That was all he would say. He retired to my sitting-room, begging me to dress quickly.

I knew Monsieur Robert Darzac from having been of great service to him in a civil action, while I was acting as secretary to Maitre Barbet Delatour. Monsieur Robert Darzac, who was at that time about forty years of age, was a professor of physics at the Sorbonne. He was intimately acquainted with the Stangersons, and, after an assiduous seven years' courtship of the daughter, had been on the point of marrying her. In spite of the fact that she has become, as the phrase goes, "a person of a certain age," she was still remarkably good-looking. While I was dressing I called out to Rouletabille, who was impatiently moving about my sitting-room:

"Have you any idea as to the murderer's station in life?"

"Yes," he replied; "I think if he isn't a man in society, he is, at least, a man belonging to the upper class. But that, again, is only an impression."

"What has led you to form it?"

"Well,—the greasy cap, the common handkerchief, and the marks of the rough boots on the floor," he replied.

"I understand," I said; "murderers don't leave traces behind them which tell the truth."

"We shall make something out of you yet, my dear Sainclair," concluded Rouletabille.

III

"A Man Has Passed Like a Shadow Through the Blinds"

Half an hour later Rouletabille and I were on the platform of the Orleans station, awaiting the departure of the train which was to take us to Epinay-sur-Orge.

On the platform we found Monsieur de Marquet and his Registrar, who represented the Judicial Court of Corbeil. Monsieur Marquet had spent the night in Paris, attending the final rehearsal, at the Scala, of a little play of which he was the unknown author, signing himself simply "Castigat Ridendo."

Monsieur de Marquet was beginning to be a "noble old gentleman." Generally he was extremely polite and full of gay humour, and in all his life had had but one passion,—that of dramatic art. Throughout his magisterial career he was interested solely in cases capable of furnishing him with something in the nature of a drama. Though he might very well have aspired to the highest judicial positions, he had never really worked for anything but to win a success at the romantic Porte-Saint-Martin, or at the sombre Odeon.

Because of the mystery which shrouded it, the case of the "Yellow Room" was certain to fascinate so theatrical a mind. It interested him enormously, and he threw himself into it, less as a magistrate eager to know the truth, than as an amateur of dramatic embroglios, tending wholly to mystery and intrigue, who dreads nothing so much as the explanatory final act.

So that, at the moment of meeting him, I heard Monsieur de Marquet say to the Registrar with a sigh:

"I hope, my dear Monsieur Maleine, this builder with his pickaxe will not destroy so fine a mystery."

"Have no fear," replied Monsieur Maleine, "his pickaxe may demolish the pavilion, perhaps, but it will leave our case intact. I have sounded the walls and examined the ceiling and floor and I know all about it. I am not to be deceived."

Having thus reassured his chief, Monsieur Maleine, with a discreet movement of the head, drew Monsieur de Marquet's attention to us. The face of that gentleman clouded, and, as he saw Rouletabille approaching, hat in hand, he sprang into one of the empty carriages saying, half aloud to his Registrar, as he did so, "Above all, no journalists!"

Monsieur Maleine replied in the same tone, "I understand!" and then tried to prevent Rouletabille from entering the same compartment with the examining magistrate.

"Excuse me, gentlemen,—this compartment is reserved."

"I am a journalist, Monsieur, engaged on the 'Epoque,'" said my young friend with a great show of gesture and politeness, "and I have a word or two to say to Monsieur de Marquet."

"Monsieur is very much engaged with the inquiry he has in hand."

"Ah! his inquiry, pray believe me, is absolutely a matter of indifference to me. I am no scavenger of odds and ends," he went on, with infinite contempt in his lower lip, "I am a theatrical reporter; and this evening I shall have to give a little account of the play at the Scala."

"Get in, sir, please," said the Registrar.

Rouletabille was already in the compartment. I went in after him and seated myself by his side. The Registrar followed and closed the carriage door.

Monsieur de Marquet looked at him.

"Ah, sir," Rouletabille began, "You must not be angry with Monsieur de Maleine. It is not with Monsieur de Marquet that I desire to have the honour of speaking, but with Monsieur 'Castigat Ridendo.' Permit me to congratulate you—personally, as well as the writer for the 'Epoque.'" And Rouletabille, having first introduced me, introduced himself.

Monsieur de Marquet, with a nervous gesture, caressed his beard into a point, and explained to Rouletabille, in a few words, that he was too modest an author to desire that the veil of his pseudonym should be publicly raised, and that he hoped the enthusiasm of the journalist for the dramatist's work would not lead him to tell the public that Monsieur "Castigat Ridendo" and the examining magistrate of Corbeil were one and the same person.

"The work of the dramatic author may interfere," he said, after a slight hesitation, "with that of the magistrate, especially in a province where one's labours are little more than routine."

"Oh, you may rely on my discretion!" cried Rouletabille.

The train was in motion.

"We have started!" said the examining magistrate, surprised at seeing us still in the carriage.

"Yes, Monsieur,—truth has started," said Rouletabile, smiling amiably,—"on its way to the Chateau du Glandier. A fine case, Monsieur de Marquet,—a fine case!"

"An obscure—incredible, unfathomable, inexplicable affair—and there is only one thing I fear, Monsieur Rouletabille,—that the journalists will be trying to explain it."

My friend felt this a rap on his knuckles.

"Yes," he said simply, "that is to be feared. They meddle in everything. As for my interest, monsieur, I only referred to it by mere chance,—the mere chance of finding myself in the same train with you, and in the same compartment of the same carriage."

"Where are you going, then?" asked Monsieur de Marquet.

"To the Chateau du Glandier," replied Rouletabille, without turning.

"You'll not get in, Monsieur Rouletabille!"

"Will you prevent me?" said my friend, already prepared to fight.

"Not I!—I like the press and journalists too well to be in any way disagreeable to them; but Monsieur Stangerson has given orders for his door to be closed against everybody, and it is well guarded. Not a journalist was able to pass through the gate of the Glandier yesterday."

Monsieur de Marquet compressed his lips and seemed ready to relapse into obstinate silence. He only relaxed a little when Rouletabille no longer left him in ignorance of the fact that we were going to the Glandier for the purpose of shaking hands with an "old and intimate friend," Monsieur Robert Darzac—a man whom Rouletabille had perhaps seen once in his life.

"Poor Robert!" continued the young reporter, "this dreadful affair may be his death,—he is so deeply in love with Mademoiselle Stangerson."

"His sufferings are truly painful to witness," escaped like a regret from the lips of Monsieur de Marquet.

"But it is to be hoped that Mademoiselle Stangerson's life will be saved."

"Let us hope so. Her father told me yesterday that, if she does not recover, it will not be long before he joins her in the grave. What an incalculable loss to science his death would be!"

"The wound on her temple is serious, is it not?"

"Evidently; but, by a wonderful chance, it has not proved mortal. The blow was given with great force."

"Then it was not with the revolver she was wounded," said Rouletabille, glancing at me in triumph.

Monsieur de Marquet appeared greatly embarrassed.

"I didn't say anything—I don't want to say anything—I will not say anything," he said. And he turned towards his Registrar as if he no longer knew us.

But Rouletabille was not to be so easily shaken off. He moved nearer to the examining magistrate and, drawing a copy of the "Matin" from his pocket, he showed it to him and said:

"There is one thing, Monsieur, which I may enquire of you without committing an indiscretion. You have, of course, seen the account given in the 'Matin'? It is absurd, is it not?"

"Not in the slightest, Monsieur."

"What! The 'Yellow Room' has but one barred window—the bars of which have not been moved—and only one door, which had to be broken open—and the assassin was not found!"

"That's so, monsieur,—that's so. That's how the matter stands."

Rouletabille said no more but plunged into thought. A quarter of an hour thus passed.

Coming back to himself again he said, addressing the magistrate:

"How did Mademoiselle Stangerson wear her hair on that evening?"

"I don't know," replied Monsieur de Marquet.

"That's a very important point," said Rouletabille. "Her hair was done up in bands, wasn't it? I feel sure that on that evening, the evening of the crime, she had her hair arranged in bands."

"Then you are mistaken, Monsieur Rouletabille," replied the magistrate; "Mademoiselle Stangerson that evening had her hair drawn up in a knot on the top of her head,—her usual way of arranging it—her forehead completely uncovered. I can assure you, for we have carefully examined the wound. There was no blood on the hair, and the arrangement of it has not been disturbed since the crime was committed."

"You are sure! You are sure that, on the night of the crime, she had not her hair in bands?"

"Quite sure," the magistrate continued, smiling, "because I remember the Doctor saying to me, while he was examining the wound, 'It is a great pity Mademoiselle Stangerson was in the habit of drawing her hair back from her forehead. If she had worn it in bands, the blow she received on the temple would have been weakened.' It seems strange to me that you should attach so much importance to this point."

"Oh! if she had not her hair in bands, I give it up," said Rouletabille, with a despairing gesture.

"And was the wound on her temple a bad one?" he asked presently.

"Terrible."

"With what weapon was it made?"

"That is a secret of the investigation."

"Have you found the weapon—whatever it was?"

The magistrate did not answer.

"And the wound in the throat?"

Here the examining magistrate readily confirmed the decision of the doctor that, if the murderer had pressed her throat a few seconds longer, Mademoiselle Stangerson would have died of strangulation.

"The affair as reported in the 'Matin,'" said Rouletabille eagerly, "seems to me more and more inexplicable. Can you tell me, Monsieur, how many openings there are in the pavilion? I mean doors and windows."

"There are five," replied Monsieur de Marquet, after having coughed once or twice, but no longer resisting the desire he felt to talk of the whole of the incredible mystery of the affair he was investigating. "There are five, of which the door of the vestibule is the only entrance to the pavilion,—a door always automatically closed, which cannot be opened, either from the outer or inside, except with the two special keys which are never out of the possession of either Daddy Jacques or Monsieur Stangerson. Mademoiselle Stangerson had no need for one, since Daddy Jacques lodged in the pavilion and because, during the daytime, she never left her father. When they, all four, rushed into the 'Yellow Room', after breaking open the door of the laboratory, the door in the vestibule remained closed as usual and, of the two keys for opening it, Daddy Jacques had one in his pocket, and Monsieur Stangerson the other. As to the windows of the pavilion, there are four; the one window of the 'Yellow Room' and those of the laboratory looking out on to the country; the window in the vestibule looking into the park."

"It is by that window that he escaped from the pavilion!" cried Rouletabille.

"How do you know that?" demanded Monsieur de Marquet, fixing a strange look on my young friend.

"We'll see later how he got away from the 'Yellow Room'," replied Rouletabille, "but he must have left the pavilion by the vestibule window."

"Once more,—how do you know that?"

"How? Oh, the thing is simple enough! As soon as he found he could not escape by the door of the pavilion his only way out was by the window in the vestibule, unless he could pass through a grated window. The window of the 'Yellow Room' is secured by iron bars, because it looks out upon the open country; the two windows of the laboratory have to be protected in like manner for the same reason. As the murderer got away, I conceive that he found a window that was not barred,—that of the vestibule, which opens on to the park,—that is to say, into the interior of the estate. There's not much magic in all that."

"Yes," said Monsieur de Marquet, "but what you have not guessed is that this single window in the vestibule, though it has no iron bars, has solid iron blinds. Now these iron blinds have remained fastened by their iron latch; and yet we have proof that the murderer made his escape from the pavilion by that window! Traces of blood on the inside wall and on the blinds as well as on the floor, and footmarks, of which I have taken the measurements, attest the fact that the murderer made his escape that way. But then, how did he do it, seeing that the blinds remained fastened on the inside? He passed through them like a shadow. But what is more bewildering than all is that it is impossible to form any idea as to how the murderer got out of the 'Yellow Room', or how he got across the laboratory to reach the vestibule! Ah, yes, Monsieur Rouletabille, it is altogether as you said, a fine case, the key to which will not be discovered for a long time, I hope."

"You hope, Monsieur?"

Monsieur de Marquet corrected himself.

"I do not hope so,—I think so."

"Could that window have been closed and refastened after the flight of the assassin?" asked Rouletabille.

"That is what occurred to me for a moment; but it would imply an accomplice or accomplices,—and I don't see—"

After a short silence he added:

"Ah—if Mademoiselle Stangerson were only well enough today to be questioned!"

Rouletabille following up his thought, asked:

"And the attic?—There must be some opening to that?"

"Yes; there is a window, or rather skylight, in it, which, as it looks out towards the country, Monsieur Stangerson has had barred, like the rest of the windows. These bars, as in the other windows, have remained intact, and the blinds, which naturally open inwards, have not been unfastened. For the rest, we have not discovered anything to lead us to suspect that the murderer had passed through the attic."

"It seems clear to you, then, Monsieur, that the murderer escaped—nobody knows how—by the window in the vestibule?"

"Everything goes to prove it."

"I think so, too," confessed Rouletabille gravely.

After a brief silence, he continued:

"If you have not found any traces of the murderer in the attic, such as the dirty footmarks similar to those on the floor of the 'Yellow Room', you must come to the conclusion that it was not he who stole Daddy Jacques's revolver."

"There are no footmarks in the attic other than those of Daddy Jacques himself," said the magistrate with a significant turn of his head. Then, after an apparent decision, he added: "Daddy Jacques was with Monsieur Stangerson in the laboratory—and it was lucky for him he was."

"Then what part did his revolver play in the tragedy?—It seems very clear that this weapon did less harm to Mademoiselle Stangerson than it did to the murderer."

The magistrate made no reply to this question, which doubtless embarrassed him. "Monsieur Stangerson," he said, "tells us that the two bullets have been found in the 'Yellow Room', one embedded in the wall stained with the impression of a red hand—a man's large hand—and the other in the ceiling."

"Oh! oh! in the ceiling!" muttered Rouletabille. "In the ceiling! That's very curious!—In the ceiling!"

He puffed awhile in silence at his pipe, enveloping himself in the smoke. When we reached Savigny-sur-Orge, I had to tap him on the shoulder to arouse him from his dream and come out on to the platform of the station.

There, the magistrate and his Registrar bowed to us, and by rapidly getting into a cab that was awaiting them, made us understand that they had seen enough of us.

"How long will it take to walk to the Chateau du Glandier?" Rouletabille asked one of the railway porters.

"An hour and a half or an hour and three quarters—easy walking," the man replied.

Rouletabille looked up at the sky and, no doubt, finding its appearance satisfactory, took my arm and said:

"Come on!—I need a walk."

"Are things getting less entangled?" I asked.

"Not a bit of it!" he said, "more entangled than ever! It's true, I have an idea—"

"What's that?" I asked.

"I can't tell you what it is just at present—it's an idea involving the life or death of two persons at least."

"Do you think there were accomplices?"

"I don't think it—"

We fell into silence. Presently he went on:

"It was a bit of luck, our falling in with that examining magistrate and his Registrar, eh? What did I tell you about that revolver?" His head was bent down, he had his hands in his pockets, and he was whistling. After a while I heard him murmur:

"Poor woman!"

"Is it Mademoiselle Stangerson you are pitying?"

"Yes; she's a noble woman and worthy of being pitied!—a woman of a great, a very great character—I imagine—I imagine."

"You know her then?"

"Not at all. I have never seen her."

"Why, then, do you say that she is a woman of great character?"

"Because she bravely faced the murderer; because she courageously defended herself—and, above all, because of the bullet in the ceiling."

I looked at Rouletabille and inwardly wondered whether he was not mocking me, or whether he had not suddenly gone out of his senses. But I saw that he had never been less inclined to laugh, and the brightness of his keenly intelligent eyes assured me that he retained all his reason. Then, too, I was used to his broken way of talking, which only left me puzzled as to his meaning, till, with a very few clear, rapidly uttered words, he would make the drift of his ideas clear to me, and I saw that what he had previously said, and which had appeared to me void of meaning, was so thoroughly logical that I could not understand how it was I had not understood him sooner.

IV

"In the Bosom of Wild Nature"

The Chateau du Glandier is one of the oldest chateaux in the Ile de France, where so many building remains of the feudal period are still standing. Built originally in the heart of the forest, in the reign of Philip le Bel, it now could be seen a few hundred yards from the road leading from the village of Sainte-Genevieve to Monthery. A mass of inharmonious structures, it is dominated by a donjon. When the visitor has mounted the crumbling steps of this ancient donjon, he reaches a little plateau where, in the seventeenth century, Georges Philibert de Sequigny, Lord of the Glandier, Maisons-Neuves and other places, built the existing town in an abominably rococo style of architecture.

It was in this place, seemingly belonging entirely to the past, that Professor Stangerson and his daughter installed themselves to lay the foundations for the science of the future. Its solitude, in the depths of woods, was what, more than all, had pleased them. They would have none to witness their labours and intrude on their hopes, but the aged stones and grand old oaks. The Glandier—ancient Glandierum—was so called from the quantity of glands (acorns) which, in all times, had been gathered in that neighbourhood. This land, of present mournful interest, had fallen back, owing to the negligence or abandonment of its owners, into the wild character of primitive nature. The buildings alone, which were hidden there, had preserved traces of their strange metamorphoses. Every age had left on them its imprint; a bit of architecture with which was bound up the remembrance of some terrible event, some bloody adventure. Such was the chateau in which science had taken refuge—a place seemingly designed to be the theatre of mysteries, terror, and death.

Having explained so far, I cannot refrain from making one further reflection. If I have lingered a little over this description of the Glandier, it is not because I have reached the right moment for creating the necessary atmosphere for the unfolding of the tragedy before the eyes of the reader. Indeed, in all this matter, my first care will be to be as simple as is possible. I have no ambition to be an author. An author is always something of a romancer, and God knows, the mystery of the "Yellow

Room" is quite full enough of real tragic horror to require no aid from literary effects. I am, and only desire to be, a faithful "reporter." My duty is to report the event; and I place the event in its frame—that is all. It is only natural that you should know where the things happened.

I return to Monsieur Stangerson. When he bought the estate, fifteen years before the tragedy with which we are engaged occurred, the Chateau du Glandier had for a long time been unoccupied. Another old chateau in the neighbourhood, built in the fourteenth century by Jean de Belmont, was also abandoned, so that that part of the country was very little inhabited. Some small houses on the side of the road leading to Corbeil, an inn, called the "Auberge du Donjon," which offered passing hospitality to waggoners; these were about all to represent civilisation in this out-of-the-way part of the country, but a few leagues from the capital.

But this deserted condition of the place had been the determining reason for the choice made by Monsieur Stangerson and his daughter. Monsieur Stangerson was already celebrated. He had returned from America, where his works had made a great stir. The book which he had published at Philadelphia, on the "Dissociation of Matter by Electric Action," had aroused opposition throughout the whole scientific world. Monsieur Stangerson was a Frenchman, but of American origin. Important matters relating to a legacy had kept him for several years in the United States, where he had continued the work begun by him in France, whither he had returned in possession of a large fortune. This fortune was a great boon to him; for, though he might have made millions of dollars by exploiting two or three of his chemical discoveries relative to new processes of dyeing, it was always repugnant to him to use for his own private gain the wonderful gift of invention he had received from nature. He considered he owed it to mankind, and all that his genius brought into the world went, by this philosophical view of his duty, into the public lap.

If he did not try to conceal his satisfaction at coming into possession of this fortune, which enabled him to give himself up to his passion for pure science, he had equally to rejoice, it seemed to him, for another cause. Mademoiselle Stangerson was, at the time when her father returned from America and bought the Glandier estate, twenty years of age. She was exceedingly pretty, having at once the Parisian grace of her mother, who had died in giving her birth, and all the splendour, all the riches of the young American blood of her parental grandfather,

William Stangerson. A citizen of Philadelphia, William Stangerson had been obliged to become naturalised in obedience to family exigencies at the time of his marriage with a French lady, she who was to be the mother of the illustrious Stangerson. In that way the professor's French nationality is accounted for.

Twenty years of age, a charming blonde, with blue eyes, milk-white complexion, and radiant with divine health, Mathilde Stangerson was one of the most beautiful marriageable girls in either the old or the new world. It was her father's duty, in spite of the inevitable pain which a separation from her would cause him, to think of her marriage; and he was fully prepared for it. Nevertheless, he buried himself and his child at the Glandier at the moment when his friends were expecting him to bring her out into society. Some of them expressed their astonishment, and to their questions he answered: "It is my daughter's wish. I can refuse her nothing. She has chosen the Glandier."

Interrogated in her turn, the young girl replied calmly: "Where could we work better than in this solitude?" For Mademoiselle Stangerson had already begun to collaborate with her father in his work. It could not at the time be imagined that her passion for science would lead her so far as to refuse all the suitors who presented themselves to her for over fifteen years. So secluded was the life led by the two, father and daughter, that they showed themselves only at a few official receptions and, at certain times in the year, in two or three friendly drawing-rooms, where the fame of the professor and the beauty of Mathilde made a sensation. The young girl's extreme reserve did not at first discourage suitors; but at the end of a few years, they tired of their quest.

One alone persisted with tender tenacity and deserved the name of "eternal fiancé," a name he accepted with melancholy resignation; that was Monsieur Robert Darzac. Mademoiselle Stangerson was now no longer young, and it seemed that, having found no reason for marrying at five-and-thirty, she would never find one. But such an argument evidently found no acceptance with Monsieur Robert Darzac. He continued to pay his court—if the delicate and tender attention with which he ceaselessly surrounded this woman of five-and-thirty could be called courtship—in face of her declared intention never to marry.

Suddenly, some weeks before the events with which we are occupied, a report—to which nobody attached any importance, so incredible did it sound—was spread about Paris, that Mademoiselle Stangerson had at last consented to "crown" the inextinguishable flame of Monsieur

Robert Darzac! It needed that Monsieur Robert Darzac himself should not deny this matrimonial rumour to give it an appearance of truth, so unlikely did it seem to be well founded. One day, however, Monsieur Stangerson, as he was leaving the Academy of Science, announced that the marriage of his daughter and Monsieur Robert Darzac would be celebrated in the privacy of the Chateau du Glandier, as soon as he and his daughter had put the finishing touches to their report summing up their labours on the "Dissociation of Matter." The new household would install itself in the Glandier, and the son-in-law would lend his assistance in the work to which the father and daughter had dedicated their lives.

The scientific world had barely had time to recover from the effect of this news, when it learned of the attempted assassination of Mademoiselle under the extraordinary conditions which we have detailed and which our visit to the chateau was to enable us to ascertain with yet greater precision. I have not hesitated to furnish the reader with all these retrospective details, known to me through my business relations with Monsieur Robert Darzac. On crossing the threshold of the "Yellow Room" he was as well posted as I was.

V

In Which Joseph Rouletabille Makes a Remark to Monsieur Robert Darzac Which Produces Its Little Effect

Rouletabille and I had been walking for several minutes, by the side of a long wall bounding the vast property of Monsieur Stangerson and had already come within sight of the entrance gate, when our attention was drawn to an individual who, half bent to the ground, seemed to be so completely absorbed in what he was doing as not to have seen us coming towards him. At one time he stooped so low as almost to touch the ground; at another he drew himself up and attentively examined the wall; then he looked into the palm of one of his hands, and walked away with rapid strides. Finally he set off running, still looking into the palm of his hand. Rouletabille had brought me to a standstill by a gesture.

"Hush! Frederic Larsan is at work! Don't let us disturb him!"

Rouletabille had a great admiration for the celebrated detective. I had never before seen him, but I knew him well by reputation. At that time, before Rouletabille had given proof of his unique talent, Larsan was reputed as the most skilful unraveller of the most mysterious and complicated crimes. His reputation was world-wide, and the police of London, and even of America, often called him in to their aid when their own national inspectors and detectives found themselves at the end of their wits and resources.

No one was astonished, then, that the head of the Surete had, at the outset of the mystery of the "Yellow Room", telegraphed his precious subordinate to London, where he had been sent on a big case of stolen securities, to return with all haste. Frederic who, at the Surete, was called the "great Frederic," had made all speed, doubtless knowing by experience that, if he was interrupted in what he was doing, it was because his services were urgently needed in another direction; so, as Rouletabille said, he was that morning already "at work." We soon found out in what it consisted.

What he was continually looking at in the palm of his right hand was nothing but his watch, the minute hand of which he appeared to be noting intently. Then he turned back still running, stopping only when he reached the park gate, where he again consulted his watch and then put it away in his pocket, shrugging his shoulders with a gesture of discouragement. He pushed open the park gate, reclosed and locked it, raised his head and, through the bars, perceived us. Rouletabille rushed after him, and I followed. Frederic Larsan waited for us.

"Monsieur Fred," said Rouletabille, raising his hat and showing the profound respect, based on admiration, which the young reporter felt for the celebrated detective, "can you tell me whether Monsieur Robert Darzac is at the chateau at this moment? Here is one of his friends, of the Paris Bar, who desires to speak with him."

"I really don't know, Monsieur Rouletabille," replied Fred, shaking hands with my friend, whom he had several times met in the course of his difficult investigations. "I have not seen him."

"The concierges will be able to inform us no doubt?" said Rouletabille, pointing to the lodge the door and windows of which were close shut.

"The concierges will not be able to give you any information, Monsieur Rouletabille."

"Why not?"

"Because they were arrested half an hour ago."

"Arrested!" cried Rouletabille; "then they are the murderers!"

Frederic Larsan shrugged his shoulders.

"When you can't arrest the real murderer," he said with an air of supreme irony, "you can always indulge in the luxury of discovering accomplices."

"Did you have them arrested, Monsieur Fred?"

"Not I!—I haven't had them arrested. In the first place, I am pretty sure that they have not had anything to do with the affair, and then because—"

"Because of what?" asked Rouletabille eagerly.

"Because of nothing," said Larsan, shaking his head.

"Because there were no accomplices!" said Rouletabille.

"Aha!—you have an idea, then, about this matter?" said Larsan, looking at Rouletabille intently, "yet you have seen nothing, young man—you have not yet gained admission here!"

"I shall get admission."

"I doubt it. The orders are strict."

"I shall gain admission, if you let me see Monsieur Robert Darzac. Do that for me. You know we are old friends. I beg of you, Monsieur

Fred. Do you remember the article I wrote about you on the gold bar case?"

The face of Rouletabille at the moment was really funny to look at. It showed such an irresistible desire to cross the threshold beyond which some prodigious mystery had occurred; it appealed with so much eloquence, not only of the mouth and eyes, but with all its features, that I could not refrain from bursting into laughter. Frederic Larsan, no more than myself, could retain his gravity. Meanwhile, standing on the other side of the gate, he calmly put the key in his pocket. I closely scrutinised him.

He might be about fifty years of age. He had a fine head, his hair turning grey; a colourless complexion, and a firm profile. His forehead was prominent, his chin and cheeks clean shaven. His upper lip, without moustache, was finely chiselled. His eyes were rather small and round, with a look in them that was at once searching and disquieting. He was of middle height and well built, with a general bearing elegant and gentlemanly. There was nothing about him of the vulgar policeman. In his way, he was an artist, and one felt that he had a high opinion of himself. The sceptical tone of his conversation was that of a man who had been taught by experience. His strange profession had brought him into contact with so many crimes and villanies that it would have been remarkable if his nature had not been a little hardened.

Larsan turned his head at the sound of a vehicle which had come from the chateau and reached the gate behind him. We recognised the cab which had conveyed the examining magistrate and his Registrar from the station at Epinay.

"Ah!" said Frederic Larsan, "if you want to speak with Monsieur Robert Darzac, he is here."

The cab was already at the park gate and Robert Darzac was begging Frederic Larsan to open it for him, explaining that he was pressed for time to catch the next train leaving Epinay for Paris. Then he recognised me. While Larsan was unlocking the gate, Monsieur Darzac inquired what had brought me to the Glandier at such a tragic moment. I noticed that he was frightfully pale, and that his face was lined as if from the effects of some terrible suffering.

"Is Mademoiselle getting better?" I immediately asked.

"Yes," he said. "She will be saved perhaps. She must be saved!"

He did not add "or it will be my death"; but I felt that the phrase trembled on his pale lips.

Rouletabille intervened:

"You are in a hurry, Monsieur; but I must speak with you. I have something of the greatest importance to tell you."

Frederic Larsan interrupted:

"May I leave you?" he asked of Robert Darzac. "Have you a key, or do you wish me to give you this one."

"Thank you. I have a key and will lock the gate."

Larsan hurried off in the direction of the chateau, the imposing pile of which could be perceived a few hundred yards away.

Robert Darzac, with knit brow, was beginning to show impatience. I presented Rouletabille as a good friend of mine, but, as soon as he learnt that the young man was a journalist, he looked at me very reproachfully, excused himself, under the necessity of having to reach Epinay in twenty minutes, bowed, and whipped up his horse. But Rouletabille had seized the bridle and, to my utter astonishment, stopped the carriage with a vigorous hand. Then he gave utterance to a sentence which was utterly meaningless to me.

"The presbytery has lost nothing of its charm, nor the garden its brightness."

The words had no sooner left the lips of Rouletabille than I saw Robert Darzac quail. Pale as he was, he became paler. His eyes were fixed on the young man in terror, and he immediately descended from the vehicle in an inexpressible state of agitation.

"Come!—come in!" he stammered.

Then, suddenly, and with a sort of fury, he repeated:

"Let us go, monsieur."

He turned up by the road he had come from the chateau, Rouletabille still retaining his hold on the horse's bridle. I addressed a few words to Monsieur Darzac, but he made no answer. My looks questioned Rouletabille, but his gaze was elsewhere.

VI

In the Heart of the Oak Grove

We reached the chateau, and, as we approached it, saw four gendarmes pacing in front of a little door in the ground floor of the donjon. We soon learned that in this ground floor, which had formerly served as a prison, Monsieur and Madame Bernier, the concierges, were confined. Monsieur Robert Darzac led us into the modern part of the chateau by a large door, protected by a projecting awning—a "marquise" as it is called. Rouletabille, who had resigned the horse and the cab to the care of a servant, never took his eyes off Monsieur Darzac. I followed his look and perceived that it was directed solely towards the gloved hands of the Sorbonne professor. When we were in a tiny sitting-room fitted with old furniture, Monsieur Darzac turned to Rouletabille and said sharply:

"What do you want?"

The reporter answered in an equally sharp tone:

"To shake you by the hand."

Darzac shrank back.

"What does that mean?"

Evidently he understood, what I also understood, that my friend suspected him of the abominable attempt on the life of Mademoiselle Stangerson. The impression of the blood-stained hand on the walls of the "Yellow Room" was in his mind. I looked at the man closely. His haughty face with its expression ordinarily so straightforward was at this moment strangely troubled. He held out his right hand and, referring to me, said:

"As you are a friend of Monsieur Sainclair who has rendered me invaluable services in a just cause, monsieur, I see no reason for refusing you my hand—"

Rouletabille did not take the extended hand. Lying with the utmost audacity, he said:

"Monsieur, I have lived several years in Russia, where I have acquired the habit of never taking any but an ungloved hand."

I thought that the Sorbonne professor would express his anger openly, but, on the contrary, by a visibly violent effort, he calmed himself, took off his gloves, and showed his hands; they were unmarked by any cicatrix.

"Are you satisfied?"

"No!" replied Rouletabille. "My dear friend," he said, turning to me, "I am obliged to ask you to leave us alone for a moment."

I bowed and retired; stupefied by what I had seen and heard. I could not understand why Monsieur Robert Darzac had not already shown the door to my impertinent, insulting, and stupid friend. I was angry myself with Rouletabille at that moment, for his suspicions, which had led to this scene of the gloves.

For some twenty minutes I walked about in front of the chateau, trying vainly to link together the different events of the day. What was in Rouletabille's mind? Was it possible that he thought Monsieur Robert Darzac to be the murderer? How could it be thought that this man, who was to have married Mademoiselle Stangerson in the course of a few days, had introduced himself into the "Yellow Room" to assassinate his fiancee? I could find no explanation as to how the murderer had been able to leave the "Yellow Room"; and so long as that mystery, which appeared to me so inexplicable, remained unexplained, I thought it was the duty of all of us to refrain from suspecting anybody. But, then, that seemingly senseless phrase—"The presbytery has lost nothing of its charm, nor the garden its brightness"—still rang in my ears. What did it mean? I was eager to rejoin Rouletabille and question him.

At that moment the young man came out of the chateau in the company of Monsieur Robert Darzac, and, extraordinary to relate, I saw, at a glance, that they were the best of friends. "We are going to the 'Yellow Room'. Come with us," Rouletabille said to me. "You know, my dear boy, I am going to keep you with me all day. We'll breakfast together somewhere about here—"

"You'll breakfast with me, here, gentlemen—"

"No, thanks," replied the young man. "We shall breakfast at the Donjon Inn."

"You'll fare very badly there; you'll not find anything—"

"Do you think so? Well, I hope to find something there," replied Rouletabille. "After breakfast, we'll set to work again. I'll write my article and if you'll be so good as to take it to the office for me—"

"Won't you come back with me to Paris?"

"No; I shall remain here."

I turned towards Rouletabille. He spoke quite seriously, and Monsieur Robert Darzac did not appear to be in the least degree surprised.

We were passing by the donjon and heard wailing voices. Rouletabille asked:

"Why have these people been arrested?"

"It is a little my fault," said Monsieur Darzac. "I happened to remark to the examining magistrate yesterday that it was inexplicable that the concierges had had time to hear the revolver shots, to dress themselves, and to cover so great a distance as that which lies between their lodge and the pavilion, in the space of two minutes; for not more than that interval of time had elapsed after the firing of the shots when they were met by Daddy Jacques."

"That was suspicious evidently," acquiesced Rouletabille. "And were they dressed?"

"That is what is so incredible—they were dressed—completely—not one part of their costume wanting. The woman wore sabots, but the man had on laced boots. Now they assert that they went to bed at half-past nine. On arriving this morning, the examining magistrate brought with him from Paris a revolver of the same calibre as that found in the room (for he couldn't use the one held for evidence), and made his Registrar fire two shots in the 'Yellow Room' while the doors and windows were closed. We were with him in the lodge of the concierges, and yet we heard nothing, not a sound. The concierges have lied, of that there can be no doubt. They must have been already waiting, not far from the pavilion, waiting for something! Certainly they are not to be accused of being the authors of the crime, but their complicity is not improbable. That was why Monsieur de Marquet had them arrested at once."

"If they had been accomplices," said Rouletabille, "they would not have been there at all. When people throw themselves into the arms of justice with the proofs of complicity on them, you can be sure they are not accomplices. I don't believe there are any accomplices in this affair."

"Then, why were they abroad at midnight? Why don't they say?"

"They have certainly some reason for their silence. What that reason is, has to be found out; for, even if they are not accomplices, it may be of importance. Everything that took place on such a night is important."

We had crossed an old bridge thrown over the Douve and were entering the part of the park called the Oak Grove, the oaks here were centuries old. Autumn had already shrivelled their tawny leaves, and their high branches, black and contorted, looked like horrid heads of hair, mingled with quaint reptiles such as the ancient sculptors have made on the head of Medusa. This place, which Mademoiselle found cheerful and in which she lived in the summer season, appeared to us as sad and funereal now. The soil was black and muddy from the recent rains and the rotting of the fallen leaves; the trunks of the trees were black and the sky above us was now, as if in mourning, charged with great, heavy clouds.

And it was in this sombre and desolate retreat that we saw the white walls of the pavilion as we approached. A queer-looking building without a window visible on the side by which we neared it. A little door alone marked the entrance to it. It might have passed for a tomb, a vast mausoleum in the midst of a thick forest. As we came nearer, we were able to make out its disposition. The building obtained all the light it needed from the south, that is to say, from the open country. The little door closed on the park. Monsieur and Mademoiselle Stangerson must have found it an ideal seclusion for their work and their dreams.

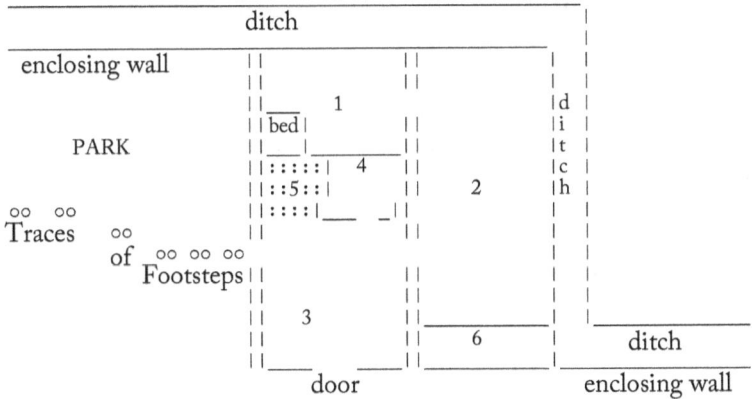

Here is the ground plan of the pavilion. It had a ground-floor which was reached by a few steps, and above it was an attic, with which we need not concern ourselves. The plan of the ground-floor only, sketched roughly, is what I here submit to the reader.

1. The "Yellow Room", with its one window and its one door opening into the laboratory.
2. Laboratory, with its two large, barred windows and its doors, one serving for the vestibule, the other for the "Yellow Room".

3. Vestibule, with its unbarred window and door opening into the park.
4. Lavatory.
5. Stairs leading to the attic.
6. Large and the only chimney in the pavilion, serving for the experiments of the laboratory.

The plan was drawn by Rouletabille, and I assured myself that there was not a line in it that was wanting to help to the solution of the problem then set before the police. With the lines of this plan and the description of its parts before them, my readers will know as much as Rouletabille knew when he entered the pavilion for the first time. With him they may now ask: How did the murderer escape from the "Yellow Room"? Before mounting the three steps leading up to the door of the pavilion, Rouletabille stopped and asked Monsieur Darzac point blank:

"What was the motive for the crime?"

"Speaking for myself, Monsieur, there can be no doubt on the matter," said Mademoiselle Stangerson's fiancé, greatly distressed. "The nails of the fingers, the deep scratches on the chest and throat of Mademoiselle Stangerson show that the wretch who attacked her attempted to commit a frightful crime. The medical experts who examined these traces yesterday affirm that they were made by the same hand as that which left its red imprint on the wall; an enormous hand, Monsieur, much too large to go into my gloves," he added with an indefinable smile.

"Could not that blood-stained hand," I interrupted, "have been the hand of Mademoiselle Stangerson who, in the moment of falling, had pressed it against the wall, and, in slipping, enlarged the impression?"

"There was not a drop of blood on either of her hands when she was lifted up," replied Monsieur Darzac.

"We are now sure," said I, "that it was Mademoiselle Stangerson who was armed with Daddy Jacques's revolver, since she wounded the hand of the murderer. She was in fear, then, of somebody or something."

"Probably."

"Do you suspect anybody?"

"No," replied Monsieur Darzac, looking at Rouletabille. Rouletabille then said to me:

"You must know, my friend, that the inquiry is a little more advanced than Monsieur de Marquet has chosen to tell us. He not only knows that Mademoiselle Stangerson defended herself with the revolver, but he knows what the weapon was that was used to attack her. Monsieur Darzac tells me it was a mutton-bone. Why is Monsieur de Marquet surrounding this mutton-bone with so much mystery? No doubt for the purpose of facilitating the inquiries of the agents of the Surete? He imagines, perhaps, that the owner of this instrument of crime, the most terrible invented, is going to be found amongst those who are well-known in the slums of Paris who use it. But who can ever say what passes through the brain of an examining magistrate?" Rouletabille added with contemptuous irony.

"Has a mutton-bone been found in the 'Yellow Room'?" I asked him.

"Yes, Monsieur," said Robert Darzac, "at the foot of the bed; but I beg of you not to say anything about it." (I made a gesture of assent.) "It was an enormous mutton-bone, the top of which, or rather the joint, was still red with the blood of the frightful wound. It was an old bone, which may, according to appearances, have served in other crimes. That's what Monsieur de Marquet thinks. He has had it sent to the municipal laboratory at Paris to be analysed. In fact, he thinks he has detected on it, not only the blood of the last victim, but other stains of dried blood, evidences of previous crimes."

"A mutton-bone in the hand of a skilled assassin is a frightful weapon," said Rouletabille, "a more certain weapon than a heavy hammer."

"The scoundrel has proved it to be so," said Monsieur Robert Darzac, sadly. "The joint of the bone found exactly fits the wound inflicted.

"My belief is that the wound would have been mortal, if the murderer's blow had not been arrested in the act by Mademoiselle Stangerson's revolver. Wounded in the hand, he dropped the mutton-bone and fled. Unfortunately, the blow had been already given, and Mademoiselle was stunned after having been nearly strangled. If she had succeeded in wounding the man with the first shot of the revolver, she would, doubtless, have escaped the blow with the bone. But she had certainly employeeed her revolver too late; the first shot deviated and lodged in the ceiling; it was the second only that took effect."

Having said this, Monsieur Darzac knocked at the door of the pavilion. I must confess to feeling a strong impatience to reach the spot where the crime had been committed. It was some time before the door was opened by a man whom I at once recognised as Daddy Jacques.

He appeared to be well over sixty years of age. He had a long white beard and white hair, on which he wore a flat Basque cap. He was dressed in a complete suit of chestnut-coloured velveteen, worn at the sides; sabots were on his feet. He had rather a waspish-looking face, the expression of which lightened, however, as soon as he saw Monsieur Darzac.

"Friends," said our guide. "Nobody in the pavilion, Daddy Jacques?"

"I ought not to allow anybody to enter, Monsieur Robert, but of course the order does not apply to you. These gentlemen of justice have seen everything there is to be seen, and made enough drawings, and drawn up enough reports—"

"Excuse me, Monsieur Jacques, one question before anything else," said Rouletabille.

"What is it, young man? If I can answer it—"

"Did your mistress wear her hair in bands, that evening? You know what I mean—over her forehead?"

"No, young man. My mistress never wore her hair in the way you suggest, neither on that day nor on any other. She had her hair drawn up, as usual, so that her beautiful forehead could be seen, pure as that of an unborn child!"

Rouletabille grunted and set to work examining the door, finding that it fastened itself automatically. He satisfied himself that it could never remain open and needed a key to open it. Then we entered the vestibule, a small, well-lit room paved with square red tiles.

"Ah! This is the window by which the murderer escaped!" said Rouletabille.

"So they keep on saying, monsieur, so they keep on saying! But if he had gone off that way, we should have been sure to have seen him. We are not blind, neither Monsieur Stangerson nor me, nor the concierges who are in prison. Why have they not put me in prison, too, on account of my revolver?"

Rouletabille had already opened the window and was examining the shutters.

"Were these closed at the time of the crime?"

"And fastened with the iron catch inside," said Daddy Jacques, "and I am quite sure that the murderer did not get out that way."

"Are there any blood stains?"

"Yes, on the stones outside; but blood of what?"

"Ah!" said Rouletabille, "there are footmarks visible on the path—the ground was very moist. I will look into that presently."

"Nonsense!" interrupted Daddy Jacques; "the murderer did not go that way."

"Which way did he go, then?"

"How do I know?"

Rouletabille looked at everything, smelled everything. He went down on his knees and rapidly examined every one of the paving tiles. Daddy Jacques went on:

"Ah!—you can't find anything, monsieur. Nothing has been found. And now it is all dirty; too many persons have tramped over it. They wouldn't let me wash it, but on the day of the crime I had washed the floor thoroughly, and if the murderer had crossed it with his hobnailed boots, I should not have failed to see where he had been; he has left marks enough in Mademoiselle's chamber."

Rouletabille rose.

"When was the last time you washed these tiles?" he asked, and he fixed on Daddy Jacques a most searching look.

"Why—as I told you—on the day of the crime, towards half-past five—while Mademoiselle and her father were taking a little walk before dinner, here in this room: they had dined in the laboratory. The next day, the examining magistrate came and saw all the marks there were on the floor as plainly as if they had been made with ink on white paper. Well, neither in the laboratory nor in the vestibule, which were both as clean as a new pin, were there any traces of a man's footmarks. Since they have been found near this window outside, he must have made his way through the ceiling of the 'Yellow Room' into the attic, then cut his way through the roof and dropped to the ground outside the vestibule window. But—there's no hole, neither in the ceiling of the 'Yellow Room' nor in the roof of my attic—that's absolutely certain! So you see we know nothing—nothing! And nothing will ever be known! It's a mystery of the Devil's own making."

Rouletabille went down upon his knees again almost in front of a small lavatory at the back of the vestibule. In that position he remained for about a minute.

"Well?" I asked him when he got up.

"Oh! nothing very important,—a drop of blood," he replied, turning towards Daddy Jacques as he spoke. "While you were washing the laboratory and this vestibule, was the vestibule window open?" he asked.

"No, Monsieur, it was closed; but after I had done washing the floor, I lit some charcoal for Monsieur in the laboratory furnace, and, as I lit it with old newspapers, it smoked, so I opened both the windows in the laboratory and this one, to make a current of air; then I shut those in the laboratory and left this one open when I went out. When I returned to the pavilion, this window had been closed and Monsieur and Mademoiselle were already at work in the laboratory."

"Monsieur or Mademoiselle Stangerson had, no doubt, shut it?"

"No doubt."

"You did not ask them?"

After a close scrutiny of the little lavatory and of the staircase leading up to the attic, Rouletabille—to whom we seemed no longer to exist—entered the laboratory. I followed him. It was, I confess, in a state of great excitement. Robert Darzac lost none of my friend's movements. As for me, my eyes were drawn at once to the door of the "Yellow Room". It was closed and, as I immediately saw, partially shattered and out of commission.

My friend, who went about his work methodically, silently studied the room in which we were. It was large and well-lighted. Two big windows—almost bays—were protected by strong iron bars and looked out upon a wide extent of country. Through an opening in the forest, they commanded a wonderful view through the length of the valley and across the plain to the large town which could be clearly seen in fair weather. Today, however, a mist hung over the ground—and blood in that room!

The whole of one side of the laboratory was taken up with a large chimney, crucibles, ovens, and such implements as are needed for chemical experiments; tables, loaded with phials, papers, reports, an electrical machine,—an apparatus, as Monsieur Darzac informed me, employeeed by Professor Stangerson to demonstrate the Dissociation of Matter under the action of solar light—and other scientific implements.

Along the walls were cabinets, plain or glass-fronted, through which were visible microscopes, special photographic apparatus, and a large quantity of crystals.

Rouletabille, who was ferreting in the chimney, put his fingers into one of the crucibles. Suddenly he drew himself up, and held up a piece of half-consumed paper in his hand. He stepped up to where we were talking by one of the windows.

"Keep that for us, Monsieur Darzac," he said.

I bent over the piece of scorched paper which Monsieur Darzac took from the hand of Rouletabille, and read distinctly the only words that remained legible:

"Presbytery—lost nothing—charm, nor the gar—its brightness."

Twice since the morning these same meaningless words had struck me, and, for the second time, I saw that they produced on the Sorbonne professor the same paralysing effect. Monsieur Darzac's first anxiety showed itself when he turned his eyes in the direction of Daddy Jacques. But, occupied as he was at another window, he had seen nothing. Then tremblingly opening his pocket-book he put the piece of paper into it, sighing: "My God!"

During this time, Rouletabille had mounted into the opening of the fire-grate—that is to say, he had got upon the bricks of a furnace—and was attentively examining the chimney, which grew narrower towards the top, the outlet from it being closed with sheets of iron, fastened into the brickwork, through which passed three small chimneys.

"Impossible to get out that way," he said, jumping back into the laboratory. "Besides, even if he had tried to do it, he would have brought all that ironwork down to the ground. No, no; it is not on that side we have to search."

Rouletabille next examined the furniture and opened the doors of the cabinet. Then he came to the windows, through which he declared no one could possibly have passed. At the second window he found Daddy Jacques in contemplation.

"Well, Daddy Jacques," he said, "what are you looking at?"

"That policeman who is always going round and round the lake. Another of those fellows who think they can see better than anybody else!"

"You don't know Frederic Larsan, Daddy Jacques, or you wouldn't speak of him in that way," said Rouletabille in a melancholy tone. "If there is anyone who will find the murderer, it will be he." And Rouletabille heaved a deep sigh.

"Before they find him, they will have to learn how they lost him," said Daddy Jacques, stolidly.

At length we reached the door of the "Yellow Room" itself.

"There is the door behind which some terrible scene took place," said Rouletabille, with a solemnity which, under any other circumstances, would have been comical.

VII

In Which Rouletabille Sets Out on an Expedition Under the Bed

Rouletabille having pushed open the door of the "Yellow Room" paused on the threshold saying, with an emotion which I only later understood, "Ah, the perfume of the lady in black!"

The chamber was dark. Daddy Jacques was about to open the blinds when Rouletabille stopped him.

"Did not the tragedy take place in complete darkness?" he asked.

"No, young man, I don't think so. Mademoiselle always had a nightlight on her table, and I lit it every evening before she went to bed. I was a sort of chambermaid, you must understand, when the evening came. The real chambermaid did not come here much before the morning. Mademoiselle worked late—far into the night."

"Where did the table with the night-light stand,—far from the bed?"

"Some way from the bed."

"Can you light the burner now?"

"The lamp is broken and the oil that was in it was spilled when the table was upset. All the rest of the things in the room remain just as they were. I have only to open the blinds for you to see."

"Wait."

Rouletabille went back into the laboratory, closed the shutters of the two windows and the door of the vestibule.

When we were in complete darkness, he lit a wax vesta, and asked Daddy Jacques to move to the middle of the chamber with it to the place where the night-light was burning that night.

Daddy Jacques who was in his stockings—he usually left his sabots in the vestibule—entered the "Yellow Room" with his bit of a vesta. We vaguely distinguished objects overthrown on the floor, a bed in one corner, and, in front of us, to the left, the gleam of a looking-glass hanging on the wall, near to the bed.

"That will do!—you may now open the blinds," said Rouletabille.

"Don't come any further," Daddy Jacques begged, "you may make marks with your boots, and nothing must be deranged; it's an idea of the magistrate's—though he has nothing more to do here."

And he pushed open the shutter. The pale daylight entered from without, throwing a sinister light on the saffron-coloured walls. The floor—for though the laboratory and the vestibule were tiled, the "Yellow Room" had a flooring of wood—was covered with a single yellow mat which was large enough to cover nearly the whole room, under the bed and under the dressing-table—the only piece of furniture that remained upright. The centre round table, the night-table and two chairs had been overturned. These did not prevent a large stain of blood being visible on the mat, made, as Daddy Jacques informed us, by the blood which had flowed from the wound on Mademoiselle Stangerson's forehead. Besides these stains, drops of blood had fallen in all directions, in line with the visible traces of the footsteps—large and black—of the murderer. Everything led to the presumption that these drops of blood had fallen from the wound of the man who had, for a moment, placed his red hand on the wall. There were other traces of the same hand on the wall, but much less distinct.

"See!—see this blood on the wall!" I could not help exclaiming. "The man who pressed his hand so heavily upon it in the darkness must certainly have thought that he was pushing at a door! That's why he pressed on it so hard, leaving on the yellow paper the terrible evidence. I don't think there are many hands in the world of that sort. It is big and strong and the fingers are nearly all one as long as the other! The thumb is wanting and we have only the mark of the palm; but if we follow the trace of the hand," I continued, "we see that, after leaving its imprint on the wall, the touch sought the door, found it, and then felt for the lock—"

"No doubt," interrupted Rouletabille, chuckling,—"only there is no blood, either on the lock or on the bolt!"

"What does that prove?" I rejoined with a good sense of which I was proud; "he might have opened the lock with his left hand, which would have been quite natural, his right hand being wounded."

"He didn't open it at all!" Daddy Jacques again exclaimed. "We are not fools; and there were four of us when we burst open the door!"

"What a queer hand!—Look what a queer hand it is!" I said.

"It is a very natural hand," said Rouletabille, "of which the shape has been deformed by its having slipped on the wall. The man dried his hand on the wall. He must be a man about five feet eight in height."

"How do you come at that?"

"By the height of the marks on the wall."

My friend next occupied himself with the mark of the bullet in the wall. It was a round hole.

"This ball was fired straight, not from above, and consequently, not from below."

Rouletabille went back to the door and carefully examined the lock and the bolt, satisfying himself that the door had certainly been burst open from the outside, and, further, that the key had been found in the lock on the inside of the chamber. He finally satisfied himself that with the key in the lock, the door could not possibly be opened from without with another key. Having made sure of all these details, he let fall these words: "That's better!"—Then sitting down on the ground, he hastily took off his boots and, in his socks, went into the room.

The first thing he did was to examine minutely the overturned furniture. We watched him in silence.

"Young fellow, you are giving yourself a great deal of trouble," said Daddy Jacques ironically.

Rouletabille raised his head and said:

"You have spoken the simple truth, Daddy Jacques; your mistress did not have her hair in bands that evening. I was a donkey to have believed she did."

Then, with the suppleness of a serpent, he slipped under the bed. Presently we heard him ask:

"At what time, Monsieur Jacques, did Monsieur and Mademoiselle Stangerson arrive at the laboratory?"

"At six o'clock."

The voice of Rouletabille continued:

"Yes,—he's been under here,—that's certain; in fact, there was no where else where he could have hidden himself. Here, too, are the marks of his hobnails. When you entered—all four of you—did you look under the bed?"

"At once,—we drew it right out of its place—"

"And between the mattresses?"

"There was only one on the bed, and on that Mademoiselle was placed; and Monsieur Stangerson and the concierge immediately carried it into the laboratory. Under the mattress there was nothing but the metal netting, which could not conceal anything or anybody. Remember, monsieur, that there were four of us and we couldn't fail to see everything—the chamber is so small and scantily furnished, and all was locked behind in the pavilion."

I ventured on a hypothesis:

"Perhaps he got away with the mattress—in the mattress!—Anything is possible, in the face of such a mystery! In their distress of mind Monsieur Stangerson and the concierge may not have noticed they were bearing a double weight; especially if the concierge were an accomplice! I throw out this hypothesis for what it is worth, but it explains many things,—and particularly the fact that neither the laboratory nor the vestibule bear any traces of the footmarks found in the room. If, in carrying Mademoiselle on the mattress from the laboratory of the chateau, they rested for a moment, there might have been an opportunity for the man in it to escape.

"And then?" asked Rouletabille, deliberately laughing under the bed.

I felt rather vexed and replied:

"I don't know,—but anything appears possible"—

"The examining magistrate had the same idea, monsieur," said Daddy Jacques, "and he carefully examined the mattress. He was obliged to laugh at the idea, monsieur, as your friend is doing now,—for whoever heard of a mattress having a double bottom?"

I was myself obliged to laugh, on seeing that what I had said was absurd; but in an affair like this one hardly knows where an absurdity begins or ends.

My friend alone seemed able to talk intelligently. He called out from under the bed.

"The mat here has been moved out of place,—who did it?"

"We did, monsieur," explained Daddy Jacques. "When we could not find the assassin, we asked ourselves whether there was not some hole in the floor—"

"There is not," replied Rouletabille. "Is there a cellar?"

"No, there's no cellar. But that has not stopped our searching, and has not prevented the examining magistrate and his Registrar from studying the floor plank by plank, as if there had been a cellar under it."

The reporter then reappeared. His eyes were sparkling and his nostrils quivered. He remained on his hands and knees. He could not be better likened than to an admirable sporting dog on the scent of some unusual game. And, indeed, he was scenting the steps of a man,—the man whom he has sworn to report to his master, the manager of the "Epoque." It must not be forgotten that Rouletabille was first and last a journalist.

Thus, on his hands and knees, he made his way to the four corners of the room, so to speak, sniffing and going round everything—everything that we could see, which was not much, and everything that we could not see, which must have been infinite.

The toilette table was a simple table standing on four legs; there was nothing about it by which it could possibly be changed into a temporary hiding-place. There was not a closet or cupboard. Mademoiselle Stangerson kept her wardrobe at the chateau.

Rouletabille literally passed his nose and hands along the walls, constructed of solid brickwork. When he had finished with the walls, and passed his agile fingers over every portion of the yellow paper covering them, he reached to the ceiling, which he was able to touch by mounting on a chair placed on the toilette table, and by moving this ingeniously constructed stage from place to place he examined every foot of it. When he had finished his scrutiny of the ceiling, where he carefully examined the hole made by the second bullet, he approached the window, and, once more, examined the iron bars and blinds, all of which were solid and intact. At last, he gave a grunt of satisfaction and declared "Now I am at ease!"

"Well,—do you believe that the poor dear young lady was shut up when she was being murdered—when she cried out for help?" wailed Daddy Jacques.

"Yes," said the young reporter, drying his forehead, "the 'Yellow Room' was as tightly shut as an iron safe."

"That," I said, "is why this mystery is the most surprising I know. Edgar Allan Poe, in 'The Murders in the Rue Morgue,' invented nothing like it. The place of that crime was sufficiently closed to prevent the escape of a man; but there was that window through which the monkey, the perpetrator of the murder, could slip away! But here, there can be no question of an opening of any sort. The door was fastened, and through the window blinds, secure as they were, not even a fly could enter or get out."

"True, true," assented Rouletabille as he kept on drying his forehead, which seemed to be perspiring less from his recent bodily exertion than from his mental agitation. "Indeed, it's a great, a beautiful, and a very curious mystery."

"The Bete du bon Dieu," muttered Daddy Jacques, "the Bete du bon Dieu herself, if she had committed the crime, could not have escaped. Listen! Do you hear it? Hush!"

Daddy Jacques made us a sign to keep quiet and, stretching his arm towards the wall nearest the forest, listened to something which we could not hear.

"It's answering," he said at length. "I must kill it. It is too wicked, but it's the Bete du bon Dieu, and, every night, it goes to pray on the tomb of Sainte-Genevieve and nobody dares to touch her, for fear that Mother Angenoux should cast an evil spell on them."

"How big is the Bete du bon Dieu?"

"Nearly as big as a small retriever,—a monster, I tell you. Ah!—I have asked myself more than once whether it was not her that took our poor Mademoiselle by the throat with her claws. But the Bete du bon Dieu does not wear hobnailed boots, nor fire revolvers, nor has she a hand like that!" exclaimed Daddy Jacques, again pointing out to us the red mark on the wall. "Besides, we should have seen her as well as we would have seen a man—"

"Evidently," I said. "Before we had seen this 'Yellow Room', I had also asked myself whether the cat of Mother Angenoux—"

"You also!" cried Rouletabille.

"Didn't you?" I asked.

"Not for a moment. After reading the article in the 'Matin,' I knew that a cat had nothing to do with the matter. But I swear now that a frightful tragedy has been enacted here. You say nothing about the Basque cap, or the handkerchief, found here, Daddy Jacques?"

"Of course, the magistrate has taken them," the old man answered, hesitatingly.

"I haven't seen either the handkerchief or the cap, yet I can tell you how they are made," the reporter said to him gravely.

"Oh, you are very clever," said Daddy Jacques, coughing and embarrassed.

"The handkerchief is a large one, blue with red stripes and the cap is an old Basque cap, like the one you are wearing now."

"You are a wizard!" said Daddy Jacques, trying to laugh and not quite succeeding. "How do you know that the handkerchief is blue with red stripes?"

"Because, if it had not been blue with red stripes, it would not have been found at all."

Without giving any further attention to Daddy Jacques, my friend took a piece of paper from his pocket, and taking out a pair of scissors, bent over the footprints. Placing the paper over one of them he began to cut. In a short time he had made a perfect pattern which he handed to me, begging me not to lose it.

He then returned to the window and, pointing to the figure of Frederic Larsan, who had not quitted the side of the lake, asked Daddy Jacques whether the detective had, like himself, been working in the "Yellow Room"?

"No," replied Robert Darzac, who, since Rouletabille had handed him the piece of scorched paper, had not uttered a word, "He pretends that he does not need to examine the 'Yellow Room'. He says that the murderer made his escape from it in quite a natural way, and that he will, this evening, explain how he did it."

As he listened to what Monsieur Darzac had to say, Rouletabille turned pale.

"Has Frederic Larsan found out the truth, which I can only guess at?" he murmured. "He is very clever—very clever—and I admire him. But what we have to do today is something more than the work of a policeman, something quite different from the teachings of experience. We have to take hold of our reason by the right end."

The reporter rushed into the open air, agitated by the thought that the great and famous Fred might anticipate him in the solution of the problem of the "Yellow Room".

I managed to reach him on the threshold of the pavilion. "Calm yourself, my dear fellow," I said. "Aren't you satisfied?"

"Yes," he confessed to me, with a deep sigh. "I am quite satisfied. I have discovered many things."

"Moral or material?"

"Several moral,—one material. This, for example."

And rapidly he drew from his waistcoat pocket a piece of paper in which he had placed a light-coloured hair from a woman's head.

VIII

THE EXAMINING MAGISTRATE QUESTIONS MADEMOISELLE STANGERSON

Two minutes later, as Rouletabille was bending over the footprints discovered in the park, under the window of the vestibule, a man, evidently a servant at the chateau, came towards us rapidly and called out to Monsieur Darzac then coming out of the pavilion:

"Monsieur Robert, the magistrate, you know, is questioning Mademoiselle."

Monsieur Darzac uttered a muttered excuse to us and set off running towards the chateau, the man running after him.

"If the corpse can speak," I said, "it would be interesting to be there."

"We must know," said my friend. "Let's go to the chateau." And he drew me with him. But, at the chateau, a gendarme placed in the vestibule denied us admission up the staircase of the first floor. We were obliged to wait down stairs.

This is what passed in the chamber of the victim while we were waiting below.

The family doctor, finding that Mademoiselle Stangerson was much better, but fearing a relapse which would no longer permit of her being questioned, had thought it his duty to inform the examining magistrate of this, who decided to proceed immediately with a brief examination. At this examination, the Registrar, Monsieur Stangerson, and the doctor were present. Later, I obtained the text of the report of the examination, and I give it here, in all its legal dryness:

QUESTION: Are you able, mademoiselle, without too much fatiguing yourself, to give some necessary details of the frightful attack of which you have been the victim?

ANSWER: I feel much better, monsieur, and I will tell you all I know. When I entered my chamber I did not notice anything unusual there.

Q: Excuse me, mademoiselle,—if you will allow me, I will ask you some questions and you will answer them. That will fatigue you less than making a long recital.

A: Do so, monsieur.

Q: What did you do on that day?—I want you to be as minute and precise as possible. I wish to know all you did that day, if it is not asking too much of you.

A: I rose late, at ten o'clock, for my father and I had returned home late on the night previously, having been to dinner at the reception given by the President of the Republic, in honour of the Academy of Science of Philadelphia. When I left my chamber, at half-past ten, my father was already at work in the laboratory. We worked together till midday. We then took half-an-hour's walk in the park, as we were accustomed to do, before breakfasting at the chateau. After breakfast, we took another walk for half an hour, and then returned to the laboratory. There we found my chambermaid, who had come to set my room in order. I went into the "Yellow Room" to give her some slight orders and she directly afterwards left the pavilion, and I resumed my work with my father. At five o'clock, we again went for a walk in the park and afterward had tea.

Q: Before leaving the pavilion at five o'clock, did you go into your chamber?

A: No, monsieur, my father went into it, at my request to bring me my hat.

Q: And he found nothing suspicious there?

A: Evidently no, monsieur.

Q: It is, then, almost certain that the murderer was not yet concealed under the bed. When you went out, was the door of the room locked?

A: No, there was no reason for locking it.

Q: You were absent from the pavilion some length of time, Monsieur Stangerson and you?

A: About an hour.

Q: It was during that hour, no doubt, that the murderer got into the pavilion. But how? Nobody knows. Footmarks have been found in the park, leading away from the window of the vestibule, but none has been found going towards it. Did you notice whether the vestibule window was open when you went out?

A: I don't remember.

MONSIEUR STANGERSON: It was closed.

Q: And when you returned?

MADEMOISELLE STANGERSON: I did not notice.

M: Stangerson. It was still closed. I remember remarking aloud: 'Daddy Jacques must surely have opened it while we were away.'

Q: Strange!—Do you recollect, Monsieur Stangerson, if during your absence, and before going out, he had opened it? You returned to the laboratory at six o'clock and resumed work?

MADEMOISELLE STANGERSON: Yes, monsieur.

Q: And you did not leave the laboratory from that hour up to the moment when you entered your chamber?

M: Stangerson. Neither my daughter nor I, monsieur. We were engaged on work that was pressing, and we lost not a moment,—neglecting everything else on that account.

Q: Did you dine in the laboratory?

A: For that reason.

Q: Are you accustomed to dine in the laboratory?

A: We rarely dine there.

Q: Could the murderer have known that you would dine there that evening?

M: Stangerson. Good Heavens!—I think not. It was only when we returned to the pavilion at six o'clock, that we decided, my daughter and I, to dine there. At that moment I was spoken to by my gamekeeper, who detained me a moment, to ask me to accompany him on an urgent tour of inspection in a part of the woods which I had decided to thin. I put this off until the next day, and begged him, as he was going by the chateau, to tell the steward that we should dine in the laboratory. He left me, to execute the errand and I rejoined my daughter, who was already at work.

Q: At what hour, mademoiselle, did you go to your chamber while your father continued to work there?

A: At midnight.

Q: Did Daddy Jacques enter the "Yellow Room" in the course of the evening?

A: To shut the blinds and light the night-light.

Q: He saw nothing suspicious?

A: He would have told us if he had seen. Daddy Jacques is an honest man and very attached to me.

Q: You affirm, Monsieur Stangerson, that Daddy Jacques remained with you all the time you were in the laboratory?

M: Stangerson. I am sure of it. I have no doubt of that.

Q: When you entered your chamber, mademoiselle, you immediately shut the door and locked and bolted it? That was taking unusual precautions, knowing that your father and your servant were there? Were you in fear of something, then?

A: My father would be returning to the chateau and Daddy Jacques would be going to his bed. And, in fact, I did fear something.

Q: You were so much in fear of something that you borrowed Daddy Jacques's revolver without telling him you had done so?

A: That is true. I did not wish to alarm anybody,—the more, because my fears might have proved to have been foolish.

Q: What was it you feared?

A: I hardly know how to tell you. For several nights, I seemed to hear, both in the park and out of the park, round the pavilion, unusual sounds, sometimes footsteps, at other times the cracking of branches. The night before the attack on me, when I did not get to bed before three o'clock in the morning, on our return from the Elysee, I stood for a moment before my window, and I felt sure I saw shadows.

Q: How many?

A: Two. They moved round the lake,—then the moon became clouded and I lost sight of them. At this time of the season, every year, I have generally returned to my apartment in the chateau for the winter; but this year I said to myself that I would not quit the pavilion before my father had finished the resume of his works on the 'Dissociation of Matter' for the Academy. I did not wish that that important work, which was to have been finished in the course of a few days, should be delayed by a change in our daily habit. You can well understand that I did not wish to speak of my childish fears to my father, nor did I say anything to Daddy Jacques who, I knew, would not have been able to hold his tongue.

Knowing that he had a revolver in his room, I took advantage of his absence and borrowed it, placing it in the drawer of my night-table.

Q: You know of no enemies you have?

A: None.

Q: You understand, mademoiselle, that these precautions are calculated to cause surprise?

M: Stangerson. Evidently, my child, such precautions are very surprising.

A: No;—because I have told you that I had been uneasy for two nights.

M: Stangerson. You ought to have told me of that! This misfortune would have been avoided.

Q: The door of the "Yellow Room" locked, did you go to bed?

A: Yes, and, being very tired, I at once went to sleep.

Q: The night-light was still burning?

A: Yes, but it gave a very feeble light.

Q: Then, mademoiselle, tell us what happened.

A: I do not know whether I had been long asleep, but suddenly I awoke—and uttered a loud cry.

M: Stangerson. Yes—a horrible cry—'Murder!'—It still rings in my ears.

Q: You uttered a loud cry?

A: A man was in my chamber. He sprang at me and tried to strangle me. I was nearly stifled when suddenly I was able to reach the drawer of my night-table and grasp the revolver which I had placed in it. At that moment the man had forced me to the foot of my bed and brandished in over my head a sort of mace. But I had fired. He immediately struck a terrible blow at my head. All that, monsieur, passed more rapidly than I can tell it, and I know nothing more.

Q: Nothing?—Have you no idea as to how the assassin could escape from your chamber?

A: None whatever—I know nothing more. One does not know what is passing around one, when one is unconscious.

Q: Was the man you saw tall or short, little or big?

A: I only saw a shadow which appeared to me formidable.

Q: You cannot give us any indication?

A: I know nothing more, monsieur, than that a man threw himself upon me and that I fired at him. I know nothing more."

Here the interrogation of Mademoiselle Stangerson concluded.

Rouletabille waited patiently for Monsieur Robert Darzac, who soon appeared.

From a room near the chamber of Mademoiselle Stangerson, he had heard the interrogatory and now came to recount it to my friend with great exactitude, aided by an excellent memory. His docility still surprised me. Thanks to hasty pencil-notes, he was able to reproduce, almost textually, the questions and the answers given.

It looked as if Monsieur Darzac were being employeeed as the secretary of my young friend and acted as if he could refuse him nothing; nay, more, as if under a compulsion to do so.

The fact of the closed window struck the reporter as it had struck the magistrate. Rouletabille asked Darzac to repeat once more Mademoiselle Stangerson's account of how she and her father had spent their time on the day of the tragedy, as she had stated it to the magistrate. The circumstance of the dinner in the laboratory seemed to interest him in the highest degree; and he had it repeated to him three times. He also wanted to be sure that the forest-keeper knew that the professor and his daughter were going to dine in the laboratory, and how he had come to know it.

When Monsieur Darzac had finished, I said: "The examination has not advanced the problem much."

"It has put it back," said Monsieur Darzac.

"It has thrown light upon it," said Rouletabille, thoughtfully.

IX

REPORTER AND DETECTIVE

The three of us went back towards the pavilion. At some distance from the building the reporter made us stop and, pointing to a small clump of trees to the right of us, said:

"That's where the murderer came from to get into the pavilion."

As there were other patches of trees of the same sort between the great oaks, I asked why the murderer had chosen that one, rather than any of the others. Rouletabille answered me by pointing to the path which ran quite close to the thicket to the door of the pavilion.

"That path is as you see, topped with gravel," he said; "the man must have passed along it going to the pavilion, since no traces of his steps have been found on the soft ground. The man didn't have wings; he walked; but he walked on the gravel which left no impression of his tread. The gravel has, in fact, been trodden by many other feet, since the path is the most direct way between the pavilion and the chateau. As to the thicket, made of the sort of shrubs that don't flourish in the rough season—laurels and fuchsias—it offered the murderer a sufficient hiding-place until it was time for him to make his way to the pavilion. It was while hiding in that clump of trees that he saw Monsieur and Mademoiselle Stangerson, and then Daddy Jacques, leave the pavilion. Gravel has been spread nearly, very nearly, up to the windows of the pavilion. The footprints of a man, parallel with the wall—marks which we will examine presently, and which I have already seen—prove that he only needed to make one stride to find himself in front of the vestibule window, left open by Daddy Jacques. The man drew himself up by his hands and entered the vestibule."

"After all it is very possible," I said.

"After all what? After all what?" cried Rouletabille.

I begged of him not to be angry; but he was too much irritated to listen to me and declared, ironically, that he admired the prudent doubt with which certain people approached the most simple problems, risking nothing by saying "that is so, or 'that is not so." Their intelligence would have produced about the same result if nature had forgotten to furnish their brain-pan with a little grey matter. As I appeared vexed, my young friend took me by the arm and admitted that he had not meant that for me; he thought more of me than that.

"If I did not reason as I do in regard to this gravel," he went on, "I should have to assume a balloon!—My dear fellow, the science of the aerostation of dirigible balloons is not yet developed enough for me to consider it and suppose that a murderer would drop from the clouds! So don't say a thing is possible, when it could not be otherwise. We know now how the man entered by the window, and we also know the moment at which he entered,—during the five o'clock walk of the professor and his daughter. The fact of the presence of the chambermaid—who had come to clean up the 'Yellow Room'—in the laboratory, when Monsieur Stangerson and his daughter returned from their walk, at half-past one, permits us to affirm that at half-past one the murderer was not in the chamber under the bed, unless he was in collusion with the chambermaid. What do you say, Monsieur Darzac?"

Monsieur Darzac shook his head and said he was sure of the chambermaid's fidelity, and that she was a thoroughly honest and devoted servant.

"Besides," he added, "at five o'clock Monsieur Stangerson went into the room to fetch his daughter's hat."

"There is that also," said Rouletabille.

"That the man entered by the window at the time you say, I admit," I said; "but why did he shut the window? It was an act which would necessarily draw the attention of those who had left it open."

"It may be the window was not shut at once," replied the young reporter. "But if he did shut the window, it was because of the bend in the gravel path, a dozen yards from the pavilion, and on account of the three oaks that are growing at that spot."

"What do you mean by that?" asked Monsieur Darzac, who had followed us and listened with almost breathless attention to all that Rouletabille had said.

"I'll explain all to you later on, Monsieur, when I think the moment to be ripe for doing so; but I don't think I have anything of more importance to say on this affair, if my hypothesis is justified."

"And what is your hypothesis?"

"You will never know if it does not turn out to be the truth. It is of much too grave a nature to speak of it, so long as it continues to be only a hypothesis."

"Have you, at least, some idea as to who the murderer is?"

"No, monsieur, I don't know who the murderer is; but don't be afraid, Monsieur Robert Darzac—I shall know."

I could not but observe that Monsieur Darzac was deeply moved; and I suspected that Rouletabille's confident assertion was not pleasing to him. Why, I asked myself, if he was really afraid that the murderer should be discovered, was he helping the reporter to find him? My young friend seemed to have received the same impression, for he said, bluntly:

"Monsieur Darzac, don't you want me to find out who the murderer was?"

"Oh!—I should like to kill him with my own hand!" cried Mademoiselle Stangerson's fiance, with a vehemence that amazed me.

"I believe you," said Rouletabille gravely; "but you have not answered my question."

We were passing by the thicket, of which the young reporter had spoken to us a minute before. I entered it and pointed out evident traces of a man who had been hidden there. Rouletabille, once more, was right.

"Yes, yes!" he said. "We have to do with a thing of flesh and blood, who uses the same means that we do. It'll all come out on those lines."

Having said this, he asked me for the paper pattern of the footprint which he had given me to take care of, and applied it to a very clear footmark behind the thicket. "Aha!" he said, rising.

I thought he was now going to trace back the track of the murderer's footmarks to the vestibule window; but he led us instead, far to the left, saying that it was useless ferreting in the mud, and that he was sure, now, of the road taken by the murderer.

"He went along the wall to the hedge and dry ditch, over which he jumped. See, just in front of the little path leading to the lake, that was his nearest way to get out."

"How do you know he went to the lake?"—

"Because Frederic Larsan has not quitted the borders of it since this morning. There must be some important marks there."

A few minutes later we reached the lake.

It was a little sheet of marshy water, surrounded by reeds, on which floated some dead water-lily leaves. The great Fred may have seen us approaching, but we probably interested him very little, for he took hardly any notice of us and continued to be stirring with his cane something which we could not see.

"Look!" said Rouletabille, "here again are the footmarks of the escaping man; they skirt the lake here and finally disappear just before this path, which leads to the high road to Epinay. The man continued his flight to Paris."

"What makes you think that?" I asked, "since these footmarks are not continued on the path?"

"What makes me think that?—Why these footprints, which I expected to find!" he cried, pointing to the sharply outlined imprint of a neat boot. "See!"—and he called to Frederic Larsan.

"Monsieur Fred, these neat footprints seem to have been made since the discovery of the crime."

"Yes, young man, yes, they have been carefully made," replied Fred without raising his head. "You see, there are steps that come, and steps that go back."

"And the man had a bicycle!" cried the reporter.

Here, after looking at the marks of the bicycle, which followed, going and coming, the neat footprints, I thought I might intervene.

"The bicycle explains the disappearance of the murderer's big footprints," I said. "The murderer, with his rough boots, mounted a bicycle. His accomplice, the wearer of the neat boots, had come to wait for him on the edge of the lake with the bicycle. It might be supposed that the murderer was working for the other."

"No, no!" replied Rouletabille with a strange smile. "I have expected to find these footmarks from the very beginning. These are not the footmarks of the murderer!"

"Then there were two?"

"No—there was but one, and he had no accomplice."

"Very good!—Very good!" cried Frederic Larsan.

"Look!" continued the young reporter, showing us the ground where it had been disturbed by big and heavy heels; "the man seated himself there, and took off his hobnailed boots, which he had worn only for the purpose of misleading detection, and then no doubt, taking them away with him, he stood up in his own boots, and quietly and slowly regained the high road, holding his bicycle in his hand, for he could not venture to ride it on this rough path. That accounts for the lightness of the impression made by the wheels along it, in spite of the softness of the ground. If there had been a man on the bicycle, the wheels would have sunk deeply into the soil. No, no; there was but one man there, the murderer on foot."

"Bravo!—bravo!" cried Fred again, and coming suddenly towards us and, planting himself in front of Monsieur Robert Darzac, he said to him:

"If we had a bicycle here, we might demonstrate the correctness of the young man's reasoning, Monsieur Robert Darzac. Do you know whether there is one at the chateau?"

"No!" replied Monsieur Darzac. "There is not. I took mine, four days ago, to Paris, the last time I came to the chateau before the crime."

"That's a pity!" replied Fred, very coldly. Then, turning to Rouletabille, he said: "If we go on at this rate, we'll both come to the same conclusion. Have you any idea, as to how the murderer got away from the 'Yellow Room'?"

"Yes," said my young friend; "I have an idea."

"So have I," said Fred, "and it must be the same as yours. There are no two ways of reasoning in this affair. I am waiting for the arrival of my chief before offering any explanation to the examining magistrate."

"Ah! Is the Chief of the Surete coming?"

"Yes, this afternoon. He is going to summon, before the magistrate, in the laboratory, all those who have played any part in this tragedy. It will be very interesting. It is a pity you won't be able to be present."

"I shall be present," said Rouletabille confidently.

"Really—you are an extraordinary fellow—for your age!" replied the detective in a tone not wholly free from irony. "You'd make a wonderful detective—if you had a little more method—if you didn't follow your instincts and that bump on your forehead. As I have already several times observed, Monsieur Rouletabille, you reason too much; you do not allow yourself to be guided by what you have seen. What do you say to the handkerchief full of blood, and the red mark of the hand on the wall? You have seen the stain on the wall, but I have only seen the handkerchief."

"Bah!" cried Rouletabille, "the murderer was wounded in the hand by Mademoiselle Stangerson's revolver!"

"Ah!—a simply instinctive observation! Take care!—You are becoming too strictly logical, Monsieur Rouletabille; logic will upset you if you use it indiscriminately. You are right, when you say that Mademoiselle Stangerson fired her revolver, but you are wrong when you say that she wounded the murderer in the hand."

"I am sure of it," cried Rouletabille.

Fred, imperturbable, interrupted him:

"Defective observation—defective observation!—the examination of the handkerchief, the numberless little round scarlet stains, the impression of drops which I found in the tracks of the footprints, at the moment when they were made on the floor, prove to me that the murderer was not wounded at all. Monsieur Rouletabille, the murderer bled at the nose!"

The great Fred spoke quite seriously. However, I could not refrain from uttering an exclamation.

The reporter looked gravely at Fred, who looked gravely at him. And Fred immediately concluded:

"The man allowed the blood to flow into his hand and handkerchief, and dried his hand on the wall. The fact is highly important," he added, "because there is no need of his being wounded in the hand for him to be the murderer."

Rouletabille seemed to be thinking deeply. After a moment he said:

"There is something—a something, Monsieur Frederic Larsan, much graver than the misuse of logic the disposition of mind in some detectives which makes them, in perfect good faith, twist logic to the necessities of their preconceived ideas. You, already, have your idea about the murderer, Monsieur Fred. Don't deny it; and your theory demands that the murderer should not have been wounded in the hand, otherwise it comes to nothing. And you have searched, and have found something else. It's dangerous, very dangerous, Monsieur Fred, to go from a preconceived idea to find the proofs to fit it. That method may lead you far astray. Beware of judicial error, Monsieur Fred, it will trip you up!"

And laughing a little, in a slightly bantering tone, his hands in his pockets, Rouletabille fixed his cunning eyes on the great Fred.

Frederic Larsan silently contemplated the young reporter who pretended to be as wise as himself. Shrugging his shoulders, he bowed to us and moved quickly away, hitting the stones on his path with his stout cane.

Rouletabille watched his retreat, and then turned toward us, his face joyous and triumphant.

"I shall beat him!" he cried. "I shall beat the great Fred, clever as he is; I shall beat them all!"

And he danced a double shuffle. Suddenly he stopped. My eyes followed his gaze; they were fixed on Monsieur Robert Darzac, who was looking anxiously at the impression left by his feet side by side with the elegant footmarks. There was not a particle of difference between them!

We thought he was about to faint. His eyes, bulging with terror, avoided us, while his right hand, with a spasmodic movement, twitched at the beard that covered his honest, gentle, and now despairing face. At length regaining his self-possession, he bowed to us, and remarking, in a changed voice, that he was obliged to return to the chateau, left us.

"The deuce!" exclaimed Rouletabille.

He, also, appeared to be deeply concerned. From his pocket-book he took a piece of white paper as I had seen him do before, and with his scissors, cut out the shape of the neat bootmarks that were on the ground. Then he fitted the new paper pattern with the one he had previously made—the two were exactly alike. Rising, Rouletabille exclaimed again: "The deuce!" Presently he added: "Yet I believe Monsieur Robert Darzac to be an honest man." He then led me on the road to the Donjon Inn, which we could see on the highway, by the side of a small clump of trees.

X

"We Shall Have to Eat Red Meat—Now"

The Donjon Inn was of no imposing appearance; but I like these buildings with their rafters blackened with age and the smoke of their hearths—these inns of the coaching-days, crumbling erections that will soon exist in the memory only. They belong to the bygone days, they are linked with history. They make us think of the Road, of those days when highwaymen rode.

I saw at once that the Donjon Inn was at least two centuries old—perhaps older. Under its sign-board, over the threshold, a man with a crabbed-looking face was standing, seemingly plunged in unpleasant thought, if the wrinkles on his forehead and the knitting of his brows were any indication.

When we were close to him, he deigned to see us and asked us, in a tone anything but engaging, whether we wanted anything. He was, no doubt, the not very amiable landlord of this charming dwelling-place. As we expressed a hope that he would be good enough to furnish us with a breakfast, he assured us that he had no provisions, regarding us, as he said this, with a look that was unmistakably suspicious.

"You may take us in," Rouletabille said to him, "we are not policemen."

"I'm not afraid of the police—I'm not afraid of anyone!" replied the man.

I had made my friend understand by a sign that we should do better not to insist; but, being determined to enter the inn, he slipped by the man on the doorstep and was in the common room.

"Come on," he said, "it is very comfortable here."

A good fire was blazing in the chimney, and we held our hands to the warmth it sent out; it was a morning in which the approach of winter was unmistakable. The room was a tolerably large one, furnished with two heavy tables, some stools, a counter decorated with rows of bottles of syrup and alcohol. Three windows looked out on to the road. A coloured advertisement lauded the many merits of a new vermouth. On the mantelpiece was arrayed the innkeeper's collection of figured earthenware pots and stone jugs.

"That's a fine fire for roasting a chicken," said Rouletabille. "We have no chicken—not even a wretched rabbit," said the landlord.

"I know," said my friend slowly; "I know—We shall have to eat red meat—now."

I confess I did not in the least understand what Rouletabille meant by what he had said; but the landlord, as soon as he heard the words, uttered an oath, which he at once stifled, and placed himself at our orders as obediently as Monsieur Robert Darzac had done, when he heard Rouletabille's prophetic sentence—"The presbytery has lost nothing of its charm, nor the garden its brightness." Certainly my friend knew how to make people understand him by the use of wholly incomprehensible phrases. I observed as much to him, but he merely smiled. I should have proposed that he give me some explanation; but he put a finger to his lips, which evidently signified that he had not only determined not to speak, but also enjoined silence on my part.

Meantime the man had pushed open a little side door and called to somebody to bring him half a dozen eggs and a piece of beefsteak. The commission was quickly executed by a strongly-built young woman with beautiful blonde hair and large, handsome eyes, who regarded us with curiosity.

The innkeeper said to her roughly:

"Get out!—and if the Green Man comes, don't let me see him."

She disappeared. Rouletabille took the eggs, which had been brought to him in a bowl, and the meat which was on a dish, placed all carefully beside him in the chimney, unhooked a frying-pan and a gridiron, and began to beat up our omelette before proceeding to grill our beefsteak. He then ordered two bottles of cider, and seemed to take as little notice of our host as our host did of him. The landlord let us do our own cooking and set our table near one of the windows.

Suddenly I heard him mutter:

"Ah!—there he is."

His face had changed, expressing fierce hatred. He went and glued himself to one of the windows, watching the road. There was no need for me to draw Rouletabille's attention; he had already left our omelette and had joined the landlord at the window. I went with him.

A man dressed entirely in green velvet, his head covered with a huntsman's cap of the same colour, was advancing leisurely, lighting a pipe as he walked. He carried a fowling-piece slung at his back. His movements displayed an almost aristocratic ease. He wore eye-glasses and appeared to be about five and forty years of age. His hair as well as his moustache were salt grey. He was remarkably handsome. As he passed near the inn, he hesitated, as if asking himself whether or no he should enter it; gave a glance towards us, took a few whiffs at his pipe, and then resumed his walk at the same nonchalant pace.

Rouletabille and I looked at our host. His flashing eyes, his clenched hands, his trembling lips, told us of the tumultuous feelings by which he was being agitated.

"He has done well not to come in here today!" he hissed.

"Who is that man?" asked Rouletabille, returning to his omelette.

"The Green Man," growled the innkeeper. "Don't you know him? Then all the better for you. He is not an acquaintance to make.—Well, he is Monsieur Stangerson's forest-keeper."

"You don't appear to like him very much?" asked the reporter, pouring his omelette into the frying-pan.

"Nobody likes him, monsieur. He's an upstart who must once have had a fortune of his own; and he forgives nobody because, in order to live, he has been compelled to become a servant. A keeper is as much a servant as any other, isn't he? Upon my word, one would say that he is the master of the Glandier, and that all the land and woods belong to him. He'll not let a poor creature eat a morsel of bread on the grass—his grass!"

"Does he often come here?"

"Too often. But I've made him understand that his face doesn't please me, and, for a month past, he hasn't been here. The Donjon Inn has never existed for him!—he hasn't had time!—been too much engaged in paying court to the landlady of the Three Lilies at Saint-Michel. A bad fellow!—There isn't an honest man who can bear him. Why, the concierges of the chateau would turn their eyes away from a picture of him!"

"The concierges of the chateau are honest people, then?"

"Yes, they are, as true as my name's Mathieu, monsieur. I believe them to be honest."

"Yet they've been arrested?"

"What does that prove?—But I don't want to mix myself up in other people's affairs."

"And what do you think of the murder?"

"Of the murder of poor Mademoiselle Stangerson?—A good girl much loved everywhere in the country. That's what I think of it—and many things besides; but that's nobody's business."

"Not even mine?" insisted Rouletabille.

The innkeeper looked at him sideways and said gruffly:

"Not even yours."

The omelette ready, we sat down at table and were silently eating, when the door was pushed open and an old woman, dressed in rags, leaning on a stick, her head doddering, her white hair hanging loosely over her wrinkled forehead, appeared on the threshold.

"Ah!—there you are, Mother Angenoux!—It's long since we saw you last," said our host.

"I have been very ill, very nearly dying," said the old woman. "If ever you should have any scraps for the Bete du Bon Dieu—?"

And she entered, followed by a cat, larger than any I had ever believed could exist. The beast looked at us and gave so hopeless a miau that I shuddered. I had never heard so lugubrious a cry.

As if drawn by the cat's cry a man followed the old woman in. It was the Green Man. He saluted by raising his hand to his cap and seated himself at a table near to ours.

"A glass of cider, Daddy Mathieu," he said.

As the Green Man entered, Daddy Mathieu had started violently; but visibly mastering himself he said:

"I've no more cider; I served the last bottles to these gentlemen."

"Then give me a glass of white wine," said the Green Man, without showing the least surprise.

"I've no more white wine—no more anything," said Daddy Mathieu, surlily.

"How is Madame Mathieu?"

"Quite well, thank you."

So the young Woman with the large, tender eyes, whom we had just seen, was the wife of this repugnant and brutal rustic, whose jealousy seemed to emphasise his physical ugliness.

Slamming the door behind him, the innkeeper left the room. Mother Angenoux was still standing, leaning on her stick, the cat at her feet.

"You've been ill, Mother Angenoux?—Is that why we have not seen you for the last week?" asked the Green Man.

"Yes, Monsieur keeper. I have been able to get up but three times, to go to pray to Sainte-Genevieve, our good patroness, and the rest of the time I have been lying on my bed. There was no one to care for me but the Bete du bon Dieu!"

"Did she not leave you?"

"Neither by day nor by night."

"Are you sure of that?"

"As I am of Paradise."

"Then how was it, Madame Angenoux, that all through the night of the murder nothing but the cry of the Bete du bon Dieu was heard?"

Mother Angenoux planted herself in front of the forest-keeper and struck the floor with her stick.

"I don't know anything about it," she said. "But shall I tell you something? There are no two cats in the world that cry like that. Well, on the night of the murder I also heard the cry of the Bete du bon Dieu outside; and yet she was on my knees, and did not mew once, I swear. I crossed myself when I heard that, as if I had heard the devil."

I looked at the keeper when he put the last question, and I am much mistaken if I did not detect an evil smile on his lips. At that moment, the noise of loud quarrelling reached us. We even thought we heard a dull sound of blows, as if some one was being beaten. The Green Man quickly rose and hurried to the door by the side of the fireplace; but it was opened by the landlord who appeared, and said to the keeper:

"Don't alarm yourself, Monsieur—it is my wife; she has the toothache." And he laughed. "Here, Mother Angenoux, here are some scraps for your cat."

He held out a packet to the old woman, who took it eagerly and went out by the door, closely followed by her cat.

"Then you won't serve me?" asked the Green Man.

Daddy Mathieu's face was placid and no longer retained its expression of hatred.

"I've nothing for you—nothing for you. Take yourself off."

The Green Man quietly refilled his pipe, lit it, bowed to us, and went out. No sooner was he over the threshold than Daddy Mathieu slammed the door after him and, turning towards us, with eyes bloodshot, and frothing at the mouth, he hissed to us, shaking his clenched fist at the door he had just shut on the man he evidently hated:

"I don't know who you are who tell me 'We shall have to eat red meat—now'; but if it will interest you to know it—that man is the murderer!"

With which words Daddy Mathieu immediately left us. Rouletabille returned towards the fireplace and said:

"Now we'll grill our steak. How do you like the cider?—It's a little tart, but I like it."

We saw no more of Daddy Mathieu that day, and absolute silence reigned in the inn when we left it, after placing five francs on the table in payment for our feast.

Rouletabille at once set off on a three mile walk round Professor Stangerson's estate. He halted for some ten minutes at the corner of a narrow road black with soot, near to some charcoal-burners' huts in the forest of Sainte-Geneviève, which touches on the road from Epinay to Corbeil, to tell me that the murderer had certainly passed that way, before entering the grounds and concealing himself in the little clump of trees.

"You don't think, then, that the keeper knows anything of it?" I asked.

"We shall see that, later," he replied. "For the present I'm not interested in what the landlord said about the man. The landlord hates him. I didn't take you to breakfast at the Donjon Inn for the sake of the Green Man."

Then Rouletabille, with great precaution glided, followed by me, towards the little building which, standing near the park gate, served for the home of the concierges, who had been arrested that morning. With the skill of an acrobat, he got into the lodge by an upper window which had been left open, and returned ten minutes later. He said only, "Ah!"—a word which, in his mouth, signified many things.

We were about to take the road leading to the chateau, when a considerable stir at the park gate attracted our attention. A carriage had arrived and some people had come from the chateau to meet it. Rouletabille pointed out to me a gentleman who descended from it.

"That's the Chief of the Surete" he said. "Now we shall see what Frederic Larsan has up his sleeve, and whether he is so much cleverer than anybody else."

The carriage of the Chief of the Surete was followed by three other vehicles containing reporters, who were also desirous of entering the park. But two gendarmes stationed at the gate had evidently received orders to refuse admission to anybody. The Chief of the Surete calmed their impatience by undertaking to furnish to the press, that evening, all the information he could give that would not interfere with the judicial inquiry.

XI

In Which Frederic Larsan Explains How the Murderer Was Able to Get Out of the "Yellow Room"

Among the mass of papers, legal documents, memoirs, and extracts from newspapers, which I have collected, relating to the mystery of the "Yellow Room", there is one very interesting piece; it is a detail of the famous examination which took place that afternoon, in the laboratory of Professor Stangerson, before the Chief of the Surete. This narrative is from the pen of Monsieur Maleine, the Registrar, who, like the examining magistrate, had spent some of his leisure time in the pursuit of literature. The piece was to have made part of a book which, however, has never been published, and which was to have been entitled: "My Examinations." It was given to me by the Registrar himself, some time after the astonishing denouement to this case, and is unique in judicial chronicles.

Here it is. It is not a mere dry transcription of questions and answers, because the Registrar often intersperses his story with his own personal comments.

The Registrar's Narrative

The examining magistrate and I (the writer relates) found ourselves in the "Yellow Room" in the company of the builder who had constructed the pavilion after Professor Stangerson's designs. He had a workman with him. Monsieur de Marquet had had the walls laid entirely bare; that is to say, he had had them stripped of the paper which had decorated them. Blows with a pick, here and there, satisfied us of the absence of any sort of opening. The floor and the ceiling were thoroughly sounded. We found nothing. There was nothing to be found. Monsieur de Marquet appeared to be delighted and never ceased repeating:

"What a case! What a case! We shall never know, you'll see, how the murderer was able to get out of this room!"

Then suddenly, with a radiant face, he called to the officer in charge of the gendarmes.

"Go to the chateau," he said, "and request Monsieur Stangerson and Monsieur Robert Darzac to come to me in the laboratory, also Daddy Jacques; and let your men bring here the two concierges."

Five minutes later all were assembled in the laboratory. The Chief of the Surete, who had arrived at the Glandier, joined us at that moment. I was seated at Monsieur Stangerson's desk ready for work, when Monsieur de Marquet made us the following little speech—as original as it was unexpected:

"With your permission, gentlemen—as examinations lead to nothing—we will, for once, abandon the old system of interrogation. I will not have you brought before me one by one, but we will all remain here as we are,—Monsieur Stangerson, Monsieur Robert Darzac, Daddy Jacques and the two concierges, the Chief of the Surete, the Registrar, and myself. We shall all be on the same footing. The concierges may, for the moment, forget that they have been arrested. We are going to confer together. We are on the spot where the crime was committed. We have nothing else to discuss but the crime. So let us discuss it freely—intelligently or otherwise, so long as we speak just what is in our minds. There need be no formality or method since this won't help us in any way."

Then, passing before me, he said in a low voice:

"What do you think of that, eh? What a scene! Could you have thought of that? I'll make a little piece out of it for the Vaudeville." And he rubbed his hands with glee.

I turned my eyes on Monsieur Stangerson. The hope he had received from the doctor's latest reports, which stated that Mademoiselle Stangerson might recover from her wounds, had not been able to efface from his noble features the marks of the great sorrow that was upon him. He had believed his daughter to be dead, and he was still broken by that belief. His clear, soft, blue eyes expressed infinite sorrow. I had had occasion, many times, to see Monsieur Stangerson at public ceremonies, and from the first had been struck by his countenance, which seemed as pure as that of a child—the dreamy gaze with the sublime and mystical expression of the inventor and thinker.

On those occasions his daughter was always to be seen either following him or by his side; for they never quitted each other, it was said, and had shared the same labours for many years. The young lady, who was then five and thirty, though she looked no more than thirty, had devoted herself entirely to science. She still won admiration for her imperial beauty which had remained intact, without a wrinkle, withstanding time and love. Who would have dreamed that I should one day be seated by her pillow with my papers, and that I should see her, on the point of death, painfully recounting to us the most monstrous and most mysterious crime I have heard of in my career? Who would have thought that I should be, that afternoon, listening to the despairing father vainly trying to explain how his daughter's assailant had been able to escape from him? Why bury ourselves with our work in obscure retreats in the depths of woods, if it may not protect us against those dangerous threats to life which meet us in the busy cities?

"Now, Monsieur Stangerson," said Monsieur de Marquet, with somewhat of an important air, "place yourself exactly where you were when Mademoiselle Stangerson left you to go to her chamber."

Monsieur Stangerson rose and, standing at a certain distance from the door of the "Yellow Room", said, in an even voice and without the least trace of emphasis—a voice which I can only describe as a dead voice:

"I was here. About eleven o'clock, after I had made a brief chemical experiment at the furnaces of the laboratory, needing all the space behind me, I had my desk moved here by Daddy Jacques, who spent the evening in cleaning some of my apparatus. My daughter had been working at the same desk with me. When it was her time to leave she rose, kissed me, and bade Daddy Jacques goodnight. She had to pass behind my desk and the door to enter her chamber, and she could do this only with some difficulty. That is to say, I was very near the place where the crime occurred later."

"And the desk?" I asked, obeying, in thus mixing myself in the conversation, the express orders of my chief, "as soon as you heard the cry of 'murder' followed by the revolver shots, what became of the desk?"

Daddy Jacques answered.

"We pushed it back against the wall, here—close to where it is at the present moment—so as to be able to get at the door at once."

I followed up my reasoning, to which, however, I attached but little importance, regarding it as only a weak hypothesis, with another question.

"Might not a man in the room, the desk being so near to the door, by stooping and slipping under the desk, have left it unobserved?"

"You are forgetting," interrupted Monsieur Stangerson wearily, "that my daughter had locked and bolted her door, that the door had remained fastened, that we vainly tried to force it open when we heard the noise, and that we were at the door while the struggle between the murderer and my poor child was going on—immediately after we heard her stifled cries as she was being held by the fingers that have left their red mark upon her throat. Rapid as the attack was, we were no less rapid in our endeavors to get into the room where the tragedy was taking place."

I rose from my seat and once more examined the door with the greatest care. Then I returned to my place with a despairing gesture.

"If the lower panel of the door," I said, "could be removed without the whole door being necessarily opened, the problem would be solved. But, unfortunately, that last hypothesis is untenable after an examination of the door—it's of oak, solid and massive. You can see that quite plainly, in spite of the injury done in the attempt to burst it open."

"Ah!" cried Daddy Jacques, "it is an old and solid door that was brought from the chateau—they don't make such doors now. We had to use this bar of iron to get it open, all four of us—for the concierge, brave woman she is, helped us. It pains me to find them both in prison now."

Daddy Jacques had no sooner uttered these words of pity and protestation than tears and lamentations broke out from the concierges. I never saw two accused people crying more bitterly. I was extremely disgusted. Even if they were innocent, I could not understand how they could behave like that in the face of misfortune. A dignified bearing at such times is better than tears and groans, which, most often, are feigned.

"Now then, enough of that sniveling," cried Monsieur de Marquet; "and, in your interest, tell us what you were doing under the windows of the pavilion at the time your mistress was being attacked; for you were close to the pavilion when Daddy Jacques met you."

"We were coming to help!" they whined.

"If we could only lay hands on the murderer, he'd never taste bread again!" the woman gurgled between her sobs.

As before we were unable to get two connecting thoughts out of them. They persisted in their denials and swore, by heaven and all the saints, that they were in bed when they heard the sound of the revolver shot.

"It was not one, but two shots that were fired!—You see, you are lying. If you had heard one, you would have heard the other."

"Mon Dieu! Monsieur—it was the second shot we heard. We were asleep when the first shot was fired."

"Two shots were fired," said Daddy Jacques. "I am certain that all the cartridges were in my revolver. We found afterward that two had been exploded, and we heard two shots behind the door. Was not that so, Monsieur Stangerson?"

"Yes," replied the Professor, "there were two shots, one dull, and the other sharp and ringing."

"Why do you persist in lying?" cried Monsieur de Marquet, turning to the concierges. "Do you think the police are the fools you are? Everything points to the fact that you were out of doors and near the pavilion at the time of the tragedy. What were you doing there? So far as I am concerned," he said, turning to Monsieur Stangerson, "I can only explain the escape of the murderer on the assumption of help from these two accomplices. As soon as the door was forced open, and while you, Monsieur Stangerson, were occupied with your unfortunate child, the concierge and his wife facilitated the flight of the murderer, who, screening himself behind them, reached the window in the vestibule, and sprang out of it into the park. The concierge closed the window after him and fastened the blinds, which certainly could not have closed and fastened of themselves. That is the conclusion I have arrived at. If anyone here has any other idea, let him state it."

Monsieur Stangerson intervened:

"What you say was impossible. I do not believe either in the guilt or in the connivance of my concierges, though I cannot understand what they were doing in the park at that late hour of the night. I say it was impossible, because Madame Bernier held the lamp and did not move from the threshold of the room; because I, as soon as the door was forced open, threw myself on my knees beside my daughter, and no one could have left or entered the room by the door, without passing over her body and forcing his way by me! Daddy Jacques and the concierge had but to cast a glance round the chamber and under the bed, as I had done on entering, to see that there was nobody in it but my daughter lying on the floor."

"What do you think, Monsieur Darzac?" asked the magistrate.

Monsieur Darzac replied that he had no opinion to express. Monsieur Dax, the Chief of the Surete who, so far, had been listening and examining the room, at length deigned to open his lips:

"While search is being made for the criminal, we had better try to find out the motive for the crime; that will advance us a little," he said. Turning towards Monsieur Stangerson, he continued, in the even, intelligent tone indicative of a strong character, "I understand that Mademoiselle was shortly to have been married?"

The professor looked sadly at Monsieur Robert Darzac.

"To my friend here, whom I should have been happy to call my son— to Monsieur Robert Darzac."

"Mademoiselle Stangerson is much better and is rapidly recovering from her wounds. The marriage is simply delayed, is it not, Monsieur?" insisted the Chief of the Surete.

"I hope so.

"What! Is there any doubt about that?"

Monsieur Stangerson did not answer. Monsieur Robert Darzac seemed agitated. I saw that his hand trembled as it fingered his watchchain. Monsieur Dax coughed, as did Monsieur de Marquet. Both were evidently embarrassed.

"You understand, Monsieur Stangerson," he said, "that in an affair so perplexing as this, we cannot neglect anything; we must know all, even the smallest and seemingly most futile thing concerning the victim— information apparently the most insignificant. Why do you doubt that this marriage will take place? You expressed a hope; but the hope implies a doubt. Why do you doubt?"

Monsieur Stangerson made a visible effort to recover himself.

"Yes, Monsieur," he said at length, "you are right. It will be best that you should know something which, if I concealed it, might appear to be of importance; Monsieur Darzac agrees with me in this."

Monsieur Darzac, whose pallor at that moment seemed to me to be altogether abnormal, made a sign of assent. I gathered he was unable to speak.

"I want you to know then," continued Monsieur Stangerson, "that my daughter has sworn never to leave me, and adheres firmly to her oath, in spite of all my prayers and all that I have argued to induce her to marry. We have known Monsieur Robert Darzac many years. He loves my child; and I believed that she loved him; because she only recently consented to this marriage which I desire with all my heart. I am an old man, Monsieur, and it was a happy hour to me when I knew that, after I had gone, she would have at her side, one who loved her and who would help her in continuing our common labours. I love and esteem Monsieur Darzac both for his greatness of heart and for his devotion to science. But, two days before the tragedy, for I know not what reason, my daughter declared to me that she would never marry Monsieur Darzac."

A dead silence followed Monsieur Stangerson's words. It was a moment fraught with suspense.

"Did Mademoiselle give you any explanation,—did she tell you what her motive was?" asked Monsieur Dax.

"She told me she was too old to marry—that she had waited too long. She said she had given much thought to the matter and while she had a great esteem, even affection, for Monsieur Darzac, she felt it would be better if things remained as they were. She would be happy, she said, to see the relations between ourselves and Monsieur Darzac become closer, but only on the understanding that there would be no more talk of marriage."

"That is very strange!" muttered Monsieur Dax.

"Strange!" repeated Monsieur de Marquet.

"You'll certainly not find the motive there, Monsieur Dax," Monsieur Stangerson said with a cold smile.

"In any case, the motive was not theft!" said the Chief impatiently.

"Oh! we are quite convinced of that!" cried the examining magistrate.

At that moment the door of the laboratory opened and the officer in charge of the gendarmes entered and handed a card to the examining magistrate. Monsieur de Marquet read it and uttered a half angry exclamation:

"This is really too much!" he cried.

"What is it?" asked the Chief.

"It's the card of a young reporter engaged on the 'Epoque,' a Monsieur Joseph Rouletabille. It has these words written on it: 'One of the motives of the crime was robbery.'"

The Chief smiled.

"Ah,—young Rouletabille—I've heard of him he is considered rather clever. Let him come in."

Monsieur Joseph Rouletabille was allowed to enter. I had made his acquaintance in the train that morning on the way to Epinay-sur-Orge. He had introduced himself almost against my wish into our compartment. I had better say at once that his manners, and the arrogance with which he assumed to know what was incomprehensible even to us, impressed him unfavourably on my mind. I do not like journalists. They are a class of writers to be avoided as the pest. They think that everything is permissible and they respect nothing. Grant them the least favour, allow them even to approach you, and you never can tell what annoyance they may give you. This one appears to be scarcely twenty years old, and the effrontery with which he dared to question us and discuss the matter with us made him particularly obnoxious to me. Besides, he had a way of expressing himself that left us guessing as to whether he was mocking us or not. I know quite well that the 'Epoque' is an influential paper with which it is well to be on good terms, but the paper ought not to allow itself to be represented by sneaking reporters.

Monsieur Joseph Rouletabille entered the laboratory, bowed to us, and waited for Monsieur de Marquet to ask him to explain his presence.

"You pretend, Monsieur, that you know the motive for the crime, and that that motive—in the face of all the evidence that has been forthcoming—was robbery?"

"No, Monsieur, I do not pretend that. I do not say that robbery was the motive for the crime, and I don't believe it was."

"Then, what is the meaning of this card?"

"It means that robbery was one of the motives for the crime."

"What leads you to think that?"

"If you will be good enough to accompany me, I will show you."

The young man asked us to follow him into the vestibule, and we did. He led us towards the lavatory and begged Monsieur de Marquet to kneel beside him. This lavatory is lit by the glass door, and, when the door was open, the light which penetrated was sufficient to light it perfectly. Monsieur de Marquet and Monsieur Joseph Rouletabille knelt down on the threshold, and the young man pointed to a spot on the pavement.

"The stones of the lavatory have not been washed by Daddy Jacques for some time," he said; "that can be seen by the layer of dust that covers them. Now, notice here, the marks of two large footprints and the black ash they left where they have been. That ash is nothing else than the charcoal dust that covers the path along which you must pass through the forest, in order to get directly from Epinay to the Glandier. You know there is a little village of charcoal-burners at that place, who make large quantities of charcoal. What the murderer did was to come here at midday, when there was nobody at the pavilion, and attempt his robbery."

"But what robbery?—Where do you see any signs of robbery? What proves to you that a robbery has been committed?" we all cried at once.

"What put me on the trace of it," continued the journalist. . .

"Was this?" interrupted Monsieur de Marquet, still on his knees.

"Evidently," said Rouletabille.

And Monsieur de Marquet explained that there were on the dust of the pavement marks of two footsteps, as well as the impression, freshly-made, of a heavy rectangular parcel, the marks of the cord with which it had been fastened being easily distinguished.

"You have been here, then, Monsieur Rouletabille? I thought I had given orders to Daddy Jacques, who was left in charge of the pavilion, not to allow anybody to enter."

"Don't scold Daddy Jacques, I came here with Monsieur Robert Darzac."

"Ah,—Indeed!" exclaimed Monsieur de Marquet, disagreeably, casting a side-glance at Monsieur Darzac, who remained perfectly silent.

"When I saw the mark of the parcel by the side of the footprints, I had no doubt as to the robbery," replied Monsieur Rouletabille. "The thief had not brought a parcel with him; he had made one here—a parcel with the stolen objects, no doubt; and he put it in this corner intending to take it away when the moment came for him to make his escape. He had also placed his heavy boots beside the parcel,—for, see— there are no marks of steps leading to the marks left by the boots, which were placed side by side. That accounts for the fact that the murderer left no trace of his steps when he fled from the 'Yellow Room', nor any in the laboratory, nor in the vestibule. After entering the 'Yellow Room' in his boots, he took them off, finding them troublesome, or because he wished to make as little noise as possible. The marks made by him in going through the vestibule and the laboratory were subsequently washed out by Daddy Jacques. Having, for some reason or other, taken off his boots, the murderer carried them in his hand and placed them by the side of the parcel he had made,—by that time the robbery had been accomplished. The man then returned to the 'Yellow Room' and slipped under the bed, where the mark of his body is perfectly visible on the floor and even on the mat, which has been slightly moved from its place and creased. Fragments of straw also, recently torn, bear witness to the murderer's movements under the bed."

"Yes, yes,—we know all about that," said Monsieur de Marquet.

"The robber had another motive for returning to hide under the bed," continued the astonishing boy-journalist. "You might think that he was trying to hide himself quickly on seeing, through the vestibule window, Monsieur and Mademoiselle Stangerson about to enter the pavilion. It would have been much easier for him to have climbed up to the attic and hidden there, waiting for an opportunity to get away, if his purpose had been only flight.—No! No!—he had to be in the 'Yellow Room'."

Here the Chief intervened.

"That's not at all bad, young man. I compliment you. If we do not know yet how the murderer succeeded in getting away, we can at any rate see how he came in and committed the robbery. But what did he steal?"

"Something very valuable," replied the young reporter.

At that moment we heard a cry from the laboratory. We rushed in and found Monsieur Stangerson, his eyes haggard, his limbs trembling, pointing to a sort of bookcase which he had opened, and which, we saw, was empty. At the same instant he sank into the large armchair that was placed before the desk and groaned, the tears rolling down his cheeks, "I have been robbed again! For God's sake, do not say a word of this to my daughter. She would be more pained than I am." He heaved a deep sigh and added, in a tone I shall never forget: "After all, what does it matter,—so long as she lives!"

"She will live!" said Monsieur Darzac, in a voice strangely touching.

"And we will find the stolen articles," said Monsieur Dax. "But what was in the cabinet?"

"Twenty years of my life," replied the illustrious professor sadly, "or rather of our lives—the lives of myself and my daughter! Yes, our most precious documents, the records of our secret experiments and our labours of twenty years were in that cabinet. It is an irreparable loss to us and, I venture to say, to science. All the processes by which I had been able to arrive at the precious proof of the destructibility of matter were there—all. The man who came wished to take all from me,—my daughter and my work—my heart and my soul."

And the great scientist wept like a child.

We stood around him in silence, deeply affected by his great distress. Monsieur Darzac pressed closely to his side, and tried in vain to restrain his tears—a sight which, for the moment, almost made me like him, in spite of an instinctive repulsion which his strange demeanour and his inexplicable anxiety had inspired me.

Monsieur Rouletabille alone,—as if his precious time and mission on earth did not permit him to dwell in the contemplation on human suffering—had, very calmly, stepped up to the empty cabinet and, pointing at it, broke the almost solemn silence. He entered into explanations, for which there was no need, as to why he had been led to believe that a robbery had been committed, which included the simultaneous discovery he had made in the lavatory, and the empty precious cabinet in the laboratory. The first thing that had struck him, he said, was the unusual form of that piece of furniture. It was very strongly built of fire-proof iron, clearly showing that it was intended for the keeping of most valuable objects. Then he noticed that the key had been left in the lock. "One does not ordinarily have a safe and leave it open!" he had said to himself. This little key, with its brass head and complicated wards, had strongly attracted him,—its presence had suggested robbery.

Monsieur de Marquet appeared to be greatly perplexed, as if he did not know whether he ought to be glad of the new direction given to the inquiry by the young reporter, or sorry that it had not been done by himself. In our profession and for the general welfare, we have to put up with such mortifications and bury selfish feelings. That was why Monsieur de Marquet controlled himself and joined his compliments with those of Monsieur Dax. As for Monsieur Rouletabille, he simply shrugged his shoulders and said: "There's nothing at all in that!" I should have liked to box his ears, especially when he added: "You will do well, Monsieur, to ask Monsieur Stangerson who usually kept that key?"

"My daughter," replied Monsieur Stangerson, "she was never without it.

"Ah! then that changes the aspect of things which no longer corresponds with Monsieur Rouletabille's ideas!" cried Monsieur de Marquet. "If that key never left Mademoiselle Stangerson, the murderer must have waited for her in her room for the purpose of stealing it; and the robbery could not have been committed until after the attack had been made on her. But after the attack four persons were in the laboratory! I can't make it out!"

"The robbery," said the reporter, "could only have been committed before the attack upon Mademoiselle Stangerson in her room. When the murderer entered the pavilion he already possessed the brass-headed key."

"That is impossible," said Monsieur Stangerson in a low voice.

"It is quite possible, Monsieur, as this proves."

And the young rascal drew a copy of the "Epoque" from his pocket, dated the 21st of October (I recall the fact that the crime was committed on the night between the 24th and 25th), and showing us an advertisement, he read:

"'Yesterday a black satin reticule was lost in the Grands Magasins de la Louvre. It contained, amongst other things, a small key with a brass head. A handsome reward will be given to the person who has found it. This person must write, poste restante, bureau 40, to this address: M. A. T. H. S. N.' Do not these letters suggest Mademoiselle Stangerson?" continued the reporter. "The 'key with a brass head'—is not this the key? I always read advertisements. In my business, as in yours, Monsieur, one should always read the personals.' They are often the keys to intrigues, that are not always brass-headed, but which are none the less interesting. This advertisement interested me specially; the woman of the key surrounded it with a kind of mystery. Evidently she valued the key, since she promised a big reward for its restoration! And I thought on these six letters: M. A. T. H. S. N. The first four at once pointed to a Christian name; evidently I said Math is Mathilde. But I could make nothing of the two last letters. So I threw the journal aside and occupied myself with other matters. Four days later, when the evening paper appeared with enormous head-lines announcing the murder of Mademoiselle Stangerson, the letters in the advertisement mechanically recurred to me. I had forgotten the two last letters, S. N. When I saw them again I could not help exclaiming, 'Stangerson!' I jumped into a cab and rushed into the bureau No. 40, asking: 'Have you a letter addressed to M. A. T. H. S. N.?' The clerk replied that he had not. I insisted, begged and entreated him to search. He wanted to know if I were playing a joke on him, and then told me that he had had a letter with the initials M. A. T. H. S. N, but he had given it up three days ago, to a lady who came for it. 'You come today to claim the letter, and the day before yesterday another gentleman claimed it! I've had enough of this,' he concluded angrily. I tried to question him as to the two persons who had already claimed the letter; but whether he wished to entrench himself behind professional secrecy,—he may have thought that he had already said too much,—or whether he was disgusted at the joke that had been played on him—he would not answer any of my questions."

Rouletabille paused. We all remained silent. Each drew his own conclusions from the strange story of the poste restante letter. It seemed, indeed, that we now had a thread by means of which we should be able to follow up this extraordinary mystery.

"Then it is almost certain," said Monsieur Stangerson, "that my daughter did lose the key, and that she did not tell me of it, wishing to spare any anxiety, and that she begged whoever had found it to write to the poste restante. She evidently feared that, by giving our address, inquiries would have resulted that would have apprised me of the loss of the key. It was quite logical, quite natural for her to have taken that course—for I have been robbed once before."

"Where was that, and when?" asked the Chief of the Surete.

"Oh! many years ago, in America, in Philadelphia. There were stolen from my laboratory the drawings of two inventions that might have made the fortune of a man. Not only have I never learnt who the thief was, but I have never heard even a word of the object of the robbery, doubtless because, in order to defeat the plans of the person who had robbed me, I myself brought these two inventions before the public, and so rendered the robbery of no avail. From that time on I have been very careful to shut myself in when I am at work. The bars to these windows, the lonely situation of this pavilion, this cabinet, which I had specially constructed, this special lock, this unique key, all are precautions against fears inspired by a sad experience."

"Most interesting!" remarked Monsieur Dax.

Monsieur Rouletabille asked about the reticule. Neither Monsieur Stangerson nor Daddy Jacques had seen it for several days, but a few hours later we learned from Mademoiselle Stangerson herself that the reticule had either been stolen from her, or she had lost it. She further corroborated all that had passed just as her father had stated. She had gone to the poste restante and, on the 23rd of October, had received a letter which, she affirmed, contained nothing but a vulgar pleasantry, which she had immediately burned.

To return to our examination, or rather to our conversation. I must state that the Chief of the Surete having inquired of Monsieur Stangerson under what conditions his daughter had gone to Paris on the 20th of October, we learned that Monsieur Robert Darzac had accompanied her, and Darzac had not been again seen at the chateau from that time to the day after the crime had been committed. The fact that Monsieur Darzac was with her in the Grands Magasins de la Louvre when the reticule disappeared could not pass unnoticed, and, it must be said, strongly awakened our interest.

This conversation between magistrates, accused, victim, witnesses and journalist, was coming to a close when quite a theatrical sensation—an incident of a kind displeasing to Monsieur de Marquet—was produced. The officer of the gendarmes came to announce that Frederic Larsan requested to be admitted,—a request that was at once complied with. He held in his hand a heavy pair of muddy boots, which he threw on the pavement of the laboratory.

"Here," he said, "are the boots worn by the murderer. Do you recognise them, Daddy Jacques?"

Daddy Jacques bent over them and, stupefied, recognised a pair of old boots which he had, some time back, thrown into a corner of his attic. He was so taken aback that he could not hide his agitation.

Then pointing to the handkerchief in the old man's hand, Frederic Larsan said:

"That's a handkerchief astonishingly like the one found in the "Yellow Room."

"I know," said Daddy Jacques, trembling, "they are almost alike."

"And then," continued Frederic Larsan, "the old Basque cap also found in the 'Yellow Room' might at one time have been worn by Daddy Jacques himself. All this, gentlemen, proves, I think, that the murderer wished to disguise his real personality. He did it in a very clumsy way—or, at least, so it appears to us. Don't be alarmed, Daddy Jacques; we are quite sure that you were not the murderer; you never left the side of Monsieur Stangerson. But if Monsieur Stangerson had not been working that night and had gone back to the chateau after parting with his daughter, and Daddy Jacques had gone to sleep in his attic, no one would have doubted that he was the murderer. He owes his safety, therefore, to the tragedy having been enacted too soon,—the murderer, no doubt, from the silence in the laboratory, imagined that it was empty, and that the moment for action had come. The man who had been able to introduce himself here so mysteriously and to leave so many evidences against Daddy Jacques, was, there can be no doubt, familiar with the house. At what hour exactly he entered, whether in the afternoon or in the evening, I cannot say. One familiar with the proceedings and persons of this pavilion could choose his own time for entering the 'Yellow Room'."

"He could not have entered it if anybody had been in the laboratory," said Monsieur de Marquet.

"How do we know that?" replied Larsan. "There was the dinner in the laboratory, the coming and going of the servants in attendance. There was a chemical experiment being carried on between ten and eleven o'clock, with Monsieur Stangerson, his daughter, and Daddy Jacques engaged at the furnace in a corner of the high chimney. Who can say that the murderer—an intimate!—a friend!—did not take advantage of that moment to slip into the 'Yellow Room', after having taken off his boots in the lavatory?"

"It is very improbable," said Monsieur Stangerson.

"Doubtless—but it is not impossible. I assert nothing. As to the escape from the pavilion—that's another thing, the most natural thing in the world."

For a moment Frederic Larsan paused,—a moment that appeared to us a very long time. The eagerness with which we awaited what he was going to tell us may be imagined.

"I have not been in the 'Yellow Room'," he continued, "but I take it for granted that you have satisfied yourselves that he could have left the room only by way of the door; it is by the door, then, that the murderer made his way out. At what time? At the moment when it was most easy for him to do so; at the moment when it became most explainable—so completely explainable that there can be no other explanation. Let us go over the moments which followed after the crime had been committed. There was the first moment, when Monsieur Stangerson and Daddy Jacques were close to the door, ready to bar the way. There was the second moment, during which Daddy Jacques was absent and Monsieur Stangerson was left alone before the door. There was a third moment, when Monsieur Stangerson was joined by the concierge. There was a fourth moment, during which Monsieur Stangerson, the concierge and his wife and Daddy Jacques were before the door. There was a fifth moment, during which the door was burst open and the 'Yellow Room' entered. The moment at which the flight is explainable is the very moment when there was the least number of persons before the door. There was one moment when there was but one person,—Monsieur Stangerson. Unless a complicity of silence on the part of Daddy Jacques is admitted—in which I do not believe—the door was opened in the presence of Monsieur Stangerson alone and the man escaped.

"Here we must admit that Monsieur Stangerson had powerful reasons for not arresting, or not causing the arrest of the murderer, since he allowed him to reach the window in the vestibule and closed it after him!—That done, Mademoiselle Stangerson, though horribly wounded, had still strength enough, and no doubt in obedience to the entreaties of her father, to refasten the door of her chamber, with both the bolt and the lock, before sinking on the floor. We do not know who committed the crime; we do not know of what wretch Monsieur and Mademoiselle Stangerson are the victims, but there is no doubt that they both know! The secret must be a terrible one, for the father had not hesitated to leave his daughter to die behind a door which she had shut upon herself,—terrible for him to have allowed the assassin to escape. For there is no other way in the world to explain the murderer's flight from the 'Yellow Room'!"

The silence which followed this dramatic and lucid explanation was appalling. We all of us felt grieved for the illustrious professor, driven into a corner by the pitiless logic of Frederic Larsan, forced to confess the whole truth of his martyrdom or to keep silent, and thus make a yet more terrible admission. The man himself, a veritable statue of sorrow, raised his hand with a gesture so solemn that we bowed our heads to it as before something sacred. He then pronounced these words, in a voice so loud that it seemed to exhaust him:

"I swear by the head of my suffering child that I never for an instant left the door of her chamber after hearing her cries for help; that that door was not opened while I was alone in the laboratory; and that, finally, when we entered the 'Yellow Room', my three domestics and I, the murderer was no longer there! I swear I do not know the murderer!"

Must I say it,—in spite of the solemnity of Monsieur Stangerson's words, we did not believe in his denial. Frederic Larsan had shown us the truth and it was not so easily given up.

Monsieur de Marquet announced that the conversation was at an end, and as we were about to leave the laboratory, Joseph Rouletabille approached Monsieur Stangerson, took him by the hand with the greatest respect, and I heard him say:

"I believe you, Monsieur."

I here close the citation which I have thought it my duty to make from Monsieur Maleine's narrative. I need not tell the reader that all that passed in the laboratory was immediately and faithfully reported to me by Rouletabille.

XII

Frederic Larsan's Cane

It was not till six o'clock that I left the chateau, taking with me the article hastily written by my friend in the little sitting-room which Monsieur Robert Darzac had placed at our disposal. The reporter was to sleep at the chateau, taking advantage of the to me inexplicable hospitality offered him by Monsieur Robert Darzac, to whom Monsieur Stangerson, in that sad time, left the care of all his domestic affairs. Nevertheless he insisted on accompanying me to the station at Epinay. In crossing the park, he said to me:

"Frederic is really very clever and has not belied his reputation. Do you know how he came to find Daddy Jacques's boots?—Near the spot where we noticed the traces of the neat boots and the disappearance of the rough ones, there was a square hole, freshly made in the moist ground, where a stone had evidently been removed. Larsan searched for that stone without finding it, and at once imagined that it had been used by the murderer with which to sink the boots in the lake. Fred's calculation was an excellent one, as the success of his search proves. That escaped me; but my mind was turned in another direction by the large number of false indications of his track which the murderer left, and by the measure of the black foot-marks corresponding with that of Daddy Jacques's boots, which I had established without his suspecting it, on the floor of the 'Yellow Room'. All which was a proof, in my eyes, that the murderer had sought to turn suspicion on to the old servant. Up to that point, Larsan and I are in accord; but no further. It is going to be a terrible matter; for I tell you he is working on wrong lines, and I—I, must fight him with nothing!"

I was surprised at the profoundly grave accent with which my young friend pronounced the last words.

He repeated:

"Yes—terrible!—terrible! For it is fighting with nothing, when you have only an idea to fight with."

At that moment we passed by the back of the chateau. Night had come. A window on the first floor was partly open. A feeble light came from it as well as some sounds which drew our attention. We approached until we had reached the side of a door that was situated just under the window. Rouletabille, in a low tone, made me understand, that this was the window of Mademoiselle Stangerson's chamber. The sounds which had attracted our attention ceased, then were renewed for a moment, and then we heard stifled sobs. We were only able to catch these words, which reached us distinctly: "My poor Robert!"—Rouletabille whispered in my ear:

"If we only knew what was being said in that chamber, my inquiry would soon be finished."

He looked about him. The darkness of the evening enveloped us; we could not see much beyond the narrow path bordered by trees, which ran behind the chateau. The sobs had ceased.

"If we can't hear we may at least try to see," said Rouletabille.

And, making a sign to me to deaden the sound of my steps, he led me across the path to the trunk of a tall beech tree, the white bole of which was visible in the darkness. This tree grew exactly in front of the window in which we were so much interested, its lower branches being on a level with the first floor of the chateau. From the height of those branches one might certainly see what was passing in Mademoiselle Stangerson's chamber. Evidently that was what Rouletabille thought, for, enjoining me to remain hidden, he clasped the trunk with his vigorous arms and climbed up. I soon lost sight of him amid the branches, and then followed a deep silence. In front of me, the open window remained lighted, and I saw no shadow move across it. I listened, and presently from above me these words reached my ears:

"After you!"

"After you, pray!"

Somebody was overhead, speaking,—exchanging courtesies. What was my astonishment to see on the slippery column of the tree two human forms appear and quietly slip down to the ground. Rouletabille had mounted alone, and had returned with another.

"Good evening, Monsieur Sainclair!"

It was Frederic Larsan. The detective had already occupied the post of observation when my young friend had thought to reach it alone. Neither noticed my astonishment. I explained that to myself by the fact that they must have been witnesses of some tender and despairing scene between Mademoiselle Stangerson, lying in her bed, and Monsieur Darzac on his knees by her pillow. I guessed that each had drawn different conclusions from what they had seen. It was easy to see that the scene had strongly impressed Rouletabille in favour of Monsieur Robert Darzac; while, to Larsan, it showed nothing but consummate hypocrisy, acted with finished art by Mademoiselle Stangerson's fiance.

As we reached the park gate, Larsan stopped us.

"My cane!" he cried. "I left it near the tree."

He left us, saying he would rejoin us presently.

"Have you noticed Frederic Larsan's cane?" asked the young reporter, as soon as we were alone. "It is quite a new one, which I have never seen him use before. He seems to take great care of it—it never leaves him. One would think he was afraid it might fall into the hands of strangers. I never saw it before today. Where did he find it? It isn't natural that a man who had never before used a walking-stick should, the day after the Glandier crime, never move a step without one. On the day of our arrival at the chateau, as soon as he saw us, he put his watch in his pocket and picked up his cane from the ground—a proceeding to which I was perhaps wrong not to attach some importance."

We were now out of the park. Rouletabille had dropped into silence. His thoughts were certainly still occupied with Frederic Larsan's new cane. I had proof of that when, as we came near to Epinay, he said:

"Frederic Larsan arrived at the Glandier before me; he began his inquiry before me; he has had time to find out things about which I know nothing. Where did he find that cane?" Then he added: "It is probable that his suspicion—more than that, his reasoning—has led him to lay his hand on something tangible. Has this cane anything to do with it? Where the deuce could he have found it?"

As I had to wait twenty minutes for the train at Epinay, we entered a wine shop. Almost immediately the door opened and Frederic Larsan made his appearance, brandishing his famous cane.

"I found it!" he said laughingly.

The three of us seated ourselves at a table. Rouletabille never took his eyes off the cane; he was so absorbed that he did not notice a sign Larsan made to a railway employeee, a young man with a chin decorated by a tiny blond and ill-kept beard. On the sign he rose, paid for his drink, bowed, and went out. I should not myself have attached any importance to the circumstance, if it had not been recalled to my mind, some months later, by the reappearance of the man with the beard at one of the most tragic moments of this case. I then learned that the youth was one of Larsan's assistants and had been charged by him to watch the going and coming of travellers at the station of

Epinay-sur-Orge. Larsan neglected nothing in any case on which he was engaged.

I turned my eyes again on Rouletabille.

"Ah,—Monsieur Fred!" he said, "when did you begin to use a walking-stick? I have always seen you walking with your hands in your pockets!"

"It is a present," replied the detective.

"Recent?" insisted Rouletabille.

"No, it was given to me in London."

"Ah, yes, I remember—you have just come from London. May I look at it?"

"Oh!—certainly!"

Fred passed the cane to Rouletabille. It was a large yellow bamboo with a crutch handle and ornamented with a gold ring. Rouletabille, after examining it minutely, returned it to Larsan, with a bantering expression on his face, saying:

"You were given a French cane in London!"

"Possibly," said Fred, imperturbably.

"Read the mark there, in tiny letters: Cassette, 6a, Opera."

"Cannot English people buy canes in Paris?"

When Rouletabille had seen me into the train, he said:

"You'll remember the address?"

"Yes,—Cassette, 6a, Opera. Rely on me; you shall have word tomorrow morning."

That evening, on reaching Paris, I saw Monsieur Cassette, dealer in walking-sticks and umbrellas, and wrote to my friend:

"A man unmistakably answering to the description of Monsieur Robert Darzac—same height, slightly stooping, putty-coloured overcoat, bowler hat—purchased a cane similar to the one in which we are interested, on the evening of the crime, about eight o'clock. Monsieur Cassette had not sold another such cane during the last two years. Fred's cane is new. It is quite clear that it's the same cane. Fred did not buy it, since he was in London. Like you, I think that he found it somewhere near Monsieur Robert Darzac. But if, as you suppose, the murderer was in the 'Yellow Room' for five, or even six hours, and the crime was not committed until towards midnight, the purchase of this cane proves an incontestable alibi for Darzac."

XIII

"THE PRESBYTERY HAS LOST NOTHING OF ITS CHARM, NOR THE GARDEN ITS BRIGHTNESS"

A week after the occurrence of the events I have just recounted—on the 2nd of November, to be exact—I received at my home in Paris the following telegraphic message: "Come to the Glandier by the earliest train. Bring revolvers. Friendly greetings. Rouletabille."

I have already said, I think, that at that period, being a young barrister with but few briefs, I frequented the Palais de Justice rather for the purpose of familiarising myself with my professional duties than for the defence of the widow and orphan. I could, therefore, feel no surprise at Rouletabille disposing of my time. Moreover, he knew how keenly interested I was in his journalistic adventures in general and, above all, in the murder at the Glandier. I had not heard from him for a week, nor of the progress made with that mysterious case, except by the innumerable paragraphs in the newspapers and by the very brief notes of Rouletabille in the "Epoque." Those notes had divulged the fact that traces of human blood had been found on the mutton-bone, as well as fresh traces of the blood of Mademoiselle Stangerson—the old stains belonged to other crimes, probably dating years back.

It may be easily imagined that the crime engaged the attention of the press throughout the world. No crime known had more absorbed the minds of people. It appeared to me, however, that the judicial inquiry was making but very little progress; and I should have been very glad, if, on the receipt of my friend's invitation to rejoin him at the Glandier, the despatch had not contained the words, "Bring revolvers."

That puzzled me greatly. Rouletabille telegraphing for revolvers meant that there might be occasion to use them. Now, I confess it without shame, I am not a hero. But here was a friend, evidently in danger, calling on me to go to his aid. I did not hesitate long; and after assuring myself that the only revolver I possessed was properly loaded, I hurried towards the Orleans station. On the way I remembered that Rouletabille had asked for two revolvers; I therefore entered a gunsmith's shop and bought an excellent weapon for my friend.

I had hoped to find him at the station at Epinay; but he was not there. However, a cab was waiting for me and I was soon at the Glandier. Nobody was at the gate, and it was only on the threshold of the chateau that I met the young man. He saluted me with a friendly gesture and threw his arms about me, inquiring warmly as to the state of my health.

When we were in the little sitting-room of which I have spoken, Rouletabille made me sit down.

"It's going badly," he said.

"What's going badly?" I asked.

"Everything."

He came nearer to me and whispered:

"Frederic Larsan is working with might and main against Darzac."

This did not astonish me. I had seen the poor show Mademoiselle Stangerson's fiance had made at the time of the examination of the footprints. However, I immediately asked:

"What about that cane?"

"It is still in the hands of Frederic Larsan. He never lets go of it."

"But doesn't it prove the alibi for Monsieur Darzac?"

"Not at all. Gently questioned by me, Darzac denied having, on that evening, or on any other, purchased a cane at Cassette's. However," said Rouletabille, "I'll not swear to anything; Monsieur Darzac has such strange fits of silence that one does not know exactly what to think of what he says."

"To Frederic Larsan this cane must mean a piece of very damaging evidence. But in what way? The time when it was bought shows it could not have been in the murderer's possession."

"The time doesn't worry Larsan. He is not obliged to adopt my theory which assumes that the murderer got into the 'Yellow Room' between five and six o'clock. But there's nothing to prevent him assuming that the murderer got in between ten and eleven o'clock at night. At that hour Monsieur and Mademoiselle Stangerson, assisted by Daddy Jacques, were engaged in making an interesting chemical experiment in the part of the laboratory taken up by the furnaces. Larsan says, unlikely as that may seem, that the murderer may have slipped behind them. He has already got the examining magistrate to listen to him. When one looks closely into it, the reasoning is absurd, seeing that the 'intimate'— if there is one—must have known that the professor would shortly leave the pavilion, and that the 'friend' had only to put off operating till after the professor's departure. Why should he have risked crossing the laboratory while the professor was in it? And then, when he had got into the 'Yellow Room'?

"There are many points to be cleared up before Larsan's theory can be admitted. I sha'n't waste my time over it, for my theory won't allow me to occupy myself with mere imagination. Only, as I am obliged for the moment to keep silent, and Larsan sometimes talks, he may finish by coming out openly against Monsieur Darzac,—if I'm not there," added the young reporter proudly. "For there are surface evidences against Darzac, much more convincing than that cane, which remains incomprehensible to me, all the more so as Larsan does not in the least hesitate to let Darzac see him with it!—I understand many things in Larsan's theory, but I can't make anything of that cane.

"Is he still at the chateau?"

"Yes; he hardly ever leaves it!—He sleeps there, as I do, at the request of Monsieur Stangerson, who has done for him what Monsieur Robert Darzac has done for me. In spite of the accusation made by Larsan that Monsieur Stangerson knows who the murderer is he yet affords him every facility for arriving at the truth,—just as Darzac is doing for me."

"But you are convinced of Darzac's innocence?"

"At one time I did believe in the possibility of his guilt. That was when we arrived here for the first time. The time has come for me to tell you what has passed between Monsieur Darzac and myself."

Here Rouletabille interrupted himself and asked me if I had brought the revolvers. I showed him them. Having examined both, he pronounced them excellent, and handed them back to me.

"Shall we have any use for them?" I asked.

"No doubt; this evening. We shall pass the night here—if that won't tire you?"

"On the contrary," I said with an expression that made Rouletabille laugh.

"No, no," he said, "this is no time for laughing. You remember the phrase which was the 'open sesame' of this chateau full of mystery?"

"Yes," I said, "perfectly,—'The presbytery has lost nothing of its charm, nor the garden its brightness.' It was the phrase which you found on the half-burned piece of paper amongst the ashes in the laboratory."

"Yes; at the bottom of the paper, where the flame had not reached, was this date: 23rd of October. Remember this date, it is highly important. I am now going to tell you about that curious phrase. On the evening before the crime, that is to say, on the 23rd, Monsieur and

Mademoiselle Stangerson were at a reception at the Elysee. I know that, because I was there on duty, having to interview one of the savants of the Academy of Philadelphia, who was being feted there. I had never before seen either Monsieur or Mademoiselle Stangerson. I was seated in the room which precedes the Salon des Ambassadeurs, and, tired of being jostled by so many noble personages, I had fallen into a vague reverie, when I scented near me the perfume of the lady in black.

"Do you ask me what is the 'perfume of the lady in black'? It must suffice for you to know that it is a perfume of which I am very fond, because it was that of a lady who had been very kind to me in my childhood,—a lady whom I had always seen dressed in black. The lady who, that evening, was scented with the perfume of the lady in black, was dressed in white. She was wonderfully beautiful. I could not help rising and following her. An old man gave her his arm and, as they passed, I heard voices say: 'Professor Stangerson and his daughter.' It was in that way I learned who it was I was following.

"They met Monsieur Robert Darzac, whom I knew by sight. Professor Stangerson, accosted by Mr. Arthur William Rance, one of the American savants, seated himself in the great gallery, and Monsieur Robert Darzac led Mademoiselle Stangerson into the conservatory. I followed. The weather was very mild that evening; the garden doors were open. Mademoiselle Stangerson threw a fichu shawl over her shoulders and I plainly saw that it was she who was begging Monsieur Darzac to go with her into the garden. I continued to follow, interested by the agitation plainly exhibited by the bearing of Monsieur Darzac. They slowly passed along the wall abutting on the Avenue Marigny. I took the central alley, walking parallel with them, and then crossed over for the purpose of getting nearer to them. The night was dark, and the grass deadened the sound of my steps. They had stopped under the vacillating light of a gas jet and appeared to be both bending over a paper held by Mademoiselle Stangerson, reading something which deeply interested them. I stopped in the darkness and silence.

"Neither of them saw me, and I distinctly heard Mademoiselle Stangerson repeat, as she was refolding the paper: 'The presbytery has lost nothing of its charm, nor the garden its brightness!'—It was said in a tone at once mocking and despairing, and was followed by a burst of such nervous laughter that I think her words will never cease to sound in my ears. But another phrase was uttered by Monsieur Robert Darzac: 'Must I commit a crime, then, to win you?' He was in an extraordinarily agitated state. He took the hand of Mademoiselle Stangerson and held it for a long time to his lips, and I thought, from the movement of his shoulders, that he was crying. Then they went away.

"When I returned to the great gallery," continued Rouletabille, "I saw no more of Monsieur Robert Darzac, and I was not to see him again until after the tragedy at the Glandier. Mademoiselle was near Mr. Rance, who was talking with much animation, his eyes, during the conversation, glowing with a singular brightness. Mademoiselle Stangerson, I thought, was not even listening to what he was saying, her face expressing perfect indifference. His face was the red face of a drunkard. When Monsieur and Mademoiselle Stangerson left, he went to the bar and remained there. I joined him, and rendered him some little service in the midst of the pressing crowd. He thanked me and told me he was returning to America three days later, that is to say, on the 26th (the day after the crime). I talked with him about Philadelphia; he told me he had lived there for five-and-twenty years, and that it was there he had met the illustrious Professor Stangerson and his daughter. He drank a great deal of champagne, and when I left him he was very nearly drunk.

"Such were my experiences on that evening, and I leave you to imagine what effect the news of the attempted murder of Mademoiselle Stangerson produced on me,—with what force those words pronounced by Monsieur Robert Darzac, 'Must I commit a crime, then, to win you?' recurred to me. It was not this phrase, however, that I repeated to him, when we met here at Glandier. The sentence of the presbytery and the bright garden sufficed to open the gate of the chateau. If you ask me if I believe now that Monsieur Darzac is the murderer, I must say I do not. I do not think I ever quite thought that. At the time I could not really think seriously of anything. I had so little evidence to go on. But I needed to have at once the proof that he had not been wounded in the hand.

"When we were alone together, I told him how I had chanced to overhear a part of his conversation with Mademoiselle Stangerson in the garden of the Elysee; and when I repeated to him the words, 'Must I commit a crime, then, to win you?' he was greatly troubled, though much less so than he had been by hearing me repeat the phrase about the presbytery. What threw him into a state of real consternation was to learn from me that the day on which he had gone to meet Mademoiselle Stangerson at the Elysee, was the very day on which she had gone to the Post Office for the letter. It was that letter, perhaps, which ended with the words: 'The presbytery has lost nothing of its charm, nor the garden its brightness.' My surmise was confirmed by my finding, if you remember, in the ashes of the laboratory, the fragment of paper dated October the 23rd. The letter had been written and withdrawn from the Post Office on the same day.

"There can be no doubt that, on returning from the Elysee that night, Mademoiselle Stangerson had tried to destroy that compromising paper. It was in vain that Monsieur Darzac denied that that letter had anything whatever to do with the crime. I told him that in an affair so filled with mystery as this, he had no right to hide this letter; that I was persuaded it was of considerable importance; that the desperate tone in which Mademoiselle Stangerson had pronounced the prophetic phrase,—that his own tears, and the threat of a crime which he had professed after the letter was read—all these facts tended to leave no room for me to doubt. Monsieur Darzac became more and more agitated, and I determined to take advantage of the effect I had produced on him. 'You were on the point of being married, Monsieur,' I said negligently and without looking at him, 'and suddenly your marriage becomes impossible because of the writer of that letter; because as soon as his letter was read, you spoke of the necessity for a crime to win Mademoiselle Stangerson. Therefore there is someone between you and her—someone who is preventing your marriage with her—someone who has attempted to kill her, so that she should not be able to marry!' And I concluded with these words: 'Now, monsieur, you have only to tell me in confidence the name of the murderer!'—The words I had uttered must have struck him ominously, for when I turned my eyes on him, I saw that his face was haggard, the perspiration standing on his forehead, and terror showing in his eyes.

"'Monsieur,' he said to me, 'I am going to ask of you something which may appear insane, but in exchange for which I place my life in your hands. You must not tell the magistrates of what you saw and heard in the garden of the Elysee,—neither to them nor to anybody. I swear to you, that I am innocent, and I know, I feel, that you believe me; but I would rather be taken for the guilty man than see justice go astray on that phrase, "The presbytery has lost nothing of its charm, nor the garden its brightness." The judges must know nothing about that phrase. All this matter is in your hands. Monsieur, I leave it there; but forget the evening at the Elysee. A hundred other roads are open to you in your search for the criminal. I will open them for you myself. I will help you. Will you take up your quarters here?—You may remain here to do as you please.—Eat—sleep here—watch my actions—the actions of all here. You shall be master of the Glandier, Monsieur; but forget the evening at the Elysee.'"

Rouletabille here paused to take breath. I now understood what had appeared so unexplainable in the demeanour of Monsieur Robert Darzac towards my friend, and the facility with which the young reporter had been able to install himself on the scene of the crime. My curiosity could not fail to be excited by all I had heard. I asked Rouletabille to satisfy it still further. What had happened at the Glandier during the past week?—Had he not told me that there were surface indications against Monsieur Darzac much more terrible than that of the cane found by Larsan?

"Everything seems to be pointing against him," replied my friend, "and the situation is becoming exceedingly grave. Monsieur Darzac appears not to mind it much; but in that he is wrong. I was interested only in the health of Mademoiselle Stangerson, which was daily improving, when something occurred that is even more mysterious than—than the mystery of the 'Yellow Room'!"

"Impossible!" I cried, "What could be more mysterious than that?"

"Let us first go back to Monsieur Robert Darzac," said Rouletabille, calming me. "I have said that everything seems to be pointing against him. The marks of the neat boots found by Frederic Larsan appear to be really the footprints of Mademoiselle Stangerson's fiance. The marks made by the bicycle may have been made by his bicycle. He had usually left it at the chateau; why did he take it to Paris on that particular occasion? Was it because he was not going to return again to the chateau? Was it because, owing to the breaking off of his marriage, his relations with the Stangersons were to cease? All who are interested in the matter affirm that those relations were to continue unchanged.

"Frederic Larsan, however, believes that all relations were at an end. From the day when Monsieur Darzac accompanied Mademoiselle Stangerson to the Grands Magasins de la Louvre until the day after the crime, he had not been at the Glandier. Remember that Mademoiselle Stangerson lost her reticule containing the key with the brass head while she was in his company. From that day to the evening at the Elysee, the Sorbonne professor and Mademoiselle Stangerson did not see one another; but they may have written to each other. Mademoiselle

Stangerson went to the Post Office to get a letter, which Larsan says was written by Robert Darzac; for knowing nothing of what had passed at the Elysee, Larsan believes that it was Monsieur Darzac himself who stole the reticule with the key, with the design of forcing her consent, by getting possession of the precious papers of her father—papers which he would have restored to him on condition that the marriage engagement was to be fulfilled.

"All that would have been a very doubtful and almost absurd hypothesis, as Larsan admitted to me, but for another and much graver circumstance. In the first place here is something which I have not been able to explain—Monsieur Darzac had himself, on the 24th, gone to the Post Office to ask for the letter which Mademoiselle had called for and received on the previous evening. The description of the man who made application tallies in every respect with the appearance of Monsieur Darzac, who, in answer to the questions put to him by the examining magistrate, denies that he went to the Post Office. Now even admitting that the letter was written by him—which I do not believe—he knew that Mademoiselle Stangerson had received it, since he had seen it in her hands in the garden at the Elysee. It could not have been he, then, who had gone to the Post Office, the day after the 24th, to ask for a letter which he knew was no longer there.

"To me it appears clear that somebody, strongly resembling him, stole Mademoiselle Stangerson's reticule and in that letter, had demanded of her something which she had not sent him. He must have been surprised at the failure of his demand, hence his application at the Post Office, to learn whether his letter had been delivered to the person to whom it had been addressed. Finding that it had been claimed, he had become furious. What had he demanded? Nobody but Mademoiselle Stangerson knows. Then, on the day following, it is reported that she had been attacked during the night, and, the next day, I discovered that the Professor had, at the same time, been robbed by means of the key referred to in the poste restante letter. It would seem, then, that the man who went to the Post Office to inquire for the letter must have been the murderer. All these arguments Larsan applies as against Monsieur Darzac. You may be sure that the examining magistrate, Larsan, and myself, have done our best to get from the Post Office precise details relative to the singular personage who applied there on the 24th of October. But nothing has been learned. We don't know where he came from—or where he went.

Beyond the description which makes him resemble Monsieur Darzac, we know nothing.

"I have announced in the leading journals that a handsome reward will be given to a driver of any public conveyance who drove a fare to No. 40, Post Office, about ten o'clock on the morning of the 24th of October. Information to be addressed to 'M. R.,' at the office of the 'Epoque'; but no answer has resulted. The man may have walked; but, as he was most likely in a hurry, there was a chance that he might have gone in a cab. Who, I keep asking myself night and day, is the man who so strongly resembles Monsieur Robert Darzac, and who is also known to have bought the cane which has fallen into Larsan's hands?

"The most serious fact is that Monsieur Darzac was, at the very same time that his double presented himself at the Post Office, scheduled for a lecture at the Sorbonne. He had not delivered that lecture, and one of his friends took his place. When I questioned him as to how he had employeeed the time, he told me that he had gone for a stroll in the Bois de Boulogne. What do you think of a professor who, instead of giving his lecture, obtains a substitute to go for a stroll in the Bois de Boulogne? When Frederic Larsan asked him for information on this point, he quietly replied that it was no business of his how he spent his time in Paris. On which Fred swore aloud that he would find out, without anybody's help.

"All this seems to fit in with Fred's hypothesis, namely, that Monsieur Stangerson allowed the murderer to escape in order to avoid a scandal. The hypothesis is further substantiated by the fact that Darzac was in the 'Yellow Room' and was permitted to get away. That hypothesis I believe to be a false one.—Larsan is being misled by it, though that would not displease me, did it not affect an innocent person. Now does that hypothesis really mislead Frederic Larsan? That is the question—that is the question."

"Perhaps he is right," I cried, interrupting Rouletabille. "Are you sure that Monsieur Darzac is innocent?—It seems to me that these are extraordinary coincidences—"

"Coincidences," replied my friend, "are the worst enemies to truth."

"What does the examining magistrate think now of the matter?"

"Monsieur de Marquet hesitates to accuse Monsieur Darzac, in the absence of absolute proofs. Not only would he have public opinion wholly against him, to say nothing of the Sorbonne, but Monsieur and Mademoiselle Stangerson. She adores Monsieur Robert Darzac.

Indistinctly as she saw the murderer, it would be hard to make the public believe that she could not have recognised him, if Darzac had been the criminal. No doubt the 'Yellow Room' was very dimly lit; but a night-light, however small, gives some light. Here, my boy, is how things stood when, three days, or rather three nights ago, an extraordinarily strange incident occurred."

XIV

"I Expect the Assassin This Evening"

I must take you," said Rouletabille, "so as to enable you to understand, to the various scenes. I myself believe that I have discovered what everybody else is searching for, namely, how the murderer escaped from the 'Yellow Room', without any accomplice, and without Mademoiselle Stangerson having had anything to do with it. But so long as I am not sure of the real murderer, I cannot state the theory on which I am working. I can only say that I believe it to be correct and, in any case, a quite natural and simple one. As to what happened in this place three nights ago, I must say it kept me wondering for a whole day and a night. It passes all belief. The theory I have formed from the incident is so absurd that I would rather matters remained as yet unexplained."

Saying which the young reporter invited me to go and make the tour of the chateau with him. The only sound to be heard was the crunching of the dead leaves beneath our feet. The silence was so intense that one might have thought the chateau had been abandoned. The old stones, the stagnant water of the ditch surrounding the donjon, the bleak ground strewn with the dead leaves, the dark, skeleton-like outlines of the trees, all contributed to give to the desolate place, now filled with its awful mystery, a most funereal aspect. As we passed round the donjon, we met the Green Man, the forest-keeper, who did not greet us, but walked by as if we had not existed. He was looking just as I had formerly seen him through the window of the Donjon Inn. He had still his fowling-piece slung at his back, his pipe was in his mouth, and his eye-glasses on his nose.

"An odd kind of fish!" Rouletabille said to me, in a low tone.

"Have you spoken to him?" I asked.

"Yes, but I could get nothing out of him. His only answers are grunts and shrugs of the shoulders. He generally lives on the first floor of the donjon, a big room that once served for an oratory. He lives like a bear, never goes out without his gun, and is only pleasant with the girls. The women, for twelve miles round, are all setting their caps for him. For the present, he is paying attention to Madame Mathieu, whose husband is keeping a lynx eye upon her in consequence."

After passing the donjon, which is situated at the extreme end of the left wing, we went to the back of the chateau. Rouletabille, pointing to a window which I recognised as the only one belonging to Mademoiselle Stangerson's apartment, said to me:

"If you had been here, two nights ago, you would have seen your humble servant at the top of a ladder, about to enter the chateau by that window."

As I expressed some surprise at this piece of nocturnal gymnastics, he begged me to notice carefully the exterior disposition of the chateau. We then went back into the building.

"I must now show you the first floor of the chateau, where I am living," said my friend.

To enable the reader the better to understand the disposition of these parts of the dwelling, I annex a plan of the first floor of the right wing, drawn by Rouletabille the day after the extraordinary phenomenon occurred, the details of which I am about to relate.

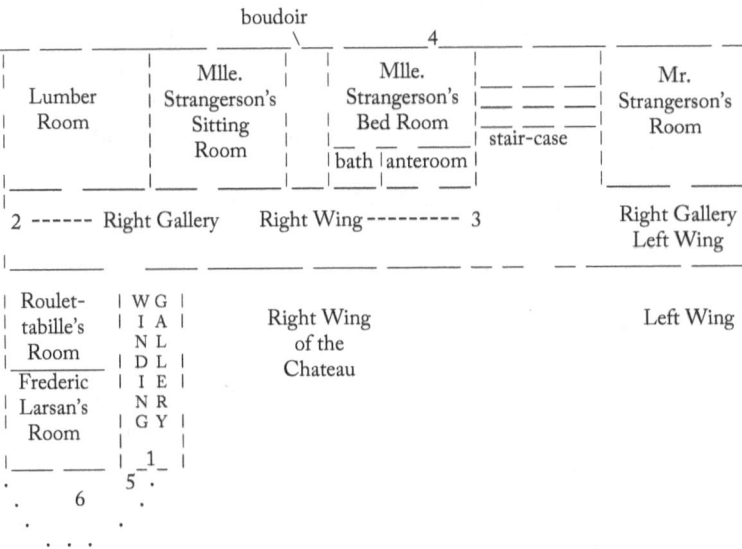

Rouletabille motioned me to follow him up a magnificent flight of stairs ending in a landing on the first floor. From this landing one could pass to the right or left wing of the chateau by a gallery opening from it. This gallery, high and wide, extended along the whole length of the building and was lit from the front of the chateau facing the north. The rooms, the windows of which looked to the south, opened out of the gallery. Professor Stangerson inhabited the left wing of the building. Mademoiselle Stangerson had her apartment in the right wing.

We entered the gallery to the right. A narrow carpet, laid on the waxed oaken floor, which shone like glass, deadened the sound of our footsteps. Rouletabille asked me, in a low tone, to walk carefully, as we were passing the door of Mademoiselle Stangerson's apartment. This consisted of a bed-room, an ante-room, a small bath-room, a boudoir, and a drawing-room. One could pass from one to another of these rooms without having to go by way of the gallery. The gallery continued straight to the western end of the building, where it was lit by a high window (window 2 on the plan). At about two-thirds of its length this gallery, at a right angle, joined another gallery following the course of the right wing.

The better to follow this narrative, we shall call the gallery leading from the stairs to the eastern window, the "right" gallery and the gallery quitting it at a right angle, the "off-turning" gallery (winding gallery in the plan). It was at the meeting point of the two galleries that Rouletabille had his chamber, adjoining that of Frederic Larsan, the door of each opening on to the "off-turning" gallery, while the doors of Mademoiselle Stangerson's apartment opened into the "right" gallery. (See the plan.)

Rouletabille opened the door of his room and after we had passed in, carefully drew the bolt. I had not had time to glance round the place in which he had been installed, when he uttered a cry of surprise and pointed to a pair of eye-glasses on a side-table.

"What are these doing here?" he asked.

I should have been puzzled to answer him.

"I wonder," he said, "I wonder if this is what I have been searching for. I wonder if these are the eye-glasses from the presbytery!"

He seized them eagerly, his fingers caressing the glass. Then looking at me, with an expression of terror on his face, he murmured, "Oh!—Oh!"

He repeated the exclamation again and again, as if his thoughts had suddenly turned his brain.

He rose and, putting his hand on my shoulder, laughed like one demented as he said:

"Those glasses will drive me silly! Mathematically speaking the thing is possible; but humanly speaking it is impossible—or afterwards—or afterwards—"

Two light knocks struck the door. Rouletabille opened it. A figure entered. I recognised the concierge, whom I had seen when she was being taken to the pavilion for examination. I was surprised, thinking she was still under lock and key. This woman said in a very low tone:

"In the grove of the parquet."

Rouletabille replied: "Thanks."—The woman then left. He again turned to me, his look haggard, after having carefully refastened the door, muttering some incomprehensible phrases.

"If the thing is mathematically possible, why should it not be humanly!—And if it is humanly possible, the matter is simply awful." I interrupted him in his soliloquy:

"Have they set the concierges at liberty, then?" I asked.

"Yes," he replied, "I had them liberated, I needed people I could trust. The woman is thoroughly devoted to me, and her husband would lay down his life for me."

"Oho!" I said, "when will he have occasion to do it?"

"This evening,—for this evening I expect the murderer."

"You expect the murderer this evening? Then you know him?"

"I shall know him; but I should be mad to affirm, categorically, at this moment that I do know him. The mathematical idea I have of the murderer gives results so frightful, so monstrous, that I hope it is still possible that I am mistaken. I hope so, with all my heart!"

"Five minutes ago, you did not know the murderer; how can you say that you expect him this evening?"

"Because I know that he must come."

Rouletabille very slowly filled his pipe and lit it. That meant an interesting story. At that moment we heard some one walking in the gallery and passing before our door. Rouletabille listened. The sound of the footstep died away in the distance.

"Is Frederic Larsan in his room?" I asked, pointing to the partition.

"No," my friend answered. "He went to Paris this morning,—still on the scent of Darzac, who also left for Paris. That matter will turn out badly. I expect that Monsieur Darzac will be arrested in the course of the next week. The worst of it is that everything seems to be in league against him,—circumstances, things, people. Not an hour passes without bringing some new evidence against him. The examining magistrate is overwhelmed by it—and blind."

"Frederic Larsan, however, is not a novice," I said.

"I thought so," said Rouletabille, with a slightly contemptuous turn of his lips, "I fancied he was a much abler man. I had, indeed, a great admiration for him, before I got to know his method of working. It's deplorable. He owes his reputation solely to his ability; but he lacks reasoning power,—the mathematics of his ideas are very poor."

I looked closely at Rouletabille and could not help smiling, on hearing this boy of eighteen talking of a man who had proved to the world that he was the finest police sleuth in Europe.

"You smile," he said? "you are wrong! I swear I will outwit him—and in a striking way! But I must make haste about it, for he has an enormous start on me—given him by Monsieur Robert Darzac, who is this evening going to increase it still more. Think of it!—every time the murderer comes to the chateau, Monsieur Darzac, by a strange fatality, absents himself and refuses to give any account of how he employs his time."

"Every time the assassin comes to the chateau!" I cried. "Has he returned then—?"

"Yes, during that famous night when the strange phenomenon occurred."

I was now going to learn about the astonishing phenomenon to which Rouletabille had made allusion half an hour earlier without giving me any explanation of it. But I had learned never to press Rouletabille in his narratives. He spoke when the fancy took him and when he judged it to be right. He was less concerned about my curiosity than he was for making a complete summing up for himself of any important matter in which he was interested.

At last, in short rapid phrases, he acquainted me with things which plunged me into a state bordering on complete bewilderment. Indeed, the results of that still unknown science known as hypnotism, for example, were not more inexplicable than the disappearance of the "matter" of the murderer at the moment when four persons were within touch of him. I speak of hypnotism as I would of electricity, for of the nature of both we are ignorant and we know little of their laws. I cite these examples because, at the time, the case appeared to me to be only explicable by the inexplicable,—that is to say, by an event outside of known natural laws. And yet, if I had had Rouletabille's brain, I should, like him, have had a presentiment of the natural explanation; for the most curious thing about all the mysteries of the Glandier case was the natural manner in which he explained them.

I have among the papers that were sent me by the young man, after the affair was over, a note-book of his, in which a complete account is given of the phenomenon of the disappearance of the "matter" of the assassin, and the thoughts to which it gave rise in the mind of my young friend. It is preferable, I think, to give the reader this account, rather than continue to reproduce my conversation with Rouletabille; for I should be afraid, in a history of this nature, to add a word that was not in accordance with the strictest truth.

XV

The Trap

(Extract from the Note-Book of Joseph Rouletabille)

L ast night—the night between the 29th and 30th of October—"
wrote Joseph Rouletabille, "I woke up towards one o'clock in the
morning. Was it sleeplessness, or noise without?—The cry of the Bete
du Bon Dieu rang out with sinister loudness from the end of the park.
I rose and opened the window. Cold wind and rain; opaque darkness;
silence. I reclosed my window. Again the sound of the cat's weird cry in
the distance. I partly dressed in haste. The weather was too bad for even
a cat to be turned out in it. What did it mean, then—that imitating
of the mewing of Mother Angenoux' cat so near the chateau? I seized
a good-sized stick, the only weapon I had, and, without making any
noise, opened the door.

"The gallery into which I went was well lit by a lamp with a reflector.
I felt a keen current of air and, on turning, found the window open, at
the extreme end of the gallery, which I call the 'off-turning' gallery, to
distinguish it from the 'right' gallery, on to which the apartment of
Mademoiselle Stangerson opened. These two galleries cross each other
at right angles. Who had left that window open? Or, who had come
to open it? I went to the window and leaned out. Five feet below me
there was a sort of terrace over the semi-circular projection of a room
on the ground-floor. One could, if one wanted, jump from the window
on to the terrace, and allow oneself to drop from it into the court of the
chateau. Whoever had entered by this road had, evidently, not had a
key to the vestibule door. But why should I be thinking of my previous
night's attempt with the ladder?—Because of the open window—left
open, perhaps, by the negligence of a servant? I reclosed it, smiling at
the ease with which I built a drama on the mere suggestion of an open
window.

"Again the cry of the Bete du Bon Dieu!—and then silence. The rain
ceased to beat on the window. All in the chateau slept. I walked with
infinite precaution on the carpet of the gallery. On reaching the corner
of the 'right' gallery, I peered round it cautiously. There was another

lamp there with a reflector which quite lit up the several objects in it,—three chairs and some pictures hanging on the wall. What was I doing there? Perfect silence reigned throughout. Everything was sunk in repose. What was the instinct that urged me towards Mademoiselle Stangerson's chamber? Why did a voice within me cry: 'Go on, to the chamber of Mademoiselle Stangerson!' I cast my eyes down upon the carpet on which I was treading and saw that my steps were being directed towards Mademoiselle Stangerson's chamber by the marks of steps that had already been made there. Yes, on the carpet were traces of footsteps stained with mud leading to the chamber of Mademoiselle Stangerson. Horror! Horror!—I recognised in those footprints the impression of the neat boots of the murderer! He had come, then, from without in this wretched night. If you could descend from the gallery by way of the window, by means of the terrace, then you could get into the chateau by the same means.

"The murderer was still in the chateau, for here were marks as of returning footsteps. He had entered by the open window at the extremity of the 'off-turning' gallery; he had passed Frederic Larsan's door and mine, had turned to the right, and had entered Mademoiselle Stangerson's room. I am before the door of her ante-room—it is open. I push it, without making the least noise. Under the door of the room itself I see a streak of light. I listen—no sound—not even of breathing! Ah!—if I only knew what was passing in the silence that is behind that door! I find the door locked and the key turned on the inner side. And the murderer is there, perhaps. He must be there! Will he escape this time?—All depends on me!—I must be calm, and above all, I must make no false steps. I must see into that room. I can enter it by Mademoiselle Stangerson's drawing-room; but, to do that I should have to cross her boudoir; and while I am there, the murderer may escape by the gallery door—the door in front of which I am now standing.

"I am sure that no other crime is being committed, on this night; for there is complete silence in the boudoir, where two nurses are taking care of Mademoiselle Stangerson until she is restored to health.

"As I am almost sure that the murderer is there, why do I not at once give the alarm? The murderer may, perhaps, escape; but, perhaps, I may be able to save Mademoiselle Stangerson's life. Suppose the murderer on this occasion is not here to murder? The door has been opened to allow him to enter; by whom?—And it has been refastened—by whom?—Mademoiselle Stangerson shuts herself up in her apartment with her nurses every night. Who turned the key of that chamber to allow the murderer to enter?—The nurses,—two faithful domestics? The old chambermaid, Sylvia? It is very improbable. Besides, they slept in the boudoir, and Mademoiselle Stangerson, very nervous and careful, Monsieur Robert Darzac told me, sees to her own safety since she has been well enough to move about in her room, which I have not yet seen her leave. This nervousness and sudden care on her part, which had struck Monsieur Darzac, had given me, also, food for thought. At the time of the crime in the 'Yellow Room', there can be no doubt that she expected the murderer. Was he expected this night?—Was it she herself who had opened her door to him? Had she some reason for doing so? Was she obliged to do it?—Was it a meeting for purposes of crime?— Certainly it was not a lover's meeting, for I believe Mademoiselle Stangerson adores Monsieur Darzac.

"All these reflections ran through my brain like a flash of lightning. What would I not give to know!

"It is possible that there was some reason for the awful silence. My intervention might do more harm than good. How could I tell? How could I know I might not any moment cause another crime? If I could only see and know, without breaking that silence!

"I left the ante-room and descended the central stairs to the vestibule and, as silently as possible, made my way to the little room on the ground-floor where Daddy Jacques had been sleeping since the attack made at the pavilion.

"I found him dressed, his eyes wide open, almost haggard. He did not seem surprised to see me. He told me that he had got up because he had heard the cry of the Bete du bon Dieu, and because he had heard footsteps in the park, close to his window, out of which he had looked and, just then, had seen a black shadow pass by. I asked him whether he had a firearm of any kind. No, he no longer kept one, since the examining magistrate had taken his revolver from him. We went out together, by a little back door, into the park, and stole along the chateau to the point which is just below Mademoiselle Stangerson's window.

"I placed Daddy Jacques against the wall, ordering him not to stir from the spot, while I, taking advantage of a moment when the moon was hidden by a cloud, moved to the front of the window, out of the patch of light which came from it,—for the window was half-open! If I could only know what was passing in that silent chamber! I returned to Daddy Jacques and whispered the word 'ladder' in his ear. At first I had thought of the tree which, a week ago, served me for an observatory; but I immediately saw that, from the way the window was half-opened, I should not be able to see from that point of view anything that was passing in the room; and I wanted, not only to see, but to hear, and—to act.

"Greatly agitated, almost trembling, Daddy Jacques disappeared for a moment and returned without the ladder, but making signs to me with his arms, as signals to me to come quickly to him. When I got near him he gasped: 'Come!'

"He led me round the château, past the don-jon. Arrived there, he said:

"'I went to the donjon in search of my ladder, and in the lower part of the donjon which serves me and the gardener for a lumber room, I found the door open and the ladder gone. On coming out, that's what I caught sight of by the light of the moon.'

"And he pointed to the further end of the chateau, where a ladder stood resting against the stone brackets supporting the terrace, under the window which I had found open. The projection of the terrace had prevented my seeing it. Thanks to that ladder, it was quite easy to get into the 'off-turning' gallery of the first floor, and I had no doubt of it having been the road taken by the unknown.

"We ran to the ladder, but at the moment of reaching it, Daddy Jacques drew my attention to the half-open door of the little semi-circular room, situated under the terrace, at the extremity of the right wing of the chateau, having the terrace for its roof. Daddy Jacques pushed the door open a little further and looked in.

"'He's not there!' he whispered.

"Who is not there?"

"The forest—keeper."

With his lips once more to my ear, he added:

"'Do you know that he has slept in the upper room of the donjon ever since it was restored?' And with the same gesture he pointed to the half-open door, the ladder, the terrace, and the windows in the 'off-turning' gallery which, a little while before, I had re-closed.

"What were my thoughts then? I had no time to think. I felt more than I thought.

"Evidently, I felt, if the forest-keeper is up there in the chamber (I say, if, because at this moment, apart from the presence of the ladder and his vacant room, there are no evidences which permit me even to suspect him)—if he is there, he has been obliged to pass by the ladder, and the rooms which lie behind his, in his new lodging, are occupied by the family of the steward and by the cook, and by the kitchens, which bar the way by the vestibule to the interior of the chateau. And if he had been there during the evening on any pretext, it would have been easy for him to go into the gallery and see that the window could be simply pushed open from the outside. This question of the unfastened window easily narrowed the field of search for the murderer. He must belong to the house, unless he had an accomplice, which I do not believe he had; unless—unless Mademoiselle Stangerson herself had seen that that window was not fastened from the inside. But, then,—what could be the frightful secret which put her under the necessity of doing away with obstacles that separated her from the murderer?

"I seized hold of the ladder, and we returned to the back of the chateau to see if the window of the chamber was still half-open. The blind was drawn but did not join and allowed a bright stream of light to escape and fall upon the path at our feet. I planted the ladder under the window. I am almost sure that I made no noise; and while Daddy Jacques remained at the foot of the ladder, I mounted it, very quietly, my stout stick in my hand. I held my breath and lifted my feet with the greatest care. Suddenly a heavy cloud discharged itself at that moment in a fresh downpour of rain.

"At the same instant the sinister cry of the Bete du bon Dieu arrested me in my ascent. It seemed to me to have come from close by me—only a few yards away. Was the cry a signal?—Had some accomplice of the man seen me on the ladder!—Would the cry bring the man to the window?—Perhaps! Ah, there he was at the window! I felt his head above me. I heard the sound of his breath! I could not look up towards him; the least movement of my head, and—I might be lost. Would he see me?—Would he peer into the darkness? No; he went away. He had seen nothing. I felt, rather than heard, him moving on tip-toe in the room; and I mounted a few steps higher. My head reached to the level of the window-sill; my forehead rose above it; my eyes looked between the opening in the blinds—and I saw—A man seated at Mademoiselle Stangerson's little desk, writing. His back was turned toward me. A candle was lit before him, and he bent over the flame, the light from it projecting shapeless shadows. I saw nothing but a monstrous, stooping back.

"Mademoiselle Stangerson herself was not there!—Her bed had not been lain on! Where, then, was she sleeping that night? Doubtless in the side-room with her women. Perhaps this was but a guess. I must content myself with the joy of finding the man alone. I must be calm to prepare my trap.

"But who, then, is this man writing there before my eyes, seated at the desk, as if he were in his own home? If there had not been that ladder under the window; if there had not been those footprints on the carpet in the gallery; if there had not been that open window, I might have been led to think that this man had a right to be there, and that he was there as a matter of course and for reasons about which as yet I knew nothing. But there was no doubt that this mysterious unknown was the man of the 'Yellow Room',—the man to whose murderous assault Mademoiselle Stangerson—without denouncing him—had had to submit. If I could but see his face! Surprise and capture him!

"If I spring into the room at this moment, he will escape by the right-hand door opening into the boudoir,—or crossing the drawing-room, he will reach the gallery and I shall lose him. I have him now and in five minutes more he'll be safer than if I had him in a cage.—What is he doing there, alone in Mademoiselle Stangerson's room?—What is he writing? I descend and place the ladder on the ground. Daddy Jacques follows me. We re-enter the chateau. I send Daddy Jacques to wake Monsieur Stangerson, and instruct him to await my coming in Mademoiselle Stangerson's room and to say nothing definite to him before my arrival. I will go and awaken Frederic Larsan. It's a bore to have to do it, for I should have liked to work alone and to have carried off all the honors of this affair myself, right under the very nose of the sleeping detective. But Daddy Jacques and Monsieur Stangerson are old men, and I am not yet fully developed. I might not be strong enough. Larsan is used to wrestling and putting on the handcuffs. He opened his eyes swollen with sleep, ready to send me flying, without in the least believing in my reporter's fancies. I had to assure him that the man was there!

"'That's strange!' he said; 'I thought I left him this afternoon in Paris.'

"He dressed himself in haste and armed himself with a revolver. We stole quietly into the gallery.

"'Where is he?' Larsan asked.

"'In Mademoiselle Stangerson's room.

"'And—Mademoiselle Stangerson?'

"'She is not in there.'

"'Let's go in.'

"'Don't go there! On the least alarm the man will escape. He has four ways by which to do it—the door, the window, the boudoir, or the room in which the women are sleeping.'

"'I'll draw him from below.'

"'And if you fail?—If you only succeed in wounding him—he'll escape again, without reckoning that he is certainly armed. No, let me direct the expedition, and I'll answer for everything.'

"'As you like,' he replied, with fairly good grace.

"Then, after satisfying myself that all the windows of the two galleries were thoroughly secure, I placed Frederic Larsan at the end of the 'off-turning' gallery, before the window which I had found open and had reclosed.

"'Under no consideration,' I said to him, 'must you stir from this post till I call you. The chances are even that the man, when he is pursued, will return to this window and try to save himself that way; for it is by that way he came in and made a way ready for his flight. You have a dangerous post.'

"'What will be yours?' asked Fred.

"'I shall spring into the room and knock him over for you.'

"'Take my revolver,' said Fred, 'and I'll take your stick.'

"'Thanks,' I said; 'You are a brave man.'

"I accepted his offer. I was going to be alone with the man in the room writing and was really thankful to have the weapon.

"I left Fred, having posted him at the window (No. 5 on the plan), and, with the greatest precaution, went towards Monsieur Stangerson's apartment in the left wing of the chateau. I found him with Daddy Jacques, who had faithfully obeyed my directions, confining himself to asking his master to dress as quickly as possible. In a few words I explained to Monsieur Stangerson what was passing. He armed himself with a revolver, followed me, and we were all three speedily in the gallery. Since I had seen the murderer seated at the desk ten minutes had elapsed. Monsieur Stangerson wished to spring upon the assassin at once and kill him. I made him understand that, above all, he must not, in his desire to kill him, miss him.

"When I had sworn to him that his daughter was not in the room, and in no danger, he conquered his impatience and left me to direct the operations. I told them that they must come to me the moment I called to them, or when I fired my revolver. I then sent Daddy Jacques to place himself before the window at the end of the 'right' gallery.

(No. 2 on my plan.) I chose that position 'for Daddy Jacques because I believed that the murderer, tracked, on leaving the room, would run through the gallery towards the window which he had left open, and, instantly seeing that it was guarded by Larsan, would pursue his course along the 'right' gallery. There he would encounter Daddy Jacques, who would prevent his springing out of the window into the park. Under that window there was a sort of buttress, while all the other windows in the galleries were at such a height from the ground that it was almost impossible to jump from them without breaking one's neck. All the doors and windows, including those of the lumber-room at the end of the 'right' gallery—as I had rapidly assured myself—were strongly secured.

"Having indicated to Daddy Jacques the post he was to occupy, and having seen him take up his position, I placed Monsieur Stangerson on the landing at the head of the stairs not far from the door of his daughter's ante-room, rather than the boudoir, where the women were, and the door of which must have been locked by Mademoiselle Stangerson herself if, as I thought, she had taken refuge in the boudoir for the purpose of avoiding the murderer who was coming to see her. In any case, he must return to the gallery where my people were awaiting him at every possible exit.

"On coming there, he would see on his left, Monsieur Stangerson; he would turn to the right, towards the 'off-turning' gallery—the way he had pre-arranged for flight, where, at the intersection of the two galleries, he would see at once, as I have explained, on his left, Frederic Larsan at the end of the 'off-turning' gallery, and in front, Daddy Jacques, at the end of the 'right' gallery. Monsieur Stangerson and myself would arrive by way of the back of the chateau.—He is ours!—He can no longer escape us! I was sure of that.

"The plan I had formed seemed to me the best, the surest, and the most simple. It would, no doubt, have been simpler still, if we had been able to place some one directly behind the door of Mademoiselle's boudoir, which opened out of her bedchamber, and, in that way, had been in a position to besiege the two doors of the room in which the man was. But we could not penetrate the boudoir except by way of the drawing-room, the door of which had been locked on the inside by Mademoiselle Stangerson. But even if I had had the free disposition of the boudoir, I should have held to the plan I had formed; because any other plan of attack would have separated us at the moment of the struggle with the man, while my plan united us all for the attack, at a spot which I had selected with almost mathematical precision,—the intersection of the two galleries.

"Having so placed my people, I again left the chateau, hurried to my ladder, and, replacing it, climbed up, revolver in hand.

"If there be any inclined to smile at my taking so many precautionary measures, I refer them to the mystery of the 'Yellow Room', and to all the proofs we have of the weird cunning of the murderer. Further, if there be some who think my observations needlessly minute at a moment when they ought to be completely held by rapidity of movement and decision of action, I reply that I have wished to report here, at length and completely, all the details of a plan of attack conceived so rapidly that it is only the slowness of my pen that gives an appearance of slowness to the execution. I have wished, by this slowness and precision, to be certain that nothing should be omitted from the conditions under which the strange phenomenon was produced, which, until some natural explanation of it is forthcoming, seems to me to prove, even better than the theories of Professor Stangerson, the Dissociation of Matter—I will even say, the instantaneous Dissociation of Matter."

XVI

STRANGE PHENOMENON OF THE DISSOCIATION OF MATTER

(Extract from the Note-Book of
Joseph Rouletabille, Continued)

I am again at the window-sill," continues Rouletabille, "and once more I raise my head above it. Through an opening in the curtains, the arrangement of which has not been changed, I am ready to look, anxious to note the position in which I am going to find the murderer,—whether his back will still be turned towards me!—whether he is still seated at the desk writing! But perhaps—perhaps—he is no longer there!—Yet how could he have fled?—Was I not in possession of his ladder? I force myself to be cool. I raise my head yet higher. I look—he is still there. I see his monstrous back, deformed by the shadow thrown by the candle. He is no longer writing now, and the candle is on the parquet, over which he is bending—a position which serves my purpose.

"I hold my breath. I mount the ladder. I am on the uppermost rung of it, and with my left hand seize hold of the window-sill. In this moment of approaching success, I feel my heart beating wildly. I put my revolver between my teeth. A quick spring, and I shall be on the window-ledge. But—the ladder! I had been obliged to press on it heavily, and my foot had scarcely left it, when I felt it swaying beneath me. It grated on the wall and fell. But, already, my knees were touching the window-sill, and, by a movement quick as lightning, I got on to it.

"But the murderer had been even quicker than I had been. He had heard the grating of the ladder on the wall, and I saw the monstrous back of the man raise itself. I saw his head. Did I really see it?—The candle on the parquet lit up his legs only. Above the height of the table the chamber was in darkness. I saw a man with long hair, a full beard, wild-looking eyes, a pale face, framed in large whiskers,—as well as I could distinguish, and, as I think—red in colour. I did not know the face. That was, in brief, the chief sensation I received from that face in the dim half-light in which I saw it. I did not know it—or, at least, I did not recognise it.

"Now for quick action! It was indeed time for that, for as I was about to place my legs through the window, the man had seen me, had bounded to his feet, had sprung—as I foresaw he would—to the door of the ante-chamber, had time to open it, and fled. But I was already behind him, revolver in hand, shouting 'Help!'

"Like an arrow I crossed the room, but noticed a letter on the table as I rushed. I almost came up with the man in the ante-room, for he had lost time in opening the door to the gallery. I flew on wings, and in the gallery was but a few feet behind him. He had taken, as I supposed he would, the gallery on his right,—that is to say, the road he had prepared for his flight. 'Help, Jacques!—help, Larsan!' I cried. He could not escape us! I raised a shout of joy, of savage victory. The man reached the intersection of the two galleries hardly two seconds before me for the meeting which I had prepared—the fatal shock which must inevitably take place at that spot! We all rushed to the crossing-place—Monsieur Stangerson and I coming from one end of the right gallery, Daddy Jacques coming from the other end of the same gallery, and Frederic Larsan coming from the 'off-turning' gallery.

"The man was not there!

"We looked at each other stupidly and with eyes terrified. The man had vanished like a ghost. 'Where is he—where is he?' we all asked.

"'It is impossible he can have escaped!' I cried, my terror mastered by my anger.

"'I touched him!' exclaimed Frederic Larsan.

"'I felt his breath on my face!' cried Daddy Jacques.

"'Where is he?'—where is he?' we all cried.

"We raced like madmen along the two galleries; we visited doors and windows—they were closed, hermetically closed. They had not been opened. Besides, the opening of a door or window by this man whom we were hunting, without our having perceived it, would have been more inexplicable than his disappearance.

"Where is he?—where is he?—He could not have got away by a door or a window, nor by any other way. He could not have passed through our bodies!

"I confess that, for the moment, I felt 'done for.' For the gallery was perfectly lighted, and there was neither trap, nor secret door in the walls, nor any sort of hiding-place. We moved the chairs and lifted the pictures. Nothing!—nothing! We would have looked into a flower-pot, if there had been one to look into!"

When this mystery, thanks to Rouletabille, was naturally explained, by the help alone of his masterful mind, we were able to realise that the murderer had got away neither by a door, a window, nor the stairs—a fact which the judges would not admit.

XVII

The Inexplicable Gallery

M ademoiselle Stangerson appeared at the door of her ante-room," continues Rouletabille's note-book. "We were near her door in the gallery where this incredible phenomenon had taken place. There are moments when one feels as if one's brain were about to burst. A bullet in the head, a fracture of the skull, the seat of reason shattered— with only these can I compare the sensation which exhausted and left me void of sense.

"Happily, Mademoiselle Stangerson appeared on the threshold of her ante-room. I saw her, and that helped to relieve my chaotic state of mind. I breathed her—I inhaled the perfume of the lady in black, whom I should never see again. I would have given ten years of my life—half my life—to see once more the lady in black! Alas! I no more meet her but from time to time,—and yet!—and yet! how the memory of that perfume—felt by me alone—carries me back to the days of my childhood.[1] It was this sharp reminder from my beloved perfume, of the lady in black, which made me go to her—dressed wholly in white and so pale—so pale and so beautiful!—on the threshold of the inexplicable gallery. Her beautiful golden hair, gathered into a knot on the back of her neck, left visible the red star on her temple which had so nearly been the cause of her death. When I first got on the right track of the mystery of this case I had imagined that, on the night of the tragedy in the 'Yellow Room', Mademoiselle Stangerson had worn her hair in bands. But then, how could I have imagined otherwise when I had not been in the 'Yellow Room'!

"But now, since the occurrence of the inexplicable gallery, I did not reason at all. I stood there, stupid, before the apparition—so pale and so beautiful—of Mademoiselle Stangerson. She was clad in a dressing-gown of dreamy white. One might have taken her to be a ghost—a lovely

---

1. When I wrote these lines, Joseph Rouletabille was eighteen years of age,—and he spoke of his "youth." I have kept the text of my friend, but I inform the reader here that the episode of the mystery of the "Yellow Room" has no connection with that of the perfume of the lady in black. It is not my fault if, in the document which I have cited, Rouletabille thought fit to refer to his childhood.

phantom. Her father took her in his arms and kissed her passionately, as if he had recovered her after being long lost to him. I dared not question her. He drew her into the room and we followed them,—for we had to know!—The door of the boudoir was open. The terrified faces of the two nurses craned towards us. Mademoiselle Stangerson inquired the meaning of all the disturbance. That she was not in her own room was quite easily explained—quite easily. She had a fancy not to sleep that night in her chamber, but in the boudoir with her nurses, locking the door on them. Since the night of the crime she had experienced feelings of terror, and fears came over her that are easily to be comprehended.

"But who could imagine that on that particular night when he was to come, she would, by a mere chance, determine to shut herself in with her women? Who would think that she would act contrary to her father's wish to sleep in the drawing-room? Who could believe that the letter which had so recently been on the table in her room would no longer be there? He who could understand all this, would have to assume that Mademoiselle Stangerson knew that the murderer was coming—she could not prevent his coming again—unknown to her father, unknown to all but to Monsieur Robert Darzac. For he must know it now—perhaps he had known it before! Did he remember that phrase in the Elysee garden: 'Must I commit a crime, then, to win you?' Against whom the crime, if not against the obstacle, against the murderer? 'Ah, I would kill him with my own hand!' And I replied, 'You have not answered my question.' That was the very truth. In truth, in truth, Monsieur Darzac knew the murderer so well that—while wishing to kill him himself—he was afraid I should find him. There could be but two reasons why he had assisted me in my investigation. First, because I forced him to do it; and, second, because she would be the better protected.

"I am in the chamber—her room. I look at her, also at the place where the letter had just now been. She has possessed herself of it; it was evidently intended for her—evidently. How she trembles!—Trembles at the strange story her father is telling her, of the presence of the murderer in her chamber, and of the pursuit. But it is plainly to be seen that she is not wholly satisfied by the assurance given her until she had been told that the murderer, by some incomprehensible means, had been able to elude us.

"Then follows a silence. What a silence! We are all there—looking at her—her father, Larsan, Daddy Jacques and I. What were we all thinking of in the silence? After the events of that night, of the mystery of the inexplicable gallery, of the prodigious fact of the presence of the murderer in her room, it seemed to me that all our thoughts might have been translated into the words which were addressed to her. 'You who know of this mystery, explain it to us, and we shall perhaps be able to save you. How I longed to save her—for herself, and, from the other!— It brought the tears to my eyes.

"She is there, shedding about her the perfume of the lady in black. At last, I see her, in the silence of her chamber. Since the fatal hour of the mystery of the 'Yellow Room', we have hung about this invisible and silent woman to learn what she knows. Our desires, our wish to know must be a torment to her. Who can tell that, should we learn the secret of her mystery, it would not precipitate a tragedy more terrible than that which had already been enacted here? Who can tell if it might not mean her death? Yet it had brought her close to death,—and we still knew nothing. Or, rather, there are some of us who know nothing. But I—if I knew who, I should know all. Who?—Who?—Not knowing who, I must remain silent, out of pity for her. For there is no doubt that she knows how he escaped from the 'Yellow Room', and yet she keeps the secret. When I know who, I will speak to him—to him!"

"She looked at us now—with a far-away look in her eyes—as if we were not in the chamber. Monsieur Stangerson broke the silence. He declared that, henceforth, he would no more absent himself from his daughter's apartments. She tried to oppose him in vain. He adhered firmly to his purpose. He would install himself there this very night, he said. Solely concerned for the health of his daughter, he reproached her for having left her bed. Then he suddenly began talking to her as if she were a little child. He smiled at her and seemed not to know either what he said or what he did. The illustrious professor had lost his head. Mademoiselle Stangerson in a tone of tender distress said: 'Father!— father!' Daddy Jacques blows his nose, and Frederic Larsan himself is obliged to turn away to hide his emotion. For myself, I am able neither to think or feel. I felt an infinite contempt for myself.

"It was the first time that Frederic Larsan, like myself, found himself face to face with Mademoiselle Stangerson since the attack in the 'Yellow Room'. Like me, he had insisted on being allowed to question the unhappy lady; but he had not, any more than had I, been permitted. To him, as to me, the same answer had always been given: Mademoiselle Stangerson was too weak to receive us. The questionings of the examining magistrate had over-fatigued her. It was evidently intended not to give us any assistance in our researches. I was not surprised; but Frederic Larsan had always resented this conduct. It is true that he and I had a totally different theory of the crime.

"I still catch myself repeating from the depths of my heart: 'Save her!—save her without his speaking!' Who is he—the murderer? Take him and shut his mouth. But Monsieur Darzac made it clear that in order to shut his mouth he must be killed. Have I the right to kill Mademoiselle Stangerson's murderer? No, I had not. But let him only give me the chance! Let me find out whether he is really a creature of flesh and blood!—Let me see his dead body, since it cannot be taken alive.

"If I could but make this woman, who does not even look at us, understand! She is absorbed by her fears and by her father's distress of mind. And I can do nothing to save her. Yes, I will go to work once more and accomplish wonders.

"I move towards her. I would speak to her. I would entreat her to have confidence in me. I would, in a word, make her understand—she alone—that I know how the murderer escaped from the 'Yellow Room'—that I have guessed the motives for her secrecy—and that I pity her with all my heart. But by her gestures she begged us to leave her alone, expressing weariness and the need for immediate rest. Monsieur Stangerson asked us to go back to our rooms and thanked us. Frederic Larsan and I bowed to him and, followed by Daddy Jacques, we regained the gallery. I heard Larsan murmur: 'Strange! strange!' He made a sign to me to go with him into his room. On the threshold he turned towards Daddy Jacques.

"'Did you see him distinctly?' he asked.

"'Who?'

"'The man?'

"'Saw him!—why, he had a big red beard and red hair.'

"'That's how he appeared to me,' I said.

"'And to me,' said Larsan.

"The great Fred and I were alone in his chamber, now, to talk over this thing. We talked for an hour, turning the matter over and viewing it from every side. From the questions put by him, from the explanation which he gives me, it is clear to me that—in spite of all our senses—he is persuaded the man disappeared by some secret passage in the chateau known to him alone.

"'He knows the chateau,' he said to me; 'he knows it well.'

"'He is a rather tall man—well-built,' I suggested.

"'He is as tall as he wants to be,' murmured Fred.

"'I understand,' I said; 'but how do you account for his red hair and beard?'

"'Too much beard—too much hair—false,' says Fred.

"'That's easily said. You are always thinking of Robert Darzac. You can't get rid of that idea? I am certain that he is innocent.'

"'So much the better. I hope so; but everything condemns him. Did you notice the marks on the carpet?—Come and look at them.'

"'I have seen them; they are the marks of the neat boots, the same as those we saw on the border of the lake.'

"'Can you deny that they belong to Robert Darzac?'

"'Of course, one may be mistaken.'

"'Have you noticed that those footprints only go in one direction?— that there are no return marks? When the man came from the chamber, pursued by all of us, his footsteps left no traces behind them.'

"'He had, perhaps, been in the chamber for hours. The mud from his boots had dried, and he moved with such rapidity on the points of his toes—We saw him running, but we did not hear his steps.'

"I suddenly put an end to this idle chatter—void of any logic, and made a sign to Larsan to listen.

"'There—below; some one is shutting a door.'

"I rise; Larsan follows me; we descend to the ground-floor of the chateau. I lead him to the little semi-circular room under the terrace beneath the window of the 'off-turning' gallery. I point to the door, now closed, open a short time before, under which a shaft of light is visible.

"'The forest-keeper!' says Fred.

"'Come on!' I whisper.

"Prepared—I know not why—to believe that the keeper is the guilty man—I go to the door and rap smartly on it. Some might think that we were rather late in thinking of the keeper, since our first business, after having found that the murderer had escaped us in the gallery, ought to have been to search everywhere else,—around the chateau,—in the park—

"Had this criticism been made at the time, we could only have answered that the assassin had disappeared from the gallery in such a way that we thought he was no longer anywhere! He had eluded us when we all had our hands stretched out ready to seize him—when we were almost touching him. We had no longer any ground for hoping that we could clear up the mystery of that night.

"As soon as I rapped at the door it was opened, and the keeper asked us quietly what we wanted. He was undressed and preparing to go to bed. The bed had not yet been disturbed.

"We entered and I affected surprise.

"'Not gone to bed yet?'

"'No,' he replied roughly. 'I have been making a round of the park and in the woods. I am only just back—and sleepy. Good-night!'

"'Listen,' I said. 'An hour or so ago, there was a ladder close by your window.'

"'What ladder?—I did not see any ladder. Good-night!'

"And he simply put us out of the room. When we were outside I looked at Larsan. His face was impenetrable.

"'Well?' I said.

"'Well?' he repeated.

"'Does that open out any new view to you?'

"There was no mistaking Larsan's bad temper. On re-entering the chateau, I heard him mutter:

"'It would be strange—very strange—if I had deceived myself on that point!'

"He seemed to be talking to me rather than to himself. He added: 'In any case, we shall soon know what to think. The morning will bring light with it.'"

XVIII

Rouletabille Has Drawn a Circle Between the Two Bumps on His Forehead

(Extract from the Note-Book of Joseph
Rouletabille, Continued)

We separated on the thresholds of our rooms, with a melancholy shake of the hands. I was glad to have aroused in him a suspicion of error. His was an original brain, very intelligent but—without method. I did not go to bed. I awaited the coming of daylight and then went down to the front of the chateau, and made a detour, examining every trace of footsteps coming towards it or going from it. These, however, were so mixed and confusing that I could make nothing of them. Here I may make a remark,—I am not accustomed to attach an exaggerated importance to exterior signs left in the track of a crime.

"The method which traces the criminal by means of the tracks of his footsteps is altogether primitive. So many footprints are identical. However, in the disturbed state of my mind, I did go into the deserted court and did look at all the footprints I could find there, seeking for some indication, as a basis for reasoning.

"If I could but find a right starting-point! In despair I seated myself on a stone. For over an hour I busied myself with the common, ordinary work of a policeman. Like the least intelligent of detectives I went on blindly over the traces of footprints which told me just no more than they could.

"I came to the conclusion that I was a fool, lower in the scale of intelligence than even the police of the modern romancer. Novelists build mountains of stupidity out of a footprint on the sand, or from an impression of a hand on the wall. That's the way innocent men are brought to prison. It might convince an examining magistrate or the head of a detective department, but it's not proof. You writers forget that what the senses furnish is not proof. If I am taking cognisance of what is offered me by my senses I do so but to bring the results within the circle of my reason. That circle may be the most circumscribed, but if it is, it has this advantage—it holds nothing but the truth! Yes, I swear that I have never used the evidence of the senses but as servants to my reason. I have never permitted them to become my master. They have not made of me that monstrous thing,—worse than a blind man,—a man who sees falsely. And that is why I can triumph over your error and your merely animal intelligence, Frederic Larsan.

"Be of good courage, then, friend Rouletabille; it is impossible that the incident of the inexplicable gallery should be outside the circle of your reason. You know that! Then have faith and take thought with yourself and forget not that you took hold of the right end when you drew that circle in your brain within which to unravel this mysterious play of circumstance.

"To it, once again! Go—back to the gallery. Take your stand on your reason and rest there as Frederic Larsan rests on his cane. You will then soon prove that the great Fred is nothing but a fool.

30th October. Noon
JOSEPH ROULETABILLE

"I acted as I planned. With head on fire, I retraced my way to the gallery, and without having found anything more than I had seen on the previous night, the right hold I had taken of my reason drew me to something so important that I was obliged to cling to it to save myself from falling.

"Now for the strength and patience to find sensible traces to fit in with my thinking—and these must come within the circle I have drawn between the two bumps on my forehead!

30th of October. Midnight
JOSEPH ROULETABILLE

XIX

ROULETABILLE INVITES ME TO BREAKFAST AT THE DONJON INN

It was not until later that Rouletabille sent me the note-book in which he had written at length the story of the phenomenon of the inexplicable gallery. On the day I arrived at the Glandier and joined him in his room, he recounted to me, with the greatest detail, all that I have now related, telling me also how he had spent several hours in Paris where he had learned nothing that could be of any help to him.

The event of the inexplicable gallery had occurred on the night between the 29th and 30th of October, that is to say, three days before my return to the chateau. It was on the 2nd of November, then, that I went back to the Glandier, summoned there by my friend's telegram, and taking the revolvers with me.

I am now in Rouletabille's room and he has finished his recital.

While he had been telling me the story I noticed him continually rubbing the glass of the eyeglasses he had found on the side table. From the evident pleasure he was taking in handling them I felt they must be one of those sensible evidences destined to enter what he had called the circle of the right end of his reason. That strange and unique way of his, to express himself in terms wonderfully adequate for his thoughts, no longer surprised me. It was often necessary to know his thought to understand the terms he used; and it was not easy to penetrate into Rouletabille's thinking.

This lad's brain was one of the most curious things I have ever observed. Rouletabille went on the even tenor of his way without suspecting the astonishment and even bewilderment he roused in others. I am sure he was not himself in the least conscious of the originality of his genius. He was himself and at ease wherever he happened to be.

When he had finished his recital he asked me what I thought of it. I replied that I was much puzzled by his question. Then he begged me to try, in my turn, to take my reason in hand "by the right end."

"Very well," I said. "It seems to me that the point of departure of my reason would be this—there can be no doubt that the murderer you pursued was in the gallery." I paused.

"After making so good a start, you ought not to stop so soon," he exclaimed. "Come, make another effort."

"I'll try. Since he disappeared from the gallery without passing through any door or window, he must have escaped by some other opening."

Rouletabille looked at me pityingly, smiled carelessly, and remarked that I was reasoning like a postman, or—like Frederic Larsan.

Rouletabille had alternate fits of admiration and disdain for the great Fred. It all depended as to whether Larsan's discoveries tallied with Rouletabille's reasoning or not. When they did he would exclaim: "He is really great!" When they did not he would grunt and mutter, "What an ass!" It was a petty side of the noble character of this strange youth.

We had risen, and he led me into the park. When we reached the court and were making towards the gate, the sound of blinds thrown back against the wall made us turn our heads, and we saw, at a window on the first floor of the chateau, the ruddy and clean shaven face of a person I did not recognise.

"Hullo!" muttered Rouletabille. "Arthur Rance!"—He lowered his head, quickened his pace, and I heard him ask himself between his teeth: "Was he in the chateau that night? What is he doing here?"

We had gone some distance from the chateau when I asked him who this Arthur Rance was, and how he had come to know him. He referred to his story of that morning and I remembered that Mr. Arthur W. Rance was the American from Philadelphia with whom he had had so many drinks at the Elysee reception.

"But was he not to have left France almost immediately?" I asked.

"No doubt; that's why I am surprised to find him here still, and not only in France, but above all, at the Glandier. He did not arrive this morning; and he did not get here last night. He must have got here before dinner, then. Why didn't the concierges tell me?"

I reminded my friend, apropos of the concierges, that he had not yet told me what had led him to get them set at liberty.

We were close to their lodge. Monsieur and Madame Bernier saw us coming. A frank smile lit up their happy faces. They seemed to harbour no ill-feeling because of their detention. My young friend asked them at what hour Mr. Arthur Rance had arrived. They answered that they did not know he was at the chateau. He must have come during the evening of the previous night, but they had not had to open the gate for him, because, being a great walker, and not wishing that a carriage should be sent to meet him, he was accustomed to get off at the little hamlet of Saint-Michel, from which he came to the chateau by way of the forest. He reached the park by the grotto of Sainte-Genevieve, over the little gate of which, giving on to the park, he climbed.

As the concierges spoke, I saw Rouletabille's face cloud over and exhibit disappointment—a disappointment, no doubt, with himself. Evidently he was a little vexed, after having worked so much on the spot, with so minute a study of the people and events at the Glandier, that he had to learn now that Arthur Rance was accustomed to visit the chateau.

"You say that Monsieur Arthur Rance is accustomed to come to the chateau. When did he come here last?"

"We can't tell you exactly," replied Madame Bernier—that was the name of the concierge—"we couldn't know while they were keeping us in prison. Besides, as the gentleman comes to the chateau without passing through our gate he goes away by the way he comes."

"Do you know when he came the first time?"

"Oh yes, Monsieur!—nine years ago."

"He was in France nine years ago, then," said Rouletabille, "and, since that time, as far as you know, how many times has he been at the Glandier?"

"Three times."

"When did he come the last time, as far as you know?"

"A week before the attempt in the 'Yellow Room'."

Rouletabille put another question—this time addressing himself particularly to the woman:

"In the grove of the parquet?"

"In the grove of the parquet," she replied.

"Thanks!" said Rouletabille. "Be ready for me this evening."

He spoke the last words with a finger on his lips as if to command silence and discretion.

We left the park and took the way to the Donjon Inn.

"Do you often eat here?"

"Sometimes."

"But you also take your meals at the chateau?"

"Yes, Larsan and I are sometimes served in one of our rooms."

"Hasn't Monsieur Stangerson ever invited you to his own table?"

"Never."

"Does your presence at the chateau displease him?"

"I don't know; but, in any case, he does not make us feel that we are in his way."

"Doesn't he question you?"

"Never. He is in the same state of mind as he was in at the door of the 'Yellow Room' when his daughter was being murdered, and when he broke open the door and did not find the murderer. He is persuaded, since he could discover nothing, that there's no reason why we should be able to discover more than he did. But he has made it his duty, since Larsan expressed his theory, not to oppose us."

Rouletabille buried himself in thought again for some time. He aroused himself later to tell me of how he came to set the two concierges free.

"I went recently to see Monsieur Stangerson, and took with me a piece of paper on which was written: 'I promise, whatever others may say, to keep in my service my two faithful servants, Bernier and his wife.' I explained to him that, by signing that document, he would enable me to compel those two people to speak out; and I declared my own assurance of their innocence of any part in the crime. That was also his opinion. The examining magistrate, after it was signed, presented the document to the Berniers, who then did speak. They said, what I was certain they would say, as soon as they were sure they would not lose their place.

"They confessed to poaching on Monsieur Stangerson's estates, and it was while they were poaching, on the night of the crime, that they were found not far from the pavilion at the moment when the outrage was being committed. Some rabbits they caught in that way were sold by them to the landlord of the Donjon Inn, who served them to his customers, or sent them to Paris. That was the truth, as I had guessed from the first. Do you remember what I said, on entering the Donjon Inn?—'We shall have to eat red meat—now!' I had heard the words on the same morning when we arrived at the park gate. You heard them also, but you did not attach any importance to them. You recollect, when we reached the park gate, that we stopped to look at a man who was running by the side of the wall, looking every minute at his watch. That was Larsan. Well, behind us the landlord of the Donjon Inn, standing on his doorstep, said to someone inside: 'We shall have to eat red meat—now.'

"Why that 'now'? When you are, as I am, in search of some hidden secret, you can't afford to have anything escape you. You've got to know the meaning of everything. We had come into a rather out-of-the-way part of the country which had been turned topsy-turvy by a crime, and my reason led me to suspect every phrase that could bear upon the event of the day. 'Now,' I took to mean, 'since the outrage.' In the course of my inquiry, therefore, I sought to find a relation between that phrase and the tragedy. We went to the Donjon Inn for breakfast; I repeated the phrase and saw, by the surprise and trouble on Daddy Mathieu's face, that I had not exaggerated its importance, so far as he was concerned.

"I had just learned that the concierges had been arrested. Daddy Mathieu spoke of them as of dear friends—people for whom one is sorry. That was a reckless conjunction of ideas, I said to myself. 'Now,' that the concierges are arrested, 'we shall have to eat red meat.' No more concierges, no more game! The hatred expressed by Daddy Mathieu for Monsieur Stangerson's forest-keeper—a hatred he pretended was shared by the concierges led me easily to think of poaching. Now as all the evidence showed the concierges had not been in bed at the time of the tragedy, why were they abroad that night? As participants in the crime? I was not disposed to think so. I had already arrived at the conclusion, by steps of which I will tell you later—that the assassin had had no accomplice, and that the tragedy held a mystery between Mademoiselle Stangerson and the murderer, a mystery with which the concierges had nothing to do.

"With that theory in my mind, I searched for proof in their lodge, which, as you know, I entered. I found there under their bed, some springs and brass wire. 'Ah!' I thought, 'these things explain why they were out in the park at night!' I was not surprised at the dogged silence they maintained before the examining magistrate, even under the accusation so grave as that of being accomplices in the crime. Poaching would save them from the Assize Court, but it would lose them their places; and, as they were perfectly sure of their innocence of the crime they hoped it would soon be established, and then their poaching might go on as usual. They could always confess later. I, however, hastened their confession by means of the document Monsieur Stangerson signed. They gave all the necessary 'proofs,' were set at liberty, and have now a lively gratitude for me. Why did I not get them released sooner? Because I was not sure that nothing more than poaching was against them. I wanted to study the ground. As the days went by, my conviction became more and more certain. The day after the events of the inexplicable gallery I had need of help I could rely on, so I resolved to have them released at once."

That was how Joseph Rouletabille explained himself. Once more I could not but be astonished at the simplicity of the reasoning which had brought him to the truth of the matter. Certainly this was no big thing; but I think, myself, that the young man will, one of these days, explain with the same simplicity, the fearful tragedy in the "Yellow Room" as well as the phenomenon of the inexplicable gallery.

We reached the Donjon Inn and entered it.

This time we did not see the landlord, but were received with a pleasant smile by the hostess. I have already described the room in which we found ourselves, and I have given a glimpse of the charming blonde woman with the gentle eyes who now immediately began to prepare our breakfast.

"How's Daddy Mathieu?" asked Rouletabille.

"Not much better—not much better; he is still confined to his bed."

"His rheumatism still sticks to him, then?"

"Yes. Last night I was again obliged to give him morphine—the only drug that gives him any relief."

She spoke in a soft voice. Everything about her expressed gentleness. She was, indeed, a beautiful woman; somewhat with an air of indolence, with great eyes seemingly black and blue—amorous eyes. Was she happy with her crabbed, rheumatic husband? The scene at which we had once been present did not lead us to believe that she was; yet there was something in her bearing that was not suggestive of despair. She disappeared into the kitchen to prepare our repast, leaving on the table a bottle of excellent cider. Rouletabille filled our earthenware mugs, loaded his pipe, and quietly explained to me his reason for asking me to come to the Glandier with revolvers.

"Yes," he said, contemplatively looking at the clouds of smoke he was puffing out, "yes, my dear boy, I expect the assassin tonight." A brief silence followed, which I took care not to interrupt, and then he went on:

"Last night, just as I was going to bed, Monsieur Robert Darzac knocked at my room. When he came in he confided to me that he was compelled to go to Paris the next day, that is, this morning. The reason which made this journey necessary was at once peremptory and mysterious; it was not possible for him to explain its object to me. 'I go, and yet,' he added, 'I would give my life not to leave Mademoiselle

Stangerson at this moment.' He did not try to hide that he believed her to be once more in danger. 'It will not greatly astonish me if something happens tomorrow night,' he avowed, 'and yet I must be absent. I cannot be back at the Glandier before the morning of the day after tomorrow.'

"I asked him to explain himself, and this is all he would tell me. His anticipation of coming danger had come to him solely from the coincidence that Mademoiselle Stangerson had been twice attacked, and both times when he had been absent. On the night of the incident of the inexplicable gallery he had been obliged to be away from the Glandier. On the night of the tragedy in the 'Yellow Room' he had also not been able to be at the Glandier, though this was the first time he had declared himself on the matter. Now a man so moved who would still go away must be acting under compulsion—must be obeying a will stronger than his own. That was how I reasoned, and I told him so. He replied 'Perhaps.'—I asked him if Mademoiselle Stangerson was compelling him. He protested that she was not. His determination to go to Paris had been taken without any conference with Mademoiselle Stangerson.

"To cut the story short, he repeated that his belief in the possibility of a fresh attack was founded entirely on the extraordinary coincidence. 'If anything happens to Mademoiselle Stangerson,' he said, 'it would be terrible for both of us. For her, because her life would be in danger; for me because I could neither defend her from the attack nor tell of where I had been. I am perfectly aware of the suspicions cast on me. The examining magistrate and Monsieur Larsan are both on the point of believing in my guilt. Larsan tracked me the last time I went to Paris, and I had all the trouble in the world to get rid of him.'

"'Why do you not tell me the name of the murderer now, if you know it?' I cried.

"Monsieur Darzac appeared extremely troubled by my question, and replied to me in a hesitating tone:

"'I?—I know the name of the murderer? Why, how could I know his name?'

"I at once replied: 'From Mademoiselle Stangerson.'

"He grew so pale that I thought he was about to faint, and I saw that I had hit the nail right on the head. Mademoiselle and he knew the name of the murderer! When he recovered himself, he said to me: 'I am going to leave you. Since you have been here I have appreciated your exceptional intelligence and your unequalled ingenuity. But I

GASTON LEROUX

ask this service of you. Perhaps I am wrong to fear an attack during the coming night; but, as I must act with foresight, I count on you to frustrate any attempt that may be made. Take every step needful to protect Mademoiselle Stangerson. Keep a most careful watch of her room. Don't go to sleep, nor allow yourself one moment of repose. The man we dread is remarkably cunning—with a cunning that has never been equalled. If you keep watch his very cunning may save her; because it's impossible that he should not know that you are watching; and knowing it, he may not venture.'

"'Have you spoken of all this to Monsieur Stangerson?'

"'No. I do not wish him to ask me, as you just now did, for the name of the murderer. I tell you all this, Monsieur Rouletabille, because I have great, very great, confidence in you. I know that you do not suspect me.'

"The poor man spoke in jerks. He was evidently suffering. I pitied him, the more because I felt sure that he would rather allow himself to be killed than tell me who the murderer was. As for Mademoiselle Stangerson, I felt that she would rather allow herself to be murdered than denounce the man of the 'Yellow Room' and of the inexplicable gallery. The man must be dominating her, or both, by some inscrutable power. They were dreading nothing so much as the chance of Monsieur Stangerson knowing that his daughter was 'held' by her assailant. I made Monsieur Darzac understand that he had explained himself sufficiently, and that he might refrain from telling me any more than he had already told me. I promised him to watch through the night. He insisted that I should establish an absolutely impassable barrier around Mademoiselle Stangerson's chamber, around the boudoir where the nurses were sleeping, and around the drawing-room where, since the affair of the inexplicable gallery, Monsieur Stangerson had slept. In short, I was to put a cordon round the whole apartment.

"From his insistence I gathered that Monsieur Darzac intended not only to make it impossible for the expected man to reach the chamber of Mademoiselle Stangerson, but to make that impossibility so visibly clear that, seeing himself expected, he would at once go away. That was how I interpreted his final words when we parted: 'You may mention your suspicions of the expected attack to Monsieur Stangerson, to Daddy Jacques, to Frederic Larsan, and to anybody in the chateau.'

"The poor fellow left me hardly knowing what he was saying. My silence and my eyes told him that I had guessed a large part of his secret.

And, indeed, he must have been at his wits' end, to have come to me at such a time, and to abandon Mademoiselle Stangerson in spite of his fixed idea as to the consequence.

"When he was gone, I began to think that I should have to use even a greater cunning than his so that if the man should come that night, he might not for a moment suspect that his coming had been expected. Certainly! I would allow him to get in far enough, so that, dead or alive, I might see his face clearly! He must be got rid of. Mademoiselle Stangerson must be freed from this continual impending danger.

"Yes, my boy," said Rouletabille, after placing his pipe on the table, and emptying his mug of cider, "I must see his face distinctly, so as to make sure to impress it on that part of my brain where I have drawn my circle of reasoning."

The landlady re-appeared at that moment, bringing in the traditional bacon omelette. Rouletabille chaffed her a little, and she took the chaff with the most charming good humour.

"She is much jollier when Daddy Mathieu is in bed with his rheumatism," Rouletabille said to me.

But I had eyes neither for Rouletabille nor for the landlady's smiles. I was entirely absorbed over the last words of my young friend and in thinking over Monsieur Robert Darzac's strange behaviour.

When he had finished his omelette and we were again alone, Rouletabille continued the tale of his confidences.

"When I sent you my telegram this morning," he said, "I had only the word of Monsieur Darzac, that 'perhaps' the assassin would come tonight. I can now say that he will certainly come. I expect him."

"What has made you feel this certainty?"

"I have been sure since half-past ten o'clock this morning that he would come. I knew that before we saw Arthur Rance at the window in the court."

"Ah!" I said, "But, again—what made you so sure? And why since half-past ten this morning?"

"Because, at half-past ten, I had proof that Mademoiselle Stangerson was making as many efforts to permit of the murderer's entrance as Monsieur Robert Darzac had taken precautions against it."

"Is that possible!" I cried. "Haven't you told me that Mademoiselle Stangerson loves Monsieur Robert Darzac?"

"I told you so because it is the truth."

"Then do you see nothing strange—"

"Everything in this business is strange, my friend; but take my word for it, the strangeness you now feel is nothing to the strangeness that's to come!"

"It must be admitted, then," I said, "that Mademoiselle Stangerson and her murderer are in communication—at any rate in writing?"

"Admit it, my friend, admit it! You don't risk anything! I told you about the letter left on her table, on the night of the inexplicable gallery affair,—the letter that disappeared into the pocket of Mademoiselle Stangerson. Why should it not have been a summons to a meeting? Might he not, as soon as he was sure of Darzac's absence, appoint the meeting for 'the coming night?"

And my friend laughed silently. There are moments when I ask myself if he is not laughing at me.

The door of the inn opened. Rouletabille was on his feet so suddenly that one might have thought he had received an electric shock.

"Mr. Arthur Rance!" he cried.

Mr. Arthur Rance stood before us calmly bowing.

XX

An Act of Mademoiselle Stangerson

Y ou remember me, Monsieur?" asked Rouletabille.

"Perfectly!" replied Arthur Rance. "I recognise you as the lad at the bar. (The face of Rouletabille crimsoned at being called a "lad.") I want to shake hands with you. You are a bright little fellow."

The American extended his hand and Rouletabille, relaxing his frown, shook it and introduced Mr. Arthur Rance to me. He invited him to share our meal.

"No thanks. I breakfasted with Monsieur Stangerson."

Arthur Rance spoke French perfectly,—almost without an accent.

"I did not expect to have the pleasure of seeing you again, Monsieur. I thought you were to have left France the day after the reception at the Elysee."

Rouletabille and I, outwardly indifferent, listened most intently for every word the American would say.

The man's purplish red face, his heavy eyelids, the nervous twitchings, all spoke of his addiction to drink. How came it that so sorry a specimen of a man should be so intimate with Monsieur Stangerson?

Some days later, I learned from Frederic Larsan—who, like ourselves, was surprised and mystified by his appearance and reception at the chateau—that Mr. Rance had been an inebriate for only about fifteen years; that is to say, since the professor and his daughter left Philadelphia. During the time the Stangersons lived in America they were very intimate with Arthur Rance, who was one of the most distinguished phrenologists of the new world. Owing to new experiments, he had made enormous strides beyond the science of Gall and Lavater. The friendliness with which he was received at the Glandier may be explained by the fact that he had once rendered Mademoiselle Stangerson a great service by stopping, at the peril of his own life, the runaway horses of her carriage. The immediate result of that could, however, have been no more than a mere friendly association with the Stangersons; certainly, not a love affair.

Frederic Larsan did not tell me where he had picked up this information; but he appeared to be quite sure of what he said.

Had we known these facts at the time Arthur Rance met us at the Donjon Inn, his presence at the chateau might not have puzzled us, but they could not have failed to increase our interest in the man himself. The American must have been at least forty-five years old. He spoke in a perfectly natural tone in reply to Rouletabille's question.

"I put off my return to America when I heard of the attack on Mademoiselle Stangerson. I wanted to be certain the lady had not been killed, and I shall not go away until she is perfectly recovered."

Arthur Rance then took the lead in talk, paying no heed to some of Rouletabille's questions. He gave us, without our inviting him, his personal views on the subject of the tragedy,—views which, as well as I could make out, were not far from those held by Frederic Larzan. The American also thought that Robert Darzac had something to do with the matter. He did not mention him by name, but there was no room to doubt whom he meant. He told us he was aware of the efforts young Rouletabille was making to unravel the tangled skein of the "Yellow Room" mystery. He explained that Monsieur Stangerson had related to him all that had taken place in the inexplicable gallery. He several times expressed his regret at Monsieur Darzac's absence from the chateau on all these occasions, and thought that Monsieur Darzac had done cleverly in allying himself with Monsieur Joseph Rouletabille, who could not fail, sooner or later, to discover the murderer. He spoke the last sentence with unconcealed irony. Then he rose, bowed to us, and left the inn.

Rouletabille watched him through the window.

"An odd fish, that!" he said.

"Do you think he'll pass the night at the Glandier?" I asked.

To my amazement the young reporter answered that it was a matter of entire indifference to him whether he did or not.

As to how we spent our time during the afternoon, all I need say is that Rouletabille led me to the grotto of Sainte-Genevieve, and, all the time, talked of every subject but the one in which we were most interested. Towards evening I was surprised to find Rouletabille making none of the preparations I had expected him to make. I spoke to him about it when night had come on, and we were once more in his room. He replied that all his arrangements had already been made, and this time the murderer would not get away from him.

I expressed some doubt on this, reminding him of his disappearance in the gallery, and suggested that the same phenomenon might occur again. He answered that he hoped it would. He desired nothing more. I did not insist, knowing by experience how useless that would have been. He told me that, with the help of the concierges, the chateau had since early dawn been watched in such a way that nobody could approach it without his knowing it, and that he had no concern for those who might have left it and remained without.

It was then six o'clock by his watch. Rising, he made a sign to me to follow him, and, without in the least trying to conceal his movements or the sound of his footsteps, he led me through the gallery. We reached the 'right' gallery and came to the landing-place which we crossed. We then continued our way in the gallery of the left wing, passing Professor Stangerson's apartment.

At the far end of the gallery, before coming to the donjon, is the room occupied by Arthur Rance. We knew that, because we had seen him at the window looking on to the court. The door of the room opens on to the end of the gallery, exactly facing the east window, at the extremity of the 'right' gallery, where Rouletabille had placed Daddy Jacques, and commands an uninterrupted view of the gallery from end to end of the chateau.

"That 'off-turning' gallery," said Rouletabille, "I reserve for myself; when I tell you you'll come and take your place here."

And he made me enter a little dark, triangular closet built in a bend of the wall, to the left of the door of Arthur Rance's room. From this recess I could see all that occurred in the gallery as well as if I had been standing in front of Arthur Rance's door, and I could watch that door, too. The door of the closet, which was to be my place of observation, was fitted with panels of transparent glass. In the gallery, where all the lamps had been lit, it was quite light. In the closet, however, it was quite dark. It was a splendid place from which to observe and remain unobserved.

I was soon to play the part of a spy—a common policeman. I wonder what my leader at the bar would have said had he known! I was not altogether pleased with my duties, but I could not refuse Rouletabille the assistance he had begged me to give him. I took care not to make him see that I in the least objected, and for several reasons. I wanted to oblige him; I did not wish him to think me a coward; I was filled with curiosity; and it was too late for me to draw back, even had I determined to do so. That I had not had these scruples sooner was because my curiosity had quite got the better of me. I might also urge that I was helping to save the life of a woman, and even a lawyer may do that conscientiously.

We returned along the gallery. On reaching the door of Mademoiselle Stangerson's apartment, it opened from a push given by the steward who was waiting at the dinner-table. (Monsieur Stangerson had, for the last three days, dined with his daughter in the drawing-room on the first floor.) As the door remained open, we distinctly saw Mademoiselle Stangerson, taking advantage of the steward's absence, and while her father was stooping to pick up something he had let fall, pour the contents of a phial into Monsieur Stangerson's glass.

XXI

On the Watch

The act, which staggered me, did not appear to affect Rouletabille much. We returned to his room and, without even referring to what we had seen, he gave me his final instructions for the night. First we were to go to dinner; after dinner, I was to take my stand in the dark closet and wait there as long as it was necessary—to look out for what might happen.

"If you see anything before I do," he explained, "you must let me know. If the man gets into the 'right' gallery by any other way than the 'off-turning' gallery, you will see him before I shall, because you have a view along the whole length of the 'right' gallery, while I can only command a view of the 'off-turning' gallery. All you need do to let me know is to undo the cord holding the curtain of the 'right' gallery window, nearest to the dark closet. The curtain will fall of itself and immediately leave a square of shadow where previously there had been a square of light. To do this, you need but stretch your hand out of the closet, I shall understand your signal perfectly."

"And then?"

"Then you will see me coming round the corner of the 'off-turning' gallery."

"What am I to do then?"

"You will immediately come towards me, behind the man; but I shall already be upon him, and shall have seen his face."

I attempted a feeble smile.

"Why do you smile? Well, you may smile while you have the chance, but I swear you'll have no time for that a few hours from now.

"And if the man escapes?"

"So much the better," said Rouletabille, coolly, "I don't want to capture him. He may take himself off any way he can. I will let him go—after I have seen his face. That's all I want. I shall know afterwards what to do so that as far as Mademoiselle Stangerson is concerned he shall be dead to her even though he continues to live. If I took him alive, Mademoiselle Stangerson and Robert Darzac would, perhaps, never forgive me! And I wish to retain their good-will and respect.

GASTON LEROUX

"Seeing, as I have just now seen, Mademoiselle Stangerson pour a narcotic into her father's glass, so that he might not be awake to interrupt the conversation she is going to have with her murderer, you can imagine she would not be grateful to me if I brought the man of the 'Yellow Room' and the inexplicable gallery, bound and gagged, to her father. I realise now that if I am to save the unhappy lady, I must silence the man and not capture him. To kill a human being is no small thing. Besides, that's not my business, unless the man himself makes it my business. On the other hand, to render him forever silent without the lady's assent and confidence is to act on one's own initiative and assumes a knowledge of everything with nothing for a basis. Fortunately, my friend, I have guessed, no, I have reasoned it all out. All that I ask of the man who is coming tonight is to bring me his face, so that it may enter—"

"Into the circle?"

"Exactly! And his face won't surprise me!"

"But I thought you saw his face on the night when you sprang into the chamber?"

"Only imperfectly. The candle was on the floor; and, his beard—"

"Will he wear his beard this evening?"

"I think I can say for certain that he will. But the gallery is light and, now, I know—or—at least, my brain knows—and my eyes will see."

"If we are here only to see him and let him escape, why are we armed?"

"Because, if the man of the 'Yellow Room' and the inexplicable gallery knows that I know, he is capable of doing anything! We should then have to defend ourselves."

"And you are sure he will come tonight?"

"As sure as that you are standing there! This morning, at half-past ten o'clock, Mademoiselle Stangerson, in the cleverest way in the world, arranged to have no nurses tonight. She gave them leave of absence for twenty-four hours, under some plausible pretexts, and did not desire anybody to be with her but her father, while they are away. Her father, who is to sleep in the boudoir, has gladly consented to the arrangement. Darzac's departure and what he told me, as well as the extraordinary precautions Mademoiselle Stangerson is taking to be alone tonight leaves me no room for doubt. She has prepared the way for the coming of the man whom Darzac dreads."

"That's awful!"

"It is!"

"And what we saw her do was done to send her father to sleep?"

"Yes."

"Then there are but two of us for tonight's work?"

"Four; the concierge and his wife will watch at all hazards. I don't set much value on them before—but the concierge may be useful after—if there's to be any killing!"

"Then you think there may be?"

"If he wishes it."

"Why haven't you brought in Daddy Jacques?—Have you made no use of him today?"

"No," replied Rouletabille sharply.

I kept silence for awhile, then, anxious to know his thoughts, I asked him point blank:

"Why not tell Arthur Rance?—He may be of great assistance to us?"

"Oh!" said Rouletabille crossly, "then you want to let everybody into Mademoiselle Stangerson's secrets?—Come, let us go to dinner; it is time. This evening we dine in Frederic Larsan's room,—at least, if he is not on the heels of Darzac. He sticks to him like a leech. But, anyhow, if he is not there now, I am quite sure he will be, tonight! He's the one I am going to knock over!"

At this moment we heard a noise in the room near us.

"It must be he," said Rouletabille.

"I forgot to ask you," I said, "if we are to make any allusion to tonight's business when we are with this policeman. I take it we are not. Is that so?"

"Evidently. We are going to operate alone, on our own personal account."

"So that all the glory will be ours?"

Rouletabille laughed.

We dined with Frederic Larsan in his room. He told us he had just come in and invited us to be seated at table. We ate our dinner in the best of humours, and I had no difficulty in appreciating the feelings of certainty which both Rouletabille and Larsan felt. Rouletabille told the great Fred that I had come on a chance visit, and that he had asked me to stay and help him in the heavy batch of writing he had to get through for the "Epoque." I was going back to Paris, he said, by the eleven o'clock train, taking his "copy," which took a story form, recounting the principal episodes in the mysteries of the Glandier. Larsan smiled at the explanation like a man who was not fooled and politely refrains from making the slightest remark on matters which did not concern him.

With infinite precautions as to the words they used, and even as to the tones of their voices, Larsan and Rouletabille discussed, for a long time, Mr. Arthur Rance's appearance at the chateau, and his past in America, about which they expressed a desire to know more, at any rate, so far as his relations with the Stangersons. At one time, Larsan, who appeared to me to be unwell, said, with an effort:

"I think, Monsieur Rouletabille, that we've not much more to do at the Glandier, and that we sha'n't sleep here many more nights."

"I think so, too, Monsieur Fred."

"Then you think the conclusion of the matter has been reached?"

"I think, indeed, that we have nothing more to find out," replied Rouletabille.

"Have you found your criminal?" asked Larsan.

"Have you?"

"Yes."

"So have I," said Rouletabille.

"Can it be the same man?"

"I don't know if you have swerved from your original idea," said the young reporter. Then he added, with emphasis: "Monsieur Darzac is an honest man!"

"Are you sure of that?" asked Larsan. "Well, I am sure he is not. So it's a fight then?"

"Yes, it is a fight. But I shall beat you, Monsieur Frederic Larsan."

"Youth never doubts anything," said the great Fred laughingly, and held out his hand to me by way of conclusion.

Rouletabille's answer came like an echo:

"Not anything!"

Suddenly Larsan, who had risen to wish us goodnight, pressed both his hands to his chest and staggered. He was obliged to lean on Rouletabille for support, and to save himself from falling.

"Oh! Oh!" he cried. "What is the matter with me?—Have I been poisoned?"

He looked at us with haggard eyes. We questioned him vainly; he did not answer us. He had sunk into an armchair and we could get not a word from him. We were extremely distressed, both on his account and on our own, for we had partaken of all the dishes he had eaten. He seemed to be out of pain; but his heavy head had fallen on his shoulder and his eyelids were tightly closed. Rouletabille bent over him, listening for the beatings of the heart.

My friend's face, however, when he stood up, was as calm as it had been a moment before agitated.

"He is asleep," he said.

He led me to his chamber, after closing Larsan's room.

"The drug?" I asked. "Does Mademoiselle Stangerson wish to put everybody to sleep, tonight?"

"Perhaps," replied Rouletabille; but I could see he was thinking of something else.

"But what about us?" I exclaimed. "How do we know that we have not been drugged?"

"Do you feel indisposed?" Rouletabille asked me coolly.

"Not in the least."

"Do you feel any inclination to go to sleep?"

"None whatever."

"Well, then, my friend, smoke this excellent cigar."

And he handed me a choice Havana, one Monsieur Darzac had given him, while he lit his briarwood—his eternal briarwood.

We remained in his room until about ten o'clock without a word passing between us. Buried in an armchair Rouletabille sat and smoked steadily, his brow in thought and a far-away look in his eyes. On the stroke of ten he took off his boots and signalled to me to do the same. As we stood in our socks he said, in so low a tone that I guessed, rather than heard, the word:

"Revolver."

I drew my revolver from my jacket pocket.

"Cock it!" he said.

I did as he directed.

Then moving towards the door of his room, he opened it with infinite precaution; it made no sound. We were in the "off-turning" gallery. Rouletabille made another sign to me which I understood to mean that I was to take up my post in the dark closet.

When I was some distance from him, he rejoined me and embraced me; and then I saw him, with the same precaution, return to his room. Astonished by his embrace, and somewhat disquieted by it, I arrived at the right gallery without difficulty, crossing the landing-place, and reaching the dark closet.

Before entering it I examined the curtain-cord of the window and found that I had only to release it from its fastening with my fingers for the curtain to fall by its own weight and hide the square of light from Rouletabille—the signal agreed upon. The sound of a footstep made me halt before Arthur Rance's door. He was not yet in bed, then! How was it that, being in the chateau, he had not dined with Monsieur Stangerson and his daughter? I had not seen him at table with them, at the moment when we looked in.

I retired into the dark closet. I found myself perfectly situated. I could see along the whole length of the gallery. Nothing, absolutely nothing could pass there without my seeing it. But what was going to pass there? Rouletabille's embrace came back to my mind. I argued that people don't part from each, other in that way unless on an important or dangerous occasion. Was I then in danger?

My hand closed on the butt of my revolver and I waited. I am not a hero; but neither am I a coward.

I waited about an hour, and during all that time I saw nothing unusual. The rain, which had begun to come down strongly towards nine o'clock, had now ceased.

My friend had told me that, probably, nothing would occur before midnight or one o'clock in the morning. It was not more than half-past eleven, however, when I heard the door of Arthur Rance's room open very slowly. The door remained open for a minute, which seemed to me a long time. As it opened into the gallery, that is to say, outwards, I could not see what was passing in the room behind the door.

At that moment I noticed a strange sound, three times repeated, coming from the park. Ordinarily I should not have attached any more importance to it than I would to the noise of cats on the roof. But the third time, the mew was so sharp and penetrating that I remembered what I had heard about the cry of the Bete du bon Dieu. As the cry had accompanied all the events at the Glandier, I could not refrain from shuddering at the thought.

Directly afterwards I saw a man appear on the outside of the door, and close it after him. At first I could not recognise him, for his back was towards me and he was bending over a rather bulky package. When he had closed the door and picked up the package, he turned towards the dark closet, and then I saw who he was. He was the forest-keeper, the Green Man. He was wearing the same costume that he had worn when I first saw him on the road in front of the Donjon Inn. There was no doubt about his being the keeper. As the cry of the Bete du Bon Dieu came for the third time, he put down the package and went to the second window, counting from the dark closet. I dared not risk making any movement, fearing I might betray my presence.

Arriving at the window, he peered out on to the park. The night was now light, the moon showing at intervals. The Green Man raised his arms twice, making signs which I did not understand; then, leaving the window, he again took up his package and moved along the gallery towards the landing-place.

Rouletabille had instructed me to undo the curtain-cord when I saw anything. Was Rouletabille expecting this? It was not my business to question. All I had to do was obey instructions. I unfastened the window-cord; my heart beating the while as if it would burst. The man reached the landing-place, but, to my utter surprise—I had expected to see him continue to pass along the gallery—I saw him descend the stairs leading to the vestibule.

What was I to do? I looked stupidly at the heavy curtain which had shut the light from the window. The signal had been given, and I did not see Rouletabille appear at the corner of the off-turning gallery. Nobody appeared. I was exceedingly perplexed. Half an hour passed, an age to me. What was I to do now, even if I saw something? The signal once given I could not give it a second time. To venture into the gallery might upset all Rouletabille's plans. After all, I had nothing to reproach myself for, and if something had happened that my friend had not expected he could only blame himself. Unable to be of any further assistance to him by means of a signal, I left the dark closet and, still in my socks, made my way to the "off-turning" gallery.

There was no one there. I went to the door of Rouletabille's room and listened. I could hear nothing. I knocked gently. There was no answer. I turned the door-handle and the door opened. I entered. Rouletabille lay extended at full length on the floor.

XXII

The Incredible Body

I bent in great anxiety over the body of the reporter and had the joy to find that he was deeply sleeping, the same unhealthy sleep that I had seen fall upon Frederic Larsan. He had succumbed to the influence of the same drug that had been mixed with our food. How was it then, that I, also, had not been overcome by it? I reflected that the drug must have been put into our wine; because that would explain my condition. I never drink when eating. Naturally inclined to obesity, I am restricted to a dry diet. I shook Rouletabille, but could not succeed in waking him. This, no doubt, was the work of Mademoiselle Stangerson.

She had certainly thought it necessary to guard herself against this young man as well as her father. I recalled that the steward, in serving us, had recommended an excellent Chablis which, no doubt, had come from the professor's table.

More than a quarter of an hour passed. I resolved, under the pressing circumstances, to resort to extreme measures. I threw a pitcher of cold water over Rouletabille's head. He opened his eyes. I beat his face, and raised him up. I felt him stiffen in my arms and heard him murmur: "Go on, go on; but don't make any noise." I pinched him and shook him until he was able to stand up. We were saved!

"They sent me to sleep," he said. "Ah! I passed an awful quarter of an hour before giving way. But it is over now. Don't leave me."

He had no sooner uttered those words than we were thrilled by a frightful cry that rang through the chateau,—a veritable death cry.

"Malheur!" roared Rouletabille; "we shall be too late!"

He tried to rush to the door, but he was too dazed, and fell against the wall. I was already in the gallery, revolver in hand, rushing like a madman towards Mademoiselle Stangerson's room. The moment I arrived at the intersection of the "off-turning" gallery and the "right" gallery, I saw a figure leaving her apartment, which, in a few strides had reached the landing-place.

I was not master of myself. I fired. The report from the revolver made a deafening noise; but the man continued his flight down the stairs. I ran behind him, shouting: "Stop!—stop! or I will kill you!" As I rushed after him down the stairs, I came face to face with Arthur Rance coming from the left wing of the chateau, yelling: "What is it? What is it?" We arrived almost at the same time at the foot of the staircase. The window of the vestibule was open. We distinctly saw the form of a man running away. Instinctively we fired our revolvers in his direction. He was not more than ten paces in front of us; he staggered and we thought he was going to fall. We had sprung out of the window, but the man dashed off with renewed vigour. I was in my socks, and the American was barefooted. There being no hope of overtaking him, we fired our last cartridges at him. But he still kept on running, going along the right side of the court towards the end of the right wing of the chateau, which had no other outlet than the door of the little chamber occupied by the forest-keeper. The man, though he was evidently wounded by our bullets, was now twenty yards ahead of us. Suddenly, behind us, and above our heads, a window in the gallery opened and we heard the voice of Rouletabille crying out desperately:

"Fire, Bernier!—Fire!"

At that moment the clear moonlight night was further lit by a broad flash. By its light we saw Daddy Bernier with his gun on the threshold of the donjon door.

He had taken good aim. The shadow fell. But as it had reached the end of the right wing of the chateau, it fell on the other side of the angle of the building; that is to say, we saw it about to fall, but not the actual sinking to the ground. Bernier, Arthur Rance and myself reached the other side twenty seconds later. The shadow was lying dead at our feet.

Aroused from his lethargy by the cries and reports, Larsan opened the window of his chamber and called out to us. Rouletabille, quite awake now, joined us at the same moment, and I cried out to him:

"He is dead!—is dead!"

"So much the better," he said. "Take him into the vestibule of the chateau." Then as if on second thought, he said: "No!—no! Let us put him in his own room."

Rouletabille knocked at the door. Nobody answered. Naturally, this did not surprise me.

"He is evidently not there, otherwise he would have come out," said the reporter. "Let us carry him to the vestibule then."

Since reaching the dead shadow, a thick cloud had covered the moon and darkened the night, so that we were unable to make out the features. Daddy Jacques, who had now joined us, helped us to carry the body into the vestibule, where we laid it down on the lower step of the stairs. On the way, I had felt my hands wet from the warm blood flowing from the wounds.

Daddy Jacques flew to the kitchen and returned with a lantern. He held it close to the face of the dead shadow, and we recognised the keeper, the man called by the landlord of the Donjon Inn the Green Man, whom, an hour earlier, I had seen come out of Arthur Rance's chamber carrying a parcel. But what I had seen I could only tell Rouletabille later, when we were alone.

Rouletabille and Frederic Larsan experienced a cruel disappointment at the result of the night's adventure. They could only look in consternation and stupefaction at the body of the Green Man.

Daddy Jacques showed a stupidly sorrowful face and with silly lamentations kept repeating that we were mistaken—the keeper could not be the assailant. We were obliged to compel him to be quiet. He could not have shown greater grief had the body been that of his own son. I noticed, while all the rest of us were more or less undressed and barefooted, that he was fully clothed.

Rouletabille had not left the body. Kneeling on the flagstones by the light of Daddy Jacques's lantern he removed the clothes from the body and laid bare its breast. Then snatching the lantern from Daddy Jacques, he held it over the corpse and saw a gaping wound. Rising suddenly he exclaimed in a voice filled with savage irony:

"The man you believe to have been shot was killed by the stab of a knife in his heart!"

I thought Rouletabille had gone mad; but, bending over the body, I quickly satisfied myself that Rouletabille was right. Not a sign of a bullet anywhere—the wound, evidently made by a sharp blade, had penetrated the heart.

XXIII

THE DOUBLE SCENT

I had hardly recovered from the surprise into which this new discovery had plunged me, when Rouletabille touched me on the shoulder and asked me to follow him into his room.

"What are we going to do there?"

"To think the matter over."

I confess I was in no condition for doing much thinking, nor could I understand how Rouletabille could so control himself as to be able calmly to sit down for reflection when he must have known that Mademoiselle Stangerson was at that moment almost on the point of death. But his self-control was more than I could explain. Closing the door of his room, he motioned me to a chair and, seating himself before me, took out his pipe. We sat there for some time in silence and then I fell asleep.

When I awoke it was daylight. It was eight o'clock by my watch. Rouletabille was no longer in the room. I rose to go out when the door opened and my friend re-entered. He had evidently lost no time.

"How about Mademoiselle Stangerson?" I asked him.

"Her condition, though very alarming, is not desperate."

"When did you leave this room?"

"Towards dawn."

"I guess you have been hard at work?"

"Rather!"

"Have you found out anything?"

"Two sets of footprints!"

"Do they explain anything?"

"Yes."

"Have they anything to do with the mystery of the keeper's body?"

"Yes; the mystery is no longer a mystery. This morning, walking round the chateau, I found two distinct sets of footprints, made at the same time, last night. They were made by two persons walking side by side. I followed them from the court towards the oak grove. Larsan joined me. They were the same kind of footprints as were made at the time of the assault in the 'Yellow Room'—one set was from clumsy boots and the other was made by neat ones, except that the big toe of one of the sets was of a different size from the one measured in the 'Yellow Room' incident. I compared the marks with the paper patterns I had previously made.

"Still following the tracks of the prints, Larsan and I passed out of the oak grove and reached the border of the lake. There they turned off to a little path leading to the high road to Epinay where we lost the traces in the newly macadamised highway.

"We went back to the chateau and parted at the courtyard. We met again, however, in Daddy Jacques's room to which our separate trains of thinking had led us both. We found the old servant in bed. His clothes on the chair were wet through and his boots very muddy. He certainly did not get into that state in helping us to carry the body of the keeper. It was not raining then. Then his face showed extreme fatigue and he looked at us out of terror-stricken eyes.

"On our first questioning him he told us that he had gone to bed immediately after the doctor had arrived. On pressing him, however, for it was evident to us he was not speaking the truth, he confessed that he had been away from the chateau. He explained his absence by saying that he had a headache and went out into the fresh air, but had gone no further than the oak grove. When we then described to him the whole route he had followed, he sat up in bed trembling.

"'And you were not alone!' cried Larsan.

"'Did you see it then?' gasped Daddy Jacques.

"'What?' I asked.

"'The phantom—the black phantom!'

"Then he told us that for several nights he had seen what he kept calling the black phantom. It came into the park at the stroke of midnight and glided stealthily through the trees; it appeared to him to pass through the trunks of the trees. Twice he had seen it from his window, by the light of the moon and had risen and followed the strange apparition. The night before last he had almost overtaken it; but it had vanished at the corner of the donjon. Last night, however, he had not left the chateau, his mind being disturbed by a presentiment that some new crime would be attempted. Suddenly he saw the black phantom rush out from somewhere in the middle of the court. He followed it to the lake and to the high road to Epinay, where the phantom suddenly disappeared.

"'Did you see his face?' demanded Larsan.

"'No!—I saw nothing but black veils.'

"'Did you go out after what passed on the gallery?'

"'I could not!—I was terrified.'

"'Daddy Jacques,' I said, in a threatening voice, 'you did not follow it; you and the phantom walked to Epinay together—arm in arm!'

"'No!' he cried, turning his eyes away, 'I did not. It came on to pour, and—I turned back. I don't know what became of the black phantom.'"

"We left him, and when we were outside I turned to Larsan, looking him full in the face, and put my question suddenly to take him off his guard:

"'An accomplice?'

"'How can I tell?' he replied, shrugging his shoulders. 'You can't be sure of anything in a case like this. Twenty-four hours ago I would have sworn that there was no accomplice!' He left me saying he was off to Epinay."

"Well, what do you make of it?" I asked Rouletabille, after he had ended his recital. "Personally I am utterly in the dark. I can't make anything out of it. What do you gather?"

"Everything! Everything!" he exclaimed. "But," he said abruptly, "let's find out more about Mademoiselle Stangerson."

XXIV

Rouletabille Knows the Two Halves of the Murderer

Mademoiselle Stangerson had been almost murdered for the second time. Unfortunately, she was in too weak a state to bear the severer injuries of this second attack as well as she had those of the first. She had received three wounds in the breast from the murderer's knife, and she lay long between life and death. Her strong physique, however, saved her; but though she recovered physically it was found that her mind had been affected. The slightest allusion to the terrible incident sent her into delirium, and the arrest of Robert Darzac which followed on the day following the tragic death of the keeper seemed to sink her fine intelligence into complete melancholia.

Robert Darzac arrived at the chateau towards half-past nine. I saw him hurrying through the park, his hair and clothes in disorder and his face a deadly white. Rouletabille and I were looking out of a window in the gallery. He saw us, and gave a despairing cry: "I'm too late!"

Rouletabille answered: "She lives!"

A minute later Darzac had gone into Mademoiselle Stangerson's room and, through the door, we could hear his heart-rending sobs.

"There's a fate about this place!" groaned Rouletabille. "Some infernal gods must be watching over the misfortunes of this family!—If I had not been drugged, I should have saved Mademoiselle Stangerson. I should have silenced him forever. And the keeper would not have been killed!"

Monsieur Darzac came in to speak with us. His distress was terrible. Rouletabille told him everything: his preparations for Mademoiselle Stangerson's safety; his plans for either capturing or for disposing of the assailant for ever; and how he would have succeeded had it not been for the drugging.

"If only you had trusted me!" said the young man, in a low tone. "If you had but begged Mademoiselle Stangerson to confide in me!—But, then, everybody here distrusts everybody else, the daughter distrusts her father, and even her lover. While you ask me to protect her she is doing all she can to frustrate me. That was why I came on the scene too late!"

At Monsieur Robert Darzac's request Rouletabille described the whole scene. Leaning on the wall, to prevent himself from falling, he had made his way to Mademoiselle Stangerson's room, while we were running after the supposed murderer. The ante-room door was open and when he entered he found Mademoiselle Stangerson lying partly thrown over the desk. Her dressing-gown was dyed with the blood flowing from her bosom. Still under the influence of the drug, he felt he was walking in a horrible nightmare.

He went back to the gallery automatically, opened a window, shouted his order to fire, and then returned to the room. He crossed the deserted boudoir, entered the drawing-room, and tried to rouse Monsieur Stangerson who was lying on a sofa. Monsieur Stangerson rose stupidly and let himself be drawn by Rouletabille into the room where, on seeing his daughter's body, he uttered a heart-rending cry. Both united their feeble strength and carried her to her bed.

On his way to join us Rouletabille passed by the desk. On the floor, near it, he saw a large packet. He knelt down and, finding the wrapper loose, he examined it, and made out an enormous quantity of papers and photographs. On one of the papers he read: "New differential electroscopic condenser. Fundamental properties of substance intermediary between ponderable matter and imponderable ether." Strange irony of fate that the professor's precious papers should be restored to him at the very time when an attempt was being made to deprive him of his daughter's life! What are papers worth to him now?

The morning following that awful night saw Monsieur de Marquet once more at the chateau, with his Registrar and gendarmes. Of course we were all questioned. Rouletabille and I had already agreed on what to say. I kept back any information as to my being in the dark closet and said nothing about the drugging. We did not wish to suggest in any way that Mademoiselle Stangerson had been expecting her nocturnal visitor. The poor woman might, perhaps, never recover, and it was none of our business to lift the veil of a secret the preservation of which she had paid for so dearly.

Arthur Rance told everybody, in a manner so natural that it astonished me, that he had last seen the keeper towards eleven o'clock of that fatal night. He had come for his valise, he said, which he was to take for him early next morning to the Saint-Michel station, and had been kept out late running after poachers. Arthur Rance had, indeed, intended to leave the chateau and, according to his habit, to walk to the station.

Monsieur Stangerson confirmed what Rance had said, adding that he had not asked Rance to dine with him because his friend had taken his final leave of them both earlier in the evening. Monsieur Rance had had tea served him in his room, because he had complained of a slight indisposition.

Bernier testified, instructed by Rouletabille, that the keeper had ordered him to meet at a spot near the oak grove, for the purpose of looking out for poachers. Finding that the keeper did not keep his appointment, he, Bernier, had gone in search of him. He had almost arrived at the donjon, when he saw a figure running swiftly in a direction opposite to him, towards the right wing of the chateau. He heard revolver shots from behind the figure and saw Rouletabille at one of the gallery windows. He heard Rouletabille call out to him to fire, and he had fired. He believed he had killed the man until he learned, after Rouletabille had uncovered the body, that the man had died from a knife thrust. Who had given it he could not imagine. "Nobody could have been near the spot without my seeing him." When the examining magistrate reminded him that the spot where the body was found was very dark and that he himself had not been able to recognise the keeper before firing, Daddy Bernier replied that neither had they seen the other body; nor had they found it. In the narrow court where five people were standing it would have been strange if the other body, had it been there, could have escaped. The only door that opened into the court was that of the keeper's room, and that door was closed, and the key of it was found in the keeper's pocket.

However that might be, the examining magistrate did not pursue his inquiry further in this direction. He was evidently convinced that we had missed the man we were chasing and we had come upon the keeper's body in our chase. This matter of the keeper was another matter entirely. He wanted to satisfy himself about that without any further delay. Probably it fitted in with the conclusions he had already arrived at as to the keeper and his intrigues with the wife of Mathieu, the landlord of the Donjon Inn. This Mathieu, later in the afternoon, was arrested and taken to Corbeil in spite of his rheumatism. He had been heard to threaten the keeper, and though no evidence against him had been found at his inn, the evidence of carters who had heard the threats was enough to justify his retention.

The examination had proceeded thus far when, to our surprise, Frederic Larsan returned to the chateau. He was accompanied by one of the employeeees of the railway. At that moment Rance and I were in the vestibule discussing Mathieu's guilt or innocence, while Rouletabille stood apart buried, apparently, in thought. The examining magistrate and his Registrar were in the little green drawing-room, while Darzac was with the doctor and Stangerson in the lady's chamber. As Frederic Larsan entered the vestibule with the railway employeee, Rouletabille and I at once recognised him by the small blond beard. We exchanged meaningful glances. Larsan had himself announced to the examining magistrate by the gendarme and entered with the railway servant as Daddy Jacques came out. Some ten minutes went by during which Rouletabille appeared extremely impatient. The door of the drawing-room was then opened and we heard the magistrate calling to the gendarme who entered. Presently he came out, mounted the stairs and, coming back shortly, went in to the magistrate and said:

"Monsieur,—Monsieur Robert Darzac will not come!"

"What! Not come!" cried Monsieur de Marquet.

"He says he cannot leave Mademoiselle Stangerson in her present state."

"Very well," said Monsieur de Marquet; "then we'll go to him."

Monsieur de Marquet and the gendarme mounted the stairs. He made a sign to Larsan and the railroad employeee to follow. Rouletabille and I went along too.

On reaching the door of Mademoiselle Stangerson's chamber, Monsieur de Marquet knocked. A chambermaid appeared. It was Sylvia, with her hair all in disorder and consternation showing on her face.

"Is Monsieur Stangerson within?" asked the magistrate.

"Yes, Monsieur."

"Tell him that I wish to speak with him."

Stangerson came out. His appearance was wretched in the extreme.

"What do you want?" he demanded of the magistrate. "May I not be left in peace, Monsieur?"

"Monsieur," said the magistrate, "it is absolutely necessary that I should see Monsieur Darzac at once. If you cannot induce him to come, I shall be compelled to use the help of the law."

The professor made no reply. He looked at us all like a man being led to execution, and then went back into the room.

Almost immediately after Monsieur Robert Darzac came out. He was very pale. He looked at us and, his eyes falling on the railway servant, his features stiffened and he could hardly repress a groan.

We were all much moved by the appearance of the man. We felt that what was about to happen would decide the fate of Monsieur Robert Darzac. Frederic Larsan's face alone was radiant, showing a joy as of a dog that had at last got its prey.

Pointing to the railway servant, Monsieur de Marquet said to Monsieur Darzac:

"Do you recognise this man, Monsieur?"

"I do," said Monsieur Darzac, in a tone which he vainly tried to make firm. "He is an employeee at the station at Epinay-sur-Orge."

"This young man," went on Monsieur de Marquet, "affirms that he saw you get off the train at Epinay-sur-Orge—"

"That night," said Monsieur Darzac, interrupting, "at half-past ten—it is quite true."

An interval of silence followed.

"Monsieur Darzac," the magistrate went on in a tone of deep emotion, "Monsieur Darzac, what were you doing that night, at Epinay-sur-Orge—at that time?"

Monsieur Darzac remained silent, simply closing his eyes.

"Monsieur Darzac," insisted Monsieur de Marquet, "can you tell me how you employeeed your time, that night?"

Monsieur Darzac opened his eyes. He seemed to have recovered his self-control.

"No, Monsieur."

"Think, Monsieur! For, if you persist in your strange refusal, I shall be under the painful necessity of keeping you at my disposition."

"I refuse."

"Monsieur Darzac!—in the name of the law, I arrest you!"

The magistrate had no sooner pronounced the words than I saw Rouletabille move quickly towards Monsieur Darzac. He would certainly have spoken to him, but Darzac, by a gesture, held him off. As the gendarme approached his prisoner, a despairing cry rang through the room:

"Robert!—Robert!"

We recognised the voice of Mademoiselle Stangerson. We all shuddered. Larsan himself turned pale. Monsieur Darzac, in response to the cry, had flown back into the room.

The magistrate, the gendarme, and Larsan followed closely after. Rouletabille and I remained on the threshold. It was a heart-breaking sight that met our eyes. Mademoiselle Stangerson, with a face of deathly pallor, had risen on her bed, in spite of the restraining efforts of two doctors and her father. She was holding out her trembling arms towards Robert Darzac, on whom Larsan and the gendarme had laid hands. Her distended eyes saw—she understood—her lips seemed to form a word, but nobody made it out; and she fell back insensible.

Monsieur Darzac was hurried out of the room and placed in the vestibule to wait for the vehicle Larsan had gone to fetch. We were all overcome by emotion and even Monsieur de Marquet had tears in his eyes. Rouletabille took advantage of the opportunity to say to Monsieur Darzac:

"Are you going to put in any defense?"

"No!" replied the prisoner.

"Very well, then I will, Monsieur."

"You cannot do it," said the unhappy man with a faint smile.

"I can—and I will."

Rouletabille's voice had in it a strange strength and confidence.

"I can do it, Monsieur Robert Darzac, because I know more than you do!"

"Come! Come!" murmured Darzac, almost angrily.

"Have no fear! I shall know only what will benefit you."

"You must know nothing, young man, if you want me to be grateful."

Rouletabille shook his head, going close up to Darzac.

"Listen to what I am about to say," he said in a low tone, "and let it give you confidence. You do not know the name of the murderer. Mademoiselle Stangerson knows it; but only half of it; but I know his two halves; I know the whole man!"

Robert Darzac opened his eyes, with a look that showed he had not understood a word of what Rouletabille had said to him. At that moment the conveyance arrived, driven by Frederic Larsan. Darzac and the gendarme entered it, Larsan remaining on the driver's seat. The prisoner was taken to Corbeil.

XXV

Rouletabille Goes on a Journey

That same evening Rouletabille and I left the Glandier. We were very glad to get away and there was nothing more to keep us there. I declared my intention to give up the whole matter. It had been too much for me. Rouletabille, with a friendly tap on my shoulder, confessed that he had nothing more to learn at the Glandier; he had learned there all it had to tell him. We reached Paris about eight o'clock, dined, and then, tired out, we separated, agreeing to meet the next morning at my rooms.

Rouletabille arrived next day at the hour agreed on. He was dressed in a suit of English tweed, with an ulster on his arm, and a valise in his hand. Evidently he had prepared himself for a journey.

"How long shall you be away?" I asked.

"A month or two," he said. "It all depends."

I asked him no more questions.

"Do you know," he asked, "what the word was that Mademoiselle Stangerson tried to say before she fainted?"

"No—nobody heard it."

"I heard it!" replied Rouletabille. "She said 'Speak!'"

"Do you think Darzac will speak?"

"Never."

I was about to make some further observations, but he wrung my hand warmly and wished me good-bye. I had only time to ask him one question before he left.

"Are you not afraid that other attempts may be made while you're away?"

"No! Not now that Darzac is in prison," he answered.

With this strange remark he left. I was not to see him again until the day of Darzac's trial at the court when he appeared to explain the inexplicable.

XXVI

In Which Joseph Rouletabille Is
Awaited with Impatience

On the 15th of January, that is to say, two months and a half after the tragic events I have narrated, the "Epoque" printed, as the first column of the front page, the following sensational article: "The Seine-et-Oise jury is summoned today to give its verdict on one of the most mysterious affairs in the annals of crime. There never has been a case with so many obscure, incomprehensible, and inexplicable points. And yet the prosecution has not hesitated to put into the prisoner's dock a man who is respected, esteemed, and loved by all who knew him—a young savant, the hope of French science, whose whole life has been devoted to knowledge and truth. When Paris heard of Monsieur Robert Darzac's arrest a unanimous cry of protest arose from all sides. The whole Sorbonne, disgraced by this act of the examining magistrate, asserted its belief in the innocence of Mademoiselle Stangerson's fiancé. Monsieur Stangerson was loud in his denunciation of this miscarriage of justice. There is no doubt in the mind of anybody that could the victim speak she would claim from the jurors of Seine-et-Oise the man she wishes to make her husband and whom the prosecution would send to the scaffold. It is to be hoped that Mademoiselle Stangerson will shortly recover her reason, which has been temporarily unhinged by the horrible mystery at the Glandier. The question before the jury is the one we propose to deal with this very day.

"We have decided not to permit twelve worthy men to commit a disgraceful miscarriage of justice. We confess that the remarkable coincidences, the many convicting evidences, and the inexplicable silence on the part of the accused, as well as a total absence of any evidence for an alibi, were enough to warrant the bench of judges in assuming that in this man alone was centered the truth of the affair. The evidences are, in appearance, so overwhelming against Monsieur Robert Darzac that a detective so well informed, so intelligent, and generally so successful, as Monsieur Frederic Larsan, may be excused for having been misled by them. Up to now everything has gone against

Monsieur Robert Darzac in the magisterial inquiry. Today, however, we are going to defend him before the jury, and we are going to bring to the witness stand a light that will illumine the whole mystery of the Glandier. For we possess the truth.

"If we have not spoken sooner, it is because the interests of certain parties in the case demand that we should take that course. Our readers may remember the unsigned reports we published relating to the 'Left foot of the Rue Oberkampf,' at the time of the famous robbery of the Credit Universel, and the famous case of the 'Gold Ingots of the Mint.' In both those cases we were able to discover the truth long before even the excellent ingenuity of Frederic Larsan had been able to unravel it. These reports were written by our youngest reporter, Joseph Rouletabille, a youth of eighteen, whose fame tomorrow will be world-wide. When attention was first drawn to the Glandier case, our youthful reporter was on the spot and installed in the chateau, when every other representative of the press had been denied admission. He worked side by side with Frederic Larsan. He was amazed and terrified at the grave mistake the celebrated detective was about to make, and tried to divert him from the false scent he was following; but the great Fred refused to receive instructions from this young journalist. We know now where it brought Monsieur Robert Darzac.

"But now, France must know—the whole world must know, that, on the very evening on which Monsieur Darzac was arrested, young Rouletabille entered our editorial office and informed us that he was about to go away on a journey. 'How long I shall be away,' he said, 'I cannot say; perhaps a month—perhaps two—perhaps three—perhaps I may never return. Here is a letter. If I am not back on the day on which Monsieur Darzac is to appear before the Assize Court, have this letter opened and read to the court, after all the witnesses have been heard. Arrange it with Monsieur Darzac's counsel. Monsieur Darzac is innocent. In this letter is written the name of the murderer; and—that is all I have to say. I am leaving to get my proofs—for the irrefutable evidence of the murderer's guilt.' Our reporter departed. For a long time we were without news from him; but, a week ago, a stranger called upon our manager and said: 'Act in accordance with the instructions of Joseph Rouletabille, if it becomes necessary to do so. The letter left by him holds the truth.' The gentleman who brought us this message would not give us his name.

"Today, the 15th of January, is the day of the trial. Joseph Rouletabille has not returned. It may be we shall never see him again. The press also counts its heroes, its martyrs to duty. It may be he is no longer living. We shall know how to avenge him. Our manager will, this afternoon, be at the Court of Assize at Versailles, with the letter—the letter containing the name of the murderer!"

Those Parisians who flocked to the Assize Court at Versailles, to be present at the trial of what was known as the "Mystery of 'The Yellow Room,' will certainly remember the terrible crush at the Saint-Lazare station. The ordinary trains were so full that special trains had to be made up. The article in the 'Epoque' had so excited the populace that discussion was rife everywhere even to the verge of blows. Partisans of Rouletabille fought with the supporters of Frederic Larsan. Curiously enough the excitement was due less to the fact that an innocent man was in danger of a wrongful conviction than to the interest taken in their own ideas as to the Mystery of the 'Yellow Room'. Each had his explanation to which each held fast. Those who explained the crime on Frederic Larsan's theory would not admit that there could be any doubt as to the perspicacity of the popular detective. Others who had arrived at a different solution, naturally insisted that this was Rouletabille's explanation, though they did not as yet know what that was.

With the day's "Epoque" in their hands, the "Larsans" and the "Rouletabilles" fought and shoved each other on the steps of the Palais de Justice, right into the court itself. Those who could not get in remained in the neighbourhood until evening and were, with great difficulty, kept back by the soldiery and the police. They became hungry for news, welcoming the most absurd rumours. At one time the rumour spread that Monsieur Stangerson himself had been arrested in the court and had confessed to being the murderer. This goes to show to what a pitch of madness nervous excitement may carry people. Rouletabille was still expected. Some pretended to know him; and when a young man with a "pass" crossed the open space which separated the crowd from the Court House, a scuffle took place. Cries were raised of "Rouletabille!—there's Rouletabille!" The arrival of the manager of the paper was the signal for a great demonstration. Some applauded, others hissed.

The trial itself was presided over by Monsieur de Rocouz, a judge filled with the prejudice of his class, but a man honest at heart. The witnesses had been called. I was there, of course, as were all who had, in any way, been in touch with the mysteries of the Glandier. Monsieur Stangerson—looking many years older and almost unrecognisable—Larsan, Arthur Rance, with his face ruddy as ever, Daddy Jacques,

Daddy Mathieu, who was brought into court handcuffed between two gendarmes, Madame Mathieu, in tears, the two Berniers, the two nurses, the steward, all the domestics of the chateau, the employeee of the Paris Post Office, the railway employeee from Epinay, some friends of Monsieur and Mademoiselle Stangerson, and all Monsieur Darzac's witnesses. I was lucky enough to be called early in the trial, so that I was then able to watch and be present at almost the whole of the proceedings.

The court was so crowded that many lawyers were compelled to find seats on the steps. Behind the bench of justices were representatives from other benches. Monsieur Robert Darzac stood in the prisoner's dock between policemen, tall, handsome, and calm. A murmur of admiration rather than of compassion greeted his appearance. He leaned forward towards his counsel, Maitre Henri Robert, who, assisted by his chief secretary, Maitre Andre Hesse, was busily turning over the folios of his brief.

Many expected that Monsieur Stangerson, after giving his evidence, would have gone over to the prisoner and shaken hands with him; but he left the court without another word. It was remarked that the jurors appeared to be deeply interested in a rapid conversation which the manager of the "Epoque" was having with Maitre Henri Robert. The manager, later, sat down in the front row of the public seats. Some were surprised that he was not asked to remain with the other witnesses in the room reserved for them.

The reading of the indictment was got through, as it always is, without any incident. I shall not here report the long examination to which Monsieur Darzac was subjected. He answered all the questions quickly and easily. His silence as to the important matters of which we know was dead against him. It would seem as if this reticence would be fatal for him. He resented the President's reprimands. He was told that his silence might mean death.

"Very well," he said; "I will submit to it; but I am innocent."

With that splendid ability which has made his fame, Maitre Robert took advantage of the incident, and tried to show that it brought out in noble relief his client's character; for only heroic natures could remain silent for moral reasons in face of such a danger. The eminent advocate however, only succeeded in assuring those who were already assured of Darzac's innocence. At the adjournment Rouletabille had not yet arrived. Every time a door opened, all eyes there turned towards it and back to the manager of the "Epoque," who sat impassive in his place. When he once was feeling in his pocket a loud murmur of expectation followed. The letter!

It is not, however, my intention to report in detail the course of the trial. My readers are sufficiently acquainted with the mysteries surrounding the Glandier case to enable me to go on to the really dramatic denouement of this ever-memorable day.

When the trial was resumed, Maitre Henri Robert questioned Daddy Mathieu as to his complicity in the death of the keeper. His wife was also brought in and was confronted by her husband. She burst into tears and confessed that she had been the keeper's mistress, and that her husband had suspected it. She again, however, affirmed that he had had nothing to do with the murder of her lover. Maitre Henri Robert thereupon asked the court to hear Frederic Larsan on this point.

"In a short conversation which I have had with Frederic Larsan, during the adjournment," declared the advocate, "he has made me understand that the death of the keeper may have been brought about otherwise than by the hand of Mathieu. It will be interesting to hear Frederic Larsan's theory."

Frederic Larsan was brought in. His explanation was quite clear.

"I see no necessity," he said, "for bringing Mathieu in this. I have told Monsieur de Marquet that the man's threats had biassed the examining magistrate against him. To me the attempt to murder Mademoiselle and the death of the keeper are the work of one and the same person. Mademoiselle Stangerson's murderer, flying through the court, was fired on; it was thought he was struck, perhaps killed. As a matter of fact, he only stumbled at the moment of his disappearance behind the corner of the right wing of the chateau. There he encountered the keeper who, no doubt, tried to seize him. The murderer had in his hand the knife with which he had stabbed Mademoiselle Stangerson and with this he killed the keeper."

This very simple explanation appeared at once plausible and satisfying. A murmur of approbation was heard.

"And the murderer? What became of him?" asked the President.

"He was evidently hidden in an obscure corner at the end of the court. After the people had left the court carrying with them the body of the keeper, the murderer quietly made his escape."

The words had scarcely left Larsan's mouth when from the back of the court came a youthful voice:

"I agree with Frederic Larsan as to the death of the keeper; but I do not agree with him as to the way the murderer escaped!"

Everybody turned round, astonished. The clerks of the court sprang towards the speaker, calling out silence, and the President angrily ordered the intruder to be immediately expelled. The same clear voice, however, was again heard:

"It is I, Monsieur President—Joseph Rouletabille!"

XXVII

In Which Joseph Rouletabille
Appears in All His Glory

The excitement was extreme. Cries from fainting women were to be heard amid the extraordinary bustle and stir. The "majesty of the law" was utterly forgotten. The President tried in vain to make himself heard. Rouletabille made his way forward with difficulty, but by dint of much elbowing reached his manager and greeted him cordially. The letter was passed to him and pocketing it he turned to the witness-box. He was dressed exactly as on the day he left me even to the ulster over his arm. Turning to the President, he said:

"I beg your pardon, Monsieur President, but I have only just arrived from America. The steamer was late. My name is Joseph Rouletabille!"

The silence which followed his stepping into the witness-box was broken by laughter when his words were heard. Everybody seemed relieved and glad to find him there, as if in the expectation of hearing the truth at last.

But the President was extremely incensed:

"So, you are Joseph Rouletabille," he replied; "well, young man, I'll teach you what comes of making a farce of justice. By virtue of my discretionary power, I hold you at the court's disposition."

"I ask nothing better, Monsieur President. I have come here for that purpose. I humbly beg the court's pardon for the disturbance of which I have been the innocent cause. I beg you to believe that nobody has a greater respect for the court than I have. I came in as I could." He smiled.

"Take him away!" ordered the President.

Maitre Henri Robert intervened. He began by apologising for the young man, who, he said, was moved only by the best intentions. He made the President understand that the evidence of a witness who had slept at the Glandier during the whole of that eventful week could not be omitted, and the present witness, moreover, had come to name the real murderer.

"Are you going to tell us who the murderer was?" asked the President, somewhat convinced though still sceptical.

"I have come for that purpose, Monsieur President!" replied Rouletabille.

An attempt at applause was silenced by the usher.

"Joseph Rouletabille," said Maitre Henri Robert, "has not been regularly subpoenaed as a witness, but I hope, Monsieur President, you will examine him in virtue of your discretionary powers."

"Very well!" said the President, "we will question him. But we must proceed in order."

The Advocate-General rose:

"It would, perhaps, be better," he said, "if the young man were to tell us now whom he suspects."

The President nodded ironically:

"If the Advocate-General attaches importance to the deposition of Monsieur Joseph Rouletabille, I see no reason why this witness should not give us the name of the murderer."

A pin drop could have been heard. Rouletabille stood silent looking sympathetically at Darzac, who, for the first time since the opening of the trial, showed himself agitated.

"Well," cried the President, "we wait for the name of the murderer." Rouletabille, feeling in his waistcoat pocket, drew his watch and, looking at it, said:

"Monsieur President, I cannot name the murderer before half-past six o'clock!"

Loud murmurs of disappointment filled the room. Some of the lawyers were heard to say: "He's making fun of us!"

The President in a stern voice, said:

"This joke has gone far enough. You may retire, Monsieur, into the witnesses' room. I hold you at our disposition."

Rouletabille protested.

"I assure you, Monsieur President," he cried in his sharp, clear voice, "that when I do name the murderer you will understand why I could not speak before half-past six. I assert this on my honour. I can, however, give you now some explanation of the murder of the keeper. Monsieur Frederic Larsan, who has seen me at work at the Glandier, can tell you with what care I studied this case. I found myself compelled to differ with him in arresting Monsieur Robert Darzac, who is innocent. Monsieur Larsan knows of my good faith and knows that some importance may be attached to my discoveries, which have often corroborated his own."

Frederic Larsan said:

"Monsieur President, it will be interesting to hear Monsieur Joseph Rouletabille, especially as he differs from me."

A murmur of approbation greeted the detective's speech. He was a good sportsman and accepted the challenge. The struggle between the two promised to be exciting.

As the President remained silent, Frederic Larsan continued:

"We agree that the murderer of the keeper was the assailant of Mademoiselle Stangerson; but as we are not agreed as to how the murderer escaped, I am curious to hear Monsieur Rouletabille's explanation."

"I have no doubt you are," said my friend.

General laughter followed this remark. The President angrily declared that if it was repeated, he would have the court cleared.

"Now, young man," said the President, "you have heard Monsieur Frederic Larsan; how did the murderer get away from the court?"

Rouletabille looked at Madame Mathieu, who smiled back at him sadly.

"Since Madame Mathieu," he said, "has freely admitted her intimacy with the keeper—"

"Why, it's the boy!" exclaimed Daddy Mathieu.

"Remove that man!" ordered the President.

Mathieu was removed from the court. Rouletabille went on:

"Since she has made this confession, I am free to tell you that she often met the keeper at night on the first floor of the donjon, in the room which was once an oratory. These meetings became more frequent when her husband was laid up by his rheumatism. She gave him morphine to ease his pain and to give herself more time for the meetings. Madame Mathieu came to the chateau that night, enveloped in a large black shawl which served also as a disguise. This was the phantom that disturbed Daddy Jacques. She knew how to imitate the mewing of Mother Angenoux' cat and she would make the cries to advise the keeper of her presence. The recent repairs of the donjon did not interfere with their meetings in the keeper's old room, in the donjon, since the new room assigned to him at the end of the right wing was separated from the steward's room by a partition only.

"Previous to the tragedy in the courtyard Madame Mathieu and the keeper left the donjon together. I learnt these facts from my examination of the footmarks in the court the next morning. Bernier, the concierge, whom I had stationed behind the donjon—as he will explain himself—

could not see what passed in the court. He did not reach the court until he heard the revolver shots, and then he fired. When the woman parted from the man she went towards the open gate of the court, while he returned to his room.

"He had almost reached the door when the revolvers rang out. He had just reached the corner when a shadow bounded by. Meanwhile, Madame Mathieu, surprised by the revolver shots and by the entrance of people into the court, crouched in the darkness. The court is a large one and, being near the gate, she might easily have passed out unseen. But she remained and saw the body being carried away. In great agony of mind she neared the vestibule and saw the dead body of her lover on the stairs lit up by Daddy Jacques' lantern. She then fled; and Daddy Jacques joined her.

"That same night, before the murder, Daddy Jacques had been awakened by the cat's cry, and, looking through his window, had seen the black phantom. Hastily dressing himself he went out and recognised her. He is an old friend of Madame Mathieu, and when she saw him she had to tell him of her relations with the keeper and begged his assistance. Daddy Jacques took pity on her and accompanied her through the oak grove out of the park, past the border of the lake to the road to Epinay. From there it was but a very short distance to her home.

"Daddy Jacques returned to the chateau, and, seeing how important it was for Madame Mathieu's presence at the chateau to remain unknown, he did all he could to hide it. I appeal to Monsieur Larsan, who saw me, next morning, examine the two sets of footprints."

Here Rouletabille turning towards Madame Mathieu, with a bow, said:

"The footprints of Madame bear a strange resemblance to the neat footprints of the murderer."

Madame Mathieu trembled and looked at him with wide eyes as if in wonder at what he would say next.

"Madame has a shapely foot, long and rather large for a woman. The imprint, with its pointed toe, is very like that of the murderer's."

A movement in the court was repressed by Rouletabille. He held their attention at once.

"I hasten to add," he went on, "that I attach no importance to this. Outward signs like these are often liable to lead us into error, if we do not reason rightly. Monsieur Robert Darzac's footprints are also like the murderer's, and yet he is not the murderer!"

The President turning to Madame Mathieu asked:

"Is that in accordance with what you know occurred?"

"Yes, Monsieur President," she replied, "it is as if Monsieur Rouletabille had been behind us."

"Did you see the murderer running towards the end of the right wing?"

"Yes, as clearly as I saw them afterwards carrying the keeper's body."

"What became of the murderer?—You were in the courtyard and could easily have seen.

"I saw nothing of him, Monsieur President. It became quite dark just then."

"Then Monsieur Rouletabille," said the President, "must explain how the murderer made his escape."

Rouletabille continued:

"It was impossible for the murderer to escape by the way he had entered the court without our seeing him; or if we couldn't see him we must certainly have felt him, since the court is a very narrow one enclosed in high iron railings."

"Then if the man was hemmed in that narrow square, how is it you did not find him?—I have been asking you that for the last half hour."

"Monsieur President," replied Rouletabille, "I cannot answer that question before half-past six!"

By this time the people in the court-room were beginning to believe in this new witness. They were amused by his melodramatic action in thus fixing the hour; but they seemed to have confidence in the outcome. As for the President, it looked as if he also had made up his mind to take the young man in the same way. He had certainly been impressed by Rouletabille's explanation of Madame Mathieu's part.

"Well, Monsieur Rouletabille," he said, "as you say; but don't let us see any more of you before half-past six."

Rouletabille bowed to the President, and made his way to the door of the witnesses' room.

I quietly made my way through the crowd and left the court almost at the same time as Rouletabille. He greeted me heartily, and looked happy.

"I'll not ask you, my dear fellow," I said, smiling, "what you've been doing in America; because I've no doubt you'll say you can't tell me until after half-past six."

"No, my dear Sainclair, I'll tell you right now why I went to America. I went in search of the name of the other half of the murderer!"

"The name of the other half?"

"Exactly. When we last left the Glandier I knew there were two halves to the murderer and the name of only one of them. I went to America for the name of the other half."

I was too puzzled to answer. Just then we entered the witnesses' room, and Rouletabille was immediately surrounded. He showed himself very friendly to all except Arthur Rance to whom he exhibited a marked coldness of manner. Frederic Larsan came in also. Rouletabille went up and shook him heartily by the hand. His manner toward the detective showed that he had got the better of the policeman. Larsan smiled and asked him what he had been doing in America, Rouletabille began by telling him some anecdotes of his voyage. They then turned aside together apparently with the object of speaking confidentially. I, therefore, discreetly left them and, being curious to hear the evidence, returned to my seat in the court-room where the public plainly showed its lack of interest in what was going on in their impatience for Rouletabille's return at the appointed time.

On the stroke of half-past six Joseph Rouletabille was again brought in. It is impossible for me to picture the tense excitement which appeared on every face, as he made his way to the bar. Darzac rose to his feet, frightfully pale.

The President, addressing Rouletabille, said gravely:

"I will not ask you to take the oath, because you have not been regularly summoned; but I trust there is no need to urge upon you the gravity of the statement you are about to make."

Rouletabille looked the President quite calmly and steadily in the face, and replied:

"Yes, Monsieur."

"At your last appearance here," said the President, "we had arrived at the point where you were to tell us how the murderer escaped, and also his name. Now, Monsieur Rouletabille, we await your explanation."

"Very well, Monsieur," began my friend amidst a profound silence. "I had explained how it was impossible for the murderer to get away without being seen. And yet he was there with us in the courtyard."

"And you did not see him? At least that is what the prosecution declares."

"No! We all of us saw him, Monsieur le President!" cried Rouletabille.

"Then why was he not arrested?"

"Because no one, besides myself, knew that he was the murderer. It would have spoiled my plans to have had him arrested, and I had then no proof other than my own reasoning. I was convinced we had the murderer before us and that we were actually looking at him. I have now brought what I consider the indisputable proof."

"Speak out, Monsieur! Tell us the murderer's name."

"You will find it on the list of names present in the court on the night of the tragedy," replied Rouletabille.

The people present in the court-room began showing impatience. Some of them even called for the name, and were silenced by the usher.

"The list includes Daddy Jacques, Bernier the concierge, and Mr. Arthur Rance," said the President. "Do you accuse any of these?"

"No, Monsieur!"

"Then I do not understand what you are driving at. There was no other person at the end of the court."

"Yes, Monsieur, there was, not at the end, but above the court, who was leaning out of the window."

"Do you mean Frederic Larsan!" exclaimed the President.

"Yes! Frederic Larsan!" replied Rouletabille in a ringing tone. "Frederic Larsan is the murderer!"

The court-room became immediately filled with loud and indignant protests. So astonished was he that the President did not attempt to quiet it. The quick silence which followed was broken by the distinctly whispered words from the lips of Robert Darzac:

"It's impossible! He's mad!"

"You dare to accuse Frederic Larsan, Monsieur?" asked the President. "If you are not mad, what are your proofs?"

"Proofs, Monsieur?—Do you want proofs? Well, here is one," cried Rouletabille shrilly. "Let Frederic Larsan be called!"

"Usher, call Frederic Larsan."

The usher hurried to the side door, opened it, and disappeared. The door remained open, while all eyes turned expectantly towards it. The clerk re-appeared and, stepping forward, said:

"Monsieur President, Frederic Larsan is not here. He left at about four o'clock and has not been seen since."

"That is my proof!" cried Rouletabille, triumphantly.

"Explain yourself?" demanded the President.

"My proof is Larsan's flight," said the young reporter. "He will not come back. You will see no more of Frederic Larsan."

"Unless you are playing with the court, Monsieur, why did you not accuse him when he was present? He would then have answered you."

"He could give no other answer than the one he has now given by his flight."

"We cannot believe that Larsan has fled. There was no reason for his doing so. Did he know you'd make this charge?"

"He did. I told him I would."

"Do you mean to say that knowing Larsan was the murderer you gave him the opportunity to escape?"

"Yes, Monsieur President, I did," replied Rouletabille, proudly. "I am not a policeman, I am a journalist; and my business is not to arrest people. My business is in the service of truth, and is not that of an executioner. If you are just, Monsieur, you will see that I am right. You can now understand why I refrained until this hour to divulge the name. I gave Larsan time to catch the 4:17 train for Paris, where he would know where to hide himself, and leave no traces. You will not find Frederic Larsan," declared Rouletabille, fixing his eyes on Monsieur Robert Darzac. "He is too cunning. He is a man who has always escaped you and whom you have long searched for in vain. If he did not succeed in outwitting me, he can yet easily outwit any police. This man who, four years ago, introduced himself to the Surete, and became celebrated as Frederic Larsan, is notorious under another name—a name well known to crime. Frederic Larsan, Monsieur President, is Ballmeyer!"

"Ballmeyer!" cried the President.

"Ballmeyer!" exclaimed Robert Darzac, springing to his feet. "Ballmeyer!—It was true, then!"

"Ah! Monsieur Darzac; you don't think I am mad, now!" cried Rouletabille.

Ballmeyer! Ballmeyer! No other word could be heard in the courtroom. The President adjourned the hearing.

Those of my readers who may not have heard of Ballmeyer will wonder at the excitement the name caused. And yet the doings of this remarkable criminal form the subject-matter of the most dramatic narratives of the newspapers and criminal records of the past twenty years. It had been reported that he was dead, and thus had eluded the police as he had eluded them throughout the whole of his career.

Ballmeyer was the best specimen of the high-class "gentleman swindler." He was adept at sleight of hand tricks, and no bolder or more ruthless crook ever lived. He was received in the best society, and was a member of some of the most exclusive clubs. On many of his depredatory expeditions he had not hesitated to use the knife and the mutton-bone. No difficulty stopped him and no "operation" was too dangerous. He had been caught, but escaped on the very morning of his trial, by throwing pepper into the eyes of the guards who were conducting him to Court. It was known later that, in spite of the keen hunt after him by the most expert of detectives, he had sat that same evening at a first performance in the Theatre Francais, without the slightest disguise.

He left France, later, to "work" America. The police there succeeded in capturing him once, but the extraordinary man escaped the next day. It would need a volume to recount the adventures of this master-criminal. And yet this was the man Rouletabille had allowed to get away! Knowing all about him and who he was, he afforded the criminal an opportunity for another laugh at the society he had defied! I could not help admiring the bold stroke of the young journalist, because I felt certain his motive had been to protect both Mademoiselle Stangerson and rid Darzac of an enemy at the same time.

The crowd had barely recovered from the effect of the astonishing revelation when the hearing was resumed. The question in everybody's mind was: Admitting that Larsan was the murderer, how did he get out of the "Yellow Room"?

Rouletabille was immediately called to the bar and his examination continued.

"You have told us," said the President, "that it was impossible to escape from the end of the court. Since Larsan was leaning out of his window, he had left the court. How did he do that?"

"He escaped by a most unusual way. He climbed the wall, sprang onto the terrace, and, while we were engaged with the keeper's body, reached the gallery by the window. He then had little else to do than to open the window, get in and call out to us, as if he had just come from his own room. To a man of Ballmeyer's strength all that was mere child's play. And here, Monsieur, is the proof of what I say."

Rouletabille drew from his pocket a small packet, from which he produced a strong iron peg.

"This, Monsieur," he said, "is a spike which perfectly fits a hole still to be seen in the cornice supporting the terrace. Larsan, who thought and prepared for everything in case of any emergency, had fixed this spike into the cornice. All he had to do to make his escape good was to plant one foot on a stone which is placed at the corner of the chateau, another on this support, one hand on the cornice of the keeper's door and the other on the terrace, and Larsan was clear of the ground. The rest was easy. His acting after dinner as if he had been drugged was make believe. He was not drugged; but he did drug me. Of course he had to make it appear as if he also had been drugged so that no suspicion should fall on him for my condition. Had I not been thus overpowered, Larsan would never have entered Mademoiselle Stangerson's chamber that night, and the attack on her would not have taken place."

A groan came from Darzac, who appeared to be unable to control his suffering.

"You can understand," added Rouletabille, "that Larsan would feel himself hampered from the fact that my room was so close to his, and from a suspicion that I would be on the watch that night. Naturally, he could not for a moment believe that I suspected him! But I might see him leaving his room when he was about to go to Mademoiselle Stangerson. He waited till I was asleep, and my friend Sainclair was busy trying to rouse me. Ten minutes after that Mademoiselle was calling out, "Murder!""

"How did you come to suspect Larsan?" asked the President.

"My pure reason pointed to him. That was why I watched him. But I did not foresee the drugging. He is very cunning. Yes, my pure reason pointed to him; but I required tangible proof so that my eyes could see him as my pure reason saw him."

"What do you mean by your pure reason?"

"That power of one's mind which admits of no disturbing elements to a conclusion. The day following the incident of 'the inexplicable gallery,' I felt myself losing control of it. I had allowed myself to be diverted by fallacious evidence; but I recovered and again took hold of the right end. I satisfied myself that the murderer could not have left the gallery, either naturally or supernaturally. I narrowed the field of consideration to that small circle, so to speak. The murderer could not be outside that circle. Now who was in it? There was, first, the murderer. Then there were Daddy Jacques, Monsieur Stangerson, Frederic Larsan, and myself. Five persons in all, counting in the murderer. And yet, in the gallery, there were but four. Now since it had been demonstrated to me that the fifth could not have escaped, it was evident that one of the four present in the gallery must be a double—he must be himself and the murderer also. Why had I not seen this before? Simply because the phenomenon of the double personality had not occurred before in this inquiry.

"Now who of the four persons in the gallery was both that person and the assassin? I went over in my mind what I had seen. I had seen at one and the same time, Monsieur Stangerson and the murderer, Daddy Jacques and the murderer, myself and the murderer; so that the murderer, then, could not be either Monsieur Stangerson, Daddy Jacques, or myself. Had I seen Frederic Larsan and the murderer at the same time?—No!—Two seconds had passed, during which I lost sight of the murderer; for, as I have noted in my papers, he arrived two seconds before Monsieur Stangerson, Daddy Jacques, and myself at the meeting-point of the two galleries. That would have given Larsan time to go through the 'off-turning' gallery, snatch off his false beard, return, and hurry with us as if, like us, in pursuit of the murderer. I was sure now I had got hold of the right end in my reasoning. With Frederic Larsan was now always associated, in my mind, the personality of the unknown of whom I was in pursuit—the murderer, in other words.

"That revelation staggered me. I tried to regain my balance by going over the evidences previously traced, but which had diverted my mind and led me away from Frederic Larsan. What were these evidences?

"1st. I had seen the unknown in Mademoiselle Stangerson's chamber. On going to Frederic Larsan's room, I had found Larsan sound asleep.

"2nd. The ladder.

"3rd. I had placed Frederic Larsan at the end of the 'off-turning' gallery and had told him that I would rush into Mademoiselle Stangerson's room to try to capture the murderer. Then I returned to Mademoiselle Stangerson's chamber where I had seen the unknown.

"The first evidence did not disturb me much. It is likely that, when I descended from my ladder, after having seen the unknown in Mademoiselle Stangerson's chamber, Larsan had already finished what he was doing there. Then, while I was re-entering the chateau, Larsan went back to his own room and, undressing himself, went to sleep.

"Nor did the second evidence trouble me. If Larsan were the murderer, he could have no use for a ladder; but the ladder might have been placed there to give an appearance to the murderer's entrance from without the chateau; especially as Larsan had accused Darzac and Darzac was not in the chateau that night. Further, the ladder might have been placed there to facilitate Larsan's flight in case of absolute necessity.

"But the third evidence puzzled me altogether. Having placed Larsan at the end of the 'off-turning gallery,' I could not explain how he had taken advantage of the moment when I had gone to the left wing of the chateau to find Monsieur Stangerson and Daddy Jacques, to return to Mademoiselle Stangerson's room. It was a very dangerous thing to do. He risked being captured,—and he knew it. And he was very nearly captured. He had not had time to regain his post, as he had certainly hoped to do. He had then a very strong reason for returning to his room. As for myself, when I sent Daddy Jacques to the end of the 'right gallery,' I naturally thought that Larsan was still at his post. Daddy Jacques, in going to his post, had not looked, when he passed, to see whether Larsan was at his post or not.

"What, then, was the urgent reason which had compelled Larsan to go to the room a second time? I guessed it to be some evidence of his presence there. He had left something very important in that room. What was it? And had he recovered it? I begged Madame Bernier who was accustomed to clean the room to look, and she found a pair of eye-glasses—this pair, Monsieur President!"

And Rouletabille drew the eye-glasses, of which we know, from his pocket.

"When I saw these eye-glasses," he continued, "I was utterly nonplussed. I had never seen Larsan wear eye-glasses. What did they mean? Suddenly I exclaimed to myself: 'I wonder if he is long-sighted?' I had never seen Larsan write. He might, then, be long-sighted. They would certainly know at the Surete, and also know if the glasses were his. Such evidence would be damning. That explained Larsan's return. I know now that Larsan, or Ballmeyer, is long-sighted and that these glasses belonged to him.

"I now made one mistake. I was not satisfied with the evidence I had obtained. I wished to see the man's face. Had I refrained from this, the second terrible attack would not have occurred."

"But," asked the President, "why should Larsan go to Mademoiselle Stangerson's room, at all? Why should he twice attempt to murder her?"

"Because he loves her, Monsieur President."

"That is certainly a reason, but—"

"It is the only reason. He was madly in love, and because of that, and—other things, he was capable of committing any crime."

"Did Mademoiselle Stangerson know this?"

"Yes, Monsieur; but she was ignorant of the fact that the man who was pursuing her was Frederic Larsan, otherwise, of course, he would not have been allowed to be at the chateau. I noticed, when he was in her room after the incident in the gallery, that he kept himself in the shadow, and that he kept his head bent down. He was looking for the lost eye-glasses. Mademoiselle Stangerson knew Larsan under another name."

"Monsieur Darzac," asked the President, "did Mademoiselle Stangerson in any way confide in you on this matter? How is it that she has never spoken about it to anyone? If you are innocent, she would have wished to spare you the pain of being accused."

"Mademoiselle Stangerson told me nothing," replied Monsieur Darzac.

"Does what this young man says appear probable to you?" the President asked.

"Mademoiselle Stangerson has told me nothing," he replied stolidly.

"How do you explain that, on the night of the murder of the keeper," the President asked, turning to Rouletabille, "the murderer brought back the papers stolen from Monsieur Stangerson?—How do you explain how the murderer gained entrance into Mademoiselle Stangerson's locked room?"

"The last question is easily answered. A man like Larsan, or Ballmeyer, could have had made duplicate keys. As to the documents, I think Larsan had not intended to steal them, at first. Closely watching Mademoiselle with the purpose of preventing her marriage with Monsieur Robert Darzac, he one day followed her and Monsieur into the Grands Magasins de la Louvre. There he got possession of the reticule which she lost, or left behind. In that reticule was a key with a brass head. He did not know there was any value attached to the key till the advertisement in the newspapers revealed it. He then wrote to Mademoiselle, as the advertisement requested. No doubt he asked for a meeting, making known to her that he was also the person who had for some time pursued her with his love. He received no answer. He went to the Post Office and ascertained that his letter was no longer there. He had already taken complete stock of Monsieur Darzac, and, having decided to go to any lengths to gain Mademoiselle Stangerson, he had planned that, whatever might happen, Monsieur Darzac, his hated rival, should be the man to be suspected.

"I do not think that Larsan had as yet thought of murdering Mademoiselle Stangerson; but whatever he might do, he made sure that Monsieur Darzac should suffer for it. He was very nearly of the same height as Monsieur Darzac and had almost the same sized feet. It would not be difficult, to take an impression of Monsieur Darzac's footprints, and have similar boots made for himself. Such tricks were mere child's play for Larsan, or Ballmeyer.

"Receiving no reply to his letter, he determined, since Mademoiselle Stangerson would not come to him, that he would go to her. His plan had long been formed. He had made himself master of the plans of the chateau and the pavilion. So that, one afternoon, while Monsieur and Mademoiselle Stangerson were out for a walk, and while Daddy Jacques was away, he entered the latter by the vestibule window. He was alone, and, being in no hurry, he began examining the furniture. One of the pieces, resembling a safe, had a very small keyhole. That interested him! He had with him the little key with the brass head, and, associating one with the other, he tried the key in the lock. The door opened. He saw nothing but papers. They must be very valuable to have been put away in a safe, and the key to which to be of so much importance. Perhaps a thought of blackmail occurred to him as a useful possibility in helping him in his designs on Mademoiselle Stangerson. He quickly made a parcel of the papers and took it to the lavatory in the vestibule. Between the time of his first examination of the pavilion and the night of the murder of the keeper, Larsan had had time to find out what those papers contained. He could do nothing with them, and they were rather compromising. That night he took them back to the chateau. Perhaps he hoped that, by returning the papers he might obtain some gratitude from Mademoiselle Stangerson. But whatever may have been his reasons, he took the papers back and so rid himself of an encumbrance."

Rouletabille coughed. It was evident to me that he was embarrassed. He had arrived at a point where he had to keep back his knowledge of Larsan's true motive. The explanation he had given had evidently been unsatisfactory. Rouletabille was quick enough to note the bad impression he had made, for, turning to the President, he said: "And now we come to the explanation of the Mystery of the 'Yellow Room'!"

A movement of chairs in the court with a rustling of dresses and an energetic whispering of "Hush!" showed the curiosity that had been aroused.

"It seems to me," said the President, "that the Mystery of the 'Yellow Room', Monsieur Rouletabille, is wholly explained by your hypothesis. Frederic Larsan is the explanation. We have merely to substitute him for Monsieur Robert Darzac. Evidently the door of the 'Yellow Room' was open at the time Monsieur Stangerson was alone, and that he allowed the man who was coming out of his daughter's chamber to pass without arresting him—perhaps at her entreaty to avoid all scandal."

"No, Monsieur President," protested the young man. "You forget that, stunned by the attack made on her, Mademoiselle Stangerson was not in a condition to have made such an appeal. Nor could she have locked and bolted herself in her room. You must also remember that Monsieur Stangerson has sworn that the door was not open."

"That, however, is the only way in which it can be explained. The 'Yellow Room' was as closely shut as an iron safe. To use your own expression, it was impossible for the murderer to make his escape either naturally or supernaturally. When the room was broken into he was not there! He must, therefore, have escaped."

"That does not follow."

"What do you mean?"

"There was no need for him to escape—if he was not there!"

"Not there!"

"Evidently, not. He could not have been there, if he were not found there."

"But, what about the evidences of his presence?" asked the President.

"That, Monsieur President, is where we have taken hold of the wrong end. From the time Mademoiselle Stangerson shut herself in the room to the time her door was burst open, it was impossible for the murderer to escape. He was not found because he was not there during that time."

"But the evidences?"

"They have led us astray. In reasoning on this mystery we must not take them to mean what they apparently mean. Why do we conclude the murderer was there?—Because he left his tracks in the room? Good! But may he not have been there before the room was locked. Nay, he must have been there before! Let us look into the matter of these traces and see if they do not point to my conclusion.

"After the publication of the article in the 'Matin' and my conversation with the examining magistrate on the journey from Paris to Epinaysur-Orge, I was certain that the 'Yellow Room' had been hermetically sealed, so to speak, and that consequently the murderer had escaped before Mademoiselle Stangerson had gone into her chamber at midnight.

"At the time I was much puzzled. Mademoiselle Stangerson could not have been her own murderer, since the evidences pointed to some other person. The assassin, then, had come before. If that were so, how was it that Mademoiselle had been attacked after? or rather, that she appeared to have been attacked after? It was necessary for me to reconstruct the occurrence and make of it two phases—each separated from the other, in time, by the space of several hours. One phase in which Mademoiselle Stangerson had really been attacked—the other phase in which those who heard her cries thought she was being attacked. I had not then examined the 'Yellow Room'. What were the marks on Mademoiselle Stangerson? There were marks of strangulation and the wound from a hard blow on the temple. The marks of strangulation did not interest me much; they might have been made before, and Mademoiselle Stangerson could have concealed them by a collarette, or any similar article of apparel. I had to suppose this the moment I was compelled to reconstruct the occurrence by two phases. Mademoiselle Stangerson had, no doubt, her own reasons for so doing, since she had told her father nothing of it, and had made it understood to the examining magistrate that the attack had taken place in the night, during the second phase. She was forced to say that, otherwise her father would have questioned her as to her reason for having said nothing about it.

"But I could not explain the blow on the temple. I understood it even less when I learned that the mutton-bone had been found in her room. She could not hide the fact that she had been struck on the head, and yet that wound appeared evidently to have been inflicted during the first phase, since it required the presence of the murderer! I thought Mademoiselle Stangerson had hidden the wound by arranging her hair in bands on her forehead.

"As to the mark of the hand on the wall, that had evidently been made during the first phase—when the murderer was really there. All the traces of his presence had naturally been left during the first phase; the mutton-bone, the black footprints, the Basque cap, the handkerchief, the blood on the wall, on the door, and on the floor. If those traces were still all there, they showed that Mademoiselle Stangerson—who desired that nothing should be known—had not yet had time to clear them away. This led me to the conclusion that the two phases had taken place one shortly after the other. She had not had the opportunity, after leaving her room and going back to the laboratory to her father, to get back again to her room and put it in order. Her father was all the time with her, working. So that after the first phase she did not re-enter her chamber till midnight. Daddy Jacques was there at ten o'clock, as he was every night; but he went in merely to close the blinds and light the night-light. Owing to her disturbed state of mind she had forgotten that Daddy Jacques would go into her room and had begged him not to trouble himself. All this was set forth in the article in the 'Matin.' Daddy Jacques did go, however, and, in the dim light of the room, saw nothing.

"Mademoiselle Stangerson must have lived some anxious moments while Daddy Jacques was absent; but I think she was not aware that so many evidences had been left. After she had been attacked she had only time to hide the traces of the man's fingers on her neck and to hurry to the laboratory. Had she known of the bone, the cap, and the handkerchief, she would have made away with them after she had gone back to her chamber at midnight. She did not see them, and undressed by the uncertain glimmer of the night light. She went to bed, worn-out by anxiety and fear—a fear that had made her remain in the laboratory as late as possible.

"My reasoning had thus brought me to the second phase of the tragedy, when Mademoiselle Stangerson was alone in the room. I had now to explain the revolver shots fired during the second phase. Cries of 'Help!—Murder!' had been heard. How to explain these? As to the cries, I was in no difficulty; since she was alone in her room these could result from nightmare only. My explanation of the struggle and noise that were heard is simply that in her nightmare she was haunted by the terrible experience she had passed through in the afternoon. In her dream she sees the murderer about to spring upon her and she cries, 'Help! Murder!' Her hand wildly seeks the revolver she had placed within her reach on the night-table by the side of her bed, but her hand, striking the table, overturns it, and the revolver, falling to the floor, discharges itself, the bullet lodging in the ceiling. I knew from the first that the bullet in the ceiling must have resulted from an accident. Its very position suggested an accident to my mind, and so fell in with my theory of a nightmare. I no longer doubted that the attack had taken place before Mademoiselle had retired for the night. After wakening from her frightful dream and crying aloud for help, she had fainted.

"My theory, based on the evidence of the shots that were heard at midnight, demanded two shots—one which wounded the murderer at the time of his attack, and one fired at the time of the nightmare. The evidence given by the Berniers before the examining magistrate was to the effect that only one shot had been heard. Monsieur Stangerson testified to hearing a dull sound first followed by a sharp ringing sound. The dull sound I explained by the falling of the marble-topped table; the ringing sound was the shot from the revolver. I was now convinced I was right. The shot that had wounded the hand of the murderer and had caused it to bleed so that he left the bloody imprint on the wall was fired by Mademoiselle in self-defence, before the second phase, when she had been really attacked. The shot in the ceiling which the Berniers heard was the accidental shot during the nightmare.

"I had now to explain the wound on the temple. It was not severe enough to have been made by means of the mutton-bone, and Mademoiselle had not attempted to hide it. It must have been made during the second phase. It was to find this out that I went to the 'Yellow Room', and I obtained my answer there."

Rouletabille drew a piece of white folded paper from his pocket, and drew out of it an almost invisible object which he held between his thumb and forefinger.

"This, Monsieur President," he said, "is a hair—a blond hair stained with blood;—it is a hair from the head of Mademoiselle Stangerson. I found it sticking to one of the corners of the overturned table. The corner of the table was itself stained with blood—a tiny stain—hardly visible; but it told me that, on rising from her bed, Mademoiselle Stangerson had fallen heavily and had struck her head on the corner of its marble top.

"I still had to learn, in addition to the name of the assassin, which I did later, the time of the original attack. I learned this from the examination of Mademoiselle Stangerson and her father, though the answers given by the former were well calculated to deceive the examining magistrate—Mademoiselle Stangerson had stated very minutely how she had spent the whole of her time that day. We established the fact that the murderer had introduced himself into the pavilion between five and six o'clock. At a quarter past six the professor and his daughter had resumed their work. At five the professor had been with his daughter, and since the attack took place in the professor's absence from his daughter, I had to find out just when he left her. The professor had stated that at the time when he and his daughter were about to re-enter the laboratory he was met by the keeper and held in conversation about the cutting of some wood and the poachers. Mademoiselle Stangerson was not with him then since the professor said: 'I left the keeper and rejoined my daughter who was at work in the laboratory.'

"It was during that short interval of time that the tragedy took place. That is certain. In my mind's eye I saw Mademoiselle Stangerson re-enter the pavilion, go to her room to take off her hat, and find herself faced by the murderer. He had been in the pavilion for some time waiting for her. He had arranged to pass the whole night there. He had taken off Daddy Jacques's boots; he had removed the papers from the cabinet; and had then slipped under the bed. Finding the time long, he had risen, gone again into the laboratory, then into the vestibule, looked into the garden, and had seen, coming towards the pavilion, Mademoiselle Stangerson—alone. He would never have dared to attack her at that hour, if he had not found her alone. His mind was made up. He would be more at ease alone with Mademoiselle Stangerson in the pavilion, than he would have been in the middle of the night, with Daddy Jacques sleeping in the attic. So he shut the vestibule window. That explains why neither Monsieur Stangerson, nor the keeper, who were at some distance from the pavilion, had heard the revolver shot.

"Then he went back to the 'Yellow Room'. Mademoiselle Stangerson came in. What passed must have taken place very quickly. Mademoiselle tried to call for help; but the man had seized her by the throat. Her hand had sought and grasped the revolver which she had been keeping in the drawer of her night-table, since she had come to fear the threats of her pursuer. The murderer was about to strike her on the head with the mutton-bone—a terrible weapon in the hands of a Larsan or Ballmeyer; but she fired in time, and the shot wounded the hand that held the weapon. The bone fell to the floor covered with the blood of the murderer, who staggered, clutched at the wall for support—imprinting on it the red marks—and, fearing another bullet, fled.

"She saw him pass through the laboratory, and listened. He was long at the window. At length he jumped from it. She flew to it and shut it. The danger past, all her thoughts were of her father. Had he either seen or heard? At any cost to herself she must keep this from him. Thus when Monsieur Stangerson returned, he found the door of the 'Yellow

Room' closed, and his daughter in the laboratory, bending over her desk, at work!"

Turning towards Monsieur Darzac, Rouletabille cried: "You know the truth! Tell us, then, if that is not how things happened."

"I don't know anything about it," replied Monsieur Darzac.

"I admire you for your silence," said Rouletabille, "but if Mademoiselle Stangerson knew of your danger, she would release you from your oath. She would beg of you to tell all she has confided to you. She would be here to defend you!"

Monsieur Darzac made no movement, nor uttered a word. He looked at Rouletabille sadly.

"However," said the young reporter, "since Mademoiselle is not here, I must do it myself. But, believe me, Monsieur Darzac, the only means to save Mademoiselle Stangerson and restore her to her reason, is to secure your acquittal."

"What is this secret motive that compels Mademoiselle Stangerson to hide her knowledge from her father?" asked the President.

"That, Monsieur, I do not know," said Rouletabille. "It is no business of mine."

The President, turning to Monsieur Darzac, endeavoured to induce him to tell what he knew.

"Do you still refuse, Monsieur, to tell us how you employeeed your time during the attempts on the life of Mademoiselle Stangerson?"

"I cannot tell you anything, Monsieur."

The President turned to Rouletabille as if appealing for an explanation.

"We must assume, Monsieur President, that Monsieur Robert Darzac's absences are closely connected with Mademoiselle Stangerson's secret, and that Monsieur Darzac feels himself in honour bound to remain silent. It may be that Larsan, who, since his three attempts, has had everything in training to cast suspicion on Monsieur Darzac, had fixed on just those occasions for a meeting with Monsieur Darzac at a spot most compromising. Larsan is cunning enough to have done that."

The President seemed partly convinced, but still curious, he asked:

"But what is this secret of Mademoiselle Stangerson?"

"That I cannot tell you," said Rouletabille. "I think, however, you know enough now to acquit Monsieur Robert Darzac! Unless Larsan should return, and I don't think he will," he added, with a laugh.

"One question more," said the President. "Admitting your explanation, we know that Larsan wished to turn suspicion on

Monsieur Robert Darzac, but why should he throw suspicion on Daddy Jacques also?"

"There came in the professional detective, Monsieur, who proves himself an unraveller of mysteries, by annihilating the very proofs he had accumulated. He's a very cunning man, and a similar trick had often enabled him to turn suspicion from himself. He proved the innocence of one before accusing the other. You can easily believe, Monsieur, that so complicated a scheme as this must have been long and carefully thought out in advance by Larsan. I can tell you that he had long been engaged on its elaboration. If you care to learn how he had gathered information, you will find that he had, on one occasion, disguised himself as the commissionaire between the 'Laboratory of the Surete' and Monsieur Stangerson, of whom 'experiments' were demanded. In this way he had been able before the crime, on two occasions to take stock of the pavilion. He had 'made up' so that Daddy Jacques had not recognised him. And yet Larsan had found the opportunity to rob the old man of a pair of old boots and a cast-off Basque cap, which the servant had tied up in a handkerchief, with the intention of carrying them to a friend, a charcoal-burner on the road to Epinay. When the crime was discovered, Daddy Jacques had immediately recognised these objects as his. They were extremely compromising, which explains his distress at the time when we spoke to him about them. Larsan confessed it all to me. He is an artist at the game. He did a similar thing in the affair of the 'Credit Universel,' and in that of the 'Gold Ingots of the Mint.' Both these cases should be revised. Since Ballmeyer or Larsan has been in the Surete a number of innocent persons have been sent to prison."

XXVIII

In Which It Is Proved That One Does Not Always Think of Everything

Great excitement prevailed when Rouletabille had finished. The court-room became agitated with the murmurings of suppressed applause. Maitre Henri Robert called for an adjournment of the trial and was supported in his motion by the public prosecutor himself. The case was adjourned. The next day Monsieur Robert Darzac was released on bail, while Daddy Jacques received the immediate benefit of a "no cause for action." Search was everywhere made for Frederic Larsan, but in vain. Monsieur Darzac finally escaped the awful calamity which, at one time, had threatened him. After a visit to Mademoiselle Stangerson, he was led to hope that she might, by careful nursing, one day recover her reason.

Rouletabille, naturally, became the "man of the hour." On leaving the Palais de Justice, the crowd bore him aloft in triumph. The press of the whole world published his exploits and his photograph. He, who had interviewed so many illustrious personages, had himself become illustrious and was interviewed in his turn. I am glad to say that the enormous success in no way turned his head.

We left Versailles together, after having dined at "The Dog That Smokes." In the train I put a number of questions to him which, during our meal, had been on the tip of my tongue, but which I had refrained from uttering, knowing he did not like to talk "shop" while eating.

"My friend," I said, "that Larsan case is wonderful. It is worthy of you."

He begged me to say no more, and humorously pretended an anxiety for me should I give way to silly praise of him because of a personal admiration for his ability.

"I'll come to the point, then," I said, not a little nettled. "I am still in the dark as to your reason for going to America. When you left the Glandier you had found out, if I rightly understand, all about Frederic Larsan; you had discovered the exact way he had attempted the murder?"

"Quite so. And you," he said, turning the conversation, "did you suspect nothing?"

"Nothing!"

"It's incredible!"

"I don't see how I could have suspected anything. You took great pains to conceal your thoughts from me. Had you already suspected Larsan when you sent for me to bring the revolvers?"

"Yes! I had come to that conclusion through the incident of the 'inexplicable gallery.' Larsan's return to Mademoiselle Stangerson's room, however, had not then been cleared up by the eye-glasses. My suspicions were the outcome of my reasoning only; and the idea of Larsan being the murderer seemed so extraordinary that I resolved to wait for actual evidence before venturing to act. Nevertheless, the suspicion worried me, and I sometimes spoke to the detective in a way that ought to have opened your eyes. I spoke disparagingly of his methods. But until I found the eye-glasses I could but look upon my suspicion of him in the light of an absurd hypothesis only. You can imagine my elation after I had explained Larsan's movements. I remember well rushing into my room like a mad-man and crying to you: 'I'll get the better of the great Fred. I'll get the better of him in a way that will make a sensation!'

"I was then thinking of Larsan, the murderer. It was that same evening that Darzac begged me to watch over Mademoiselle Stangerson. I made no efforts until after we had dined with Larsan, until ten o'clock. He was right there before me, and I could afford to wait. You ought to have suspected, because when we were talking of the murderer's arrival, I said to you: 'I am quite sure Larsan will be here tonight.'

"But one important point escaped us both. It was one which ought to have opened our eyes to Larsan. Do you remember the bamboo cane? I was surprised to find Larsan had made no use of that evidence against Robert Darzac. Had it not been purchased by a man whose description tallied exactly with that of Darzac? Well, just before I saw him off at the train, after the recess during the trial, I asked him why he hadn't used the cane evidence. He told me he had never had any intention of doing so; that our discovery of it in the little inn at Epinay had much embarrassed him. If you will remember, he told us then that the cane had been given him in London. Why did we not immediately say to ourselves: 'Fred is lying. He could not have had this cane in London. He was not in London. He bought it in Paris'? Then you found out, on inquiry at Cassette's, that the cane had been bought by a person dressed very like Robert Darzac, though, as we learned later, from Darzac himself, it was not he who had made the purchase. Couple this with the fact we already knew, from the letter at the poste restante, that there was actually a man in Paris who was passing as Robert Darzac, why did we not immediately fix on Fred himself?

"Of course, his position at the Surete was against us; but when we saw the evident eagerness on his part to find convicting evidence against Darzac, nay, even the passion he displayed in his pursuit of the man, the lie about the cane should have had a new meaning for us. If you ask why Larsan bought the cane, if he had no intention of manufacturing evidence against Darzac by means of it, the answer is quite simple. He had been wounded in the hand by Mademoiselle Stangerson, so that the cane was useful to enable him to close his hand in carrying it. You remember I noticed that he always carried it?

"All these details came back to my mind when I had once fixed on Larsan as the criminal. But they were too late then to be of any use to me. On the evening when he pretended to be drugged I looked at his hand and saw a thin silk bandage covering the signs of a slight healing wound. Had we taken a quicker initiative at the time Larsan told us that lie about the cane, I am certain he would have gone off, to avoid suspicion. All the same, we worried Larsan or Ballmeyer without our knowing it."

"But," I interrupted, "if Larsan had no intention of using the cane as evidence against Darzac, why had he made himself up to look like the man when he went in to buy it?"

"He had not specially 'made up' as Darzac to buy the cane; he had come straight to Cassette's immediately after he had attacked Mademoiselle Stangerson. His wound was troubling him and, as he was passing along the Avenue de l'Opera, the idea of the cane came to his mind and he acted on it. It was then eight o'clock. And I, who had hit upon the very hour of the occurrence of the tragedy, almost convinced that Darzac was not the criminal, and knowing of the cane, I still never suspected Larsan. There are times. . ."

"There are times," I said, "when the greatest intellects— . . ." Rouletabille shut my mouth. I still continued to chide him, but, finding he did not reply, I saw he was no longer paying any attention to what I was saying. I found he was fast asleep.

XXIX

The Mystery of Mademoiselle Stangerson

During the days that followed I had several opportunities to question him as to his reason for his voyage to America, but I obtained no more precise answers than he had given me on the evening of the adjournment of the trial, when we were on the train for Paris. One day, however, on my still pressing him, he said:

"Can't you understand that I had to know Larsan's true personality?"

"No doubt," I said, "but why did you go to America to find that out?"

He sat smoking his pipe, and made no further reply. I began to see that I was touching on the secret that concerned Mademoiselle Stangerson. Rouletabille evidently had found it necessary to go to America to find out what the mysterious tie was that bound her to Larsan by so strange and terrible a bond. In America he had learned who Larsan was and had obtained information which closed his mouth. He had been to Philadelphia.

And now, what was this mystery which held Mademoiselle Stangerson and Monsieur Robert Darzac in so inexplicable a silence? After so many years and the publicity given the case by a curious and shameless press; now that Monsieur Stangerson knows all and has forgiven all, all may be told. In every phase of this remarkable story Mademoiselle Stangerson had always been the sufferer.

The beginning dates from the time when, as a young girl, she was living with her father in Philadelphia. A visitor at the house, a Frenchman, had succeeded by his wit, grace and persistent attention, in gaining her affections. He was said to be rich and had asked her of her father. Monsieur Stangerson, on making inquiries as to Monsieur Jean Roussel, found that the man was a swindler and an adventurer. Jean Roussel was but another of the many names under which the notorious Ballmeyer, a fugitive from France, tried to hide himself. Monsieur Stangerson did not know of his identity with Ballmeyer; he learned that the man was simply undesirable for his daughter. He not only refused to give his consent to the marriage but denied him admission into the house. Mathilde Stangerson, however, had fallen in love. To her Jean Roussel was everything that her love painted him. She was indignant at her father's attitude, and did not conceal her feelings. Her father sent her to stay with an aunt in Cincinnati. There she was joined by Jean Roussel and, in spite of the reverence she felt for her father, ran away with him to get married.

They went to Louisville and lived there for some time. One morning, however, a knock came at the door of the house in which they were and the police entered to arrest Jean Roussel. It was then that Mathilde Stangerson, or Roussel, learned that her husband was no other than the notorious Ballmeyer!

The young woman in her despair tried to commit suicide. She failed in this, and was forced to rejoin her aunt in Cincinnati, The old lady was overjoyed to see her again. She had been anxiously searching for her and had not dared to tell Monsieur Stangerson of her disappearance. Mathilde swore her to secrecy, so that her father should not know she had been away. A month later, Mademoiselle Stangerson returned to her father, repentant, her heart dead within her, hoping only one thing: that she would never again see her husband, the horrible Ballmeyer. A report was spread, a few weeks later, that he was dead, and she now determined to atone for her disobedience by a life of labour and devotion for her father. And she kept her word.

All this she had confessed to Robert Darzac, and, believing Ballmeyer dead, had given herself to the joy of a union with him. But fate had resuscitated Jean Roussel—the Ballmeyer of her youth. He had taken steps to let her know that he would never allow her to marry Darzac—that he still loved her.

Mademoiselle Stangerson never for one moment hesitated to confide in Monsieur Darzac. She showed him the letter in which Jean Roussel asked her to recall the first hours of their union in their beautiful and charming Louisville home. "The presbytery has lost nothing of its charm, nor the garden its brightness," he had written. The scoundrel pretended to be rich and claimed the right of taking her back to Louisville. She had told Darzac that if her father should know of her dishonour, she would kill herself. Monsieur Darzac had sworn to silence her persecutor, even if he had to kill him. He was outwitted and would have succumbed had it not been for the genius of Rouletabille.

Mademoiselle Stangerson was herself helpless in the hands of such a villain. She had tried to kill him when he had first threatened and then attacked her in the "Yellow Room". She had, unfortunately, failed, and felt herself condemned to be for ever at the mercy of this unscrupulous wretch who was continually demanding her presence at clandestine interviews. When he sent her the letter through the Post Office, asking her to meet him, she had refused. The result of her refusal was the tragedy of the "Yellow Room". The second time he wrote asking for a meeting, the letter reaching her in her sick chamber, she had avoided him by sleeping with her servants. In that letter the scoundrel had warned her that, since she was too ill to come to him, he would come to her, and that he would be in her chamber at a particular hour on a particular night. Knowing that she had everything to fear from Ballmeyer, she had left her chamber on that night. It was then that the incident of the "inexplicable gallery" occurred.

The third time she had determined to keep the appointment. He asked for it in the letter he had written in her own room, on the night of the incident in the gallery, which he left on her desk. In that letter he threatened to burn her father's papers if she did not meet him. It was to rescue these papers that she made up her mind to see him. She did not for one moment doubt that the wretch would carry out his threat if she persisted in avoiding him, and in that case the labours of her father's lifetime would be for ever lost. Since the meeting was thus inevitable, she resolved to see her husband and appeal to his better nature. It was for this interview that she had prepared herself on the night the keeper was killed. They did meet, and what passed between them may be imagined. He insisted that she renounce Darzac. She, on her part, affirmed her love for him. He stabbed her in his anger, determined to convict Darzac of the crime. As Larsan he could do it, and had so managed things that Darzac could never explain how he had employeeed the time of his absence from the chateau. Ballmeyer's precautions were most cunningly taken.

Larsan had threatened Darzac as he had threatened Mathilde—with the same weapon, and the same threats. He wrote Darzac urgent letters, declaring himself ready to deliver up the letters that had passed between him and his wife, and to leave them for ever, if he would pay him his price. He asked Darzac to meet him for the purpose of arranging the matter, appointing the time when Larsan would be with Mademoiselle Stangerson. When Darzac went to Epinay, expecting to find Ballmeyer or Larsan there, he was met by an accomplice of Larsan's, and kept waiting until such time as the "coincidence" could be established.

It was all done with Machiavellian cunning; but Ballmeyer had reckoned without Joseph Rouletabille.

Now that the Mystery of the "Yellow Room" has been cleared up, this is not the time to tell of Rouletabille's adventures in America. Knowing the young reporter as we do, we can understand with what acumen he had traced, step by step, the story of Mathilde Stangerson and Jean Roussel. At Philadelphia he had quickly informed himself as to Arthur William Rance. There he learned of Rance's act of devotion and the reward he thought himself entitled to for it. A rumour of his marriage with Mademoiselle Stangerson had once found its way into the drawing-rooms of Philadelphia. He also learned of Rance's continued attentions to her and his importunities for her hand. He had taken to drink, he had said, to drown his grief at his unrequited love. It can now be understood why Rouletabille had shown so marked a coolness of demeanour towards Rance when they met in the witnesses' room, on the day of the trial.

The strange Roussel-Stangerson mystery had now been laid bare. Who was this Jean Roussel? Rouletabille had traced him from Philadelphia to Cincinnati. In Cincinnati he became acquainted with the old aunt, and had found means to open her mouth. The story of Ballmeyer's arrest threw the right light on the whole story. He visited the "presbytery"—a small and pretty dwelling in the old colonial style—which had, indeed, "lost nothing of its charm." Then, abandoning his pursuit of traces of Mademoiselle Stangerson, he took up those of Ballmeyer. He followed them from prison to prison, from crime to crime. Finally, as he was about leaving for Europe, he learned in New York that Ballmeyer had, five years before, embarked for France with some valuable papers belonging to a merchant of New Orleans whom he had murdered.

And yet the whole of this mystery has not been revealed. Mademoiselle Stangerson had a child, by her husband,—a son. The infant was born in the old aunt's house. No one knew of it, so well had the aunt managed to conceal the event.

What became of that son?—That is another story which, so far, I am not permitted to relate.

About two months after these events, I came upon Rouletabille sitting on a bench in the Palais de Justice, looking very depressed.

"What's the matter, old man?" I asked. "You are looking very downcast. How are your friends getting on?"

"Apart from you," he said, "I have no friends."

"I hope that Monsieur Darzac—"

"No doubt."

"And Mademoiselle Stangerson—How is she?"

"Better—much better."

"Then you ought not to be sad."

"I am sad," he said, "because I am thinking of the perfume of the lady in black—"

"The perfume of the lady in black!—I have heard you often refer to it. Tell me why it troubles you."

"Perhaps—some day; some day," said Rouletabille.

And he heaved a profound sigh.

THE PERFUME OF THE LADY IN BLACK

I

Which Begins Where Most Romances End

The marriage of Mr. Robert Darzac and Miss Mathilde Stangerson took place in Paris, at the Church of St. Nicolas du Chardonnet, on April 6, 1895, everything connected with the occasion being conducted in the quietest fashion possible. A little more than two years had rolled by since the events which I have recorded in a previous volume—events so sensational that it is not speaking too strongly to say that an even longer lapse of time would not have sufficed to blot out the memory of the famous "Mystery of the Yellow Room."

There was no doubt in the minds of those concerned that, if the arrangements for the wedding had not been made almost secretly, the little church would have been thronged and surrounded by a curious crowd, eager to gaze upon the principal personages of the drama which had aroused an interest almost world wide and the circumstances of which were still present in the minds of the sensation-loving public. But in this isolated little corner of the city, in this almost unknown parish, it was easy enough to maintain the upmost privacy. Only a few friends of M. Darzac and the Professor Stangerson, on whose discretion they felt assured that they might rely, had been invited. I had the honour to be one of the number.

I reached the church early, and naturally, my first thought was to look for Joseph Rouletabille there. I had been somewhat surprise at not seeing him, but, having no doubt that he would arrive shortly, and, I entered the pew and already occupied by M. Henri-Robert and M. Andre Hesse, who, in the quiet shades of the little chapel, exchanged the undertones reminiscences of the strange affair at Versailles, which the approaching ceremony brought to their memories. I listened without paying much attention to what they were saying, glancing from time to time carelessly around me.

A dreary place enough is the Church of St. Nicolas du Chardonnet. With its cracked walls, the lizards running from every corner and dirt— not the beautiful dust of ages, but the common, ill-smelling, germ-laden dust of today—everywhere, this church, so dark and forbidding on the outside, is equally dismal within. The sky, which seems rather to be withdrawn from the above the edifice, sheds a miserly light which seems to find the greatest difficulty in penetrating through the dusty panes of unstained glass. Have you read Renan's "Memories of Childhood and Youth?" Push the door of St. Nicolas du Chardonnet and you will understand how the author of the "Life of Jesus" longed to die, when as a lad he was a pupil in the little seminary of the Abbe Duplanloup, close by, and could only leave the school to come to pray in this church. And it is in this funeral darkness, in a scene which seemed to have been painted only for mourning and for all rites consecrated to sorrow, that the marriage of Robert Darzac and Mathilde Stangerson was to be solemnised. I could not cast aside the feeling of foreboding that came over me in these dreary surroundings.

Beside me, M. Henri-Robert and M. André Hesse continued to chat, and my wandering attention was arrested by a remark made by the former:

"I never felt quite easy about Robert and Mathilde," he said—"not even after the happy termination of the affair at Versailles—until I know that the information of the death of Frederic Larsan had been officially confirmed. That man was a pitiless enemy."

It will be remembered, perhaps, by the readers of "The Mystery of the Yellow Room" that a few months after the acquittal of the Professor in Sorbonne, there occurred the terrible catastrophe of La Dordogne, a transatlantic steamers, running between Havre and New York. In the broiling heat of a summer night, upon the coast of the New Worl, La Dordogne had caught fire from an overheated boiler. Before help could reach her, the steamer was utterly destroyed. Scarcely thirty passengers were able to leap into the life boats, and these were picked up the next day by a merchant vessel, which conveyed them to the nearest port. For days thereafter, the ocean cast up on the beach hundreds of corpses. And among these, they found Larsan.

The papers which were found carefully hidden in the clothing worn by the dead man, proved beyond a doubt his identity. Mathilde Stangerson was at last delivered from this monster of a husband to whom, through the facility of the American laws, she had given her hand in secret, in the unthinking ardour of girlish romance. This wretch, whose real name, according to court records, was Ballmeyer, and who had married her under the name of Jean Rouseel, could no longer rise like a dark shadow between Mathilde and the man whom she had loved so long and so well, without daring to become his bride. In "The Mystery of the Yellow Room," I have related all the details of this remarkable affair, one of the strangest which has ever been known in the annals of the Court of Assizes, and which, without doubt, would have had a most tragic denouncement, had it not been for the extraordinary party played by a boy reporter, scarcely eighteen years old, Joseph Rouletabille, who was the only one to discover that Frederic Larsan, the celebrated Secret Service agent, was none other than Ballmeyer himself. The accidental— one might almost say "providential"—death of this villain, had seemed to assure a happy termination to the extraordinary story, and it must be confessed that it was undoubtedly one of the chief factors in the rapid recovery of Mathilde Stangerson, whose reason had been almost overturned by the mysterious horrors at the Glandier.

"You see, my dear friend," said M. Henri-Robert to M. André Hesse, whose eyes were roving restlessly about the church, "you see, in this world, one can always find the bright side. See how beautifully everything has turned out—even the troubles of Mlle. Stangerson. But why are you constantly looking around you? What are you looking for? Do you expect anyone?"

"Yes," replied M. Hesse. "I am waiting for Frédéric Larsan!"

M. Henri-Robert laughed—a decorous little laugh, in deference to the sanctity of the surroundings. But I felt no inclination to join in his mirth. I was an hundred leagues from foreseeing the terrible experience which was even then approaching us; but when I recall that moment and seek to blot out of my mind all that has happened since—all those events which I intend to relate in the course of this narrative, letting the circumstances come before the reader as they came before us during their development—I recollect once more the curious unrest which thrilled me at the mention of Larsan's name.

"What's the matter, Sainclair?" whispered M. Henri-Robert, who had noticed Something odd in my expression. "You know that Hesse was only joking."

"I don't know anything about it," I answered. And I looked attentively around me, as M. Andre Hesse had done. And, indeed, we had believe Larsan dead so often when he was known as Ballmeyer, that it seemed quite possible that he might be once more brought to life in the guise of Larsan.

"Here comes Rouletabille, remarked M. Henri-Robert. "I'll wager that he isn't worried about anything."

"But how pale he is!" exclaimed M. Andre Hesse in an undertone.

The young reporter joined us and pressed our hands in an absent-minded manner.

"Good morning, Sainclair. Good morning, gentlemen. I am not late, I hope?"

It seemed to me that his voice trembled. He left our pew immediately and withdrew to a dark corner, where I beheld him kneel down like a child. He hid his face, which was indeed very pale, in his hands, and prayed. I had never guessed that Rouletabille was of a religious turn of mind, and his fervent devotion astonished me. When he raised his head, his eyes were filled with tears. He did not even try to hide them. He paid no attention to anything or anyone around him. He was lost completely in his prayers, and, one might imagine, his grief.

But what could be the occasion of his sorrow? Was he not happy at the prospect of the union so ardently desired by everyone? Had not the good fortune of Mathilde Stangerson and Robert Darzac been in a great measure brought about by his efforts? After all, it was perhaps from joy, that the lad had wept. He rose from his knees, and was hidden behind a pillar. I made no endeavour to join him, for I could see that he was anxious to be alone.

And the next moment, Mathilde Stangerson made her entrance into the church upon the arm of her father, Robert Darzac walking behind them. Ah, the drama of the Glandier had been a sorrowful one for these three! But, strange as it may seem, Mathilde Strangerson appeared only the more beautiful, for all that she had passed through. True, she was no longer the beautiful statue, the living marble, the ancient goddess, the cold Pagan divinity, who, at the official functions at which her father's position had forced her to appear, had excited a flutter of admiration whenever she was seen. It seen, on the contrary, that fate, in making her expiate for so many long years and imprudence committed in early youth, had cast her into the depths of madness and despair, only to tear away the mask of stone, which hid from sight the tender, delicate spirit. And it was this spirit which shone forth on her wedding day, in the sweetest and most charming smile, playing on her curved lips, hiding in her eyes, filled with pensive happiness, and leavings its impress on her forehead, polished like ivory, where one might read the love of all that was beautiful and all that was good.

As to her gown, I must acknowledge that I remember nothing at all about it, and am unable even to say of what colour it was. But what I do remember, is the strange expression which came over her visage when she looked through the rows of faces in the pews without seeming to discover the one she sought. In a moment she had regained her composure, and was mistress of herself once more. She had seen Rouletabille behind his pillar. She smiled at him and my companions and I smiled in our turn.

"She has the eyes of a mad woman!"

I turned around quickly to see who had uttered the heartless words. It was a poor fellow whom Robert Darzac, out of the kindness of his heart, had made his assistant in the laboratory at the Sorbonne. The man was named Brignolles, and was a distant cousin of the bridegroom. We knew of no other relative of M. Darzac, whose family came originally from the Midi. Long ago he had lost both father and mother; he had neither brother nor sister, and seemed to have broken off all intercourse with his native province, from which he had brought an eager desire for success, an exceptional ability to work, a strong intellect and natural need for affection, which had satisfied itself in his relations with Professor Stangerson and his daughter. He had also as a legacy from Provence, his native place, a soft voice and slight accent, which had often brought a smile to the lips of his pupils at the Sorbonne, who, nevertheless, loved it as they might have loved a strain of music, which made the necessary dryness of their studies a little less arid.

One beautiful morning, in the preceeding spring, and consequently a year after the occurrences in the yellow room, Robert Darzac had presented Brignolles to his pupils. The new assistant had come direct from Aix, where he had been a tutor in the natural sciences, and where he had committed some fault of discipline which had caused his dismissal. But he had remembered that he was related to M. Darzac, the famous chemist, had taken the train to Paris, and had told such a piteous tale to the fiancé of Mlle. Stangerson that the Darzac, out of pity, had found the means to associate his cousin with him in his work. At this time, the health of Robert Darzac had been far from flourishing. He was suffering from the reaction following the strong emotions which had nearly weighed him down at the Glandier and at the Court of Assizes; but one might have thought that the recovery, now assured, of Mathilde, and the prospect of their marriage would have had a happy influence both upon the mental and physical condition of the professor. We, however, remarked on the contrary, that from the day that Brignolles came to him—Brignolles, whose friendship should have been a precious solace, the weakness of M. Darzac seemed to increase. However, we are obliged to acknowledge that Brignolles was not to blame for that, for two unfortunate and unforeseen accidents had occurred in the course of some experiments, which would have seemed, on the face of them, not at all dangerous. The first resulted from the unexpected explosion of a Gessler tube, which might have severely injured M. Darzac, but which only injured Brignolles, whose hands were badly scarred. The second, which might have been extremely grave, happened through the explosion of a tiny lamp against which M. Darzac was leaning. Happily, he was not hurt, but his eyebrows were scorched, and for some time after his sight was slightly impaired, and he was unable to stand much sunlight.

Since the Glandier mysteries, I had been in such a state of mind that I often found myself attaching importance to the most simple happenings. At the time of the second accident I was present, having come to seek M. Darzac at the Sorbonne. I myself led our friend to a druggist and then to a doctor, and I (rather dryly, I own) begged Brignolles, when he wished to accompany us, to remain at his post. On the way, M. Darzac asked me why I had wounded the poor fellow's feelings. I had told him that I did not care for Brignolles's society, for the abstract reason that I did not care for his manners, and for that concrete reason, on this special occasion, that I believed him to be responsible for the accident. M. Darzac demanded why I thought so, and I did not know how to answer, and he began to laugh—a laugh that was quickly silence, however, when the doctor told him that he might easily have been made entirely blind, and that he might consider himself very lucky in having gotten off so well.

My suspicions of Brignolles were, doubtless, ridiculous, and no more accidents happened. All the same, I was so strongly prejudiced against the ridiculous, and the accidents never happened again. All of the same, I was so strongly prejudiced against the young man that, at the bottom of my heart, I blamed him for the slow improvement in M. Darzac's physical condition. At the beginning of winter, Darzac had such a bad cough that I entreated him to ask for leave of absence and to take a trip to the Midi—a prayer in which all his friends joined. The physicians advised San Remo. He went thither, and a week later he wrote us that he felt much better—that it seemed to him as though a heavy weight had been lifted from his breast. "I can breathe here," he wrote. "When I left Paris, I seemed to be stifling."

This letter from M. Darzac gave me much food for thought, and I no longer hesitated to take Rouletabille into my confidence.

He agreed with me that it was a most peculiar coincidence that M. Darzac was so ill when Brignolles was with him and so much better when he and his young assistant were separated. The impression that this was actually fact was so strong in my mind that I would on no account have permitted myself to lose sight of Brignolles. No, indeed. I verily believe that if he had attempted to leave Paris, I should have followed him. But he made no such attempt. On the contrary, he haunted the footsteps of M. Stangerson. Under the pretext of asking news of M. Darzac, he presented himself at the house of the Professor almost every day. Once he made an effort to see Mlle. Stangerson, but I had painted his portrait to M. Darzac's fiancée in such unflattering terms, that I had succeeding in dusting her with him completely—a fact on which I congratulated myself in my innermost soul.

M. Darzac remained four months in San Remo and returned home at the end of that time almost completely restored to health. His eyes, however, were still weak, and he was under the necessity of taking the greatest care of them. Rouletabille and myself had resolved to keep a close watch on Brignolles, but we were satisfied that everything would be right when we were informed that the long-deferred marriage was to occur almost immediately and that M. Darzac would take his wife away on a long honeymoon trip far from Paris—from Brignolles.

Upon his return from San Remo, M. Darzac had asked me:

"Well, how are you getting on with poor Brignolles? Have you decided that you were wrong with him?"

"Indeed, I have not," was my response.

And Darzac turned away, laughing at me, and uttering one of the Provencal jests which he affected when circumstances allowed him to be gay, and which found on his lips a new freshness since his visit to the Midi had accustomed him again to the accents of his childhood.

We knew that he was happy. But we had formed no real idea of how happy he was—for between the time of his return and the wedding day we had had few chances to see him—until we beheld him walking up the aisle of the church, his face fairly transformed. His slight erect figure bore itself as proudly as though he were an Emperor. Happiness had made him another being.

"Anyone could guess that he was a bridegroom!" tittered Brignolles.

I left the neighbourhood of the man who was so repulsive to me, and stepped behind poor M. Stangerson, who stood through the entire ceremony with his arms crossed on his breast, seeing nothing and hearing nothing. I was obliged to touch him on the shoulder when all was over to arouse him from his dream.

As they passed into sacristy, M. Andre Hesse heaved a deep sigh.

"I can breathe again," he murmured.

"Why couldn't you breathe before, my friend?" asked M. Henri-Robert.

And M. Andre Hesse confessed that he had feared up to the last moment that the dead man would reappear.

"I can't help it," was the only response he would make when his friend rallied him. "I cannot bring myself to the idea that Frederic Larsan will stay dead for good."

And now we all—a dozen or so persons—were gathered in the sacristy. The witness signed the register, and the rest of us congratulated the newly wedded pair. The sacristy was yet more dismal than the church, and I might have thought that it was on account of the darkness that I could not perceive Joseph Rouletabille, if the room had not been so small. But, assuredly, he was not there. Mathilde had already asked for him twice, and M. Darzac requested me to go and look for him. I did so, but returned to the vestry without him. He had disappeared from the church.

"How strange it is!" examined M. Darzac. "I can't understand it. Are you sure that you looked everywhere? He may be in some corner dreaming."

"I looked everywhere, and I called his name," I told him.

But M. Darzac was still not satisfied. He wanted to look through the church for himself. His search was better rewarded than mine, for learned from a beggar, who was sitting in the porch with a tambourine, that Rouletabille has left the church a few minutes before and had been driven away in a hack. When the bridegroom brought this news to his wife, she appeared to be both pained and anxious. She called me to her side and said:

"My dear M. Sainclair, you know that we are to take the train in two hours. Will you hunt up our little friend and bring him to me, and tell him that his strange behaviour is grieving me very much?"

"Count upon me," I said.

And I began a wild goose chase after Rouletabille. But I appeared at the station without him. Neither at his home, nor at the office of his paper, nor at the Café du Barreau, where the necessities of his work often called him at this hour of the day, could I lay my hand on him. None of his comrades could tell me where I might chance to find him. I leave you to think how unwillingly I turned my steps in the direction of the railroad station. M. Darzac was greatly disturbed, but as he had to look after the comfort of his fellow travellers (for Professor Stangerson, who was on his way to Mentone, was to accompany his daughter and her husband to Dijon, changing cars there, while the Darzacs continued their trips to Culoz and Mt. Cenis,) he asked me to break the bad news to his bride. I performed the commission, adding that Rouletabille would, without doubt, present himself before the train started. At these words, Mathilde began to cry softly, and shook her head:

"No—no!" she whispered. "It is all over. He will never come again."

And she stepped into the railway carriage.

It was at this point that the insufferable Brignolles, seeing the emotion of the newly-made bride, whispered again to M. Andre Hesse, "Look! Look! Hasn't she the eyes of a maniac? Ah, Robert has done wrong. It would have been better for him to wait." M. Hesse gave him a disdainful glance, and bade him to be silent.

I can still see Brignolles as he spoke those words, and can recall as vividly as though it were yesterday the feeling of horror with which he inspired me. There was no longer any doubt in my mind that he was an evil and a jealous man, and that he would never forgive his relative for having placed him in a position which might be considered subordinate. He had a yellow face and long features that looked as if they had been drawn down from forehead to chin. Everything about him seemed to diffuse bitterness and everything about him was long. He had a long figure, long arms, long legs and a long head. However, to this general rule of length, there were exceptions—the feet and the hands. He had extremities small and almost beautiful.

After having been so rudely silence for his malicious words by the young lawyer, Brignolles immediately took offense and left the statin, after having paid his respects to the bride and bridegroom. At least, I believe that he left the station, for I did not see him again.

There were three minutes yet before the departure of the train. We still hoped that Rouletabille would appear, and we looked across the quay, thinking once or twice that we saw the form of our young friend approaching, among the hurrying throng of travellers. How could it be that he would not advance, as we were so used to seeing him, in his quick, boyish fashion, rushing through the crows, paying no heed to the cries and protestations that his method of pushing his way usually evoked while he seemed to be hurrying faster than any one else? What could he be doing that detained him?

Already the doors were closed. The bell on the engine began to sound its first slow strokes, and the calls of hack driver began to arise: "Carriage, Monsieur? Carriage?" And then the quick last word which gave the signal for the departure. But no Rouletabille. We were all so grieved, and moreover, so surprised, that we remained on the platform, looking at Mme. Darzac, without thinking to wish her a pleasant journey. Professor Stangerson's daughter cast a long glance upon the quay, and, at the moment that the speed of the train began to accelerate, certain now that she was not to see her "little friend" again, she threw me an envelope from the car window.

"For him," she said.

An almost as though moved by an irresistible impulse, her face wearing an expression of something that resembled terror, she added in a tone so strange that I could not help recalling the horrible speeches of Brignolles:

"Au revoir, my friends—or adieu."

II

In Which There is Question of the Changing Rumours of Joseph Rouletabille

In returning alone from the station I could not help feeling some surprise at the singular sensation of sad ness which oppressed me, and of the cause of which I had not the least idea. Since the affair at Versailles, with the details of which my existence had become so strangely intermingled, I had enjoyed the closest in timacy with Professor Stangerson, his daughter, and Robert Darzac. I ought to have been completely happy on the day of this wedding, which seemed in every way so satisfactory. I wondered whether the unexplained absence of the young reporter did not account in some measure for my strange depression. Rouletabille had been treated by the Stangersons and by M. Darzac as their deliverer. And especially since Mathilde had left the sanitarium, in which, for several months, her shat tered nervous system had needed and received the most assiduous care—since the daughter of the famous professor had been able to understand the eextraordinary part which the boy had played in the drama that, with out his help, would inevitably have ended in the bitterest grief for all those whom she loved—since she had read by the light of her restored reason the short-hand reports of the trial, at which Rouletabille appeared at the last moment like some hero of a miracleshe had surrounded the youngster with an affection little less than maternal. She interested herself in everything which concerned him; she begged for his confidence: she wanted to know more about him than I knew, and, perhaps, more even than he knew himself. She had shown an unobtrusive but strong curiosity in regard to the mystery of his birth, of which all of us were ignorant, and on which the young man had kept silence with a sort of savage pride. Although he fully realised the tender friendship which the poor soul felt for him, Rouletabille maintained his reserve and in his dealings with her affected a formal politeness which astonished me, coming from the boy whom I had known so exuberant, so whole-hearted, so strong in his likes and dislikes. More than once I had mentioned the matter to him, and he had answered me in an evasive manner, laying great stress, however, upon his sentiments of devotion for "a lady whom he esteemed beyond anyone in the world, and for whom he would have been ready to sacrifice his all, if fate or fortune had given him anything to sacrifice for anyone." He would take strange whims at such times. For instance, after having made, in my presence, a promise to take a holiday and remain all day with the Stangersons, who had rented for the summer (for they did not wish to live at the Glandier again) a pretty little place at Chennevieres, on the borders of the Marne, and after having shown an almost childish joy at the prospect, he suddenly and without any reason refused to accompany me. And I was obliged to set out alone, leaving him in his little room, in the corner of the Boulevard St. Michel and the Rue Monsieur-le-Prince. I wished as I departed that he might experience as much pain as I knew that he would cause Mlle. Stangerson. One Sunday, she, vexed at the lad's behavior, made up her mind to go with me to his den in the Latin Quarter, and surprise him.

When we reached his lodgings, Rouletabille, who had answered our knock with an energetic "Come in," sat working at a little table. He arose as we entered, and turned so pale that we believed that he was about to fall in a faint.

"Good heavens!" cried Mlle. Stangerson, hastening toward him. But he was quicker than she, and before she reached the table on which he leaned, he had thrown a cover over the papers which were spread over the surface, hiding them entirely.

Mathilde had, of course, noticed the action. She paused in amazement.

"We are disturbing you," she said.

"Oh, not at all," replied Rouletabille. "I have finished my work. I will show it to you sometime. It is a masterpiece—a piece in five acts, for which I am not able to find the denouement."

And he smiled. Soon he was again entirely master of himself, and made us a hundred droll speeches, thanking us for having come to cheer him in his solitude. He insisted on inviting us to dinner, and we three ate our evening meal in a Latin Quarter restaurant—Foyot's. It was a happy evening. Rouletabille telephoned for Robert Darzac, who joined us at dessert. At this time M. Darzac was not ill, and the amazing Brignolles had not yet made his appearance in Paris. We played like children. That summer night was so beautiful in the solitude of the Luxembourg!

Before bidding adieu to Mlle. Stangerson, Roulet abille begged her pardon for the strange humor which he evinced at times, and accused himself of being at bottom a very disagreeable person. Mathilde kissed him and Robert Darzac put his arm affectionately around the lad's shoulders. And Rouletabille was so moved that he never uttered a word while I walked with him to his door; but at the moment of our parting, he pressed my hand more tenderly than he had ever done before. Poor little fellow! Ah, if I had known How I re proach myself in the light of the present for having judged him with too little patience!

Thus, sad at heart, assailed by premonitions which I tried in vain to drive away, I returned from the railway station at Lyons, pondering over the numerous fanta sies, the strange caprices of Rouletabille during the last two years. But nothing that entered my mind could have warned me of what had happened, or still less have explained it to me. Where was Rouletabille? I went to his rooms in the Boulevard St. Michel, telling myself that if I did not find him there, I could, at least, leave Mme. Darzac's letter. What was my astonish ment when I entered the building to see my own servant carrying my bag. I asked him to tell me what he was doing and why, and he replied that he did not know—that I must ask M. Rouletabille.

The boy had been, as it turned out, while I had been seeking him everywhere (except, naturally, in my own house), in my apartments in the Rue de Rivoli. He had ordered my servant to take him to my rooms, and had made the man fill a valise with everything necessary for a trip of three or four days. Then he had directed the man to bring the bag in about an hour to the hotel in the "Boul' Mich."

I made one bound up the stairs to my friend's bed chamber, where I found him packing in a tiny hand satchel an assortment of toilet articles, a change of linen and a night shirt. Until this task was ended, I could obtain no satisfaction from Rouletabille, for in regard to the little affairs of everyday life, he was extremely particular, and, despite the modesty of his means, succeeded in living very well, having a horror of everything which could be called bohemian. He finally deigned to announce to me that "we were going to take our Easter vacation," and that, since I had nothing to do, and the *Epoch* had granted him a three days' holiday, we couldn't do better than to go and take a short rest at the seaside. I made no reply, so angry was I at this high-handed method, and all the more because I had not the least desire to contemplate the beauties of the ocean upon one of the abominable days of early spring, which for two or three weeks every year makes us regret the winter. But my silence did not disturb Rouletabille in the least, and taking my valise in one hand, his satchel in the other, he hustled me down the stairs and pushed me into a hack which awaited us before the door of the hotel. Half an hour later, we found ourselves in a first-class carriage of the Northern Railway, which was carrying us toward Trepot by way of Amiens. As we entered the station, he said:

"Why don't you give me the letter that you have for me?"

I gased at him in amazement. He had guessed that Mme. Darzac would be greatly grieved at not seeing him before her departure, and would write to him. He had been positively malicious. I answered:

"Because you don't deserve it."

And I gave him a good scolding, to which he inter posed no defense. He did not even try to excuse himself, and that made me angrier than ever. Finally, I handed him the letter. He took it, looked at it and in haled its fragrance. As I sat looking at him curiously, he frowned, trying, as I could see, to repress some strong feeling. But he could no longer hide it from me when he turned toward the window, his forehead against the glass, and became absorbed in a deep study of the landscape. His face betrayed the fact that he was suffering profoundly.

"Well?" I said. "Aren't you going to read the letter?"

"No," he replied. "Not here. When we are yonder."

We arrived at Trepot in the blackest night that I remember, after six hours of an interminable trip and in wretched weather. The wind from the sea chilled us to the bone and swept over the deserted quay with weird sounds of lamentation. We met only a watch man, wrapped in his cloak and hood, who paced the banks of the canal. Not a cab, of course. A few gas jets, trembling in their glass globes, reflected their light in the mud puddles formed by the falling rain. We heard in the distance the clicking noise of the little wooden shoes of some Trepot woman who was out late. That we did not fall into a huge watering trough was due to the fact that we were warned by the hoofs of a stray horse, which passed that way to drink. I walked behind Rouletabille, who made his way with difficulty in this damp obscurity. However, he appeared to know the place, for we finally arrived at the door of a queer little inn, which remained open during the early spring for the fishermen. Rouletabille demanded supper and a fire, for we were half starved and half frozen.

"Ah, now, my friend," I said, when we were settled after a fashion. "Will you condescend to explain to me what we have come to look for in this place, aside from rheumatism and pneumonia?"

But Rouletabille, at this moment, coughed and turned toward the fire to warm his hands again.

"Oh, yes," he answered. "I am going to tell you. We have come to look for the perfume of the Lady in Black."

This phrase gave me so much to think about that I scarcely slept at all that night. Besides, the wind howled continuously, sending its wails over the water, then swallowing itself up in the little streets of the town as if it were entering corridors. I heard someone mov ing about in the room next to mine, which was occupied by my friend: I arose and tried his door. In spite of the cold and the wind, he had opened the window, and I could see him distinctly waving kisses toward the shad ows. He was embracing the night.

I closed the door again and went quictly back to bed. Early in the morning I was awakened by a changed Rouletabille. His face was distorted with grief as he handed me a telegram which had come to him at the Bourg, having been forwarded from Paris, in accordance with the orders that he had left.

Here is the dispatch:

"Come immediately without losing a minute. We have given up our trip to the Orient, and will join M. Stangerson at Mentone, at the home of the Rances at Rochers Rouges. Let this message remain a secret between us. It is not necessary to frighten anyone. You may pretend that you are on your vacation, or make any other excuse that you like, but come. Telegraph me general delivery, Mentone. Quickly, quickly, I am waiting for you.

Yours in despair
Darzac

III

The Perfume

W ell!" I cried, leaping out of bed. "It doesn't surprise me!"

"You never believed that *he* was dead?" demanded Rouletabille, in a tone filled with an emotion that I could not explain to myself, for it seemed greater even than was warranted by the situation, admitting that the terms of M. Darzac's telegram were to be taken literally.

"I never felt quite sure of it," I answered. "It was too useful for him to pass for dead to permit him to hesitate at the sacrifice of a few papers, however important those were which were found upon the victim of the Dordogne disaster. But what is the matter with you, my boy? You look as though you were going to faint. Are you ill?"

Rouletabille had let himself sink into a chair. It was in a voice which trembled like that of an old man that he confided to me that, even while the marriage ceremony of our friends was going on, he had become possessed with a strong conviction that Larsan was not dead. But after the ceremony was at an end, he had felt more secure. It seemed to him that Larsan would never have permitted Mathilde Stangerson to speak the vows that gave her to Robert Darzac if he were really alive. Larsan would only have had to show his face to stop the marriage; and, however dangerous to himself such an act might have been, he would not, the young reporter believed, have hesitated to deliver himself up to the danger, knowing as he did the strong religious convictions of Professor Stangerson's daughter, and knowing, too, that she would never have consented to enter into an alliance with another man while her first husband was alive, even had she been freed from the latter by human laws. In vain had everyone who loved her attempted to persuade her that her first marriage was void, according to French statute. She persisted in declaring that the words pronounced by the priest had made her the wife of the miserable wretch who had victimised her, and that she must remain his wife so long as they both should live.

Wiping the perspiration from his forehead, Rouletabille remarked:—

"Sainclair, can you ever forget Larsan's eyes? Do you remember, 'The Presbytery has not lost its charm or the garden its brightness?'"

I pressed the boy's hand; it was burning hot. I tried to calm him, but he paid no attention to anything I said.

"And it was after the wedding—just a few hours after the wedding, that he chose to appear!" he cried. "There isn't anything else to think, is there, Sainclair? You took M. Darzac's wire just as I did? It could mean nothing else except that that man has come back?"

"I should think not—but M. Darzac may be mistaken."

"Oh, M. Darzac is not a child to be frightened at bogies. But we must hope—we must hope, mustn't we, Sainclair, that he is mistaken? Oh, it isn't possible that such a fearful thing can be true. Oh, Sainclair, it would be too terrible!"

I had never seen Rouletabille so deeply agitated, even at the time of the most terrible events at the Glandier. He arose from his chair and walked up and down the room, casting aside any object which came in his way and repeating over and over: "No, no! It's too terrible—too terrible!"

I told him that it was not sensible to put himself in such a state merely upon the receipt of a telegram which might mean nothing at all, or might be the result of some delusion. And there, too, I added, that it was not at this time, when we needed all our strength and fortitude, that we ought to give way to imaginary fears which were particularly inexcusable in a lad of his practical temperament.

"Inexcusable! I am glad you think so, Sainclair."

"But, my dear boy, you frighten me. What is there you know that you have not told me?"

"I am going to tell you. The situation is horrible. Why didn't that villain die?"

"And, after all, how do you know that he is not dead?"

"Look here, Sainclair—Don't talk—Be quiet, please—You see, if he is alive, I wish to God that I were dead!"

"You are crazy. It is if he is alive that you have all the more reason to live to defend that poor woman."

"Ah, that is true! That is true! Thanks, old fellow! You have said the only thing that makes me want to live. To defend her! I will not think of myself any longer—never again."

And Rouletabille smiled—a smile which almost frightened me. I threw my arm around him and begged him to tell me why he was so terrified, why he spoke of his own death and why he smiled so strangely.

Rouletabille laid his hand on my shoulder, and I went on:

"Tell your friend what it is, Rouletabille. Speak out. Relieve your mind. Tell me the secret that is killing you. I would tell you anything."

Rouletabille looked down and steadily into my eyes.

Then he said:

"You shall know all, Sainclair. You shall know as much as I do, and when you do, you will be as unhappy as I am, for you are kind and you are fond of me."

Then he straightened back his shoulders as though he had already cast off a burden and pointed in the direction of the railway.

"We shall leave here in an hour," he said. "There is no direct train from Eu to Paris in the winter: we shall not reach Paris until 7 o'clock. But that will give us plenty of time to pack our trunks and take the train that leaves the Lyons station at nine o'clock for Marscilles and Mentone."

He did not ask my opinion on the course which he had laid out. He was taking me to Mentone, just as he had brought me to Trepot. He was well aware that in the present crisis I could refuse him nothing. Besides, he was in such a state of mental strain that even if he had wished it, I should scarcely have left him. And it was not hard for me to accompany him, for we were just beginning our long vacations, and my affairs were so arranged that I felt entirely at liberty.

"Then we are going to Eu?" I inquired.

"Yes: we will take the train from there. It will scarcely take half an hour to drive over."

"We shall have spent only a little time in this part of the country," I remarked."Enough, I hope—enough for me to find what I am looking for."

I thought of the perfume of the Lady in Black, but I kept silence. Had he not said that he was going to tell me everything? He led me out to the jetty. The wind was still blowing a gale, and we were almost taken off our feet. Rouletabille stood for an instant as if lost in thought, closing his eyes as if in a dream.

"It was here," he said, "that I last saw her."

He looked down at the stone bench beside which we were standing.

"We were sitting there. She held me to her heart. I was a very little fellow, even for nine years old. She told me to stay there—on this bench—and then she went away, and I never saw her again. It was night—a soft summer evening—the evening of the distribution of prizes. She had not assisted at the distribution, but I knew that she would come that night—that night full of stars and so clear that I hoped every moment that I would be able to distinguish her face. But she covered it with her veil and breathed a heavy sigh. And then she went away. And I have never seen her since."

"And you, my friend?"

"I?"

"Yes, what happened to you? Did you sit on the bench for very long?"

"I would have—but the coachman came to look for me and I went in."

"Where?"

"Into the school."

"Is there a boarding school at Trepot?"

"No, but there is one at Eu—I went to the school at Eu."

He motioned me to follow him.

"We will go there," he said. "I can't talk here. There is too much of a storm."

In another half hour we were at Eu. At the foot of the Rue des Marroniers our carriage rolled over the pavements of the big, cold, empty place, as the coachman announced his arrival by cracking his whip, filling the dead town with the noise of the snapping leather.

Soon we heard the sound of a bell—that of the school, Rouletabille told me—and then everything was quiet again. We alighted and the horse and carriage stood motionless upon the street. The driver had gone into a saloon. We entered the cool shades of a high Gothic church which faced upon the square. Rouletabille cast a glance at the castle—a red brick structure, crowned with an immense Louis XIII roof—a mournful facade which seemed to weep over the glory of departed princes. The young reporter gased sorrowfully at the square battlements of the City Hall, which extended toward us the hostile lance of its soiled and weather-beaten flag: at the Cafe de Paris; at the silent houses; at the shops and the library. Was it there that the boy had bought those first new books for which the Lady in Black had paid?

"Nothing has changed."

An old dog, colourless and shaggy, upon the library steps, stretched himself lazily on his frozen paws.

"Cham! Cham!" called Rouletabille. "Oh, I remember him well. It is Cham—it is my old Cham."

And he called him again, "Cham! Cham!"

The dog got upon his feet, turned toward us, listening to the voice that called him. He took a few steps, wagged his tail, and stretched himself out in the sun again.

"He doesn't remember me," said Rouletabille sadly.

He drew me into a little street which had a steep down grade, and was paved with sharp pebbles. As we went down the hill he took my hand and I could feel the fever in his. We stopped again in front of a tiny temple of the Jesuit style, which raised in front of us its porch, ornamented with semicircles of stone, the "reversed consoles" which are the characteristic features of an architecture which contributed nothing to the glory of the Seventeenth Century. After having pushed open a little low door, Rouletabille bade me enter, and we found ourselves inside a beautiful mortuary chapel, upon the stone floor of which were kneeling, beside their empty tombs, magnificent marble statues of Catherine of Cleves and Guise le Balafre.

"The college chapel," whispered Rouletabille.

There was no person in the chapel. We crossed the room hastily. On the left wall, Rouletabille tapped very gently a kind of drum, which gave out a queer, muffled sound.

"We are in luck!" he said. "Everything is going well. We are inside the college and the concierge has not seen me. He would surely have remembered me."

"What harm would that have done?"

Just at that moment a man with bare head and a bunch of keys at his side passed through the room and Rouletabille drew me into the shadow.

"It is Pere Simon. Ah, how old he has grown He is almost bald. Listen: this is the hour when he goes to superintend the study hour of the younger boys. Everyone is in the classroom at this time. Oh, we are very lucky! There is only Mere Simon in the lodge—that is, if she is not dead. At any rate, she can't see us from here. But wait—here is Pere Simon back again!"

Why was Rouletabille so anxious to hide himself? Decidedly, I knew very little of the lad whom I believed that I knew so well. Every hour that I had spent with him of late had brought me some new surprise. While we were waiting for Pere Simon to leave us a clear field once more, Rouletabille and I managed to slip out of the chapel without being seen, and hid ourselves in the corner of a tiny garden, laid out in the middle of a stone court, behind the shrubbery of which we could, leaning over, contemplate at our leisure the grounds and buildings of the school. Rouletabille hung on to my arm as though he were afraid of falling. "Good Heavens!" he murmured, in a voice broken with emotion. "How things are changed! They have torn down the old study where I found the knife and the leather hangings where the money was hidden have, doubtless, been destroyed. But the chapel walls are just the same. Look, Sainclair: lean over the hedge. That door that opens in the rear of the chapel is the door of the infant class room. But never, never did I leave that class room so gladly, even in my happiest play hours, as when Pere Simon came to fetch me to the parlour where the Lady in Black was waiting for me. Ah—suppose that they have destroyed the parlour!"

And he cast a quick look toward the building behind him.

"No—no: it is all right—beside the mortuary. There is the same door at the right through which she came. We shall go there as soon as Pere Simon is out of the way."

And he set his teeth.

"I believe that I am going crazy!" he said with a short laugh. "But I can't help my feelings. They are stronger than I. To think that I am going to see the parlour—where she waited for me! I had been living only in the hope of seeing her, and after she had gone, although I had promised to be good and sensible, I fell into such a despondent state that after each of her visits, they feared for my health. They were only able to save me from utter prostration by telling me that if I fell ill they would not let me see her any more. So from one visit to another, I had her memory and her perfume to comfort me. Never having seen her dear face distinctly, and being so weak that I was ready to swoon with joy every time she pressed me to her heart, I lived less with her image than with the heavenly odour. Often on the days after she had come and gone, I would escape from my comrades during the recreation hours and steal to the parlour, and when I found it empty, I would draw deep breaths of the air which she had breathed and remain there like a little devotee, and leave with a heart filled with the sense of her presence. The perfume which she always used and which was indissolubly associated in my mind with her, was the most delicate, the most subtle, and the sweetest odour I have ever known, and I never breathed it again in all the years which followed until the day I spoke of it to you, Sainclair. You remember—the day we first went to the Glandier?"

"You mean the day that you met Mathilde Stanger son?"

"That is what I mean," responded the lad in a trembling voice.

(Ah, if I had known at that moment that Professor Stangerson's daughter, as the result of her first marriage in America, had had a child, a son, who would have been, if he had lived, the same age as Rouletabille, perhaps I would have at last comprehended his emotion and grief, and the strange reluctance which he showed to pronounce the name of Mathilde Stangerson there at the school, to which, in the past, had come so often the Lady in Black!)

There was a long silence, which I finally broke.

"And you have never known why the Lady in Black did not return?"

"Oh!" cried Rouletabille. "I am sure that she did return. It was I who was not here."

"Who took you away?"

"No one: I ran away."

"Why? To look for her?"

"No—no! To flee from her—to flee from her, I tell you, Sainclair. But she came back—I know that she came back."

"She may have been broken hearted at not finding you."

Rouletabille raised his arms toward the sky and shook his head.

"I don't know—how can I know? Ah, what an unhappy wretch I am! But, hush, Sainclair! Here comes Pere Simon! Now, he's gone again. Quick—to the parlour!"

We were there in three seconds. It was a common place room enough, rather large, with cheap white curtains in front of the shadeless windows. It was furnished with six leather chairs placed against the wall, a mantel mirror, and a clock. The whole appearance of the place was sombre.

As we entered the room, Rouletabille uncovered his head with an appearance of respect and reverence which one rarely assumes except in a sacred place. His face became flushed, he advanced with short steps, rolling his travelling cap in his hands as if he were embarrassed. He turned to me and said in low tones—far lower than he used in the chapel:

"Oh, Sainclair, this is it—the parlour. Feel how my hands burn. My face is flushed, is it not? I was always flushed when I came here, knowing that I should find her. I used to run. I felt smothered—I do now. I was not able to wait. Oh, my heart beats just as it used when I was a little lad! I would come to the door—right here—and then I would pause, bashful and shame faced. But I would see her dark shadow in the corner: she would take me in her arms and hold me there in silence, and before we knew it, we were both weeping, as we clung together. How dear those meetings were. She was my mother, Sainclair. Oh, she never told me so: on the contrary, she used to say that my mother was dead, and that she had been her friend. But she told me to call her Mamma—and when she wept as I kissed her, I knew that she really was my mother. See—she always sat there in the dark corner, and she came always at nightfall, when the parlour had not yet been lit up for the evening. And every time she came, she would place on the window sill a big, white package, tied with pink cord. It was a fruit cake. I have loved fruit cake ever since, Sainclair!"

The poor lad could no longer contain himself. He rested his arms on the mantel and wept like a little child. When he was able to control himself a little, he raised his head and looked at me with a sad smile. And then he sank into a chair as though he were tired out. I had not had the heart to say one word to him during his reminiscences. I knew well that he was not talking with me, but with his memories.

I saw him draw from his breast the letter which he had placed there in the train, and tear it open with trembling fingers. He read it slowly. Suddenly his hand fell, and he uttered a groan. His flushed face grew pallid—so pallid that it seemed as though every drop of blood had left his heart. I stepped toward him, but he waved me away and closed his eyes. He looked almost as though he were sleeping. I walked across the room, moving as softly as one does in the chamber of death. I looked up at the wall, where hung a heavy wooden crucifix. How long did I stand gazing on the cross? I have no idea. Nor do I know what we said to someone belonging to the house, who came into the parlour. I was pondering with all my strength of concentration on the strange and mysterious destiny of my friend—on this mysterious woman who might or might not have been his mother. Rouletabille had been so young in those school days. He longed so for a mother, that he might have imagined that he had found one in his visitor. Rouletabille—what other name did we know him by? Joseph Josephin. It was without doubt under that name that he had pursued his early studies here. Joseph Josephin, the queer appellation of which the editor of the *Epoch* had said to him, "It is no name at all!" And now, what was he about to do here? Seek the trace of a perfume? Revive a memory—an illusion? I turned as I heard him stir. He was standing erect and seemed quite calm. His features had taken on the serenity which comes from assurance of victory.

"We must go now, Sainclair. Come, my friend."

And he left the parlour without even looking back. I followed him.

In the deserted street, which we regained without meeting anyone, I stopped him by asking anxiously:

"Well—did you find the perfume of the Lady in Black?"

He must have seen that all my heart was in the question and that I was filled with an ardent desire that this visit to the scenes of his childhood might have brought a little peace to his soul.

"Yes," he said, very gravely. "Yes, Sainclair, I found it."

And he handed me the letter from Professor Stangerson's daughter.

I looked at him, doubting the evidence of my own senses—not understanding, because I knew nothing. Then he took my two hands and looked into my eyes.

"I am going to confide a secret to you, Sainclair—the secret of my life, and perhaps some day the secret of my death. Let what will come, it must die with you and me. Mathilde Stangerson had a child—a son. He is dead—is dead to everyone except to the two of us who stand here."

I recoiled, struck with horror under such a revelation. Rouletabille the son of Mathilde Stangerson! And then suddenly I received a still more violent shock. In that case, Rouletabille must be the son of Larsan.

Oh, I understood now, all the wretchedness of the boy. I understood why he had said this morning: "Why did he not die? If he is living, I wish to God that I were dead!"

Rouletabille must have read my thoughts in my eyes, and he simply made a gesture which seemed to say, "And now you understand, Sainclair." Then he finished his sentence aloud. The word which he spoke was "Silence!"

When we reached Paris we separated, to meet again at the train. There, Rouletabille handed me a new dispatch, which had come from Valence, and which was signed by Professor Stangerson. It said, "M. Darzac tells me that you have a few days' leave. We should all be very glad if you could come and spend them with us. We will wait for you at Arthur Rance's place, Rochers Rouges—he will be delighted to present you to his wife. My daughter will be pleased to see you. She joins me in kindest greetings."

Just as the train was starting, a concierge from Rouletabille's hotel came rushing up and handed us a third dispatch. This one was sent from Mentone, and signed by Mathilde. It contained two words: "Rescue us."

IV

En Route

N ow I knew all. As we continued on our journey, Rouletabille related to me the remarkable and adventurous story of his childhood, and I knew, also, why he dreaded nothing so much as that Mme. Darzac should penetrate the mystery which separated them. I dared say nothing more—give my friend no advice. Ah, the poor unfortunate lad! When he read the words "Rescue us," he carried the dispatch to his lips, and then, pressing my hand, he said: "If I arrive too late, I can avenge her, at least." I have never heard anything more filled with resolution than the cold determination of his tone. From time to time a quick movement betrayed the passion of his soul, but for the most part he was calm—terribly calm. What resolution had he taken in the silence of the parlour, when he sat motionless and with closed eyes in the shadow of the corner where he had used to see the Lady in Black?

While we journeyed toward Lyons, and Rouletabille lay dreaming, stretched out fully dressed in his berth, I will tell you how and why the child that he had been ran away from school at Eu, and what had happened to him.

Rouletabille had fled from the school like a thief. There was no need to seek for another expression, because he had been accused of stealing. This was how it happened.

At the age of nine, he had already an extraordinarily precocious intelligence, and could arrive easily at the solution of the most perplexing problems. By logical deductions of an almost amazing kind, he astonished his professor of mathematics by his philosophical method of work. He had never been able to learn his multiplication tables, and always counted upon his fingers. He would usually get the answers to the problems himself, leaving the working out to be done by his fellow pupils, as one will leave an irksome task to a servant. But first, he would show them exactly how the example ought to be done. Although as yet ignorant of the rudiments of algebra, he had invented for his own personal use a system of algebra carried on with queer signs, looking like hieroglyphics, by the aid of which he marked all the steps of his mathematical reasoning, and thus he was able to write down the general formulae so that he alone could interpret them. His professor used proudly to compare him to Pascal, discovering for himself without knowledge of geometry, the first propositions of Euclid. He applied his admirable faculties of reasoning to his daily life, as well as to his studies, using the rules both materially and morally. For example, an act had been committed in the school—I have forgotten whether it was of cheating or talebearing—by one of ten persons whom he knew, and he picked out the right one with a divination which seemed almost supernatural, simply by using the powers of reasoning and deduction, which he had practiced to such an extent. So much for the moral aspect of his strange gift, and as for the material, nothing seemed more simple to him than to find any lost or hidden object—or even a stolen one. It was in the detection of thefts especially that he displayed a wonderful resourcefulness, as if nature, in her wondrous fitting together of the parts that make an equal whole, after having created the father a thief of the worst kind, had caused the son to be born the evil genius of thieves.

THIS STRANGE APTITUDE, AFTER HAVING won for the boy a sort of fame in the school, on account of his detection of several attempts at pilfering, was destined one day to be fatal to him. He found in this abnormal fashion a small sum of money which had been stolen from the superintendent, who refused to believe that the discovery was due only to the lad's intelligence and clearness of insight. This hypothesis, indeed, appeared impossible to almost everyone who knew of the matter, and, thanks to an unfortunate coincidence of time and place, the affair finished up by having Rouletabille himself accused of being the thief. They tried to make him acknowledge his fault; he defended himself with such indignation and anger that it drew upon him a severe punishment. The principal held an investigation and a trial, at which Joseph Josephin was accused by some of his youthful comrades in that spirit of falsehood which children sometimes possess. Some of them complained of having had books, pencils, and tablets stolen at different times, and declared that they believed that Joseph had taken them. The fact that the boy seemed to have no relatives, and that no one knew where he came from, made him particularly likely, in that little world, to be suspected of crime. When the boys spoke of him, it was as "that thief." The contempt in which he was held preyed upon him, for he was not a strong child at best, and he was plunged in despair. He almost prayed to die. The principal, who was really the most kind hearted of men, was persuaded that he had a vicious little creature to deal with, because he was unable to produce an impression on the child, and make him comprehend the horror of what he had done. Finally, he told the lad that if he did not confess his guilt, it had been decided not to keep him in the school any longer, and that a letter would be written to the lady who interested herself in him—Mme. Darbel was the name which she had given—to tell her to come after him.

The child made no reply and allowed himself to be taken to his little room, where he had been kept a prisoner. Upon the morrow he had disappeared. He had run away. He had felt that the principal, to whose care he had been entrusted during the earliest years of his childhood (for in all his little life he could remember no other home than the school), and who had always been so kind to him, was no longer his friend, since he believed him guilty of theft. And he could see no reason why the Lady in Black would not believe it, too—that he was a thief. To appear as a thief in the sight of the Lady in Black He would far rather have died.

And he made his escape from the place by climbing over the wall of the garden at night. He rushed to the canal, sobbing, and, with a prayer, uttered as much to the Lady in Black as to God Himself, threw himself in the water. Happily, in his despair, the poor child had forgotten that he knew how to swim.

If I have reported this passage in the life of Rouletabille at some length, it is because it seems to me that it is all important to the thorough comprehension of his future. At that time, of course, he was ignorant that he was the son of Larsan. Rouletabille, even as a child of nine years, could not without agony harbour the idea that the Lady in Black might believe him to be a thief, and thus, when the time came that he imagined—an imagination too well founded, alas!—that he was bound by ties of blood to Larsan, what infinite misery he experienced His mother, in hearing of the crime of which he had been accused, must have felt that the criminal instincts of the father were coming to light in the son, and, perhaps—thought more cruel than death itself—she may have rejoiced in believing him dead.

For everyone believed him dead. They found his footsteps leading to the canal, and they fished out his cap. How had he lived after leaving the school? In a most singular fashion. After swimming to dry land and making up his mind to fly the country, the lad, while they were searching for him everywhere in the canal and out of it, devised a most original plan for travelling to a distance without being disturbed. He had not read that most interesting tale, *The Stolen Letter*. His own invention served him. He reasoned the thing out, as he always did.

He knew—for he had often heard them told by the heroes themselves—many stories of little rascals who had run away from their parents in search of adventures, hiding themselves by day in the fields and the wood, and travelling by night—only to find themselves speedily captured by the gendarmes, or forced to return home because they had no money and no food, and dared not ask for anything to eat along the road which they followed, and which was too well guarded to admit of their escape if they applied for aid. Our little Rouletabille slept at night like everyone else, and travelled in broad daylight, without hiding himself. But, after having dried his garments (the warm weather was coming on, and he did not suffer from cold), he tore them to tatters. He made rags of them, which barely covered him, and begged in the open streets, dirty and unkempt, holding out his hands and declaring to passers-by that if he did not bring home any money his parents would beat him. And everyone took him for some gypsy child, hordes of which constantly roamed through the locality. Soon came the time of wild strawberries. He gathered the fruit and sold it in little baskets of leaves. And he assured me, in telling the story, that if it had not been for the terrible thought that the Lady in Black must believe that he was a thief, that time would have been the happiest of his life. His astuteness and natural courage stood him well in stead through these wanderings, which lasted for several months. Where was he going? To Marseilles. This was his plan:

He had seen in his illustrated geography views of the Midi, and he had never looked at those pictures without breathing a sigh and wishing that he might some day visit that enchanted country. Through his gypsy-like manner of living, he had made the acquaintance of a little caravan load of Romanies, who were following the same route as himself, and who were journeying to Ste. Marie's of the Sea to render homage to a new king of their tribe. The lad had an opportunity to render them some small service, and finding him a pleasant, well-mannered little fellow, these people, not being in the habit of asking everyone whom they met for his history, desired to know nothing more about him. They believed that, on account of ill treatment, the child had run away from some troop of wandering mountebanks, and they invited him to travel with them. Thus he arrived in the Midi.

In the neighbourhood of Arles, he separated himself from his travelling companions, and at last came to Marseilles. There was his paradise! Eternal summer—and the port.

The port was the favourite resort of all the gamins of the locality, and this fact was the greatest safeguard for Rouletabille. He roamed over the docks as he chose, and served himself according to the measure of his needs, which were not great. For example, he made of himself an "orange fisher." It was at the time that he exercised this lucrative calling that, one beautiful morning upon the quay, he made the acquaintance of M. Gaston Leroux, a journalist from Paris, and this acquaintance was destined to have such an influence upon the future of Rouletabille that I do not consider it out of place to transcribe here in full the article in which the editor of *Le Matin* recorded that first memorable interview.

The Little Orange Fisher.

As the sun, piercing through the cloudless heavens, struck with its ardent rays the golden robe of Notre-Dame-de-la-Garde, I descended toward the quay. The scene which met my eyes was one which was worth going far to see. Townfolk, sailors and workmen were moving about, the former idly looking on, while the others tugged at the pulleys and drew up the cables of their vessels. The great merchant vessels glided like huge beasts of burden between the tower of St. Jean and the fort of St. Nicholas, caressing the sparkling waters of the Old Port in their onward motion. Side by side, shoulder to shoulder, the smaller barks seemed to hold out their arms to each other. To throw aside their veils of mist and to dance upon the water. Beside them, tired with the long journey, worn out from ploughing for so many days and nights over unknown seas, the heavy laden East Indiamen rested peacefully, lifting their great, motionless sails in rags toward the skies.

My eyes, sweeping swiftly over the scene through the forest of masts and sails paused at the tower which commemorated the fact that it was twenty-five centuries since the children of Ancient Phoenicia first cast anchor upon this happy shore, and that they had come by the water ways of Ionia. Then my attention returned to the border of the quay, and I perceived the little orange fisher.

He was standing erect, clad in the rags of a man's coat which hung down almost to his feet, bareheaded and barefooted, with blonde curly locks and black eyes, and I should think that he was about nine years old. A string passed around his shoulder supported a big sailcloth sack. His left hand rested on his waist and his right hand held a stick three times as tall as himself, which was surmounted by a little wooden hook. The child stood motionless and lost in thought. When I asked him what he was doing there, he told me that he was an orange fisher.

He seemed very proud of being an orange fisher and did not ask me for a penny, as the little vagabonds of the neighbourhood are accustomed to demand toll of every bystander. I spoke to him again, but this time he made no answer, for he was too intent on watching the water. On one side of us was the beautiful steamer Fides, in from Castellmare and on the other a three masted schooner from Genoa. Further off were two ships loaded with fruits which had just arrived from Baleares that morning, and I saw that they were spilling a part of their cargo. Oranges were bobbing up and down upon the water and the light current sent them in our direction. My "fisher" leaped into a little canoe, came quickly to the vessel, and, armed with his stick and hook, waited. Then he began his gathering. The hook on his stick brought him one orange, then a second, a third and a fourth. They disappeared in the sack. The boy gathered a fifth, jumped upon the quay and tore open the golden fruit. He plunged his little teeth in the pulp and devoured it in an instant.

"You have a good appetite," I told him.

"Monsieur," he replied, flushing slightly as he spoke, "I don't care for any food but fruit."

"That is a very good diet," I replied as gravely as he had spoken. "But what do you do when there are no oranges?"

"I pick up coal."

And his little hand, diving into the sack, brought out an enormous piece of coal.

The orange juice had rolled down his chin to his coat. The coat had a pocket. The little fellow took a clean handkerchief from this pocket and carefully wiped both chin and coat. Then he proudly put the handkerchief back.

"What is your father's work?" I asked.

"He is poor."

"Yes, but what does he do?"

The orange fisher shrugged his shoulders.

"He doesn't do anything, he is poor."

My inquiries into his family affairs did not seem to please him. He turned away from the quay and I followed him. We came in a moment to the "shelter," a little square of sea which holds the small pleasure yachts—the neat little boats all polished wood and brass, the neat little sailors in their irreproachable toilettes. My ragamuffin looked at them with the eye of a connoisseur and seemed to find a keen enjoyment in the spectacle. A new yacht had just been launched and her immaculate sail looked like a white veil against the blue sky.

"Isn't it pretty?" exclaimed my little companion.

The next moment he fell over a board covered with fresh tar and when he picked himself up, he looked with dismay at the stain on his coat which seemed to be his proudest possession. What a disaster! He looked as if he could have burst into tears. But quick as thought he drew out his handkerchief and rubbed and rubbed the spot, then he looked at me piteously and said:

"Monsieur, are there any other stains? Did I get anything on my back?"

I assured him that he had not, and with an expression of satisfaction, he put the handkerchief back in his pocket once more.

A few steps further on, upon the walk which stretches in front of the red and yellow, and blue houses, the windows of which are brave with wares of many kinds, we found an oyster stand. Upon the little tables were displayed piles of oysters in their shells, and flasks of vinegar.

When we passed by the oyster stand, as the fish appeared fresh and appetizing, I said to the orange fisher.

"If you cared for anything to eat except fruit, I might ask you to have some oysters with me."

His black eyes glistened and we sat down together to eat our oysters. The merchant opened them for us while we waited. He started to bring us vinegar, but my companion stopped him with an imperious gesture. He opened his bag carefully and triumphantly produced a lemon. The lemon, having been in close contact with the bit of coal, might have passed for black itself. But my guest took out his handkerchief and wiped it off. Then he cut the fruit and offered me half, but I like oysters without other flavour, so I declined with thanks.

After our luncheon we went back to the quay. The orange fisher asked me for a cigarette and lighted it with a match which he had in another pocket of his coat.

Then, the cigarette between his lips, puffing rings toward the sky like a man, the little creature threw himself down on the ground and with his eyes fixed upon the statue of Notre-Dame-de-la-Garde, took the very pose of the boy who is the most beautiful ornament of the Brussels tower. He did not lose a line of the attitude, and seemed very proud of the fact and apparently desired to play the part exactly.

Upon the following day Joseph Josephin met M. Gaston Leroux once more upon the quay, and the man handed him a newspaper which he carried in his hand. The boy read the article pointed out to him, and the journalist gave him a bright new 100-sous piece. Rouletabille made no difficulties about accepting it, and seemed to even find the gift a natural one. "I take your money," he said to Gaston Leroux, "because we are collaborators." With his hundred sous he bought himself a fine new bootblack's box and installed himself in business opposite the Bregaillon. For two years he polished the boots of those who came to eat the traditional bouillabaisse at this hostelry. When he was not at work, he would sit on his box and read. With the feeling of ownership which his box and his business had brought him, ambition had entered his mind. He had received too good an education and had been too well instructed in rudimentary things not to understand that if he did not himself finish what others had begun for him, he would be deprived of the best chance which he had of making for himself a place in the world.

His customers grew interested in the little bootblack, who always had on his box some work of history or mathematics, and a harness maker became so attached to him that he took him into his shop.

Soon Rouletabille was promoted to the dignity of working in leather, and was able to save. At the age of sixteen years, having a little money in his pocket, he took the train for Paris. What did he intend to do there? To look for the Lady in Black.

Not one day had passed without his having thought of the mysterious visitor to the parlour of the boarding school, and, although no one had ever told him that she lived in Paris, he was persuaded that no other city in the world was worthy to contain a lady who wore so sweet a perfume. And then his little schoolmates, who had been able to see her form when she glided out of the parlour, had often said: "See the Parisienne is here again today!" It would have been difficult to exactly define the ideas in Rouletabille's head, and perhaps he himself scarcely knew what they were. His longing was merely to see the Lady in Black—to watch her reverently—at a distance, as a devotee watches the image of a saint. Would he dare to speak to her? The importance of the accusation of theft which had been brought against him had only grown greater in Rouletabille's imagination as time had gone by, and he believed that it would always be a barrier between himself and the Lady in Black, which he had not the right to try to throw down. Perhaps even—but, come what might, he longed to see her. That was the only thing of which he was sure.

As soon as he reached the capital, he looked up M. Gaston Leroux, and recalled himself to the latter's memory, telling him that, although he felt no particular liking for the life, which he considered rather a lazy one for a man who liked to be up and doing, he had decided to become a journalist. And he fairly demanded that his old acquaintance should at once give him a trial as a reporter.

Leroux tried to turn the youth from his project. At last, tired of his persistent requests, the editor said:

"Well, my lad, since you have nothing special to do just now, go and find the left foot of the body in the Rue Oberkampf."

And with these words, M. Leroux turned away, leaving poor Rouletabille standing there with half a dozen young reporters tittering around him. But the boy was not daunted in the least. He searched through the files of the paper and found out that the *Epoch* was offering a large reward to the person who would bring to its office the foot which was missing from the mutilated body of a woman, which had been found in the Rue Oberkampf.

The rest we know. In "The Mystery of the Yellow Room," I have told how Rouletabille succeeded on this occasion, and in what manner there revealed itself to him his own singular calling—that of always beginning to reason a matter out from the point where others had finished.

I have told, too, by what chance he was led one evening to the Elysee, where he inhaled as he passed by the perfume of the Lady in Black. He realised then that it was Mlle. Stangerson who had been his visitor at the school, and for whom he had been seeking so long. What more need I add: Why speak of the sensations which his knowledge as to the wearer of the perfume aroused in the heart of Rouletabille during the events at the Glandier, and, above all, after his trip to America? They may be easily guessed. How simple a thing now to understand his hesitations and his whims! The proofs brought by him from Cincinnati in regard to the child of the woman who had been Jean Roussel's wife had been sufficiently explicit to awaken in his mind a suspicion that he himself might be that child, but not enough so to render him certain of the fact. However, his instinct drew him so strongly to the professor's daughter that he could scarcely resist his longing to throw himself into her arms and press her to his heart and cry out to her: "You are my mother! you are my mother!"

And he fled from her presence just as he had fled from the vestry on the day of her wedding, in order that there should not escape from him any sign of the secret tenderness that had burned in his breast through so many long years. For horrible thoughts dwelt in his mind. Suppose he were to make himself known to her, and she were to repulse him—cast him off—turn from him in horror—from him, the little thief of the boarding school—the son of Roussel—Ballmeyer—the heir of the crimes of Larsan! Suppose she were to order him to get out of her sight, never to come near her again, nor to breathe the same air which brought back to him, whenever he came near her, the perfume of the Lady in Black Ah, how he had fought, on account of these frightful visions, to restrain himself from yielding to the almost overwhelming impulse to ask each time that he came near her, "Is it you? Are you the Lady in Black?" As to her, she had seemed fond of him from the first, but, doubtless, that was because of the Glan dier affair. If she were really the Lady in Black, she must believe that the child whom he had been was dead. And if it were not she—if by some fatality which set at naught both his instincts and his powers of reasoning, it were not she Could he, through any imprudence, risk having her discover that he had fled from the school at Eu under ban as a thief? No, no—not that! She had often said to him:

"Where were you brought up, my boy? What school did you attend when you were a child?" And he had replied: "I was in school at Bordeaux."

He might as well have answered, "At Pekin."

However, this torture could not last always, he told himself. If it were she, he would know how to say things to her that must open her heart. Anything would be better than to be sure that she was not the Lady in Black, but some stranger who had never held him to her heart. But he must be certain—certain beyond any doubt, and he knew how to place himself in the presence of his memories of the Lady in Black, just as a dog is sure of finding its master. The simile which presented itself quite naturally to his imagination was simply that of "following the scent." And this led us, under the circumstances which I have narrated, to Trepot and to Eu. However, it is by no means certain that decisive results would have been gained from this expedition—at least in the eyes of a third person, like myself—had it not been for the influence of the odour—if the letter from Mathilde, which I had handed to Rouletabille in the train, had not suddenly, with its faint, sweet perfume, brought to us directly the evidence which we were seeking. I have never read this letter. It is a document so sacred in the eyes of my friend, that other eyes will never behold it, but I know that the gentle reproaches which it contained for the boy's rudeness and lack of confidence in the writer, had been so tender that Rouletabille could no longer deceive himself, even if the daughter of Professor Stanger son had not concluded the note with a final sentence, through which throbbed the heart of a despairing mother, and which said that "the interest which she felt in him arose less from the services he had rendered her, than because of the memories which she had of a little boy, the son of a friend, whom she had loved very dearly, and who had killed himself 'like a little man with a broken heart' at the age of nine years, and whom Rouletabille greatly resembled."

V

PANIC

Dijon—Macon—Lyons—certainly the boy could not be sleeping all this time. I called him softly and he did not reply, but I would have wagered my hand that he was not sleeping. What was he planning? How quiet he was! What could it be that had given him such a strange calmness? I seemed to see him again as he had been in the parlour, suddenly standing erect as he said: "Let us go on!" in that voice so composed and tranquil and resolute. Go on to whom? Toward what was he resolved to go? Toward Her, evidently, who was in danger, and who could be rescued only by him—toward her who was his mother and who did not know it.

"It is a secret which must remain between you and me! That child is dead to the whole world, except to us two!"

That was his decision, taken almost in a single moment, never to reveal himself to her. And the poor child had come to seek the certainty that she was indeed the Lady in Black, only to have the right to speak to her! In the very moment that the assurance which he sought was his, he had determined to forget it; he condemned himself to endless silence. Poor little hero soul, which had understood that the Lady in Black, who had such dire need of his help, would have shrunk from a safety bought by the warfare of a son against his father! Where might not such warfare lead? To what bloody conflict? Everything must be expected, no matter how terrible, and Rouletabille must have his hands free to fight to the death for the Lady in Black.

The boy was so quiet that I could not even hear him breathing. I leaned over him; his eyes were open.

"Do you know what I have been thinking of?" he said. "Of the dispatch that came to us from Bourg and was signed 'Darzac,' and the other dispatch which came from Valence and was signed 'Stangerson.'"

"And the more I think of them, the stranger they seem to me. At Bourg, M. and Mme. Darzac were not with M. Stangerson, who left them at Dijon. Besides, the dispatch says: 'We are going to rejoin M. Stangerson.' But the Stangerson dispatch proves that M. Stangerson, who had continued on his journey toward Marseilles, is again with the

Darzacs. The Darzacs might have rejoined M. Stargerson on the way to Marseilles; but if that were so, the Professor must have stopped on the road. Why was this? He did not expect to do so. At the train, he said: 'Tomorrow at ten o'clock, I shall be at Mentone.' Look at the hour that the dispatch was sent from Valence, and then we'll look in the time table and find out the hour at which M. Stangerson would have passed through Valence if he had not stopped upon the journey."

We consulted the time table. M. Stangerson should have passed through Valence at 12:44 o'clock in the morning, and the dispatch was sent at 12:47 o'clock. It had, therefore, been sent by M. Stangerson while he was continuing on the trip which he had planned. At that moment he must have been with M. and Mme. Darzac. Still poring over the time table, we endeavoured to solve the mystery of this re-encounter. M. Stangerson had left the Darzacs at Dijon, where the whole party had arrived at twenty-seven minutes after six o'clock in the evening. The Professor had then taken the train which leaves Dijon at eight minutes past seven, and had arrived at Lyons at four minutes after ten and at Valence at forty-seven minutes after midnight. During the same time the Darzacs, leaving Dijon at seven o'clock, continued on their way to Modane, and, by way of Saint-Amour, reached Bourg at three minutes past nine in the evening, on the train which was scheduled to leave at eight minutes past nine. M. Darzac's dispatch was sent from Bourg, and had left the telegraph office at the station at 9:28. The Darzacs, therefore, must have left their train at Bourg, and remained there. Or, it might have happened that the train was late. In any case, we must seek the reason for M. Darzac's telegram somewhere between Dijon and Bourg, after the departure of M. Stangerson. One might even go further, and say 'between Louhans and Bourg,' for the train stops at Louhans, and if anything had happened before he reached there, at eight o'clock, it is altogether likely that M. Darzac would have sent his message from that station.

Finally, seeking the correspondence between Bourg and Lyons, we reasoned that M. Darzac must have sent his wire from Bourg one minute before leaving for Lyons by the 9:29 train. But this train reached Lyons at 10:23 o'clock, while M. Stangerson's train reached Lyons at 10:24. After changing their plans and leaving the train at Bourg, M. and Mme. Darzac must have rejoined M. Stangerson at Lyons, which they reached one minute before him. Now, what had upset their plans? We could only think of the most terrible hypotheses, every one of which, alas! had as its basis the reappearance of Larsan. The fact which gave the greatest colour to this idea was the desire expressed by each of our friends, *not to frighten anyone*. M. Darzac in his message, Mme. Darzac in hers, had not endeavoured to conceal the gravity of the situation. As to M. Stangerson, we asked ourselves whether he had been made aware of the new developments, whatever they might be.

Having thus approximately settled the question of time and distance, Rouletabille invited me to profit by the luxurious accommodations which the International Sleeping Car company places at the disposal of those who wish to sleep while on a journey, and he himself set me the example by making as careful a night toilet as he would have done in his own room at his hotel. A quarter of an hour later he was snoring, but I believed the snores to be feigned. At any rate, I could not sleep.

At Avignon Rouletabille jumped up from his cot, hastily donned his trousers and coat, and rushed out to the refreshment rooms to get a cup of chocolate. I was not hungry. From Avignon to Marseilles, in our anxiety and suspense, neither of us desired to talk, and the journey was continued almost in silence, but at the sight of the city in which he had led such a chequered existence, Rouletabille, doubtless to keep from showing the emotion which he felt, and to lighten the heaviness of both our hearts as we drew near our journey's end, began to tell funny stories, in the narration of which, however, he did not seem to find the least amusement. I scarcely heard what he was saying. And at last we reached Toulon.

What a trip! And it might have been so beautiful!

Ordinarily, it is always with an almost boyish enthusiasm that I come within sight of this marvellous country, with its azure shores, like a bit of dreamland or a corner of paradise after the horrible departure from Paris in the snow and rain and darkness and dampness and dirt. With what joy that night, had things been otherwise, would I have set my foot upon the quay, sure of finding the glorious friend who would be waiting for me in the morning at the end of those two iron rails—the wonderful southern sun!

When we left Toulon, our impatience became extreme. And at Cannes, we were scarcely surprised at all to see M. Darzac upon the platform of the station, anxiously looking for us. He could scarcely have received the dispatch which Rouletabille had sent him from Dijon, announcing the hour at which we would reach Mentone. Having arrived there with Mme. Darzac and M. Stangerson the day before, at ten o'clock in the morning, he must have left Mentone almost at once, and have come to meet us at Cannes, for we could understand from his dispatch that he had something to say to us in confidence. His face looked worn and sad. Somehow, it frightened us only to look at him.

"Trouble?" questioned Rouletabille, briefly.

"No, not yet," was the reply.

"God be praised" exclaimed Rouletabille, having a deep sigh. "We have come in time!"

M. Darzac said simply:

"I thank you for coming."

And he pressed both our hands in silence, following us into our compartment, in which we locked ourselves, taking care to draw the curtains and so isolate ourselves completely. When we were comfortably settled, and the train had begun to move on, our friend spoke again. His voice trembled so that he could scarcely utter the words.

"Well," he said: "he is not dead."

"We suspected it!" interrupted Rouletabille. "But are you sure?"

"I have seen him as surely as I have seen you."

"And has Mme. Darzac seen him?"

"Alas, yes! But it is necessary that we should use every means to make her believe that it was an illusion. I could not bear it if she were to lose her mind again, poor, innocent, wretched girl! Ah, my friends, what a fatality pursues us! What has this man come back to do to us? What does he want now?"

I looked at Rouletabille. His face was even more full of grief than that of M. Darzac. The blow which he feared had fallen. He leaned back against the cushions as though he were going to faint. There was a brief pause, and then M. Darzac spoke again:

"Listen This man must disappear—he must be gotten rid of! We must go to him and ask what it is that he wants. If it is money, he may take all that I have. If he will not go, I shall kill him. It is very simple—after all, I think that would be the simplest way. Don't you think so, too?"

We could not answer. It was too pitiful. Rouletabille, overcoming his own feelings by a visible effort, engaged M. Darzac in conversation, endeavouring to calm him, and asking him to tell us what had happened since his departure from Paris.

And he told us that the event which had changed the face of his existence had taken place at Bourg, just as we had thought. Two compartments of the sleeping car had been reserved by M. Darzac, and these compartments were joined by a little dressing room. In one had been placed the travelling bag with the toilet articles of Mme. Darzac, and in the other the smaller packages. It was in the latter compartment that the Darzacs and Professor Stangerson had travelled from Paris to Dijon, where the three had left the train, and had dined at the buffet. They had arrived at 6:27 o'clock, exactly on time, and M. Stangerson had left Dijon at eight minutes after seven, and the Darzacs at just seven o'clock.

The Professor had bidden adieu to his daughter and his son-in-law upon the platform of the station after dinner. M. and Mme. Darzac had returned to their compartment—the one in which the small parcels had been deposited—and remained at the window, chatting with the Professor until the train started. As it steamed out of the station, the newly wedded pair looked back and waved their hands to M. Stangerson, who was still standing upon the platform, throwing kisses at them from the distance.

From Dijon to Bourg neither M. nor Mme. Darzac had occasion to enter the adjacent compartment, where Mme. Darzac's night bag had been placed. The door of this compartment, opening upon the vestibule, had been closed at Paris, as soon as the baggage had been brought there. But the door had not been locked, either upon the outside with a key by the porter, nor on the inside with the bolt by the Darzacs. The curtain of the glass door had been drawn over the pane from the inside by M. Darzac in such a way that no one could look into the compartment from the corridor. But the curtain between the two compartments had not been drawn. All of these circumstances were brought out by the questions asked by Rouletabille of M. Darzac, and, although I could not understand his reasons for going into such minute detail, I give the facts in order to make the condition under which the journey of the Darzacs to Bourg and of M. Stangerson to Dijon was accomplished.

When they reached Bourg our travellers learned that, on account of an accident on the line at Culoz, the train would be delayed for an hour and a half. M. and Mme. Darzac alighted and took a stroll on the platform. M. Darzac, while talking with his wife, mentioned the fact that he had forgotten to write some important letters before leaving Paris. Both entered the buffet, and M. Darzac asked for writing materials. Mathilde sat beside him for a few moments and then remarked that she would take a little walk through the station while he finished his letters.

"Very well," replied M. Darzac. "As soon as I have finished, I will join you."

From that point, I will quote M. Darzac's own words:

"I had finished writing," he said. "And I arose to go and look for Mathilde, when I saw her approaching the buffet, pallid and trembling. As soon as she perceived me, she uttered a shriek and threw herself into my arms. 'Oh, my God!' she cried. 'Oh, my God!' It seemed impossible for her to utter any other words. She was shaking from head to foot. I tried to calm her. I assured her that she had nothing to fear when I was with her, and I strove as gently and patiently as I could to draw from her the cause of her sudden terror. I made her sit down, for her limbs seemed too weak to support her, and I begged her to take some restorative, but she told me that she could not even swallow a drop of water. Her teeth chattered as though she had an ague. At length she was able to speak, and she told me, interrupting herself at almost every other word, and looking about her as though she expected to encounter something which she dreaded, that she had started to walk about the station, as she had said she intended to do, but that she had not dared to go far, lest I should finish my writing and look for her. Then she went through the station and out upon the platform. She decided to come back to the buffet, when she noticed through the lighted windows of the cars, the sleeping car porters, who were making up the bed in a berth near our own. She remembered immediately that her night travelling bag, in which she had put her jewels, was standing unlocked, and she decided to go and lock it up without delay, not because she suspected the honesty of the employees, but through a natural instinct of prudence on a journey. She entered the car, walked down the corridor and came to the glass door of the compartment which had been reserved for her, and which neither of us had entered since leaving Paris. She opened the door and instantly uttered a cry of horror. No one heard her, for there was no one in that part of the car, and a train which passed at that moment drowned the sound of her voice with the clamour of the locomotive. What had happened to alarm her? The most terrible, ghastly, monstrous thing that the imagination could devise.

"Within the compartment, the little door opening upon the dressing cabinet was half drawn toward the interior of the section, cutting off diagonally the view of whoever might enter. This little door was ornamented by a mirror. There, in the glass, Mathilde beheld the face of Larsan! She flung herself backward, shrieking for help, and fled so precipitately that, in leaping down from the platform of the car, she fell on her knees in the train shed. Regaining her feet with difficulty, she dragged herself toward the buffet, which she reached in the condition which I have described.

"When she had told me these things, my first care was to try to convince her that she was labouring under some hideous delusion— partly because I prayed that this might be the case, and that the horrible thing which she believed had not happened, but mainly because I felt that it was my duty, if I wished to prevent Mathilde from going mad, to make her think that she must have been mistaken. Wasn't Larsan dead and buried?

A s I soothed her thus, I really believed what I said, and I continued to reassure her until there remained no doubt in my mind, at least, that what she had seen was merely a phantom, conjured up by fear and imagination. Naturally, I wished to make an investigation for myself, and I offered to accompany Mathilde at once to the compartment, in order to prove to her that she had been the victim of an hallucination. She was bitterly opposed to the idea, crying out that neither she nor I must ever enter the compartment again, and, not only that, but she refused to continue our journey that night. She said all these things in little halting phrases—she could hardly breathe—and it caused me the most intense pain to look at her and listen to her. The more I told her that such an apparition was an impossibility, the more she insisted that it was a reality. I tried to remind her of how seldom she had seen Larsan while the events at the Glandier were going on—which was true—and to persuade her that she could not be certain that it was his face which she had beheld, and not that of some one who might resemble him. She replied that she remembered Larsan's face perfectly—that it had appeared before her twice under such circumstances as would impress it indelibly upon her memory, even if she were to live for a century—once during the strange scene in the gallery, and again at the moment when they came into her sick room to place me under arrest. And then, now that she knew who Larsan was, it was not only the features of the Secret Service agent that she had recognised, but the dreaded countenance of the man who had not ceased pursuing her for so many years.

"She cried out that she could swear on her life and on mine that she had seen Ballmeyer—that Ballmeyer was alive—alive in the glass, with the smooth face of Larsan and his high, bald forehead. She clung to me, crouching upon the ground like a helpless wild animal, as though she feared a separation yet more terrible than the others. She drew me from the buffet where, fortunately, we had been entirely alone, out upon the platform, and then, suddenly she released my arm, and hiding her face in her hands, rushed into the superintendent's office. The man was as alarmed as myself when he saw the poor soul, and I could only repeat under my breath to myself, 'She is going mad again! She will lose her reason!'

"I explained to the superintendent that my wife had been frightened at something she fancied that she had seen while alone in our compartment, and I begged him to keep her in his office while I went myself to discover what it was that she had seen.

GASTON LEROUX

"And then, my friends," continued Robert Darzac, his voice beginning to tremble, "I left the superintendent's office, but I had no sooner gotten out of the room than I went back and slammed the door behind me. My face must have looked strange enough, to judge from the expression of the superintendent's face when I reappeared. But there was reason for it. *I, too, had seen Larsan*. My wife had had no illusion. *Larsan was there*—in the station—upon the platform outside that door!"

Robert Darzac paused for an instant, as though the remembrance overcame him. He passed his hand over his forehead, heaved a sigh and resumed: "He was there, in front of the superintendent's door, standing under a gas jet. Evidently, he expected us and was waiting for us. For, extraordinarily enough, he made no effort to hide himself. On the contrary, anyone would have declared that he had stationed himself there for the express purpose of being seen. The gesture which had made me close the door upon this apparition was purely instinctive. When I opened it again, intending to walk straight up to the miserable wretch, he had disappeared.

"The superintendent must have thought that he had fallen in with two lunatics. Mathilde was staring at me, her great eyes wide open, speechless, as though she were a somnambulist. In a moment, however, she came back to herself sufficiently to ask me whether it were far from Bourg to Lyons, and what was the next train which would take us there. At the same time, she begged me to give orders about our baggage, and asked me to accede to her desire to rejoin her father as soon as possible. I could see no other means of calming her, and, far from making any objection to the new project, I immediately entered into her plans. Besides, now that I had seen Larsan with my own eyes—yes, with my own eyes—I knew well that the long honeymoon trip which we had planned must be given up, and, my dear boy," went on M. Darzac, turning to Rouletabille, "I became possessed with the idea that we were running the risk of some mysterious and fantastic danger, from which you alone could rescue us, if it were not already too late. Mathilde was grateful to me for the readiness with which I fell in with her wish to join her father, and she thanked me fervently, when I told her that in a few minutes we would be on board the 9:29 train, which reaches Lyons at about ten o'clock, and when we consulted the time table, we discovered that we would overtake M. Stangerson himself at that point. Mathilde showed as much gratitude toward me as though I were personally responsible for this lucky chance. She had regained her composure to a certain extent when the nine o'clock train arrived in the station, but at the moment that we boarded the train, as we rapidly crossed the platform and passed beneath the gas jet where I had seen Larsan, I felt her arm trembling in my own. I looked around, but could not see any sign of our enemy. I asked her whether she had seen anything, and she made no reply. Her agitation seemed to increase, however, and she begged me not to take her into a private car, but to enter a car the berths of which were already two-thirds filled with passengers. Under pretext of making some inquiries about the baggage, I left her for an instant, and went to the telegraph office, where I sent the telegram to you. I said nothing to Mathilde of this dispatch, because I continued to assure her that her eyes must have deceived her, and because on no account did I wish her to believe that I placed any faith in such a resurrection. When my wife opened her travelling bag, she found that no one had touched her jewels.

"The few words which we exchanged concerning the secret were in relation to the necessity for concealing it from M. Stangerson, to whom it might have dealt a mortal blow. I will pass over his amazement when he beheld us upon the platform of the station at Lyons. Mathilde explained to him that on account of a serious accident, which had closed the line at Culoz, we had decided, since a change of plans had to be made, that we would join him, and to spend a few days with him at the home of Arthur Rance and his young wife, as we had before been entreated to do by this faithful friend of ours."

At this time, it might be well for me to interrupt M. Darzac's narrative to recall to the memory of the reader of "The Mystery of the Yellow Room" the fact that M. Arthur William Rance had for many years cherished a hopeless devotion for Mlle. Stangerson, but had at last overcome it, and married a beautiful American girl, who knew nothing of the mysterious adventures of the Professor's daughter.

After the affair at the Glandier, and while Mlle. Stangerson was still a patient in a private asylum near Paris, where the treatment restored her to health and reason, we heard one fine day that M. Arthur William Rance was about to wed the niece of an old professor of geology at the Academy of Science in Philadelphia.

Those who had known of his luckless passion for Mathilde, and had gauged its depths by the excess with which it was displayed (for it had seemed at one time to rob the man of sense and reason and turn him into a maniac)—such persons, I say, believed that Rance was marrying in desperation, and prophesied little happiness for the union. Stories were told that the match—which was a good one for Arthur Rance, for Miss Edith Prescott was rich—had been brought about in a rather singular fashion. But these are stories which I may tell at some future time. You will learn then by what chain of circumstances the Rances had been led to locate at Rochers Rouges in the old castle, on the peninsula of Hercules, of which they had become the owners the preceding autumn.

But at present I must give place to M. Darzac, who continued his story, as follows:

"When we had given these explanations to M. Stangerson, my wife and I saw that he seemed to understand very little of what we had said, and that, instead of being glad to have us with him again, he appeared very mournful. Mathilde tried in vain to seem happy. Her father saw that something had happened since we had left him which we were concealing from him. Mathilde began to talk of the ceremony of the morning, and in that way the conversation came around to you, my young friend"—and again M. Darzac addressed himself to Rouletabille—"and I took the occasion to say to M. Stangerson that since your vacation was just beginning at the time that we were all going to Mentone, you might be pleased with an invitation that would give you the chance of spending your holiday in our society. There was, I said, plenty of room at Rochers Rouges, and I was certain that M. Arthur Rance and his bride would extend to you a cordial welcome. While I was speaking, Mathilde looked gratefully at me and pressed my hand tenderly with an effusion which showed me what gladness she was experiencing at the proposition. Thus it happened that when we reached Valence, I had M. Stangerson write the dispatch which you must have received. All night long we did not sleep. While her father rested in his compartments next to ours, Mathilde opened my travelling bag and took out my revolver. She requested me to put it in my overcoat pocket, saying: 'If *he* should attack us, you must defend yourself.' Ah, what a night we passed! We kept silence, each attempting to deceive the other into the belief that we were resting, our eyes closed, with the light burning full force, for we did not dare to sit in the darkness. The doors of our compartment were locked and bolted, but yet, every moment, we dreaded to see *his* face appear. When we heard a step in the corridor, our hearts beat wildly. We seemed to recognize it. And Mathilde had put a cover over the mirror, for fear of glancing toward it and seeing the reflection of that face again. 'Had he followed us?' 'Could we have been mistaken?' 'Would we escape from him?' 'Had he gone on to Culoz on the train which we had left?' 'Could we hope for any such good fortune?' For my own part, I did not believe that we could. And she—she! Ah, how my heart bled for her, wrapped in a silence like that of death, sitting there in her corner. I knew how she was weighed down by despair and agony—how far more unhappy she was even than myself, because of the misery which it seemed to be her lot to bring upon those whom she loved most dearly. I longed to console her, to comfort her, but I found no words. And when once I attempted to speak, she made a gesture so full of misery and desolation that I realised that I would be far kinder if I kept silence. Then, like her, I closed my eyes."

This was M. Darzac's story, although I have shortened it in a certain degree. We felt, Rouletabille and myself, that the narrative was so important that we both resolved on arriving at Mentone, that we would write it down from memory as faithfully as possible. We did as we agreed, and where our versions did not agree, or halted a little, we submitted them to M. Darzac, who made a few unimportant changes, after which the story read just as I have given it here.

The rest of the journey taken by the Darzacs and M. Stangerson presented no incident worthy of note. At the station of Mentone Garavan, they found M. Arthur Rance, who was astonished at beholding the bride and bridegroom; but when he was told that they intended to spend a few days with him, and to accept the invitation which M. Darzac, under various pretexts, had always declined, he was delighted, and declared that his wife would be as glad as himself. He was pleased, too, to learn that Rouletabille might soon join the party. M. Arthur Rance had not, even after his marriage to Miss Edith Prescott, been able to overcome the extreme reserve with which M. Darzac had always treated him. When, during his last trip to San Remo, the young Professor of the Sorbonne had been urged in passing to make a visit at the Château Hercules, he had made his excuses in the most ceremonious manner. But when he met Rance in the station at Mentone Garavan, M. Darzac greeted him most cordially, and complimented him upon his appearance, saying that the air of the country seemed to agree with him perfectly.

We have seen how the apparition of Larsan in the station at Bourg had overthrown all the plans of M. and Mme. Darzac, and had completely overwhelmed them both with grief and consternation, and had made them turn to the Rances' home as to a refuge, casting them, figuratively speaking, into the arms of these people who were not especially congenial to them, but whom they believed to be honest, loyal and willing to protect them. We know that M. Stangerson, to whom nothing had been told of what had occurred, was beginning to suspect something, and we know that all three of the party had called Rouletabille to their aid. It was a veritable panic. And, so far as M. Darzac was concerned, the terror which he felt was increased by news brought to us by M. Arthur Rance when he met us at Nice. But before this there had occurred a little incident which I cannot pass by in silence. As soon as we reached the Nice station, I had jumped from the train and hurried into the telegraph office to ask whether there was any message for me. A dispatch was handed to me, and, without opening it, I went back to M. Darzac and Rouletabille.

"Read this!" I said to the young reporter.

Rouletabille opened the envelope and read:

"Brignolles has not been away from Paris since April 6th. This is an absolute certainty."

Rouletabille looked at me for a moment and then said:

"Well, what does this amount to, now that you have it? What did you suspect, anyway?"

"It was at Dijon," I rejoined, vexed at the attitude of the lad toward the affair, "that the idea came to me that Brignolles might be in some way concerned in the misfortunes that seem to be crowding upon us, and of which warning was given by the telegrams that you received. I wired one of my friends to make inquiries for me in regard to the movements of the fellow during the last few days. I was anxious to learn whether he had left Paris."

"Well," said Rouletabille. "You have your inquiries answered. Are you willing to admit now that Brignolles is not and has never been Larsan in disguise?"

"I never thought of any such thing as that!" I exclaimed with some vexation, for I suspected that Rouletabille was laughing at me.

The truth was that the idea, absurd as it was, had actually entered my mind.

"Will you never stop thinking ill of poor Brignolles?" asked M. Darzac, with a sad smile at me. "He is quiet and shy, I grant you, but he is a good lad, just the same."

"That's where we differ," I retorted.

And I retired to my own corner of the railway carriage. In general my personal intuitions in regard to things were poor enough guides compared to the wonderful insight of Rouletabille, but in this case, we were to receive proof, only a few days later, that even if the personality of Brignolles were not another of Larsan's disguises, the laboratory assistant was nevertheless a miserable wretch. And this time both M. Darzac and Rouletabille begged my pardon and paid their respects to my despised intuitions. But there is no use of anticipating. If I mention this incident here, it is for the purpose of showing to how great an extent I was haunted by the image of Larsan, hiding under some new form, and lurking unknown among us. Dear Heaven! Larsan had so often proved his talent—I may even say his genius—in this respect, that I felt that he was quite capable of defying us now, and of mingling with us while we thought that he was a stranger—or, perhaps, even a friend.

I was soon to change my ideas, however, and to believe that this time Ballmeyer had altered his usual tactics, and the unexpected arrival of M. Arthur Rance was to go far in leading me to this opinion. Instead of hiding himself, the bandit was showing himself openly—at least, to some of us—with an audacity that staggered belief. After all, what had he to fear in this part of the country? He was well aware that neither M. Darzac nor his wife would be likely to denounce him, nor, consequently, would their friends do so. His bold revelation of his presence seemed to have but one end in view—that of ruining the happiness of the couple who had believed that his death had opened the way for their marriage. But an objection arose to that conjecture. Why should he have chosen such a means of vengeance? Would it not have been a better plan to let himself be seen before the marriage had taken place? He would certainly have prevented it by so doing. Yes, but in that case, he would have found it necessary to appear in his own person in Paris. But when had any thought of danger or risk been able to deter Larsan from an undertaking upon which he had determined? Who dared affirm that he knew of one such case?

But now let me tell you of the news brought by Arthur Rance when he joined the three of us on the train at Nice. Rance, of course, knew nothing of what had happened at Bourg, nothing of the appearing of Larsan to Mme. Darzac on the train and to her husband in the station, but he brought alarming tidings. If we had retained the slightest hope that we had lost Larsan on the road to Culoz, Rance's words obliterated it, for he, too, had seen the man whom we so feared, face to face. And he had come to warn us, before we reached his home, so that we might decide upon some plan of action.

"When we were about to return home after having taken you to the station," said Rance to Darzac.; "after the train had pulled out, your wife, M. Stangerson and myself thought that we would leave the carriage for a little while and take a stroll on the promenade walk. M. Stangerson gave his arm to his daughter. I was at the right of M. Stangerson, who, therefore, was walking between the two of us. Suddenly, as we paused for a moment near a sort of public garden to let a tramcar pass, I brushed against a man who said to me, 'I beg your pardon, sir.' The sound of the voice made me tremble and I knew as well beforehand as I did when I raised my head that it was Larsan. The voice was the voice I had heard at the Court of Assizes. He cast a long, calm look upon the three of us. I do not know how I was able to restrain the exclamation which rose to my lips,—how I kept from crying aloud his miserable name! Happily M. Stangerson and Mme. Darzac had not seen him and I hurried them rapidly away. I made them walk around the garden and listen to the music in the park and then we returned to where the carriage was waiting. Upon the sidewalk in front of the station, there was Larsan again! I do not know—I cannot understand how M. Stangerson and Mme. Darzac could have helped but see him—"

"Are you sure that they did not see him?" interrupted Robert Darzac.

"Absolutely sure. I feigned a sudden attack of illness. We got into the carriage and ordered the coachman to drive as fast as he could. The man was still standing on the sidewalk, staring after us with his cold, cruel eyes when we drove away."

"And are you certain that my wife did not see him?" repeated Darzac, who was growing more and more agitated.

"Certain, I assure you."

"But, Good God, M. Darzac!" interposed Rouletabille. "How long do you think you can deceive your wife as to the fact that Larsan has reappeared and that she actually saw him? If you imagine that you can keep her in ignorance for very long, you are greatly mistaken."

"But," replied Darzac, "while we were ending our journey, the idea that she had been the victim of a delusion seemed to grow in her mind and by the time we reached Garavan, she seemed to be quite calm."

"At the time you reached Garavan," said Rouletabille, quietly, "your wife sent me the telegram I am going to ask you to read."

And the reporter held out to M. Darzac the paper which bore the two words, "Save us."

M. Darzac read it with the blood seeming to die away from his face as we looked at him.

"She will go mad again," was all that he said.

That was what he dreaded—all of us—and, strangely enough, when we arrived at the station of Mentone Garavan and found M. Stangerson and Mme. Darzac (who were awaiting us in spite of the promise which the Professor had made to Arthur Rance not to leave Rochers Rouges nor allow his daughter to do so until we came, for reasons which their host said he would tell them later, not being able to invent them on the spur of the moment) it was with a phrase which seemed the echo of our terror that Mme. Darzac greeted Rouletabille. As soon as she perceived the young man, she rushed toward him and it seemed to us that she was making a great effort not to throw her arms around him. I saw that her spirit was clinging to him as a shipwrecked sailor grips at the hand which is stretched out to save him from drowning. And I heard the words that she whispered to him:

"I know that I am going mad!"

As to Rouletabille, I may have seen his face as pale before, but I had never seen it look like that of a man stricken with his death blow.

VI

The Fort of Hercules

When he alights at the Garavan station, whatever may be the season of the year in which he visits that enchanted country, the traveller might almost fancy himself in the Garden of Hesperides whose golden apples excited the desire of the conqueror of the Nemean lion. I might not perhaps, however, have recalled to mind the son of Jupiter and Alcmene merely because of the numerous lemon and orange trees which in the balmy air let their ripened fruit hang heavily on their boughs if everything about the scene had not spoken of his mythological glories and his fabled promenade upon these fair shores. You remember how the Phoenicians in transporting their penates to the shadow of the rocks which were one day to become the abode of the Grimaldi, gave to the little port in which they anchored and to other natural features all along the shore—a mountain, a cape, and an islet—the name of Hercules whom they looked upon as their god—the name which they have always retained. But I like to fancy that the Phoenicians found the name here already, and indeed, if the divinities, fatigued by the white dust of the roads of Hellas, went to seek for a marvellous spot, warm and perfumed, to rest after their strenuous adventures, they could not have found a more beautiful scene. The gods, to my mind, were the first tourists of the Riviera. The Garden of the Hesperides was nowhere else and Hercules had made the place ready for his Olympian comrades by destroying the evil dragon with an hundred heads who wanted to keep the azure shore for himself, all alone. And I am not at all certain that the bones of the ancient elephant discovered a few years ago in the neighbourhood of Rochers Rouges were not those of the dragon himself!

When, after alighting from the train, we came in silence to the bank of the sea, our eyes were immediately struck by a dazzling silhouette of a castle standing upon the peninsula of Hercules, which the works accomplished on the frontier have, alas, nearly destroyed. The oblique rays of the sun which were falling upon the walls and the old Square Tower made the reflection of the tower glisten in the waters like a breastplate. The tower seemed to stand guard like an old sentinel, over the Bay of Garavan which lay before us like a blue lake of fire. And as we advanced nearer, the tower gleaming in the water seemed to grow longer. The sky behind us leaned toward the crest of the mountains; the promontories to the west were already wrapped in clouds at the approach of night and by the time we crossed the threshold of the actual structure the castle in the water was only a menacing hade.

Upon the lower steps of the stairway which led up to one of the towers, we beheld a slender, charming figure. It was Arthur Rance's wife, who had been the beautiful and brilliant Edith Prescott. Certainly the Bride of Lammermoor was not more pale on the day when the black-eyed stranger from Ravenswood first crossed her path, O Edith! Ah, when one wishes to present a romantic figure in a mediaeval frame, the figure of a princess, lost in dreams, plaintive and melancholy, one should not have such eyes, my lady! And your hair was as black as the raven's wing. Such colouring is not of the kind which one is used to attribute to the angels. Are you an angel, Edith? Is this gentle, plaintive little manner natural or acquired? Is the sweet expression that your face wears today an entirely truthful one? Pardon that I ask you all these questions, Edith; but when I beheld you for the first time, after having been entranced by the delicate harmony of your white figure, standing motionless upon the stone stair, I followed the quick, lowering glance of your dark eyes in the direction of the daughter of Professor Stangerson, and it had a cruel look which accorded ill with the sweet tones of your voice and the bright smile on your lips.

The voice of the young wife was her greatest charm although the grace of her entire being was perfect. At the introductions which were, of course, performed by her husband, she greeted us in the simplest and sweetest fashion imaginable—the fashion of the ideal hostess. Rouletabille and myself made an effort to tell her that we had intended to look for a stopping place in the village instead of trespassing upon her hospitality. She made a delicious little grimace, lifted her shoulders with a gesture that was almost childish, said that our rooms were all ready for us and changed the subject.

"Come, come! You haven't seen the château. You must see it—all of you. Oh, I will show you "la Louve" another time. It is the only gloomy corner in the place. It is horrible—so cold and dismal. It makes me shiver. But, do you know I love to shiver! Oh, M. Rouletabille, you'll tell me stories that will make me shiver someday, won't you?"

And chattering thus, she glided in front of us in her white gown. She walked like an actress. She made a singularly pretty picture in this garden of the Orient, between the threatening old tower and the carved stone flowers of the ruined chapel. The vast court which we were crossing was so completely covered on every side with grass, shrubs and foliage plants, with cactus and aloes, mountain laurel, wild roses and marguerites that one might have sworn that an eternal spring had found its habitation in this enclosure, formerly the drilling ground of the château when the soldiers assembled in time of war. This court, through the help of the winds of heaven and the neglect of man had naturally become a garden, a beautiful wild garden in which one saw that the chatelaine had interfered as little as possible and which she had in no way attempted to restore to the beaten track. Behind all this verdure and this wealth of bloom one could see the most exquisite sight which could be imagined in dead architecture. Figure to yourself the perfect arches of gothic brought up to the doors of the old Roman chapel; the pillars twined with climbing plants, rose geranium and vervain uniting their sweet perfume and raising to the azure heavens their broken arch, which nothing seems to support. There is no longer a roof on the chapel. And there are no more walls. There remains of it only the bit of lace work in stone, which a miracle of equilibrium keeps suspended in the air.

And at our left is the immense tower of the Twelfth Century, which, Mme. Edith tells us, the natives call "la Louve" and which nothing— neither time, nor man, nor peace, nor war, nor cannon, nor tempest has ever been able to destroy. It is just as it appeared in 1107, when the Saracens, who sowed devastation in their wake, were able to make no headway in their attacks upon the château of Hercules,—just as it was seen by Salageri and his corsairs of Genoa, when, after they had seised the fort and the Square Tower and even the castle itself, it resisted attack and its defenders held it until the arrival of the troops of the Princes of Provence, who delivered them. It was there that Mme. Edith had chosen to have her own rooms.

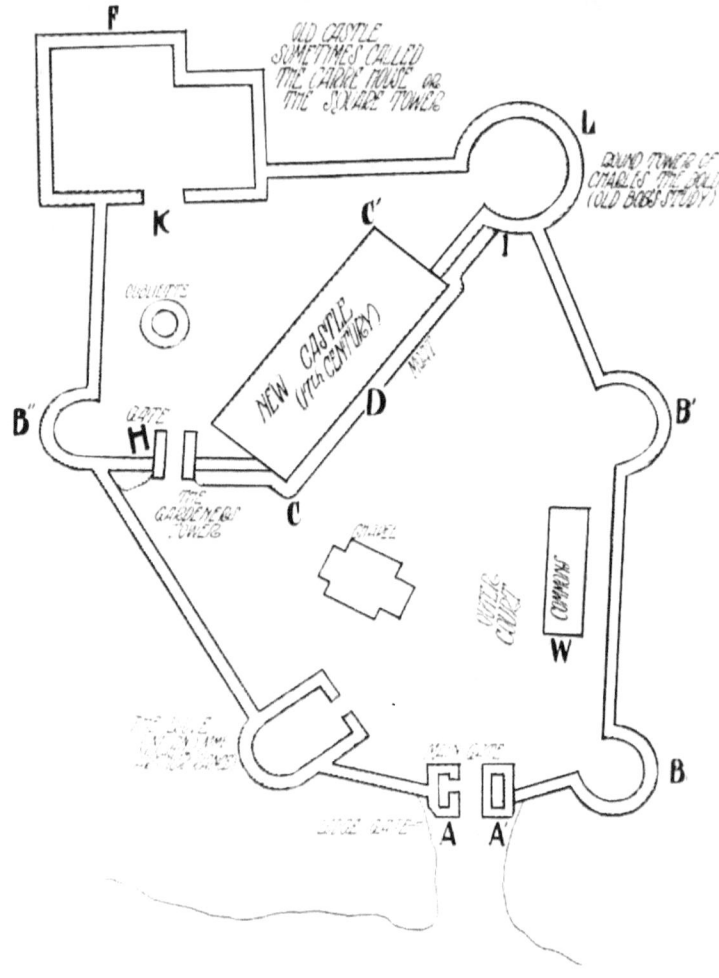

The Plan of the Fort of Hercules

But while she spoke to us in her sweet, clear voice, I stopped looking at the objects around us to look at the people. Arthur Rance was gazing at Mme. Darzac, when my eyes fell upon them, and Rouletabille seemed to be lost in thought, and far, far away from us all. M. Darzac and M. Stangerson were talking in low tones. The same thought was filling the minds of each one of these people—both those who kept silence and those who, if they spoke, were careful to say nothing which could give a clue to the thoughts. We reached the postern. "This is what we call the Gardener's Tower," said Edith, childishly. "From this gate one may see all the fort, and all the castle, both north and south. See!"

And she stretched her arms wide to emphasize her words.

"Every stone has its history. I'll tell them to you some day, if you are good."

"How gay Edith is!" murmured her husband. I thought to myself that she was the only one who was gay in the party.

We had passed through the postern and found ourselves in another court. Opposite us was the old donjon. Its appearance was more than impressive. It was high and square, and it was on account of its shape that it was known as the Square Tower. And, as this tower occupies the most important corner of the fortification, it was also known as the Corner Tower. It was the most extraordinary and the most important part of this agglomeration of defensive works. The walls were heavier and higher than those anywhere else, and half way up they were still sealed with the Roman cement with which Caesar's own columns had welded together the stones.

"That tower yonder, in the opposite corner," went on Edith, "is the Tower of Charles the Bold, so called because he was the Duke who furnished the plans when it became necessary to transform the defences of the château, so as to make them resist the attacks of the artillery. Don't you think I am very learned? Old Bob has made this tower his study. It is too bad, for we might have a magnificent dining hall there. But I have never been able to refuse old Bob anything he wanted. Old Bob," she added, with a charming smile, "is my uncle—that is the name he taught me to call him by when I was a little thing. He is not here just now. He went to Paris on the five o'clock train, but he will be back tomorrow. He is going to compare some of the anatomical specimens which he found at Rochers Rouges with those in the Museum of Natural History in Paris. Ah—here is an oubliette!"

And she showed us in the centre part of the second court a small shaft, which she called, romantically, an oubliette, and above which a eucalyptus tree, with its white blossoms and its leafless limbs, leaned like a woman over a fountain.

Since we had entered the second court, we understood better—or at least I did, for Rouletabille, every moment more deeply lost in his own thoughts, seemed neither to see nor to hear—the topographical plan of the Fort of Hercules. As this plan is of the greatest importance in the proper understanding of the incredible events which were to occur so soon after our arrival at Rochers Rouges, I shall place at once before the eyes of the reader the general scheme of the buildings as it was traced later by Rouletabille and myself.

The castle had been built in 1140 by the Seigneurs of Mortola. In order to isolate it completely from the land, they had not hesitated to make an island of the peninsula by cutting away the narrow isthmus which connected it with the mainland. Upon the mainland itself, they had built a barricade in the form of a semicircular fortification, designed to protect the approaches to the drawbridge and the two entrance towers. Not a trace of this fortification was left. And the isthmus, in the course of the centuries, had again resumed its old form, the drawbridge had been thrown down and the trenches had filled up. The walls of the Château of Hercules followed the outline of the peninsula, which was that of an irregular hexagon. The walls were built upon the rocks, and the latter, in some places, extended over the waters in such a manner that a little ship might have taken shelter beneath them, fearing no enemy, while it was protected by this natural ceiling. This design of building was marvellously well adapted for defence, and gave the inmates of the fort ress little reason to fear an attack, no matter from what quarter it might come.

The fort was entered by way of the north gate, which guarded the two towers, A and A', connected by a passageway. These towers which had suffered greatly during the last sieges of the Genoese, had been repaired to some slight extent some time afterward, and had, shortly before we came to Rochers Rouges, been made habitable by Mrs. Rance, who used them as servants' quarters. The front of the tower A served as the keeper's lodge. A little door opened in the side of the tower upon the passageway, and enabled anyone looking out to observe all those who came or went. A heavy double door of oak, with bands of iron, was no longer in use, its twin portals having stood for uncounted years open against the inner walls of the two towers, on account of the difficulty which had been experienced in managing them; and the entrance to the castle was only closed by a little gate, which anyone might open at will. This entrance was the only one by which it was possible to get into the château. As I have said, in passing through this gate, one found himself in the first court, closed in on all sides by the walls and the towers. These walls were by no means as high as when they were built. The old high courtyards which connected the towers had been rased to the ground and replaced by a sort of circular boulevard, from which one mounted toward the first court by means of a little terrace. The boulevards were still crowned by a parapet. For the changes which I have described took place in the Fifteenth Century, at the time when every lord of the manor was obliged to consider the possibility of being obliged to meet an attack of artillery. As to the towers B, B' and B", which had for a considerable time longer preserved their uniformity and their first height, and the pointed roofs of which had been replaced by a platform designed to support the artillery, they had later been rased to the height of the boulevard parapets, and their shape seemed almost like that of a half moon. These alterations had taken place in the Seventeenth Century, at the time of the construction of a modern castle, still known as the New Castle, although it had been in ruins for years when we first saw it. The New Castle on the plan is at C C'.

Upon the flat platform roofs of these old towers—roofs which were surrounded by a parapet—palm trees had been planted, which had thriven ill, swept as they were by the sea winds and burned by the sun. When one leaned over the circular parapet which surrounded the whole domain, it seemed to him as though the château were still as completely closed in as it was in the days when the courtyards reached to the second stories of the old towers. "La Louve," as I have said, had not been changed at all, but still reared its dark hulk against the blue waters of the Mediterranean, a strange, weird figure, looking thousands of years old. I have spoken also of the ruins of the chapel. The ancient commons (shown on the map by W), near the parapet between B and B', had been transformed into the stables and the kitchens.

I am describing now all the anterior portion of the Château of Hercules. One could only penetrate into the second enclosure through the postern (indicated by H), which Mrs. Arthur Rance called "the tower of the gardener," and which was actually only a pavilion, formerly defended by the tower B", and by another tower situated at C, and which had entirely disappeared at the time of the erection of the New Castle (shown at C C'). A moat and a wall started from B" to abut on I at the Tower of Charles the Bold, advancing at C in the form of a spur to the midst of the first court, and entirely isolating the court, which they completely closed in. The moat still exists, wide and deep, but the walls had been torn down all the length of the New Castle and replaced by the walls of the castle itself. A central door at D, now condemned, opened upon a bridge, which had been thrown over the moat, and which formerly permitted direct communication with the outer court. But this bridge had been torn down or was swallowed up in the waters, and as the windows of the castle, rising high above the moat, were still guarded by their heavy iron bars, one might readily believe that the inner court still remained as impenetrable as when it was entirely shut in by its enclosing walls at the time when the New Castle did not exist.

The pavement of the inner court—the Court of Charles the Bold, as the old guide books of the country call it still—was a little higher than that of the outer court. The rocks formed there a very high seat, a natural pedestal of that colossal black column, the Old Castle, standing square and erect, as though it had been carved from a single block of stone, stretching its awesome shadow over the blue waters. One could only penetrate into the Old Castle (designated by F) by a little door, K. The old inhabitants of the country never spoke of it except as the Square Tower, to distinguish it from the Round Tower, or the Tower of Charles the Bold, as they sometimes called the latter. A parapet similar to the one which closed in the outer court was built between the towers B", F and L, closing the inner court as firmly as the outer.

We have seen that the Round Tower had been in years past torn down to half its former height, as it had been built by the Mortola, according to plans drawn by Charles the Bold himself, to whom the Seigneur had been of some service in the Helvetian war. This tower had a number of tiny chambers above, and an immense octagon chamber below. One descended into this chamber by a steep and narrow stairway. The ceiling of the octagon room was supported by four great cylindrical pillars, and from its walls opened three enormous embrasures for three enormous cannons. It was of this room that Mme. Edith had wished to make a dining room, for it was in an admirable state of preservation, on account of the thickness of the walls, and the light could still penetrate through the great windows, which had been enlarged and made square, although they, too, were still guarded by barriers of iron. This tower (shown on the map at L) was the spot chosen by Mme. Edith's uncle for a workshop, and the abiding place of his collection. Its roof was a beautiful little garden, to which the mistress of the domain had had transported fertile soil and wonderful plants and flowers. I have marked upon the map in array all the portions of the buildings which Mme. Edith had restored, improved and put in shape for habitation.

Of the château of the Seventeenth Century, known as the New Castle, they had only repaired two bed chambers on the first floor and a little sitting room for guests. It was to these that Rouletabille and myself were assigned, while M. and Mme. Robert Darzac were lodged in the Square Tower, of which I shall have to give a more special description.

Two rooms, the windows of which opened upon the balcony, were reserved in this Square Tower for "Old Bob," who slept there. M. Stangerson was upon the first floor of "la Louve," in the rear of the suite occupied by the Rances.

Mme. Edith herself showed us to our rooms. She made us cross over the sunken ceilings of ruined apartments, over broken railings and tumble-down walls; but here and there some mouldy hangings, a broken statue or a ragged bit of tapestry, bore witness to the ancient splendors of the New Castle, born of the fantasies of some Mortola of the wonderful Seventeenth Century. But when we reached them, our little rooms recalled to us nothing of that magnificent past. They had been swept and garnished with a care that was almost touching. Clean and hygienic, without carpets, hangings or upholstered chairs, furnished in the simplest of modern styles, they pleased us very much. As I have already said, the two sleeping rooms were separated by a little parlour.

As I tied my cravat, after dressing for dinner, I called Rouletabille to ask him if he were ready. There was no answer. I went into his room and discovered with surprise that he had already gone out. I went to the window of his room, which opened like my own upon the court of Charles the Bold. The court was empty, inhabited only by a large eucalyptus, the fragrance of which mounted to my nostrils. Above the parapet of the boulevard I saw the vast stretch of the silent waters. The blue of the sea had grown dark at the fall of evening, and the shades of night were visible on the horizon of the Italian shore, reaching already to the pointe d'Ospedaletti. Not a sound, not a breath on the land or in the heavens! I have never yet noticed such a silence and such a complete repose of nature except at the moment which precedes the most violent storms and the unchaining of the elements. But now I felt that we had nothing of the sort to fear. The whole appearance of the night was of the calmest, most serene beauty—

But what was that dark shadow? From whence had come that spectre which glided over the waters? Standing erect at the prow of a little boat which a fisherman was rowing, keeping rhythmic time with the two oars, I recognised the form of Larsan. Why should I try to deceive myself by saying even for one moment that I was wrong? He was only too easily to be recognised. And if those who beheld him should have had the slightest doubt as to his identity, he seemed to desire to set it entirely at rest by this open display of himself, utterly without disguise, as entirely convincing as though he had shouted aloud, "It is I!"

Oh, yes! it was he! It was "the great Fred," as we used to call him when we looked upon him only as the wonderfully resourceful and brilliant Secret Service agent. The boat, silent, with its motionless statue at the prow, rowed completely around the peninsula. It passed beneath the windows of the Square Tower and then directed its course to the shores of the Pointe de Garibaldi. And the man still stood erect, his arms folded, his face turned toward the tower, a diabolical apparition on the threshold of the night, which slowly crept up behind him, enveloped him in its shades and carried him away.

When he had vanished, I lowered my eyes and beheld two figures in the court of Charles the Bold. They were at the corner of the railing near the little door of the Square Tower. One of these forms—the taller—was supporting the other and speaking in tones of entreaty. The smaller attempted to break away—one would have said that it wished to throw itself into the sea. And I heard the voice of Mme. Darzac say:

"Be careful. It is a gage of defiance which he has thrown down. You shall not leave me this evening."

And then came Rouletabille's voice answering:

"He must land upon the bank! Let me hurry to the bank."

"What will you do there?" moaned Mathilde.

"Whatever may be necessary."

And then Mathilde spoke again, and her voice was terrible to hear.

"I forbid you to touch that man!"

And I heard no more.

I descended to the court, where I found Rouletabille alone, seated upon the edge of the oubliette. I spoke to him, but he did not answer. I felt no surprise, for this had often happened of late. I went on into the outer court, and I saw M. Darzac coming toward me, evidently in the greatest excitement. Before I came up to him, he called out:

"Did you see him?"

"Yes, I saw him," I replied.

"And she—my wife—do you know whether she saw him?"

"She saw him, too. She was with Rouletabille when he passed. What bravado the creature showed!"

Robert Darzac was trembling like an aspen leaf from the shock which he had just experienced. He told me that as soon as he had caught sight of the boat and its passenger, he had rushed like a madman to the shore, but that before he had reached the Pointe de Garibaldi the bark had disappeared as if by enchantment. But even before he finished speaking, Darzac left me and hurried away to seek Mathilde, dreading the thought of the state of mind in which he felt that he would find her. But he returned almost immediately, gloomy and grieved. The door of his wife's apartment was locked, and she had said to him that she wished to be alone for awhile.

"And Rouletabille?" I asked.

"I have not seen him."

We remained together upon the rampart gazing at the night which had carried Larsan away. Robert Darzac was infinitely sorrowful. In order to change the direction of his thoughts, I asked him a few questions regarding the Rance household. Here is in substance the information which I succeeded in extracting from him little by little:

After the trial at Versailles, Arthur Rance had returned to Philadelphia, and there, one evening, at a family dinner party, he had found himself seated beside a charming young girl, who had interested him at once by a display of interest in literature and art, the like of which he had not often seen in his beautiful countrywomen. She was not in the least like the quick, independent and audacious type of young women who are often found in America, nor was she of the "Fluffy Ruffles" variety, so much in favour at present. Somewhat haughty in mien, yet gentle and melancholy, she at once recalled to the young man the heroines of Walter Scott, who he soon learned was her favourite author. From the first, she attracted him strongly. How could this delicate little creature so quickly have impressed Arthur Rance, who had been madly in love with the majestic Mathilde? Of such are the mysteries of the heart. Now, fortunately or unfortunately, as you prefer, Arthur Rance had upon that evening so far forgotten himself as to drink considerably more wine than was good for him. He never realised what his offense had been, but he knew that he must have committed some frightful blunder or breach of politeness, when Miss Edith in a low voice and with heightened colour, requested him not to address her again. Upon the morrow, Arthur Rance went to call on the young lady and entreated her pardon, swearing that he would never permit wine to pass his lips again.

Arthur Rance had already known for some time Miss Prescott's uncle, the fine old man who still bore among his friends the nickname of "Old Bob," which had been given him in his college days, and who was as celebrated for his adventures as an explorer as for his discoveries as a geologist. He seemed as gentle as a sheep, but he had hunted many a tiger through the pampas of South America. He had spent half his life south of the Rio Negro among the Patagonians, in seeking for the man of the tertiary period—or, at least, for his fossils, not as the anthropological relic or some other pithecanthropus, approaching in a greater or less extent the race of monkeys, but as the real living man, stronger, more powerful, than those who inhabit this planet in our own day—the man, to speak clearly, who must have been contemporaneous with the immense mammoths and mastodons, which appeared upon the globe before the quarternary epoch. He generally returned from these expeditions with closely filled notebooks and a respectable collection of tibias and femurs, which may or may not have belonged to the aboriginal man, and also with a rich display of skins of wild beasts, which showed that the spectacled old savant knew how to use more modern arms than the stone ax and bow and arrow. As soon as he was back in Philadelphia, he would dispose of his treasures either in his private cabinets or in those of the Museum, and, opening his notebooks, would resume his lectures, amusing himself as he talked by making the splinters from the long pencils, which he was always sharpening but had never been seen to use, fly almost into the eyes of the students on the front benches. All these details were given me later by Arthur Rance himself. He had been one of "Old Bob's" pupils, but had not seen him in many years until he made the acquaintance of Miss Edith. If I have seemed to dwell too minutely on such apparently unimportant things, I have done so because, by quite a natural train of events, we were to make "Old Bob's" acquaintance at Rochers Rouges.

Miss Edith, upon the occasion when Arthur Rance had been presented to her and had forgotten himself on account of overindulgence in wine, had seemed somewhat more melancholy than she usually was, because she had received disquieting news of her uncle. The latter for four years back had been absent on a trip to Patagonia. In his last letter, he had told his niece that he was ill, and that he feared that he should not live to see her again. One might be tempted to wonder why so tender-hearted a niece, under such circumstances, had not refrained from attending a dinner, no matter how quiet, but Miss Edith, during her uncle's many absences from home, had so frequently received such communications from him and had afterward seen him return in such perfect health that she could scarcely be blamed for not having remained at home to mourn that evening. Three months later, however, laying received another letter, she suddenly resolved to go all alone to South America and join her uncle. During those three months important events had transpired. Miss Edith had been touched by the remorse of Arthur Rance, and when Miss Prescott departed for Patagonia, no one was astonished to find that "Old Bob's" old pupil was going to accompany her. If the engagement was not officially announced, it was because the pair preferred to wait for the consent of the geologist. Miss Edith and Arthur Rance were met at St. Louis by the young woman's uncle. He was in excellent health and in a charming humour. Rance, who had not seen him in years, declared to him that he had grown younger— the easiest of compliments to pay and the pleasantest to receive. When his niece informed him of her engagement to this fine young fellow, the uncle manifested the greatest delight. The three returned to Philadelphia, where the wedding took place. Miss Edith had never been in France, and Arthur determined that their honeymoon should be spent there. And it was thus that they found, as will be told a little later, a scientific reason for locating in the neighbourhood of Mentone, not exactly in France, but an hundred meters from the frontier, in Italy, at Rochers Rouges.

The gong had sounded for dinner, and Arthur Rance was coming to look for us, so we repaired to "la Louve," in the lower hall of which we were to dine. When we were all assembled (save "Old Bob," who, as has been mentioned, was absent), Mme. Edith asked whether any of us had noticed a little boat which had made the circle of the fortress, and in which a man was standing erect. The man's strange attitude had struck her, she said. No one replied, and she added:

"Oh, I know who it is, for I know the fisherman who rowed the boat. He is a great friend of Old Bob."

"Ah, then you know the fisherman, madame?" asked Rouletabille.

"He comes to the castle sometimes to sell fish. The people around the village have given him an odd name, which I don't know how to say in their impossible patois, but I can translate it. They call him, 'the hangman of the sea.' A pretty name, isn't it?"

VII

WHICH TELLS OF SOME PRECAUTIONS TAKEN BY JOSEPH ROULETABILLE TO DEFEND THE FORT OF HERCULES AGAINST THE ATTACK OF AN ENEMY

Rouletabille had not even the politeness to inquire into the explanation of this amazing sobriquet. He appeared to be plunged in the deepest meditation. A strange dinner! a strange castle! strange guests! All the graces and coquetries of Mme. Edith had no effect in awakening us to any semblance of life. There were two newly married pairs, four lovers, who ought to have been radiant with the joy of life, and to have made the hours pass gayly and happily. But the repast was one of the most gloomy at which I have ever been present. The spectre of Larsan hovered about our festivities, and it seemed almost as though the man whom we knew to be so near was actually among us.

It is as well to say here that Professor Stangerson, since he had learned the cruel, the miserable truth, had not for one moment been able to free himself from the thought of it. I do not think that I am saying too much in declaring that the first victim of the affair at the Glandier, and the most unfortunate of all, was this good old man. He had lost everything—his faith in science, his love of work, and—more bitter than all the rest—his belief in his daughter. His faith in her had been his religion. She had been such an object of joy and pride. He had thought of her for so many years as a vestal virgin, seeking, with him, the unknown in the world of higher things. He had been so marvellously dazzled with the thought of her angelic purity, and had believed that her reason for having remained unmarried was that she was unwilling to resign herself to any life which would withdraw her from science and her father, to both of which she had dedicated her existence. And while he was thinking of her almost with reverence, he discovered that the reason that his daughter refused to marry was because she was already the wife of Ballmeyer. The day in which Mathilde had decided to confess everything to her father, and to tell him the story of the past, which must clear up the present with a tragic light to the eyes of the professor, already warned by the mysteries of the Glandier—the day when, falling at his feet and embracing his knees, she had told him the story of her youth, Professor Stangerson had raised the form of his beloved child from the ground and had pressed her to his heart; he had placed a kiss of pardon on her brow: he had mingled his tears with the sobs of her whose fault had been so bitterly expiated, and he had sworn to her that she had never been more precious than since he had known how she had suffered. And by these words, she was a little comforted. But he, when she left his presence, was another man—a man alone, all alone—. Professor Stangerson had lost his daughter and his goddess.

He had experienced only indifference in regard to her marriage to Robert Darzac, although the latter had been the best beloved of his pupils. In vain Mathilde, with the warmest tenderness, had endeavoured to rekindle the old feeling in the heart of her father. She knew well that he had changed toward her, that his glance never dwelt upon her in the old fond way, and that his weary eyes were looking back into the past at an image which he had only dreamed was her own. And she knew, too, that when those eyes rested upon her—upon her, Mathilde Darzac—it was to see at her side, not the honoured figure of a good man and tender husband, but the shadow, eternally living, eternally infamous, of the other—the man who had stolen his daughter. The Professor could work no longer. The great secret of the dissolution of matter which he had promised to reveal to mankind, had returned to the unknown from which, for a moment, the scientist had drawn it, and men will go on, repeating for centuries to come the imbecile phrase, "From nothing, nothing."

The evening meal was rendered still more doleful by the setting in which it was served—the sombre hall, lighted by a gothic lamp, with old candelabra of wrought iron, and the walls of the fortress adorned with oriental tapestries, against which were ranged the old suits of armour dating back to the first Saracen invasion and the sieges of Dagobert.

I looked at the members of the party, and it seemed to me that I was able to see reason enough for the general sadness. M. and Mme. Darzac were seated beside each other. The mistress of the house had evidently not desired to separate a bridal pair, whose union only dated back to yesterday. Of the two, I must say that the more unhappy looking was, beyond a doubt, our friend, Robert. He never spoke one word. Mme. Darzac joined to some extent in the conversation, exchanging now and then a few commonplaces with Arthur Rance. Is it necessary for me to add that at this time, after the scene between Rouletabille and Mathilde, which I had witnessed from my window, I expected to see her in a most wretched state—almost overcome by the vision of Larsan, which had surged up in front of her eyes? But no: on the contrary, I discovered a remarkable difference between the terrified aspect with which she had approached us at the station, for instance, and the easy, composed manner which was hers, at present. One would have said that she had been relieved by the sight of the apparition, and when I expressed my opinion to Rouletabille later in the evening, I discovered that he shared it, and he explained the reason for Mathilde's change of manner in the simplest possible fashion. The unhappy woman had dreaded nothing so much as the thought that she was going mad, and the certainty that she had not been the victim of a mental delusion, cruel as that certainty was, had served to make her a little more calm. She preferred to fight even against the living Larsan than against a phantom. In the first interview which she had had with Rouletabille in the Square Tower, while I was dressing for dinner, she had, my young friend told me, been completely possessed by the dread that insanity was coming upon her. Rouletabille, in telling me of this interview, acknowledged to me that he had taken altogether different means to calm Mathilde from those which Robert Darzac had employed—that is, he made no effort to conceal from her that her eyes had seen clearly and had seen Frederic Larsan. When she was told that Robert Darzac had only denied the truth to her because he feared for its effect upon her, and that he had been the first to telegraph to Rouletabille to come to their aid, she heaved a sigh so long and so deep that it was almost a sob. She took Rouletabille's hands in her own and covered them with kisses, just as a mother kisses the hands of her little child. Evidently she was instinctively drawn toward the youth by all the mysterious forces of maternal affection, in spite of the fact that she had every reason to believe that her child had died years before. It was just at this point that the two had first noticed through the window of the tower the form of Frederic Larsan, standing erect in the boat. At first, both had remained, stupefied, motionless and mute at the sight. Then a cry of rage escaped from the agonised heart of Rouletabille, and he longed to pursue the man and reckon with him, face to face. I have told how Mathilde held him back, clinging to him upon the parapet. In her mind, apparently, horrible as was this resurrection of Larsan, it was less horrible than the continual and supernatural resurrection of a Larsan who had no existence save in her own diseased brain. She no longer saw Larsan everywhere around her. She saw him in the flesh, as he was.

At one moment trembling with nervousness, the next gentle and composed, now patient and in another instant impatient, Mathilde, even while conversing with Arthur Rance, showed for her husband the most charming and sweetest solicitude imaginable. She was attentive to him at every moment, serving him herself, and smiling gently at him as she did so, watching him carefully, to be sure that he was not overtired and that the light did not strike too near his eyes. Robert thanked her for her cares, but seemed none the less frightfully unhappy. And his demeanour compelled me to recollect the fact that the resuscitation of Larsan would undoubtedly recall to Mme. Darzac that before she was Mme. Darzac, she had been Mme. Jean Roussel Ballmeyer Larsan before God and herself, and even, so far as the transatlantic laws are concerned, before men as well.

If the design of Larsan in showing himself had been to deal a frightful blow to a happiness which had yet scarcely begun, he had completely succeeded. And, perhaps, as the historian of all parts of this strange affair, I ought to mention the fact that Mathilde had given Robert Darzac at once to understand that she did not regard herself as his wife, since the man to whom she had pledged herself in her early girlhood was still living. I have said that Mathilde Stangerson had been brought up in a very religious manner, not by her father, who cared little for such things, but by her female relatives, especially her old aunt in Cincinnati. The scientific studies which she had pursued with her father had in no wise impaired her faith, while the latter had taken care never to speak against religion to his daughter. She had preserved it, even in the deepest researches into the professor's theory of the creation. She said to him that no matter how plausibly he might prove that everything came from nothingness, that is to say, from the atmosphere, and returned to nothingness in the end, it remained to prove that that nothing, originating from nothing, had not been created by God. And, as she was a good Catholic, she believed that the Vicar of Christ on earth was the Pope. I might have perhaps passed over these religious beliefs of Mathilde in silence, if they had not had so strong an influence on the resolution which she had taken in regard to her second husband, when she discovered that her first husband was still alive. It had seemed to her that Larsan's death had been proven beyond the slightest doubt, and she had gone to her new husband as a widow with the approval of her confessor. And now she learned that in the sight of Heaven, she was not a widow, but a bigamist But, at all events, the catastrophe might not be irremediable, and she herself proposed to poor M. Darzac that the case should be propounded to the ecclesiastical courts of Rome for a settlement as quickly as possible. Thus it was that M. and Mme. Robert Darzac, forty-eight hours after their marriage in the Church of St. Nicolas du Chardonnet, were separated by a gulf over which one could not and the other would not pass. The reader will comprehend from this brief explanation the mournful demeanour of Robert and the gentle sweetness displayed toward him by Mathilde.

Without being entirely conversant with all these details on the evening of which I write, I nevertheless suspected most of them. Leaving the Darzacs, my eyes wandered to the neighbour of Mme. Darzac, M. Arthur William Rance, and my thoughts were taking a new turn, when they were suddenly arrested by the butler's coming to say that Bernier, the concierge, requested to speak to M. Rouletabille. My friend arose, excused himself, and left the room.

"What!" I cried. "The Berniers are no longer at the Glandier?"

Readers of "The Mystery of the Yellow Room" will recall that these Berniers—the man and his wife—were the concierges of M. Stangerson at Ste. Geneviève-des Bois. I have told in that work how Rouletabille had had them set at liberty when they were accused of complicity in the attempt made at the pavilion de la Chenaie. Their gratitude to the young reporter on this account had been of the greatest, and Rouletabille had been ever since the object of their devotion. M. Stangerson replied to my exclamation by informing me that all the servants had left the Glandier at the time that he himself had abandoned it. As the Rances had need of concierges for the Fort of Hercules, the Professor had been glad to send them his faithful domestics, of whom he had never had reason to complain except for one slight infraction of the game laws, which had turned out most unfortunately for them. Now they were lodged in one of the towers of the postern, where they kept the gate, and from which they admitted those who entered and dismissed those who wished to go out of the fort.

Rouletabille had not appeared in the least astonished when the butler announced that Bernier wished to say a word to him, and from that fact, I drew the conclusion that he must be already aware of his presence at Rochers Rouges. So I discovered, without being very greatly surprised at it, that Rouletabille had made excellent use of the few minutes during which I believed him to be in his room, and which I had given up to my toilet and to chatting with M. Darzac.

The unexpected exit of Rouletabille sent a chill to my heart and seemed to spread a general sensation of alarm throughout the company. Every one of us who was in the secret asked himself whether this summons had not something to do with some important event connected with the return of Larsan. Mme. Darzac was very restless. And because Mathilde showed herself to be disturbed and nervous, I fancied that M. Arthur Rance thought that it behooved him to display some little anxiety. And it may be as well to say at this point that M. Arthur Rance and his wife were not aware of the whole of the unfortunate story of Professor Stangerson's daughter. It had seemed useless to inform them of the fact of Mathilde's secret marriage to Jean Roussel, afterward known as Larsan. That was something which concerned only the family. But they were fully aware—Arthur Rance from having been mixed up in the Glandier business, and his wife from what he had told her—of the way in which the Secret Service agent had pursued the young woman who was now Mme. Darzac. The crimes of Larsan were explained in the eyes of Arthur Rance by a mad passion for Mathilde, and this was by no means surprising to the young American who had been for so long in love with her himself, and who perceived in all of Larsan's acts merely the indications of an insane and hopeless love. As to Mme. Edith, I soon found out why the events which had transpired at the Glandier had not seemed so simple to her when they were related to her as they had to her husband. For her to share his opinions on the subject, it would have been necessary for her to have seen Mathilde with eyes as enthusiastic as those of Arthur Rance, and, on the contrary, her thoughts (which I had good opportunities to read without her suspecting it) ran about in this way: "But what on earth is there about this woman which could inspire such an insane passion, lasting for years and years in the heart of any man! Here is a woman for whose sake a detective officer becomes a murderer; for whom a temperate man becomes a drunkard, and for whom an innocent man permits himself to be pronounced guilty of a felony. What is there about her more than there is about myself who owe my husband to the fact that she refused him before he ever saw me? What is the charm about her? She isn't even young. And yet even now my husband forgets all about me while he is looking at her." That is what I read in Edith's eyes as she watched her husband gazing at Mathilde. Ah, those black eyes of the gentle, languid Mme. Edith!

I am congratulating myself upon the explanations which I have made to the reader. It is as well that he should know the sentiments which dwelt in the heart of each one concerned at the moment when all were about to have their own parts to play in the strange and awful drama which was already drawing near in the shadow which enveloped the Fort of Hercules. As yet, I have said nothing of Old Bob nor of Prince Galitch, but, never fear, their turn will come! I have taken as a rule in the narration of this affair to paint things and people as nearly as possible as they appeared to me in the development of events. Thus the reader will pass through all the phases of the tragedy as we ourselves passed through them—anguish and peace, mysteries and their unravelling, misunderstanding and comprehension. If the light breaks upon the mind of the reader before the hour when it broke upon mine, so much the better. As he will be conversant with the same circumstances, neither more nor less, which came under our observation, he will prove to himself if he solves the mystery before it is revealed to him, that he possesses a brain worthy to rank with that of Rouletabille.

We finished our repast without our young friend having reappeared, and we arose from the table without having mentioned to each other any of the thoughts which troubled us. Mathilde immediately asked me where I thought Rouletabille had gone. As she left the dining room, and I walked with her as far as the entrance to the fort; M. Darzac and Mme. Edith followed us. M. Stangerson had bidden us good-night. Arthur Rance, who had disappeared for a moment, joined us while we were at the passageway. The night was clear and the moon shone brightly. Someone had lighted the lanterns in the archway, however, in spite of the fact that their rays were not needed for seeing. As we passed beneath the arch, we heard Rouletabille speaking, as though he were encouraging those whom he addressed.

"Come on! One more effort!" he cried, and the voice which answered him was husky and panting, like that of a sailor who was working with his fellows to bring his bark into port. Finally, a great tumult filled our ears. It was the two portals of the immense iron doors, which were being closed for the first time in more than an hundred years.

Mme. Edith looked astonished at the act of her guest, and asked what had happened to the gate, which had always served in place of the doors since she had been mistress of the place. But Arthur Rance caught her arm, and she seemed to understand that he was impressing upon her that she must keep silence. But that did not keep her from exclaiming in a not-too-well pleased tone:

"Really! Anyone would think that we expected to undergo a siege!"

But Rouletabille beckoned our group into the garden and announced to us in a jesting tone that if any of us had any desire to make a trip to the village, we must give it up for that evening, for the order had gone forth and no one could leave the château or enter it. Pere Jacques, he added, still pretending to jest, was charged with the carrying out of the command, and everyone knew that it was impossible to bribe the faithful old servitor. It was then that I learned for the first time that Pere Jacques, whom I had known so well at the Glandier, had accompanied Professor Stangerson on his visit and was acting as his valet. That night he was sleeping in a tiny closet in "la Louve," near his master's bed room, but Rouletabille had changed that, and it was Pere Jacques who took the place of the concierges in the tower marked A.

"But where are the Berniers?" cried Mme. Edith.

"They are installed in the Square Tower, in the room on the left, near the entrance; they are to act as caretakers of the Square Tower," replied Rouletabille.

"But the Square Tower doesn't need any caretakers!" exclaimed Edith, whose vexation was plainly visible.

"That, Madame," returned the young reporter, "is what we cannot be sure of."

He made no further explanations, but he took M. Arthur Rance to one side and informed him that he ought to tell his wife about the reappearance of Larsan. If there was to be the slightest chance of hiding the truth from M. Stangerson, it could scarcely be accomplished without the aid and intelligence of Mme. Edith. And, then, too, it would be as well, henceforward, for all of those in the Fort of Hercules to be prepared for everything, *and surprised at nothing*!

The next act of Rouletabille was to make us walk across the court and place ourselves at the postern of the gardener. I have said that this postern (H) commanded the entrance to the inner court; but at that point the moat had been filled up a long time ago. Rouletabille, to our amazement, declared that the next day he intended to have the moat dug out and to replace the drawbridge. For the present, he busied himself with ordering the postern to be closed more securely by the servants of the château by means of a sort of fortification built from the boards and bricks which had been used in the repairs of the château, and which had not yet been taken away by the workmen. Thus the château was barricaded and Rouletabille laughed softly to himself, for Mme. Edith, having been apprised by her husband of the facts of the case, made no further objection, but contented herself with smiling a little contemptuously at the timidity of her guests, who were transforming the old stronghold into an absolutely impenetrable spot, because they were afraid of just one man—one man, all alone. But Mme. Edith did not know what manner of man this was. She had not lived through the mysteries of the yellow room.

As to the others—Arthur Rance among them—they found it perfectly natural and reasonable that Rouletabille should fortify the place against that which was unknown and mysterious and invisible, and which plotted in the night they knew not what against the Fort of Hercules.

At the newly fortified postern, Rouletabille had stationed no one, for he reserved that place that night for himself. From there he could obtain a complete view of both the inner and outer courts. It was a strategic point which commanded a view of the whole château. One could reach the apartment of the Darzacs only after passing by Pere Jacques in A; by Rouletabille at H, and by the Berniers, who guarded the Square Tower at the door marked K. The young man had decided that it would be better for those on guard not to retire that night. As we passed by the "oubliette" in the Court of Charles the Bold, I saw by the light of the moon that someone had displaced the circular board which covered it. I saw also on the margin a flask attached to a cord. Rouletabille explained to me that he had wished to know if this old oubliette (which was really nothing but a well) corresponded with the sea, and that he had found that the water was clear and sweet—a proof that it had nothing to do with the Mediterranean.

The young man walked for a few steps with Mme. Darzac, who immediately took leave of us and entered the Square Tower. M. Darzac and Arthur Rance, at the request of Rouletabille, remained with us. Some words of excuse addressed to Mme. Edith made her understand that she was being politely asked to retire, and she bade us good-night with a nonchalant grace, flinging the words, "Good-night, M. le Captain," at Rouletabille over her shoulder as she passed him.

When we were alone, we men, Rouletabille beckoned us toward the postern into the little room of the gardener, a dark, low-ceiled apartment, where we were surprised to find how easily we could see anything that passed near by without being seen ourselves. There, Arthur Rance, Robert Darzac, Rouletabille and myself, without even lighting a lamp, held our first council of war. In truth, I know not what other name to give to this reunion of frightened men, hidden behind the stones of this old fortress.

"We may make our plans here in tranquillity," began Rouletabille. "No one can hear us, and we shall not be surprised by anyone. If any person should attempt to pass the first gate which Jacques is guarding without the old man's seeing him, we shall be immediately warned by the sentinel whom I have stationed in the very middle of the court, hidden in the ruins of the chapel. I have placed your gardener, Mattoni, at that point, M. Rance. I believe from what I have been told that you can depend upon the man. Is not that your opinion?"

I listened to Rouletabille with admiration. Mme. Edith was right. He had indeed constituted himself a captain, and he had not left one impregnable spot without defence, and had neglected nothing in his cogitations. I felt certain that he would never surrender, no matter on what terms, and that he would prefer death to capitulation, either for himself or for any of the rest of us. What a brave little commander he was And, indeed, it seemed to me that he displayed more bravery in undertaking the defence of the Fort of Hercules against Larsan than the Lords of Mortola had shown in holding the castle against a thousand of the enemy. For they had fought merely against shot and shell and spears. And what had we to fight against? The darkness. Where was our enemy? Everywhere and nowhere. We were able neither to see him, nor to know his whereabouts, nor to guess his designs, nor to take the offensive ourselves, ignorant as we were of where our blows might fall. There remained for us only to be on guard, to shut ourselves in, to watch and to wait.

M. Arthur Rance assured Rouletabille that he could answer for his gardener, Mattoni, and our young man proceeded to explain to us in a general fashion the situation. He lit his pipe, took three or four puffs, and said:

"Well, here we are. Can we hope that Larsan, after having so insolently flaunted himself before us, at our very doors, in order to defy us, will confine himself to such a platonic manifestation? Will he consider that he has accomplished enough in bringing trouble, terror and consternation among the members of the besieged party in the garrison? And content with what he has done, will he go away? I hardly think so. First, because such a thing would be foreign to his character—for he loves a fight, and is never satisfied with a partial success; and, secondly, because no one of us has the power to drive him off. Consider that he can do anything that he will to injure us, but that we can make no move against him save to defend ourselves if he strikes, provided we are able when it may suit him to do so. We have, of course, no hope of any help from outside. And he knows it well; that is what makes him so bold and audacious. Whom can we call to our aid?"

"The authorities," suggested Arthur Rance. He spoke with some hesitation, for he felt that if this plan had not been entertained by Rouletabille, there must be some reason for it.

The young reporter looked at his host with an air of pity, which was not entirely free from reproach. And he said in a chilly tone, which showed plainly to Arthur Rance how little value there was in his proposition:

"You ought to understand, Monsieur, that I did not save Larsan from French justice at Versailles to deliver him over to Italian justice at Rochers Rouges."

M. Arthur Rance, who was, as I have said, ignorant of the first marriage of Professor Stangerson's daughter, could not understand, as did the rest of us, the impossibility of revealing the existence of Larsan without stirring up (especially after the ceremony at St. Nicolas du Chardonnet) the worst of scandals and the most dreadful of catastrophes: but certain inexplicable incidents of the trial at Versailles had impressed him sufficiently to make him realize that we dreaded above all things to bring again to the public mind what someone had called "The Mystery of Mlle. Stangerson."

He comprehended this on the evening of which I speak better than he had ever done before, and knew that Larsan must hold one of those terrible secrets on which life and honour depend, and with which the magistrates of the world can have no concern.

M. Rance bowed to M. Robert Darzac without uttering a word: but the salute signified the declaration that M. Arthur Rance was ready to combat for the cause of Mathilde, whatever it might be, as a noble chevalier, who does not bother himself about the reason of the battle in the moment when he dies for his lady. At least, I thus interpreted his gesture, and I felt certain that, in spite of his recent marriage, the American had by no means forgotten his old love.

M. Darzac said:

"This man must disappear, but in silence, whether we move him by our entreatics, or bribe him or kill him. But the first condition of his disappearance is to keep the fact that he has reappeared at all a secret. Above all—and I am speaking of the heartfelt wish of Mme. Darzac as well as my own—M. Stangerson must never know that we are menaced by the blows of this monster."

"Mme. Darzac's wishes are commands," replied Rouletabille. "M. Stangerson shall know nothing."

We went on to discuss the situation in regard to the servants and to what one might expect from them. Happily, Pere Jacques and the Berniers were already partly in the secret and would be astonished at nothing. Mattoni was devoted enough to render unquestioning obedience to Mme. Edith. The others did not count. Later there would be Walter, the servant of Old Bob, but he had accompanied his master to Paris, and would not return until he did.

Rouletabille arose, exchanged through the window a signal with Bernier, who was standing erect upon the threshold of the Square Tower. Then he came back to us and sat down again.

"Larsan probably is not far off," he said. "During dinner I made a tour of observation around the place. We possess at the North gate a natural means of defence which is really marvellous, and which completely replaces the old fortifications of the château. We have there fifty paces away, at the western shore, the two frontier posts of the French and Italian revenue officers, whose untiring vigilance may be of the greatest assistance to us. Pere Bernier is on the most friendly terms with these worthy people, and I am going with him to talk to them. The Italian customs officer speaks only Italian, but the French officer speaks both languages, as well as the patois of the country, and it is this man, whom Bernier tells me is called Michael, to whom I look to be of the greatest use to us. Through his means we have already learned that the two revenue posts are much interested in the strange manoeuvres of the little boat, which belongs to Tullio, the fisherman, whom they call 'the hangman of the sea.' Old Tullio is one of the former acquaintances of the customs men. He is the most skillful smuggler on the coast. He had with him this evening in his boat an individual whom the revenue officers had never seen. The boat, Tullio and the passenger, all disappeared at the Pointe de Garibaldi. I have been there with Pere Bernier, and we found nothing, any more than M. Darzac, who visited the spot before us. However, Larsan must have landed.

I have a presentiment of the fact. In any case, I am sure that Tullio's little boat is anchored near the Pointe de Garabaldi."

"You are sure of that?" cried M. Darzac.

"What reason have you for thinking so?" I demanded.

"Bah!" exclaimed Rouletabille. "It left the marks of the keel in the sand on the bank, and when they anchored, they let fall a little lantern, which I picked up and which the revenue officers recognised as the one used by Tullio when he fishes in the waters on calm nights."

"Larsan certainly landed!" repeated M. Darzac. "He is at Rochers Rouges."

"In any case, if the boat has been left at Rochers Rouges, he has not come back here," exclaimed Rouletabille. "The two revenue posts are situated upon the narrow road which leads from Rochers Rouges to France, and are placed in such a manner that no one can pass by whether by day or by night without being seen. You know besides that the Red Rocks from which the village takes its name from a cul de sac, and that a sentinel is on guard in front of these rocks every hundred meters around the frontier. The sentinel passes between the rocks and the sea. The rocks are steep and form a terrace sixty meters high."

"That is true," said Arthur Rance, who had not recently spoken, and who seemed greatly interested. "It is not easy to scale the rocks."

"He will have hidden himself in the grottoes," said Darzac. "There are some deep pockets in the terrace."

"I thought of that," said Rouletabille. "And I went back alone to Rochers Rouges, after I left Pere Bernier."

"That was very imprudent!" I said.

"It was very prudent," corrected Rouletabille. "I had some things to say to Larsan which I did not wish a third party to hear. Well, I went back to Rochers Rouges and called Larsan's name through all the caves."

"You called him?" cried Arthur Rance.

"Yes, I shouted into the gathering night; I waved my handkerchief as the soldiers wave their flag of truce. But whether it was that he heard me and saw my white flag or not, he did not answer."

"Perhaps he was not there," I suggested.

"Perhaps not: I don't know. I heard a noise in the grotto."

"And you did not enter?" demanded Arthur Rance.

"No," replied Rouletabille, quietly. "But you do not think that it was because I was afraid of him, do you?"

"Let us run!" we all cried in one breath, rising at the same moment. "Let us go and finish up the business immediately."

"I don't think that we shall ever have a better chance of meeting Larsan," said Arthur Rance. "We can do what we like with him at the bottom of Rochers Rouges."

Darzac and Arthur Rance were already starting off; I waited to see what Rouletabille would say. He calmed the two men with a gesture, and begged them to be seated again.

"It is necessary to remember," he said, "that Larsan would have acted exactly as he has done if he had wished to lure us tonight to the grotto of Rochers Rouges. He has shown himself to us; he has landed almost under our eyes at the Point of Garabaldi; he might as well have shouted under our windows, "You know I am at Rochers Rouges. I'll wait for you there." He would have been neither more explicit or more eloquent."

"You went to Rochers Rouges," resumed Arthur Rance, who I saw was deeply impressed with the arguments of Rouletabille—"and he did not show himself. He hid himself, meditating on some horrible crime to be committed tonight. We must have him out of that grotto."

"Doubtless," replied Rouletabille, "my promenade to Rochers Rouges produced no result because I was all alone—but if we all go, I can assure you that we shall find some results on our return."

"On our return?" echoed Darzac who did not understand.

"Yes," explained Rouletabille: "on our return to the château, where we have left Mne. Darzac all alone—and where, perhaps, we may not find her. Oh, of course," he added, as a general silence fell upon his companions, "it is only a hypothesis. But at this time we have no other means of reasoning than by hypothesis."

We looked at each other and this hypothesis over whelmed us. Evidently, without Rouletabille, we should have committed a terrible blunder and perhaps have been responsible for a terrible disaster.

Rouletabille arose and continued, thoughtfully:

"You see, tonight there is nothing that we can do except to barricade ourselves. It is only a temporary barricade, for I want the place put in an absolutely unassailable state tomorrow. I have had the iron doors closed and Pere Jacques is guarding them. I have stationed Mattoni as sentinel at the chapel. I have established a barrier under the postern, the only vulnerable point of the inner court, and I will guard that myself. Pere Bernier will watch all night at the door of the Square

Tower, and Mere Bernier, who has a good pair of eyes, and to whom I have given a spyglass, will remain until morning on the platform of the tower. Sainclair will station himself in the little palm leaf pavilion upon the terrace of the Round Tower. From the height of this terrace he will watch as I do all the inner court and the boulevards and parapets. M. Rance and M. Darzac will go into the garden and walk until daylight, the one toward the boulevard on the west, the other toward the boulevard on the east—the two boulevards which are at the edge of the outer court near the sea. The vigil will be hard tonight, because we are not yet organised. Tomorrow we shall draw up a set of rules for our little garrison, and a list of the trustworthy domestics upon whom we may depend with security.

"If there is one on the place who could come under the slightest suspicion, he must be dismissed at once. You will bring here to this cell all the arms which you can gather—rifles and revolvers. We will divide them among those who do guard duty. The sentinel is to draw upon every person who does not reply to 'Who goes there?' and who is not recognised. There is no need of a password, it would be useless. Let the countersign be to utter one's name and to show one's face. Besides, it is only ourselves who have the right to pass. Beginning tomorrow morning I will have raised at the inner entrance of the North gate the grating which until today formed its exterior entrance—the entrance which is closed, henceforth, by the iron doors; and in the daytime the commissaires can come as far as this grating with their provisions. They will place their wares in the little lodge in the tower where I have stationed Pere Jacques. At seven o'clock every night, the iron doors will be closed. Tomorrow morning M. Arthur Rance will send for builders, masons and carpenters. Every person on the place will be counted, and no one allowed, under any pretext, to pass the door of the second court. Before seven o'clock in the evening every one will be counted again, and the workpeople will be allowed to go out. In this one day the men must completely finish their work, which will consist of making a door for my postern, repairing a small breach in the wall which joins the New Castle to the Tower of Charles the Bold and another little break near the Round Tower (B in the plan), which defends the northeast corner of the outer court. After that, I shall be tranquil, and Mme. Darzac, who is forbidden to leave the château under the new order, having been placed in security, I may attempt a sortie and enter seriously into the search for the camp of Larsan. Come, M. Rance, to arms' Bring me some weapons to pass around this evening. I have loaned my own revolver to Pere Bernier, who is keeping guard before the door of Mme. Darzac's apartments."

Anyone not knowing of the events at the Glandier who had heard the words spoken by Rouletabille would have considered both him who spoke and us who listened to be beside ourselves. But, I repeat, if anyone had lived, like myself, through that terrible and mysterious time, he would have done what I did—loaded his revolver and waited for dawn without uttering a word.

VIII

Which Contains Some Pages From the History of Jean Roussel-Larsan Ballmeyer

A n hour later, we were all at our posts, passing along the parapets in the moonlight, keeping close watch upon the land, the sky and the water, and listening anxiously to the slightest sounds of the night— the sighing of the sea and the voices of the birds which began to sing at about three o'clock in the morning. Mme. Edith, who said that she could not sleep, came out and talked to Rouletabille at his postern. The lad called me, placed me in charge of his postern and of Mrs. Rance, and made his rounds. The fair Edith was in the most charming humour. She looked as fresh as a rose washed in dew, and she seemed to be greatly amused at the wan countenance of her husband, to whom she had brought out a glass of whisky.

"It's the funniest thing I ever heard of," she exclaimed, clapping her tiny hands. "All of you keeping watch out here like this! How I wish I knew your Larsan I'm sure I should adore him!"

I shuddered involuntarily at the words she uttered so lightly. Beyond a doubt there do exist romantic little creatures who fear nothing, and who in their carelessness jest at fate. Ah! if the unhappy girl had only realised what was to come!

I spent two delightful hours with Mme. Edith, during the greater part of which I related to her some facts regarding the history of Ballmeyer. And since this occasion presents itself, I will at this time relate to the reader, in historical order—if I may use an expression which perfectly interprets my meaning—the characteristics and circumstances in the career of Larsan-Ballmeyer, some of which had been sufficient to make it doubtful whether he still lived at the time that he appeared to play so unexpected a part in "The Mystery of the Yellow Room." As this man's powers will be seen to extend in "The Perfume of the Lady in Black" to heights which some may believe inaccessible, I judge it to be my duty to prepare the mind of the reader to admit in the end that I am only the transcriber of an affair the like of which never has been known before, and that I have invented nothing. And, moreover, Rouletabille, in the event that I might have the hardihood to add to such a wonderful and veracious history any rhetorical ornaments or exaggerations, would certainly contradict me and riddle my story as with bullets. The great interests at stake are such that the slightest exaggeration would assuredly entail the most terrible consequences, so that I shall keep strictly to the exact details of my narrative, even at the risk of making it seem a little dry and methodical. I will refer those who believe in actual records to the stenographic reports of the trial at Versailles. M. Andre-Hesse and M. Henri Robert, who appeared for M. Robert Darzac, made admirable addresses, to which the public may easily obtain access. And it must not be forgotten that before destiny had brought Larsan-Ballmeyer and Joseph Rouletabille into contact, the elegantly mannered bandit had given considerable trouble to the authorities. We have only to open the files of the *Gazette les Tribuneaux* and to read the account of the day when Larsan was condemned by the Court of Assizes to ten years at hard labour, to be assured on this score. Then, one will understand that there is no need of inventing anything about a man concerning whom one can with truth relate such a history: and thus the reader, knowing the sort of man that he is—that is to say, his manner of working and his incredible audacity—will refrain from smiling because Joseph Rouletabille placed a drawbridge between Larsan-Ballmeyer and Mathilde Darzac.

M. Albert Bataille of *le Figaro*, who has published an admirable work on "Criminal and Civil Causes," has devoted some interesting pages to Ballmeyer.

Ballmeyer had a happy childhood and youth. He did not become a criminal as so many others have done because driven to evil doing by the hard blows of poverty and misery. The son of a rich broker in the Rue Molay, he might have chosen any vocation that he desired, but his preferred calling was to lay hands upon the money of other people. At an early age, he decided to become a swindler, just as another lad might have decided to become an engineer. His debut was a stroke of genius, and the history of it is almost incredible. Ballmeyer stole a letter addressed to his father containing a considerable sum of money. Then he took the train for Lyons and from there wrote his parent as follows:

"Monsieur, I am an old soldier, retired and with a medal of honour to show that I have served my country. My son, a post office clerk, has stolen in the mails a letter addressed to you and containing money, to pay a gambling debt. I have called the members of the family together. In a few days we shall be able to raise the sum necessary to repay you. You are a father. Have pity upon a father. Do not bring me down in sorrow and shame to my grave."

M. Ballmeyer willingly granted the petition. He is still waiting for his first remittance—or, rather, he has ceased to expect it, for the law apprised him ten years ago of the identity of the culprit.

Ballmeyer, relates M. Albert Bataille, seems to have received from nature all the gifts which go to make the successful swindler: a wonderful diversity, the talent of persuading new acquaintances to believe in him, the careful attention to the smallest details, the genius for completely disguising himself (he even took the precaution along this line of having his linen marked with different initials every time that he judged it expedient to change his name). But his strongest characteristic of all was his astonishing aptitude for evasion—for coquetting with fraud, for mocking at and defying justice. This was evinced in the malignant pleasure which he took in speaking of himself at Parquet as among those who might have been guilty, knowing how little importance would be attached by the magistrate by the clues which he gave.

This delight in jesting at the judges was apparent in every act of his life.

While he was doing military duty, Ballmeyer stole his companion's box and accused the captain.

He committed a theft of forty thousand francs from the Maison Furet, and immediately afterward denounced M. Furet as having stolen it himself.

THE FURET AFFAIR REMAINED FOR a long time celebrated among judicial records under the appellation of "the coup of the telephone." Science, applied as an aid to knavery, has never given anything better.

Ballmeyer appropriated a draft for six thousand livres sterling from the messenger of Messrs. Furet, brothers, who were note brokers in the Rue Poissoniere, and who allowed him desk room in their offices.

He went to the Rue Poissoniere, into the house of M. Furet, and, imitating the voice of M. Edouard Furet, asked over the telephone of M. Cohen, a banker, whether he would be willing to discount the draft. M. Cohen replied in the affirmative, and ten minutes later, Ballmeyer, after having cut the telephone wire to prevent further communication and possible explanations, sent for the money by a companion named Rigaud, whom he had known not long before in the African battalion, where their common interests had made them useful to each other.

Ballmeyer kept the lion's share for himself: then he rushed to the court to denounce Rigaud, and, as I have said, M. Furet himself.

A dramatic scene took place when accuser and accused were confronted with each other in the cabinet of M. Espierre, the judge of instruction who had charge of the affair.

"You know, my dear Furet," said Ballmeyer to the amased broker, "I am heart-broken at being obliged to expose you, but you must tell the Justice the truth. It is not an affair from which you need fear serious consequences. Why don't you confess? You needed forty thousand francs to pay a little debt incurred at the race track and you intended to pay back the sum. It was you who telephoned?"

"I! I!" stammered M. Edouard Furet, almost breathless with rage and astonishment.

"You may as well confess," said Ballmeyer. "No one could mistake your voice."

The bold thief was detected within eight days and was caught; and the police furnished such a report upon him that M. Cruppi, then attorney general, now Minister of Commerce, presented to M. Furet the most humble excuses of the Department of Justice. Rigaud was also tried and condemned to twenty years at hard labour.

One might go on relating this kind of stories about Ballmeyer indefinitely. At that time, before he had entered upon the darker and more horrible pages of his career, he played a comedy—and what a comedy! It may be as well to give in detail the history of one of his escapes. Nothing could be more immensely comical than the adventure of the prisoner composing a long memorial during his trial for the sole purpose of hanging over the table of the judge, M. Villars, and of turning over the papers in order to obtain a glimpse of the formula of orders of discharge.

When he was sent back to jail at Mazas, the fellow wrote a letter signed "Villars," in which, according to the prescribed formula, M. Villars requested the superintendent of the prison to set the prisoner, Ballmeyer, at liberty without delay. But he had no paper of the kind used by the Judge for such matters.

However, so small a thing as that scarcely embarrassed Ballmeyer. He went back to the courthouse in the morning, hiding the letter in his sleeve, protested his innocence and feigning great indignation and anger. He picked up the seal that lay on the table and gesticulated with it in expressing his wrath, and he knocked the inkstand over on the blue trousers of his guard. While the poor fellow, surrounded by the inmates of the court-room, who condoled with him on his ill luck, was sadly sponging off his "Number One," Ballmeyer profited by the general diversion to apply a strong pressure of the stamp upon the order of discharge, and then began loudly excusing himself to the soldier.

The trick succeeded. The thief made his way out amid the confusion, and, negligently tossing the signed and sealed paper to the guards, remarked carelessly:

"What is M. Villars thinking of to order me to carry his papers? Does he take me for his servant?"

Then he went back to his seat. The guards picked up the paper, and one of them carried it to the warden at Mazas, to whom it was addressed. It was the order to set Ballmeyer at liberty without delay. The same night, Ballmeyer was free.

This was his second escape. Arrested for the Furet affair, he had gotten away once by throwing pepper in the eyes of the guard who was taking him to the station, and that same evening he was present in evening dress at a first night at the Comedie Francaise. Prior to this, at the time when he had been sentenced by court martial to five years' imprisonment because he had robbed his companion, he had made his way out of the Cherche Midi by having one of his comrades forge an order of release for him. A variation of the same plan had served him well once more.

But one would never finish if one tried to relate all the amazing adventures of Ballmeyer.

Known at various times as the Count de Maupas, Vicomte Drouet d'erion, Comte de Motteville, Comte de Bonneville, and under many other aliases, as an elegant man about town, setting the fashion, he frequented the summer resorts and watering places—Biarritz, Aix les Bains, Luchon, losing in play at the club as much as ten thousand francs in one evening, surrounded by pretty women, who envied each other his attentions—for this fellow was extremely popular with the fair sex. In his regiment, he had made a con quest—happily platonic—of the Colonel's daughter. Do you know the type now?

Well, it was with this man that Joseph Rouletabille was going to fight.

I thought that morning that I had sufficiently informed Mme. Edith in regard to the personality of the bandit. She listened so silently that my attention was finally drawn to the fact that she had not uttered a remark in some time, and, bending down, I saw that she was fast asleep. This circumstance should not have given me a very good opinion of the little creature. But, as I watched her sleeping face at my leisure, I felt springing up in my soul feelings which I later endeavoured in vain to chase away from my mind.

The night passed without any event. When the day dawned, I saluted it with a deep sigh of relief. Nevertheless, Rouletabille did not permit me to retire until eight o'clock in the morning, after he had settled on how matters should go on through the day. He was already in the midst of the workmen whom he had summoned, and who were labouring actively in repairing the breaches of the tower B. The work was done so expeditiously and so promptly that the strong château of Hercules was soon sealed as hermetically close as it was possible for a building to be. Seated on a big boulder in the bright sunlight, Rouletabille began to draw upon his note book the plan which I have submitted to the reader, and he said to me while I, worn out with my vigil, was making absurd efforts to keep my eyes open:

"You see, Sainclair, these people believe that I am fortifying the place to defend myself. Well, that is merely a small part of the truth, for I am fortifying the place because reason bids me do so. And, if I close up the breaches, it is less in order that Larsan cannot get in than for the sake of depriving my reason of any chance of accusing me of carelessness. For instance, I can never reason in a forest. How will you reason in a forest? There, reason flies away on every side. But in a closed up château! My friend, it is like a sealed casket. If you are inside and are not insane, your reasoning powers must come back to you."

"Yes, yes," I murmured sleepily, nodding.

"That's it—your reason will come back to you—"

"Well, well, never mind!" answered Rouletabille. "Go to bed, old fellow. You are walking in your sleep now."

IX

In Which "Old Bob" Unexpectedly Arrives

When I heard a knock at my door about eleven o'clock in the morning and the voice of Mere Bernier told me that Rouletabille wanted me to get up, I threw my window wide open and looked out in delight. The bay was of an incomparable beauty, and the sea was so transparent that the rays of the sun pierced through it as they would have done through a mirror without quicksilver, so that one could perceive the rocks, the anemones and the moss in the sea bottom just as if the waters had ceased to cover them and left them bared to the eye. The harmonious curve of the bank on the Mentone side enclosed the sea like a flowery frame. The villas of Garavan, white and rose, looked like fresh flowers which had blossomed over night. The peninsula of Hercules was a bouquet which floated upon the waters and perfumed the old stones of the château.

Never had nature appeared to me more sweet, more delightful, more exquisite, nor, above all, more worthy of being loved. The serene air, the beautiful shore, the balmy sea, the purple mountains, all this picture to which my Northern senses were so little accustomed, evoked in my mind the thought of some tender, caressing human being. As these thoughts passed through my mind, I noticed a man who was lashing the sea. Oh! he gave it a box on the ear! I could have wept if I had been a poet! The miserable wretch appeared to be furiously angry. I could not understand what had excited his wrath in this tranquil spot, but he evidently felt that he had some serious cause for vexation, for he never ceased his blows. He was armed with an enormous cudgel, and, standing erect in a tiny boat, into which a timid child might have feared to entrust its weight, he administered to the sea, with the fiercest splashings, such a castigation as provoked the mute indignation of some strangers who were standing on the shore. But as everyone under all circumstances dreads to mix himself in what is none of his affairs, these persons made no protest. What was it that could have so deeply excited the savage? Perhaps it might have been the very calm of the sea which, after having been for a moment disturbed by the insult of the madman, resumed its peaceful tranquillity.

At this point, I was interrupted by the voice of Rouletabille, who told me that breakfast was nearly ready. Rouletabille appeared in the garb of a plasterer, his clothing showing plainly that he had been working in the fresh mortar. In one hand he held a foot rule and in the other a file. I asked him whether he had seen the man who was beating the water, and he told me that it was Tullio who was frightening the fishes to drive them into his nets. It was for this reason, I realised, that Tullio had obtained the nickname of the "hangman of the sea."

Rouletabille went on to tell me that he had asked Tullio that morning about the stranger whom he had rowed about in his boat the night before, and whom he had taken all around the peninsula of Hercules. Tullio had replied that he had no knowledge whatever of whom the man might be; that he was a crazy sort of fellow whom he had taken in as a passenger at Men tone, and who had given him five francs to land him at the point of Rochers Rouges.

I dressed myself quickly and joined Rouletabille, who told me that we were to have a new guest at luncheon, in the person of "Old Bob." We waited for a few moments for him to come to the table, and then, as he did not appear, we began our repast without him in the flowery frame of the round terrace of Charles the Bold.

There was served to us a delicious bouillabaisse, smoking hot, which seemed to have drawn the best of their flavors from fishes of all species, and was tinted by a little *vino del Paese*, and which, in the light and brightness of the daytime, contributed as much as all the precaution of Rouletabille toward making us feel serene and secure. In truth, we felt not the slightest fear of the dreaded Larsan under the beautiful sunshine of the brilliant heavens, whatever we may have felt in the pale gleam of the moon and stars. Ah, how forgetful and easily impressed human nature is 'I am ashamed to say it, but we were feeling rather proud (I speak for Arthur Rance and myself, and also for Edith, whose romantic and languid nature was superficial, as such are likely to be) of the fact that we could smile and speak with scorn of our nocturnal vigils and of our armed guard upon the boulevards of the citadel—when Old Bob made his appearance. And—let me say it: let me say it here—it was not this apparition which could have turned our thoughts toward anything dark or gloomy. I have rarely seen anything more droll than Old Bob walking in the blinding sun of the springtime in the Midi, with a tall hat of black beaver; his black trousers, his black spectacles, his white hair and his rosy cheeks. Yes, yes, we sat there and laughed in the tower of Charles the Bold. And Old Bob laughed with us. For Old Bob was as gay as a child.

What was this old savant doing at the Château of Hercules? Perhaps this is as good a time as any to explain. How could he have made up his mind to quit his collections in America and his work and his drawings and his museum in Philadelphia? For these reasons: The reader will not have forgotten that M. Arthur Rance was already looked upon in his own country as the anthropologist of the future at the time when his un happy infatuation for Mlle. Stangerson had weaned him away from his studies and made them almost distasteful to him. After his marriage to Miss Prescott, who was deeply interested in such matters, he felt that he could resume with pleasure his researches in the science of Gall and Lavater. But at the self-same time that they visited the azure shores in the autumn which preceded the events of this history, there was much discussion in regard to the new discoveries which M. Abbo had just made at Rochers Rouges. M.M. Julien, Riviere, Girardin, Delesot had come to the spot to work, and had succeeded in interesting the Institute and the Minister of Public Instruction in their discoveries. These discoveries soon created a profound sensation, for they proved beyond the shadow of a doubt that primeval man had lived in this spot before the glacial epoch. Without doubt, the proof of the existence of the man of the quarternary epoch had been found long before; but this epoch, extending certainly two hundred thousand years into the past, was interesting in that it fixed the quarternary epoch in the proper period. Learned men were always digging at Rochers Rouges, and they came upon surprise after surprise. However, the most beautiful of the grottoes—the Barma Grande, as they called it in the country side—had remained intact, for it was the private property of M. Abbo, who kept the "Restaurant of the Grotto" not far away on the sea shore. M. Abbo was determined to dig in his own grotto himself. But now, public report (for the event had passed the bounds of the scientific world and interested people generally) said that in the Barma Grande there had been found extraordinary human bones, skeletons remarkably preserved by the ferruginous earth, contemporaneous with the mammoths of the beginning of the quarternary epoch, or even of the end of the tertiary epoch.

Arthur Rance and his wife hastened to Mentone, and while the husband passed his days in antiquarian researches, going back two hundred thousand years, digging up with his own hands the humerus of the Barma Grande and measuring the skulls of his ancestors, his young wife seemed to experience an ever renewed pleasure in rambling over the mediaeval ruins of an old fortress which reared its massive silhouette above a little peninsula, united to Rochers Rouges by a few crumbling stones. The most romantic legends were attached to this relic of the old Genoese wars; and it seemed to Edith, pensively leaning from the highest terrace, in the most beautiful scene in the world, that she was one of those noble demoiselles of ancient times, whose romantic adventures she had so dearly loved to read in the pages of her favourite romances. The castle was for sale and the price was very reasonable. Arthur Rance purchased it, and by doing so made his wife the happiest of women. She sent for masons and furnishers, and within three months she had succeeded in transforming the old fortress into an exquisite nest of love—an ideal abode for a young person who revelled in "The Lady of the Lake," or "The Bride of Lammermoor."

When Arthur Rance had found himself standing beside the last skeleton discovered in the Barma Grande, and knew that the *elephus antiquus* had come out of the same bed of earth, he was beside himself with enthusiasm, and his first impulse had been to telegraph to Old Bob and tell him that it might be that someone had discovered, a few kilometers from Monte Carlo, the relics which the old savant had been seeking for so many years in the mountains of Patagonia. But the telegram never reached its destination, for Old Bob, who had previously promised to join his nephew and niece after they had been married for awhile, had already taken the steamer for Europe. Evidently report had already brought to him the story of the treasures of the Rochers Rouges. A few days after the cable had been dispatched, he landed at Marseilles and arrived at Mentone, where he became the companion of Arthur Rance and his wife in the Château of Hercules, which his very presence seemed to fill with life and gayety.

The gayety of Old Bob appeared to us a little theatrical, but that feeling arose without doubt from the effects of our apprehensions of the evening before. The Old Bob had the soul of a child; he was as much of a coquette as an old woman (that is to say, that his coquetries frequently changed their object), and, having once for all adopted a garb of the most severe—black coat, black waistcoat, black trousers, white hair and rosy cheeks—there was constantly attached to him the idea of complete harmony. It was in this professional uniform that Old Bob had chased the tigers in the pampas and this he wore at the present time while he dug in the grottoes of Rochers Rouges in his search for the missing bone of the *elephus antiquus*.

Mrs. Rance presented him to us, and he uttered a few polite phrases, after which he opened his wide mouth in a great hearty laugh. He was jubilant, and we were soon to learn the reason why. He had brought back from his visit to the Museum of Paris the certainty that the skeleton of the Barma Grande was no more ancient than the one which he had discovered in his last expedition to Terra del Fuego. All the Institute was of this opinion, and took for the basis of its reasonings the fact that the bone of the spine of the *elephus* which Old Bob had carried to Paris, and which the owner of the Barma Grande had loaned him after having declared to him that he had found it in the same bed of earth as the famous skeleton—that this spinal bone belonged, let us say, to an *elephus* of the middle of the quarternary period. Ah, it would have done your heart good to hear the joyous contempt with which Old Bob spoke of the middle of the quarternary period. At the very thought of a spinal bone of the middle of the quarternary period, he laughed as heartily as though some one had told him the finest joke in the world. Could it be that in this day and age, a savant, worthy of being dignified by the name, could find anything to interest him in a skeleton of the middle of the quarternary period! His own skeleton (or, to be more exact, that which he had brought from Terra del Fuego) dated from the commencement of this period, and, in consequence, was older by two thousand years—you hear? *two thousand years*—! And he was sure, because of this shoulder blade having belonged to the cave bear, the shoulder blade which he had found, he, Old Bob, between the arms of his own skeleton. (He said "my own skeleton" in his enthusiasm, making no distinction between the living skeleton which he was carrying about under his black coat, his black trousers, his white hair and his rosy cheeks, and the prehistoric skeleton of Terra del Fuego.)

"Therefore, my skeleton dates from the cave. But that of Baousse-Raousse! Oh, no, no, my children! at furthest from the epoch of the mammoth, and yet—no—no—from the rhinoceros with the cloven nostrils. Therefore—One has nothing left to discover, ladies and gentlemen, in the period of the rhinoceros with the cleft nostrils.—I swear it, upon the honour of Old Bob. My skeleton comes from the chelleenne epoch, as you say in France. Well, what are you laughing at? I am not even sure that the *elephus* of Rochers Rouges dates from the Mousterian epoch. And why not from the Silurian epoch—or yet—or yet—from the Magdalenian epoch? No, no—that's too much. An *elephus antiquus* from the Magdalenian epoch would be an impossibility.

That *elephus* will drive me mad! Ah, I shall die of joy. Poor Baousse-Raousse!"

Mme. Edith had the unkindness to interrupt the jubilations of her uncle by announcing to him that Prince Galitch, who had purchased the Grotto of Romeo and Juliet at Rochers Rouges, must have made some sensational discovery, for she had seen him, the very morning of Old Bob's departure for Paris, passing by the Fort of Hercules, carrying under his arm a little box which he had touched as he went by, calling out to her, "See, Mrs. Rance! I have found a treasure!" She said that she had asked him what the treasure was, but he had walked on laughing, with the remark that he would have a surprise for Old Bob on his return. And later, she had heard that Prince Galitch had declared that he had discovered "the oldest skull in the history of the human race."

Mrs. Rance had scarcely pronounced these last words when every vestige of gayety fled from Old Bob's face and manner. His eyes shot fire and his voice was husky with passion as he exclaimed:

"That is a lie—an infernal lie! The oldest skull in the history of the human race is Old Bob's skull—do you understand me?—it is Old Bob's skull."

And he shouted out:

"Mattoni! Mattoni! Bring my trunk here at once!"

Almost as soon as the words were spoken, we saw Mattoni crossing the Court of Charles the Bold with Old Bob's trunk on his shoulder. He obeyed the professor to the letter, and carried the trunk through the room and up to his master. Old Bob took his bunch of keys, got down on his knees and opened the box. From this receptacle, which contained his clothing and piles of clean linen, neatly folded, he took a hat box, and from the hat box he drew out a skull, which he placed in the middle of the table among our coffee cups.

"The oldest skull in the history of humanity!" he echoed. "Here it is! It is Old Bob's skull! Look at it! Oh, I can tell you, Old Bob never goes anywhere without his skull!"

And he took up the frightful object and began to caress it, his eyes sparkling and his thick lips parting once more in a broad smile. If you will represent to yourself that Old Bob knew French only imperfectly and pronounced it like English or Spanish (he spoke Spanish like a native), you will see and hear the scene. Rouletabille and I were unable longer to control ourselves, and nearly split our sides with laughter—all the more, because Old Bob every few moments would interrupt himself in the midst of a peal of merriment to demand of us what was the object of our mirth. His wrath was almost as funny as his mirth, and even Mme. Darzac could not refrain from laughter, for, in truth, Old Bob, with his "oldest skull of the human race," was a droll sight to see. I must acknowledge, too, that a skull two hundred thousand years old is not such an unpleasant sight as one might expect it to be, especially when, like this one, it has all its teeth.

Suddenly Old Bob grew serious. He lifted the skull in his right hand and placed the forefinger of the left hand upon the forehead of his ancestor.

"When one looks at the skull from above, one notices very clearly a pentagonal formation which is due to the notable development of the parietal bumps and the jutting out of the shell of the occipitals. The great breadth of the face comes from the exaggerated development of the zygomatic proportions. While in the head of the troglodytes of the Baousse-Raousse, what do we find?"

I shall never know what it was that Old Bob found in the head of the troglodytes, for I did not listen to him, *but I looked at him*. And I had no further inclination for laughter. Old Bob seemed to me terrifying, horrible, as false as the Father of Lies, with his counterfeit gayety and his scientific jargon. My eyes remained fixed upon him as if they were fascinated. It seemed to me that I could see his hair move, just as a wig might do. One thought—the thought of Larsan, which never left me completely, seemed to expand until it filled my entire brain. I felt as if I must speak it out, when all at once, I felt an arm locked in mine, and I saw Rouletabille looking at me with an expression which I did not know how to read.

"What is the matter, Sainclair?" whispered the lad, anxiously.

"My friend," I returned in a tone as low as his own. "I dare not tell you; you would make sport of me."

He drew me away from the table and we walked toward the west boulevard. After he had looked closely on every side and made sure that no one was near us, he said:

"No, Sainclair, no: I won't make sport of you, for you are in the right in seeing *him* everywhere around us. If he were not there a little while ago, he is perhaps there now. Ah, he is stronger than the stones! He is stronger than anything else in the world. I fear him less within than without. And I should be very glad if the stones which I have called to my aid in hindering his entrance shall aid me to hold him inside. For, Sainclair, *I feel that he is here!*"

I pressed Rouletabille's hand, for, strange as it may seem, I shared the same impression—I felt that the eyes of Larsan were upon me—I could hear him breathe. When and how this sensation had first come over me, I was unable to say. But it seemed to me that it had come with the appearance of Old Bob.

I said to Rouletabille, scarcely daring to put into words what was in my mind:

"Old Bob?"

He did not answer. At the end of a few moments, he said:

"Hold your left hand in your right for five minutes and then ask yourself: *'Is it you, Larsan?' And when you have replied to yourself, do not feel too sure, for he may, perhaps, have lied to you, and he may be in your own skin without your knowing it.*"

With these words, Rouletabille left me alone in the west boulevard. It was there that Pere Jacques came to look for me. He brought me a telegram. Before reading it, I congratulated him on his appearance, for he showed no trace of the fact that, like all the rest of us, he had passed a sleepless night; but he informed me that the pleasure he experienced in seeing his "dear Mlle. Mathilde" happy had made him ten years younger. Then he tried to obtain from me some information in regard to the motives for the strange vigil of the night before, and the reason for the events which had occurred at the château since Rouletabille's arrival and for the exceptional precautions which had been taken to prevent the entrance of any stranger. He added that if "that monster, Larsan," were not dead, it would seem as if we dreaded his return. I told him that this was not the moment for explanations and reasoning, and that, as he was a worthy man, he ought, like all other soldiers, to observe the rules without seeking to understand them or to discuss them. He saluted me with a military gesture and started off, shaking his head. The old man was evidently puzzled, and it did not displease me at all that, since he had the watch of the North Gate, he had thought of Larsan. He also had narrowly escaped being one of Larsan's victims; he had not forgotten the fact. It would make him a better sentinel.

I was not in much of a hurry to open the dispatch which Pere Jacques had brought me, and in this I was wrong, for as soon as I cast my eyes over the words which it contained, I realised that it was of the deepest importance. My friend at Paris, whom I had requested to keep an eye upon Brignolles, sent me word that the said Brignolles had left Paris the evening before for the Midi. He had taken the 10:35 train. My friend informed me that he had reason to believe that Brig nolles had taken a ticket for Nice.

What should Brignolles be doing in Nice? That was the question which I propounded to myself, and which I have since so often regretted that a foolish impulse of self-esteem kept me from putting to Rouletabille. The young reporter had made so much fun of me when I showed him the first dispatch, which stated that Brignolles had not quitted Paris, that I resolved to tell him nothing about the one which announced his departure. Since Brignolles amounted to so little, in his opinion, I would not bother him with Brignolles. And I kept Brignolles to myself, all alone and so well, that when, assuming my most indifferent air, I rejoined Rouletabille in the Court of Charles the Bold, I never mentioned the subject.

Rouletabille was ready to fasten down with bars of iron the heavy circularly cut oak board which closed the opening to the "oubliette," and he showed me that even if the shaft communicated with the sea, it would be impossible for anyone to succeed in an attempt to introduce himself into the château by this means, for the reason that he could not raise the board and would be driven to give up his plan. His brow was dripping with perspiration, his arms were bared, his collar thrown off, a heavy hammer was in his hand. It seemed to me that he was devoting considerable time and energy to a comparatively simple task, and, like a fool who does not see beyond the end of his own nose, I could not refrain from telling him so. How could I have helped guessing that the boy was voluntarily exerting himself beyond necessity, and that he was delivering himself up to all sorts of physical fatigue in order to efface the memory of the grief which filled his poor heart? But no! I was only able to understand that, half an hour later, when I came upon him lying beside the ruins of the chapel, murmuring in his dreams the one word which betrayed the sorrow of his heart—"Mother." Rouletabille was dreaming of the Lady in Black! He dreamed, perhaps, that her arms were around him as in days gone by, when he was a little fellow and came into the school parlour, flushed and breathless with running. I waited beside him for a moment, asking myself nervously if I ought to leave him in there, or whether there was any danger of anyone's else passing by and discovering his secret. But, after having relieved his overcharged heart with that one word, the lad left nothing more to be heard except his heavy breathing. He was completely exhausted. I believe that it was the first time that the boy had really slept since we had come from Paris.

I profited by his slumbers to leave the château with out informing anyone of my intention, and soon, my dispatch in my pocket, I took the train for Nice. On the way, I chanced to read this item on the first page of the *Petit Nicois*: "Professor Stangerson has arrived at Garavan, where he will spend a few weeks with M. Arthur Rance, the recent purchaser of the Fort of Hercules, who, aided by the beautiful Mme. Arthur Rance, will dispense the most gracious hospitality to his friends in this fine old medieval stronghold. As we go to press, we learn that Professor Stangerson's daughter, whose marriage to M. Robert Darzac has just taken place in Paris, has also arrived at the Fort of Hercules with her husband, the brilliant young professor of la Sorbonne. These new guests descend upon us from the North at the time when strangers usually leave us. How wise they are! There is no more beautiful springtime in the world than that of the 'azure shore.'"

At Nice, hidden behind the blinds of a buffet, I awaited the arrival of the train from Paris, by which Brignolles was due to arrive. And the next moment I saw him alighting from a car. Ah, how my heart beat, for I knew that there must be some strange reason for this journey of which he had not informed M. Darzac beforehand. And I knew that the trip was a secret one, when I saw that Brignolles was trying to avoid observation, was bending his hand as he hurried along, gliding rapidly as a pickpocket among the passengers, so that he was soon lost to sight. But I was behind him. He jumped into a closed hack and I hastily got into another closed just as tightly. At the Place Massena he left his carriage and turned toward the Jetee Promenade, where he took another cab. I still followed him. These maneuvers seemed to me more and more ambiguous. Finally, Brignolles' carriage came out upon the road de la Corniche, and I directed my coachman to take the same way. The numerous windings of this road, its accentuated curves, permitted me to see without being seen. I had promised my coachman a large tip if he helped me to keep in sight of my quarry, and he did his very best. Finally, we reached the Beaulieu railway station, where I was astonished to see Brignolles' carriage stop and the man himself get out, pay the driver and enter the waiting room. He was going to take the train. For what purpose? If I should attempt to get into the same car as he, would he not be certain to see me in this little station or on the almost deserted platform? But I decided to try it anyway. If he were to see me, I could get out of the difficulty by feigning surprise at his presence, and by sticking to him until I was sure of what he was going to do in this part of the world. But luck was with me and Brignolles did not see me. He got into a passenger coach which was bound for the Italian frontier. I realised that all his movements were bringing him nearer to the Fort of Hercules. I got in the car behind his and watched from my window all the travellers who got out at every station.

Brignolles did not get off until we reached Mentone. He certainly had some reason for reaching there by a different train than the one from Paris, and at an hour when there was little chance of his seeing any acquaintances at the station. I saw him alight: he had turned up the collar of his overcoat and pulled his hat down over his eyes. He cast a stealthy glance around the quay, and then, as if reassured, mingled with the other passengers. Once outside the train shed, he got into a shabby old stage coach which was standing by the sidewalk. I watched him from the corner of the waiting room. What was he doing here? And where was he going in that rackety old vehicle? I inquired of an employé, who told me that that carriage was the stage to Sospel.

Sospel is a picturesque little city lost between the last counterfores of the Alps, two hours and a half from Mentone by coach. No railroad passes through there. It is one of the most retired and quietest corners of France, the most dreaded by revenue officers and by the Alpine hunters. But the road which leads to it is one of the most beautiful in the world, for, in order to reach Sospel, it is necessary to wind through I do not know how many mountain passes, to climb countless precipices, and to follow, until one reaches Castillon, the deep and narrow valley of Carei, as wild as a field in Judaea, but covered with luxuriant herbage, bright with beautiful flowers, fertile and beautiful with the shimmering gold of its forests of olive trees, which descend from the heights to the clear bed of the stream by the terraces of a giant staircase formed by nature. I had been at Sospel a few years previously with a party of English tourists in an immense carriage, drawn by eight horses, and I had brought from the trip a remembrance of vertigo which came over my mind in the future every time the name was mentioned. Why was Brignolles going to Sospel? I must find out. The diligence was crowded and had already started on its way with a loud noise of creaking springs and of shaking window panes. I hired a carriage from the station and in a few moments I, too, was climbing over the rocks to the valley of Carei.

How I regretted not having spoken of my telegram to Rouletabille! The strange behaviour of Brignolles would have given him ideas, useful and reasonable, while, for my part, I had not the slightest idea of how to reason. I only knew how to follow this Brignolles as a dog follows his master or a policeman follows his quarry by the clues which he finds. And yet, had I followed them well, these clues? It was at the moment that I felt certain that nothing in the world in regard to this man's movements could be small enough to escape me that I made a formidable discovery. I had let the diligence keep a little way in advance, a precaution which I deemed necessary, and I reached Castillon ten minutes later than Brignolles. Castillon is at the highest point of the road between Mentone and Sospel. My driver asked my permission to let his horse rest for a moment, and while he watered the beast, I descended from the carriage, and, at the entrance of a tunnel through which it was necessary to pass to reach the opposite turn of the mountain, I beheld Brignolles and Frederic Larsan!

I stood staring at them, my feet as helpless as though they had taken root in the soil. I could not utter a sound nor make a gesture. Upon my honour, I was completely stupefied by the revelation. Then I recovered my wits, and at the same time felt myself overwhelmed by a feeling of horror for Brignolles, and by a feeling of admiration for my own intuition in regard to him. Ah, I had known from the start! I had been the only one to guess that the companionship of this devil of a Brignolles had been of the gravest danger to Robert Darzac. If they would have listened to me, the Professor of la Sarbonne would have gotten rid of the creature's presence long ago. Brignolles, the tool of Larsan—the accomplice of Larsan—what a discovery! Why, I had known all along that those accidents in the laboratory had not happened by chance! They would believe me now! I had seen with my own eyes Larsan and Brignolles, talking and consulting together at the entrance of the Castillon tunnel. I *had* seen them—but where were they gone now? For I saw them no longer. They must be in the tunnel. I hastened my steps, leaving my coachman behind me, and reached the tunnel in a few moments, drawing my revolver from my pocket. My state of mind was beyond description. What would Rouletabille say when I told him all about my adventure? It was I—I—who had discovered Brignolles and Larsan.

But where were they? I walked through the dark tunnel—no Larsan, no Brignolles! I looked down the road which descends toward Sospel.

Not a living creature! But upon my left, toward ancient Castillon, it seemed to me that I could perceive two forms that hastened. They disappeared. I ran after them. I arrived at the ruins. I stopped. Who could say that those two figures were not lying in wait for me behind a wall?

The old Castillon was no longer inhabited, and for a good reason. It had been entirely ruined—destroyed by the earthquake of 1887. Nothing of it remained but a few piles of stone and a few mural windows, gently covered with dust by time; some headless statues, a few isolated pillars which remained standing upright, spired by the shock, and leaning sorrowfully toward the earth, melancholy at having nothing to support. What a silence there was all around me! With a thousand precautions I searched through the ruins, contemplating with horror the depth of the crevices which the earthquake of 1887 had opened in the rocks. One of these in particular seemed to be a shaft without a bottom, and as I leaned above it, hanging on to an olive tree to keep from falling in, I was almost swept into the abyss by a gust of wind. I felt the draught on my face and recoiled with a cry. An eagle darted out of the abyss, quick as a flash. He rose straight to the sun, and then I saw him descend toward me, and describe some menacing circles above my head, uttering savage shrieks, as though he reproached me for having come to trouble him in his realm of solitude and of death which the elements had given him.

Had I been the victim of an illusion? I could no longer see my two shadows. Was I also the plaything of my imagination, when I stooped and picked up from the road a bit of letter paper which looked to me singularly like that which M. Robert Darzac used at la Sarbonne?

Upon this bit of paper I deciphered two syllables which I believed Brignolles had written. These syllables seemed to be the end of a word the beginning of which was missing. All that it was possible to make out was "bonnet."

Two hours later I reëntered the Fort of Hercules and told my story to Rouletabille, who placed the bit of paper in his portfolio and entreated me to be as silent as the grave in regard to my expedition.

Astonished at having produced so different an effect from the one which I had anticipated at a discovery which I believed so important, I stared at Rouletabille. He turned his head away, but not quickly enough to hide from me that his eyes were filled with tears.

"Rouletabille!" I exclaimed.

But again, he motioned me not to speak.

"Silence, Sainclair!"

I took his hand; it was burning with fever. And I thought that this agitation could not come entirely from his apprehensions in regard to Larsan. I reproached him with concealing from me what had passed between him and the Lady in Black, but, as often happened, he made me no answer, and turned away, heaving a deep sigh.

They had waited dinner for me. It was late. The dinner was a dismal affair, in spite of the gayety of Old Bob. We scarcely attempted to hide the deep anxiety which froze our hearts. One would have said that each one of us was resigned to the blow which was threatening and that we had lost hope that it might be averted. M. and Mme. Darzac ate nothing. Mme. Edith kept looking at me with a strange expression. At ten o'clock I went to take up my station at the tower of the gardener, almost with relief. While I was in the little room where we had consulted together the night before, the Lady in Black and Rouletabille passed beneath the arch. The glimmer of the lantern fell on their faces. Mme. Darzac appeared to me to be in a state of the greatest excitement. She was urging Rouletabille to something which I could not hear. The conversation between them looked like an argument and I caught only one word of Rouletabille, "Thief!" The two entered the Court of the Bold. The Lady in Black stretched her arm toward the young man, but he did not see it, for he left her immediately and went toward his own room. She remained standing alone for a moment in the court, leaning against the trunk of the eucalyptus tree in an attitude of unutterable sadness, then, with slow steps, she entered the Square Tower.

It was now the tenth of April. The attack of the Square Tower occurred on the night between the eleventh and twelfth.

X

The Events of The Twelfth of April

This attack took place under circumstances so mysterious and so inexplicable, to all appearances, under any reasonable hypothesis, that the reader will permit me, in order to make him comprehend the issue more fully, to dwell upon certain details in regard to the manner in which we spent our time on the eleventh day of April, 1895.

(1) *The Morning*.

The day, almost from the rising of the sun, was intolerably hot and the hours on guard were almost overpowering. The sun was as torrid as in the heart of Africa and it would have blinded us to keep watch over the waters which burned like a sheet of steel, brought to a white heat, if we had not been furnished with eyeglasses of crooked glass, without which it is difficult to pass the—a son of departing winter in this part of the country.

At nine o'clock, I came down from my room and went to the postern and entered the room which we had styled "the hall of counsel" to relieve Rouletabille of his guard. I had no time to say a single word to him before M. Darzac appeared, following almost upon my heels, and announcing that he had something very important to communicate to us. We inquired anxiously the cause of his agitation and he replied that he intended to quit the Fort of Hercules at once, taking his wife with him. This declaration left Rouletabille and myself dumb with surprise. I was the first to speak and endeavoured to dissuade M. Darzac from even thinking of such an imprudence. Rouletabille frigidly inquired the reason for our friend's sudden resolution and the latter replied by informing us of a scene which had occurred during the previous evening at the château and which revealed to us in how difficult a position the Darzacs were placed by remaining at the Fort of Hercules. The story may be summed up in a few words: Mme. Edith had had a nervous attack. We understood the reason at once for there was no doubt in the mind of either Rouletabille or myself that Mrs. Rance's jealousy of Mme. Darzac was increasing every hour and that each act of courtesy performed by the husband toward the former object of his admiration was positively insupportable to his wife. The sounds of the fit of hysterics to which she had treated M. Rance and the words which she had spoken the night before had penetrated even through the heavy walls of "la Louve," and M. Darzac, who was doing sentinel duty in the outer court, had been unable to help hearing some of the echoes of the young woman's anger.

Rouletabille implored M. Darzac to endure the situation with fortitude, unpleasant as were the circumstances. He assured him that he agreed with his feeling that the stay of himself and Mme. Darzac at the Fort of Hercules must be made as brief as possible: but he also assured him that the security of both de pended in great measure on their remaining in their present quarters for the time being. A new struggle had been begun between them on the one side and Larsan on the other. If they were to go away Larsan would know on the moment how to overtake them and in a time and place that they expected him the least. Here, they were forewarned, they were upon their guard, for they *knew*. Elsewhere, they would be at the mercy of everything and every person that surrounded them, for they would not have the ramparts of the Fort of Hercules to defend them. Certainly, this situation could not endure very long, but Rouletabille asked M. Darzac to wait eight days longer— not a single one more. "Eight days," said Columbus long ago, "and I will give you a new world." "Give me eight days and I will deliver Larsan into your hands," was not what Rouletabille said, but it was what we knew that he was thinking.

M. Darzac left us, shaking his head, doubtfully. He was angrier than we had ever seen him. Rouletabille remarked:

"Mme. Darzac will not leave us and M. Darzac will stay if she does."

And he started off on his rounds.

A few moments later, I caught sight of Mme. Edith. She was charmingly dressed, with a simplicity which suited her marvellously. She smiled at me coquettishly, but her gayety seemed a little forced as she jested at my "new trade." I answered her, perhaps a little too quickly, that she was uncharitable in her jests, because she knew quite well that all the trouble which we were taking and the careful watch which we were maintaining might be the means, at any moment, of saving the sweetest of women from untold misery and danger.

She looked at me mockingly and cried with a sharp little laugh:

"Oh, surely. "The Lady in Black!" She has you all under her spell."

What a ringing laugh she had! At another time, rest assured, I would not have allowed anyone to speak so lightly of "the Lady in Black," but this morning I had not the strength of mind to assert myself. On the contrary, I laughed, too.

"Perhaps, there is a little truth in that speech," I returned.

"My husband is crazy about her! I never would have believed that he could be so romantic. But, then," she went on, with a droll little sigh, "I am romantic, too!"

And she turned upon me that same curious look which had disturbed me before.

"Ah?" That was all that I could find to answer.

"And, therefore," she continued, "I take very great pleasure in the conversation of Prince Galitch, who is more romantic than all the rest of you put together."

Whereupon I asked her who was this Prince Galitch of whom I had heard so much but had not yet seen. She told me that he was coming to luncheon—that she had invited him on our accounts; and she gave me a few particulars in regard to him from which I learned that Prince Galitch was one of the richest landholders in his own part of Russia— that portion called the "Black Lands," fertile above all others, and situated between the forests of the North and the steppes of the Midi.

Fallen heir, at the age of twenty, to one of the greatest of Muscovite estates, he had increased his patrimony by economical and intelligent management of which no one would have believed a man so young to be capable—especially one who had heretofore had his hounds and his books as his principal objects in life. He was called a hermit, a miser and a poet. He had inherited from his father a high position at court. He was a chamberlain to His Majesty and, on account of the immense services rendered by the parent, the Emperor was supposed to regard the son with a great deal of affection. He was at once as gentle as a woman and as strong as a Turk—in brief, a thorough Russian gentleman.

I cannot tell why, but I felt a singular antipathy for the Prince without ever having set eyes on him.

His relations with the Rances were those of friendly neighbourliness. Having purchased two years before the magnificent property whose hanging gardens, flowery terraces, and beautiful balconies had made it known at Garavan as "the Garden of Babylon," he had had the opportunity to be of assistance to Edith when she had begun to make the outer court of the Château of Hercules into an exotic garden. He had presented her with certain plants which had revived, in some corners of the Fort of Hercules, a tropical vegetation hitherto scarcely known except on the banks of the Tigris and the Euphrates. M. Rance sometimes invited the Prince to dinner, and always after one of these functions the Prince would send to his hostess a wonderful palm tree from Nineveh or a cactus, fabled to have belonged to Semiramis. He declared that they cost him nothing. He had too many; he was tired of them and he did not want them among his roses. Edith said that she was interested in the young Russian because he dedicated such beautiful verses to her. After he had repeated them in Russian, he would translate them into English and he had even composed them in English for her and for her alone. Verses—the verses of a real poet, dedicated to Mme. Edith! This had so flattered her that she had requested the poet to compose English verses for her and translate them into Russian. This "literary game" greatly amused Mme. Edith, but Arthur Rance cared for it not at all. The young anthropologist did not attempt to conceal that his feelings toward Prince Galitch were not of the most friendly, and I felt assured that the traits which the husband disliked most heartily were those which the wife found most attractive in the Russian, for M. Rance had no use for "verse writing fellows," nor did he care for those who were quite so prudent in their expenditures. He could not understand how a poet could be something very like a miser. The Prince kept no carriage nor motor car. He used the street cars and often did his own marketing, attended by his servant, Ivan, who carried a basket for the provisions. And—so said Mrs. Edith, who had heard these details from the cook—he haggled over prices with the fishwife when there was only two sous between what she asked and what he offered. Strangely enough, this avariciousness did not seem in the least dis tasteful to Mme. Edith, who appeared to consider it a mark of originality. And, she finished by saying, "No one has ever set foot within his doors. He has never even invited us to come and see his gardens."

"Isn't it beautifully fascinating?" demanded the young woman when she had completed her description.

"Too beautifully fascinating!" I replied. "You will see!"

I do not know why this answer should have displeased my hostess, but I could see that it did so. Mme. Edith turned away and left me and I finished my guard duty which was an hour and a half long.

The first stroke of the luncheon bell sounded: I hurried to my room to bathe my hands and face and make a hasty toilet and I mounted the steps of "la Louve" rapidly fearing that I should be late; but I paused in the vestibule, amased to hear the sound of music. Who, under the present circumstances, cared or dared to play a piano in the Fort of Hercules? And, hark someone was singing. It was a voice at once soft and sonorous singing a strange song which sounded now plaintive, now threatening! I know the song now by heart; I have often heard it since. Ah, reader, you, too, know it well, perhaps, if you have ever passed the frontiers of chill Lithuania, if you have ever entered the vast empires of the North. It is the song of the virgins who surround the traveller as he sails and destroy him without pity; it is the song that Sienkiewicz, one immortal day, made for Michel Vereszezaka. Listen.

"If you approach the Swiss lakes at the hour of night fall, the face turned toward the lake, the stars above Ayour head, the stars beneath your feet, and two moons shining before your eyes— you shall see this plant that caresses the bank—the wives and daughters of the Swiss whom God has changed into flowers. They balance their forms above the abyss, their heads white like the moths; their leaves are green as the needle of the maize tipped with gold.

"Images of innocence during life, they have kept their virginal robe after death; they live in the shadow and no blemish comes near them; mortal hands dare not touch them,

"The Tsar and his guard one day made the attempt when, after having gathered the beautiful flowers, they wished to wreath their brows and adorn their swords with them.

"All those who had gathered the blossoms were smitten with great ill or struck with sudden death.

"When time would have effaced these things from the memory of the people, the memory of the punishment is preserved, and in perpetuating it, the flowers are still called the doom of the Tsars.

"Thus saying the lady of the lake departed slowly; the lake opened for her the most profound of its depths; but the eye seeks in vain for the fair unknown whose face was born out of the mist and whose voice the traveller never heard again."

These were the words, translated into our language, of the song which was sung by the soft yet resonant voice while the piano played a weird accompaniment. I opened the door and found myself face to face with a young man who was standing. I heard the footsteps of Mme. Rance behind me and the next moment she was introducing me to Prince Galitch.

The Prince was of the type that one reads of in romances, "handsome, pensive young man"; his clear cut and rather stern profile might have given a somewhat severe expression to his face if his eyes, as mild and clear as those of a child, and with an expression of perfect candour, had not told an altogether different story. They were framed in long black lashes so black that they almost looked as though they had been touched with a pencil; and when one had noticed this peculiarity, one realised why it was that his countenance looked so strange. His skin was fresh and rosy, almost like that of a young girl. Such was my first impression of him but I felt the prejudice which I had experienced before I saw him rise up in my heart again. But it seemed to me, in spite of this, that he was too young to be of any special importance.

I could find nothing to say to this beautiful youth who chanted foreign poems. Mme. Edith smiled at my embarassment, took my arm (which gave me great satisfaction) and led me away to walk in the perfumed gardens of the outer court while we waited for the second bell for luncheon which was to be served to us in the cabin of palm trees on the platform of the Tower of the Bold.

(2) *The Luncheon and What Followed—A Contagious Terror Spreads Through Our Midst.*

At noon we seated ourselves at the table on the terrace of Charles the Bold, the view from which was incomparable. The palm leaves covered us with their grateful shade, for the heat of the earth and the heavens was so intense that our eyes would not have been able to endure the glare if we had not taken the precaution to put on the smoked spectacles of which I have spoken before.

Those of us at the table were M. Stangerson, Mathilde, Old Bob, M. Darzac, M. Arthur Rance, Edith, Rouletabille, Prince Galitch and myself. Rouletabille, turning his back to the sea, concerned himself very little with his companions and had placed himself in such a position that he could observe everything which transpired along the entire length of the fort. The servants were at their posts. Pere Jacques was at the entrance gate, Mattoni at the postern of the gardener, and the Berniers in the Square Tower before the door of the apartments occupied by M. and Mme. Darzac.

The first part of the meal was rather silent. I looked at the others. We were rather a solemn sight to contemplate around a table spread for good cheer—mute, and turning upon each other our dark smoked glasses behind which it was as impossible to see our eyes as to read our thoughts.

Prince Galitch was the first to make a remark. He spoke politely to Rouletabille mentioning the fame which the young reporter had won. This appeared to embarrass the lad a little and he made a confused and rather ungracious reply. The Prince did not seem to feel rebuffed, but went on to explain that he was particularly interested in the exploits of my friend for the reason that, as a subject of the Tsar, he knew that Rouletabille would shortly be sent to Russia. But the reporter replied that nothing had yet been decided and that he would prefer to say nothing on the subject until he had received his directions from his paper; whereupon, the Prince astonished us by drawing a newspaper from his pocket. It was a journal of his own country from which he translated to us a few lines announcing the fact that Rouletabille was soon to be in St. Petersburg. There was occurring in that city, the Prince went on to read to us, a series of events so strange and inexplicable in high governmental circles that, upon the advice of the Chief of the Secret Service at Paris, the Superintendent of Police had decided to ask the Epoch to lend him the young reporter. Prince Galitch had presented the affair so vividly that Rouletabille blushed to the roots of his hair as he replied dryly that he had never in the course of his short life done detective work and that the Chief of the Secret Service at Paris and the Superintendent of Police at St. Petersburg were two idiots. The Prince showed his fine teeth in a hearty laugh and it seemed to me that his laughter was not pleasant but cruel and savage. He seemed to be of Rouletabille's opinion in regard to the Government officers, and, as if to prove the fact, he added:

"It sounds good to hear anyone talk like that, for now one expects tasks of journalists which have nothing in the world to do with their profession."

Rouletabille made no reply and the subject was abandoned.

Mme. Edith arose from her chair, speaking ecstatically of the beauty of nature. But, in her opinion, she declared, there was nothing more beautiful anywhere near than the "Gardens of Babylon." She added, mischievously: "They seem so much more beautiful, because one may only see them from a distance!"

The attack was so direct that it seemed as though the Prince must reply to it by an invitation. But he said nothing. Mme. Edith looked vexed and a moment later, said suddenly:

"I'm not going to deceive you any longer, Prince. I have seen your gardens."

"Indeed! And how was that?" inquired Galitch, not losing his presence of mind for an instant.

"Yes, I have been there, and I'll tell you all about it."

And she related while the Prince listened with an air of cold imperturbability the story of her visit to the "Gardens of Babylon."

She had come upon them, inadvertently, from the rear, in climbing over a hillock which separated the gardens from the mountains. She had wandered from enchantment to enchantment, but without being in the least astonished. When she had walked upon the seashore, she had seen enough of the "Gardens of Babylon." to prepare her for the marvels, the secrets of which she had so audaciously stolen. She had finally reached the edge of a little pond, black as ink, upon the bank of which she saw a great water lily and a little old woman with a long, peaked chin. When they saw her the water lily and the little old woman had fled away, the latter so light on her feet in running that she fairly skimmed over the ground. Mme. Edith had laughed and had called after her:

"Madame! Madame!"

But the little old woman had seemed only more terrified and had disappeared with her lily behind the barberry hedge. Mme. Edith had continued her stroll but not quite so carelessly. Suddenly she had heard a rustle in the bushes and the strange cry which is made by wild birds when, surprised by the hunter, they escape from the prison of verdure in which they have hidden themselves. It was another little old woman, still more shrivelled and wrinkled than the first, but heavier of build and who carried her cane like a battle axe. She vanished—that is to say, Edith lost sight of her in a turn of the path. And a third little old woman, leaning on two canes appeared a little further on in the mysterious garden: she escaped behind the trunk of a giant eucalyptus tree and she went so much the faster than she had done before, by running on her hands and knees so rapidly that it was amazing that she did not get all tangled up. Mme. Edith still went on. And at last she came to the marble steps of the villa with their climbing roses over head, but the three little old women were standing guard on the highest step like three rooks on a branch and they opened their threatening beaks from which escaped threatening sounds. It was then Mme. Edith's turn to flee.

The little woman had related her adventure in a manner so charming and with such grace, borrowed as it was from the fairy tales of childhood, that I was enraptured and began to comprehend how certain women who have nothing natural about them can supplant in the heart of men those whose gifts are only those of nature.

The Prince did not seem in the least embarrassed by the little history. He said without a smile:

"Those are my three fairy godmothers. They have never left me since the hour of my birth. I can neither work nor live without them, I can only leave them when they permit it and they watch over my verse making with a fierce jealousy."

The Prince had scarcely ceased giving us this fantastic explanation of the presence of the three old women in the "Gardens of Babylon" when Walter, Old Bob's man servant, brought a dispatch to Rouletabille. The latter asked permission to open it and read aloud:

"Return as soon as possible. We are waiting for you very anxiously. A magnificent assignment at St. Petersburg."

This dispatch was signed by the Editor in chief of the Epoch.

"Well, what do you say to that, M. Rouletabille?" demanded the Prince. "Will you admit now that I was pretty well informed?"

The Lady in Black could not repress a sigh. "I shall not go to St. Petersburg!" declared Rouletabille.

"They will regret your decision at the Court," said the Prince. "I am certain of that, and, allow me to say, young man, that you are missing a wonderful opportunity."

The term "young man" seemed extremely displeasing to Rouletabille, who opened his lips as though to answer the Prince, but closed them again, to my great surprise, without uttering a word. Galitch went on:

"You would have found an adventure worthy of your skill. One may hope for everything when one has been strong enough to unmask a Larsan!"

The word fell into the midst of us like a bombshell and, as if by a common impulse, we took refuge behind our smoked glasses. The silence which followed was horrible. We sat as motionless as statues. *Larsan!* Why should this name which we ourselves had so often pronounced within the last forty-eight hours and which represented a danger with which we were commencing to almost feel familiar— why, I say, should that name, spoken at that precise moment, have produced an effect upon us, which, speaking for myself, was like nothing ever felt before? It seemed to me as though I had been struck by a thunderbolt. An indefinable terror glided through my body. I longed to flee but it seemed to me that if I were to stand up my limbs would not be able to support me. The unbroken silence on every hand contributed to increase this indescribable state of hypnosis. Why did no one speak? Where had old Bob's gayety vanished? He had scarcely uttered a word during the meal. And why did all the others sit so silent and so motionless behind their dark glasses? All at once, I turned my head and looked behind me. Then I understood, more by instinct than anything else, that I was the object of a common psychical attraction. Someone was looking at me. Two eyes were fixed upon me—*weighing* upon me. I could not see the eyes and I did not know from where the glance fixed upon me came, but it was there. I knew it—and it was *his* glance. But there was no one behind me, nor at the right, nor the left, nor in front, except the people who were seated at the table, motionless, behind their dark glasses. And then—then I knew that Larsan's eyes were glaring at me from behind a pair of those glasses—ah! the dark glasses—the dark glasses behind which were hidden Larsan's eyes.

And then, all at once, the sensation passed. The eyes, doubtless, were turned away from me. I drew a long breath. Another sigh echoed my own. Was it from the breast of Rouletabille—was it the Lady in Black, who perhaps, had at the same time as myself endured the weight of those piercing eyes?

Old Bob spoke:

"Prince, I do not believe that your last spinal bone goes any further back than the middle of the quaternary period."

And all the black spectacles turned in his direction. Rouletabille arose and made a sign to me. I hastened to the council room where he was waiting for me. As soon as I appeared, he closed the door and whispered:

"Well, did you fuel it, too?"

I felt smothered. I could scarcely articulate.

"He was there—at that table—unless we are going mad."

There was a pause and then I resumed, more calmly:

"You know, Rouletabille, that it is quite possible that we are going mad. This phantasm of Larsan will land us all in a madhouse yet! We have been shut up here only two days and see the state we are in!"

Rouletabille interrupted me.

"No, no; I felt him. He is there. I could have touched him! But where—but when? Since I came into that room, I have known that it was not necessary for me to go further. I will not fall into his trap. I will not go and look for him outside the castle even though I have seen him outside with my own eyes—even though you saw him with yours."

All in a moment he seemed to grow perfectly calm, passed his hand across his eyebrows, lighted his pipe and said, as he had so often said before, in happier hours when his reasoning powers, which were yet ignorant of the ties which united him to the Lady in Black, were not disturbed by the tumult of his heart:

"Let us reason it out!"

And he returned on the instant to that argument which had already served us and which he repeated again and again to himself (in order that, he said, he should not be lured away by the outer appearance of things): "Do not look for Larsan in that place where he reveals himself; seek for him everywhere else where he hides himself."

This he followed up with the supplementary argument:

"He never shows himself where he seems to be except to prevent us from seeing him where he really is."

And he resumed:

"Ah! the outer appearance of things! Look here, Sainclair! There are moments when, for the sake of reasoning clearly, I want to get rid of my eyes! Let us get rid of our eyes, Sainclair, for five minutes—just five minutes, and, perhaps, we shall see more clearly."

He seated himself, placed his pipe on the table, buried his face in his hands and said:

"Now, I have no eyes. Tell me, Sainclair—*who is within these walls?*"

"What do I see within these walls?" I echoed stupidly.

"No, no! You have no eyes at all; you see nothing. Enumerate them without seeing. Count them ALL."

"There is, first of all, you and I," I said, understanding, at last, what he wished to reach.

"Very well."

"Neither you nor I," I continued, "is Larsan."

"Why?"

"Why?" I echoed.

"Yes, why. Tell me. You must give a reason why you believe so. I acknowledge that I am not Larsan; I am sure of that, for I am Rouletabille; but, face to face with Rouletabille, tell me why you cannot be Larsan?"

"Because you saw him—"

"Idiot!" exclaimed Rouletabille closing his eyes in with his clasped hands more firmly than before. "I have no eyes. I can't see anything! If Jerry, the croupier at Monte Carlo, had not seen the Comte de Maupas sit down at his table, he would have sworn that the man who picked up the cards was Ballmeyer! If Noblet at the garrison had not found himself face to face one evening at the Troyons, with a man whom he recognised as the Vicomte Drouet d'Eslon, he would have sworn that the man whom he came to arrest and whom he did not arrest because he had *seen* him, was Ballmeyer. If Inspector Giraud, who knew the Comte de Motteville as well as you know me, had not *seen* him one afternoon at the race course at Longchamps, chatting with two of his friends—had not *seen*, I say, the Comte de Motteville, he would have arrested Ballmeyer. Ah, you see, Sainclair!" exclaimed the lad in a voice shaken with sobs, "my father was born before I was! One will have to be very strong and very shrewd to capture my father!"

The words were uttered so despairingly that the little force of reasoning I possessed vanished completely. I threw out my hands before me, a gesture which Rouletabille did not see, for he saw nothing.

"No—no! It isn't necessary to *see* any of them " he repeated. "Neither you, nor M. Stangerson, nor M. Darzac, nor Arthur Rance, nor Old Bob, nor Prince Galitch. But we must know some good reason why each of these cannot be Larsan. Only when that is accomplished shall I be able to breathe freely behind these stone walls!"

There was no freedom in my breathing. We could hear, under the arch of the postern, the regular steps of Mattoni as he kept guard.

"Well, how about the servants?" I asked, with an effort. "Mattoni and the others?"

"I am absolutely certain that none of them was absent from the Fort of Hercules when Larsan appeared to Mme. Darzac and to M. Darzac at the railway station at Bourg." "Own up, Rouletabille!" I cried. "That you don't trouble yourself about them because none of their eyes were behind the black spectacles."

Rouletabille tapped the ground impatiently with his foot and said:

"Be quiet, please, Sainclair. You make me more nervous than my mother."

This phrase, uttered in vexation, struck me strangely.

I would have questioned Rouletabille in regard to the state of mind of the Lady in Black, but he resumed, meditatively:

"First, Sainclair is not Larsan, because Sainclair was at Trepot with me while Larsan was at Bourg."

"Second: Professor Stangerson is not Larsan because he was on his way from Dijon to Lyons while Larsan was at Bourg. As a fact, reaching Lyons one minute before him, M. and Mme. Darzac saw him alight from the train."

"But all the others, if it is necessary to prove that they were not at Bourg at that moment, might be Larsan, for all of them might have been at Bourg."

"First M. Darzac was there. Arthur Rance was away from home during the two days which preceded the arrival of the Professor and of M. Darzac. He arrived at Mentone just in time to receive them (Mme. Edith herself informed me in reply to a few careless questions of mine that her husband had been absent those two days on business). Old Bob made his journey to Paris. Prince Galitch was not seen at the grottoes nor outside the Gardens of Babylon.

"First, let us take M. Darzac."

"Rouletabille!" I cried. "That is a sacrilege."

"I know it."

"And it is a piece of the grossest stupidity."

"I know that, too. But why?"

"Because," I exclaimed, almost beside myself, "Larsan is a genius, we are aware; he might be able to deceive a detective, a journalist, a reporter, and even a Rouletabille—he might even deceive a friend, under some circumstances, I admit. But he could never deceive a daughter so far that she would take him for her father. That ought to reassure you as to M. Stangerson. Nor would he deceive a woman to the point of taking him for her betrothed. And, my friend, Mathilde Stangerson knew M. Darzac and threw herself into his arms at the railway station."

"And she knew Larsan, too!" added Rouletabille coldly. "Well, my dear fellow, your reasons are powerful but as I do not know at present what form the genius of my father has assumed as a disguise, I prefer rather to bestow, for the sake of supposition, a personality on

M. Robert Darzac which I have never expected to fasten upon him, in order to base my argument against the possibility a little more solidly: If Robert Darzac were Larsan, Larsan would not have appeared on several occasions to Mathilde Stangerson, for it is the apparition of Larsan that has created a gulf between Mathilde Stangerson and Robert Darzac."

"Pshaw!" I cried. "Of what use are such vain reasonings when one has only to open his eyes—open them, Rouletabille!"

He opened them.

"Upon whom?" he asked with a trace of bitterness in his voice. "Upon Prince Galitch?"

"Why not? Do you like him, this prince from the Black Lands who sings Lithuanian folk songs?"

"No," replied Rouletabille. "But he entertains Mme. Edith."

And he smiled. I pressed his hand. He acted as though he had not felt the touch, but I knew that he did.

"Prince Galitch is a Nihilist and I am not troubled over him in the least degree," he said, tranquilly. "Are you sure of it? Who told you?"

"Bernier's wife, who knows one of the three old women whom Mrs. Edith told about at luncheon. I have made an investigation. She is the mother of one of the three men hanged at Kazan for the attempted assassination of the Emperor. I have seen the photograph of the poor wretches. The other two old women are the other two mothers. There's nothing interesting about that!"

I could not refrain from a gesture of admiration.

"Ah, you haven't lost any time."

"Neither has *he*!" he muttered.

I folded my arms.

"And Old Bob?" I asked.

"No, dear boy, no!" scoffed Roultubille, almost angrily. "Not he, either. You have noticed that he wears a wig, I suppose. Well, I assure you that when my father wears a wig, it will fit him."

He spoke so mechanically that I rose to leave him, thinking he had no more to say to me. He stopped me:

"Wait a minute. We have said nothing of Arthur Rance."

"Oh, he has not changed at all since we were at Glandier," I exclaimed. "That is out of the question." "Always the eyes! Take care of your eyes, Sainclair!"

And he put his hand on my shoulder for a moment as I turned away. Through my clothing I felt that his flesh was burning. He left the room and I remained for a moment where I stood, lost in thought. In thought of what? Of the fact that I had been wrong in saying that Arthur Rance had not changed at all. For one thing, now, he wore a slight moustache, something very rarely seen in an American of his type; next, his hair had grown longer with a lock falling over the forehead. And again, I had not seen him in two years—and everyone changes in two years—and again, Arthur Rance, who had used to drink heavily, now tasted only water. But then, there was Edith—what about Edith? Ah! was I going insane, I, too? Why do I say, "I, too," like—like the Lady in Black; like—like Rouletabille. Did I believe that Rouletabille's brain was becoming slightly turned? Ah, the Lady in Black had us all under her spell. Because the Lady in Black lived in the perpetual fear of her memories, here were we all trembling with the same horror as she. Fear is as contagious as the cholera.

(3) *How I Spent My Afternoon up to Five O'clock.*

I profited by the fact that I was not on guard to go to my room for a little rest; but I slept badly and dreamed that Old Bob, M. Rance and Mme. Edith had formed themselves into a band of brigands who had sworn death to Rouletabille and myself. And when I awakened under this pleasant impression and saw the old towers and the old château with their menacing walls rising before me, I came near thinking that my nightmare was real and I said to myself half aloud: "It's a fine place in which we have taken refuge!" I put my head out of the window. Mrs. Edith was walking in the Court of the Bold, chatting carelessly with Rouletabille and twisting the stem of a beautiful rose between her pretty fingers. I went down immediately. But when I reached the court, I found no one there. I followed Rouletabille whom I saw on his way to make his inspection of the Square Tower.

I found him quite calm and entirely master of him self—and also, entirely the master of his eyes, which were not closed now but open wide and keenly on the watch for anything that might turn up. Ah, it was worth while to see the manner in which he looked at everything around him! Nothing escaped him. And the Square Tower, the abode of the Lady in Black, was the object of his constant surveillance.

And at this point, it seems to me opportune, a few hours before the moment at which that most mysterious attack occurred, to present to the reader the interior plan of the inhabited story of the Square Tower the story which was on a level with the Court of Charles the Bold.

When one entered the Square Tower by the only door (K) one found himself in a large corridor which had previously formed a part of the guard room. The guard room had formerly taken up all the space at O, O, O" and O" and was shut in by walls of stone which still existed with their doors opening upon the other rooms of the Old Castle. It was Mrs. Arthur Rance who in this guard room had had wooden partitions raised to make quite a large room which she wished to use for a bathroom. This room, also, was now surrounded by the two passages at right angles to each other. The door of the room which served as the lodge of the Berniers was situated at S. It was necessary to pass in front of this door to reach R, where was the only door affording admission to the apartment of the Darzacs. One or other of the Berniers was always in the lodge. And no one save themselves had a right to enter it. From this lodge one could easily see from a little window at Y, the door V which opened off the suite of Old Bob. When M. and Mme. Darzac were not in their apartment, the only key which opened the door R was in the keeping of the Berniers; and it was a special kind of key made purposely for the room within the last twenty-four hours in a place which no one but Rouletabille knew. The young reporter had let no one into the secret.

Rouletabille would have wished that the watch which he had had placed upon the rooms of the Darzacs might have been kept also upon those of Old Bob, but the latter had opposed such an idea with an earnestness so comical that it was necessary to abandon it. Old Bob swore that he would not be treated like a prisoner and he said that on no account would he give up the privilege of going and coming to his own rooms when he saw fit without asking the keys from the lodge-keepers. His door must remain unlocked so that he might go as many times as he liked to his rooms, whether it might be to his bed chamber or to his sitting room in the Tower of Charles the Bold, without disturbing or worrying himself or anyone else. On account of his insistence, it was necessary to leave the door at K open. He demanded it and Mme. Edith upheld her uncle in so intense a manner and spoke so pertly to Rouletabille that he knew she was seeking to convey the idea that she believed that Rouletabille was treating Old Bob with discourtesy at the instigation of Professor Stangerson's daughter. So he had not insisted on what he believed to be best. Mme. Edith had said with her lips pressed together in a narrow little line: "But, M. Rouletabille, my uncle doesn't think that anyone is coming to carry *him* away!" And Rouletabille had realised that there was nothing for him to do save to laugh with the Old Bob over this absurd idea that one could be trying to steal as they would a pretty woman, the man who had the oldest skull in the world. And so he had laughed—had laughed even louder than Old Bob, but had imposed the condition that the door at K should be locked with a key after 10 o'clock at night and that the key should be left in the keeping of the Berniers, who would come and open it whenever anyone desired. Even this was against the inclination of Old Bob, who sometimes worked very late in the Tower of Charles the Bold. But, nevertheless, he declared, he would submit to it for he did not wish to have the appearance of opposing the worthy M. Rouletabille, who had told him that he was afraid of robbers. For, be it said in exculpation of Old Bob, that, if he lent himself so ungraciously to the defensive plans of our young friend it was because it had not been judged expedient to inform him in regard to the resurrection of Larsan. He had, of course, heard of the extraordinary series of fatalities which had formerly occurred in the history of poor Mlle. Stangerson; but he was a thousand miles from doubting that all her troubles had ceased long before she had become Mme. Darzac. And then, too, Old Bob was an egoist, like nearly all savants. Happy because he possessed the oldest skull in the history of the human race, he could not conceive that the whole world did not revolve around his treasure.

Rouletabille, after having politely inquired after the health of Mere Bernier, who was gathering up potatoes and putting them in a bag at her side, requested Pere Bernier to open the door of the Darzacs' room for us.

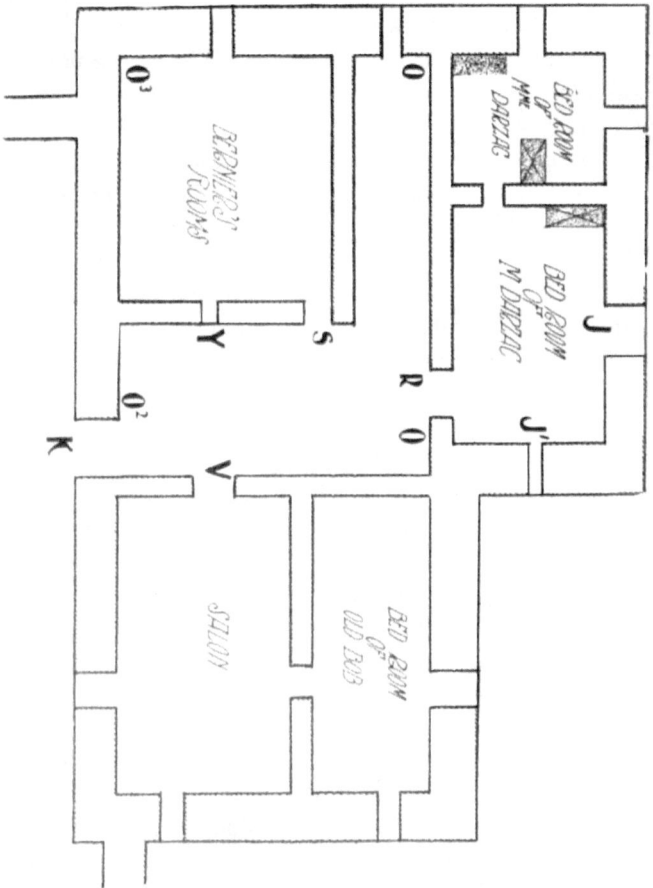

The Plan of the Inhabitied | Loot of the Square Tower

This was the first time that I had entered the apartment. The atmosphere was almost freezing, and the whole place seemed to me cold and sombre. The room, very large, was furnished with extreme simplicity, containing an oak bed, and a toilet table which was placed at one of the two openings in the wall around which there had formerly been loopholes. So thick was the wall and so large the opening that this embrasure (J) formed a kind of little room beside the big one and of this M. Darzac had made his dressing closet. The second window (J') was smaller. The two windows were fitted with bars of iron between which one could scarcely pass one's arm. The high bedstead had its back to the outer wall and had been drawn up against the partition of stone which separated M. Darzac's apartment from that of his wife. Opposite in the angle of the tower was a panel. In the centre of the room was a reading table on which were some scientific books and writing materials. And there was an easy chair and three straight-backed chairs. That was all. It would have been absolutely impossible for anyone to hide in this chamber, unless, of course, behind the panel. And then, too, Pere and Mere Bernier had received orders to look every time they visited the room both behind the panel and in the closet where M. Darzac hung his clothes, and Rouletabille himself, who, during the absence of the Darzacs often came to cast his eye around this room, never neglected to search it thoroughly.

He did so now, as I stood there. When we at length passed into the sleeping room of Mme. Darzac, we were absolutely certain that we had left nothing behind us of which we did not know. As soon as we entered the room, Bernier, who had followed us, had taken care, as he always did, to draw the bolt which closed from the inside the only door by which the apartment communicated with the corridor.

Mme. Darzac's room was smaller than that of her husband. But it was bright and well lighted from the way that the windows were placed. As soon as we set foot over the threshold, I saw Rouletabille turn pale and he turned to me and said:

"Sainclair, do you perceive the perfume of the Lady in Black?"

I did not. I perceived nothing at all. The window, barred, like all the others which looked out on the sea, was wide open and a light breeze rustled the hangings which had been drawn in front of a set of hooks for gowns which had been placed in one corner. The other corner was occupied by the bed. The hooks were placed so high that the gowns and peignoir which they held were covered by the hangings in front scarcely more than half way down, so that it would have been entirely out of the question for any person to conceal himself there without leaving his legs exposed to view from the knees to the feet. Nor would anyone have been able to hide in the corner where the portmanteaux and trunks were placed, although, nevertheless, Rouletabille examined it with the greatest care. There was no panel in this room. Toilet table, bureau, an easy chair, two other chairs, and the four walls between which there was no one but ourselves, as we could have sworn by all that we held most sacred.

Rouletabille, after having looked under the bed, gave the signal for departure and motioned us from the room. He lingered for a moment, but no longer. Bernier locked the door with the tiny key which he put in his inside pocket and tightly buttoned his coat over it. We made the tour of the corridors and also that of Old Bob's apartment which consisted of a bedroom and sitting room as easy to examine and as incapable of hiding anyone as those of the Darzacs. No one was in the suite, which was furnished rather carelessly, the chief article noticeable being an almost empty bookcase with the doors standing open. When we left the room Mere Bernier brought up her chair and placed it on the threshold where she could see clearly and still go on with her work, which seemed to be always that of paring potatoes.

We entered the rooms occupied by the Berniers and found them like all the others. The other stories were inhabited and communicated with the ground floor by a little inner stairway which began at the angle O' and ascended to the summit of the tower. A trap door in the ceiling of the Berniers' room closed this stairway. Rouletabille asked for a hammer and nails and nailed up the trap door, thus making the stairway unusable.

One might say, in short and in fact, that nothing escaped Rouletabille and that when we had made the rounds of the Square Tower we had left no one behind us save M. and Mme. Bernier. One would have said, too, that there could have been no human being in the apartment of the Darzacs before Bernier, a few minutes later, opened the door to M. Darzac himself as I am now about to relate.

It was about five minutes before five o'clock when, leaving Bernier in his corridor in front of the door of the Darzacs' room, Rouletabille and myself found ourselves again in the Court of the Bold.

At that moment we climbed to the platform of the ancient tower at B". We seated ourselves upon the parapet, our eyes looking down to the ground, attracted by the echoes of the Rochers Rouges. At that moment, we noticed upon the edge of the Barma Grande which opened its mysterious mouth in the flaming face of Baousse Raousse, the disturbed and wrathful countenance of Old Bob. His shadow was the only dark thing about. The red cliff's rose from the waters with such a vivid radiance that one might have readily believed that they were still glowing with the same fires which are found in the interior of the earth. By what a prodigious anachronism it was that this modern scholar with his coat and hat in the height of fashion should be moving about, grotesque and ghoulish, in front of this cavern three hundred thousand years old formed by the ardent lava to serve as the first roof for the first family in the first days of the world! Why this sinister gravedigger in this beautiful corner of the earth? We could see him brandishing his skull as he had done at the table and we could hear him laugh—laugh—laugh! Ah, his laughter made us ill even to think of it! It tore our ears and our hearts.

From Old Bob our attention was drawn to M. Darzac, who was coming through the postern of the gardener and crossing the Court of the Bold. He did not see us. Ah, he was not laughing! Rouletabille felt the deepest pity for him for he saw that he was at the end of his endurance. In the afternoon he had said to my friend, who now repeated the words to me: "Eight days is too much! I do not believe that I can bear this torment for eight days!"

"And where would you go?" Rouletabille had asked him.

"To Rome," he had replied. Evidently Professor Stangerson's daughter would accompany him nowhere else and Rouletabille believed that it was the idea that the Pope could arrange the affair which was driving him wild with grief that had put the journey to Rome into the mind of poor M. Darzac. Poor, poor M. Darzac! No, in truth, his face wore no smile.

We followed him with our eyes to the door of the Square Tower. We could see from his looks that he could endure no more. His head was moodily bent toward the ground; his hands were in his pockets. He had the air of a man fatigued and disgusted with the whole world. Yes, with his hands buried in his pockets, he looked out of humour with everything. But, patience! he will take his hands out of his pockets and one will not smile at him always. I confess that I smiled. Well, M. Darzac a little after this gave me cause to experience the most frightful thrill of terror which could freeze human bones! And I did not smile then.

M. Darzac went straight to the Square Tower, where, of course, he found Bernier, who opened the door for him. As Bernier had been keeping constant guard before the door of the room, as he had kept the key in his pocket and as we had proven by our investigation that the place was empty when we had left it, we had established the fact that *when M. Darzac entered his room, there could be no one else there*. And this is the truth.

Everything that I have said could have been sworn to "after" by each one of us. If I tell it to you "before," it is that I am haunted by the mystery which lurks in the shadow and makes ready to reveal itself.

At the moment that we saw M. Darzac go to his room, we heard a clock strike five.

(4) *What Happened from Five O'clock that Night Until the Moment When the Attack on the Square Tower Began.*

Rouletabille and I remained chatting, or, rather, trying to reason things out, upon the platform of the Tower B for another hour. Suddenly, my friend struck me a little tap on the shoulder and exclaimed, "For my part, I think—" and then, without completing the sentence, he started for the Square Tower. I followed him.

I was a thousand miles from guessing what he thought. He thought of Mere Bernier's bag of potatoes which he emptied out on the white floor of the room to the great amazement of the good woman: then, satisfied with this act which evidently corresponded to the state of his mind, he returned with me to the Court of the Bold, while, behind us, we could hear Pere Bernier laughing as he picked up the potatoes.

As we reached the court we saw the face of Mme. Darzac appearing for a moment at the window of the room occupied by her father on the first story of "la Louve."

The heat had become insupportable. We were threatened with a violent storm and we believed that it would begin to lighten immediately.

Ah, how much the storm would relieve us, we thought. The sea had a thick and heavy quietude as though it had been saturated with oil. The sea was heavy and the air was heavy and our hearts were heavy. No one or nothing on the earth or in the heavens was lighter than Old Bob, whose form had appeared again at the edge of the Barma Grande and who was still moving around agitatedly. One would have said that he was dancing. No, he was making a speech To whom? We leaned over the railing to see. There was apparently someone upon the strand to whom Old Bob was addressing some long-winded scientific discourse. But the palm leaves hid his auditor from us. Finally, the listener moved and advanced, and approached the "black professor," as Rouletabille called him. And we saw that Old Bob's congregation was composed of two persons. One was Mme. Edith—we could easily recognize her with her languishing graces, clinging like a vine to her husband's arm. To her husband's arm! But this was not her husband? Who, then, was the young man upon whom Mme. Edith was playing off so many pretty airs?

Rouletabille turned around, looking for someone of whom to make inquiries—either Mattoni or Bernier.

We saw Bernier upon the threshold of the door of the Square Tower and Rouletabille beckoned him. Bernier approached and his eye followed the direction indicated by Rouletabille's finger.

"Who is that with Mme. Rance?" asked the young reporter.

"The young man?" responded Bernier without hesitation. "That is Prince Galitch."

Rouletabille and I looked at each other. It is true that we had never seen Prince Galitch walking at a distance, but I would not have imagined that his manner of walking would be like this, and he had not seemed to me to be so tell. Rouletabille understood my thoughts, I knew. He shrugged his shoulders.

"All right," he said to Bernier. "Thanks."

And we continued to gaze at Mme. Edith and her Prince.

"I can only say one thing," said Bernier as he turned to leave us. "And that is that I don't care for this prince at all. He is too soft spoken and too blonde and his eyes are too blue. They say that he is a Russian. That may be, but there are some who leave the country because they have to. But he comes and goes in a strange fashion and takes no leave beforehand. The time before the last that he was invited here to luncheon Madame and Monsieur waited and waited for him and dared not begin without him. Well, after an hour or two they received a wire, begging them to excuse him because he had missed the train. The dispatch was sent from Moscow."

And Bernier, chuckling, returned to his vantage post.

Our eyes remained fixed upon the beach. Mme. Edith and her prince continued their stroll toward the grotto of Romeo and Juliet; Old Bob suddenly ceased to gesticulate, descended from the Barma Grande and came toward the château, entered the gate, crossed the outer court, and we saw, even from the height of the plat form of the tower, that he had ceased to smile. Old Bob's face had become sadness itself. He was silent. He passed beneath the arch of the postern. We called him, he did not seem to hear us. He carried before him in the crook of his arm his "oldest skull in the world," and all at once we saw him fly into the fiercest of passions. He addressed the worst of insults to the skull. He descended into the Round Tower and we heard the mutterings of his wrath for moments after he was out of sight. Then heavy blows resounded. One would have said that he was hurling himself against the wall.

At this moment six strokes resounded from the old clock of the New Castle. And at almost the same instant a clap of thunder echoed over the sea. And the line of the horizon grew black.

Then a groom of the stables, Walter, a brave, stupid fellow who was incapable of a single idea, but who had shown for years past the blind devotion of a brute toward his master, Old Bob, passed under the postern of the gardener, entered into the Court of Charles the Bold, and came to us. He held in his hand a letter which he gave to Rouletabille. He handed me another and continued on his way toward the Square Tower.

Rouletabille, calling after him, inquired what errand was taking him to the Square Tower. He answered that he was taking the mail for M. and Mme. Darzac to Pere Bernier. He spoke in English for Walter understood no other language; but we spoke it well enough to understand him and make him understand. Walter was charged with distributing the mail because Pere Jacques had no right to leave his lodge on any account. Rouletabille took the letters from the man's hands and said to him that he would take it in himself.

A few drops of water had begun to fall.

We turned to the door of M. Darzac's room. Bernier was smoking his pipe in the corridor, sitting astride a chair.

"Is M. Darzac still there?" asked Rouletabille.

"He hasn't stirred since he went in," Bernier replied.

We knocked. We heard the heavy bolt drawn from the inside. (These bolts can only be used by the person within the room.)

M. Darzac was writing letters when we entered. He had been seated beside the little reading table facing the door R. Now mark well all our movements. Rouletabille complained that the letter which he held in his hand confirmed the telegram which he had received in the morning and pressed him to return to Paris. His paper insisted upon his proceeding at once to Russia.

M. Darzac read indifferently the two or three letters which we had brought him and put them in his pocket. I held out to Rouletabille the letter which I had received. It was from my friend in Paris who, after having given me some important details regarding the departure of Brignolles, informed me that the laboratory assistant had left his address for mail to be forwarded to Sospel, the Hotel des Alps. This was extremely interesting and M. Darzac and Rouletabille were greatly excited over it. We decided to go to Sospel as soon as it could be arranged and, after talking of the matter for a few minutes, we went out of the room. The door of Mme. Darzac's sleeping room was not closed. Here is what we noticed as we passed out:

I have mentioned that Mme. Darzac was not in her own room. As soon as we made our exit, Pere Bernier immediately—immediately, I say, for I saw him—turned the key in the lock and then took it out and put it in his pocket—in the little inside pocket of his waistcoat. Ah, I can still see him putting the key into his inside pocket—I swear it!—and he buttoned his coat over it!

Then the three of us went out of the Square Tower, leaving Pere Bernier in his corridor like the good watch dog that he never ceased to be until the last day of his life. One may be a poacher and a good watch dog into the bargain, you know. Even watch dogs poach sometimes. And I bear witness here and now, among all the events which followed, Pere Bernier always did his duty and never told lies. And his wife, Mere Bernier, was an excellent servant, faithful, intelligent and not too talkative. Since she has been a widow, I have had her in my service. She will be glad to read here the tribute which I pay to her and to her husband. They both deserved it.

It was about half past six o'clock when, in emerging from the Square Tower, we went to pay a visit to Old Bob in the Round Tower, Rouletabille, M. Darzac and I. As soon as we entered the low basement M. Darzac uttered an exclamation of surprise and indignation at seeing the destruction which had been wrought upon a wash drawing upon which he had been working ever since the evening before in the endeavour to distract his mind, and which represented the plan for a great scaling ladder for the Fort of Hercules of the kind which had existed in the Fifteenth Century and of which Arthur Rance had shown us the pictures. This drawing had been gashed with a knife and paint had been smeared over it. He endeavoured in vain to obtain some explanation from Old Bob, who was kneeling beside a box containing a skeleton and was so wrapped up in a shoulder blade that he did not even answer us.

I desire here, by way of parenthesis, to ask the pardon of the reader for the mathematical precision with which for the last few pages, I have enumerated our every act and movement, but I will assure him, once and for all, that even the smallest circumstances have in reality a considerable importance, for everything which we did at this time was done, though alas, we did not guess it, on the brink of a precipice.

As Old Bob seemed to be in a churlish humour, we left him—that is, Rouletabille and myself did. M. Darzac remained gazing at his spoiled drawing, but thinking, doubtless, of altogether different things.

As we went out of the Round Tower, Rouletabille and I raised our eyes to the sky which was rapidly becoming covered with great, black clouds. The tempest was near at hand. In the meantime, the air seemed to grow more and more stifling.

"I am going to lie down in my room," I said. "I can't stand any more of this. Perhaps it may be cooler there with all the windows open."

Rouletabille followed me into the New Castle. Suddenly, as we reached the first landing of our winding staircase, he stopped me:

"Ah," he said in a low voice; "*she* is there!"

"Who?"

"The Lady in Black. Can't you smell the perfume?"

And he hid himself behind a door, motioning me to continue without waiting for him. I obeyed.

What was my amazement in opening the door of my room to find myself face to face with Mathilde!

She uttered a low cry and disappeared in the shadow, gliding away like a surprised bird. I rushed to the staircase and leaned over the balustrade. She swept down the steps like a ghost. She soon gained the ground floor and I saw below me the face of Rouletabille, who, leaning over the rail of the first landing, looked at her, too.

He mounted the steps to my side.

"Oh, my God!" he cried. "What did I tell you! Poor, poor soul!"

He seemed to be in the greatest agitation.

"I asked M. Darzac for eight days!" he went on.

"But this thing must be ended in twenty-four hours or I shall no longer have strength to act."

He entered my room and threw himself into a chair as if exhausted. "I am smothering!" he moaned. "I can't breathe!" He tore his collar away from his throat. "Water!" he entreated. "Water!"

I started to fetch some, but he stopped me.

"No—I want the water from the heavens! I must have it!" and he waved his hands toward the dark skies from which huge drops were slowly beginning to fall.

For ten minutes he remained stretched out in the chair, thinking. What surprised me was that he asked no question or uttered no conjecture as to what the Lady in Black had been seeking in my room. I would not have known how to answer, if he had done so. At length, he rose.

"Where are you going?" I asked.

"To take the guard at the postern."

He would not even come in to dinner and sent word to have some soup brought out to him as though he were a soldier. The dinner was served in la Louve at half past eight. Darzac, who came to the table from Old Bob's workroom, said that the latter refused to dine also. Mme. Edith, fearing that her uncle might be ill, went immediately to the Round Tower. She would not even allow her husband to accompany her—indeed, she seemed to be much out of humour with him.

The Lady in Black came in on the arm of her father. She cast on me a look of sorrowful reproach which disturbed me greatly. Her eyes seemed never to wander from me.

It was a gloomy meal enough. No one ate much. Arthur Rance looked every moment in the direction of the Lady in Black. All the windows were open. The atmosphere was suffocating. A flash of lightning and a heavy clap of thunder came in rapid succession—and then, the deluge! A sigh of relief issued from our over charged breasts. Mme. Faith reappeared just in time to escape being drenched by the furious rain which beat down like cannon balls upon the peninsula.

The young woman told us in excited tones and with her hands clasped, how she had found Old Bob bending over his desk with his head buried in his hands. He had refused to have anything to say to her. She had spoken to him affectionately and he had treated her like a bear. Then, as he had obstinately held his hands to his ears, she had pricked one of his fingers with a little pin set with rubies which she used to fasten the lace scarf which she wore in the evening over her shoulders. Her uncle, she said, had turned upon her like a mad man, had snatched the little pin from her and thrown it upon the desk. And then he had spoken to her—"brutally, rudely as he had never done before in his life!" she exclaimed. "Get out of here and leave me alone!" was what he had said to her. Mme. Edith had been so much pained that she went out without saying a word, promising herself, however, that she would not soon set foot again in the Round Tower. But she had turned her head for a last look at her old uncle and had been almost struck dumb by what she saw.

The "oldest skull in the history of the human race" was upon the desk, and Old Bob, a handkerchief stained with blood in his hand, was spitting in the skull. He had always treated it with the most severe respect and had insisted that others should do the same. Edith had hurried away, almost frightened.

Robert Darzac reassured her by telling her that what she had taken for blood was only paint and that Old Bob's skull had been spattered by the paints which had been used in the wash drawing.

I left the table to hurry out to Rouletabille and also to escape from Mathilde's glances. What had the Lady in Black been doing in my bedroom? I was not to wait long to know!

When I started out the thunder was pealing loudly and the rain falling with redoubled force. It took me only one bound to reach the postern. No Rouletabille was there! I found him on the terrace B", watching the entrance to the Square Tower and receiving the full strength of the storm at his back.

I entreated him to take shelter under the arch.

"Leave me alone!" he said impatiently. "Leave me alone. This is the deluge. Ah, how good it is! how good—all this anger of the heavens! Have you ever had a desire to roar with the thunder? I have—and I am roaring now. Listen, while I cry out—alas! alas! alas! My voice is stronger than the thunder!"

And he plunged into the darkness making the shadows resound with his savage clamours. I believed this time that he had surely gone mad! But in my heart I knew that the unhappy lad was breathing forth in these indistinct articulations of frightful anguish the misery that burned him, and which he was constantly trying to hinder from burning up the heart and the soul in his body—the misery of being the son of Larsan.

I turned helplessly and as I did so, I felt a hand seize my wrist and a dark form cried out to me above the tempest:

"Where is he?"

It was Mme. Darzac who was also seeking Rouletabille. A new peal of thunder burst and we heard the boy in his mad delirium hurling wild shouts of defiance to the heavens. She heard him. She saw him. We were drenched with water from the rain and the breaking of the sea on the terrace. Mme. Darzac's clothing clung around her like a rag and her skirt dripped as she walked. I took the wretched woman's arm and held her up, for I saw that she was about to fall, and at that moment, in the midst of that terrible unchaining of the elements, in that mad tempest, under this terrible downpour on the breast of the raging sea, I all at once breathed the perfume—the odour so sweet and penetrating and haunting that its fragrance has remained with me ever since—the Perfume of the Lady in Black. Ah, I understood now how Rouletabille had remembered it all these years.

Yes, it was a fragrance full of sadness—something like the perfume of an isolated flower which has been condemned to be seen by no one but to blossom for itself all alone. It was a fragrance which set such ideas as these running through my brain, although I did not analyse them at the time—a sweet, soft and yet insistent perfume which seemed to steal away my senses in the midst of this battle of the elements, as soon as I perceived it. A strange perfume! Surely it was that, for I had seen the Lady in Black hundreds of times without noticing it, and now that I had done so, it was everywhere and above all things and I knew that the memory of it would abide with me while life should last. I understood how when one had—I will not say smelled but seised (for I do not think that everyone would have been able to catch the subtle fragrance of the perfume of the Lady in Black, any more than I myself had done before this night in which my senses seemed to have become sharpened to the keenest point)—yes, when one had seised this adorable and captivating odour, it was for life. And the heart would be perfumed by it, whether it was the heart of a son, like Rouletabille: or the heart of a lover, like M. Darzac.; or the heart of a villain, like Larsan. No, no—the knowledge of it could never pass. And now, by some sudden insight, I seemed to understand Rouletabille and Darzac and Larsan and all the misfortunes which had attended the daughter of Professor Stangerson.

There in the night and the tempest, the Lady in Black called aloud to Rouletabille and he fled from us and rushed further into the night, shrieking aloud, "The perfume of the Lady in Black! The perfume of the Lady in Black!"

The unhappy woman sobbed. She drew me toward the tower. She struck with desperate hands at the door which Bernier opened to us and her weeping would have melted the heart of a stone.

I could only utter the veriest commonplaces, begging her to calm herself, although I would have given everything I had in the world to find words which, without betraying anyone, might perhaps have made her understand my own part in the sorrowful drama which was being played out between the mother and the child.

Suddenly she seemed to recover herself in some degree and she motioned me to enter the little parlour at the right which was just outside the bed chamber of Old Bob. The door stood open but there we were as much alone as we could have been in her own room, for we knew that Old Bob worked late in the Tower of Charles the Bold.

I can assure you that in my memories of that horrible night the thought of the moments which I spent in the company of the Lady in Black are not the least sorrowful. I was put to a proof which I had not expected, and it was like a blow full in the face when, without even taking time to speak of the way in which we had been treated by the elements, Mme. Darzac looked me full in the eyes and demanded: "How long is it, M. Sainclair, that you were at Trepot?"

I was struck dumb—overpowered more completely than I had been by the fury of the storm. And I felt that, at the moment when nature, wearied out, was beginning to grow more quiet, I was to suffer a more dangerous assault than that of thunderbolts or lightning flashes. I must, by my expression, have betrayed the agitation which was aroused in my mind by this unexpected remark, for I could see by her eyes as she looked at me that she was aware how deeply I was moved. At first I made no answer: then I stammered out some disconnected words of which I remember nothing, save that they were ridiculous. It is years now since that night, but as I write I am living over the scene as if I were a spectator instead of the actor which I actually was, and as if it were even now going on in front of my eyes.

There are people who may be drenched to the skin and yet not look in the least ridiculous. The Lady in Black was one of them. Although, like myself, she had experienced the full fury of the storm, she was majestic and beautiful with her dishevelled locks, her bare neck and magnificent shoulders which, through the thin silk which clothed them seemed to have merely a light veil thrown across the flesh. She seemed to be a sublime statue, carved by Phidias from the immortal clay to which his chisel has given form and beauty. I am well aware that, even after all the years which have elapsed, my description sounds too glowing and I will not linger on the subject. But those who have known Professor Stangerson's daughter will understand me, I think, and I desire, here, with Rouletabille near me, to affirm the sentiments of respectful admiration which filled my heart at the sight of this mother, so divinely beautiful, who, in the state of disorder to which the fearful tempest had brought her, and with her whole heart filled with agony, was endeavouring to make me break the oath that I had sworn to the lad who was my friend.

She took both my hands in hers and said in a voice which I shall never forget:

"You are his friend. Tell him, then, that he is not the only one who has suffered." And she added with a sob which shook her whole frame:

"Why will he insist on not telling me the truth!"

I had not a word to say. What could I have answered? This woman had always seemed so cold and formal to the world in general and (as I had thought) to me in particular that it was as if I had not existed for her, and now she was laying bare her heart before me as though I were an old friend. And I had breathed the perfume of the Lady in Black.

Yes, she treated me as an old friend. She told me everything that I already knew in a few sentences as piteous and as simple as a mother's love itself—and she told me other things which Rouletabille had kept a secret from me. Evidently the game of hide and seek could not have lasted long. The relationship between them had been guessed by the one as surely as by the other. Led by a sure instinct Mme. Darzac had resolved to take means to learn who was this Rouletabille who had saved her from death and who was of the age of her own son—and who resembled the lad whom she had mourned as dead. And since her arrival at Mentone, a letter had reached her containing the proof that Rouletabille had lied to her in regard to his early life and had never set foot in any school at Bordeaux. Immediately, she had sought the youth and had asked for an explanation, but he had hurried away without replying. But he had seemed disturbed when she spoke to him of Trepot and of the school at Eu, and the trip which we had made there before coming to Mentone.

"How did you know?" I exclaimed, betraying my secret without realizing that I was doing so. She showed no sign of triumph at my involuntary confession, and in a few words went on to reveal to me her stratagem. That evening when I had taken her by surprise, it was not the first time that she had been in my room. My luggage bore the labels of the hotels at which we had stopped on our recent journey.

"Why did he not throw himself into my arms when I opened them to him?" she moaned. "Ah, my God! If he refuses to be Larsan's son, will he never consent to be mine!"

As she told me her story, it seemed to me that Rouletabille had conducted himself in an atrocious fashion toward this poor woman who had believed him dead, who had mourned for him in despair, and who, in the midst of her terrible dread and mortal anguish, experienced a thrill of the keenest joy in realizing that her son was still alive. Ah, the poor mother! The evening before, he had mocked at her when she had cried out to him with all her soul that she had a son and that that son was he! He had mocked her, even while the tears had streamed down his cheeks. I could never have believed that Rouletabille could have been so cruel or so heartless—or, even, so ill-bred!

Certainly he behaved in an abominable fashion! He had told her with a sardonic smile that "he was nobody's son—not even the son of a thief." It was these words that had sent her flying to her room in the Square Tower and had made her long to die. But she had not found her son only to give him up so easily and she would—she must have him acknowledge her!

I was almost beside myself. I kissed her hands and entreated pardon for Rouletabille. Here was the result of my friend's schemes to save her pain. Under the pretext of saving her from Larsan, he had plunged a knife into her heart. I felt as though I had no wish to know any more of the story. I knew too much already and I longed to run away. I hastened out of the room and called Bernier, who opened the door for me. I went out of the Square Tower, cursing Rouletabille roundly. I went to the Court of the Bold to look for him, but found it deserted.

At the postern gate Mattoni had come to take the ten o'clock watch. I saw a light in Rouletabille's room and I hastened up the rickety stairway of the New Castle and quickly found myself outside his door. I opened it without knocking. Rouletabille looked up.

"What do you want, Sainclair?"

I told him all that I had heard and my opinion of him for his actions which had so deeply wounded Mme. Darzac.

"She didn't tell you everything, my friend," he replied, coldly. "She did not tell you that she forbade me to touch that man."

"That is true!" I cried. "I heard her."

"Well, what have you come here to tell me then?" he went on, roughly. "Do you know what she said to me yesterday? She ordered me to go away. She would rather die than see me take issue *against my father*."

And he laughed—laughed. Such laughter, I hope not to hear again.

"Against my father! She thinks, I suppose, that he is stronger than I!"

His face was not a pleasant sight to see as he uttered the words.

But suddenly it seemed to be transformed and to glow with unearthly beauty.

"She is afraid for me!" he said, softly. "And I—I am afraid for her—only for her. And I do not know my father. And, God help me! I do not know my mother!"

At that moment the sound of a shot rang out on the night, followed by a cry of mortal agony! Ah, it was again the cry that I had heard two years ago in the "inexplicable gallery." My hair rose on my scalp and Rouletabille tottered as though the bullet had struck himself.

And then he bounded toward the open window, filling the fortress with a despairing burst of anguish:

"Mother! Mother! Mother!"

XI

The Attack of the Square Tower

I leaped after him and threw my arms around his body, dreading what he might attempt. There was in that cry, "Mother! Mother! Mother!" such a madness of despair, a call, or rather, an assurance of coming aid so beyond the realization of human strength, that I was obliged to fear that the young fellow had forgot ten that he was only a man and had not the power to fly straight out of the window of the tower and to traverse, like a bird or a flash of lightning, the black space which separated him from the crime which had been committed and which he filled with his frightful cries. Quickly, he turned on me, threw me off, and precipitated himself wildly, through corridors, apartments, stairways and courts toward the accursed tower from which had come that same death cry that we both had heard—a moment ago, and also two years before when it had resounded through the "inexplicable gallery."

As for me, I had thus far only had the time to gaze out of the window, rooted to my place by the horror of that cry. I was still there when the door of the Square Tower opened, and in its frame of light, there appeared the form of the Lady in Black. She was standing upright, living and unharmed, in spite of that cry of death, but her pale and ghastly visage reflected a terror like that of death itself. She stretched out her arms toward the night and the darkness cast Rouletabille into them, and the arms of the Lady in Black closed around him and I heard no more only sobs and moans and again the two syllables which the night repeated over and over, "Mother! Mother!"

I descended from my tower into the court, my temples throbbing, my heart beating so fast that it almost stifled me. What I had seen on the threshold of the Square Tower had not by any means assured me that nothing terrible had taken place. It was in vain that I attempted to reason with myself and to say: "Nonsense! At the very moment when we believed that all was lost, is not, on the contrary, everything found? Are not the mother and son united?"

But why, then, this cry of death when she was alive and well? Why that scream of agony before she had appeared standing on the threshold of the tower?

Strange to say, I found no one in the Court of the Bold when I crossed it. No one then had heard the pistol shot! No one had heard the cries! Where was M. Darzac? Where was Old Bob? Was he still working in the lower basement of the Round Tower? I might have believed so, for I perceived a light in the window of the tower. But Mattoni—Mattoni—had he heard nothing, either?—Mattoni, who kept watch at the postern of the gardener? And the Berniers? I saw neither of them. And the door of the Square Tower still stood open. Ah, the soft murmur, "Mother! Mother! Mother!" And I heard her voice answer back, tenderly, though choked with sobs, "My boy! My little one!" They had not even taken the precaution to close the door of Old Bob's parlour. It was into that room where I had talked with her a little while before that she had led her child.

And they were there alone, clasped in each other's arms, repeating over and over again, "Mother!" and "My little one!" And then they murmured broken sentences, phrases without end—with the divine foolishness of a mother and her child. "Then, you were not dead!" That was sufficient to make them both fall to sobbing. And then, how they embraced each other, as though to make up for all the years they had lost. I heard him murmur, "You know, mamma, it was not true that I stole!" And one would have thought from the sound of his voice that he was still the little lad of nine years—my poor Rouletabille. "No, my darling—you never stole! My little boy! my little boy!" Ah, it was not my fault that I heard—but my heart was torn in two as I listened.

B ut where was Bernier? I entered the lodge from the left, for I wished to know the meaning of the cry and of the shot which I had heard.

Mere Bernier was at the back of the room which was lighted only by a tiny taper. She was like a black bundle on a sofa. She must have been in bed when the shot was heard and she had hastily donned some clothing. I picked up the taper and brought it near. Her features were distorted with fear.

"Where is Bernier?" I asked.

"He is there," she replied, trembling.

"There. Where is that?"

But she made no answer.

I took a few steps toward the interior of the lodge and I stumbled. I bent down to know what I had stepped upon and found out that it was Mere Bernier's potatoes. I lowered the light and looked at the floor; it was strewn with potatoes; they had rolled everywhere. Could it be that Mme. Bernier had not gathered them up after Rouletabille had emptied out the bag?

I arose and turned to Mere Bernier.

"Someone fired off a pistol!" I said. "What has happened?"

"I do not know," she responded.

And, at that moment, I heard someone open the door of the tower and Pere Bernier stood on the threshold.

"Ah! it is you, M. Sainclair?"

"Bernier! What has happened?"

"Oh, nothing very serious, M. Sainclair, I am glad to say." (But his voice was too palpably endeavouring to sound strong and brave for me to feel as reassured as he was trying to make me!) "An accident without any importance whatever. M. Darzac, while placing his revolver on the stand beside his bed, accidentally fired it off. Madame, naturally, was frightened, and screamed; and, as the window of their room was open, she thought that you and M. Rouletabille might have heard something and started out to tell you that it was nothing." "M. Darsac has come in, then?"

"He got here almost as soon as you had left the tower, M. Sainclair. And the shot was fired almost immediately after he entered his bedroom. You can guess that I had a pretty fright! I rushed to the door! M. Darzac opened it, himself. Happily, no one was injured!"

"Did Mme. Darzac go to her own room as soon as I left the tower?"

"At once. She heard M. Darzac when he came in and followed him directly to their apartments. They went in almost at the same moment."

"And M. Darzac? Is he still in his room?"

"Here he is now."

"I turned and saw Robert Darzac; despite the gloom of the place, I saw that his face was ghastly pale. He made me a sign and then said very calmly and quietly:

"Listen, Sinclair! Bernier told you about their little accident. It is not worth mentioning to anyone, unless someone should speak of it to you. The others, perhaps, have not heard the shot. It would be useless to frighten all these good people; don't you think so? Now I have a little favour to ask of you."

"Speak, my friend," I bade him. "Whatever it is, I will do it: you know that without my saying so. Make any use of me that you like."

"Thanks; but it is only to persuade Rouletabille to go to bed: when he is gone, my wife will calm herself and will try to get the rest that she needs. Every one of use has need of rest and calmness, Sainclair. We all need calm and silence."

"Surely, my friend: you may count upon me."

I pressed his hand with a force which attested my sentiments towards him. I was persuaded that both he and Bernier were concealing something from us—something very grave!

Darzac reached his room and I went to find Rouletabille in the sitting room of Old Bob.

But upon the threshold of the apartment, I jostled against the Lady in Black and her son who were passing out. They were both so silent and wore an expression unexpected to me who had overheard their exclamations of love and joy only a few moments before that I stood before them without saying a word or making a movement. The extremity which induced Mme. Darzac to leave Rouletabille so soon under such extraordinary circumstances as those which had attended their reunion, puzzled me so greatly that I could not find words to say what I thought and the submission of Rouletabille in taking leave of her so quickly amased me. Mathilde pressed a kiss upon the lad's forehead and murmured: "Good-night, my darling," in a voice so soft, so sweet and at the same time so solemn that it seemed to me that it must resemble the leave-taking of one who was about to die. Rouletabille, without answering his mother, took my arm and led me out of the tower. He was trembling like a leaf.

It was the Lady in Black herself who closed the door of the Square Tower. I was sure that something strange was passing within those walls.

The account of the pistol shot which had been given me satisfied me not at all: and it is not to be doubted that Rouletabille would have agreed with me if his reasoning powers and his heart had not been giddy from the scene which had taken place between the Lady in Black and himself. And then, after all, how did I know that Rouletabille did not agree with me? We had scarcely gotten outside the Square Tower before I demanded of Rouletabille the meaning of his strange manner. I drew him into that corner of the parapet which joins the Square Tower to the Round Tower in the angle formed by the jutting out of the Square Tower upon the court.

The reporter, who had allowed me as docilely as a little child to lead him wherever I would, spoke to me in a low tone:

"Sainclair, I have sworn to my mother that I will see nothing or hear nothing of that which may pass this night in the Square Tower. It is the first promise that I have made to my mother, Sainclair; but I will break it for her sake just as I would give up my hope of heaven for her. I must see and I must hear!"

We were at that moment not far from a window in which a light was still burning and which opened upon the sitting room of Old Bob and sloped out upon the sea. This window was not closed, and it was this, doubtless, which had permitted us to hear so distinctly in spite of the thickness of the walls of the tower, the pistol shot and the cry of agony that had followed it. From the spot where we were now stationed, we could see nothing through this window, but was it not something to be able to hear? The storm was past, but the waters were not yet appeased and the waves broke on the rocks of the peninsula with a violence that would have rendered the approach of any vessel impossible. The thought of a vessel crossed my mind because I believed for an instant that I could see the shadow of a vessel of some sort appearing or disappearing in the gloom. But what could it be? Evidently a delusion of my mind which beheld hostile shades everywhere—an illusion of a mind which was assuredly more agitated than the waters themselves.

We stood there, motionless, for more than five minutes, before we heard a sigh—ah, how long it was, that mournful sound!—a groan, deep as an expiration, like a moan of agony, a heavy sob, like the last breath of a departing soul—which reached our ears from that window, and brought the sweat of terror to our brows. And then, nothing more—nothing except the intermit tent sobbings of the sea.

And suddenly the light in the window went out. The outline of the Square Tower blended with the blackness of the night.

My friend and I grasped each other's hand as if instinctively, commanding each other, by this mute communication, to remain motionless and silent. *Someone was dying, there, in that tower!* Someone whom they had hidden. Why? And who? Someone who was neither M. Darzac nor Mme. Darzac, nor Pere Bernier, nor Mere Bernier, nor—almost beyond the shadow of a doubt, Old Bob; *someone who could not have been in the tower.*

Leaning against the parapet to support ourselves, our necks stretched toward that window through which there had come to us that sigh of agony, we listened. A quarter of an hour passed thus—it might have been a century! Rouletabille pointed out to me the window of his own room in the New Castle which was still illuminated. I understood: it was necessary to extinguish this light and return. I took a thousand precautions. Five minutes later, I was back again with Rouletabille. There was now no other light in the Court of the Bold than the feeble ray which told of the late vigil of Old Bob in the lower basement of the Round Tower and the light at the gardener's postern where Mattoni was standing sentinel. In truth, considering the positions which they occupied, one might easily understand how it was that neither Old Bob nor Mattoni had heard anything that had passed in the Square Tower, nor even, in the heart of the storm, could the clamours of Rouletabille have reached their ears. The walls of the postern were heavy and Old Bob was entombed in a veritable subterranean cavern.

I had scarcely time to steal back to Rouletabille in the corner of the parapet, the post of observation which he had not quitted, before we distinctly heard the door of the Square Tower moving softly upon its hinges. As I attempted to lean further out of my corner, and see further down into the court, Rouletabille pushed me back and allowed only his own head to look over the wall; but as he was leaning far over, I allowed myself to violate his command and looked over his head; and this is was I saw.

First, Pere Bernier, perfectly recognizable, in spite of the darkness, who came out of the tower and directed his steps noiselessly to the gardener's postern. In the middle of the court, he paused, looked up at the side where our windows were, and then returned to the side of the court and made a signal which we interpreted as a sign that all was well.

To whom was this signal addressed? Rouletabille leaned further over; but he quickly retreated, pushing me back with him.

When we hared to look out in the court again, no one was there. But in a few moments, we again beheld Pere Bernier (or, rather, we heard him first, for there ensued between him and Mattoni a brief conversation the echoes of which were carried to us.) And then we heard something which climbed under the arch of the gardener's postern and Pere Bernier reappeared with the black and softly rolling form of a carriage beside him. We could see that it was the little English cart drawn by Toby, Arthur Rance's pony. The Court of the Bold was of beaten earth and the little equipage made no more sound than as if it were gliding over a carpet. Toby was so intelligent and so quiet that one would have said that he had received his instructions from Pere Bernier. The latter, reaching, at length, the "oubliette," raised again his face toward our windows, and then, still holding Toby by the bridle, came to the door of the Square Tower. Leaving the little equipage before the door, he entered the tower. A few moments passed by which seemed to us like hours, particularly to Rouletabille, who was seised with a fit of trembling which shook his frame like an aspen leaf. Pere Bernier reappeared. He crossed the court alone and returned to the postern. It was then that we were obliged to lean further out and, certainly, the persons who were now upon the threshold of the Square Tower might have perceived us, if they had looked up at our side, but they were not thinking of us. The night had become clear and a beautiful moon had arisen which threw its rays over the sea and stretched its radiance across the Court of the Bold. The two persons who came out of the tower and approached the carriage appeared so surprised that they almost recoiled at what they saw. But we could hear the Lady in Black repeating again and again in low, firm tones: "Courage, Robert, courage! You must be brave now!"

And Robert Darzac replied in a voice which froze my blood: "It is not courage which I lack!" He was bending over something which he dragged before him and then raised in his arms as though it were a heavy burden and tried to slip under the long seat of the English cart. Rouletabille had taken off his cap. His teeth were chattering. As well as we could distinguish, the thing was in a sack. To move this sack M. Darzac was making the greatest efforts and we heard him breathe a sigh of exhaustion. Leaning against the wall of the tower, the Lady in Black watched him without offering any assistance. And, suddenly, at the moment that M. Darzac had succeeded in loading the sack into the cart, Mathilde pronounced these words in a voice shaken with horror:

"It is *moving*."

"It is the end!" said M. Darzac, wiping his forehead with his pocket handkerchief. Then he took Toby by the bridle and started off, making a sign to the Lady in Black, but she, still leaning against the wall, as though she had been placed there for some punishment, made no signal in reply. M. Darzac seemed to us to be quite calm. His figure straightened up: his step grew firm—one might almost say that his manner was that of an honest man who has done his duty. Still with the greatest precaution, he disappeared with his carriage beneath the postern of the gardener and the Lady in Black went back into the Square Tower.

After this, I wished to emerge from our corner, but Rouletabille restrained me. It was well that he did so, for Bernier came up to the postern and crossed the court, directing his way again toward the Square Tower. When he was not more than two meters from the door, which was closed, Rouletabille glided softly from the corner of the parapet, stepped between the door and the figure of Bernier, who was struck with terror. He put his hands upon the shoulders of the concierge.

"Come with me!" he commanded.

Bernier seemed absolutely powerless. I, too, came out of my hiding place. The old man looked at us both standing there in the moonlight: his face was sorrowful and he murmured sadly:

"This is a great misfortune!"

XII

The Impossible Body

I t will be a great misfortune if you don't tell the truth," muttered Rouletabille, in smothered tones. "But if you conceal nothing, the trouble may not be so great. Come this way."

And he drew him, clasping him by the fist, toward the New Château, I following. I saw that a great change had come over Rouletabille. He was completely his old self again. Now that he was so happily relieved of the sorrow of separation from his mother which had pressed on his mind ever since his early childhood, now that he had again found the perfume of the Lady in Black, he seemed to have reconquered all the forces of his spirit and was ready to enter eagerly into the strife against the mysteries which surrounded us. And, until the day when all was ended—until the last supreme moment—the most dramatic that I have ever lived through in the whole course of my existence—*the moment in which life and death spoke out and were explained by his lips*—he never again made a sign of hesitation in the forward march: he never spoke another word which could have been taken as an attempt to warn us against the dreadful situation which arose from the siege of the Square Tower by the attack of that night between the twelfth and thirteenth of April.

Bernier resisted him no further. When others tried to do so, he held them in his grasp until they cried for mercy.

Bernier walked in front of us, his head bent, looking like an accused man who is being led on his way to trial. And when we reached Rouletabille's room, the young reporter bade Bernier sit down facing us. I lighted the lamp. Rouletabille sat silent for a moment, looking at Bernier, lighting his pipe the while, and evidently seeking to read in the face of the concierge all the honesty which he could find. Soon his knitted brows relaxed, his eye grew clearer and, after he had blown a few rings of smoke toward the ceiling, he said:

"Well, Bernier, how did they kill him?"

Bernier shook his shaggy head.

"I have sworn to say nothing and I will say nothing, monsieur. And, upon my word of honour, I know nothing."

"All right," went on Rouletabille, unconcernedly. "Tell me what you don't know. For if you do not tell me what you don't know, Bernier, I will be responsible for nothing, no matter what happens."

"And for what could you be responsible in any case, monsieur?"

"For one thing, I won't answer for your safety, Bernier."

"For my safety? I have done nothing."

"For the safety of all of us, then for our lives, even!" replied Rouletabille, arising from his chair and pacing restlessly across the room, in order, doubtless, to give himself an opportunity to perform some necessary mental algebraic operation. Then he paused and went on, "Where was he? In the Square Tower?"

Bernier did not speak but he nodded assent.

"Where? In Old Bob's bedroom?"

"No," Bernier shook his head. "Hidden in your rooms?"

Bernier shook his head vehemently.

"Well, where was he then? He could certainly not have been in the apartments of M. and Mme. Darzac!"

Bernier bowed his head.

"Miserable hound!" cried Rouletabille and he leaped at Bernier's throat. I rushed to the rescue of the concierge and snatched him from the young man's clutches. As soon as he could breathe, the old servant looked up, piteously.

"Why did you try to strangle me, M. Rouletabille?" he asked.

"How dare you ask, Bernier? How dare you? And you acknowledge that *he* was in the apartment of M. and Mme. Darzac! Who, then, gained him entrance to that apartment? No one but yourself. You, the only person who had the key when the Darzacs were not there!"

Bernier arose to his feet. He was as pale as a ghost, but his look and attitude were full of dignity.

"M. Rouletabille, do you accuse me of being an accomplice of Larsan?"

"I forbid you to pronounce that name!" shouted the reporter. "You know very well that Larsan is dead—and has been dead for months!"

"For months!" echoed Bernier, ironically. "Yes, that is true—I was wrong to forget it. When one devotes oneself to his masters and permits himself to be beaten and abused for them, it is necessary to ignore everything, no matter what they may do to you. I beg your pardon, sir."

"Listen to me, Bernier. I know that you are a brave man and I respect you. It is not your good faith that I am questioning, but I am censuring your negligence."

"My negligence!" Bernier, as pale as his face had been, flushed crimson. "My negligence! I have not budged from my lodge—not even from the corridor. I have always worn the key in my breast pocket and I swear to you that no one entered that room—no one at all—after you were there at five o'clock, except M. and Mme. Darzac, themselves. I do not count, of course, the few moments that you and M. Sainclair were there at about six o'clock."

"What!" exclaimed Rouletabille. "Do you want me to believe that this individual—you have forgotten his name, I think, Bernier—let us call him 'the Man'—that the man was killed in M. Darzac's rooms if he was not there?"

"I do not. And, furthermore, I can swear to you that he *was* there."

"Yes, but how could he have been?" That is what I ask you, Bernier. And you are the only one who can answer because you alone had the key in the absence of M. and Mme. Darzac. And M. Darzac never took the key with him when he left the room and no one could have gotten into the room to hide while he was there."

"That is the mystery, monsieur. That is what puzzles M. Darzac more than all the rest. But I have only been able to answer him as I have answered you. There is the mystery."

"When you left the room with M. Darzac, M. Sainclair and myself at about a quarter after six, did you lock the door immediately?"

"Yes, monsieur."

"When did you open it after that?"

"Not at all."

"And where were you in the meantime?"

"In front of the door of my lodge, watching the door of the apartment. My wife and I took our dinner in that same spot at about half after six, on a little table in the corridor, because, on account of the door of the tower being open, it was quite light and was pleasanter. After dinner, I sat in the doorway of the lodge, smoking a cigarette and chatting with my wife. We were so seated that, even if we had wished to do so, we would not have been able to withdraw our eyes from M. Darzac's rooms. It is a mystery!—a mystery more extraordinary than the mystery of the Yellow Room. For, in the former case, we did not know of what had passed *before*. But now, monsieur, one knows all that happened beforehand since you yourself visited the apartment at 5 o'clock and saw that no person was there: one knows all that passed during the interim, for either I had the key in my pocket, or M. Darzac was in his room and must have seen the man who opened his door and entered the room for the purpose of assassinating him. And while I was sitting in the corridor before the door, I must have seen the man pass! And we know what took place *after*. After, there was the death of the man and that proved that the man was there. Ah, it is a mystery!"

"And from five o'clock until the moment of the tragedy, you declare that you never quitted the corridor?"

"I swear it."

"You are absolutely certain?" persisted Rouletabille.

"Ah, pardon, monsieur—there was one moment—the moment that you called me."

"That is good, Bernier. I wanted to see if you remembered that."

"But I was not away from my post more than an instant or two, and M. Darzac was in his room then. He did not leave it while I was gone. Ah! what a mystery!"

"How do you know that M. Darzac didn't go out during those moments?"

"Why, because if he had done so, my wife, who was in the lodge, must have seen him! And then all would be explained and we would not be so puzzled, nor Madame either. Ah! must I say it to you over again? No one has entered that room except M. Darzac at five o'clock and you two at six, and no person got in between the time that M. Darzac went out and the time when he came in at night with Mme. Darzac. He was like you—he didn't want to believe me. I swore it to him upon the corpse that lay before us!"

"Where was the corpse?"

"In M. Darzac's bedroom."

"It was really a dead body?"

"Oh, he was breathing still—I heard him."

"Then it was not a corpse, Pere Bernier."

"Oh, M. Rouletabille, where was the difference? He had a bullet in his heart."

At last, Pere Bernier was going to tell us of the body. Had he seen it? Who was it? One would have said that this seemed of secondary importance in the eyes of Rouletabille. The reporter seemed engrossed only with the problem of finding how the body had come to be there. How had that man happened to be killed? But, indeed, Pere Bernier knew only very little. The whole thing had been as sudden as a rifle shot—so it seemed to him—and he was behind the door. He told us that he was going to his lodge and felt so drowsy that he had intended to throw himself down on the bed for a few moments, when he and Mere Bernier heard such a commotion issue from the apartment of M. Darzac that they were seised with terror. It was as if the furniture were being thrown about and blows were rained upon the walls.

"What is the matter?" cried Mere Bernier, and the same instant they heard the voice of Mme. Darzac, shouting, "Help! help!" This was the cry that we, too, had heard in the New Château. Pere Bernier, leaving his wife almost fainting from horror, rushed to the door of M. Darzac's room and beat against it, crying aloud to him to open, but obtaining no reply. The struggle within was still going on. Bernier heard the laboured breathing of two men and he recognised the voice of Larsan when he heard the words: "With this blow, I shall have your life!" Then he heard M. Darzac, who called his wife to his aid in a voice almost stifled, as though he were gagged, "Mathilde! Mathilde!" Evidently he and Larsan must have been engaged in a life and death struggle when, suddenly, the pistol shot had saved him. This pistol shot had frightened Pere Bernier less than the cry which had followed it. One would have thought that Mme. Darzac, who had uttered the cry, had been mortally wounded. Bernier was unable to understand Mme. Darzac's attitude in the matter. Why did she not open the door and admit him to help her husband? Why did she not draw the shades? Finally, almost immediately after the pistol shot, the door, upon which Pere Bernier had not stopped knocking all the time, was opened. The room was wrapped in darkness, which did not surprise the concierge, for the light of the chandelier which he had perceived under the door during the fight had been suddenly extinguished and at the same moment he had heard the chandelier itself fall heavily to the floor. It was Mme. Darzac who had opened the door and Bernier could distinguish through the gloom the form of M. Darzac leaning over something which the concierge knew was a dying man. Bernier had called to his wife to bring a light, but Mme. Darzac had cried: "No, no! No light! no light! And, above all, be sure that *he* knows nothing." And immediately she had rushed to the door of the tower, calling out, "He is coming! he is coming! I hear him Open the door, Pere Bernier' I must go and meet him!" And Pere Bernier had opened the door, the while she kept on moaning, "Hide yourselves! Go in Don't let him know anything!"

Pere Bernier went on:

"You came like a waterspout, M. Rouletabille. And she drew you into Old Bob's sitting room. You saw nothing. I stayed with M. Darzac. The rattle in the throat of the man on the floor had ceased. M. Darzac still bending over him said to me: "Get a sack, Bernier, a sack and a stone, and we will throw him into the sea and no one will ever hear his voice again!"

"Then," Bernier went on, "I thought of my sack of potatoes; my wife had gathered them up and put them back in the sack after you had emptied them out; I emptied the bag again and brought it to him. We made as little noise as possible. During this time, Madame was, I suppose, telling you the story in Old Bob's sitting room and we heard M. Sainclair questioning my wife in the lodge. Moving very quietly, we had slipped the body, which M. Darzac had tied up, into the sack. But I said to M. Darzac: 'Let me beg of you not to throw it into the water. It is not deep enough to hide it. There are days when the sea is so clear that one may look down to the bottom.' 'What shall we do, then?' whispered M. Darzac. I answered: 'Heaven help us, I don't know, monsieur! All that I could do for you and for Madame and for humanity against a villain like Frederic Larsan, I have done and willingly. But don't ask any more of me and may God protect you!' And I went out of the room and found you in the lodge, M. Sainclair. And then you went for M. Rouletabille at the request of M. Darzac, who had come out of his own apartment. As for my wife, she was almost swooning with terror when she suddenly saw that both M. Darzac and myself were covered with blood. See, messieurs, my hands are red Pray Heaven, it doesn't bring us misfortune! But we have done our duty. Oh, he was a miserable wretch!—But do you want me to tell you?—well, one could never keep such a history secret—and, in my opinion, it would be better to go immediately with it to the justice. I have promised to keep silence and I did keep silence so long as I was able, but I'm glad enough to relieve myself of such a burden before you gentlemen who are the friends of Monsieur and Madame—and who may, perhaps, be able to make them listen to reason. Why should they hide the facts? Isn't it an honour to have killed Larsan!—Pardon me for having spoken his name—I know well, it was not right—but is it not an honour to have saved the whole world from a scoundrel in saving oneself? Ah! hold! a fortune! Mme. Darzac promised me a fortune, if I would keep silence. What do I care for that? Could one have a better fortune than to be of service to the poor lady who has had so many troubles? Never in the world' But, how she looked! Why should she have feared? I asked her when we thought that you had gone to bed and that we three were all alone in the Square Tower with our corpse. I said to her, 'Tell everyone that you have killed him All the world will praise you!' She answered: 'There has been too much scandal already, Bernier: and as much as it depends on me to do, and as much as is possible, I will hide this new horror forever! It would kill my father!' I had nothing to say to that, but I wanted to speak. It was upon the tip of my tongue to say, 'If the business comes out later, one will believe that you did something wrong and monsieur, your father, will die just as surely.' But it was her idea. She wished that all should be concealed! Well, I promised her. That's all!"

Bernier turned toward the door, showing us his hands.

"I must rid myself of the blood of the accursed pig!" he said, dryly.

Rouletabille stopped him.

"And what was M. Darzac saying all this time? What was his opinion?"

"He repeated: 'What Mme. Darzac says is right. She must be obeyed implicitly.' His shirt was torn and he had a slight wound in his throat, but it did not seem to bother him at all, and, indeed, there was only one thing in which he seemed interested, and that was as to how the miserable wretch had gotten into his rooms. I told him what I have told you—that he could not have entered without my seeing him, and I told him just how I had passed every moment of my time. His first words on the subject had been: 'But when I came in a little while ago, there was no one in my room and I shut and bolted the door.'"

"Where did this conversation take place?"

"In the lodge, in the presence of my wife, who was nearly frightened to death, poor thing!"

"And the body? Where was that?"

"It lay in the sleeping room of M. Darzac."

"And how was it decided that it should be disposed of?"

"I can't say as to that for certain, but their resolution was taken, for Mme. Darzac said to me: 'Bernier, I am going to ask of you one last service: go and bring the English cart from the stable and harness Toby to it. Don't waken Walter, if you can help it. If you wake him and he asks for any explanations, say this to him and also to Mattoni, who has the watch at the postern: "It is for M. Darzac, who must be at Castelar at four o'clock in the morning to see the tournament in the Alps."' Mme. Darzac said also: 'If you meet M. Sainclair, bring him to me, but if you meet M. Rouletabille, say nothing to him and do nothing that may attract his attention.' Ah, Monsieur! Madame did not let me go out until the window of your room was closed and your light extinguished! And, then, we were not entirely certain in regard to the body which we believed to be dead, before it sighed once more—and, my God! what a sigh! The rest, Monsieur, you saw for yourself and now you know as much as I. God help us!"

When Bernier had finished relating this incredible story, Rouletabille put his hand on his arm, thanking him most earnestly for his great devotion to his master and mistress, and begged him to use the utmost discretion. The young reporter entreated the old servant to pardon his roughness and ordered him to say nothing to Mme. Darzac of anything that had passed between them. Bernier extended his hand in token of fidelity, but Rouletabille drew back:

"No—I can't, Bernier! You are covered with blood."

Bernier left us to look for the Lady in Black.

"Well!" I said when we were alone. "Larsan is dead!"

"Yes," answered Rouletabille. "I fear so!"

"You fear so why, in Heaven's name?"

"Because," he answered in a strange tone, which I could scarcely recognize as his. "Because the death of Larsan, who is carried out dead from a place which he never entered dead or alive, terrifies me more than his life itself!"

XIII

In Which the Fears of Rouletabille Assume Alarming Proportions

I t was literally true that he was frightened. And I was more terrified myself than words could express. I had never seen him in such a state of mental inquietude. He walked up and down the room nervously, occasionally stopping in front of the mirror and passing his hand over his forehead, as if he were asking his own image, "Can it be you, Rouletabille, who have such thoughts? How dare you harbour them?" What thoughts? He seemed rather to be upon the point of thinking than to be actually doing so, and to be using every means of driving thought away. He shook his head savagely and started for the window as though he meant to leap out, leaning forth into the night, listening for the slightest noise on the distant bank of the sea, expecting, perhaps, to hear the wheels of the little carriage and the echo of Toby's shoes. One might have thought him a beast at bay. The surf was quiet; the waves had grown entirely appeased. A white ray appeared suddenly shining over the black waters. It was the dawn. And in a moment the old château seemed to rise out of the night, pale and livid with the same pallor as our own—the pallor of one who has not slept. "Rouletabille," I asked, trembling as I spoke, for I felt that I was intruding upon ground where my feet had no right to tread; "your interview with your mother was very brief and you separated in silence. I want to ask you, my boy, whether she told you the story of the accident with the revolver on the night stand that Bernier told me?"

"No," he answered without turning his face toward me.

"She told you nothing of that kind?"

"No."

"And you did not ask her for any explanation of the pistol shot nor of the death cry—the cry that was the echo of the one which we heard two years ago from her lips in the 'inexplicable gallery'?"

"Sainclair, you are too curious—you are more curious than I. I asked her nothing."

"And you swore to see nothing and to hear nothing without her saying anything to you about the pistol shot and the cry?"

"Truly, Sainclair, it was necessary for me to believe—for my part, I respected the secrets of the Lady in Black. I had nothing to ask of her when she said to me, 'We must leave each other now, my child, but nothing can ever separate us again!'"

"Ah, she said that to you—'Nothing can ever separate us again'?"

"Yes, my friend—and there was blood upon her hands."

We looked at each other in silence. I was now at the window and beside the reporter. Suddenly his hand touched mine. Then he pointed to the little taper which was burning at the entrance to the subterranean door which led to Old Bob's study in the Tower of the Bold.

"It is dawn," said Rouletabille. "And Old Bob is still at work. This old fellow is certainly industrious and we will go and have a peep at him at his labours. That will change our current of thought and I shall be able to get away from these horrors that are smothering me and driving me half wild."

And he heaved a long sigh.

"Will Darzac never return!" he murmured, more as though he were speaking to himself than to me.

A few moments later we had crossed the court and had descended into the octagon room of the Tower of Charles the Bold. It was empty. The lamp was burning on the work table, but there was no sign of Old Bob.

"Oh!" cried Rouletabille. He picked up the lamp and carried it from place to place examining everything around him. He tried in turn the lock of every little window which opened from the walls of the basement. Nothing had changed its place, and all was arranged in order and scientific etiquette. While we were looking around at the bones and shells and horns of the prehistoric ages, the "hanging crystals," the rings made out of bone, the buckles formed from teeth, and the other treasures of the savant, we came to the little desk table. There we found the "oldest skull in the history of humanity"; and it was true that it had been spattered with the red paint of the wash drawing which M. Darzac had set to dry upon that part of the desk which faced the window and was exposed to the sun. I went from one window to the other and shook the iron bars in order to assure myself that they had not been touched nor tampered with in any way. Rouletabille saw what I was doing and said:

"What are you about? Before thinking about how he could have gotten out at the windows, wouldn't it be better to find out whether he went by the door?"

He set the lamp upon the parapet and looked for traces of footprints. Then Rouletabille said:

"Go and knock at the door of the Square Tower and ask Bernier whether Old Bob has come in. Ask Mattoni at the postern and Pere Jacques at the iron gate. Go, Sainclair—quick!"

Five minutes after I went out I was back with the information. No one had seen Old Bob in any part of the fortress. He had not passed by anywhere. Rouletabille had his face close to the parapet. He said:

"He left this lamp burning in order to make people believe that he was at work." And then he added, softly: "There is no sign of a struggle of any sort and in the sand I find the traces of the footprints of only M. Arthur Rance and M. Robert Darzac, who came to this room during the storm last night and have brought on their feet a little earth from the court of the Bold and also of the claylike soil of the outer court. There is no footprint which could be Old Bob's. Old Bob reached here before and, perhaps, went out while the tempest was raging, but, in any case, he has not come in since." Rouletabille stood erect. He replaced upon the desk the lamp the rays of which fell directly upon the skull which had been splashed by the red paint in a frightful fashion. Around us there were dozens of skeletons but certainly their presence was less alarming to me than the absence of Old Bob.

Rouletabille stood for a moment staring at the crimson skull, then he took it in his hands and held his eyes close to its empty orbits. Then he raised the skull higher and held it at arms' length, gazing at it with an almost breathless interest; he looked at the profile. Then he placed the hideous object in my hands and told me to raise it to the level of my head, as carefully as thought it were the most precious of burdens while Rouletabille brought the lamp very close to it.

Like a flash an idea pierced through my brain. I let the skull fall on the desk and rushed through the court till I came to the oubliette. I discovered that the iron bars which closed it were still fast. If anyone had fled by that way or had fallen into the shaft or had thrown himself down, the bars would have been opened. I hurried back, more anxious than ever.

"Rouletabille! Rouletabille! There is no way that Old Bob could have gotten out except in the sack!"

I repeated the sentence, but my friend was not listening and I was surprised to see him deeply engrossed in a task of which I found it impossible to guess the meaning. How, at a time as tragic as the present, while we were awaiting only the return of M. Darzac to complete the circle in which the impossible body was found—while in the Square Tower, the Lady in Black, like Lady MacBeth, must be occupied in effacing from her hands the stains of the strangest of crimes, Rouletabille seemed to be amusing himself by making drawings with a foot rule, a square, a measure and a compass. There he was, seated in the old geologist's easy chair with Robert Darzac's drawing board before him and he also was making a plan—quiet and imperturbable as an architect's clerk.

He had pricked the paper with one of the points of his compass while the other point traced the circle which might represent the Tower of the Bold as we could see it in the design of M. Darzac. Then, dipping his brush into a tiny dish half full of the red pain which M. Darzac had been using he carefully spread the paint over the entire space occupied by the circle. In doing this, he was extremely particular, giving the greatest attention to seeing that the paint was of the same thickness at every point, just as a student might have done in preparing a lesson. He bent his head first to the right and then to the left as though to see the effect, moistening his lips with his tongue as though he were meditating earnestly. In a moment he gave a little start and then sat motionless. His eyes were fixed on the drawing as thought they had been glued to it. They did not even move in their sockets. The stillness was horrible, but it was not much better when his lips opened to utter an exclamation of breathless horror. His face looked like that of a maniac. And he turned toward me so quickly that he upset the great easy chair in which he had been seated.

"Sainclair! Sainclair! Look at the red paint! Look at the red paint!"

I leaned over the drawing breathless terrified of the savage exultation of his tone. But I could see a little drawing carefully done. "The red paint! The red paint!" he kept groaning, his eyes staring in his head as though he were witnessing some frightful spectacle.

"But what—what is it?" I stammered.

"'*What is it?*' My god, man, can't you see? Don't you know that that is *blood*?"

No, I did not know it indeed. I was quite sure that it wasn't blood. It was merely red paint. But I took care not to contradict Rouletabille. I feigned to be interested in this idea of blood.

"Whose blood?" I inquired. "Do you think that it can be Larsan's?"

"Oh! oh! oh! Larsan's blood? Who knows anything about Larsan's blood? Who has ever seen the colour of it? To see that, it would be necessary to open my own veins, Sainclair. That's the only way!"

I was completely overwhelmed and astonished. "My father would not let his blood be spilled like that!"

He was speaking again with that strange, desperate pride of his father.

"When my father wears a wig, it will fit! My father would not let his blood be spilled like that!"

"Bernier's hands were covered with it and you yourself saw it upon the hand of the Lady in Black."

"Yes, yes! That is true—that is true! But they could never kill my father like that!"

He seemed to grow more excited every moment and he never ceased gazing on the little wash drawing. At last he spoke, his breast shaken with a great sob.

"O, God! O God! O God, have pity on us! That would be too frightful!"

He ceased for a moment and then spoke again:

"My poor mother did not deserve this I did not deserve it—nor any one in the world!" A tear ran down his cheek and fell into the little dish of paint.

"Ah!" he cried. "It isn't necessary to fill it any fuller." And he picked up the tiny cup with infinite care and carried it to the cabinet.

Then he took me by the hand and bade me look at him carefully—carefully—and tell him whether he had not really gone suddenly insane.

"Let us go! let us go!" he said, drearily, at last. "The time is come, Sainclair. No matter what happens, we can never turn back now! The Lady in Black must tell us everything—*everything about the man who is in that sack*! Ah, if M. Darzac were to return immediately—immediately—it might be less painful—but I dare wait no longer!"

Wait for what? Wait for whom? And why should he be so terrified now? What fear had made his eyes so wild? Why did his teeth chatter?

I could not restrain myself from asking him again: "What are you afraid of: Do you think that Lar san is not dead?"

And he answered, gripping my hand as though he would never release it :"I tell you I fear his death more than I fear his life!"

And he knocked at the door of the Square Tower before which we were standing as he spoke. I asked him whether he did not wish me to leave him alone with his mother. But, to my great surprise, he begged me not to abandon him "for anything in the world—so that the circle should not be closed." And he added mournfully. "Perhaps it may never be!"

The door of the Tower remained closed. He knocked again; then it was opened and we saw Bernier's face appear. He seemed embarrassed at the sight of us. "What do you want? What are you doing here again?" he demanded. "Speak low. Madame is in Old Bob's sitting room. And the old man has not come in yet."

"Let us enter, Bernier" said Rouletabille. And he pushed the door further open.

"But whatever you do, don't let Madame suspect—"

"No, no!" replied Rouletabille, impatiently.

We were in the vestibule of the Tower. The darkness was almost impenetrable.

"What is Madame doing in Old Bob's sitting room?" asked the reporter in a low voice.

"She is waiting—waiting for the return of M. Darzac. She dare not reënter *the room* until he comes—nor I, either!"

"Well, go back into your lodge, Bernier!" ordered Rouletabille. "And wait until I call you."

The young reporter opened the door of Old Bob's salon, and we saw the form of the Lady in Black, or, rather, her shadow, for the apartment was very dark and the first faint rays of the sun had scarcely penetrated it. The tall, sombre silhouette of Mathilde was standing but it leaned against the corner of the window which looked out upon the court of Charles the Bold. She never moved at our entrance, but her lips opened and a voice that I should never have recognised as hers, murmured:

"Why are you come? I saw you crossing the court. You have been there all night. You know all. What do you want now?"

And she added in a tone of unutterable misery:

"You swore to me that you would seek to know nothing."

Rouletabille went to her side and took her hand reverently.

"Come, Mother, dearest!" he said and the simple words upon his lips sounded like a prayer, tender and imploring. "Come—come!"

And he drew her away. She did not resist in the least. It was as though as soon as he touched her hand, he could bend her to his will. But when he led her to the door of the fatal chamber, her whole frame seemed to recoil. "Not there!" she moaned.

And she reeled against the wall to keep herself from falling. Rouletabille tried the door. It was locked. He called Bernier, who opened the door and then hurried away as though he were bent on escaping from some deadly peril.

Once the door was opened, we looked into the room. What a spectacle we beheld! The chamber was in the most frightful disorder. And the crimson dawn which entered through the vast embrasures rendered the disorder still more sinister. What an illumination for a chamber of horrors! Blood was upon the walls and upon the floor and upon the furniture! The blood of the rising sun and the blood of him whom Toby had carried off in the sack, no one knew whither—in the potato bag! The tables, the chairs, the sofas were all overturned. The curtains of the bed to which the man in his death agony had tried desperately to cling were half torn down and one could distinguish upon one of them the mark of a bloody hand.

It was into this scene that we entered, supporting the Lady in Black, who seemed ready to swoon, while Rouletabille kept murmuring to her in his gentle and pleading tones: "It has to be done, Mother! It has to be done!" And as soon as he had placed her upon a couch which I had turned right side up, he began to question her. She answered in monosyllables, by signs of the head or movements of the hands. And I saw that the further the examination progressed, the more troubled and restless Rouletabille became. He was visibly affected. He endeavoured to regain his composure and to help his mother maintain hers but it was difficult for him to succeed in either effort. He spoke to the unhappy woman as though he were still her little child. He called her "mamma" and tried in every way to show his reverence and love for her. But she had utterly lost courage. He held out his arms and she threw herself into them; the son and mother embraced and that seemed to give her a little more strength and she burst into a fit of weeping which seemed to relieve a little the terrible weight upon her breast. I made a movement as if to retire, but both sought to detain me and I saw that they did not wish to be left alone in this room red with blood.

Mme. Darzac, after her sobs had ceased, murmured:

"We are delivered!"

Rouletabille had fallen upon his knees at her side and, as she uttered the words, he said entreatingly: "Mother, dearest, in order that we may be sure of that—quite sure—you must tell me all that happened—everything that you saw."

Then she told us the story. She looked at the closed door; she looked with what seemed to be new horror at the overturned furniture and the blood-spattered walls and floor and she narrated the details of the frightful scene through which she had passed in a voice so low as to be almost inaudible, and I was obliged to bring my ear close to her to hear at all. In short, halting phrases, she told us that as soon as M. Darzac had entered his room, he had drawn the bolt and had walked straight to the little table which was placed in the centre of the room. The Lady in Black was standing a little nearer the left, ready to pass into her own sleeping room. The apartment was lighted only by a wax candle placed on the night commode, at the left, near Mathilde's door. And this is what happened:

The silence of the room was suddenly broken by a loud crash, like that of a piece of furniture falling to the ground, which made both M. and Mme. Darzac quickly raise their heads while their hearts were struck at the same moment by the same thrill of terror. The crash came from the little panel. And then all was silent. The pair looked at each other without daring to utter a word, perhaps without being able to do so. Darzac made a movement toward the panel which was situated at the back of the room on the right hand side. He was nailed to the spot where he stood by a second crash, louder than the first, and this time it seemed to Mathilde that she could see the panel move. The Lady in Black asked herself whether she were the victim of a hallucination, or if she had really seen the panel move. But Darzac had seen the same thing, for he made a hasty step in that direction. But at that very moment, the panel swung open before them. Pushed by an invisible hand it turned on its hinges. The Lady in Black tried to cry out, but her tongue clove to the roots of her mouth. But she made a gesture of terror and bewilderment which threw the wax candle to the ground at the very moment when a shadowy form issued from the panel. Uttering a cry of rage, Robert Darzac rushed upon the figure.

"And that shadow—that shadow had a face that you could see?" interrupted Rouletabille. "Mamma, why did you not see the face? You have killed the shadow, but how do we know that it was Larsan, if you did not see his face? Perhaps you have not even killed Larsan's shadow."

"Oh, yes," she replied, almost listlessly. "He is dead." And then for a moment, she said no more.

And I looked at Rouletabille, asking myself: Who could have been killed if it were not Larsan? If Mathilde had not seen his face, she had certainly heard his voice. She shuddered yet at the recollection—she heard it yet. And Bernier, too, had heard the voice and recognised it—that terrible voice of Larsan's—the voice of Ballmeyer, who in that fearful conflict in the middle of the night, had promised death to Robert Darzac. "This blow will end your life!" while Darzac could only groan in the tones of a dying man, "Mathilde! Mathilde!" Ah, how he had cried to her!—how he had called with the rattle in his throat, as he lay already vanquished and in the shadow of death! And she—she had only to throw her own shadow, swooning with terror, into the midst of those two other shadows, while the man she loved called upon her for the aid she could not give and which could not come from elsewhere. And then, suddenly, there had come the pistol shot and she had uttered that terrible shriek—as though she had been wounded, herself. "Who was dead? Who was living? Who was speaking? Whose voice would she hear?"

And then it was Robert who spoke.

Rouletabille took the Lady in Black into his arms once more, lifted her up and carried her tenderly to the door of her own room. And there, he said to her: "Mamma, you must leave me now. I have work to do—for you, for M. Darzac and for myself."

"Don't leave me! I beg of you not to leave me until Robert comes back!" she cried in terror. Rouletabille begged her to try and take some rest and promised to remain near her if she would close her door, when someone knocked at the door of the corridor. Rouletabille asked who was there and the voice of Darzac answered.

"At last!" cried Rouletabille, and he threw the door open.

The man who entered looked like a corpse. Never was human face so pallid, so bloodless, so devoid of all semblance of life. So many emotions had ravaged his visage that it expressed not a single one.

"Ah! you were there!" he said. "Well, it is over." And he fell into the chair from which Rouletabille had just raised the Lady in Black. He looked up at her.

"Your wish is realised," he said. "It is where you wished it to be."

"Did you see his face?" questioned Rouletabille excitedly.

"No," answered Darzac, wearily. "I have not seen it. Did you think that I was going to open the sack?"

I thought that Rouletabille would have shown discomfiture at this answer but, on the contrary, he turned to M. Darzac and said:

"Ah, you did not see his face. That's very good, indeed." And he pressed his hand affectionately.

"The important thing now," he went on, "is not that, at all. It is necessary that we should close the circle. And you will help us do that, M. Darzac. Wait a moment."

And almost joyously, he threw himself down on all fours and crawled around among the furniture and under the bed as I had seen him do in the Yellow Room. And from time to time, he raised his head to say:

"Ah, I shall find something—something that will save us."

I answered, looking at M. Darzac: "Aren't we saved already?"

"Which will save our brains," Rouletabille went on.

"The boy is right!" exclaimed M. Darzac. "It is absolutely necessary for us to know how that man got into the room."

Suddenly Rouletabille rose to his feet, holding in his hand a revolver which he had found under the panel.

"Ah! you have found his revolver!" cried M. Darzac.

"Fortunately, he did not have time to use it." As he spoke M. Darzac took from his pocket his own revolver—the revolver which had saved his life—and held it out to the young man.

"This is a good weapon!" he said.

Rouletabille examined it closely and looked into the empty barrel out of which had sped the ball which had dealt death; then he compared the pistol with that which he had found under the panel and which had fallen from the hand of the assassin. The latter was a "bull dog" and bore the mark of a London gunsmith; it seemed to be quite new, every barrel was filled and Rouletabille declared that it had never been fired.

"Larsan only avails himself of firearms in the last extremity," said the young man. "He hates noise of any kind. You may be sure that he intended merely to frighten you with his revolver, otherwise he would have fired it immediately."

And Rouletabille returned M. Darzac's revolver and put Larsan's in his pocket.

"Of what use is it to be armed now?" cried M. Darzac, shaking his head. "I assure you it is quite futile."

"You believe so?" demanded Rouletabille.

"I am certain of it."

Rouletabille made a few steps through the room and said:

"With Larsan, one can never be sure of anything. Where is the body?"

M. Darzac replied.

"Ask my wife. I want to forget all about it. I know nothing more about this horrible thing. When the remembrance of that dreadful journey shall return to me, I shall try to make myself believe that it was a nightmare. And I will drive it away. Never speak to me of it again. No one save Mme. Darzac knows where the body is. She may tell you, if she likes."

"I have forgotten, too!" said Mathilde. "I was obliged to do so."

"Nevertheless," insisted Rouletabille, shaking his head, "you must tell me. You said that he was in his agony. Are you sure that he is dead now?"

"I am perfectly sure," replied M. Darzac, simply.

"Oh, it is finished. Is it not entirely ended?" pleaded Mathilde. She arose and walked to the window. "See! there is the sun! This horrible night is dead—dead, forever! Everything is over!"

Poor Lady in Black! The yearnings of her soul revealed themselves in her words. "It is finished!" And the fact, as she believed it, made her forget all the horror of the scene which had passed in this room. Larsan no more! Larsan buried! Buried in the potato sack!

And we all started up in affright, when the Lady in Black began to laugh—the frantic laugh of a mad woman! She ceased as suddenly as she had begun and a horrible stillness followed. We dared look neither at her nor at each other she was the first to speak.

"It is all over!" she said. "Forgive me: I won't laugh again."

And then Rouletabille said, speaking in a very low tone:

"It will be over when we know how he got in."

"What good would it do?" replied the Lady in Black.

"It is a question to which he alone knows the answer. He is the only one who could tell us and he is dead."

"He will not be truly dead for us until we know that," responded Rouletabille.

"Evidently," said M. Darzac, "so long as we do not know that, we shall be uneasy and he will be there in our minds. He must be driven away! he must be!"

"Let us try to drive him away then," said Rouletabille.

And he went to the Lady in Black and gently took her hand in his and attempted to draw her into the next room, begging her to lie down and rest. But Mathilde declared that she would not go. She said: "What! you would drive Larsan away and I not here!" And her voice sounded as though she were about to laugh again. I made a sign to Rouletabille not to insist upon her absence.

Rouletabille opened the door leading into the corridor and called

Bernier and his wife. They did not wish to enter, but we insisted on their doing so, and a general consultation took place from which we deduced the following facts:

(1) Rouletabille had visited the apartment at five o'clock and searched behind the panel and at that time there was no one in the room.

(2) After five o'clock, the door of the apartment had been twice opened by Pere Bernier, who alone had the right to open it in the absence of M. and Mme. Darzac. The first time was at five o'clock to permit M. Darzac to enter; the next at eleven o'clock to admit M. and Mme. Darzac.

(3) Bernier had locked the door of the apartment when M. Darzac went out with us between a quarter past and half past six.

(4) The door of the apartment had been locked and bolted by M. Darzac as soon as he entered his room, both in the afternoon and in the evening.

(5) Bernier had stood guard before the door of the apartment from five o'clock till eleven o'clock with a brief interruption of not more than two minutes at six o'clock.

When we had discussed and fully established these facts, Rouletabille, who was sitting at M. Darzac's desk taking notes, arose and said:

"So far, it is very simple. We have only one hope. It is in the few moments that Bernier was off guard about six o'clock. At least, at that time, no one was in front of the door. But there was someone behind it. It was you, M. Darzac. Can you reiterate, after having thoroughly searched your memory, that when you went into your room, you instantly closed the door and drew the bolt?"

"I can!" replied M. Darzac, solemnly; and he added:

"And I opened that door only when you and Sainclair knocked upon it. I swear it."

And in saying this, as later events proved, the man spoke the truth.

Rouletabille thanked the Berniers and dismissed them to get some rest. Then, his voice trembling, the lad said:

"It is well, M. Darzac, you have closed the circle. The apartment in the Square Tower is now closed as firmly as was the Yellow Room which was like a strong box, or as the 'inexplicable gallery.'"

"One would guess immediately that Larsan was mixed up in the affair!" I exclaimed. "It is the same mode of procedure!" "Yes," observed Mme. Darzac. "Yes, M. Sainclair, it is the same mode of procedure." And she unfastened her husband's collar to show the wounds hidden beneath it.

"See!" she said. "They are the same nail prints. I know them well."

There was a sorrowful silence.

M. Darsac, caring only to solve this strange problem, reviewed the crime of the Glandier. And he repeated what he had said in the Yellow Room:

"There must be a passage in the floor, in the ceiling or in the walls."

"There is not," replied Rouletabille.

"Then he must have found some way to make one," persisted M. Darzac.

"Why?" asked Rouletabille. "Did he do anything of the sort in the Yellow Room?"

"Oh, this isn't the same thing at all!" I exclaimed. "This apartment is more firmly closed than the Yellow Room since no one could have gotten into it before nor after."

"No, it is not the same thing," pronounced Rouletabille. "It is just the opposite. In the Yellow Room, there was a body missing: in the room in the Round Tower, there is a body too many."

And he tottered out, leaning on my arm so as not to fall. The Lady in Black rushed toward him. He had strength enough left to stop her with a gesture.

"Oh—this is nothing!" he said. "I'm a little tired, that's all!"

XIV

The Sack of Potatoes

While M. Darzac, with the assistance of Bernier, busied himself, as Rouletabille advised, with obliterating all signs of the tragedy, the Lady in Black, who had hastily changed her dress, hurried to her father's rooms in order not to run the risk of encountering any of the other members of the party. Her last word was to counsel us to prudence and silence. Rouletabille also took leave of us.

It was now about seven o'clock in the morning and things began to stir in and about the château. We could hear the fishermen singing in their boats. I threw myself upon my bed, and in a few moments I was sleeping profoundly, vanquished by the physical weariness which was stronger than my powers of resistance. When I awakened, I lay for a few moments on my couch in a pleasant bewilderment, but as the events of the night dawned on my remembrance, I started up in terror.

"Ah!" I cried out, "A body too many! No, no! It can't be! It's impossible!"

It was this which surged across the dark gulf of my thoughts, above the abyss of my memory; this impossibility of "a body too many." And the horror which I found in my heart at my awakening was not confined to myself—far from it! All those who had mingled, near or far, in this strange drama of the Square Tower, shared it; and even though the horror of the event itself were appeased—the horror of the body in its last throes of agony thrown into a sack which a man carried off at night to cast it into who knows what far off and profound and mysterious tomb where it might gasp out its last breath of life—even if, I say, this horror should be forgotten and blotted out of the mind, and effaced from the vision, yet still the impossibility of this "body too many" grew and increased and rose up before us higher and higher and more threatening and more dreadful. Certain persons there are—like Mme. Edith, for example—who deny almost from habit, anything which they cannot understand—who deny the presentation of the problem which destiny holds for us (such as we have established in the preceding chapter) even while every event and every circumstance among those which had the Fort of Hercules for their theatre rendered proof of the exactitude of the presentation.

First of all, the attack! How had the attack been made? At what moment? By what means of approach? What mines, trenches, covered paths, breaches—in the domains of the mental fortifications—have served the assailant and delivered the château over into his hands? Yes, under the existing conditions, where was the attack? The answer is—silence. And yet, the facts must be brought to light. Rouletabille has said so: he ought to know. In a siege as mysterious as this, the attack may be in everything or in nothing. The assailant is as still as the grave itself and the assault is made without clamour and the enemy approaches the walls walking in his stocking feet. The *attack*? It is, perhaps, in the very stillness itself, but again, it may, perhaps, be in the spoken word. It is in a tone, in a sigh, in a breath. It is in a gesture, but if perhaps it may be in all which is hidden, it may be, also, in all that is revealed—in *everything which one sees and which one does not see.*

Eleven o'clock! Where was Rouletabille? His bed had not been disturbed. I dressed myself hurriedly and went to look for my friend, whom I found in the outer court. He took me by the arm and led me into the vast drawing room of "la Louve." There, I was surprised to find, although it was not yet time for luncheon, everybody assembled. M. and Mme. Darzac were there. It seemed to me that M. Rance's manner was rather frigid. When he shook my hand in wishing me good morning, he barely touched my fingers. As soon as we entered the room Mme. Edith, from the dark corner where she was reclining carelessly on a sofa, saluted us with the words:

"Ah, here is M. Rouletabille with his friend, Sainclair. Now we shall know why we have all been summoned here!"

To this remark, Rouletabille responded by first excusing himself for having requested us all to gather at so early an hour; but he had, he went on to say, such a serious and important communication to make to us that he had not wished to delay it one moment longer than was absolutely necessary. His tone was so grave that Edith pretended to shiver and counterfeited an infantile terror. But Rouletabille, without noticing her, continued: "Before you shiver, Madame, wait until you know what you have to be afraid of. I have some news for you which is very far from pleasant."

We all looked at him, and then at each other! What was he about to say? I endeavoured to read in the faces of M. and Mme. Darzac what they thought of the matter. Both showed remarkably little evidence of last night's horrors! But what was it that Rouletabille had to say to us? He entreated those who were standing to be seated and then he began to speak. He addressed himself to Mme. Rance.

"First of all, Madame, permit me to inform you that I have decided to suppress the 'guard' which surrounded the Château of Hercules, like an inner wall, and which I judged necessary for the protection of M. and Mme. Darzac which you kindly allowed me to establish, although it vexed you, showing the most charming of good humour and accommodating spirit."

This direct allusion to the mocking remarks and innuendos of Mme. Edith at the time when we mounted guard made Mr. Rance and his wife both smile. But no smile arose to the lips of M. or Mme. Darzac nor myself, for we had begun to ask ourselves anxiously what the boy was preparing to say.

"Ah, really, are you going to withdraw the guard for the château, M. Rouletabille? Well, I am very glad to hear it, although I assure you that it did not vex me in the least!" exclaimed Mme. Edith with an affectation of gayety. "On the contrary, it had interested me very much, because, you know, I am of a very romantic nature, and if I rejoice at the change, it is because the fact proves to me that M. and Mme. Darzac are no longer in any danger."

"This is true, Madame," replied Rouletabille, "since last night."

Mme. Darzac could not refrain from a hasty movement which no one save myself perceived.

"So much the better!" cried Mme. Edith. "May Heaven be praised! But how is it that my husband and I are the last to hear the news? Interesting things must have been happening last night! The nocturnal trip of M. Darzac to Castelar was one of them, without doubt!" As she spoke, I could see the embarrassment of M. and Mme. Darzac. The former, after a glance at his wife, started to speak, but Rouletabille would not permit him to do so.

"Madame, I do not know where M. Darzac went last night, but it is necessary that you should know one thing: and that is the reason why M. and Mme. Darzac have ceased to run any danger. Your husband, Madame, has told you of the frightful tragedy of the Glandier two years ago and of the villainous part played in it by—"

"Frederic Larsan—yes, monsieur, I know all that."

"You know also, of course, that the reason why we have placed such a strong guard here around M. Darzac and his wife was because we had seen this man again?"

"I do."

"Well, M. and Mme. Darzac are no longer in danger because this man cannot appear again ever."

"What has become of him?"

"He is dead."

"When did he die?"

"Last night."

"And how did he die last night?"

"He was killed, madame."

"And where was he killed?"

"In the Square Tower."

We all sprang to our feet at this declaration in the greatest agitation. M. and Mme. Rance seemed completely stupefied by the words which they had heard and M. and Mme. Darzac and myself were plunged into the most profound agitation by the fact that Rouletabille had not hesitated to reveal the secret.

"In the Square Tower?" cried Mme. Edith. "And who, then, has killed him?"

"M. Robert Darzac," replied Rouletabille. "And he entreats everyone to sit down."

It was astonishing how we seated ourselves with one accord, as though, at such a moment, we had nothing to do except to obey this youngster. But almost immediately Mme. Edith arose and seizing M. Darzac by the hand, she exclaimed with an emphasis which made me decide that I had judged her wrongly when I called her affected:

"Bravo, Monsieur Robert! All right! You are a gentleman!" Then she paid some exaggerated compliments—for after all, it was her nature to exaggerate things—to Mme. Darzac. She swore eternal friendship for her; she declared that she and her husband were ready, under all circumstances, to stand by the Darzacs and that the latter might count upon their zeal and their devotion and that they would swear whatever one liked before all the judges in the tribunal.

"Gently, dear Madame," interrupted Rouletabille. "There is no question of judges and we hope that there may not be. There's no need of it. Larsan was a dead man in the eyes of the whole world long before he was killed last night—he will continue to be dead, that is all! We have decided that it would be useless to reopen a scandal of which M. and Mme. Darzac have already been made the innocent victims and we have counted upon your assistance. The affair has happened in so mysterious a fashion that even you, if we had not informed you in regard to it, would never have suspected. But M. and Mme. Darzac are endowed with sentiments too noble to permit them to forget what they owe to their hosts. The most simple rules of hospitality ordered them to tell you that they killed a man in your house last night. How foolish it would be to lay bare this unfortunate story to some Italian police officer and subject you to the inconvenience of having your names coupled with the miserable business, and, it might easily be, to have a search made of your house and hired servants of the law under your roof! M. and Mme. Darzac, for your sakes alone, are anxious that you should not run the risk of being the object of idle gossip, or, perhaps, of having the police descend upon your home."

M. Arthur Rance, who up to this time had remained speechless, arose and said, his face as pallid as though he had seen a ghost:

"Frederic Larsan is dead. Well, so far so good, and no one is more rejoiced than myself to know it. And if he has received the punishment due to his crimes from the hand of M. Darsac, no one is more to be congratulated than M. Darzac. But I consider that it would be wrong for M. Darzac to make any attempt to conceal an act which is an honour to himself. It would be better to inform the authorities and without delay. If they should come to learn of this affair from others, rather than by our means, think of what the situation would be! If we give out the information ourselves, we shall show that an act of justice has been committed. If we conceal anything, we shall place ourselves in the category of malefactors. People might even suppose—"

To listen to M. Rance's stammering speech and to observe his demeanour, one might almost have imagined that he was the slayer of Frederic Larsan—he who was in danger of being accused of murder and dragged to prison.

"It is necessary to think of everything, gentlemen," he concluded. And Edith added: "I believe that my husband is right. But before we come to a decision, we ought to know just what has happened."

And she addressed herself directly to M. and Mme. Darzac. But both of the latter were still under the spell of surprise which Rouletabille had caused them by his remarks—Rouletabille who that very morning, in my presence, had promised to be silent and had sworn us all to silence.

Neither the one nor the other had a word to say. M. Rance repeated, nervously: "Why should we conceal anything? Why should we? We must tell everything."

All at once, the reporter seemed to take a sudden resolution. I understood by the expressions which chased themselves over his face in rapid succession that something of considerable moment was passing through his mind. He leaned toward Arthur Rance, whose right hand was resting on a cane, the head of which was carved in ivory, beautifully cut by a famous carver at Dieppe. Rouletabille took the cane in his hand.

"May I look at it?" he asked. "I am an amateur ivory carver myself and my friend, Sainclair, here, has told me about this beautiful cane. I had not noticed it before. It is really very beautiful. It is a figure by Lambesse and there is no better workman on the Norman shore."

The young man seemed to be entirely engrossed in studying the cane. As he touched the carving, the stick fell from his hand and rolled toward M. Darzac. I picked it up and returned it immediately to M. Rance. Rouletabille cast a withering look at me, and I read in that glance that, somehow or other, I had shown myself an idiot.

Mme. Edith rose to her feet, tapping her little foot impatiently and seemingly very nervous at the tension of the situation—by the carelessness of Rouletabille and the silence of M. and Mme. Darzac.

"Dearest," she said to Mme. Darzac, in the sweetest tones. "You are completely tired out. The experiences of this horrible night have overpowered you. Let me take you into my own room so that you may rest a little."

"Pardon me for asking you to wait a few moments, Madame," interrupted Rouletabille. "What I have yet to say may be of special interest to you."

"Very well, monsieur, but speak out, please. Don't drag the recital along so."

She was perfectly justified in her remarks. Did Rouletabille realize it? At all events, he certainly made up for his previous deliberation by the rapidity and clearness with which he retraced the events of the night. In no other words could the problem of the "body too many" have been presented before us with such mysterious horror. Mme. Edith shivered—and if her shudder was counterfeit, I never saw a real one! As for Arthur Rance, he sat with his chin resting on the head of his cane, murmuring with a truly American coolness, but in accents of the strongest conviction: "What a devilish history! The story of the body which could not have gotten into the room is a page from the notebook of Satan himself!"

While he was speaking, he was gazing at the tip of Mme. Darzac's shoe which peeped out from the hem of her gown. In the moment which followed the closing of Rouletabille's narration, conversation became a little more general; but it was less a conversation than such a confused mixture of exclamations and interruptions, of interjections and indignation and demands for explanations on one point or another that the confusion seemed more increased than ever before. They spoke also of the horrible departure of "the body too many" in the potato sack, and at this point, Mme. Edith took occasion to once more express her admiration for M. Robert Darzac as a hero and a gentleman. Rouletabille never opened his lips during this torrent of words. It was plain to be seen that he despised this verbal manifestation of perturbation of spirits, but he endured it with the air of a professor who permits a few moments relaxation to pupils who have been well behaved in school. This was a mannerism of his which often vexed me and with which I sometimes reproached him, but without having any effect on him, for Rouletabille was likely to give himself whatever airs he chose.

At length—probably when it appeared to him that the recreation had lasted long enough, he asked abruptly of Mrs. Rance:

"Well, Madame, do you think we ought to inform the authorities?"

"I think so more than ever," she replied. "That which we are powerless to discover, they would certainly find out." (This allusion to the intellectual incapacity of my friend left him profoundly indifferent). "And I warn you of one thing, M. Rouletabille, and that is that we may already be too late in seeking out the officers of justice. If we had told them of our fears at the very beginning, you would have been spared some long hours of watching and sleepless nights which have profited you nothing, since, as now appears, they did not prevent what you dreaded from coming to pass."

Rouletabille seated himself, evidently conquering some strong emotion which made him tremble as though he were chilled to the bone. Then with a wave of the hand which he strove to render careless, he motioned Mme. Edith to a chair and again picked up the cane which M. Rance had laid down upon a sofa. I said to myself: "What is he trying to do with that stick? This time, I won't touch it, I'm certain. I must keep a lookout."

Playing with the cane, Rouletabille replied to Mme. Edith with an attack almost as sharp as her own.

"Madame, you are wrong in asserting that all the precautions which I had taken for the safety of M. and Mme. Darzac have been useless. If I am obliged to acknowledge the unexplainable presence of one body too many, I am also compelled to refer to the absence—perhaps less inexplicable—of one member of our own party."

We stared at each other, some of us seeking to understand, the others dreading to do so.

"What is that?" inquired Mme. Edith, with a mocking little smile. "In such a case, I fail to see how you find any mystery at all." And she added with a flippant imitation of the reporter's words and manner: "A body too many on the one side; an unexplained absence on the other! Everything is for the best."

"Perhaps," rejoined Rouletabille. "But the most frightful thing of all is that the unexplained disappearance comes just at the right time to make known to us, apparently, the identity of the 'body too many.' Madame, I deeply regret to tell you that the person for whose whereabouts we are unable to account, is none other than your uncle, Monsieur Bob."

"Old Bob!" screamed the young woman. "Old Bob has disappeared!"

And we all cried out with her:

"Old Bob has disappeared?"

"Unfortunately, it is true!" said Rouletabille.

And he let the cane drop to the ground.

But the news of the sudden disappearance of Old Bob had so seised the Rances and the Darzacs that no one paid any attention to the cane as it fell.

"My dear Sainclair, will you be kind enough to pick up that cane?" asked Rouletabille.

I did as I was ordered and quickly, too, but Rouletabille did not even deign to thank me. Mme. Edith turned like a lioness upon Robert Darzac, who recoiled from her almost in fear as she shrieked:

"You have killed my uncle!"

Her husband and myself, with difficulty, prevented her from flying at him. We entreated her to be calm and to remember that because her uncle had absented himself from the peninsula did not necessarily mean that he had disappeared in the potato sack and we reproached Rouletabille with his brutality in blurting out an idea which could only be, at the present time, at all events, an hypothesis of his uneasy mind. And we added, imploring Mme. Edith to listen to us, that this hypothesis could under no circumstances be looked upon by her either as an injury or an insult, even admitting that it might be the true one, as it would only show the superhuman cunning of Larsan, who must, in that case, have taken the place of her respected uncle. But the young woman ordered her husband to be quiet, and said, turning scornfully to me:

"M. Sainclair, I sincerely hope that my uncle's absence from here will only be of short duration; for if it should turn out otherwise, I should accuse you of being an accomplice in the most cowardly of murders. As to you, monsieur," and she turned to Rouletabille, "the mere idea that you have ever dared to compare a man like Larsan with my uncle, the gentlest, kindliest soul and the greatest scholar of his time, forbids me to ever again consider you in the light of a friend, and I hope that you will have the courtesy to relieve me of your presence as soon as possible."

"Madame," replied Rouletabille, bowing very low, "I was just about to ask your permission to take leave of you. I have a short journey of twenty-four hours to take. At the expiration of that time, I shall return, ready to be of any possible assistance to you in whatever difficulties may arise in accounting for the disappearance of your uncle."

"If my uncle has not returned within twenty-four hours, I shall lodge a complaint in the hands of the police, monsieur."

"It is a good plan, Madame; but before having recourse to it, I advise you to question all the servants in whom you have confidence— particularly Mattoni. You trust Mattoni, do you not?"

"Yes, monsieur, I trust Mattoni."

"Well, then, Madame, question him—question him. Ah—before I take my departure, allow me to leave with you this excellent and historical book." And Rouletabille drew a small volume from his pocket.

"What foolery is this?" demanded Mme. Edith, superbly disdainful.

"This, Madame, is a work of M. Albert Bataille, a copy of his 'Civil and Criminal Cases,' in which I advise you to read the adventures, disguises, travesties and deceptions wrought by an illustrious swindler whose true name was Ballmeyer."

Rouletabille entirely ignored the fact that he had only the day before spent two hours in recounting to Mme. Edith the exploits of Ballmeyer.

"After having read this," he went on, "ask yourself carefully whether the cleverness of such an individual would have found very great difficulty in presenting himself before your eyes under the guise of an uncle whom you had not seen in four years—for it was four years, Madame, since you had seen Old Bob, until that time that you started out to the heart of the Pampas to look for him. As to the memory of M. Arthur Rance, who started out with you on that journey, it would be even less distinct than your own and he would be more capable of being deceived than yourself with your intuition of kinship added to your recollections of your relative. I implore you on my knees, Madame, do not lose patience with us. The situation, Heaven knows, is grave enough for each and every one of us. Let us remain united. You tell me to rid you of my presence. I am going but I shall return; for if it is necessary, taking everything into consideration, to arrive at the intolerable conclusion that Larsan has assumed the name and likeness of Monsieur Bob, it will remain for us only to seek Monsieur Bob himself, in which case, Madame, I shall be at your disposal and your most humble and obedient servant."

Mme. Edith assumed the attitude of an outraged tragedy queen and Rouletabille, turning to Arthur Rance, continued:

"For all that has happened, M. Rance, I make you my humblest excuses and also to your wife. And I count upon you as the loyal gentleman that you are and always have been to persuade her to have patience a little longer. I realize that you feel that you have reason to reproach me with having stated my hypothesis too quickly and too abruptly, but, please remember, it is only a few moments since Madame reproached me with being too slow."

But Arthur Rance seemed to have ceased to listen. He took his wife's arm and both moved toward the door and were about to leave the room when the portals flew open and the stable boy, Walter, Old Bob's faithful servant, rushed into our midst. His clothing was torn, muddy and covered with burs and thistles. Perspiration was streaming down his forehead and cheeks, his hair was in disorder and his face wore an expression of rage mingled with terror which made us fear some new misfortune. He carried in his hand a dirty rag which he threw upon the table. This repulsive object, stained with great blotches of reddish brown was (as we divined immediately, recoiling from it in horror) nothing other than the sack which had served to carry off the mysterious body.

With a harsh voice and savage gestures, Walter howled forth a thousand incomprehensible things in his broken jumble of French and English and all of us with the exception of Arthur Rance and Mme. Edith, asked each other, "What is he saying? What is he saying?"

Arthur Rance interrupted him from time to time, while Walter shook his fists menacingly at the rest of us and cast fiery glances at Robert Darzac. Once, for a moment, it seemed as though he intended to seize Darzac by the throat, but a gesture from Mme. Edith restrained him. When he finished speaking, Arthur Rance translated his words for us.

"He says that this morning he noticed blood stains on the English cart and saw that Toby seemed very greatly fatigued. This puzzled him so much that he decided to speak of it at once to Old Bob, but he sought his master in vain. Then, seised by a dark foreboding, he followed the prints of the horse's feet and the wheels of the vehicle which he could easily do because the road was muddy and the wheels had sunk deep. Finally he reached the old Castillon and noticed that the wheels led up to a deep chasm into which he descended, believing that he should find the body of his master; but he saw merely this empty sack which may have contained the corpse of Old Bob, and now, having caught a ride in a peasant's wagon, he has returned to ask for his master, to learn whether anyone has seen him, and, if he is not found, to accuse Robert Darzac of having caused his death."

We stood confounded. But, to our great astonishment, Mme. Edith was the first to recover her self-possession. She spoke a few words to Walter which appeared to quiet him, promising him that she would soon bring him face to face with Old Bob, who was perfectly safe and well. And she said to Rouletabille:

"You have twenty-four hours, Monsieur; make the best use of it."

"Thanks, Madame," said Rouletabille. "But if your uncle should not return in that time, it will be because my idea was correct."

"But where can he be!" she cried. "I cannot tell you, Madame. He is not in the sack now, at all events."

Mme. Edith cast a withering glance at him and left the room, followed by her husband. The sight of the sack seemed to have stricken Robert Darzac speech less. He had thrown the bag into an abyss and it was brought back empty. After a moment's pause, Rouletabille spoke:

"Larsan is not dead, be sure of that! Never has the situation been so frightful as it is today and I must hurry away at once. I have not a minute to lose. Twenty-four hours—in twenty-four hours, I shall be back. But promise me—swear to me, both of you, that you will not quit the château. Swear to me, M. Darzac, that you will watch over your wife—that you will prevent her from leaving these walls, even by force, if it is necessary. Ah—and again—it is no longer necessary that you should sleep in the Square Tower. No, you ought not to do so. In the same wing where M. Stangerson is lodged, there are two empty rooms. You must occupy them. It is absolutely necessary that you should. Sainclair, you will see that this change is made. After my departure, see that neither the one nor the other of them shall set foot in the Square Tower. Adieu! Ah, wait!—let me embrace you—all three."

He pressed us to his heart: M. Darzac first, then myself, and then, falling into the arms of the Lady in Black, he burst into a passion of sobs. This show of weakness and of grief on the part of Rouletabille, in spite of the gravity of the circumstances of his departure, appeared to me very strange. Alas! how easy it was for me to understand it afterward!

XV

THE SIGHS OF THE NIGHT

Two o'clock in the morning! Every person and everything in the castle seemed wrapped in slumber. Silence brooded over the heavens and the earth. While I stood at my window, my forehead burning and my heart frozen, the sea yielded its last sigh and in a moment the moon appeared riding like a queen in the cloudless sky. Shadows no longer veiled the stars of the night. There, in that vast, motionless slumber which seemed to envelope all the world, I heard the words of the Lithuanian folk song: "But his glance seeks in vain for the beautiful unknown who has covered her head with a veil and whose voice he has never heard." The words were carried to my ear, clear and distinct, in the still air of the night. Who had pronounced them? Was the voice that of a man or a woman? or was the song only an hallucination evoked by my memories? What should the Prince from the Black lands be doing on the Azure shore with his Lithuanian melodies? And why should his image and his songs pursue me thus?

Why was Mme. Edith attracted toward him? He was ridiculous with his melancholy eyes and his long lashes and his Lithuanian songs! And I—I was ridiculous, too. Had I the heart of a college boy? I think not. I would rather believe that the emotion which was excited in me by the personality of Prince Galitch rose less from my knowledge of the interest which Mme. Edith felt in him than from the thought of *that other*. Yes, it was surely that. In my mind the thought of the Prince and that of Larsan somehow went together. And the Prince had not returned to the château since the famous luncheon at which he was presented to us—that is to say since the day before yesterday.

The afternoon following Rouletabille's departure had brought us nothing new. We received no news from him nor from Old Bob. Mme. Edith had locked herself up in her own apartments, after having questioned the domestics and visiting her uncle's rooms and the Round Tower. She made no effort to penetrate into the apartments of the Darzacs in the Square Tower. "That is an affair for the police," she had said. Arthur Rance had walked for an hour on the western boulevard, his manner restless and impatient. No one had spoken a word to me. Neither M. nor Mme. Darzac had stirred out of "la Louve." All of us had dined in our own rooms. No one had seen Professor Stangerson.

And now, so far as the eye could see, everyone in the château seemed to be lost in dreams. But a shadow appeared on the bosom of the starry night—the shadow of a canoe which slowly detached itself from the shadow of the fort and glided out upon the silvery water. Whose is this silhouette, which arises proudly in the front of the boat while another shade bends over a silent oar? It is yours, Feodor Feodorowitch! Ah, here is a mystery which might be easier to solve than that of the Square Tower, O Rouletabille! And I who believed that Mme. Edith had too good a brain and too fine a mind to lend herself to a vulgar intrigue!

What a hypocrite is the night! Everything seems to sleep and all the while slumber is far from all eyes! Who was there that might be sleeping among those in the château of Hercules? Was Mme. Edith sleeping, perhaps? Or M. or Mme. Darzac" And how could M. Stangerson, who seemed to have been slumbering all day, be dreaming away the night also?—he whose couch, ever since the revelation of the Glandier, had not ceased to be haunted by the pale ghost of insomnia? And I—could I sleep?

I left my bedchamber and went down into the court of the Bold and my feet bore me rapidly over to the boulevard of the Round Tower—so rapidly that I arrived there in time to see the bark of Prince Galitch landing on the strand in front of the "Gardens of Babylon." He leaped out of the boat and his man, having picked up the oars, followed. I recognised the master and servant. It was Feodor Feodorowitch and his serf, Jean. A few seconds later, they disappeared in the protecting shade of the century plants and the giant eucalypti.

I turned and walked around the boulevard of the court. And then my heart beating wildly, I directed my steps toward the outer court. The stone slabs of the walks resounded under my tread and I seemed to see a form arise in a listening attitude from beneath the arch of the ruined chapel. I paused in the thick darkness of the shadow cast by the gardener's tower and drew my revolver from my pocket. The form did not move. Was it really a human creature who stood there listening? I glided behind a hedge of vervain which bordered the path that led directly to "la Louve" through bushes and thickets, heavy with the perfume of the flowers of the spring. I had made no noise, and the shadow, doubtless reassured, made a slight movement. It was the Lady in Black. The moon, under the half ruined arch, showed me that she was as pale as death. And suddenly her figure vanished as if by enchantment. I approached the chapel and as I diminished the space which lay between me and the ruins, I heard a soft murmur of words mingled with such bitter sobs that my own eyes grew moist as I listened. The Lady in Black was weeping there behind that pillar. Was she alone? Had she not chosen in this night of anguish to come to this altar decked with flowers there to pour out her prayers in solitude to the balmy air?

Suddenly I perceived a shadow beside the Lady in Black and I recognised Robert Darzac. From the corner where I was I could now hear all that they were saying. I knew that my behaviour in listening was degraded and shameless, but, curiously enough, it was borne upon me that it was my duty to listen. Now I thought no longer of Edith and her Prince Galitch. I thought only of Larsan. Why? Why was it on account of Larsan that I bent my ears so anxiously to hear all that went on between those two? I learned from their words that Mathilde had descended stealthily from la Louve to be alone in the garden with her agony and that her husband had followed her. The Lady in Black was weeping. And she took Robert Darzac's hands and said to him:

"I know, dear—I know all your grief. You need not speak of it to me when I see you so changed-so wretched I accuse myself of being the cause of your sorrow. But do not tell me that I no longer love you. Oh, I will love you dearly, Robert—just as I have always done. I promise you."

And she seemed to sink into a deep fit of thought, while he, almost as though incredulous, still stood as though he were listening to her. In a moment, she looked up again and repeated in a tone of firm conviction: "Yes—I promise you."

She pressed his hand and turned away, casting upon him a smile so sweet and yet so sorrowful that I wondered how this woman could speak to a man of future happiness. She brushed past me without seeing me. She passed with her perfume and I no longer smelled the laurel bushes behind which I was hidden.

M. Darzac remained standing in the same spot, looking after her. Suddenly he said aloud with a violence which startled me:

"Yes, happiness must come! It must!"

Assuredly, he was at the end of his patience. And before withdrawing in his turn, he made a gesture of protest—against fate, it seemed to me—a gesture of defiance to destiny—a gesture which snatched the Lady in Black through the space which divided them and caught her to his breast and held her there.

He had scarcely made this gesture when my thought took form—my thought which had been wandering about Larsan stopped at Darzac. Oh, how well I remember that instant! The fancy was gone in a moment, but as I beheld gesture of defiance and rapture, I dared to say to myself, "If HE should be Larsan!"

And in looking back to the depths of my memory, I realize now that my thought was even stronger than that. To the gesture of this man, my mind answered with the cry, "This is Larsan!"

I was white with terror and when I saw Robert Darzac coming in my direction, I could not refrain from a movement which revealed my presence while I was trying to conceal it. He saw me and recognised me, and, grasping me by the arm, he exclaimed:

"You were there, Sainclair: you were watching. We are all watching, my friend. And you heard what she said. Sainclair, her grief is too great. I can bear no more. We would have been so happy. She began to believe that misfortune had forgotten her when that man reappeared. Then all was finished; she had no longer strength to desire love or to feel it. She is bowed down by destiny. She imagines that she is to be pursued by eternal punishment. It was necessary for the frightful tragedy of last night to prove to me that this woman did love me—once. Yes, for one moment, all her fears were for me—and I, alas, have blood on my hands only because of her. Now she has returned to her old indifference. She cares no longer—her only desire is that the old man shall be kept in ignorance."

He sighed so sorrowfully and so sincerely that the abominable idea which it had harboured fled from my mind. I thought only of what he was saying to me—of the sorrow of this man who seemed to have lost completely the woman whom he loved in the moment when the woman had found a son of whose existence the husband continued to be ignorant. In fact, he had in no way been able to understand the attitude of the Lady in Black as regards the facility with which she had detached herself from him—and he found no explanation for this cruel metamorphosis other than the love heightened by remorse of Professor Stangerson's daughter for her father.

"What good did it do me to kill him?" groaned M. Darzac. "Why did I fire the shot? Why did she impose upon me such a criminal, horrible silence if she did not intend to recompense me for it by her love? Did she fear arrest for me? Ah, no! Not even that, Sainclair, not even that! She fears only the agony of her father and the danger that he will succumb entirely under this new disgrace. Her father! Always her father! I do not exist for her. I have loved her for twenty years and when I believe at last that I have won her, the thought of her father takes my place."

And I said to myself: "The thought of her father—and of her child."

He seated himself on an old moss grown boulder by the chapel and said again, as if speaking to himself: "But I will snatch her away from this place—I cannot see her roaming about on the arm of her father—as if I were not in the world."

And, while he said this, I looked up and I fancied that I beheld the shadow of the father and the daughter passing and repassing in the dawn, beneath the sombre height of the Tower of the North, and I likened them in my mind to the old Oedipus and his daughter, Antigone, walking under the walls of Colone, dragging with them the weight of a grief beyond human endurance.

And then suddenly, without my being able to recall myself to reason, perhaps because Darzac made again the gesture which had startled me before, the same frightful fancy assailed me, and I demanded:

"How did it happen that the sack was empty?"

He was not in the least confused or taken aback.

He replied simply:

"Rouletabille must tell us that." Then he pressed my hand and wandered away through the undergrowth of the garden. I looked after him and said to myself:

"I have gone mad!"

XVI

Discovery of "Australia"

The moon was shining full on his face. He believed himself to be alone in the night and certainly it was one of the moments in which he would cast aside the mask of the day. First the black glasses had ceased to shade his eyes. And if his figure, during the hours of disguise, was more bent than nature had made it, if his shoulders were rounded by pretence instead of study, this was the moment when the magnificent body of Larsan, away from all observers, must relax itself. Would it relax now? I hid in the ditch behind the barberry hedge. Not one of his movements escaped me.

Now he was standing erect upon the western boulevard which looked like a pedestal beneath his feet; the rays of the moon enveloped him with a cold and mournful light. Is it you, Darzac? or your spectre? or the ghost of Larsan, come back from the house of the dead?

I felt that I had gone mad. What a piteous state was ours—all of us madmen! We saw Larsan everywhere, and, perhaps, Darzac himself might more than once have gased at me, Sainclair, saying to himself: "Suppose that he were Larsan!" More than—once! I speak as though it were years since we had been locked up in the château and it was now just four days. We came here on the eighth of April in the evening.

It is true that my heart had never beaten so wildly when I had asked myself the same terrible question about the others; perhaps, because it was less terrible when there was question of any of the others. And then, how strange that such a thought should have come to me! Instead of my spirit recoiling in affright before the black abyss of such an incredible hypothesis, it was, on the contrary, attracted, enchained, horribly bewitched by it. It was as though struck with vertigo which it could do nothing to evade. It glued my eyes to that figure standing upon the western boulevard, making me find the attitudes, the gestures, a strong resemblance from the rear—and then, the profile—and even the face. Yes, all—all. He did look like Larsan. Yes, but just as strongly did the face and figure resemble Darzac.

How was it that this idea had come to me that night for the first time? Now that I thought of it—it should have been our first hypothesis of all. Was it not true that, at the time of "The Mystery of the Yellow Room," the silhouette of Larsan had been confounded at the moment of the crime with that of Darzac" Was it not true that the man who was believed to be Darzac, who had come to inquire for Mlle. Stangerson's answer at Post Office Box No. 40, had really been Larsan himself? Was it not true that this emperor of disguises had already undertaken with success to appear to be Darzac?—and to such good purpose that Mlle. Stangerson's fiancé had been accused of being the perpetrator of the crimes committed by the other?

It was true—all true—and yet when I ordered my restless heart to be quiet and listen to reason, I knew that my hypothesis was absurd. Absurd? Why? Look at him there, the ghost of Larsan which strides session. She spoke a few words to Walter which appeared to quiet him, promising him that she would soon bring him face to face with Old Bob, who was perfectly safe and well. And she said to Rouletabille:

"You have twenty-four hours, Monsieur; make the best use of it."

"Thanks, Madame," said Rouletabille. "But if your uncle should not return in that time, it will be because my idea was correct."

"But where can he be!" she cried. "I cannot tell you, Madame. He is not in the sack now, at all events."

Mme. Edith cast a withering glance at him and left the room, followed by her husband. The sight of the sack seemed to have stricken Robert Darzac speech less. He had thrown the bag into an abyss and it was brought back empty. After a moment's pause, Rouletabille spoke:

"Larsan is not dead, be sure of that! Never has the situation been so frightful as it is today and I must hurry away at once. I have not a minute to lose. Twenty-four hours—in twenty-four hours, I shall be back. But promise me—swear to me, both of you, that you will not quit the château. Swear to me, M. Darzac, that you will watch over your wife—that you will prevent her from leaving these walls, even by force, if it is necessary. Ah—and again—it is no longer necessary that you should sleep in the Square Tower. No, you ought not to do so. In the same wing where M. Stangerson is lodged, there are two empty rooms. You must occupy them. It is absolutely necessary that you should. Sainclair, you will see that this change is made. After my departure, see that neither the one nor the other of them shall set foot in the Square Tower. Adieu! Ah, wait!—let me embrace you—all three."

He pressed us to his heart: M. Darzac first, then myself, and then, falling into the arms of the Lady in Black, he burst into a passion of sobs.

This show of weakness and of grief on the part of Rouletabille, in spite of the gravity of the circumstances of his departure, appeared to me very strange. Alas! how easy it was for me to understand it afterward!

Those shoulders are those of Darzac.

I must admit that my suspicions are absurd. I say absurd because anyone who was not Darzac might have passed for him in the shade and the mystery that surrounded the drama of the Glandier. But here we have lived with the man. We have talked with him—touched him.

We have lived with him? No!

To begin with, he was rarely there among us. Always locked in his own room or bending over that useless work in the Tower of the Bold. A fine pretext, that of drawing, to prevent anyone's seeing your face and to make it appear natural to answer questions without turning the head!

But he was not drawing all the time! Yes, but at other times, always, except tonight, he wore his dark glasses. Ah! that accident in the laboratory had been well contrived. That little lamp which exploded knew—I have always thought so, it seems to me—the service which it was going to do for Larsan when Larsan should have taken the place of Darzac. It permitted him to evade always and everywhere the full light of day—because of the weakness of his eyes. How then! Was it not always Mlle. Stangerson or Rouletabille who had managed to find dark corners where M. Darzac's eyes could not be exposed to the sun? But, lately, he himself, more than anyone else now that I reflected upon it, had been careful to keep in the shadow—we have seen him seldom and always in the shadow. That little "hall of counsel" was very dark, "la Louve" was dark, and he had chosen the two rooms in the Square Tower which are plunged in semi-darkness.

But still—still—Rouletabille could not be deceived like that—even for three days. But, as the lad himself said, Larsan was born before Rouletabille and was his father.

And suddenly there recurred to my mind the first act of Darzac when he came to meet us at Cannes and entered our compartment with us. He drew the curtain. The shadow—always the shadow!

The figure on the western boulevard is still standing there. I can look him full in the face. No spectacles now! He was not moving. He stood as if he were posing for a photograph. Do not stir There! that is he! Yes, it is Robert Darzac—only Robert Darzac!

He began to walk again—I was certain no longer. There is something in his walk which is not Darzac's—something in which I seem to recognize Larsan—but what?

Yes, Rouletabille must have seen! And yet—Rouletabille reasons more often than he looks! And has he ever had a chance to look at him like this?

No! We must not forget that Darzac went to spend three months in the Midi—That is true! Ah, what might not have happened in that time! Three months during which none of us saw him. He went away ill; he returned almost well. There could be nothing astonishing in the fact that a man's appearance should be changed when he went away with the look of a dead man and returned with the look of one living and strong!

And the wedding had taken place immediately after that. How little any of us had seen of him before the ceremony! And, besides, a week had not yet elapsed since the marriage. A Larsan could easily wear his mask for so short a time.

The man—was it Darzac or was it Larsan?—descended from his pedestal and came straight toward me. Had he seen me? I crouched down behind my barberries.

(Three months of absence during which Larsan might have had a chance to study every gesture, every mannerism of Darzac! And then—how easy to put Darzac out of the way and to take his place and his bride! Not a difficult trick—for a Larsan!)

The voice? What more easy than to imitate the voice of a native of the Midi? One has a little more or a little less of accent than the other, that is all. Occasionally I have fancied that *his* accent was a little stronger than before the wedding.

He was almost upon me. He passed by. He had not Seen me.

"It is Larsan! I could swear that it was Larsan!" But he paused for a second and gased sorrowfully upon all nature slumbering around him—him whose suffering was in loneliness and solitude, and a groan escaped his lips, unhappy soul that he was!

"It is Darzac!"

And then he was gone—and I remained there behind my hedge overwhelmed with the horror of the thought which I had dared to harbour.

How long did I remain thus, lying on the ground? One hour? Two? When I arose, I was so stiff that I could scarcely stir and my mind was as worn out as my body—worn out and distracted. In the course of my unthinkable hypotheses, I had even gone so far as to ask myself whether, by chance (by chance!) the Larsan who had been in the potato sack had not succeeded in substituting himself for Darzac who had carried him off in the little English cart with Toby drawing it, meaning to throw him into the gulf of Castillon. I could picture the body of the victim rising up suddenly and ordering M. Darzac to take its place. So far from all reason had my wild supposition driven me, that in order to drive away from my mind this ridiculous idea, I was compelled to recall word by word a private conversation that had occurred between M. Darzac and myself that morning when we went out from the terrible session in the Square Tower at which had been so clearly presented the problem of the "body too many." In this conversation, I had received an absolute proof of the impossibility of my supposition. I had, while we talked, proposed to M. Darzac a few questions in relation to Prince Galitch, whose image would not cease to pursue me, and my friend had answered by making allusion to another conversation, involving certain scientific facts, which had taken place between us the night previous, and which could not possibly have been heard by any other person than our two selves and which had also concerned Prince Galitch. On this account, there could be no real doubt in my mind that the Darzac whom I had talked with in the garden was none other than the same man I had seen the evening before.

As senseless as was the idea of this substitution, it was, nevertheless, in a certain degree, pardonable. Rouletabille was a little to blame for it by his fashion of talking of Larsan as a very god of metamorphosis. And after casting it aside, I returned to the sole possible idea under which Larsan could have taken the place of Darzac—the idea of a substitution before the marriage ceremony at the time when Mlle. Stangerson's fiancé returned to Paris after three months absence in the Midi.

The despairing plaint which Robert Darzac, believing himself alone, had allowed to escape his lips only a little while before, in my hearing, could not entirely banish this supposition from my head. I saw him again entering the church of St. Nicolas du Chardonnet, in which parish he had requested that the wedding should take place—perhaps, thought I, because there is no darker nor more gloomy church in all Paris.

Ah, one's fancy plays strange tricks on a moon light night, when one is lurking behind a barberry hedge, with a mind and brain filled with Larsan!

"I am a veritable imbecile!" I told myself, beginning to wish that I were in the quiet little room in the New Castle, where my undisturbed bed awaited me. "For if Larsan had been masquerading as Darzac, he would have been satisfied with carrying off Mathilde and he would not have reappeared in his own likeness to frighten her and he would not have brought her to the Château of Hercules and he would not have com mitted the foolhardy act of showing himself again in the bark of Tullio. For at that moment, Mathilde belonged to him and it was from that moment that she had cast him off. The reappearance of Larsan had divided the Lady in Black from Darzac, and, therefore, Darzac could not be Larsan."

Dear Heaven, how my head ached! It was the moon light above which must have turned my brain—I was moonstruck.

And then, too, had not *he* appeared to Arthur Rance himself in the gardens at Mentone after he had accompanied Darzac to the train which had taken him to Cannes, where he met us. If Arthur Rance had spoken the truth, I might go to my couch in tranquility. And why should he have lied?—Arthur Rance who had been in love with the Lady in Black and who had not ceased to love her. Mme. Edith was not a fool—she knew that Mme. Darzac still held the heart of the young American. Well, it was time for me to go to bed!

I was still beneath the arch of the gardener's postern and I was just about to enter the Court of the Bold when it seemed to me that I heard something moving—it sounded as though a door might have been closed. Then there was a sound as of wood striking on iron. I thrust my head out from under the arch and I believed that I could see the shadow of a person near the door of the New Castle—a shadow which somehow seemed to mingle with that of the castle itself. I snatched my revolver from my pocket and with three steps was at the place where I believed I had seen the shape. But it was there no longer. I could see nothing but darkness. The door of the castle was closed and I was certain that I had left it open. I was disturbed and anxious. I felt that I was not alone—who, then, could be near me? Evidently if that shadow had existed elsewhere than in my imagination, it could have vanished only within the New Castle or must still be in the court.

And the court was deserted.

I listened attentively for more than five minutes without making the slightest sound. Nothing! I must have been mistaken. But, nevertheless, I did not even strike a match, and as silently as I could, I ascended the staircase which led to my chamber. When I reached it, I locked myself in and only then began to breathe freely.

This vision or whatever it had been continued to disturb me more than I was willing to confess to myself, and even after I had gotten into bed I could not sleep. Without my being able to account for it at all this vision and the thought of Darzac-Larsan began to mingle strangely in my restless spirit.

The effect on my mind was so strong that, at last, I said to myself: "I shall never know peace again until I am certain that M. Darzac is not Larsan. And I shall take means to make myself certain, one way or the other, on the first occasion." Yes, but how? Pull his beard off? If my suspicion was baseless, he would take me for a madman, or else he would guess what I was thinking of and such a knowledge would add yet another to the load of misfortunes, already too heavy for him to bear. Only this misery was lacking to him still—to know that he was suspected of being Larsan.

Suddenly I threw off the bedclothes, jumped up and cried almost aloud:

"Australia!"

An episode had returned to my mind of which I have spoken at the beginning of this story. The reader may remember that, at the time of the accident in the laboratory, I had accompanied M. Robert Darzac to a druggist. While his injuries were being attended to, he had been obliged to remove his study coat, and the sleeve of his shirt had fallen back, leaving his arm bare through the entire session with the druggist, and placing in full view just above the right elbow, a large birth mark, the shape of which resembled that of Australia as it appears on the maps in the geographies. Mentally, while the chemist was at work, I had amused myself by trying to locate upon the arm in the positions which they occupied on an actual map, the cities of Melbourne, Sydney, Adelaide, etc.; and directly beneath this large mark, there was another smaller one which was situated like the country known as Tasmania.

And when, by any chance, the thought of that accident had happened to recur to my mind, I had always thought of the half hour at the chemist's and the birth mark shaped like the outlines of Australia.

And in this sleepless night, it was the thought of Australia that came to me.

Seated on the edge of my bed, I had scarcely had time to congratulate myself upon having found a means to prove decisively the identity of Robert Darzac and to try to devise some way of bringing it to an immediate test, when a singular sound made me prick up my ears. The sound was repeated—one would have said that gravel was cracking beneath slow and cautious footsteps.

Breathless, I hurried to my door and, with my ear at the keyhole, I listened. Silence for a moment and then once more the same sound—footsteps, beyond a doubt. Someone was now ascending the staircase—and someone who desired his presence to be unknown. I thought of the shadow which I had believed I saw as I was entering the Court of the Bold—whose could this shadow be and what was it doing on the staircase? Was it coming up or going down?

Silence again! I profited by it to hastily don my trousers and, armed with my revolver, I succeeded in opening my door without letting it creak on its hinges. Holding my breath, I advanced to the head of the stairs and waited. I have told of the state of dilapidation of the New Castle. The pale rays of the moon light entered obliquely through the high windows which opened at each landing, cutting with exact squares of soft light the black darkness of the stairway which was very wide and high. The ruined condition of the château, thus lighted up in spots, only appeared more complete. The broken balustrade and railings of the staircase, the walls overrun with lizards over which here and there hung floating rags of once priceless tapestry—all these things which I had scarcely noticed in the daylight, struck me strangely in this lonely night and my whirling brain felt quite prepared to find in this gloomy scene the fit setting for the appearance of a phantom. Indeed and in truth, I was afraid. The shadow which I had seen a little while ago had practically slipped between my fingers—for I had been near enough to have touched it. But, surely a phantom might walk in an empty house without making any sound. Though the footsteps were silent now!

All at once, as I was leaning on the broken balustrade, I saw the shadow again—it was lighted up by the moonbeams as though it were a flambeau. And I recognised Robert Darzac.

He had reached the ground floor, and, crossing the vestibule, raised his head and looked in my direction as though he felt the weight of my eyes upon him. Instinctively, I drew back. And then I returned to my post of observation just in time to see him disappear into a corridor which led to another staircase winding up to the battlements. What could this mean? Was Robert Darzac spending the night in the New Castle? Why did he take such precautions not to be seen? A thousand suspicions crossed my mind—or rather all the terrible thoughts that had come to haunt me since we had been in the Fort of Hercules seised me again in their grasp and I felt that I must set my spirit at rest, immediately. I must follow Robert Darzac and discover "Australia."

I had reached the corridor almost as soon as he quitted it and I saw him beginning to climb very quietly the moth-eaten wood of the stairway. I saw him pause at the first landing and push open a door. Then I saw nothing more. He had been swallowed up by the darkness—and, perhaps, by the room of which he had opened the door. I reached this door and finding it locked, I gave three little taps, certain that he was inside. And I waited. My heart was beating wildly. All these rooms were uninhabited—abandoned. What should M. Darzac be doing in one of these haunted chambers!

I waited for a few moments which seemed to me like hours and as no one answered and the door did not open, I knocked again and waited again. Then the door was opened and I heard Darzac's voice saying:

"Is it you, Sainclair? What is it, my friend?"

"I wanted to know what you could be doing here at such an hour?" I replied, and it seem d to me that my voice was that of another man, so great was my terror.

Tranquilly, he struck a match and said:

"You see. I am preparing for bed."

And he lit a candle which was placed on a chair, for there was no night stand in this dilapidated apartment. A bed in one corner—an iron bed which must have been brought there during the day, and a single chair, comprised all the furnishings.

"I thought that you were going to sleep near Mme. Darzac and the Professor on the first floor of 'la Louve'?"

"The rooms are too small. I was afraid of inconveniencing Mme. Darzac," answered the unhappy man, bitterly. "I asked Bernier to fetch me a bed here. And then what difference does it make where I am, since I do not sleep?"

We were both silent for a moment. I was ashamed of myself and of my wretched suspicions. And, frankly, my remorse was so great that I could not refrain from giving it expression. I confessed everything to him; my infamous ideas and how I had even believed when I saw him wandering so mysteriously over the New Castle that it was upon some evil errand; and so had decided to go and look for the "Australia" birthmark. For I did not conceal from him that for a moment, I had placed all my hopes upon the Australia.

He listened to me with such an expression of reproachful sorrow that it wrung my heart; then he quietly rolled up his shirt sleeve and bringing his bare arm close to the light, he showed me the birthmark, which made a sane man of me once more. I did not wish to look at it, but he even insisted upon my touching it and I knew beyond a doubt that it was a natural scar upon which one might place little dots with the names of the cities, "Sydney," "Melbourne," "Adelaide." And beneath it there was another little blotch shaped like Tasmania.

"You may rub it as much as you choose," said Darzac, gently, "It will not come off."

I begged his pardon a thousand times over, with tears in my eyes, but he would not forgive me until he had made me pull at his beard which remained firmly attached to his chin, instead of coming off in my hand.

Then, only, he allowed me to go back to my room, which I did, cursing myself for an idiot.

XVII

Old Bob's Terrible Adventure

When I awakened my thoughts were still dwelling on Larsan. And, in truth, I did not know what to think either of myself or any other person—of Larsan's death or of his life. Had he been wounded less seriously than we had believed? Or shall I say, "Was he *less dead* than we had thought?" Had he been able to extricate himself from the sack which Darzac had cast in the gulf of Castillon? After all, the thing was not impossible, or, rather, the possibility was not altogether without the bounds of what might be looked for from the superhuman cunning and prowess of a Larsan—particularly since Walter had explained that he had found the sack three meters from the mouth of the abyss upon a natural landing place the existence of which M. Darzac assuredly did not suspect when he believed that he was throwing Larsan's body into the orifice.

My second thoughts turned to Rouletabille. What was he doing now? Why had he gone away? Never had his presence at the Fort of Hercules been so necessary as now. If he delayed his return, this day could scarcely pass without bringing the unfriendly feeling between the Rances and the Darzacs to an open issue.

As I lay there puzzling my brain over the outcome of the affair, I heard someone knocking at my door. It was Pere Bernier, who brought me a brief note from my friend which had been handed to Pere Jacques by a little lad from the village. Rouletabille wrote: "I shall return early in the morning. Get up as soon as this reaches you and be good enough to go fishing for my breakfast and catch some of the fine trout which are so plentiful among the rocks near the Point of Garibaldi. Do not lose an instant. Thanks and remembrances.—Rouletabille."

This communication gave me more food for thought, for I knew by experience that whenever Rouletabille seemed most occupied with trivial matters, his activity was really most thoroughly engaged with important subjects.

I dressed myself in haste, provided myself with some old tackle which was furnished me by Bernier, and set out to obey the request of my young friend. As I went out of the North gate, having encountered nobody at that early hour of the morning (it was about seven o'clock), I was joined by Mme. Edith, to whom I showed what Rouletabille had written. The young woman was greatly dejected over the unexplained absence of her uncle, remarked that the letter was "so queer that it made her nervous," and she informed me that she intended to follow me to the trout streams. On the way, she confided to me the fact that her uncle had not an enemy in the world, so far as she knew, and she said that she had been hoping against hope that he would yet return and that everything would be satisfactorily explained, but now the idea had entered her brain that by some frightful mistake, Old Bob had fallen a victim to the vengeance of Darzac and she was nearly wild with apprehension.

And she added, between her pretty teeth, a few words of contempt and wrath for the Lady in Black. "My patience can hold out until noon, I hope!" she said, and then was silent.

We started to fish for Rouletabille's trout. Mrs. Rance and I both removed our shoes and stockings, but I concerned myself more about the dainty bare feet of my pretty hostess than about my own. The fact is, that Edith's feet, as I discovered in the Bay of Hercules, were as beautifully shaped and pink as flowers and they made me forget the trout of my poor Rouletabille to such an extent that he must certainly have gone without his breakfast if Edith had not shown more energy than I. She clambered into the pools and crept among the rocks with a grace which enchanted me more than I dared express. Suddenly we both desisted from our task and pricked up our cars at the same moment. We heard cries from the shore where the grottoes are. Upon the very threshold of the Grotto of Romeo and Juliet we distinguished a little group, the persons in which were making gestures of appeal. Urged on by the same presentiment, we hastily rushed to the beach and in a few seconds we learned that, attracted by moans, two fishermen had just discovered in a cave in the Grotto of Romeo and Juliet an unfortunate human being who had fallen into the chasm and who must have been there helpless for several hours.

The quick conjecture which rushed into both our minds at once proved to be the right one. It was Old Bob who had been fished out of the cave. When he had been drawn up on the beach in the full light of day, he certainly presented a pitiable spectacle. His beautiful black coat was torn and covered with mud and his white shirt was as black as tar. Mme. Edith burst into tears and nearly went into hysterics when she found that the old man had a torn collarbone and a sprained foot, and was so pale that he looked as if he were about to die.

Happily, the old man's injuries were far less serious than it at first had seemed. He was, according to his own account, on his bed in his room in the Square Tower. Would anyone believe that he absolutely refused to become undressed, even so far as to have his coat on before the arrival of the doctors? And Mrs. Rance, increasingly nervous, installed herself next to his bedside until the physicians came, and Old Bob instructed her not only to leave his room but to go outside of the Square Tower altogether. And he insisted that the door should be locked after her.

The precaution was a great surprise to us all. We stood assembled in the Court of the Bold, M. and Mme. Darzac, M. Arthur Rance and myself, as well as Bernier who haunted my footsteps, waiting the news. When Mme. Edith quitted the tower after the dismissal of the medical men, she came to us and said:

"Let us hope that his injuries won't be serious. Old Bob is solid as a rock. What did I tell you about him? I made him confess, the old sinner! He was trying to steal Prince Galitch's skull which he believe to be more ancient than his own. Just the jealousy of one savant toward another. We shall all laugh at him when he is cured!"

At that moment the door of the Square Tower opened and Walter, Old Bob's faithful servant, appeared. His face was pale and he seemed very nervous.

"Oh, Miss Edith!" he cried out. "He is covered with blood! He doesn't want anything to be said about it, but he must be saved—"

Edith had already rushed into the Square Tower. As to us we dared not utter a word. Soon the young woman returned.

"Oh!" she sobbed. "It is frightful. His whole breast is torn open!" I started to offer her the support of my arm, for, strangely enough M. Arthur Rance had withdrawn to some distance and was walking upon the boulevard, whistling and with his hands behind his back. I tried to comfort and to soothe Mme. Edith, but neither M. nor Mme. Darzac uttered a word.

Rouletabille reached the castle about an hour after these events. I watched for his return from the highest part of the western boulevard and as soon as I saw his form appearing in the distance I hurried to meet him. He cut short my demands for an explanation and asked me immediately if I had made a good catch, but I was not at all deceived by the expression of his countenance, and wishing to reply to him in his own style of banter, I replied:

"Oh, yes: a very good catch. I fished up Old Bob."

He started violently. I shrugged my shoulders, for I believed that he was counterfeiting surprise, and I went on :

"Oh, go on! You knew very well what kind of fish I should find when you sent your message!"

He fixed an astonished glance on me.

"You certainly must be unaware of the purport of your words, my dear Sainclair, or else you would have spared me the trouble of protesting against such an accusation."

"What accusation?" I cried.

"That of having left Old Bob in the Grotto of Romeo and Juliet, knowing that he might be dying there."

"Oh, nonsense!" I cried. "Old Bob is far from dying. He has a sprained foot and a broken collar bone, and his story of his misfortune is perfectly plain and straightforward. He declares that he was trying to steal Prince Galitch's skull."

"What a funny idea!" exclaimed Rouletabille, bursting out laughing. He leaned toward me and looked full into my eyes.

"Do you believe that story? And—and that is all? No other injuries?"

"Yes," I replied. "There is another injury, but the doctors declare that it is not at all serious. He has a wound in the breast."

"A wound in the breast!" repeated Rouletabille, touching my hand, nervously. "And how was this wound made?"

"We do not know. None of us have seen it. Old Bob is strangely modest. He would not even permit his coat to be taken off in our presence; and the coat hid the wound so well that we should never have suspected it was there if Walter had not come to tell us, frightened at the sight of the blood."

As soon as we came to the château, we encountered Mme. Edith, who appeared to have been watching for us.

"My uncle won't have me near him," she said, regarding Rouletabille with an air of anxiety different from anything I had ever noticed in her before. "It's in comprehensible!"

"Ah, Madame," replied the reporter, making a low bow to his hostess. "I assure you that nothing in the world is incomprehensible, when one is willing to take a little trouble to understand it." And he offered her his congratulations upon having had her uncle restored to her at the moment when she was ready to despair of ever seeing him again.

Mme. Edith seemed about to inquire into the purport of the enigmatical words at the beginning of my friend's remarks when we were joined by Prince Galitch. He had come to ask for news of his old friend, Bob, of whose misfortune he had learned. Mme. Edith reassured him as to her uncle's condition and entreated the Prince to pardon her relative for his too excessive devotion to the "oldest skulls in the history of humanity." The Prince smiled graciously and with the utmost kindliness when he was told that Old Bob had been attempting to steal his skull.

"You will find your skull," Mrs. Rance told him, "in the bottom of the cave in the grotto where it rolled down with him. Your collection will be unimpaired, Prince."

The Prince asked for the details. He seemed very curious about the affair. And Mme. Edith told how her uncle had acknowledged to her that he had quitted the Fort of Hercules by way of the air shaft which communicated with the sea. As soon as she said this, I recalled the experience of Rouletabille with the flask of water and also the close iron bars, and the falsehoods which Old Bob had uttered assumed gigantic proportions in my mind, and I was sure that the rest of the party must hold the same opinion as myself. Mme. Edith told us that Tullio had been waiting with his boat at the opening of the gallery abutting on the shaft, to row the old savant to the bank in front of the Grotto of Romeo and Juliet.

"Why so many twists and turnings when it was so simple to go out by the gate?" I could not restrain myself from exclaiming.

Mme. Edith looked at me reproachfully and I regretted having even seemed to have taken part against her in any way.

"And this is stranger yet!" said the Prince. "Day before yesterday, the 'hangman of the sea' came to bid me adieu, saying that he was going to leave the country, and I am sure that he took the train for Venice, his native city, at five o'clock in the afternoon. How then could he have conveyed your uncle in his boat late that night? In the first place, he was not in this part of the world; in the second, he had sold his boat. He told me so, adding that he would never return to this country."

There was a dead silence and Prince Galitch continued:

"All this is of little importance—provided that your uncle, Madame, recovers speedily from his injuries and, again," he added with another smile, more charming than those which had preceded it—"if you will aid me in regaining a poor piece of flint which has disappeared from the grotto and of which I will give you the description. It is a sharp piece of flint, twenty-five centimeters long and shaped at one end to the form of a dagger—in brief, the oldest dagger of the human race. I value it greatly and, perhaps you may be able to learn, Madame, through your uncle, Bob, what has become of it."

Mme. Edith at once gave her promise to the Prince, with a certain air of haughtiness which pleased me greatly, that she would do everything possible to obtain for him news of so precious an object. The Prince bowed low and left us. When we had finished returning his parting salutes, we saw M. Arthur Rance before us. He must have heard the conversation for he seemed very thoughtful. He had his ivory-headed cane in his hand, and was whistling, according to his habit. And he looked at Mme. Edith with an expression so strange that she appeared somewhat exasperated.

"I know exactly what you are thinking, sir!" she said. "It does not astonish me in the least. And you may keep on thinking so, if it amuses you, for aught I care.

"And she stepped nearer Rouletabille, smiling nervously.

"At all events," she exclaimed. "You can never explain to me how, when *he* was outside the Square Tower, *he* could have hidden behind that panel."

"Madame," said Rouletabille, slowly and impressively, looking at the young woman as though he were trying to hypnotize her, "have patience and have courage. If God is with me, before night I shall explain to you all that you wish to know."

XVIII

How Death Stalked Abroad
at Noon Day

A little later, I found myself in the lower parlour of "la Louve," tete-a-tete with Mme. Edith. I attempted to reassure her, seeing how restless and nervous she was; but she buried her pale face in her hands and her trembling lips allowed the confession of her fears to escape them.

"I am frightened" she murmured. I asked her what frightened her and she looked at me wildly and said, "And aren't you afraid, too?" I kept silence, for I was afraid, myself. She said again. "You know something of what is going on—here or there or all around us! Ah, I am all alone! all alone! And I am so frightened."

She turned toward the door.

"Where are you going?" I asked.

"I am going to look for someone. I won't stay here alone."

"For whom are you going to look?"

"For Prince Galitch."

"Your 'Feodor Feodorowitch,'" I cried. "What do you want with him? Am I not here?"

Her nervousness, unfortunately, seemed to increase in proportion to my efforts to drive it away and I began to realize that a fearful doubt as to the personality of her uncle, Old Bob, had entered her mind.

"Let us go out into the air!" she said, impatiently. "I can't breathe in this place." We left "la Louve" and entered the garden. It was approaching the hour of noontide and the court was a dream of perfumed beauty. As we had not donned our smoked spectacles, we were obliged to put our hands before our eyes in order to shield them from the glaring rays of the sun and the too glowing hues of the flowers. The giant geraniums struck on our eyeballs like bleeding wounds. When we had grown a little more used to the dazzling sight, we advanced over the shining sands, Edith clinging to my hand like a little child. Her hand burned hotter than the sun and seemed like a veritable flame. We looked down at our feet in order to prevent our eyes from falling on the blinding expanse of the waters and also, it may be, in order not to glance toward the buildings in which so many strange things had taken place—perhaps, were taking place even now.

"I am afraid!" murmured Edith once more. And I, too, was afraid—overwhelmed after the mysteries of the night by the vast, desolate silence of the noon.

The broad glare of daylight in which one knows that something strange and terrible is going on is more awful than the deepest and darkest night. Everything sleeps and yet everything wakes. Everything is dead and everything is living. Everything is wrapped in silence and still there are sounds everywhere. Listen to your own ear. It sounds as loud as a conch shell filled with the most mysterious sounds of the sea. Close your lids and look into your own eyes; you will find there a throng of crowding visions more mysterious than the phantoms of the night.

I looked at Mme. Edith. Beads of perspiration stood out on her forehead and her face was pale as death. I was trembling and chilled, for, alas! I could do nothing to help her and destiny was weaving its inexorable web all around us and that nothing which we could say or do would hinder in the slightest degree its slow, undeviating march. Edith led the way toward the postern gate which opens upon the Court of the Bold. The vault of this postern formed a black arch in the light and at the extremity of this tunnel, we perceived, facing us, Rouletabille and M. Darzac, who were standing at the edge of the inner court, like two white statues. Rouletabille was holding in his hand Arthur Rance's ivory-headed cane. Why this latter fact should have disturbed me, I do not know, but so it was. Motioning with the cane, he showed Robert Darzac something on the summit of the vault which we could not see and then he pointed us out in the same way. We could not hear what he said. The two talked together for a few moments with their lips scarcely moving, like two accomplices in some dark secret. Mme. Edith paused, but Rouletabille beckoned to her, repeating the signal with his cane.

"Oh, what does he want with me now?" she cried like a frightened child. "Oh, M. Sainclair, I am so miserable. I am going to tell my uncle everything and we shall see what will happen them."

We went on until we reached the vault and the others watched us without making a movement to meet us. They stood like two statues, and I said aloud in a voice which sounded strangely in my own ears:

"What are you two doing here?"

We had come up close to them by this time, upon the threshold of the Court of the Bold, and they bade us turn around with our backs toward the court so that we could see what they were looking at. There was on top of the arch, an escutcheon, the shield of the Mortola, barred with the mark of the cadet branch. This escutcheon had been carved in a stone now loose, which seemed in imminent danger of falling and crushing the heads of the passersby. Rouletabille had without doubt noticed this danger, and he asked Mme. Edith if she had any objections to its being pulled down until it could be replaced more solidly.

"I am sure that it will fall before long and it might do serious damage," he said, touching it with the end of his cane, and then passing the stick to Mme. Edith.

"You are taller than I," he went on. "See if you can reach it."

But both she and I tried in vain to touch the stone; it was too high for us and I was about to inquire what was the meaning of this singular exercise when all at once, behind my back, *I heard the cry of a dying man in his last agony*.

We turned with one impulse, uttering an exclamation of horror. Ah, that cry of mortal agony which rang out on the air of the noonday just as it had through the night! Would we never be free from murder? When would that fearful sound which I had heard for the first time that night at the Glandier, never be done with announcing to us that a new victim had been struck down among us? that one of our own number had fallen beneath some fatal blow, as suddenly as though by some frightful pestilence? Surely, the mark of the epidemic itself is less invisible and terrible than that of the hand which kills.

We all stood there, shivering, our eyes wide with horror, questioning the deeps of the sky still vibrating from that cry of death. Who was dead? Who was dying? What expiring breath had emitted that terrible sound? One might have thought that it was the clearness of the day itself which cried out in suffering.

Rouletabille was the most terrified of us all. I have seen him, under the most untoward circumstances, maintain a composure which seemed greater than any human creature could hold; I have seen him, at a like horrible cry of death, rush into the danger of the darkness and cast himself like a heroic rescuer into the sea of shadows. Why should he tremble so today in the full splendour of the noon? He remained fixed to the spot, as weak as a baby, he, who a little while ago, declared that he would prove himself the master of the hour. He had not foreseen this moment then? this moment in which a human life had been snatched away under the noonday sun!

Mattoni, who was passing through the garden, and who had also heard the cry, rushed up. At a gesture from Rouletabille he stood rooted to the spot an immovable sentinel; and now the young man had gained sufficient power to advance toward the cry—or, at least, toward the centre of the cry, for it seemed still to echo everywhere around us and to circle about in the all embracing space. And we hurried behind him, our breath coming fast, our arms stretched out, as one holds them when one is groping in the dark and fears to stumble against something which one does not see.

We approached the place from which the shriek had come and when we had passed the shade of the eucalyptus we found the cause. The cry had come, indeed, from a soul passing into the unknown. It was Bernier—Bernier in whose throat sounded the death rattle, who was trying in vain to rise and who was at the last gasp of his life. It was Bernier from whose breast flowed a stream of blood—Bernier over whom we leaned, and who, with one last, fearful struggle, summoned strength enough to utter the two words: "Frederic Larsan!"

Then his head fell back and he was dead. Frederic Larsan! Frederic Larsan! He who was everywhere and nowhere! He always and forever. Here, yet again, was his mark. A dead body—and no one anywhere near who could have committed the murder, by any possibility of human reason. For the only means of egress from the spot on which the crime had occurred was by this postern where we four had been standing. And we had turned, with one impulse and one movement, at the very instant that the cry rang out—so quickly that we had almost seen the stroke of death given. And when we looked, there had not even been a shadow before our eyes—nothing but the light! We rushed, moved by the same sentiment, it seemed to me, into the Square Tower, the door of which still stood open; we entered in a body the bedroom of Old Bob, passing through the empty sitting room. The injured man was lying quietly on his bed within, and near him a woman was watching—Mere Bernier. Both were as calm and still as the day itself. But when the wife of the dead concierge saw our faces she uttered a cry of affright, as though smitten by the knowledge of some calamity. She had heard nothing. She knew nothing. But she rushed into the air like a streak of lightning and went straight, as though impelled by some hidden force, directly to the place where the body was lying.

And now it was her groans that sounded on the air, under the terrible sun of the Midi, over the bleeding corpse. We tore the shirt from the dead man's breast and found a gaping wound just above the heart. Rouletabille looked up with the same expression which I had seen at the Glandier when he came to examine the wound of the "inexplicable body."

"One would say that it was the same stroke of the knife!" he said. "It is the same measurement. But where is the knife?"

We looked for the weapon everywhere without finding it. The man who had struck the blow had carried the knife away. Where was the man? Who was he? What we did not know, Bernier had known before he died and it was, perhaps, because of that knowledge that his life had been forfeited. "Frederic Larsan!" We repeated the last words of the dying man in fear and trembling.

Suddenly on the threshold of the postern, we saw the Prince Galitch, a newspaper in his hand. He was reading as he came toward us. His air was jovial and his face wore a smile. But Mme. Edith rushed up to him, snatched the paper from his hands, pointed to the corpse and cried out:

"A man has been murdered! Send for the police!"

The Prince stared at the body and then at us without uttering a word and then turned hastily away, saying that he would send for the authorities immediately, Mere Bernier kept up her wild lamentations. Rouletabille seated himself on the edge of the shaft. He seemed to have lost all his strength. He spoke to Mme. Edith in a low tone:

"Let the police come then, Madame, but remember, it is you who have insisted upon it!"

Mrs. Rance gave him a withering glance from her black eyes. And I knew what her thoughts were as well as though she had spoken them out. She felt that she hated Rouletabille, who had for a single moment been able to make her suspect Old Bob. While Bernier had been assassinated, had not Old Bob been quietly in his chamber, watched over by Mere Bernier herself?

Rouletabille was examining the iron bars and heavy lid which closed the shaft, but his manner was distrait and discouraged. After he had finished what seemed to be a very careless inspection he stretched himself out on the ground as if it were a couch in which he was trying to get some rest. Turning once more to his hostess, he said in the same low voice:

"And what will you tell the police when they get here?"

"Everything!"

Mrs. Rance fairly snapped out the word between her teeth, her eyes flashing fire. Rouletabille shook his head sorrowfully and closed his eyes. He seemed utterly exhausted and vanquished. Robert Darzac touched him on his shoulder. M. Darzac wanted to search through the Square Tower, the Tower of the Bold, the New Castle—all the dependencies of the fort from which no one could have made his escape, and where, therefore, the assassin must still be concealed. The reporter shook his head drearily, and said that it would be of no use. Rouletabille and I knew only too well that any search would be in vain. Had we not made a search at the Glandier after the phenomenon of the dissolution of matter, for the man who had disappeared in the inexplicable gallery? No, no! I had learned that there was no use in looking for Larsan with one's eyes.

A man had been murdered just behind our backs. We had heard him cry out when the blow struck him down. We had turned around and had seen nothing except the daylight. To see clearly, it was better to close the eyes as Rouletabille was doing at this moment.

And when he opened them, he was another man! A new energy animated his features. He stood erect as though he had thrown off a weight. He clenched his fist and raised it toward the heavens.

"That is not possible!" he cried. "Or there is no more good in reasoning."

And he threw himself on the ground, creeping on his hands and knees, his nose to the earth, like a hound following the scent, going round the body of poor Bernier and around Mere Bernier, who had blankly refused to leave her husband—around the shaft—around each of us. He moved about like a pig, nosing its nourishment out of the mire, and we all stood still, looking at him curiously and half in alarm. Suddenly he started to his feet, almost white with dust and uttered a shout of triumph as though he had found Larsan himself in the gravel. What new victory did the boy feel that he had achieved over the mystery? What had given this new firmness to his step and steadiness to his glance? What had given back to him the strength of his voice? For when he addressed M. Robert Darzac his tones were full of vigour and resolution.

"It's all right, Monsieur! *Nothing is changed*!"

And, turning to Mme. Edith—

"There is nothing more to do, Madame, except to wait for the police. I hope that they will not be long."

The unhappy woman shuddered. I knew that she was again struck with mortal fear.

"Yes, let them come!" she cried, taking my arm. "And let them attend to everything! Let them think for us! Whatever may happen, let it come as soon as it will."

Attracted by the sound of voices we looked around and saw Pere Jacques approaching, followed by two gendarmes. It was the brigadier of la Mortola, who, summoned by Prince Galitch, had hurried to the scene of the crime.

"The gendarmes! the gendarmes! They say that murder has been done!" exclaimed Pere Jacques, who as yet knew nothing of what had happened.

"Be calm, Pere Jacques!" exhorted Rouletabille, and when the old man, panting and breathless, drew near to the reporter, the latter said to him in low tones:

"*Nothing is changed*, Pere Jacques!"

But Pere Jacques was gazing at Bernier's body.

"Only one more dead man!" he sighed. "This is Larsan's work again!"

"It is the work of destiny!" answered Rouletabille. Larsan and destiny—both were as one. But what did Rouletabille mean by his "Nothing is changed," if not that, despite the incidental murder of Bernier, everything which we dreaded, which made us shudder and which we had no understanding of, continued just as before?

The gendarmes were busy examining the body and chattering over it in their uncomprehensible jargon. The brigadier informed us that they had telephoned to the Garibaldi Tavern, a few steps away, where at this moment the delegato, or special commissioner, stationed at Vintimille, was even now breakfasting. The delegato would have power to begin the investigation, which would be continued when the examining magistrate had been notified.

The delegato arrived. It was easily to be seen that he was enchanted, even though he had not had the time to finish his repast. A crime! actually a crime! And in the Château of Hercules. He was fairly radiant; his eyes shone. He was full of business, full of importance. He ordered the brigadier to station one of his men at the gate of the château with directions to permit no person to pass in or out. Then he knelt down beside the body while a gendarme, despite her protestations and tears, led Mere Bernier away to the Square Tower, where her groans sounded louder than ever. The delegato examined the wound and said in very good French:

"That was a magnificent stroke!"

The man was enchanted. If he had had the assassin under arrest, he would assuredly have paid him his compliments. He looked at us. Then he looked at us again. Perhaps he was seeking among us for the criminal to tell him of his admiration. At last he rose from his knees.

"And now how did all this happen?" he asked encouragingly, smacking his lips as though in the anticipation of hearing a story of thrilling interest. "It is terrible!" he added—"terrible! In the five years that I have been delegato, we have never had a murder, Monsieur the examining magistrate—." Here he checked himself but we knew well what he had been on the point of saying: "Monsieur the examining magistrate will be very much pleased." He brushed away the white dust which covered his knees, wiped the perspiration from his forehead and repeated "It is terrible!" his Southern accent seeming to grow stronger.

And at that moment, he noticed in a new arrival who entered the court, a doctor from Mentone who had come to continue his treatment of Old Bob.

"Ah, doctor, I am glad that you are here! Just look at this wound and tell me what you think of such a knife stroke. But be as careful as possible about changing the position of the corpse before the arrival of the examining magistrate."

The doctor sounded the depth of the wound and gave us all the technical details which we could desire. There was no doubt about it at all. It was a truly magnificent stroke of the knife which had penetrated from high to low in the cardiac region and the point of the knife had certainly opened a ventricle. During the colloquy between the delegato and the doctor, Rouletabille never took his eyes off Mme. Edith, who was still clinging to my arm as though she knew that I was her only refuge. Her eyes fell before the eyes of Rouletabille which seemed to hypnotize her and to command her to be silent. But I knew that she was trembling with the desire to speak.

At the request of the delegato, we all entered the Square Tower. We took our places in Old Bob's sitting room, where the inquest was to be held and where each of us in turn recounted what we had seen and heard. Mere Bernier was first questioned, but little or nothing could be gained from her testimony. She declared that she knew nothing about anything. She had been in Old Bob's bedroom, attending to the needs of the injured man, when we had rushed madly into the room. She had been with Old Bob for an hour, having left her husband in the lodge of the Square Tower, ready to work at making a rope.

It was a curious fact, but I was less interested at that moment in what was going on under my eyes than in what I could not see and yet knew *that I expected*.

Would Edith speak? She was looking out of the open window, her lips compressed, her brows drawn. A gendarme was standing near the corpse over the face of which a handkerchief had been laid. Edith, like myself, was paying very little heed to what was going on inside the room. Her eyes were fixed upon Bernier's body.

An exclamation from the delegato struck upon our ears. The further the evidence of the witnesses progressed, the greater became the amazement of the Commissioner, and the more and more inexplicable he found the crime. He was on the point of finding it impossible that it should have been committed at all, when it came Mme. Edith's turn to be interrogated.

They questioned her. Her lips were already opened to answer the first question when Rouletabille's quiet voice was heard:

"Look at the end of the shadow of the eucalyptus." "What is there at the end of the shadow of the eucalyptus?" demanded the delegato. "The weapon with which the crime was committed," replied the reporter.

He jumped out of the window to the court and picked up from the bloody stones a sharp, shining piece of flint. He brandished it in our eyes. We all recognised it. It was "the oldest dagger of the human race."

XIX

In Which Rouletabille Orders the Iron Doors to Be Closed

The weapon belonged to Prince Galitch, but there was no doubt in the mind of any one of us that it had been stolen by Old Bob, and we could not forget that with his latest breath Bernier had accused Larsan of being his assassin. Never had the image of Old Bob and that of Larsan been so inextricably confounded in our restless spirits as since Rouletabille had found "the oldest dagger known to the human race" dripping with the blood of Bernier. Mme. Edith had at once realised that henceforth the fate of Old Bob lay in the hands of Rouletabille. The latter had only to say a few words to the delegato relative to the singular incidents which had accompanied the fall of Old Bob into the cave in the "Grotto of Romeo and Juliet, enumerating the reasons which had given occasion for fear that Old Bob and Larsan were one and the same, and, finally, repeating the accusation made by the last victim of Larsan, in order to fix the suspicions of the delegato firmly upon the wigged head of the professor of geology. And, therefore, Mme. Edith, who in her filial affection had not ceased to believe that the man who lay on his bed in the Square Tower was really her uncle, had begun to imagine, thanks to the bloody weapon, that the invisible Larsan had woven so strong a web of circumstantial evidence around old Bob that it could scarcely be broken, with the design, doubtless, of making the old man suffer the punishment for the wretch's own crimes and also the dangerous weight of his personality. Mme. Edith trembled for Old Bob and for herself. She trembled with fear, like an insect in the centre of the web in which it has lost itself—this mysterious web woven by Larsan, attached by invisible threads to the old walls of the Château of Hercules. She felt as though if she were to make a sudden movement—to say anything even—both she and her uncle would be lost, and that some horrible beast of prey awaited only this signal to spring upon and devour her. So she who had been so anxious to speak out stood silent and when Rouletabille was called upon, it was her turn to fear. She told me afterward of her state of mind at this time and she acknowledged to me that her terror of Larsan had reached such a pitch as even we, who had known so much of his evil power already, had never experienced. This were wolf whose name she had so often heard spoken in accents of horror which had made her smile, had begun to interest her, when she learned of the events of the Yellow Room, because of the impossibility of the police discovering the manner of his exit. Her interest had increased when she had heard the story of the attack of the Square Tower because of the impossibility of anyone's explaining how Larsan could have entered; but, now—now, in the full glare of the noonday sun, Larsan had killed a man almost under her own eyes, and within a radius in which there was at the time only herself, Robert Darzac, Rouletabille, myself, Old Bob and Mere Bernier, each and every one of them far enough away from the body so that not one could have struck Bernier down. And Bernier had accused Larsan! Where was Larsan? *In whose body?*—according to the reasoning which I had set forth to her myself in telling her the story of the "inexplicable gallery"? She had been under the arch with Darzac and myself, standing between us, with Rouletabille in front of us, when the death cry had resounded at the end of the shadow of the eucalyptus tree—that is to say, at least, seven meters away. As to Old Bob and Mere Bernier, they had not been separated; the one had watched over the other. If she placed them outside the realms of possibility, there was no one left to kill Bernier. Not alone this time was everyone ignorant how *he* had departed but also of *how he had been present*. Ah, she understood now that when one thought of Larsan there were moments in which one shivered to the marrow of one's bones! Nothing! Nothing anywhere around the corpse but the stone knife which Old Bob had stolen! It was frightful—it was reason enough for us to think of everything—to imagine everything!

She read the certainty of this conviction in the eyes and in the manner of Rouletabille and of Robert Darzac. But she understood as soon as the young man began speaking that he seemed to have no other end in view than to save Old Bob from the suspicions of the authorities.

Rouletabille was given a seat between the delegato and the examining magistrate who had arrived while Mme. Edith had been testifying, and he gave his evidence (or rather, reasoned the matter out) holding the "oldest knife known to the human race" in his hand. It seemed definitely established that the guilty person could have been no other than one of the living men and women who were near the dead man and whom I have enumerated above, when Rouletabille proved with a logical accuracy that overwhelmed the examining magistrate and plunged the delegato into despair that the deed could only have been committed by the dead man himself. The four persons at the postern gate and the two persons in Old Bob's room had each been looking at the others and had not lost sight of each other while *someone* was killing Bernier a few steps away, so it was impossible to believe that the killing could have been done by any other than the victim.

To this the examining magistrate, greatly interested, replied by inquiring whether any of us had reason to suspect any motive for suicide on the part of Bernier, to which Rouletabille answered that the supposition of suicide might easily be laid aside and that of accident substituted for it. "The weapon of the crime," as he called ironically the "oldest knife known to the human race," testified to the truth of this theory by its presence. Rouletabille declared that there would be no chance of an assassin meditating the commission of a murder with an old piece of stone as an instrument. And still less could one believe that Bernier, if he had resolved upon suicide, would not have found another means toward his end than the one which had been used. But if, on the contrary, that stone, which might have attracted his attention by its strange form, had been picked up by Pere Bernier, and if he had happened to slip and fall while holding it in his hand, everything would be explained and very simply. Pere Bernier, undoubtedly, must have thus unfortunately fallen upon this triangular flint which had pierced his heart.

After Rouletabille had stated this hypothesis, the physician was recalled, the wound examined once more and confronted with the fatal object from which the scientific conclusion was reached that the wound was made by the object. From this to the theory of accident, as stated by Rouletabille, there was only a step. The judges spent six hours in clearing up the matter—six hours during which they questioned us without weariness but without result.

As to Mme. Edith and your humble servant, after some futile and useless questions, asked while the doctors were at the bedside of Old Bob, we were allowed to leave the room and we went to sit in the little parlour just outside the bedroom and were there when the magistrates were ready to depart. The door of this parlour which opened upon the corridor of the Square Tower had not been closed. We could hear the sobs and groans of Mere Bernier, who was watching beside the body of her husband which had been carried into the lodge. Between this body and the wounded man, the injury to one as inexplicable as the death of the other, the situation of both Mrs. Rance and myself had become extremely painful, in spite of Rouletabille's efforts, and all the terrors which we had experienced before grew pale and simple before the thought of what might be yet to come. Edith suddenly seised me by the hand and cried out:

"Do not leave me! I beg of you, don't leave me! I have only you left. I do not know where Prince Galitch is—I do not know anything about my husband. That is what makes this so horrible. Arthur sent me a message, saying that he was going in search of Tullio. He does not know even yet that Bernier has been murdered. Has he found the 'hangman of the sea'? It is from this man—from Tullio now that I expect the truth! And not a word has come! It is horrible!"

As she took my hand so confidingly and held it for a moment in her own, I felt that I was for Mme. Edith with all my heart and soul and I assured her that she might rely upon my devotion. We murmured a few words of trust and eternal fidelity to each other in low voices while there in the corridor we could see, passing back and forth, the dark forms of the emissaries of justice, now preceded, now followed by Rouletabille and M. Darzac. Rouletabille never failed to cast a glance in our direction every time he had the opportunity. The window remained open.

"Ah, he is watching us!" exclaimed Mme. Edith.

"Why is that, I wonder? Probably we are in his way and M. Darzac's when we remain here. But, whatever may happen, we shall not stir, shall we, M. Sainclair?"

"You ought to be grateful to Rouletabille," I ventured to remind her; "for his intervention and his silence relative to the 'oldest knife known to the human race.' If the officers had learned that this stone dagger belonged to your uncle, Bob, what could have hindered them from placing him under arrest? Or if they knew that Bernier in dying had accused Larsan of his murder, the story of the accident would have found very little credence."

I placed an emphasis upon these last words.

"Oh!" she cried, bitterly. "Your friend has as many good reasons to keep silence as I have! And I dread only one thing, M. Sainclair—I dread only one thing!"

"And what is that?"

She arose, her eyes shining with fever.

"I fear lest he has saved my uncle from the authorities only to ruin him more completely."

"How can you think such a thing for a moment?" I asked her, convinced that her fears were robbing her of her senses.

"I am sure that I could read some such plan in the eyes of your friend a little while ago. If I were sure that I were right, I would rather hand my uncle over to the mercies of the authorities."

I managed to quiet her a little and to make her cast aside such an impossible supposition, and, at length, she said:

"At all events, it is necessary to be ready for anything, and I know how to defend him so long as I draw breath."

And she showed me a tiny revolver which was hidden in her gown.

"Ah!" she cried again. "Why is Prince Galitch not here?"

"Again?" I exclaimed, angrily.

"Is it actual truth that you are ready to defend me?" she demanded, turning her beautiful eyes full upon my own."

"I am ready."

"Against the whole world?"

I hesitated. She repeated the words again:

"Against the whole world?"

"Yes."

"Against your friend even?"

"If it should be necessary," I answered with a sigh, passing my hand across my forehead.

"Very well: I believe you!" she answered. "In that case. I will leave you here for a few minutes. You will guard this door for *me*!"

And she pointed to the door behind which Old Bob was resting. Then she ran out of the room. Where was she going? She confessed to me later. She was going to look for the Prince Galitch! Oh, woman, woman!

She had scarcely disappeared under the arch when Rouletabille and M. Darzac entered the room. They had heard all that had passed. Rouletabille advanced to my side and told me quietly that he was aware that I had betrayed him.

"You are using a large word, Rouletabille!" I exclaimed. "You know that I am not in the habit of betraying anyone! Mme. Edith is really very much to be pitied and you do not pity her enough, my friend."

"Ah, well! you pity her too much!"

I blushed to the roots of my hair. I started to make some reply but Rouletabille cut short my words with a dry gesture.

"I ask you only one thing—only one, you understand. It is that, no matter what may happen—*no matter what may happen*—you shall not address one word to either M. Darzac or to myself."

"That will be a very easy thing to promise!" I replied, foolishly irritated, and I turned my back upon him. It seemed to me that it was with difficulty that he refrained from uttering some angry speech.

But at the same moment, the officers, coming out of the New Castle, called to us. The inquest was at an end. There was no doubt, in their eyes, after the declaration of the doctors, that the affair had been an accident and that was the verdict which they felt obliged to render. M. Darzac and Rouletabille accompanied them to the outer gate. And as I stood leaning on my elbows, at the window which opens upon the Court of the Bold, assailed by a thousand sinister presentiments and awaiting with an increasing anxiety for the return of Mme. Edith, while a few steps away in the lodge, where the candles had been lighted around Bernier's bier, Mere Bernier kept on sobbing and praying beside the corpse of her husband, I suddenly heard a sound which fell upon the evening air like the blow of an immense gong; and I knew that it was Rouletabille who had ordered the iron gates to be closed.

Not a single minute passed after that when I saw Mme. Edith rush into the room and hurry to me as though I were her only refuge.

Then I saw M. Darzac appear—

Then Rouletabille, and leaning on his arm was the Lady in Black.

XX

In Which Rouletabille Gives a Corporeal Demonstration of the Possibility of "The Body of Too Many"

Through the window I could see Rouletabille and the Lady in Black entering the Square Tower. Never had the young reporter walked with such solemn stateliness. His demeanour might have made one smile, if instead, at this tragic moment, it had not added to our apprehensions. Never had magistrate or counsellor, wearing the purple or the ermine, entered the court room where the accused waited him with more of threatening yet tranquil majesty. But I fancy, too, that never had a judge looked so pale.

As to the Lady in Black, it could easily be seen that she was making a powerful effort to hide the sentiments of horror which, in spite of all, pierced through her troubled glance, and to hide from us the emotion which made her cling feverishly to the arm of her young companion. Robert Darzac, too, had the sombre and resolute mien of a judge. But that which most of all added to our surprise and affright was the entrance of Pere Jacques, Walter and Mattoni into the Square Tower. All three were armed with muskets, and placed themselves in silence before the door, where they stood with military precision while they received from the lips of Rouletabille the order to let no person *go out* from the Old château. Edith was overwhelmed with terror, and demanded of Mattoni and Walter, both of whom were greatly attached to her, what their presence signified and what their weapons threatened; but, to my great astonishment, they returned no answer. Then the little woman rushed to the door which gave access to Old Bob's room, and, extending her two arms across the threshold, as if to bar the passage, she cried:

"What are you going to do? You do not mean to kill *him*?"

"No, Madame," replied Rouletabille, gravely. "We are going to judge him. And in order to be sure that the judges shall not be executioners we are all going to swear upon the body of Pere Bernier, after having laid down our arms, that each of us will keep guard over himself."

And he led us into the chamber where Mere Bernier continued to groan beside the bier of her spouse whom "the oldest knife known to the human race" had smitten. There we laid aside our revolvers and took the oath which Rouletabille exacted. Mrs. Rance alone made some difficulties about giving up the weapon which Rouletabille was well aware that she had concealed in her clothing. But upon the urging of the reporter who made her understand that the general disarming ought to reassure her, she finally consented.

The oath having been taken, Rouletabille, with the Lady in Black still on his arm, went from the funereal chamber into the corridor; but instead of directing our steps toward the apartment of Old Bob as we expected him to do, he went straight to the door which afforded entrance to the chamber of "the body too many." And, drawing from his pocket the little special key of which I have spoken, he opened the door.

We were all astonished in entering the rooms which had been occupied by M. and Mme. Darzac to see upon M. Darzac's desk the drawing board, the wash drawing upon which our friend had worked at the side of Old Bob in the latter's workshop in the Court of the Bold, and also the little dish full of red paint and the tiny brush drenched with the paint. And, lastly, in the middle of the desk, there was placed, appearing very much at its ease, upon its bloody jaws, "the oldest skull of humanity."

Rouletabille locked and bolted the door and said to us, himself greatly affected, while we listened with stupe faction:

"Sit down, if you please, ladies and gentlemen."

Some chairs were arranged around the table and in these we seated ourselves, a prey to the most disquieting fancies—I might almost say to an agony of suspense. A secret presentiment warned us that all the familiar appurtenances of drawing which were displayed before us might hide, under their apparent common place tranquility, the terrible causes which helped to bring about this most fearful of dramas. And as we looked upon it, the skull seemed to smile like Old Bob.

"You will acknowledge," began Rouletabille, "that there is here, around this table one chair too many, and, in consequence, one person too few—to particularize, M. Arthur Rance, for whom we cannot wait much longer."

"Perhaps at this very moment my husband possesses the proofs of Old Bob's innocence!" observed Mme. Edith, whom all these preparations had disturbed more than anyone else. "I entreat Mme. Darzac to join me in imploring these gentlemen to do nothing until Arthur's return."

The Lady in Black had no opportunity to intervene, for before Mme. Edith finished speaking, we heard a loud noise outside the door of the corridor. A knock came at the door and we heard the voice of Arthur Rance begging us to open immediately.

He cried:

"*I have brought the pin with the ruby head*!"

Rouletabille opened the door.

"Arthur Rance, you are come then at last!" he exclaimed.

Edith's husband seemed plunged in the deepest melancholy.

"What have you to tell me? What has happened? Some new misfortune? Ah, I feared so—feared that I had arrived too late when I saw the iron gate closed and heard the prayers for the dead chanted in the tower. Yes—I knew that you had *executed* Old Bob!"

Rouletabille, who had closed and bolted the door behind Arthur Rance turned to the American and said:

"Old Bob is alive and Pere Bernier is dead. Be seated, Monsieur."

Arthur Rance stared at the speaker in amazement; then looked in consternation at the drawing board, the dish of paint and the bloody skull and demanded:

"Who killed him?"

Then, condescending to notice that his wife was there, he pressed her hand, but his eyes were fixed upon the Lady in Black.

"Before his death, Bernier accused Frederic Larsan," answered M. Darzac.

"Do you mean to say by that that he accused Old Bob?" interrupted M. Rance indignantly, "I will not suffer that. I, too, had some doubts in regard to the personality of our beloved uncle, but I tell you that I have the ruby-headed pin!"

What was he talking about with his "little ruby headed pin"? I remembered that Mme. Edith had told us that Old Bob had snatched one from her hand when she had playfully pricked him with it on the night of the drama of the Square Tower. But what relation could there be between this pin and the adventure of Old Bob Arthur Rance did not wait for us to ask him, but hurried on to tell us that this little pin had disappeared at the same time as Old Bob and that he had found it in the possession of "the Hangman of the Sea," fastening a sheaf of bank notes which the old uncle had paid him on that fated night for his complicity and his silence in having brought him in the fisher boat to the grotto of Romeo and Juliet. And M. Rance told us moreover that

Tullio had withdrawn from the spot at dawn, greatly disquieted at the non appearance of his passenger. Rance concluded, triumphantly:

"A man who gives a ruby pin to another man in a boat cannot be at the same moment tied up in a potato sack in the Square Tower."

Upon which Mrs. Rance inquired:

"What gave you the idea of going to San Remo: Did you know that Tullio was to be found there?"

"I received an anonymous letter informing me of his whereabouts."

"It was I who sent it to you," said Rouletabille, tranquilly. And, then, turning to the rest of us, he said in frigid tones:

"Ladies and gentlemen, I congratulate myself upon the prompt return of M. Arthur Rance. At the present moment there are reunited around this table all the members of the house party of the Château of Hercules for whom my corporeal demonstration of the possibility of the 'body too many' may have some interest. I entreat you to give me your undivided attention."

But Arthur Rance halted him with a quick movement.

"What do you mean by the expression: 'There are united around this table all the members of the party for whom the corporeal demonstration of the possibility of the body too many can have any interest'?"

"I mean," declared Rouletabille, "all those among whom we may hope to find Larsan."

The Lady in Black, who had up to this time not uttered a word, arose trembling to her feet.

"Do you mean," she breathed, her eyes filled with agonised apprehension, "that Larsan is now among us?"

"I am sure of it," Rouletabille replied, gravely.

There was an awful silence during which none of us dared look at each other.

The reporter continued, still in the same frigid tone:

"I am sure of it—and there is no reason why the idea should surprise you, Madame, since it has not for a moment left your own mind. As to the rest of us, is it not true, gentlemen, that the idea has occurred to each one of us at the same moment on the day when we took luncheon on the terrace of the Bold when all our eyes were hidden by the black glasses? If I except Mrs. Rance, who is there among us that did not feel the presence of Larsan at that time?"

"That is a question which ought to be propounded to Professor Stangerson as well as to the rest of us," interposed Arthur Rance, instantly. "For from the moment when we begin any course of reasoning along these lines, I can see no object in not having the Professor, who was at the table at luncheon with us on that day, here at this time also."

"Mr. Rance!" cried the Lady in Black.

"Yes, I must repeat it, if you will pardon me," replied Edith's husband, haughtily. "Monsieur Rouletabille was wrong to generalize when he said, 'All the members of the house party—'"

"Professor Stangerson is so far from us in spirit that I have no need of his presence here," pronounced Rouletabille in a tone so stern and solemn that it fell impressively on the ears of each and every one among us. "Although Professor Stangerson had lived with us in the Château of Hercules, he was not one of us in regard to feeling the presence of Larsan on that day. And Larsan is here among us."

This time we stole stealthy glances at each other as though we suspected each other of stealing, and the idea that Larsan might really be among us appeared to me so mad that I exclaimed, forgetting that I had promised not to address Rouletabille:

"But at that luncheon on the terrace, there was still another person whom I do not see here."

Rouletabille cast an angry look at me as he answered: "Still Prince Galitch! I have already told you, Sainclair, with what task the Prince is occupying himself on this frontier and I swear to you that it is not the trouble of Professor Stangerson's daughter which concerns him. Leave Prince Galitch to his humanitarian labours!"

"All that is not reasonable," I remarked almost mechanically.

"To tell the truth, Sainclair, your nonsense prevents me from reasoning."

But I had launched out, and, forgetting that I had promised Mme. Edith to defend Old Bob, started in to attack him for the pleasure of proving Rouletabille in the wrong—and, besides, I felt, Edith would not bear to rancor against me for very long.

"Old Bob," I began, in the clearest and most assured tones I could command, "was also at the luncheon on the terrace and you take him entirely out of your calculations on account of this little ruby pin. But of what use is this little pin to prove to us that Old Bob was rowed away by Tullio, who waited for him at the orifice of a gallery leading from the shaft to the sea, if we cannot discover how Old Bob could, as he said, have gone by way of the shaft which we found closed from above and on the outside?"

"Which *you* found closed, you mean," returned Rouletabille, fixing his eyes upon me with a strange expression which somehow embarrassed me. "I, on the contrary, found the shaft open. I had sent you after Mattoni and Pere Jacques. When you came back, you found me in the same place in the Court of the Bold, but I had time to run to the shaft and find out that it had been opened."

"And to lose it again!" I cried. "And why did you close it? Whom did you wish to deceive?"

"*You, monsieur!*"

He pronounced these two words with a contempt so crushing that the blood rushed to my face. I arose. Every eye was turned upon me and as I remembered the rudeness with which Rouletabille had treated me a little while before M. Darzac, I had trouble feeling that every eye was suspecting me—accusing me! *Yes! I felt myself entirely wrapped around by the atrocious fancy in the mind of each and all that I might be Larsan!*

I! Larsan!

I looked at each one in turn. Rouletabille did not lower his eyes while my own were seeking to make him feel the fierce protestation of my whole being and my indignation against such a monstrous supposition. Anger ran through my veins like a flame. "Now, it is high time to end this farce!" I cried. "If Old Bob is removed from consideration and Professor Stangerson and Prince Galitch, there remain only ourselves—we who are locked up in this room—and if Larsan is among us, show us to him, Rouletabille!"

I repeated the words furiously, for the eyes of the boy, although they were piercing through me, seemed to be fixed upon something outside of and apart from me.

"Show him to us! Name him! You are as slow here as you were at the Court of Assizes."

"Had I not good reason at the Court of Assizes for being as slow as I was?" he replied, without betraying any emotion.

"You want him to escape this time, too, then?"

"No! I swear to *you* that this time he shall *not* escape."

Why did his voice continue to be so threatening when he addressed me? Could it be really—*really* that he suspected me of being Larsan? My eyes wandered to those of the Lady in Black. She was gazing on me in terror.

"Rouletabille!" I cried madly, feeling my voice almost smothered in my throat. "You do not—you cannot suspect!"

GASTON LEROUX

At this moment, a pistol shot sounded outside, very near to the Square Tower. We all leaped to our feet, remembering the order given by the reporter to the three servants to fire upon anyone who should attempt to go out of the Square Tower. Edith uttered a cry and tried to run out of the room, but Rouletabille, who had not made so much as a gesture, calmed her with a word.

"If anyone had drawn upon *him*," he said, "the three men would have fired together. That pistol shot was merely a signal—a direction for me to begin."

Turning to me, he continued:

"M. Sainclair, you ought to know that I never suspect any person or anything without previously having satisfied myself upon the 'ground of pure reason.' That is a solid staff which has never yet failed me on the road and on which I invite you all to lean with me. Larsan is here among us, and the power of pure reason is going to show him to you; so be seated again, if you please, and do not take your eyes from me, for I am going to begin on this paper the corporeal demonstration of the possibility of 'the body too many'!"

First of all, he investigated to make sure that the bolts of the door behind him were closely drawn; then, returning to the table, he took up a compass.

"I have the intention of making my demonstration," he said, "along the same lines on which the "body too many has produced itself. It will be, thereby, only the more irrefutable."

And, with his compass, he took, upon M. Darzac's drawing, the measure of the radius of the circle which represented the space occupied by the Tower of the Bold, so that he was immediately afterward able to trace the same circle upon an immaculate piece of white paper which he had fastened with copper-headed nails to another drawing board.

When the circle was traced, Rouletabille, putting down his compass, picked up the tiny dish of red paint and asked M. Darzac whether he recognised it as the colouring matter he had used. M. Darzac, who, from all appearances, understood the significance of the young man's words and actions no better than the rest of us, replied that, to the best of his belief, it was the same paint which he had mixed for his wash drawing.

A good half of the paint had dried up in the bottom of the dish, but, according to the opinion expressed by M. Darzac, the part which remained would, upon paper, give nearly the same tint with which he had "washed" the drawing of the peninsula of Hercules.

"No one has touched it," said Rouletabille very gravely, "and nothing has been added to it, save a single tear. Besides, you will see that a tear more or less in the paint cup would detract nothing from the value of my demonstration."

Thus saying, he dipped the brush in the paint and began carefully to "wash" all the space occupied by the circle which he had previously traced. He did this with the care and exactitude which had already astonished me in the Tower of the Bold when I had been nearly stupefied in seeing him absorbed in a drawing when we knew that someone had been assassinated.

When he had finished he looked at his immense silver watch and said:

"You may see, ladies and gentlemen, that the coating of paint which covers my circle is neither more nor less thick than that which covers the circle of M. Darzac. It is almost the same thing—the same tint."

"Undoubtedly," rejoined M. Darzac. "But what does all this signify?"

"Wait!" replied the reporter. "It is understood, then, that it is you who have made this plan and this painting?"

"I was certainly in enough of an ill humour when I found the state it was in that time I went with you into Old Bob's cabinet when we came out of the Square Tower. Old Bob had ruined my drawing by letting his skull roll over it."

"We are there!" spoke up Rouletabille, quick as a flash. And he lifted from the bureau the "oldest skull of the human race." He turned it over and showed the crimsoned jaws to M. Darzac. Then he inquired:

"Is it your opinion that the red which we see upon that under jaw is no different from the red which would be taken off by any object coming in contact with your plan?"

"I don't see how there could be any doubt of it! The skull was upside down on my drawing when we entered the workshop."

"Let us continue then to remain of the same opinion!" said the reporter.

Then he arose, holding the skull in the crook of his arm, and went into the alcove in the wall, lighted by a large window and crossed by bars, which had been a loophole for cannon in the ancient times, and which M. Darzac had used as a dressing room. There he struck a match and lighted a lamp filled with spirits of wine which stood upon a little table. Upon this lamp he set a little pot which he had previously filled with water. The skull still lay in the crook of his arm.

During this weird cookery, we never took our eyes off him. Never had Rouletabille's behaviour appeared to us so incomprehensible nor so mysterious nor so disturbing. The more he explained matters to us and the more he did, the less we understood. And we were afraid because we felt that someone—*someone among us—one of ourselves*—had reason for fear. Who was this one? Perhaps the most calm of us all!

But the calmest of all was Rouletabille between his skull and his casserole.

But what? Why did we all suddenly recoil with a single movement? Why were the eyes of M. Darzac wide with a new terror—why did the Lady in Black—Arthur Rance—I, myself—utter the same syllable—a name which expired on our lips: "*Larsan!*"?

Where had we seen him? Where had we discovered him this time, we who were gazing at Rouletabille? Ah, that profile, in the red shadow of the approaching twilight, that brow in the background of the alcove upon which the sunset rays stream as did the dawn on the morning of the crime! Oh, that stern jaw, bespeaking an iron will, which appeared before us, not, as in the light of day, gentle though a little bitter, but evil and threatening. How like Rouletabille was to Larsan! How in that moment the son resembled his father! It was Larsan's very self!

Another transformation. At a moan from his mother Rouletabille came out of his funereal frame and appeared before us as a bandit, and as he hurried toward us, he was Rouletabille once more. Mme. Edith, who had never seen Larsan, could not understand. She whispered to me, "What is going on?"

Rouletabille was there before us with his hot water in the casserole, a napkin and his skull. And he washed the skull.

It was soon done. The paint disappeared. He made us bear witness to the fact. Then, placing himself in front of the bureau, he stood in mute contemplation before his own drawing. This lasted for ten minutes, during which he had, by a sign, ordered us to keep silence—ten minutes which seemed as long as the same number of hours. What was he waiting for? What did he expect? Suddenly, he seised the skull in his right hand, and with the gesture familiar to those who play at bowling, he tossed it about so that it rolled hither and yon over the drawing; then he showed us the skull and bade us notice that it bore no trace of red paint. Rouletabille drew out his watch again.

"The paint has dried upon the plan," he said. "It has taken a quarter of an hour to dry. Upon the 11th of April we saw at five o'clock in the afternoon, M. Darzac entering the Square Tower and coming from out of doors. But M. Darzac, after having entered the Square Tower, and after having fastened behind him the bolts of his door, as he tells us, has not gone out again until we came to fetch him after six o'clock. As to Old Bob, we had seen him enter the Square Tower at six o'clock and there was no paint on this skull then!"

"How was this paint which has taken only a quarter of an hour to dry upon this plan, fresh enough still—more than an hour after M. Darzac had left it—to stain Old Bob's skull when the savant, with a movement of anger, threw it down on the plan as he entered the Round Tower? There is only one explanation of this, and I defy you to find another—and that is that the Robert Darzac who entered the Square Tower at five o'clock and whom no one has seen going out again, was not the same as the one who came to paint in the Round Tower before the arrival of Old Bob at six o'clock and whom we found in the room in the Square Tower without having seen him enter there and with whom we went out. In one word—he was not the same man as the M. Darzac here present before us. The testimony of pure reason shows that there are two personalities appearing in the guise of Robert Darzac!"

And Rouletabille turned his eyes full upon the man whose name he had uttered.

Darzac, like all the rest of us, was under the spell of the luminous demonstration of the young reporter. We were all divided between a new horror and a bound less admiration. How clear was every word that Rouletabille had uttered! How clear—and how terrible! Here again we found the mark of his prodigious and logical mathematical intelligence!

M. Darzac cried out:

"It was thus, then, that *he* was able to enter the Square Tower under a disguise which made him, without doubt, my very image! It was thus that he was able to hide behind the panel in such a way that I did not see him myself when I came here to write my letters after quitting the Tower of the Bold, where I left my drawing. But how could Pere Bernier have opened to him?"

"Doubtless," replied Rouletabille, who had taken the hand of the Lady in Black in both his own as though he wished to give her courage, "he must have believed that it was yourself."

"That then explains the fact that when I reached my door I had only to push it open. Pere Bernier believed that I was within." "Exactly: that is good reasoning!" declared Rouletabille. "And Pere Bernier, who had opened to Darzac No. 1, had not troubled himself about No. 2, since he did not see him any more than yourself. You certainly reached the Square Tower at the moment that Sainclair and myself called Bernier 'to the parapet to see whether he could help us in understanding the strange gesticulations of Old Bob, talking at the threshold of the Barma Grande to Mrs. Rance and Prince Galitch."

"But More Bernier" cried M. Darzac. "She had gone into her lodge. Was she not astonished to see M. Darzac come in a second time when she had not seen him go out?"

"Let us suppose," replied the young reporter with a sad smile; "let us suppose, M. Darzac, that Mere Bernier at that moment—the moment when you passed into your apartments—that is to say, when the second apparition of Darzac passed in—was occupied in picking up the potatoes and putting them back into the sack which I had emptied upon her floor—and we shall suppose the truth."

"Well, then, I can congratulate myself on the fact that I am still upon earth!"

"Congratulate yourself, M. Darzac? congratulate yourself!"

"When I remember that as soon as I entered my room, I drew the bolts as I have told you that I did, that I began to work and that this wretch was hidden behind my back. Why, he might have killed me without hindrance!"

Rouletabille stepped close to M. Darzac and fixed his eyes upon him with a look that seemed to read his soul.

"Why did he not kill you then?" he asked.

"You know very well that he was waiting for someone else," replied M. Darzac, turning his face sorrow fully toward the Lady in Black.

Rouletabille was now so close to M. Darzac that their shadows on the floor looked like that of one strangely formed being. The lad put his two hands on the older man's shoulders.

"M. Darzac," he said, his voice again clear and strong, "I have a confession to make to you. When I began to understand how the 'body too many' had effected an entrance and when I had discovered that you did nothing to undeceive us in regard to the hour of five o'clock at which we had believed—at which everyone, rather, except myself, believed—that you had entered the Square Tower, I felt that I had the right to suspect that the murderer was not the man who at five o'clock entered the Square Tower under the form of Darzac. I thought, on the contrary, that that Darzac might be the true Darzac and you might be the false one. Ah, my dear M. Darzac, how I have suspected you!"

"That was madness!" cried M. Darzac. "If I did not tell you the exact hour at which I entered the Square Tower it was because the time was somewhat vague in my own mind and I did not attach any importance to it."

"In such a manner, M. Darzac," continued Rouletabille, without paying any attention to the interruptions of his interlocutor, the emotion of the Lady in Black and our attitude, more than over filled with terror. "In such a manner as that you could have stolen away the true Darzac when he came from outside and, by your own carefulness and the too faithful help of the Lady in Black, could have taken his place and have been perfectly able to defy detection of your audacious enterprise. This was my imagination—only my imagination, M. Darzac; don't let it disturb you. But in such a manner as this, I had thought that, you being Larsan, the man who was put in the sack was Darzac. Ah! the fancies that I have had! and the useless suspicions!"

"Bah!" responded Mathilde's husband, gloomily. "We are all suspicious here!"

Rouletabille turned his back upon M. Darzac, put his hands in his pocket and said, addressing himself to Mathilde, who seemed ready to swoon before the horror of Rouletabille's imaginings:

"Courage for a little while longer, Madame!"

And he began speaking again, in his "teacher's" voice which I knew so well, and with the air of a professor of mathematics propounding or resolving a theorem:

"You see, M. Darzac, there are two manifestations of Robert Darzac. To know which was the true one and which was the one which formed a disguise for Larsan—my duty, M. Darzac—that which the power of pure reason showed me—was to examine, without fear or reproach, both of these manifestations—*in all impartiality*. Thus, I begin with you—M. Darzac."

M. Darzac replied: "It does not matter since you suspect me no longer. But you must tell me immediately who is Larsan. I insist upon it—I demand it!"

"We all demand it—and at once!" we all cried, turning upon both of them. Mathilde rushed up to her child and placed herself in front of him, as if to protect him. We felt the pathos of her attitude but the scene had endured too long and we were beyond the limits of patience.

"If he knows who is Larsan let him speak out and make an end of this!" exclaimed Arthur Rance.

And suddenly, just as the thought crossed my mind that I had heard the same cries of anger and impatience two years before at the Court of Assizes, another pistol shot sounded outside the door of the Square Tower, and we were all so seised with consternation that our anger fell away in a moment and we found ourselves not threatening Rouletabille but entreating him to put an end as soon as possible to this intolerable situation. At this moment, it actually seemed as though we were each imploring him to speak out, as though we calculated that by doing so, we would prove, not only to the others but to ourselves, that we were not Larsan.

As soon as the second shot was heard, the countenance of Rouletabille changed completely. His face seemed transformed and his whole being appeared to vibrate with a savage energy. Laying aside the half bantering manner which he had used toward M. Darzac and which we had all found extremely disagreeable, he gently released himself from the clasp of the Lady in Black, who still clung to him, walked toward the door, folded his arms and said:

"You see, my friends, in an affair like this, it does not do to neglect any point. There were two manifestations of Robert Darzac which entered the Square Tower. There were two manifestations which came out— and one of these was in the sack! That is where one loses oneself. And *even now*, I do not wish to make any mistakes! Will M. Darzac, here present, permit me to say that I had a hundred excuses for suspecting him?"

Then I thought to myself: "How unlucky that he did not mention his suspicions to me! I would have told him about the map of Australia!"

M. Darzac strode across the room and planted himself in front of the young reporter and said in a tone nearly inaudible from anger:

"What excuses? I ask you, what excuses?"

"You will soon understand, my friend," said the reporter with the utmost calmness. "The first thing that I said to myself while I was examining the conditions surrounding *your* manifestation of Larsan, was this: 'Nonsense! if he were Larsan, would not Professor Stangerson's daughter have perceived it?' That is self evident—the common sense of that thought—is it not? But when I tried to look into the mind of the lady who has become Mme. Darzac, I discovered beyond a doubt, Monsieur, that all the while she could not free herself from just this fear—the fear that you might be Larsan!"

Mathilde, who had fallen half fainting into a chair, gathered strength enough to start up and to protest against the words with a frightened, despairing gesture.

As for M. Darzac, his face was a picture of hopeless anguish. He sank upon a couch and said in a voice so low that it was scarcely audible and so full of wretchedness that it pierced our hearts:

"And could you have thought that, Mathilde?"

His wife dropped her eyes and spoke not a word. Rouletabille, still merciless, continued:

"When I recall all the acts of Mme. Darzac after your return from San Remo, I can see now in each one of them an expression of the terror which she experienced from her fear that she should allow the secret of her suspicion and her constant agony to escape her. Ah, let me speak, M. Darzac! Everything must be said—everything must be explained here and now if there is to be peace in the future! We are about to clear up the situation. To go on then, there was nothing natural or happy in Mlle. Stangerson's behaviour. The very eagerness with which she assented to your desire to hasten the marriage ceremony proved the longing which she felt to definitely banish the torment of her soul. Her eyes—I remember it now!—used to say at that time—how often and how clearly 'Is it possible that I continue to see Larsan everywhere, even in the face of the man who is at my side, who is going to lead me to the altar and to take me away with him?'"

"From the moment of your return from the South until the apparition at the railroad station, monsieur, she lived in the most utter misery. She was already crying for help-for help against herself—against her thoughts—and, perhaps, even against *you*! But she dared not reveal her thought to any person because she dreaded that any confidant might say to her—"

And Rouletabille leaned over and said in M. Darzac's ear, not so low that I could not hear, but so softly that the words did not reach Mathilde: "Are you going mad again?"

Then, lifting his head again, he continued:

"You ought to understand everything better now, my dear M. Darzac—both the strange coldness with which you were treated occasionally and also the fits of remorseful tenderness which, in the doubt which filled her brain, would impel Mme. Darzac to surround you with every evidence of attention and affection. And, furthermore, allow me to tell you that I myself have sometimes found you so gloomy and *distrait* that I have fancied that you must have discovered that whenever Mme. Darzac looked at you, she could not, in spite of herself, chase from her mind the image of Larsan. It came upon her when she spoke to you and when she was silent—when you were beside her and when you were at a distance. And, consequently—let us understand each other completely—it was *not* the belief that Professor Stangerson's daughter would have known it' which removed my suspicions, since, in spite of herself, she entertained the fear all the while that you and Larsan were one. No! no my suspicions were removed by another cause!"

"They might have been removed," exclaimed M. Darzac, at once ironically and despairingly—"they might have been removed, it would seem, by the simple course of reasoning that if I had been Larsan, wedded to Mlle. Stangerson, having her for my wife, I would have had every cause for making her believe in Larsan's death! And I would have never resuscitated myself! Was it not upon the day that Larsan returned to earth that I lost Mathilde?"

"Pardon, monsieur, pardon" replied Rouletabille, whose face had grown as white as a sheet. "You are abandoning now, if I may say so, the directions of pure reason. The facts which you mentioned show us just the contrary of that which you believe we should see. For my part, it seems to me that when one has a wife who believes, or who comes very near to believing, that one is Larsan, one has every interest in showing her that *Larsan exists outside of oneself*!"

As Rouletabille uttered these words, the Lady in Black, supporting herself by groping with her hands against the wall as she walked, came stumblingly to the side of Rouletabille, and devoured with her eyes the face of M. Darzac which had grown frightfully harsh and strained. As to the rest of us, we were so struck by the novelty and the irrefutability of Rouletabille's reasoning, that we experienced no other emotion than an ardent desire to know what was to follow, and we took care not to interrupt, asking ourselves to what such a formidable hypothesis might not lead. The young man, imperturbably, went on:

"And, if you had an interest in showing her that Larsan existed elsewhere than in your body, there arose an exigency in which that interest was transformed into an immediate necessity. Imagine—I say *imagine*, M. Darzac, that you had really brought Larsan to life once—once only—in spite of yourself—in your own rooms—before the eyes of Professor Stangerson's daughter—and you will be, I repeat, under the necessity of bringing him to life again and yet again—outside of yourself, in order to prove to your wife that the Larsan whom she has seen returned to life is not you! Ah, calm yourself, my dear M. Darzac, I entreat you. Have I not told you that my suspicion has been banished—completely banished? But it is as well that we should divert ourselves for a few moments in reasoning the matter out a little, after these long hours of anguish when it seemed as though there would never be any place for reasoning again. See, then, where I am obliged to come in considering this hypothesis as realised (these are the procedures of mathematics which you know better than I—you who are a scholar!)—in considering, as I said, as realised the hypothesis that you are the counterfeit Darzac, the one which hides Larsan. According to my reasoning, then, you are Larsan! And I asked myself what could have happened in the railway station at Bourg to make you appear in the form of Larsan before the eyes of your wife. The fact of such an appearance is undeniable. It exists. And its occurrence at that moment cannot be explained by any desire on your part to have Larsan seen!"

He paused for a moment, but Robert Darzac did not utter a word.

"As you were saying, M. Darzac," Rouletabille went on, "it was because of this apparition of Larsan that your cup of happiness was dashed empty to the ground. Therefore, if this resurrection should not have been voluntary there is only one other way in which it could have happened—through accident. And now just let us consider how this latter supposition clears up the entire situation. Oh, I have spent a lot of thought upon the incident at Bourg—you see, I am still reasoning out the problem! You (the you who is Larsan, be it understood) are at Bourg in the buffet. You believe that your wife is waiting for you somewhere in the station as she told you she would do. After having finished your letters, you wish to go to your compartment in the car in order to attend to some detail of your toilet—or, shall we say to cast a critical eye over your disguise to see if in any point it might be lacking? You think to yourself: 'A few more hours of this comedy and we shall have passed the frontier, she will be all my own—entirely alone with me, and I will throw aside this mask'—for the mask wearies you a little, we may imagine—so much so, indeed, that, once arrived in your compartment, you grant yourself the grace of a few moments of repose. You cast away your assumed character and your disguise. You relieve yourself of the false beard and the spectacles—and at that very moment the door of the section opens. Your wife, thrown into a spasm of terror at the sight of Larsan's smooth, beardless face in the glass, does not wait to make any further investigation and rushes out into the night, her screams drowned by the noise of another train. You comprehend the danger at once. You realize that everything is lost unless you can *immediately* arrange matters so that your wife shall see Darzac somewhere else. You quickly resume the mask; you hurry out of the compartment and reach the buffet by a shorter route than that taken by your wife, who rushes there to look for you. She finds you standing up. You have not even had time enough to seat yourself before she enters. Is everything safe now? Alas, no! Your troubles are only beginning. For the fearful thought that you may be at one and the same time both Darzac and Larsan will not leave her mind. Upon the platform of the station, while passing beneath the gas jet, she casts a frightened glance at you, lets go your hand and runs wildly into the office of the station master. You read her thought as though she had spoken it. The abominable idea must be banished without a moment's delay. You quit the office, leaving the lady in the care of the superintendent, and immediately return, closing the door quickly, seeking to give the impression that you, too, have seen Larsan. In order to ease her mind, and, also, for the purpose of deceiving us all, in case she dared reveal her suspicions to anyone, you are the first to warn me that something unforeseen has happened—to send me a dispatch. See how clear and plain as the day your every act becomes! You cannot refuse to take her to rejoin her father. She would go without you. And, since nothing is yet really lost, you have the hope that everything may be regained. In the course of the journey, your wife continues to have alternating periods of faith in you and of fear of you. She gives you her revolver, in a sort of half delirium, which might sum itself up in some such phrase as this: 'If he is Darzac, let him protect me; if he is Larsan, let him kill me! But in pity, let me know which he is.' At Rochers Rouges, you realised once more how utterly she had withdrawn herself from you and in order to reassure her as to your identity, you showed her Larsan again."

S ee how in accordance with reason such a proceeding would be, my dear M. Darzac! Every fact would fit perfectly into every other under the supposition which I am placing before you. There is not a single point up to your appearance as Larsan at Mentone, during your journey as Darzac to Cannes, at the time when you came to meet us, which cannot be explained in the easiest way imaginable. You had taken the train at Mentone-Garavan before the eyes of your friends, but you alighted from the train at the next station, which is Mentone, and there, after a short stay for the purpose of altering your looks, you appeared in the image of Larsan to the same friends who were promenading in the gardens at Mentone. The following train brought you to Cannes, where you met Sainclair and myself. Only, as you had on this occasion the vexation of hearing from the lips of Arthur Rance when he met us at the station at Nice, the news that Mme. Darzac had not, on this occasion, caught sight of Larsan, you were under the necessity that same evening of showing her Larsan under the very windows of the Square Tower, standing erect in the prow of Tullio's boat. So, you see, my dear M. Darzac, how even those things which appear most complicated would have become entirely simple and logically explicable, if, by chance, my suspicions should have been confirmed."

At these words, I myself, who had seen and touched "the map of Australia," was unable to repress a shudder as I looked pityingly at Robert Darzac, just as one might look at some poor man who is on the point of becoming the victim of some hideous judicial error. And all the others, seated around me, shuddered as well, whether for him or on account of him, for the arguments of Rouletabille were becoming so terribly *possible* that each of us was asking himself how, after having so completely established the possibility of guilt, the young reporter could prove Darzac's innocence. As to Robert Darzac, after having at first evinced the deepest agitation, he had grown quite tranquil and calm, as he listened attentively to every word that escaped the young man's lips. And it seemed to me that his eyes held the same expression of astonishment, amased and frightened, and yet full of breathless interest, which I had seen in the eyes of accused men at the bar of the Assizes when they had heard the Procurer General de liver one of his wonderful disquisitions which almost convinced the prisoners themselves that they were guilty of a crime which sometimes they had never committed.

"But since you no longer have these suspicions, monsieur!" he exclaimed, his intonation singularly calm, in spite of the fact that his voice was raised, "I should be glad to know, after all this exercise of your talent of reasoning, what could have driven them away?"

"In order to have them driven away, monsieur, one thing was essential—an *absolute certitude*! And I found it—a simple but conclusive proof which showed me in a manner complete and undeniable which of the two manifestations of Darzac was in reality Larsan. That proof, monsieur, was, happily, furnished me by yourself at the very moment when you *closed the circle*—the circle in which there had been found the 'body too many'!—the time when, after having sworn that which was the truth—that you had drawn the bolt of your apartment as soon as you had entered your sleeping room, *you had lied to us in concealing from us that you had entered that room at six o'clock instead of at five o'clock as Pere Bernier said and as we ourselves could have proved. You were then the only person except myself who knew that the Darzac who had entered at five o'clock and of whom we had spoken to you as yourself was in reality another man. But you said nothing. And you need not pretend that you did not attach any importance to that hour of five o'clock. What interest could the real Darzac have in hiding the fact that another Darzac, who might be Larsan, had come and hidden in the Square Tower before you came in? Larsan was the only one who could have a reason for concealing the knowledge that there was another Darzac besides himself. Of the two, false and the real Darzac, the false one was necessarily the one who lied. Thus were my suspicions dispelled by a certainty. You were Larsan, and the man in the wardrobe was Darzac!*"

"You are a liar!" howled the man as he sprang at Rouletabille.

But we got between them, and Rouletabille, who was not in the least disturbed, pointed at the cupboard and said:

"*He is in there now!*"

None of us will ever forget what followed. Just as on the memorable night, an invisible hand opened the door of the cupboard, and the body appeared before us again.

Exclamations of surprise, excitement and fear rang through the Square Tower. The voice of the Lady in Black rose above all the others.

"Robert! Robert! Robert!"

And it was a cry of joy! Two Darzacs before us so exactly similar that every one of us save the Lady in Black might have been deceived. But her heart told her the truth, even admitting that her reason, not withstanding the triumphant conclusion of Rouletabille, might have hesitated. Her arms outstretched, her eyes alight with love and joy, she rushed toward the second manifestation of Darzac—the one which had descended from the panel. Mathilde's face was radiant with new life; her sorrowful eyes which I had so often beheld fixed with sombre gloom upon *that other*, were shining upon this one with a joy as glorious as it was tranquil and assured. It was he! It was he whom she had believed lost—whom she had sought in vain in the visage of the other and had not found there and, therefore, had accused herself, during the weary hours of day and night, of folly which was akin to madness.

As to the man who, up to the last moment I had not believed to be guilty—as to that wretch who, un veiled and tracked to earth, found himself suddenly face to face with the living proof of his crimes, he attempted yet again, one of the daring coups which had so often saved him. Surrounded on every side, he yet endeavoured to flee. Then we understood the audacious drama which in the last few moments, he had played for our benefit. When he could no longer have any doubt as to the issue of the discussion which he was holding with Rouletabille, he had had the incredible self control to permit nothing of his emotions to appear, and had also been able to prolong the situation, permitting Rouletabille to pursue at leisure the thread of the argument at the end of which he knew that he would find his doom, but during the progress of which he might discover perchance some means of escape. And he had effected his manoeuvers so well that at the moment when we beheld the other Darzac advancing toward us, we could not hinder the imposter from disappearing at one bound within the room which had served as the bedchamber of Mme. Darzac and closing the door violently behind him with a rapidity which was nothing less than marvellous. We only knew that he had vanished when it was too late to stop his flight.

Rouletabille, during the scene which had passed had thought only of guarding the door opening into the corridor and he had not noticed that every movement of the false Darzac, as soon as he realised that he was being convicted of his imposture, had been in the direction of Mme. Darzac's room. The reporter had attached no importance to these movements, knowing as he did that this room did not offer any way by which Larsan might escape. But, however, when the scoundrel was behind the door which afforded his last refuge, our confusion increased beyond all proportions. One might have thought that we had become suddenly bereft of our senses. We knocked on the door. We cried out. We thought of all his strokes of genius—of his marvellous escapes in the past!

"He will escape us! He will get away from us again!"

Arthur Rance was the most enraged of us all. Mme. Faith, who was clinging to my arm, drove her fingernails into my hand in a paroxysm of nervous fear. None of us paid any heed to the Lady in Black and Robert Darzac who, in the midst of this tempest, seemed to have forgotten everything, even the clamour and confusion around them. Neither one had spoken a word but they were looking into each other's eyes as though they had discovered another world—the world which is love. But they had not discovered it; they had merely found it again, thanks to Rouletabille.

The latter had opened the door of the corridor and summoned the three domestics to our assistance. They entered with their rifles. But it was axes that were needed. The door was solid and barricaded with heavy bolts. Pere Jacques went out and fetched a beam which served us as a battering ram. Each of us exerted all his strength and, finally, we saw the door beginning to give way. Our anxiety was at its height. In vain, we told ourselves that we were about to enter a room in which there were only walls and barred windows. We expected anything—or, rather, we expected nothing, for in the mind of each and every one of us was the recollection of the disappearances, the flights, the actual "dissolution of matter" which Larsan had brought about in times past and which at this moment haunted us and drove us nearly mad.

When the door had commenced to yield, Rouletabille directed the servants to take up their guns, with the order, however, that the weapons were to be used only in case it should be impossible to capture Larsan living. Then the young reporter set his shoulder to the door with one last powerful effort and as the boards, wrenched from their hinges, fell to the ground, he was the first to enter the room.

We followed him. And behind him, upon the threshold, we all halted, stupefied by the sight which met our eyes. Larsan was there—plainly to be seen by everyone. And this time there was no difficulty in recognizing him. He had removed his false beard; he had put aside his "Darzac mask"; he had resumed once more the pale, clean-shaven face of that Frederic Larsan whom we had known at the Château of Glandier. And his presence seemed to fill the entire room. He was lying back comfortably in an easy chair in the centre of the room and was looking at us with his great, calm eyes. His arm was stretched along the arm of the chair. His head was resting on the cushion at the back. One would have said that he was giving us an audience and was waiting for us to make known our business. It seemed to me that I could even discern an ironical smile on his lips.

Rouletabille advanced toward him.

"Larsan," he said in a voice which was not quite steady, "Larsan, do you give yourself up?"

But Larsan did not reply.

Then Rouletabille touched the man's face and his hand and we saw that Larsan was dead.

Rouletabille pointed to a ring on the middle finger. The collet was open and showed a hollow cup which was empty. It must have contained a deadly poison.

Arthur Rance put his head against the man's chest and assured us that all was over. And Rouletabille entreated us to leave him alone in the Square Tower and to try and forget the terrible events which had passed there.

"I will charge myself with everything," he asserted gravely. "Here is the 'body too many.' No one will inquire into the disposition which may be made of it."

And he gave an order to Walter which Arthur Rance translated into English. "Walter, bring me the sack which you found at the Castillon yesterday."

Then he made a gesture to which we were all obedient—a gesture of dismissal. And we left the son face to face with the corpse of the father.

The next moment we saw that M. Darzac was swooning and we were obliged to carry him into Old Bob's sitting room. But it was only a passing faintness and soon he opened his eyes again and smiled at Mathilde when he saw her beautiful face bending over him with the look of dread in which we read the fear of losing her beloved husband at the very moment in which she had, through a chain of circumstances which still remained wrapped in mystery, found him again. He succeeded in convincing her that his life was not in any danger and he added his entreaties to those of Mme. Edith that she would go away for a little while and try to get some rest. When the two women had left us, Arthur Rance and myself turned our attention to our friend, inquiring of him, first of all, in regard to his curious state of health. For how could a man whom all of us had believed to be dead, and who had been, with the death rattle in his throat, tied up in a sack and carried away, have been able to rise again and step-down living from the fateful panel? But when we had opened his shirt and discovered the bandage which hid the wound that he bore in his breast, we recognised the fact that this injury, by a chance so rare that one would scarcely believe that it could exist, after having brought about an almost immediate state of coma, was not a very serious one. The ball which had struck Darzac in the midst of the savage fight which he had been obliged to make against Larsan, had planted itself in the sternum, causing a bad external hemorrhage and weakening the entire organism, but, fortunately, suspending none of the vital functions.

As we finished the task of dressing the wound Pere Jacques came to close the door of the parlour which had remained open and I wondered what might be the reason which had led the old man to this precaution until I heard steps in the corridor and a strange noise—the sound that one hears when a body is carried away on a stretcher. And I thought of Larsan and of the sack which was holding now for the second time "the body too many."

Leaving Arthur Rance to watch over M. Darzac I hurried to the window. I had not been mistaken. I beheld the sinister funeral cortege in the court outside.

It was nearly nightfall. A gathering gloom surrounded everything. But I could distinguish Walter, who had been stationed as a sentinel under the arch of the gardener's postern. He was looking toward the outer court, ready, evidently, to bar the passage of anyone who might desire to penetrate into the Court of the Bold.

Moving onward in the direction of the oubliette, I saw Rouletabille and Pere Jacques—two dark shadows bending over another shadow—a shadow which I recognised and which, on that other night of horror, I had believed to contain another dead body. The sack seemed heavy. The two men were scarcely able to lift it to the edge of the shaft. And I could see that the little passageway was open—yes, the heavy wooden lid which ordinarily closed it had been removed and was lying on the ground. Rouletabille leaped lightly over the edge of the oubliette and then made a step downward. He showed no hesitation; the way seemed to be familiar to him. In a few moments his figure vanished from sight. Then Pere Jacques pushed the sack into the passageway and leaned over the edge, apparently still holding on to his burden which I could no longer see. Then he stood back, closed up the opening and adjusted the iron bars and in doing so made a sound which I suddenly remembered—the sound which had puzzled me so much that evening when, before the "discovery of Australia," I had rushed in pursuit of a shadow which had suddenly disappeared and which I had searched for up to the very door of the New Castle.

I felt that I must see—up to the very last moment. I must know all! Too many strange and inexplicable things were filling my soul with anxiety already. I had learned the most important part of the truth, but I had not all of the truth—or, rather, something which would explain the truth was still lacking.

I left the Square Tower: I went to my own room in the New Castle, I stationed myself at the window and my eyes lost themselves in the depths of the shadows which covered the sea. Thick darkness: jealous shadows. Nothing more. And then I strained my ears to listen, although I knew that there was not the faintest sound of the strokes of the oar.

All at once—far–very far off—it seemed to me that all this was passing so far over the sea that it crossed the horizon—or, rather, approached the horizon—I fancied that I could see in the narrow red band which was all that remained of the setting sun something that seemed more unreal than a vision.

Into that narrow red band an object entered—something dark and very small, but to my eyes, which were fixed upon it in breathless suspense, it seemed the greatest and most formidable sight that I had ever beheld. It was the shadow of a fishing smack which glided over the waters as automatically as though it were propelled by machinery and as its movements became slower, and I saw it emerging from the gloom, I recognised the form of Rouletabille. The oars ceased to move and I saw my friend rise to his feet. I could recognize him and see everything which he did as clearly as if he had not been ten yards away from me. His gestures were out lined against the red background of the sunset with a fantastic precision.

What he had to do did not take long. He leaned over and got up again, lifting in his arms something which seemed to mix with his form and become a part of himself in the darkness. And then the burden glided down into the water and the man's figure reappeared alone, still bending, still leaning over the edge of the boat, remaining thus for an instant motionless, and then once more picking up the oars of the bark which resumed its automatic motion until it had disappeared completely from the dying glare of the ever narrowing band of red. And then the band of red, too, vanished.

Rouletabille had consigned the body of Larsan to the waves of Hercules.

Epilogue

Nice–Cannes–Saint-Raphael—Toulon. I saw without regret all the stages of my return trip passing before my eyes. Upon the very day which had followed all the horrible things I have related, I hastened to quit the Midi, anxious to find myself once more in Paris and to plunge into my business affairs—and anxious also to find myself alone with Rouletabille, who was now only a few feet away from me, locked up in a private compartment with the Lady in Black. Up to the very last moment—that is to say, as far as Marseilles, where they were obliged to separate, I was unwilling to interrupt their tender and sorrowful confidences, their plans for the future, their fond farewells. Despite all the prayers of Mathilde Rouletabille was determined to leave her, to return to Paris and to his paper. The son had the superb heroism of effacing himself for the sake of the husband. The Lady in Black had not been able to resist Rouletabille and the boy had dictated exactly what should be done. He had directed that *M. and Mme. Darzac* must continue their honeymoon trip as if nothing remarkable had happened at Rochers Rouges. It was one Darzac who had begun the journey; it was another Darzac who was to finish it—this trip which had become such a happy one—but in the eyes of all the world Darzac would be the same man without any suspicion that things had ever been otherwise.

M. and Mme. Darzac were married. The civil law united them. As to the religious law, as Rouletabille said, the affair might easily be laid before the Pope while the couple were in Rome and there would, without doubt, be found means of regularizing the situation, if there was found to be need of it or if the conscientious scruples of the couple desired it. And Robert Darzac and his wife were happy—completely happy. They belonged to each other.

At Rochers Rouges—at the "Louve" itself, we had said adieu to Professor Stangerson. Robert Darzac had departed immediately for Bordighera, where Mathilde was to join him. Arthur Rance and Mme. Edith accompanied us to the railroad station. My charming hostess, contrary to my hope, evinced no great amount of concern at my departure. I attributed this indifference to the fact that Prince Galitch had come to the quay to see us off. Mme. Edith was giving him the latest bulletin from Old Bob's bedside (which was excellent, by the way), and paid no further attention to me. I felt a real pang of-was it grief or wounded self love? And here and now, I have a confession to make to the reader. Never would I have allowed myself to betray the sentiments which I had entertained toward her, if, several years later, after the death of Arthur Rance, which was surrounded and followed by a most terrible tragedy of which I may relate the history one day, I had not married the dark eyed, melancholy, romantic Edith!

We were approaching Marseilles.

Marseilles!

The farewells were heart rending, although neither Rouletabille nor the Lady in Black uttered a word. And as the train bore us away we saw her standing on the platform in the station, without a movement or gesture, her arms hanging at her side, looking in her sombre draperies like a statue of mourning and of sorrow.

I saw in front of me Rouletabille's shoulders shaken with sobs.

L yons. We could not sleep. We alighted from the train and walked about the station. Both of us recalled the moment when we had been there before—only a few days past—when we were rushing to the rescue of the most unhappy of women. My thoughts plunged once more into the memories of the tragedy and I knew that Rouletabille's were following the same track. And now Rouletabille spoke—spoke in a voice which he tried to make sound careless and light hearted and which made me understand that he was endeavouring to efface from his mind the thought of the grief which had made him sob like a little child only a short while ago.

"Old man!" he said, with a smile, throwing his arm across my shoulder. "That Brignolles was really a beast!" and he looked at me with such an air of reproach that he almost succeeded in making me believe for a moment that I had ever taken the creature for an honest man.

And then he told me everything—all the marvellous, horrible story which I am compressing here into a few lines. Larsan had had need of some relative of Darzac in order that he might obtain the necessary signature for the incarceration of the Sorbonne professor in a madhouse. And he discovered Brignolles. He could not have fallen upon a better man for his purpose. Everyone knows how simple it is, even today, to have a human being, no matter who he may be, locked up in a cell. The desire of a relative and the signature of a medical man is sufficient in France, impossible as the thing appears, for the accomplishment of this task which may be performed with the utmost celerity. The matter of a signature never embarrassed Larsan in his life. He forged one—that of an eminent alienist—and Brignolles, richly reimbursed, charged himself with the rest. When Brignolles came to Paris, he was already a party to the combination. Larsan had formed his plan—to take Darzac's place before the wedding. The accident to the young professor's eyes had been, as I had believed from the first, the result of design. Brignolles had been directed to manage in some manner so that Darzac's eyes might be sufficiently injured that Larsan, when he took his place, might have in his trickery the important adjunct of dark spectacles, or, failing spectacles, which one cannot wear always, the right to sit in the shadow without arousing suspicion.

The departure of Darzac for the Midi must have strangely facilitated the plans of the two villains. It was not until the end of his sojourn at San Remo that Darzac had been, by the efforts of Larsan who had never ceased to spy upon him, actually dragged to the lunatic asylum.

He had been assisted materially in this affair by that "special police force" which has nothing to do with police officials and which puts itself at the disposal of families in certain disagreeable cases which demand as much discretion as rapidity in their execution.

One day M. Darzac was taking a walk in the mountains. The asylum was not far away—in fact, only a few steps from the Italian frontier—and every prep a ration for the reception of "the unfortunate man" had been made some time before hand. Brignolles, before leaving for Paris at all, had made arrangements with the proprietor and had presented to him his proofs of relationship, and his representative—Larsan himself. There are certain directors of such institutions who do not ask for explanations, provided that the provisions of the law are complied with—and that one pays well. And both these conditions were easily carried out. And such things are done everyday!

"But how did you find out all these things?" I demanded of Rouletabille.

"You remember, my friend," the reporter replied, "that little piece of paper which you brought back to the Château of Hercules on the day when, without giving me any warning, you took it upon yours. If to follow the trail of the excellent Brignolles, who had come to make a short stay in the Midi? That bit of paper, which bore the heading of the Sorbonne and the two syllables, *bonnet*, gave me the most important assistance. First of all, the circumstances under which you found it—you recollect that you picked it up after you had seen Larsan and Brignolle?—rendered it precious to me. And thin the place where it had been thrown was nearly a revelation for me when I began to take up the search for the real Darzac, after I had gained the conviction that his was 'the body too many' which had been tied up in the sack and carried out in it."

And Rouletabille went on in the simplest manner possible, taking me in his narrative over the different phases necessary for my comprehension of the mysteries which, up to that time, had remained so inexplicable to every one of us. The first step in his reasoning had come from the conclusions which he had drawn from the fact that the paint on the drawing would dry less than fifteen minutes after it had been laid on, and following that, the other formidable fact that a lie must have been told by one of the two manifestations of Darzac. Bernier, under the cross examination to which Rouletabille subjected him before the return of the man who had carried the sack, had reported the lying words of the man whom everyone had believed to be Darzac. That was what had astonished Bernier—that the man who had come in at six o'clock had not told him that the man who had entered at six o'clock *was not he*! He was trying to conceal the fact that there existed a second manifestation of Darzac and he would have had no interest in concealing it, if his own personality had been the true one. That was clear as the light of day! When the horror of the thing dawned upon Rouletabille, he nearly swooned. His limbs refused to support him: his teeth chattered; everything grew black in front of his eyes. But he was not entirely without hope, even yet. Bernier might have been mistaken. Perhaps he had not correctly understood the words which M. Darzac had spoken in his amazement and confusion' Rouletabille decided that he himself would question M. Darzac. Then he would soon see. How he longed for his return! It would be for M. Darzac himself to "close the circle." He waited impatiently—and when Darzac returned how the young reporter's feeble hopes were crushed! "Did you look at the man's face?" he had asked: and when the so-called Darzac replied, "No, I did not look at him!" Rouletabille could hardly hide his joy.

It would have been so easy for Larsan to have answered, "I saw him. The face was that of Larsan!" And the young man had not understood that this was the last piece of malice, the furthest limit of hatred in the mind of the villain, and too, one which fitted so well into his role. The real Darzac would not have acted otherwise. He would have gotten rid of his frightful booty as soon as possible without wishing to look at it. But what could all the articles of a Larsan accomplish against the reasonings of a Rouletabille? The false Darzac, under the questionings of Rouletabille had "closed the circle." He had lied. Now Rouletabille *knew*! And besides his eyes, which always looked *behind* the reason, could see now.

But what was to be done? Could he expose Larsan and in doing so, perhaps, give him a chance to escape? Could he reveal to his mother the fact that she was married to Larsan and had helped him to kill Darzac? He felt the need of reflection of combining circumstances and possibilities. He wish to strike a blow when he was ready to strike at all. He asked for twenty-four hours. He made sure of the safety of the Lady in Black by begging her to take the unoccupied room in Professor Stangerson's suite and he made her take a secret oath that she would not leave the chateu. He deceived Larsan by making him think that he was firmly convinced of the guilt of Old Bob. And when Walter rushed into the chateu with his empty sack the first gleam of hope that Darzac might still be alive dawned upon his mind. At last, he rushed off to find him, dead or living. He had in his possession the revolver belonging to the real Darzac which he had found in the Square Tower—a new revolver of which he had noticed the style in a shop at Mentone. He went to that shop; he showed the clerk the revolver; he learned that the weapon had been purchased a few days before by a man of whom he was given a description—a soft hat, a loose grey overcoat and a heavy beard. From there he lost all trace of the man, but he was not discouraged. He took up another trail, or, rather, he resumed that one which had led Walter to the gulfs of Castillon. When he arrived there, he did what Walter had not done. The latter, as soon as he had found the sack, looked for nothing more but hurried back to the Fort of Hercules. But Rouletabille, on the contrary, continued to follow the scent—and he perceived that this scent (which consisted of the exceptional clearness of the impressions left by the two wheels of the little English cart) instead of going back toward Mentone, after having stopped at the abyss of Castillon, went toward the other side, crossing by the mountain toward Sospel. Sospel! Had not Brignolles been reported as having gone to Sospel? Brignolles! Rouletabille remembered my sudden and interrupted journey. What could Brignolles be doing in these parts? His presence might be closely allied to the solution of the mystery. Certainly, the reappearance and disappearance of the true Darzac suggested the idea that he must have been kept some where in confinement. But where? Brignolles, who was undoubtedly in the confidence of Larsan, had not made the journey from Paris for nothing. Perhaps he had come at that critical moment to watch over this place of confinement.

Meditating thus and pursuing the logical tenor of his reasoning, Rouletabille had questioned the landlord of the inn near the Castillon tunnel, who had acknowledge to him that he had been very much puzzled the day before by the passage through the tunnel of a man who perfectly answered the description which had been given by the gunsmith. This man had entered the tavern to drink. His manner and appearance were so strange that the landlord had feared that he might have escaped from the sanatorium. Rouletabille felt that he was right on track and asked as indifferently as he could, "You have a sanatorium near here then?" "Oh, yes," replied the landlord; "the Mount Barbonnet sanatorium for mental diseases." It was at this point that the memory of the two syllables "bonnet" flashed in full significance upon the brain of Rouletabille. Henceforth, he had no longer any doubt that the real Darzac had been immolated by the false one as a madman in the sanatorium of Mount Barbonnet. He was resolved to know everything and to venture everything! He was certain that as a reporter of the Epoch he possessed the means of loosening the tongue of proprietors of sanatoriums of the kind which take college professors as patients and ask no questions. He hired a carriage and had himself driven to Sospel, which is at the foot of the mountains. He realised that he was running the change of encountering Brignolles. But, fortunately, nothing of the kind happened and the young man reached Mount Barbonnet and the sanatorium in safety. His mind was filled now with the thought that he was at least definitely to learn what had become of Robert Darzac! For at the moment that the sack had been found without the corpse— from the moment that the tracks of the little carriage descended toward Soepl or elsewhere and lost themselves; from the moment he had discovered that Larsan had not considered it prudent to relieve himself of Darzac by throwing him in the sack into one of the gulfs of Castillon, Rouletabille had believed that Larsan might have been found it to his interest to return the living Darzac to the madhouse at Sospel. And the reasoning powers of Rouletabille showed him that this might well be so. Darzac living might be more useful to Larsan than Darzac dead. What hostage would he have otherwise on the day when Mathilde should discover his imposture?

And Rouletabille had guessed right. At the very door of the asylum, he had encountered Brignolles. Immediately, without warning, he had seised him by the throat and threatened him with his revolver. Brignolles was a coward. He entreated Rouletabille to spare him, vowed that Darzac was living. A quarter of an hour later, Rouletabille knew the whole story. But the revolver had not sufficed, for Brignolles, who feared and hated the thought of death, loved life and everything which renders life desirable, particularly money. Rouletabille had not much trouble to convince him that he was lost if he did not betray Larsan and that he had much to gain if he helped the Darzac family to extricate itself from the present situation without scandal. At the close of the interview, both men entered the institution and were received by the director, who listened to what they had to say with an amazement which soon transformed into terror and later to the greatest affability which showed itself in immediate preparations for the release of Robert Darzac.

Darzac, by the miraculous chance which I have already explained, had sustained only a very slight injury from a wound which might easily have been mortal. Rouletabille, almost wild with joy, took him at once to Mentone. I will pass over the transports of both the rescuer and the rescued. They had disposed of Brignolles by agreeing to meet him in Paris for the settling of the accounts. On the journey, Rouletabille learned from the lips of Darzac that the Sorbonne Professor in his prison had a few days before happened to see the newspaper which spoke of the fact that M. and Mme. Darzac, whose wedding had just taken place in Paris, were guests at the Fort of Hercules. He had no further to look in order to comprehend why all his misfortunes had taken place and it was not difficult to guess who had had the fantastic audacity to take his place at the side of the unfortunate woman whose still wavering mind would have rendered so wild an enterprise not impossible. This discovery seemed to give him strength which he had not guessed that he possessed. After having stolen the overcoat of the director in order to conceal his asylum garb and having found a purse containing an hundred francs in the pocket, he had succeeded, at the risk of his life, in scaling a wall which under any other circumstances he would certainly have found insurmountable, and he had gone to Mentone. He had hastened to the Fort of Hercules. And he had seen Darzac with his own eyes! He had seen his very self. He spent a few hours in making himself so like his double in dress and appearance that the other Darzac himself might have been puzzled to find out which was which. His plan was simple. He would make his way into the Fort of Hercules in his own proper person—would enter the apartment of Mathilde and show himself to the other man in Mathilde's presence, confounding him with the truth. He had questioned the people of the coast and had learned that the Darzacs' suite was located at the back part of the Square Tower. "The Darzacs' suite"! All that he had suffered up to that time seemed like nothing in comparison with what he felt at those words. And this suffering had been without surcease until he had seen with his own eyes, at the time of the corporeal demonstration of the possibility of the "body too many," the Lady in Black. Then he had understood all. Never would she have dared to look at him like that, never would have so joyously flown to the refuge of his arms, if for a single instant, in body or in spirit, she had been the victim of the machinations of that other man and had belonged to him as his wife. Robert Darzac and Mathilde had been separated—but they had never lost each other!

Before putting his project into execution, Darzac had purchased a revolver at Mentone, had disembarrassed himself of his overcoat which he had managed to lose, believing that it would be a means of identification, had procured a suit of clothes which in colour and in cut was the counterpart of that worn by the other Darzac and had waited until five o'clock—the hour at which he had resolved to act. He had hidden himself behind the Villa Lucie, high up on the boulevard at Garavan, at the top of a little hillock from which he could see plainly all that was passing in the château. When he had passed by us and we had both seen him he had had a fierce desire to cry out and tell us who he was, but he had strength of mind enough to contain himself, desiring to be recognised first of all by the Lady in Black. This hope alone sustained his steps. This only was worth the trouble of living and an hour afterward, when he had had the life of Larsan at his disposal while the latter sat in the same room with his back turned to him, writing letters, he had not even been tempted by the idea of vengeance. After so many sorrows, there was no room in Robert Darzac's heart for hatred of Larsan; it was too full of love for the Lady in Black. Poor dear pitiful M. Darzac!

We know the rest of the adventure. That which I did not know was the way in which the true M. Darzac had penetrated a second time into the Fort of Hercules and had obtained entrance a second time into the recess hidden by the panel. And Rouletabille told me how on the same night that he had taken M. Darzac to Mentone, he had learned through the flight of Old Bob that there existed an entrance to the castle through the oubliette and so he had, by the help of a little boat, smuggled M. Darzac into the château by the way which Old Bob had taken in going out. Rouletabille wish d to be master of the hour when he came to confound Larsan and strike him down. On that night it was too late to act, but he felt that he could count upon finishing up the affair on the night following. The only thing was how to hide M. Darzac on the peninsula. And with the aid of Bernier, he had found him a quiet, deserted little corner in the New Château.

At this point of the narrative, I could not hinder myself from interrupting Roultabille with a cry which had the effect of sending him into a burst of laughter.

"It was really he then!" I exclaimed.

"It really was!" answered my friend. "That was how I was able to find the 'map of Australia'! It was the true Darzac with whom I stood face to face that night! And I who understood nothing that was going on! For it was not only the 'Australia'—it was the beard as well. And it did not come off—it was natural!" "Oh, now, I understand everything!"

"You've taken time enough about it!" replied Rouletabille, tranquilly. "That night, old fellow, you caused us a lot of trouble. When you made your appearance in the Court of the Bold, M. Darzac had come to take me back to my underground passage. I had only time enough to close the wooden lid above my head, while M. Darzac rushed back to the New Castle. But when you had retired, after your experience with the beard, he came back to me and we were bothered enough, I assure you. If, by chance, you should speak of this adventure upon the morrow to the other M. Darzac, believing that he was the same man you had seen in the New Château, there would be a catastrophe. But I dared not yield to the pleadings of M. Darzac, who begged me to go to you and tell you the whole truth. I was afraid that, knowing how matters stood, you would be unable to hide your feelings during the following day. You have a rather impulsive nature, Sainclair, and the sight of a bad man usually arouses in you a praiseworthy irritation which at such a moment might have ruined us. And then, the other Darzac was so cunning and so clever! I resolved to bring about the climax without saying anything to you! I would return to the château the next morning. And from that time on it was necessary to manage things so that you should not speak to Darzac. That was why, as soon as it was daylight, I sent you word to go fishing for brook—"

"Oh, I understand!"

"You always finish by understanding, Sainclair! I hope that you have forgiven me for that fault which gave you such a charming hour with Mme. Edith!"

"Apropos of Mme. Edith, why did you take such a mischievous pleasure in putting me into such a fit of anger?" I demanded.

"In order to have the right to abuse you and to forbid you to speak henceforward, one word to me *or to M. Darzac*! I repeat to you that, after your adventure of the night before, it would not have done to let you talk to M. Darzac. Try to understand the position, Sainclair!"

"I'll try, my friend!"

"Much obliged!"

"And still there is one thing that I don't understand!" I exclaimed. "The death of Pere Bernier. Who killed Bernier?"

"It was the cane!" said Rouletabille, gloomily. "It was that damned cane!"

"I thought that it was 'the oldest dagger known to humanity.'"

"It was both of them; the cane and the flint. But it was the cane which decided his death; the stone was only his executioner." I stared at Rouletabille, asking myself whether, this time, I had not come to the end of his intelligence.

"You never understood, Sainclair—among other things—why upon the morrow of the day on which I had come to comprehend everything, I had let fall Arthur Rance's ivory-headed cane in front of M. and Mme. Darzac. It was because I hoped that M. Darzac would pick it up. You remember, Sainclair, the ivory headed cane which Larsan used to carry and the gestures he was in the habit of making with it while we were at the Glandier? He had a fashion of holding his cane which was all his own. I wanted to see whether Darzac would hold an ivory-headed cane as Larsan had used to do. And this fixed idea pursued me until the morrow, even after my visit to the insane asylum. Even after I had seen and felt the true Darzac, I longed to see the imposter make the gestures of Larsan. Ah, to see him suddenly brandish his cane like a bandit—forget the disguise of his figure for one single moment! throw back his falsely stooped shoulders. 'Knock it, please! Knock at the shield of the Mortolas with heavy blows of the cane, dear, dear M. Darzac!' And he knocked it—and I saw his form—erect—undisguised and another man saw it and he is dead! It was poor Bernier, who was so horrified at the sight that he stumbled and fell so unfortunately on the 'oldest dagger' that the wound killed him. He is dead because he picked up the flint which, doubtless, had fallen out of Old Bob's overcoat and which Bernier had intended to take to the workshop of the Professor in the Round Tower! He is dead, because at the same moment that he picked up the flint he saw Larsan brandishing his cane—saw the scoundrel's figure and his gestures'. All battles, Sainclair, have their innocent victims!"

We were both silent for a moment. And I could not keep myself from mentioning the bitterness which I felt at the knowledge that he had had so little confidence in me. I could not pardon him for having deceived me as he had done everyone else in regard to Old Bob.

He smiled.

"That was something that didn't bother me at all. I was certain enough that he was not in the sack! However on the night before he was fished out of the grotto after I had hidden the true Darzac, under the guidance of Bernier, in the New Château, and had left the gallery of the underground passage after having left there my boat in readiness for my projects of the morrow—my boat which had belonged to Paolo, a fisherman, and a friend of 'the Hangman of the Sea,' I regained the bank by my oars. I was undressed and carried my clothing in a package on my head. As I went on, I met Paolo who was amased to see me taking a bath at such an hour and invited me to go fishing with him. I accepted. And then I learned that the bark which I had used belonged to Tullio. The 'Hangman of the Sea' had suddenly become rich and had announced to everyone that he was about to return to his native country. He said that he had sold some precious shells to the old professor for a very great deal of money and, in fact, for many days past, he had been seen a great deal in the old professor's company. Paolo knew that before going to Venice, Tullio intended to stop at San Remo. When I heard all this, I had a clear insight into Old Bob's behaviour and disappearance. He had needed a boat in quitting the château and this boat was that of the 'Hangman of the Sea.' I asked him for the address of Tullio in San Remo and sent it to Arthur Rance in an anonymous letter. Rance started for San Remo, believing that Tullio could inform him as to the fate of Old Bob. And, in fact, Old Bob had paid Tullio to take him to the grotto and then to disappear. It was out of pity for the old savant that I had decided to warn Arthur Rance; for I feared that some accident might have befallen his relative. As for myself, all that I could ask was that the old dandy would not put in an appearance before I had finished with Larsan, for I wanted the false Darzac to believe that Old Bob was occupying my mind to the exclusion of everything else. And when I learned that he really had returned, I was, at first, only half pleased, but I confess that the news of the wound in his breast (because of the wound in the breast of the man in the sack) did not cause me any pain at all. Thanks to that injury, I might hope to continue my game a few hours longer."

"And why should you not have abandoned it immediately."

"Don't you understand that it would have been impossible for me to have gotten rid of the body of Larsan in the daylight? A whole day was necessary to prepare for the disappearance by night. But what a day we had with the death of Bernier! The arrival of the gendarmes only served to simplify the affair. I waited until I knew that they were gone. The first rifle shot that you heard when we were in the Square Tower was to inform me that the last gendarme had quitted the tavern at Albo, at the Point of Garibaldi: the second told me that the customs officers had gone into their cabins and were at supper and that the *sea was free!*"

"Tell me, Rouletabille," I said, looking into his clear eyes. "When you left Tullio's boat at the end of the gallery of the passageway, for the carrying out of your plans, did you know already *what that boat would carry away on the morrow?*"

Rouletabille bowed his head.

"No," he answered, sadly and slowly. "No—do not think that, Sainclair! I did not expect that it would carry away a corpse. After all—he was my father! *I believed that the boat would carry the 'body too many' to the madhouse!* You understand, Sainclair? I would only have condemned him to prison—forever. But he killed himself. It is God who did it. May God forgive him!"

We never spoke again of that night.

At Laroche I was anxious for a hot supper, but Rouletabille refused to join me. He bought all the Paris papers and buried himself in the events of the day. The journals were filled with news from Russia. A great conspiracy against the Czar had been discovered at St. Petersburg. The facts related were so wonderful that they were almost incredible.

I unfolded the Epoch and I read in great black letters on the first column of the first page:

"Departure of Joseph Rouletabille for Russia."

And underneath:

"The Czar Implores His Aid."

I passed the paper to Rouletabille, who shrugged his shoulders and said: "That's a nice thing! Without even asking my opinion! What does that fool of an editor think that I am going to do out there? I'm not interested in the Czar. Let him and his Nihilists settle their squabbles for themselves! It is their affair, not mine! To Russia? I shall apply for a vacation—that's what I'll do! I need rest. I'll tell you,

Sainclair, you and I will go somewhere together. We'll take a nice, quiet rest—"

"Not if I know it!" I cried hastily. "Thanks very much but I have had enough of your kind of 'nice, quiet rest!' I have a wild desire to work!"

"Just as you like. I won't insist."

As we drew nearer Paris, he bathed his hands and face, combed his hair and turned out his pockets. And in one of them he was surprised to find a red envelope which had come there without anyone knowing how.

"What nonsense is this?" he remarked carelessly, tearing it open.

Then he burst into a peal of laughter. I had found my gay Rouletabille again and I was anxious to know the reason for this hilarity.

"Why, I'm going, old man!" he exclaimed. "I'm going to start immediately! When things begin to come like this, it's a little different. I shall take the train tonight."

"Where to?"

"To St. Petersburg."

He handed me the letter and I read:

> "We know, monsieur, that your paper has decided to send you to Russia, on account of the incidents which are at this time disturbing the court of Turkoie-Selo. *We are obliged to warn you that you will not reach St. Petersburg alive.*"
>
> (Signed)
> THE CENTRAL REVOLUTIONARY COMMITTEE

I looked at Rouletabille, whose eyes were shining with delight. "Prince Galitch was at the station," I remarked. He understood me and shrugging his shoulders indifferently, he repeated:

"Ah, now, old fellow, this begins to be amusing!"

And this was all that I could get out of him, in spite of my protestations. And that night when, at the Northern station, I put my arms around him and begged him not to go, the tears in my eyes as I spoke—he laughed again and repeated:

"This is just beginning to be amusing!"

And that was his farewell.

The following day I took up the work which was waiting for me at the Palace. The first of my colleagues whom I saw were M.M. Henri Robert and Andre Hesse.

"Did you have a pleasant holiday?" they asked me.

"Delightful!" I responded.

But I made such a grimace as I spoke that they both dragged me off to take a drink with them.

THE END

THE SECRET OF THE NIGHT

I

Gayety and Dynamite

"B arinia, the young stranger has arrived."

"Where is he?"

"Oh, he is waiting at the lodge."

"I told you to show him to Natacha's sitting-room. Didn't you understand me, Ermolai?"

"Pardon, Barinia, but the young stranger, when I asked to search him, as you directed, flatly refused to let me."

"Did you explain to him that everybody is searched before being allowed to enter, that it is the order, and that even my mother herself has submitted to it?"

"I told him all that, Barinia; and I told him about madame your mother."

"What did he say to that?"

"That he was not madame your mother. He acted angry."

"Well, let him come in without being searched."

"The Chief of Police won't like it."

"Do as I say."

Ermolai bowed and returned to the garden. The "barinia" left the veranda, where she had come for this conversation with the old servant of General Trebassof, her husband, and returned to the dining-room in the datcha des Iles, where the gay Councilor Ivan Petrovitch was regaling his amused associates with his latest exploit at Cubat's resort. They were a noisy company, and certainly the quietest among them was not the general, who nursed on a sofa the leg which still held him captive after the recent attack, that to his old coachman and his two piebald horses had proved fatal. The story of the always-amiable Ivan Petrovitch (a lively, little, elderly man with his head bald as an egg) was about the evening before. After having, as he said, "recure la bouche" for these gentlemen spoke French like their own language and used it among themselves to keep their servants from understanding—after having wet his whistle with a large glass of sparkling rosy French wine, he cried:

"You would have laughed, Feodor Feodorovitch. We had sung songs on the Barque[1] and then the Bohemians left with their music and we went out onto the river-bank to stretch our legs and cool our faces in the freshness of the dawn, when a company of Cossacks of the Guard came along. I knew the officer in command and invited him to come along with us and drink the Emperor's health at Cubat's place. That officer, Feodor Feodorovitch, is a man who knows vintages and boasts that he has never swallowed a glass of anything so common as Crimean wine. When I named champagne he cried, 'Vive l'Empereur!' A true patriot. So we started, merry as school-children. The entire company followed, then all the diners playing little whistles, and all the servants besides, single file. At Cubat's I hated to leave the companion-officers of my friend at the door, so I invited them in, too. They accepted, naturally. But the subalterns were thirsty as well. I understand discipline. You know, Feodor Feodorovitch, that I am a stickler for discipline. Just because one is gay of a spring morning, discipline should not be forgotten. I invited the officers to drink in a private room, and sent the subalterns into the main hall of the restaurant. Then the soldiers were thirsty, too, and I had drinks served to them out in the courtyard. Then, my word, there was a perplexing business, for now the horses whinnied. The brave horses, Feodor Feodorovitch, who also wished to drink the health of the Emperor. I was bothered about the discipline. Hall, court, all were full. And I could not put the horses in private rooms. Well, I made them carry out champagne in pails and then came the perplexing business I had tried so hard to avoid, a grand mixture of boots and horse-shoes that was certainly the liveliest thing I have ever seen in my life. But the horses were the most joyous, and danced as if a torch was held under their nostrils, and all of them, my word! were ready to throw their riders because the men were not of the same mind with them as to the route to follow! From our window we laughed fit to kill at such a mixture of sprawling boots and dancing hoofs. But the troopers finally got all their horses to barracks, with patience, for the Emperor's cavalry are the best riders in the world, Feodor Feodorovitch. And we certainly had a great laugh!—Your health, Matrena Petrovna."

---

1. The "Barque" is a restaurant on a boat, among the isles, near the Gulf of Finland, on a bank of the Neva.

These last graceful words were addressed to Madame Trebassof, who shrugged her shoulders at the undesired gallantry of the gay Councilor. She did not join in the conversation, excepting to calm the general, who wished to send the whole regiment to the guard-house, men and horses. And while the roisterers laughed over the adventure she said to her husband in the advisory voice of the helpful wife:

"Feodor, you must not attach importance to what that old fool Ivan tells you. He is the most imaginative man in the capital when he has had champagne."

"Ivan, you certainly have not had horses served with champagne in pails," the old boaster, Athanase Georgevitch, protested jealously. He was an advocate, well-known for his table-feats, who claimed the hardest drinking reputation of any man in the capital, and he regretted not to have invented that tale.

"On my word! And the best brands! I had won four thousand roubles. I left the little fete with fifteen kopecks."

Matrena Petrovna was listening to Ermolai, the faithful country servant who wore always, even here in the city, his habit of fresh nankeen, his black leather belt, his large blue pantaloons and his boots glistening like ice, his country costume in his master's city home. Madame Matrena rose, after lightly stroking the hair of her step-daughter Natacha, whose eyes followed her to the door, indifferent apparently to the tender manifestations of her father's orderly, the soldier-poet, Boris Mourazoff, who had written beautiful verses on the death of the Moscow students, after having shot them, in the way of duty, on their barricades.

Ermolai conducted his mistress to the drawing-room and pointed across to a door that he had left open, which led to the sitting-room before Natacha's chamber.

"He is there," said Ermolai in a low voice.

Ermolai need have said nothing, for that matter, since Madame Matrena was aware of a stranger's presence in the sitting-room by the extraordinary attitude of an individual in a maroon frock-coat bordered with false astrakhan, such as is on the coats of all the Russian police agents and makes the secret agents recognizable at first glance. This policeman was on his knees in the drawing-room watching what passed in the next room through the narrow space of light in the hinge-way of the door. In this manner, or some other, all persons who wished to approach General Trebassof were kept under observation without their knowing it, after having been first searched at the lodge, a measure adopted since the latest attack.

Madame Matrena touched the policeman's shoulder with that heroic hand which had saved her husband's life and which still bore traces of the terrible explosion in the last attack, when she had seized the infernal machine intended for the general with her bare hand. The policeman rose and silently left the room, reached the veranda and lounged there on a sofa, pretending to be asleep, but in reality watching the garden paths.

Matrena Petrovna took his place at the hinge-vent. This was her rule; she always took the final glance at everything and everybody. She roved at all hours of the day and night round about the general, like a watch-dog, ready to bite, to throw itself before the danger, to receive the blows, to perish for its master. This had commenced at Moscow after the terrible repression, the massacre of revolutionaries under the walls of Presnia, when the surviving Nihilists left behind them a placard condemning the victorious General Trebassof to death. Matrena Petrovna lived only for the general. She had vowed that she would not survive him. So she had double reason to guard him.

But she had lost all confidence even within the walls of her own home.

Things had happened even there that defied her caution, her instinct, her love. She had not spoken of these things save to the Chief of Police, Koupriane, who had reported them to the Emperor. And here now was the man whom the Emperor had sent, as the supreme resource, this young stranger—Joseph Rouletabille, reporter.

"But he is a mere boy!" she exclaimed, without at all understanding the matter, this youthful figure, with soft, rounded cheeks, eyes clear and, at first view, extraordinarily naive, the eyes of an infant. True, at the moment Rouletabille's expression hardly suggested any superhuman profundity of thought, for, left in view of a table, spread with hors-d'oeuvres, the young man appeared solely occupied in digging out with a spoon all the caviare that remained in the jars. Matrena noted the rosy freshness of his cheeks, the absence of down on his lip and not a hint of beard, the thick hair, with the curl over the forehead. Ah, that forehead—the forehead was curious, with great over-hanging cranial lumps which moved above the deep arcade of the eye-sockets while the mouth was busy—well, one would have said that Rouletabille had not eaten for a week. He was demolishing a great slice of Volgan sturgeon, contemplating at the same time with immense interest a salad of creamed cucumbers, when Matrena Petrovna appeared.

He wished to excuse himself at once and spoke with his mouth full.

"I beg your pardon, madame, but the Czar forgot to invite me to breakfast."

Madame Matrena smiled and gave him a hearty handshake as she urged him to be seated.

"You have seen His Majesty?"

"I come from him, madame. It is to Madame Trebassof that I have the honor of speaking?"

"Yes. And you are Monsieur—?"

"Joseph Rouletabille, madame. I do not add, 'At your service—because I do not know about that yet. That is what I said just now to His Majesty."

"Then?" asked Madame Matrena, rather amused by the tone the conversation had taken and the slightly flurried air of Rouletabille.

"Why, then, I am a reporter, you see. That is what I said at once to my editor in Paris, 'I am not going to take part in revolutionary affairs that do not concern my country,' to which my editor replied, 'You do not have to take part. You must go to Russia to make an inquiry into the present status of the different parties. You will commence by interviewing the Emperor.' I said, 'Well, then, here goes,' and took the train."

"And you have interviewed the Emperor?"

"Oh, yes, that has not been difficult. I expected to arrive direct at St. Petersburg, but at Krasnoie-Coelo the train stopped and the grand-marshal of the court came to me and asked me to follow him. It was very flattering. Twenty minutes later I was before His Majesty. He awaited me! I understood at once that this was obviously for something out of the ordinary."

"And what did he say to you?"

"He is a man of genuine majesty. He reassured me at once when I explained my scruples to him. He said there was no occasion for me to take part in the politics of the matter, but to save his most faithful servant, who was on the point of becoming the victim of the strangest family drama ever conceived."

Madame Matrena, white as a sheet, rose to her feet.

"Ah," she said simply.

But Rouletabille, whom nothing escaped, saw her hand tremble on the back of the chair.

He went on, not appearing to have noticed her emotion:

"His Majesty added these exact words: 'It is I who ask it of you; I and Madame Trebassof. Go, monsieur, she awaits you.'"

He ceased and waited for Madame Trebassof to speak.

She made up her mind after brief reflection.

"Have you seen Koupriane?"

"The Chief of Police? Yes. The grand-marshal accompanied me back to the station at Krasnoie-Coelo, and the Chief of Police accompanied me to St. Petersburg station. One could not have been better received."

"Monsieur Rouletabille," said Matrena, who visibly strove to regain her self-control, "I am not of Koupriane's opinion and I am not"—here she lowered her trembling voice—"of the opinion His Majesty holds. It is better for me to tell you at once, so that you may not regret intervening in an affair where there are—where there are—risks—terrible risks to run. No, this is not a family drama. The family is small, very small: the general, his daughter Natacha (by his former marriage), and myself. There could not be a family drama among us three. It is simply about my husband, monsieur, who did his duty as a soldier in defending the throne of his sovereign, my husband whom they mean to assassinate! There is nothing else, no other situation, my dear little guest."

To hide her distress she started to carve a slice of jellied veal and carrot.

"You have not eaten, you are hungry. It is dreadful, my dear young man. See, you must dine with us, and then—you will say adieu. Yes, you will leave me all alone. I will undertake to save him all alone. Certainly, I will undertake it."

A tear fell on the slice she was cutting. Rouletabille, who felt the brave woman's emotion affecting him also, braced himself to keep from showing it.

"I am able to help you a little all the same," he said. "Monsieur Koupriane has told me that there is a deep mystery. It is my vocation to get to the bottom of mysteries."

"I know what Koupriane thinks," she said, shaking her head. "But if I could bring myself to think that for a single day I would rather be dead."

The good Matrena Petrovna lifted her beautiful eyes to Rouletabille, brimming with the tears she held back.

She added quickly:

"But eat now, my dear guest; eat. My dear child, you must forget what Koupriane has said to you, when you are back in France."

"I promise you that, madame."

"It is the Emperor who has caused you this long journey. For me, I did not wish it. Has he, indeed, so much confidence in you?" she asked naively, gazing at him fixedly through her tears.

"Madame, I was just about to tell you. I have been active in some important matters that have been reported to him, and then sometimes your Emperor is allowed to see the papers. He has heard talk, too (for everybody talked of them, madame), about the Mystery of the Yellow Room and the Perfume of the Lady in Black."

Here Rouletabille watched Madame Trebassof and was much mortified at the undoubted ignorance that showed in her frank face of either the yellow room or the black perfume.

"My young friend," said she, in a voice more and more hesitant, "you must excuse me, but it is a long time since I have had good eyes for reading."

Tears, at last, ran down her cheeks.

Rouletabille could not restrain himself any further. He saw in one flash all this heroic woman had suffered in her combat day by day with the death which hovered. He took her little fat hands, whose fingers were overloaded with rings, tremulously into his own:

"Madame, do not weep. They wish to kill your husband. Well then, we will be two at least to defend him, I swear to you."

"Even against the Nihilists!"

"Aye, madame, against all the world. I have eaten all your caviare. I am your guest. I am your friend."

As he said this he was so excited, so sincere and so droll that Madame Trebassof could not help smiling through her tears. She made him sit down beside her.

"The Chief of Police has talked of you a great deal. He came here abruptly after the last attack and a mysterious happening that I will tell you about. He cried, 'Ah, we need Rouletabille to unravel this!' The next day he came here again. He had gone to the Court. There, everybody, it appears, was talking of you. The Emperor wished to know you. That is why steps were taken through the ambassador at Paris."

"Yes, yes. And naturally all the world has learned of it. That makes it so lively. The Nihilists warned me immediately that I would not reach Russia alive. That, finally, was what decided me on coming. I am naturally very contrary."

"And how did you get through the journey?"

"Not badly. I discovered at once in the train a young Slav assigned to kill me, and I reached an understanding with him. He was a charming youth, so it was easily arranged."

Rouletabille was eating away now at strange viands that it would have been difficult for him to name. Matrena Petrovna laid her fat little hand on his arm:

"You speak seriously?"

"Very seriously."

"A small glass of vodka?"

"No alcohol."

Madame Matrena emptied her little glass at a draught.

"And how did you discover him? How did you know him?"

"First, he wore glasses. All Nihilists wear glasses when traveling. And then I had a good clew. A minute before the departure from Paris I had a friend go into the corridor of the sleeping-car, a reporter who would do anything I said without even wanting to know why. I said, 'You call out suddenly and very loud, "Hello, here is Rouletabille."' So he called, 'Hello, here is Rouletabille,' and all those who were in the corridor turned and all those who were already in the compartments came out, excepting the man with the glasses. Then I was sure about him."

Madame Trebassof looked at Rouletabille, who turned as red as the comb of a rooster and was rather embarrassed at his fatuity.

"That deserves a rebuff, I know, madame, but from the moment the Emperor of all the Russias had desired to see me I could not admit that any mere man with glasses had not the curiosity to see what I looked like. It was not natural. As soon as the train was off I sat down by this man and told him who I thought he was. I was right. He removed his glasses and, looking me straight in the eyes, said he was glad to have a little talk with me before anything unfortunate happened. A half-hour later the entente-cordiale was signed. I gave him to understand that I was coming here simply on business as a reporter and that there was always time to check me if I should be indiscreet. At the German frontier he left me to go on, and returned tranquilly to his nitro-glycerine."

"You are a marked man also, my poor boy."

"Oh, they have not got us yet."

Matrena Petrovna coughed. That *us* overwhelmed her. With what calmness this boy that she had not known an hour proposed to share the dangers of a situation that excited general pity but from which the bravest kept aloof either from prudence or dismay.

"Ah, my friend, a little of this fine smoked Hamburg beef?"

But the young man was already pouring out fresh yellow beer.

"There," said he. "Now, madame, I am listening. Tell me first about the earliest attack."

"Now," said Matrena, "we must go to dinner."

Rouletabille looked at her wide-eyed.

"But, madame, what have I just been doing?"

Madame Matrena smiled. All these strangers were alike. Because they had eaten some hors-d'oeuvres, some zakouskis, they imagined their host would be satisfied. They did not know how to eat.

"We will go to the dining-room. The general is expecting you. They are at table."

"I understand I am supposed to know him."

"Yes, you have met in Paris. It is entirely natural that in passing through St. Petersburg you should make him a visit. You know him very well indeed, so well that he opens his home to you. Ah, yes, my step-daughter also"—she flushed a little—"Natacha believes that her father knows you."

She opened the door of the drawing-room, which they had to cross in order to reach the dining-room.

From his present position Rouletabille could see all the corners of the drawing-room, the veranda, the garden and the entrance lodge at the gate. In the veranda the man in the maroon frock-coat trimmed with false astrakhan seemed still to be asleep on the sofa; in one of the corners of the drawing-room another individual, silent and motionless as a statue, dressed exactly the same, in a maroon frock-coat with false astrakhan, stood with his hands behind his back seemingly struck with general paralysis at the sight of a flaring sunset which illumined as with a torch the golden spires of Saints Peter and Paul. And in the garden and before the lodge three others dressed in maroon roved like souls in pain over the lawn or back and forth at the entrance. Rouletabille motioned to Madame Matrena, stepped back into the sitting-room and closed the door.

"Police?" he asked.

Matrena Petrovna nodded her head and put her finger to her mouth in a naive way, as one would caution a child to silence. Rouletabille smiled.

"How many are there?"

"Ten, relieved every six hours."

"That makes forty unknown men around your house each day."

"Not unknown," she replied. "Police."

"Yet, in spite of them, you have had the affair of the bouquet in the general's chamber."

"No, there were only three then. It is since the affair of the bouquet that there have been ten."

"It hardly matters. It is since these ten that you have had. . ."

"What?" she demanded anxiously.

"You know well—the flooring."

"Sh-h-h."

She glanced at the door, watching the policeman statuesque before the setting sun.

"No one knows that—not even my husband."

"So M. Koupriane told me. Then it is you who have arranged for these ten police-agents?"

"Certainly."

"Well, we will commence now by sending all these police away."

Matrena Petrovna grasped his hand, astounded.

"Surely you don't think of doing such a thing as that!"

"Yes. We must know where the blow is coming from. You have four different groups of people around here—the police, the domestics, your friends, your family. Get rid of the police first. They must not be permitted to cross your threshold. They have not been able to protect you. You have nothing to regret. And if, after they are gone, something new turns up, we can leave M. Koupriane to conduct the inquiries without his being preoccupied here at the house."

"But you do not know the admirable police of Koupriane. These brave men have given proof of their devotion."

"Madame, if I were face to face with a Nihilist the first thing I would ask myself about him would be, 'Is he one of the police?' The first thing I ask in the presence of an agent of your police is, 'Is he not a Nihilist?'"

"But they will not wish to go."

"Do any of them speak French?"

"Yes, their sergeant, who is out there in the salon."

"Pray call him."

Madame Trebassof walked into the salon and signaled. The man appeared. Rouletabille handed him a paper, which the other read.

"You will gather your men together and quit the villa," ordered Rouletabille. "You will return to the police Headguarters. Say to M. Koupriane that I have commanded this and that I require all police service around the villa to be suspended until further orders."

The man bowed, appeared not to understand, looked at Madame Trebassof and said to the young man:

"At your service."

He went out.

"Wait here a moment," urged Madame Trebassof, who did not know how to take this abrupt action and whose anxiety was really painful to see.

She disappeared after the man of the false astrakhan. A few moments afterwards she returned. She appeared even more agitated.

"I beg your pardon," she murmured, "but I cannot let them go like this. They are much chagrined. They have insisted on knowing where they have failed in their service. I have appeased them with money."

"Yes, and tell me the whole truth, madame. You have directed them not to go far away, but to remain near the villa so as to watch it as closely as possible."

She reddened.

"It is true. But they have gone, nevertheless. They had to obey you. What can that paper be you have shown them?"

Rouletabille drew out again the billet covered with seals and signs and cabalistics that he did not understand. Madame Trebassof translated it aloud: "Order to all officials in surveillance of the Villa Trebassof to obey the bearer absolutely. Signed: Koupriane."

"Is it possible!" murmured Matrena Petrovna. "But Koupriane would never have given you this paper if he had imagined that you would use it to dismiss his agents."

"Evidently. I have not asked him his advice, madame, you may be sure. But I will see him tomorrow and he will understand."

"Meanwhile, who is going to watch over him?" cried she.

Rouletabille took her hands again. He saw her suffering, a prey to anguish almost prostrating. He pitied her. He wished to give her immediate confidence.

"We will," he said.

She saw his young, clear eyes, so deep, so intelligent, the well-formed young head, the willing face, all his young ardency for her, and it reassured her. Rouletabille waited for what she might say. She said nothing. She took him in her arms and embraced him.

II

NATACHA

I n the dining-room it was Thaddeus Tchnichnikoff's turn to tell
hunting stories. He was the greatest timber-merchant in Lithuania.
He owned immense forests and he loved Feodor Feodorovitch[1] as a
brother, for they had played together all through their childhood, and
once he had saved him from a bear that was just about to crush his skull
as one might knock off a hat. General Trebassof's father was governor
of Courlande at that time, by the grace of God and the Little Father.
Thaddeus, who was just thirteen years old, killed the bear with a single
stroke of his boar-spear, and just in time. Close ties were knit between
the two families by this occurrence, and though Thaddeus was neither
noble-born nor a soldier, Feodor considered him his brother and felt
toward him as such. Now Thaddeus had become the greatest timber-
merchant of the western provinces, with his own forests and also with
his massive body, his fat, oily face, his bull-neck and his ample paunch.
He quitted everything at once—all his affairs, his family—as soon as
he learned of the first attack, to come and remain by the side of his dear
comrade Feodor. He had done this after each attack, without forgetting
one. He was a faithful friend. But he fretted because they might not
go bear-hunting as in their youth. 'Where, he would ask, are there any
bears remaining in Courlande, or trees for that matter, what you could
call trees, growing since the days of the grand-dukes of Lithuania, giant
trees that threw their shade right up to the very edge of the towns?
Where were such things nowadays? Thaddeus was very amusing, for it
was he, certainly, who had cut them away tranquilly enough and watched
them vanish in locomotive smoke. It was what was called Progress. Ah,
hunting lost its national character assuredly with tiny new-growth trees
which had not had time to grow. And, besides, one nowadays had not
time for hunting. All the big game was so far away. Lucky enough if
one seized the time to bring down a brace of woodcock early in the

---

1. In this story according to Russian habit General Trebassof is called alternately by that
name or the family name Feodor Feodorovitch, and Madame Trebassof by that name or
her family name, Matrena Petrovna.—Translator's Note.

morning. At this point in Thaddeus's conversation there was a babble of talk among the convivial gentlemen, for they had all the time in the world at their disposal and could not see why he should be so concerned about snatching a little while at morning or evening, or at midday for that matter. Champagne was flowing like a river when Rouletabille was brought in by Matrena Petrovna. The general, whose eyes had been on the door for some time, cried at once, as though responding to a cue:

"Ah, my dear Rouletabille! I have been looking for you. Our friends wrote me you were coming to St. Petersburg."

Rouletabille hurried over to him and they shook hands like friends who meet after a long separation. The reporter was presented to the company as a close young friend from Paris whom they had enjoyed so much during their latest visit to the City of Light. Everybody inquired for the latest word of Paris as of a dear acquaintance.

"How is everybody at Maxim's?" urged the excellent Athanase Georgevitch.

Thaddeus, too, had been once in Paris and he returned with an enthusiastic liking for the French demoiselles.

"Vos gogottes, monsieur," he said, appearing very amiable and leaning on each word, with a guttural emphasis such as is common in the western provinces, "ah, vos gogottes!"

Matrena Perovna tried to silence him, but Thaddeus insisted on his right to appreciate the fair sex away from home. He had a turgid, sentimental wife, always weeping and cramming her religious notions down his throat.

Of course someone asked Rouletabille what he thought of Russia, but he had no more than opened his mouth to reply than Athanase Georgevitch closed it by interrupting:

"Permettez! Permettez! You others, of the young generation, what do you know of it? You need to have lived a long time and in all its districts to appreciate Russia at its true value. Russia, my young sir, is as yet a closed book to you."

"Naturally," Rouletabille answered, smiling.

"Well, well, here's your health! What I would point out to you first of all is that it is a good buyer of champagne, eh?"—and he gave a huge grin. "But the hardest drinker I ever knew was born on the banks of the Seine. Did you know him, Feodor Feodorovitch? Poor Charles Dufour, who died two years ago at fete of the officers of the Guard. He wagered at the end of the banquet that he could drink a glassful of champagne to the health of each man there. There were sixty when you came to count them. He commenced the round of the table and the affair went splendidly up to the fifty-eighth man. But at the fifty-ninth—think of the misfortune!—the champagne ran out! That poor, that charming, that excellent Charles took up a glass of vin dore which was in the glass of this fifty-ninth, wished him long life, drained the glass at one draught, had just time to murmur, 'Tokay, 1807,' and fell back dead! Ah, he knew the brands, my word! and he proved it to his last breath! Peace to his ashes! They asked what he died of. I knew he died because of the inappropriate blend of flavors. There should be discipline in all things and not promiscuous mixing. One more glass of champagne and he would have been drinking with us this evening. Your health, Matrena Petrovna. Champagne, Feodor Feodorovitch! Vive la France, monsieur! Natacha, my child, you must sing something. Boris will accompany you on the guzla. Your father will enjoy it."

All eyes turned toward Natacha as she rose.

Rouletabille was struck by her serene beauty. That was the first enthralling impression, an impression so strong it astonished him, the perfect serenity, the supreme calm, the tranquil harmony of her noble features. Natacha was twenty. Heavy brown hair circled about er forehead and was looped about her ears, which were half-concealed. Her profile was clear-cut; her mouth was strong and revealed between red, firm lips the even pearliness of her teeth. She was of medium height. In walking she had the free, light step of the highborn maidens who, in primal times, pressed the flowers as they passed without crushing them. But all her true grace seemed to be concentrated in her eyes, which were deep and of a dark blue. The impression she made upon a beholder was very complex. And it would have been difficult to say whether the calm which pervaded every manifestation of her beauty was the result of conscious control or the most perfect ease.

She took down the guzla and handed it to Boris, who struck some plaintive preliminary chords.

"What shall I sing?" she inquired, raising her father's hand from the back of the sofa where he rested and kissing it with filial tenderness.

"Improvise," said the general. "Improvise in French, for the sake of our guest."

"Oh, yes," cried Boris; "improvise as you did the other evening."

He immediately struck a minor chord.

Natacha looked fondly at her father as she sang:

"When the moment comes that parts us at the close of day,
when the Angel of Sleep covers you with azure wings;
"Oh, may your eyes rest from so many tears, and your oppressed
heart have calm;
"In each moment that we have together, Father dear, let our
souls feel harmony sweet and mystical;
"And when your thoughts may have flown to other worlds, oh, may
my image, at least, nestle within your sleeping eyes."

Natacha's voice was sweet, and the charm of it subtly pervasive. The words as she uttered them seemed to have all the quality of a prayer and there were tears in all eyes, excepting those of Michael Korsakoff, the second orderly, whom Rouletabille appraised as a man with a rough heart not much open to sentiment.

"Feodor Feodorovitch," said this officer, when the young girl's voice had faded away into the blending with the last note of the guzla, "Feodor Feodorovitch is a man and a glorious soldier who is able to sleep in peace, because he has labored for his country and for his Czar."

"Yes, yes. Labored well! A glorious soldier!" repeated Athanase Georgevitch and Ivan Petrovitch. "Well may he sleep peacefully."

"Natacha sang like an angel," said Boris, the first orderly, in a tremulous voice.

"Like an angel, Boris Nikolaievitch. But why did she speak of his heart oppressed? I don't see that General Trebassof has a heart oppressed, for my part." Michael Korsakoff spoke roughly as he drained his glass.

"No, that's so, isn't it?" agreed the others.

"A young girl may wish her father a pleasant sleep, surely!" said Matrena Petrovna, with a certain good sense. "Natacha has affected us all, has she not, Feodor?"

"Yes, she made me weep," declared the general. "But let us have champagne to cheer us up. Our young friend here will think we are chicken-hearted."

"Never think that," said Rouletabille. "Mademoiselle has touched me deeply as well. She is an artist, really a great artist. And a poet."

"He is from Paris; he knows," said the others.

And all drank.

Then they talked about music, with great display of knowledge concerning things operatic. First one, then another went to the piano and ran through some motif that the rest hummed a little first, then shouted in a rousing chorus. Then they drank more, amid a perfect fracas of talk and laughter. Ivan Petrovitch and Athanase Georgevitch walked across and kissed the general. Rouletabille saw all around him great children who amused themselves with unbelievable naivete and who drank in a fashion more unbelievable still. Matrena Petrovna smoked cigarettes of yellow tobacco incessantly, rising almost continually to make a hurried round of the rooms, and after having prompted the servants to greater watchfulness, sat and looked long at Rouletabille, who did not stir, but caught every word, every gesture of each one there. Finally, sighing, she sat down by Feodor and asked how his leg felt. Michael and Natacha, in a corner, were deep in conversation, and Boris watched them with obvious impatience, still strumming the guzla. But the thing that struck Rouletabille's youthful imagination beyond all else was the mild face of the general. He had not imagined the terrible Trebassof with so paternal and sympathetic an expression. The Paris papers had printed redoubtable pictures of him, more or less authentic, but the arts of photography and engraving had cut vigorous, rough features of an official—who knew no pity. Such pictures were in perfect accord with the idea one naturally had of the dominating figure of the government at Moscow, the man who, during eight days—the Red Week—had made so many corpses of students and workmen that the halls of the University and the factories had opened their doors since in vain. The dead would have had to arise for those places to be peopled! Days of terrible battle where in one quarter or another of the city there was naught but massacre or burnings, until Matrena Petrovna and her step-daughter, Natacha (all the papers told of it), had fallen on their knees before the general and begged terms for the last of the revolutionaries, at bay in the Presnia quarter, and had been refused by him. "War is war," had been his answer, with irrefutable logic. "How can you ask mercy for these men who never give it?" Be it said for the young men of the barricades that they never surrendered, and equally be it said for Trebassof that he necessarily shot them. "If I had only myself to consider," the general had said to a Paris journalist, "I could have been gentle as a lamb with these unfortunates, and so I should not now myself be condemned to death. After all, I fail to see what they reproach me with. I have served my master as a brave and loyal subject, no more, and, after the fighting, I have let others ferret out the children that had hidden under their mothers' skirts. Everybody talks of the repression of Moscow, but let us speak, my friend, of the Commune.

There was a piece of work I would not have done, to massacre within a court an unresisting crowd of men, women and children. I am a rough and faithful soldier of His Majesty, but I am not a monster, and I have the feelings of a husband and father, my dear monsieur. Tell your readers that, if you care to, and do not surmise further about whether I appear to regret being condemned to death."

Certainly what stupefied Rouletabille now was this staunch figure of the condemned man who appeared so tranquilly to enjoy his life. When the general was not furthering the gayety of his friends he was talking with his wife and daughter, who adored him and continually fondled him, and he seemed perfectly happy. With his enormous grizzly mustache, his ruddy color, his keen, piercing eyes, he looked the typical spoiled father.

The reporter studied all these widely-different types and made his observations while pretending to a ravenous appetite, which served, moreover, to fix him in the good graces of his hosts of the datcha des Iles. But, in reality, he passed the food to an enormous bull-dog under the table, in whose good graces he was also thus firmly planting himself. As Trebassof had prayed his companions to let his young friend satisfy his ravening hunger in peace, they did not concern themselves to entertain him. Then, too, the music served to distract attention from him, and at a moment somewhat later, when Matrena Petrovna turned to speak to the young man, she was frightened at not seeing him. Where had he gone? She went out into the veranda and looked. She did not dare to call. She walked into the grand-salon and saw the reporter just as he came out of the sitting-room.

"Where were you?" she inquired.

"The sitting-room is certainly charming, and decorated exquisitely," complimented Rouletabille. "It seems almost a boudoir."

"It does serve as a boudoir for my step-daughter, whose bedroom opens directly from it; you see the door there. It is simply for the present that the luncheon table is set there, because for some time the police have pre-empted the veranda."

"Is your dog a watch-dog, madame?" asked Rouletabille, caressing the beast, which had followed him.

"Khor is faithful and had guarded us well hitherto."

"He sleeps now, then?"

"Yes. Koupriane has him shut in the lodge to keep him from barking nights. Koupriane fears that if he is out he will devour one of the police who watch in the garden at night. I wanted him to sleep in the house, or by his master's door, or even at the foot of the bed, but Koupriane said, 'No, no; no dog. Don't rely on the dog. Nothing is more dangerous than to rely on the dog.' Since then he has kept Khor locked up at night. But I do not understand Koupriane's idea."

"Monsieur Koupriane is right," said the reporter. "Dogs are useful only against strangers."

"Oh," gasped the poor woman, dropping her eyes. "Koupriane certainly knows his business; he thinks of everything."

"Come," she added rapidly, as though to hide her disquiet, "do not go out like that without letting me know. They want you in the dining-room."

"I must have you tell me right now about this attempt."

"In the dining-room, in the dining-room. In spite of myself," she said in a low voice, "it is stronger than I am. I am not able to leave the general by himself while he is on the ground-floor."

She drew Rouletabille into the dining-room, where the gentlemen were now telling odd stories of street robberies amid loud laughter. Natacha was still talking with Michael Korsakoff; Boris, whose eyes never quitted them, was as pale as the wax on his guzla, which he rattled violently from time to time. Matrena made Rouletabille sit in a corner of the sofa, near her, and, counting on her fingers like a careful housewife who does not wish to overlook anything in her domestic calculations, she said:

"There have been three attempts; the first two in Moscow. The first happened very simply. The general knew he had been condemned to death. They had delivered to him at the palace in the afternoon the revolutionary poster which proclaimed his intended fate to the whole city and country. So Feodor, who was just about to ride into the city, dismissed his escort. He ordered horses put to a sleigh. I trembled and asked what he was going to do. He said he was going to drive quietly through all parts of the city, in order to show the Muscovites that a governor appointed according to law by the Little Father and who had in his conscience only the sense that he had done his full duty was not to be intimidated. It was nearly four o'clock, toward the end of a winter day that had been clear and bright, but very cold. I wrapped myself in my furs and took my seat beside him, and he said, 'This is fine, Matrena; this will have a great effect on these imbeciles.' So we started. At first we drove along the Naberjnaia. The sleigh glided like the wind. The general hit the driver a heavy blow in the back, crying, 'Slower, fool; they will think we are afraid,' and so the horses were almost walking when, passing behind the Church of Protection and intercession, we reached the Place Rouge. Until then the few passers-by had looked at us, and as they recognized him, hurried along to keep him in view. At the Place Rouge there was only a little knot of women kneeling before the Virgin. As soon as these women saw us and recognized the equipage of the Governor, they dispersed like a flock of crows, with frightened cries. Feodor laughed so hard that as we passed under the vault of the Virgin his laugh seemed to shake the stones. I felt reassured, monsieur. Our promenade continued without any remarkable incident. The city was almost deserted. Everything lay prostrated under the awful blow of that battle in the street. Feodor said, 'Ah, they give me a wide berth; they do not know how much I love them," and all through that promenade he said many more charming and delicate things to me.

"As we were talking pleasantly under our furs we came to la Place Koudrinsky, la rue Koudrinsky, to be exact. It was just four o'clock, and a light mist had commenced to mix with the sifting snow, and the houses to right and left were visible only as masses of shadow. We glided over the snow like a boat along the river in foggy calm. Then, suddenly, we heard piercing cries and saw shadows of soldiers rushing around, with movements that looked larger than human through the mist; their short whips looked enormous as they knocked some other shadows that we saw down like logs. The general stopped the sleigh and got out to see what was going on. I got out with him. They were soldiers of the famous Semenowsky regiment, who had two prisoners, a young man and a child. The child was being beaten on the nape of the neck. It writhed on the ground and cried in torment. It couldn't have been more than nine years old. The other, the young man, held himself up and marched along without a single cry as the thongs fell brutally upon him. I was appalled. I did not give my husband time to open his mouth before I called to the subaltern who commanded the detachment, 'You should be ashamed to strike a child and a Christian like that, which cannot defend itself.' The general told him the same thing. Then the subaltern told us that the little child had just killed a lieutenant in the street by firing a revolver, which he showed us, and it was the biggest one I ever have seen, and must have been as heavy for that infant to lift as a small cannon. It was unbelievable.

"'And the other,' demanded the general; 'what has he done?'

"'He is a dangerous student,' replied the subaltern, 'who has delivered himself up as a prisoner because he promised the landlord of the house where he lives that he would do it to keep the house from being battered down with cannon.'

"'But that is right of him. Why do you beat him?'

"'Because he has told us he is a dangerous student.'

"'That is no reason,' Feodor told him. 'He will be shot if he deserves it, and the child also, but I forbid you to beat him. You have not been furnished with these whips in order to beat isolated prisoners, but to charge the crowd when it does not obey the governor's orders. In such a case you are ordered "Charge," and you know what to do. You understand?' Feodor said roughly. 'I am General Trebassof, your governor.'

"Feodor was thoroughly human in saying this. Ah, well, he was badly compensated for it, very badly, I tell you. The student was truly dangerous, because he had no sooner heard my husband say, 'I am General Trebassof, your governor,' than he cried, 'Ah, is it you, Trebassoff' and drew a revolver from no one knows where and fired straight at the general, almost against his breast. But the general was not hit, happily, nor I either, who was by him and had thrown myself onto the student to disarm him and then was tossed about at the feet of the soldiers in the battle they waged around the student while the revolver was going off. Three soldiers were killed. You can understand that the others were furious. They raised me with many excuses and, all together, set to kicking the student in the loins and striking at him as he lay on the ground. The subaltern struck his face a blow that might have blinded him. Feodor hit the officer in the head with his fist and called, 'Didn't you hear what I said?' The officer fell under the blow and Feodor himself carried him to the sleigh and laid him with the dead men. Then he took charge of the soldiers and led them to the barracks. I followed, as a sort of after-guard. We returned to the palace an hour later. It was quite dark by then, and almost at the entrance to the palace we were shot at by a group of revolutionaries who passed swiftly in two sleighs and disappeared in the darkness so fast that they could not be overtaken. I had a ball in my toque. The general had not been touched this time either, but our furs were ruined by the blood of the dead soldiers which they had forgotten to clean out of the sleigh. That was the first attempt, which meant little enough, after all, because it was fighting in the open. It was some days later that they commenced to try assassination."

At this moment Ermolai brought in four bottles of champagne and Thaddeus struck lightly on the piano.

"Quickly, madame, the second attempt," said Rouletabille, who was aking hasty notes on his cuff, never ceasing, meanwhile, to watch the convivial group and listening with both ears wide open to Matrena.

"The second happened still in Moscow. We had had a jolly dinner because we thought that at last the good old days were back and good citizens could live in peace; and Boris had tried out the guzla singing songs of the Orel country to please me; he is so fine and sympathetic. Natacha had gone somewhere or other. The sleigh was waiting at the door and we went out and got in. Almost instantly there was a fearful noise, and we were thrown out into the snow, both the general and me. There remained no trace of sleigh or coachman; the two horses were disemboweled, two magnificent piebald horses, my dear young monsieur, that the general was so attached to. As to Feodor, he had that serious wound in his right leg; the calf was shattered. I simply had my shoulder a little wrenched, practically nothing. The bomb had been placed under the seat of the unhappy coachman, whose hat alone we found, in a pool of blood. From that attack the general lay two months in bed. In the second month they arrested two servants who were caught one night on the landing leading to the upper floor, where they had no business, and after that I sent at once for our old domestics in Orel to come and serve us. It was discovered that these detected servants were in touch with the revolutionaries, so they were hanged. The Emperor appointed a provisional governor, and now that the general was better we decided on a convalescence for him in the midi of France. We took train for St. Petersburg, but the journey started high fever in my husband and reopened the wound in his calf. The doctors ordered absolute rest and so we settled here in the datcha des Iles. Since then, not a day has passed without the general receiving an anonymous letter telling him that nothing can save him from the revenge of the revolutionaries. He is brave and only smiles over them, but for me, I know well that so long as we are in Russia we have not a moment's security. So I watch him every minute and let no one approach him except his intimate friends and us of the family. I have brought an old gniagnia who watched me grow up, Ermolai, and the Orel servants. In the meantime, two months later, the third attempt suddenly occurred. It is certainly of them all the most frightening, because it is so mysterious, a mystery that has not yet, alas, been solved."

But Athanase Georgevitch had told a "good story" which raised so much hubbub that nothing else could be heard. Feodor Feodorovitch was so amused that he had tears in his eyes. Rouletabille said to himself as Matrena talked, "I never have seen men so gay, and yet they know perfectly they are apt to be blown up all together any moment."

General Trebassof, who had steadily watched Rouletabille, who, for that matter, had been kept in eye by everyone there, said:

"Eh, eh, monsieur le journaliste, you find us very gay?"

"I find you very brave," said Rouletabille quietly.

"How is that?" said Feodor Feodorovitch, smiling.

"You must pardon me for thinking of the things that you seem to have forgotten entirely."

He indicated the general's wounded leg.

"The chances of war! the chances of war!" said the general. "A leg here, an arm there. But, as you see, I am still here. They will end by growing tired and leaving me in peace. Your health, my friend!"

"Your health, general!"

"You understand," continued Feodor Feodorovitch, "there is no occasion to excite ourselves. It is our business to defend the empire at the peril of our lives. We find that quite natural, and there is no occasion to think of it. I have had terrors enough in other directions, not to speak of the terrors of love, that are more ferocious than you can yet imagine. Look at what they did to my poor friend the Chief of the Surete, Boichlikoff. He was commendable certainly. There was a brave man. Of an evening, when his work was over, he always left the bureau of the prefecture and went to join his wife and children in their apartment in the ruelle des Loups. Not a soldier! No guard! The others had every chance. One evening a score of revolutionaries, after having driven away the terrorized servants, mounted to his apartments. He was dining with his family. They knocked and he opened the door. He saw who they were, and tried to speak. They gave him no time. Before his wife and children, mad with terror and on their knees before the revolutionaries, they read him his death-sentence. A fine end that to a dinner!"

As he listened Rouletabille paled and he kept his eyes on the door as if he expected to see it open of itself, giving access to ferocious Nihilists of whom one, with a paper in his hand, would read the sentence of death to Feodor Feodorovitch. Rouletabille's stomach was not yet seasoned to such stories. He almost regretted, momentarily, having taken the terrible responsibility of dismissing the police. After what Koupriane had confided to him of things that had happened in this house, he had not hesitated to risk everything on that audacious decision, but all the same, all the same—these stories of Nihilists who appear at the end of a meal, death-sentence in hand, they haunted him, they upset him. Certainly it had been a piece of foolhardiness to dismiss the police!

"Well," he asked, conquering his misgivings and resuming, as always, his confidence in himself, "then, what did they do then, after reading the sentence?"

"The Chief of the Surete knew he had no time to spare. He did not ask for it. The revolutionaries ordered him to bid his family farewell. He raised his wife, his children, clasped them, bade them be of good courage, then said he was ready. They took him into the street. They stood him against a wall. His wife and children watched from a window. A volley sounded. They descended to secure the body, pierced with twenty-five bullets."

"That was exactly the number of wounds that were made on the body of little Jacques Zloriksky," came in the even tones of Natacha.

"Oh, you, you always find an excuse," grumbled the general. "Poor Boichlikoff did his duty, as I did mine.

"Yes, papa, you acted like a soldier. That is what the revolutionaries ought not to forget. But have no fears for us, papa; because if they kill you we will all die with you."

"And gayly too," declared Athanase Georgevitch.

"They should come this evening. We are in form!"

Upon which Athanase filled the glasses again.

"None the less, permit me to say," ventured the timber-merchant, Thaddeus Tchnitchnikof, timidly, "permit me to say that this Boichlikoff was very imprudent."

"Yes, indeed, very gravely imprudent," agreed Rouletabille. "When a man has had twenty-five good bullets shot into the body of a child, he ought certainly to keep his home well guarded if he wishes to dine in peace."

He stammered a little toward the end of this, because it occurred to him that it was a little inconsistent to express such opinions, seeing what he had done with the guard over the general.

"Ah," cried Athanase Georgevitch, in a stage-struck voice, "Ah, it was not imprudence! It was contempt of death! Yes, it was contempt of death that killed him! Even as the contempt of death keeps us, at this moment, in perfect health. To you, ladies and gentlemen! Do you know anything lovelier, grander, in the world than contempt of death? Gaze on Feodor Feodorovitch and answer me. Superb! My word, superb! To you all! The revolutionaries who are not of the police are of the same mind regarding our heroes. They may curse the tchinownicks who execute the terrible orders given them by those higher up, but those who are not of the police (there are some, I believe)—these surely recognize that men like the Chief of the Surete our dead friend, are brave."

"Certainly," endorsed the general. "Counting all things, they need more heroism for a promenade in a salon than a soldier on a battle-field."

"I have met some of these men," continued Athanase in exalted vein. "I have found in all their homes the same—imprudence, as our young French friend calls it. A few days after the assassination of the Chief of Police in Moscow I was received by his successor in the same place where the assassination had occurred. He did not take the slightest precaution with me, whom he did not know at all, nor with men of the middle class who came to present their petitions, in spite of the fact that it was under precisely identical conditions that his predecessor had been slain. Before I left I looked over to where on the floor there had so recently occurred such agony. They had placed a rug there and on the rug a table, and on that table there was a book. Guess what book. 'Women's Stockings,' by Willy! And—and then—Your health, Matrena Petrovna. What's the odds!"

"You yourselves, my friends," declared the general, "prove your great courage by coming to share the hours that remain of my life with me."

"Not at all, not at all! It is war."

"Yes, it is war."

"Oh, there's no occasion to pat us on the shoulder, Athanase," insisted Thaddeus modestly. "What risk do we run? We are well guarded."

"We are protected by the finger of God," declared Athanase, "because the police—well, I haven't any confidence in the police."

Michael Korsakoff, who had been for a turn in the garden, entered during the remark.

"Be happy, then, Athanase Georgevitch," said he, "for there are now no police around the villa."

"Where are they?" inquired the timber-merchant uneasily.

"An order came from Koupriane to remove them," explained Matrena Petrovna, who exerted herself to appear calm.

"And are they not replaced?" asked Michael.

"No. It is incomprehensible. There must have been some confusion in the orders given." And Matrena reddened, for she loathed a lie and it was in tribulation of spirit that she used this fable under Rouletabille's directions.

"Oh, well, all the better," said the general. "It will give me pleasure to see my home ridded for a while of such people."

Athanase was naturally of the same mind as the general, and when Thaddeus and Ivan Petrovitch and the orderlies offered to pass the night at the villa and take the place of the absent police, Feodor Feodorovitch caught a gesture from Rouletabille which disapproved the idea of this new guard.

"No, no," cried the general emphatically. "You leave at the usual time. I want now to get back into the ordinary run of things, my word! To live as everyone else does. We shall be all right. Koupriane and I have arranged the matter. Koupriane is less sure of his men, after all, than I am of my servants. You understand me. I do not need to explain further. You will go home to bed—and we will all sleep. Those are the orders. Besides, you must remember that the guard-post is only a step from here, at the corner of the road, and we have only to give a signal to bring them all here. But—more secret agents or special police—no, no! Good-night. All of us to bed now!"

They did not insist further. When Feodor had said, "Those are the orders," there was room for nothing more, not even in the way of polite insistence.

But before going to their beds all went into the veranda, where liqueurs were served by the brave Ermolai, as always. Matrena pushed the wheel-chair of the general there, and he kept repeating, "No, no. No more such people. No more police. They only bring trouble."

"Feodor! Feodor!" sighed Matrena, whose anxiety deepened in spite of all she could do, "they watched over your dear life."

"Life is dear to me only because of you, Matrena Petrovna."

"And not at all because of me, papa?" said Natacha.

"Oh, Natacha!"

He took both her hands in his. It was an affecting glimpse of family intimacy.

From time to time, while Ermolai poured the liqueurs, Feodor struck his band on the coverings over his leg.

"It gets better," said he. "It gets better."

Then melancholy showed in his rugged face, and he watched night deepen over the isles, the golden night of St. Petersburg. It was not quite yet the time of year for what they call the golden nights there, the "white nights," nights which never deepen to darkness, but they were already beautiful in their soft clarity, caressed, here by the Gulf of Finland, almost at the same time by the last and the first rays of the sun, by twilight and dawn.

From the height of the veranda one of the most beautiful bits of the isles lay in view, and the hour was so lovely that its charm thrilled these people, of whom several, as Thaddeus, were still close to nature. It was he, first, who called to Natacha:

"Natacha! Natacha! Sing us your 'Soir des Iles.'"

Natacha's voice floated out upon the peace of the islands under the dim arched sky, light and clear as a night rose, and the guzla of Boris accompanied it. Natacha sang:

"This is the night of the Isles—at the north of the world. The sky presses in its stainless arms the bosom of earth, Night kisses the rose that dawn gave to the twilight. And the night air is sweet and fresh from across the shivering gulf, Like the breath of young girls from the world still farther north. Beneath the two lighted horizons, sinking and rising at once, The sun rolls rebounding from the gods at the north of the world. In this moment, beloved, when in the clear shadows of this rose-stained evening I am here alone with you, Respond, respond with a heart less timid to the holy, accustomed cry of 'Good-evening.'"

Ah, how Boris Nikolaievitch and Michael Korsakoff watched her as she sang! Truly, no one ever can guess the anger or the love that broods in a Slavic heart under a soldier's tunic, whether the soldier wisely plays at the guzla, as the correct Boris, or merely lounges, twirling his mustache with his manicured and perfumed fingers, like Michael, the indifferent.

Natacha ceased singing, but all seemed to be listening to her still— the convivial group on the terrace appeared to be held in charmed attention, and the porcelain statuettes of men on the lawn, according to the mode of the Iles, seemed to lift on their short legs the better to hear pass the sighing harmony of Natacha in the rose nights at the north of the world.

Meanwhile Matrena wandered through the house from cellar to attic, watching over her husband like a dog on guard, ready to bite, to throw itself in the way of danger, to receive the blows, to die for its master—and hunting for Rouletabille, who had disappeared again.

III

The Watch

She went out to caution the servants to a strict watch, armed to the teeth, before the gate all night long, and she crossed the deserted garden. Under the veranda the schwitzar was spreading a mattress for Ermolai. She asked him if he had seen the young Frenchman anywhere, and after the answer, could only say to herself, "Where is he, then?" Where had Rouletabille gone? The general, whom she had carried up to his room on her back, without any help, and had helped into bed without assistance, was disturbed by this singular disappearance. Had someone already carried off "their" Rouletabille? Their friends were gone and the orderlies had taken leave without being able to say where this boy of a journalist had gone. But it would be foolish to worry about the disappearance of a Journalist, they had said. That kind of man—these journalists—came, went, arrived when one least expected them, and quitted their company—even the highest society—without formality. It was what they called in France "leaving English fashion." However, it appeared it was not meant to be impolite. Perhaps he had gone to telegraph. A journalist had to keep in touch with the telegraph at all hours. Poor Matrena Petrovna roamed the solitary garden in tumult of heart. There was the light in the general's window on the first floor. There were lights in the basement from the kitchens. There was a light on the ground-floor near the sitting-room, from Natacha's chamber window. Ah, the night was hard to bear. And this night the shadows weighed heavier than ever on the valiant breast of Matrena. As she breathed she felt as though she lifted all the weight of the threatening night. She examined everything—everything. All was shut tight, was perfectly secure, and there was no one within excepting people she was absolutely sure of—but whom, all the same, she did not allow to go anywhere in the house excepting where their work called them. Each in his place. That made things surer. She wished each one could remain fixed like the porcelain statues of men out on the lawn. Even as she thought it, here at her feet, right at her very feet, a shadow of one of the porcelain men moved, stretched itself out, rose to its knees, grasped her skirt and spoke in the voice of

Rouletabille. Ah, good! it was Rouletabille. "Himself, dear madame; himself."

"Why is Ermolai in the veranda? Send him back to the kitchens and tell the schwitzar to go to bed. The servants are enough for an ordinary guard outside. Then you go in at once, shut the door, and don't concern yourself about me, dear madame. Good-night."

Rouletabille had resumed, in the shadows, among the other porcelain figures, his pose of a porcelain man.

Matrena Petrovna did as she was told, returned to the house, spoke to the schwitzar, who removed to the lodge with Ermolai, and their mistress closed the outside door. She had closed long before the door of the kitchen stair which allowed the domestics to enter the villa from below. Down there each night the devoted gniagnia and the faithful Ermolai watched in turn.

Within the villa, now closed, there were on the ground-floor only Matrena herself and her step-daughter Natacha, who slept in the chamber off the sitting-room, and, above on the first floor, the general asleep, or who ought to be asleep if he had taken his potion. Matrena remained in the darkness of the drawing-room, her dark-lantern in her hand. All her nights passed thus, gliding from door to door, from chamber to chamber, watching over the watch of the police, not daring to stop her stealthy promenade even to throw herself on the mattress that she had placed across the doorway of her husband's chamber. Did she ever sleep? She herself could hardly say. Who else could, then? A tag of sleep here and there, over the arm of a chair, or leaning against the wall, waked always by some noise that she heard or dreamed, some warning, perhaps, that she alone had heard. And tonight, tonight there is Rouletabille's alert guard to help her, and she feels a little less the aching terror of watchfulness, until there surges back into her mind the recollection that the police are no longer there. Was he right, this young man? Certainly she could not deny that some way she feels more confidence now that the police are gone. She does not have to spend her time watching their shadows in the shadows, searching the darkness, the arm-chairs, the sofas, to rouse them, to appeal in low tones to all they held binding, by their own name and the name of their father, to promise them a bonus that would amount to something if they watched well, to count them in order to know where they all were, and, suddenly, to throw full in their face the ray of light from her little dark-lantern in order to be sure, absolutely sure, that she was face to face with them, one of the police, and not with some other, some other with an infernal machine under his arm. Yes, she surely had less work now that she had no longer to watch the police. And she had less fear!

She thanked the young reporter for that. Where was he? Did he remain in the pose of a porcelain statue all this time out there on the lawn? She peered through the lattice of the veranda shutters and looked anxiously out into the darkened garden. Where could he be? Was that he, down yonder, that crouching black heap with an unlighted pipe in his mouth? No, no. That, she knew well, was the dwarf she genuinely loved, her little domovoi-doukh, the familiar spirit of the house, who watched with her over the general's life and thanks to whom serious injury had not yet befallen Feodor Feodorovitch—one could not regard a mangled leg that seriously. Ordinarily in her own country (she was from the Orel district) one did not care to see the domovoi-doukh appear in flesh and blood. When she was little she was always afraid that she would come upon him around a turn of the path in her father's garden. She always thought of him as no higher than that, seated back on his haunches and smoking his pipe. Then, after she was married, she had suddenly run across him at a turning in the bazaar at Moscow. He was just as she had imagined him, and she had immediately bought him, carried him home herself and placed him, with many precautions, for he was of very delicate porcelain, in the vestibule of the palace. And in leaving Moscow she had been careful not to leave him there. She had carried him herself in a case and had placed him herself on the lawn of the datcha des Iles, that he might continue to watch over her happiness and over the life of her Feodor. And in order that he should not be bored, eternally smoking his pipe all alone, she had surrounded him with a group of little porcelain genii, after the fashion of the Jardins des Iles. Lord! how that young Frenchman had frightened her, rising suddenly like that, without warning, on the lawn. She had believed for a moment that it was the domovoi-doukh himself rising to stretch his legs. Happily he had spoken at once and she had recognized his voice. And besides, her domovoi surely would not speak French. Ah! Matrena Petrovna breathed freely now. It seemed to her, this night, that there were two little familiar genii watching over the house. And that was worth more than all the police in the world, surely. How wily that little fellow was to order all those men away. There was something it was necessary to know; it was necessary therefore that nothing should be in the way of learning it. As things were now, the mystery could operate without suspicion or interference. Only one man watched it, and he had not the air of watching. Certainly Rouletabille had not the air of constantly watching anything. He had the manner, out in the night, of an easy little man in porcelain, neither more nor less, yet he could see everything—if anything were there to see—and he could hear everything—if there were anything to hear. One passed beside him without suspecting him, and men might talk to each other without an idea that he heard them, and even talk to themselves according to the habit people have sometimes when they think themselves quite alone. All the guests had departed thus, passing close by him, almost brushing him, had exchanged their "Adieus," their "Au revoirs," and all their final, drawn-out farewells. That dear little living domovoi certainly was a rogue! Oh, that dear little domovoi who had been so affected by the tears of Matrena Petrovna! The good, fat, sentimental, heroic woman longed to hear, just then, his reassuring voice.

"It is I. Here I am," said the voice of her little living familiar spirit at that instant, and she felt her skirt grasped. She waited for what he should say. She felt no fear. Yet she had supposed he was outside the house. Still, after all, she was not too astonished that he was within. He was so adroit! He had entered behind her, in the shadow of her skirts, on all-fours, and had slipped away without anyone noticing him, while she was speaking to her enormous, majestic schwitzar.

"So you were here?" she said, taking his hand and pressing it nervously in hers.

"Yes, yes. I have watched you closing the house. It is a task well-done, certainly. You have not forgotten anything."

"But where were you, dear little demon? I have been into all the corners, and my hands did not touch you."

"I was under the table set with hors-d'oeuvres in the sitting-room."

"Ah, under the table of zakouskis! I have forbidden them before now to spread a long hanging cloth there, which obliges me to kick my foot underneath casually in order to be sure there is no one beneath. It is imprudent, very imprudent, such table-cloths. And under the table of zakouskis have you been able to see or hear anything?"

"Madame, do you think that anyone could possibly see or hear anything in the villa when you are watching it alone, when the general is asleep and your step-daughter is preparing for bed?"

"No. No. I do not believe so. I do not. No, oh, Christ!"

They talked thus very low in the dark, both seated in a corner of the sofa, Rouletabille's hand held tightly in the burning hands of Matrena Petrovna.

She sighed anxiously. "And in the garden—have you heard anything?"

"I heard the officer Boris say to the officer Michael, in French, 'Shall we return at once to the villa?' The other replied in Russian in a way I could see was a refusal. Then they had a discussion in Russian which I, naturally, could not understand. But from the way they talked I gathered that they disagreed and that no love was lost between them."

"No, they do not love each other. They both love Natacha."

"And she, which one of them does she love? It is necessary to tell me."

"She pretends that she loves Boris, and I believe she does, and yet she is very friendly with Michael and often she goes into nooks and corners to chat with him, which makes Boris mad with jealousy. She has forbidden Boris to speak to her father about their marriage, on the pretext that she does not wish to leave her father now, while each day, each minute the general's life is in danger."

"And you, madame—do you love your step-daughter?" brutally inquired the reporter.

"Yes—sincerely," replied Matrena Petrovna, withdrawing her hand from those of Rouletabille.

"And she—does she love you?"

"I believe so, monsieur, I believe so sincerely. Yes, she loves me, and there is not any reason why she should not love me. I believe—understand me thoroughly, because it comes from my heart—that we all here in this house love one another. Our friends are old proved friends. Boris has been orderly to my husband for a very long time. We do not share any of his too-modern ideas, and there were many discussions on the duty of soldiers at the time of the massacres. I reproached him with being as womanish as we were in going down on his knees to the general behind Natacha and me, when it became necessary to kill all those poor moujiks of Presnia. It was not his role. A soldier is a soldier. My husband raised him roughly and ordered him, for his pains, to march at the head of the troops. It was right. What else could he do? The general already had enough to fight against, with the whole revolution, with his conscience, with the natural pity in his heart of a brave man, and with the tears and insupportable moanings, at such a moment, of his daughter and his wife. Boris understood and obeyed him, but, after the death of the poor students, he behaved again like a woman in composing those verses on the heroes of the barricades; don't you think so? Verses that Natacha and he learned by heart, working together, when they were surprised at it by the general. There was a terrible scene. It was before the next-to-the-last attack. The general then had the use of both legs. He stamped his feet and fairly shook the house."

"Madame," said Rouletabille, "a propos of the attacks, you must tell me about the third."

As he said this, leaning toward her, Matrena Petrovna shouted "Listen!" that made him rigid in the night with ear alert. What had she heard? For him, he had heard nothing.

"You hear nothing?" she whispered to him with an effort. "A tick-tack?"

"No, I hear nothing."

"You know—like the tick-tack of a clock. Listen."

"How can you hear the tick-tack? I've noticed that no clocks are running here."

"Don't you understand? It is so that we shall be able to hear the tick-tack better."

"Oh, yes, I understand. But I do not hear anything."

"For myself, I think I hear the tick-tack all the time since the last attempt. It haunts my ears, it is frightful, to say to one's self: There is clockwork somewhere, just about to reach the death-tick—and not to know where, not to know where! When the police were here I made them all listen, and I was not sure even when they had all listened and said there was no tick-tack. It is terrible to hear it in my ear any moment when I least expect it. Tick-tack! Tick-tack! It is the blood beating in my ear, for instance, hard, as if it struck on a sounding-board. Why, here are drops of perspiration on my hands! Listen!"

"Ah, this time someone is talking—is crying," said the young man.

"Sh-h-h!" And Rouletabille felt the rigid hand of Matrena Petrovna on his arm. "It is the general. The general is dreaming!"

She drew him into the dining-room, into a corner where they could no longer hear the moanings. But all the doors that communicated with the dining-room, the drawing-room and the sitting-room remained open behind him, by the secret precaution of Rouletabille.

He waited while Matrena, whose breath he heard come hard, was a little behind. In a moment, quite talkative, and as though she wished to distract Rouletabille's attention from the sounds above, the broken words and sighs, she continued:

"See, you speak of clocks. My husband has a watch which strikes. Well, I have stopped his watch because more than once I have been startled by hearing the tick-tack of his watch in his waistcoat-pocket. Koupriane gave me that advice one day when he was here and had pricked his ears at the noise of the pendulums, to stop all my watches and clocks so that there would be no chance of confusing them with the tick-tack that might come from an infernal machine planted in some corner. He spoke from experience, my dear little monsieur, and it was by his order that all the clocks at the Ministry, on the Naberjnaia, were stopped, my dear little friend. The Nihilists, he told me, often use clockworks to set off their machines at the time they decide on. No one can guess all the inventions that they have, those brigands. In the same way, Koupriane advised me to take away all the draught-boards from the fireplaces. By that precaution they were enabled to avoid a terrible disaster at the Ministry near the Pont-des-chantres, you know, petit demovoi? They saw a bomb just as it was being lowered into the fire-place of the minister's cabinet.[1] The Nihilists held it by a cord and were up on the roof letting it down the chimney. One of them was caught, taken to Schlusselbourg and hanged. Here you can see that all the draught-boards of the fireplaces are cleared away."

"Madame," interrupted Rouletabille (Matrena Petrovna did not know that no one ever succeeded in distracting Rouletabille's attention), "madame, someone moans still, upstairs."

"Oh, that is nothing, my little friend. It is the general, who has bad nights. He cannot sleep without a narcotic, and that gives him a fever. I am going to tell you now how the third attack came about. And then you will understand, by the Virgin Mary, how it is I have yet, always have, the tick-tack in my ears.

"One evening when the general had got to sleep and I was in my own room, I heard distinctly the tick-tack of clockwork operating. All the clocks had been stopped, as Koupriane advised, and I had made an excuse to send Feodor's great watch to the repairer. You can understand how I felt when I heard that tick-tack. I was frenzied. I turned my head in all directions, and decided that the sound came from my husband's chamber. I ran there. He still slept, man that he is! The tick-tack was there. But where? I turned here and there like a fool. The chamber was in darkness and it seemed absolutely impossible for me to light a

---

1. Actual attack on Witte.

lamp because I thought I could not take the time for fear the infernal machine would go off in those few seconds. I threw myself on the floor and listened under the bed. The noise came from above. But where? I sprang to the fireplace, hoping that, against my orders, someone had started the mantel-clock. No, it was not that! It seemed to me now that the tick-tack came from the bed itself, that the machine was in the bed. The general awaked just then and cried to me, 'What is it, Matrena? What are you doing?' And he raised himself in bed, while I cried, 'Listen! Hear the tick-tack. Don't you hear the tick-tack?' I threw myself upon him and gathered him up in my arms to carry him, but I trembled too much, was too weak from fear, and fell back with him onto the bed, crying, 'Help!' He thrust me away and said roughly, 'Listen.' The frightful tick-tack was behind us now, on the table. But there was nothing on the table, only the night-light, the glass with the potion in it, and a gold vase where I had placed with my own hands that morning a cluster of grasses and wild flowers that Ermolai had brought that morning on his return from the Orel country. With one bound I was on the table and at the flowers. I struck my fingers among the grasses and the flowers, and felt a resistance. The tick-tack was in the bouquet! I took the bouquet in both hands, opened the window and threw it as far as I could into the garden. At the same moment the bomb burst with a terrible noise, giving me quite a deep wound in the hand. Truly, my dear little domovoi, that day we had been very near death, but God and the Little Father watched over us."

And Matrena Petrovna made the sign of the cross.

"All the windows of the house were broken. In all, we escaped with the fright and a visit from the glazier, my little friend, but I certainly believed that all was over."

"And Mademoiselle Natacha?" inquired Rouletabille. "She must also have been terribly frightened, because the whole house must have rocked."

"Surely. But Natacha was not here that night. It was a Saturday. She had been invited to the soiree du 'Michel' by the parents of Boris Nikolaievitch, and she slept at their house, after supper at the Ours, as had been planned. The next day, when she learned the danger the general had escaped, she trembled in every limb. She threw herself in her father's arms, weeping, which was natural enough, and declared that she never would go away from him again. The general told her how I had managed. Then she pressed me to her heart, saying that she never would forget such an action, and that she loved me more than if I were truly her mother. It was all in vain that during the days following we sought to understand how the infernal machine had been placed in the bouquet of wild flowers. Only the general's friends that you saw this evening, Natacha and I had entered the general's chamber during the day or in the evening. No servant, no chamber-maid, had been on that floor. In the day-time as well as all night long that entire floor is closed and I have the keys. The door of the servants' staircase which opens onto that floor, directly into the general's chamber, is always locked and barred on the inside with iron. Natacha and I do the chamber work. There is no way of taking greater precautions. Three police agents watched over us night and day. The night of the bouquet two had spent their time watching around the house, and the third lay on the sofa in the veranda. Then, too, we found all the doors and windows of the villa shut tight. In such circumstances you can judge whether my anguish was not deeper than any I had known hitherto. Because to whom, henceforth, could we trust ourselves? what and whom could we believe? what and whom could we watch? From that day, no other person but Natacha and me have the right to go to the first floor. The general's chamber was forbidden to his friends. Anyway, the general improved, and soon had the pleasure of receiving them himself at his table. I carry the general down and take him to his room again on my back. I do not wish anyone to help. I am strong enough for that. I feel that I could carry him to the end of the world if that would save him. Instead of three police, we had ten; five outside, five inside. The days went well enough, but the nights were frightful, because the shadows of the police that I encountered always made me fear that I was face to face with the Nihilists. One night I almost strangled one with my hand. It was after that incident that we arranged with Koupriane that the agents who watched at night, inside, should stay placed in the veranda, after having, at the end of the evening, made complete examination of everything. They were not to leave the veranda unless they heard a suspicious noise or I called to them. And it was after that arrangement that the incident of the floor happened, that has puzzled so both Koupriane and me."

"Pardon, madame," interrupted Rouletabille, "but the agents, during the examination of everything, never went to the bedroom floor?"

"No, my child, there is only myself and Natacha, I repeat, who, since the bouquet, go there."

"Well, madame, it is necessary to take me there at once."

"At once!"

"Yes, into the general's chamber."

"But he is sleeping, my child. Let me tell you exactly how the affair of the floor happened, and you will know as much of it as I and as Koupriane."

"To the general's chamber at once."

She took both his hands and pressed them nervously. "Little friend! Little friend! One hears there sometimes things which are the secret of the night! You understand me?"

"To the general's chamber, at once, madame."

Abruptly she decided to take him there, agitated, upset as she was by ideas and sentiments which held her without respite between the wildest inquietude and the most imprudent audacity.

IV

"The Youth of Moscow is Dead"

Rouletabille let himself be led by Matrena through the night, but he stumbled and his awkward hands struck against various things. The ascent to the first floor was accomplished in profound silence. Nothing broke it except that restless moaning which had so affected the young man just before.

The tepid warmth, the perfume of a woman's boudoir, then, beyond, through two doors opening upon the dressing-room which lay between Matrena's chamber and Feodor's, the dim luster of a night-lamp showed the bed where was stretched the sleeping tyrant of Moscow. Ah, he was frightening to see, with the play of faint yellow light and diffused shadows upon him. Such heavy-arched eyebrows, such an aspect of pain and menace, the massive jaw of a savage come from the plains of Tartary to be the Scourge of God, the stiff, thick, spreading beard. This was a form akin to the gallery of old nobles at Kasan, and young Rouletabille imagined him as none other than Ivan the Terrible himself. Thus appeared as he slept the excellent Feodor Feodorovitch, the easy, spoiled father of the family table, the friend of the advocate celebrated for his feats with knife and fork and of the bantering timber-merchant and amiable bear-hunter, the joyous Thaddeus and Athanase; Feodor, the faithful spouse of Matrena Petrovna and the adored papa of Natacha, a brave man who was so unfortunate as to have nights of cruel sleeplessness or dreams more frightful still.

At that moment a hoarse sigh heaved his huge chest in an uneven rhythm, and Rouletabille, leaning in the doorway of the dressing-room, watched—but it was no longer the general that he watched, it was something else, lower down, beside the wall, near the door, and it was that which set him tiptoeing so lightly across the floor that it gave no sound. There was no slightest sound in the chamber, except the heavy breathing lifting the rough chest. Behind Rouletabille Matrena raised her arms, as though she wished to hold him back, because she did not know where he was going. What was he doing? Why did he stoop thus beside the door and why did he press his thumb all along the floor at the doorway? He rose again and returned. He passed again before the bed, where rumbled now, like the bellows of a forge, the respiration of the sleeper. Matrena grasped Rouletabille by the hand. And she had already hurried him into the dressing-room when a moan stopped them.

"The youth of Moscow is dead!"

It was the sleeper speaking. The mouth which had given the stringent orders moaned. And the lamentation was still a menace. In the haunted sleep thrust upon that man by the inadequate narcotic the words Feodor Feodorovitch spoke were words of mourning and pity. This perfect fiend of a soldier, whom neither bullets nor bombs could intimidate, had a way of saying words which transformed their meaning as they came from his terrible mouth. The listeners could not but feel absorbed in the tones of the brutal victor.

Matrena Petrovna and Rouletabille had leant their two shadows, blended one into the other, against the open doorway just beyond the gleam of the night-lamp, and they heard with horror:

"The youth of Moscow is dead! They have cleared away the corpses. There is nothing but ruin left. The Kremlin itself has shut its gates— that it may not see. The youth of Moscow is dead!"

Feodor Feodorovitch's fist shook above his bed; it seemed that he was about to strike, to kill again, and Rouletabille felt Matrena trembling against him, while he trembled as well before the fearful vision of the killer in the Red Week!

Feodor heaved an immense sigh and his breast descended under the bed-clothes, the fist relaxed and fell, the great head lay over on its ear. There was silence. Had he repose at last? No, no. He sighed, he choked anew, he tossed on his couch like the damned in torment, and the words written by his daughter—by his daughter—blazed in his eyes, which now were wide open—words written on the wall, that he read on the wall, written in blood.

> "The youth of Moscow is dead! They had gone so young into the fields
> and into the mines,
> And they had not found a single corner of the Russian land where
> there were not moanings.
> Now the youth of Moscow is dead and no more moanings are heard,
> Because those for whom all youth died do not dare even to moan
> any more.

But—what? The voice of Feodor lost its threatening tone. His breath came as from a weeping child. And it was with sobs in his throat that he said the last verse, the verse written by his daughter in the album, in red letters:

"*The last barricade had standing there the girl of eighteen*
winters, the virgin of Moscow, flower of the snow.
Who gave her kisses to the workmen struck by the bullets
from the soldiers of the Czar;
"*She aroused the admiration of the very soldiers who, weeping,*
killed her:
"*What killing! All the houses shuttered, the windows with heavy*
eyelids of plank in order not to see!—
"*And the Kremlin itself has closed its gates—that it may not see.*
"*The youth of Moscow is dead!*"

"Feodor! Feodor!"

She had caught him in her arms, holding him fast, comforting him while still he raved, "The youth of Moscow is dead," and appeared to thrust away with insensate gestures a crowd of phantoms. She crushed him to her breast, she put her hands over his mouth to make him stop, but he, saying, "Do you hear? Do you hear? What do they say? They say nothing, now. What a tangle of bodies under the sleigh, Matrena! Look at those frozen legs of those poor girls we pass, sticking out in all directions, like logs, from under their icy, blooded skirts. Look, Matrena!"

And then came further delirium uttered in Russian, which was all the more terrible to Rouletabille because he could not comprehend it.

Then, suddenly, Feodor became silent and thrust away Matrena Petrovna.

"It is that abominable narcotic," he said with an immense sigh. "I'll drink no more of it. I do not wish to drink it."

With one hand he pointed to a large glass on the table beside him, still half full of a soporific mixture with which he moistened his lips each time he woke; with the other hand he wiped the perspiration from his face. Matrena Petrovna stayed trembling near him, suddenly overpowered by the idea that he might discover there was someone there behind the door, who had seen and heard the sleep of General Trebassof! Ah, if he learned that, everything was over. She might say her prayers; she should die.

But Rouletabille was careful to give no sign. He barely breathed. What a nightmare! He understood now the emotion of the general's friends when Natacha had sung in her low, sweet voice, "Good-night. May your eyes have rest from tears and calm re-enter your heart oppressed." The friends had certainly been made aware, by Matrena's anxious talking, of the general's insomnia, and they could not repress their tears as they listened to the poetic wish of charming Natacha. "All the same," thought Rouletabille, "no one could imagine what I have just seen. They are not dead for everyone in the world, the youths of Moscow, and every night I know now a chamber where in the glow of the night-lamp they rise—they rise—they rise!" and the young man frankly, naively regretted to have intruded where he was; to have penetrated, however unintentionally, into an affair which, after all, concerned only the many dead and the one living. Why had he come to put himself between the dead and the living? It might be said to him: "The living has done his whole heroic duty," but the dead, what else was it that they had done?

Ah, Rouletabille cursed his curiosity, for—he saw it now—it was the desire to approach the mystery revealed by Koupriane and to penetrate once more, through all the besetting dangers, an astounding and perhaps monstrous enigma, that had brought him to the threshold of the datcha des Iles, which had placed him in the trembling hands of Matrena Petrovna in promising her his help. He had shown pity, certainly, pity for the delirious distress of that heroic woman. But there had been more curiosity than pity in his motives. And now he must pay, because it was too late now to withdraw, to say casually, "I wash my hands of it." He had sent away the police and he alone remained between the general and the vengeance of the dead! He might desert, perhaps! That one idea brought him to himself, roused all his spirit. Circumstances had brought him into a camp that he must defend at any cost, unless he was afraid!

The general slept now, or, at least, with eyelids closed simulated sleep, doubtless in order to reassure poor Matrena who, on her knees beside his pillow, had retained the hand of her terrible husband in her own. Shortly she rose and rejoined Rouletabille in her chamber. She took him then to a little guest-chamber where she urged him to get some sleep. He replied that it was she who needed rest. But, agitated still by what had just happened, she babbled:

"No, no! after such a scene I would have nightmares myself as well. Ah, it is dreadful! Appalling! Appalling! Dear little monsieur, it is the secret of the night. The poor man! Poor unhappy man! He cannot tear his thoughts away from it. It is his worst and unmerited punishment, this translation that Natacha has made of Boris's abominable verses. He knows them by heart, they are in his brain and on his tongue all night long, in spite of narcotics, and he says over and over again all the time, 'It is my daughter who has written that!—my daughter!—my daughter!' It is enough to wring all the tears from one's body—that an aide-de-camp of a general, who himself has killed the youth of Moscow, is allowed to write such verses and that Natacha should take it upon herself to translate them into lovely poetic French for her album. It is hard to account for what they do nowadays, to our misery."

She ceased, for just then they heard the floor creak under a step downstairs. Rouletabille stopped Matrena short and drew his revolver. He wished to creep down alone, but he had not time. As the floor creaked a second time, Matrena's anguished voice called down the staircase in Russian, "Who is there?" and immediately the calm voice of Natacha answered something in the same language. Then Matrena, trembling more and more, and very much excited keeping steadily to the same place as though she had been nailed to the step of the stairway, said in French, "Yes, all is well; your father is resting. Good-night, Natacha." They heard Natacha's step cross the drawing-room and the sitting-room. Then the door of her chamber closed. Matrena and Rouletabille descended, holding their breath. They reached the dining-room and Matrena played her dark-lantern on the sofa where the general always reclined. The sofa was in its usual place on the carpet. She pushed it back and raised the carpet, laying the floor bare. Then she got onto her knees and examined the floor minutely. She rose, wiping the perspiration from her brow, put the carpet hack in place, adjusted the sofa and dropped upon it with a great sigh.

"Well?" demanded Rouletabille.

"Nothing at all," said she.

"Why did you call so openly?"

"Because there was no doubt that it could only be my step-daughter on the ground-floor at that hour."

"And why this anxiety to examine the floor again?"

"I entreat you, my dear little child, do not see in my acts anything mysterious, anything hard to explain. That anxiety you speak of never leaves me. Whenever I have the chance I examine the flooring."

"Madame," demanded the young man, "what was your daughter doing in this room?"

"She came for a glass of mineral water; the bottle is still on the table."

"Madame, it is necessary that you tell me precisely what Koupriane has only hinted to me, unless I am entirely mistaken. The first time that you thought to examine the floor, was it after you heard a noise on the ground-floor such as has just happened?"

"Yes. I will tell you all that is necessary. It was the night after the attempt with the bouquet, my dear little monsieur, my dear little domovoi; it seemed to me I heard a noise on the ground-floor. I hurried downstairs and saw nothing suspicious at first. Everything was shut tight. I opened the door of Natacha's chamber softly. I wished to ask her if she had heard anything. But she was so fast asleep that I had not the heart to awaken her. I opened the door of the veranda, and all the police—all, you understand—slept soundly. I took another turn around the furniture, and, with my lantern in my hand, I was just going out of the dining-room when I noticed that the carpet on the floor was disarranged at one corner. I got down and my hand struck a great fold of carpet near the general's sofa. You would have said that the sofa had been rolled carelessly, trying to replace it in the position it usually occupied. Prompted by a sinister presentiment, I pushed away the sofa and I lifted the carpet. At first glance I saw nothing, but when I examined things closer I saw that a strip of wood did not lie well with the others on the floor. With a knife I was able to lift that strip and I found that two nails which had fastened it to the beam below had been freshly pulled out. It was just so I could raise the end of the board a little without being able to slip my hand under. To lift it any more it would be necessary to pull at least half-a-dozen nails. What could it mean? Was I on the point of discovering some new terrible and mysterious plan? I let the board fall back into place. I spread the carpet back again carefully, put the sofa in its place, and in the morning sent for Koupriane."

Rouletabille interrupted.

"You had not, madame, spoken to anyone of this discovery?"

"To no one."

"Not even to your step-daughter?"

"No," said the husky voice of Matrena, "not even to my step-daughter."

"Why?" demanded Rouletabille.

"Because," replied Matrena, after a moment's hesitation, "there were already enough frightening things about the house. I would not have spoken to my daughter any more than I would have said a word to the general. Why add to the disquiet they already suffered so much, in case nothing developed?"

"And what did Koupriane say?"

"We examined the floor together, secretly. Koupriane slipped his hand under more easily than I had done, and ascertained that under the board, that is to say between the beam and the ceiling of the kitchen, there was a hollow where any number of things might be placed. For the moment the board was still too little released for any maneuver to be possible. Koupriane, when he rose, said to me, 'You have happened, madame, to interrupt the person in her operations. But we are prepared henceforth. We know what she does and she is unaware that we know. Act as though you had not noticed anything; do not speak of it to anyone whatever—and watch. Let the general continue to sit in his usual place and let no one suspect that we have discovered the beginnings of this attempt. It is the only way we can plan so that they will continue. All the same,' he added, 'I will give my agents orders to patrol the ground-floor anew during the night. I would be risking too much to let the person continue her work each night. She might continue it so well that she would be able to accomplish it—you understand me? But by day you arrange that the rooms on the ground-floor be free from time to time—not for long, but from time to time.' I don't know why, but what he said and the way he said it frightened me more than ever. However, I carried out his program. Then, three days later, about eight o'clock, when the night watch was not yet started, that is to say at the moment when the police were still all out in the garden or walking around the house, outside, and when I had left the the ground-floor perfectly free while I helped the general to bed, I felt drawn even against myself suddenly to the dining-room. I lifted the carpet and examined the floor. Three more nails had been drawn from the board, which lifted more easily now, and under it, I could see that the normal cavity had been made wider still!"

When she had said this, Matrena stopped, as if, overcome, she could not tell more.

"Well?" insisted Rouletabille.

"Well, I replaced things as I found them and made rapid inquiries of the police and their chief; no one had entered the ground-floor. You understand me?—no one at all. Neither had anyone come out from it."

"How could anyone come out if no one had entered?"

"I wish to say," said she with a sob, "that Natacha during this space of time had been in her chamber, in her chamber on the ground-floor."

"You appear to be very disturbed, madame, at this recollection. Can you tell me further, and precisely, why you are agitated?"

"You understand me, surely," she said, shaking her head.

"If I understand you correctly, I have to understand that from the previous time you examined the floor until the time that you noted three more nails drawn out, no other person could have entered the dining-room but you and your step-daughter Natacha."

Matrena took Rouletabille's hand as though she had reached an important decision.

"My little friend," moaned she, "there are things I am not able to think about and which I can no longer entertain when Natacha embraces me. It is a mystery more frightful than all else. Koupriane tells me that he is sure, absolutely sure, of the agents he kept here; my sole consolation, do you see, my little friend can tell you frankly, now that you have sent away those men—my sole consolation since that day has been that Koupriane is less sure of his men than I am of Natacha."

She broke down and sobbed.

When she was calmed, she looked for Rouletabille, and could not find him. Then she wiped her eyes, picked up her dark-lantern, and, furtively, crept to her post beside the general.

For that day these are the points in Rouletabille's notebook:

"Topography: Villa surrounded by a large garden on three sides. The fourth side gives directly onto a wooded field that stretches to the river Neva. On this side the level of the ground is much lower, so low that the sole window opening in that wall (the window of Natacha's sitting-room on the ground-floor) is as high from the ground as though it were on the next floor in any other part of the house. This window is closed by iron shutters, fastened inside by a bar of iron.

"Friends: Athanase Georgevitch, Ivan Petrovitch, Thaddeus the timber-merchant (peat boots), Michael and Boris (fine shoes). Matrena, sincere love, blundering heroism. Natacha unknown. Against Natacha: Never there during the attacks. At Moscow at the time of the bomb in the sleigh, no one knows where she was, and it is she who should have accompanied the general (detail furnished by Koupriane that Matrena generously kept back). The night of the bouquet is the only night Natacha has slept away from the house. Coincidence of the disappearance of the nails and the presence all alone on the ground-floor of Natacha, in case, of course, Matrena did not pull them out herself. For Natacha: Her eyes when she looks at her father."

And this bizarre phrase:

"We mustn't be rash. This evening I have not yet spoken to Matrena Petrovna about the little hat-pin. That little hat-pin is the greatest relief of my life."

V

BY ROULETABILLE'S ORDER
THE GENERAL PROMENADES

G ood morning, my dear little familiar spirit. The general slept splendidly the latter part of the night. He did not touch his narcotic. I am sure it is that dreadful mixture that gives him such frightful dreams. And you, my dear little friend, you have not slept an instant. I know it. I felt you going everywhere about the house like a little mouse. Ah, it seems good, so good. I slept so peacefully, hearing the subdued movement of your little steps. Thanks for the sleep you have given me, little friend."

Matrena talked on to Rouletabille, whom she had found the morning after the nightmare tranquilly smoking his pipe in the garden.

"Ah, ah, you smoke a pipe. Now you do certainly look exactly like a dear little domovoi-doukh. See how much you are alike. He smokes just like you. Nothing new, eh? You do not look very bright this morning. You are worn out. I have just arranged the little guest-chamber for you, the only one we have, just behind mine. Your bed is waiting for you. Is there anything you need? Tell me. Everything here is at your service."

"I'm not in need of anything, madame," said the young man smilingly, after this outpouring of words from the good, heroic dame.

"How can you say that, dear child? You will make yourself sick. I want you to understand that I wish you to rest. I want to be a mother to you, if you please, and you must obey me, my child. Have you had breakfast yet this morning? If you do not have breakfast promptly mornings, I will think you are annoyed. I am so annoyed that you have heard the secret of the night. I have been afraid that you would want to leave at once and for good, and that you would have mistaken ideas about the general. There is not a better man in the world than Feodor, and he must have a good, a very good conscience to dare, without fail, to perform such terrible duties as those at Moscow, when he is so good at heart. These things are easy enough for wicked people, but for good men, for good men who can reason it out, who know what they do and that they are condemned to death into the bargain, it is terrible, it is terrible! Why, I told him the moment things began to go wrong in

Moscow, 'You know what to expect, Feodor. Here is a dreadful time to get through—make out you are sick.' I believed he was going to strike me, to kill me on the spot. 'I! Betray the Emperor in such a moment! His Majesty, to whom I owe everything! What are you thinking of, Matrena Petrovna!' And he did not speak to me after that for two days. It was only when he saw I was growing very ill that he pardoned me, but he had to be plagued with my jeremiads and the appealing looks of Natacha without end in his own home each time we heard any shooting in the street. Natacha attended the lectures of the Faculty, you know. And she knew many of them, and even some of those who were being killed on the barricades. Ah, life was not easy for him in his own home, the poor general! Besides, there was also Boris, whom I love as well, for that matter, as my own child, because I shall be very happy to see him married to Natacha—there was poor Boris who always came home from the attacks paler than a corpse and who could not keep from moaning with us."

"And Michael?" questioned Rouletabille.

"Oh, Michael only came towards the last. He is a new orderly to the general. The government at St. Petersburg sent him, because of course they couldn't help learning that Boris rather lacked zeal in repressing the students and did not encourage the general in being as severe as was necessary for the safety of the Empire. But Michael, he has a heart of stone; he knows nothing but the countersign and massacres fathers and mothers, crying, 'Vive le Tsar!' Truly, it seems his heart can only be touched by the sight of Natacha. And that again has caused a good deal of anxiety to Feodor and me. It has caught us in a useless complication that we would have liked to end by the prompt marriage of Natacha and Boris. But Natacha, to our great surprise, has not wished it to be so. No, she has not wished it, saying that there is always time to think of her wedding and that she is in no hurry to leave us. Meantime she entertains herself with this Michael as if she did not fear his passion, and neither has Michael the desperate air of a man who knows the definite engagement of Natacha and Boris. And my step-daughter is not a coquette. No, no. No one can say she is a coquette. At least, no one had been able to say it up to the time that Michael arrived. Can it be that she is a coquette? They are mysterious, these young girls, very mysterious, above all when they have that calm and tranquil look that Natacha always has; a face, monsieur, as you have noticed perhaps, whose beauty is rather passive whatever one says and does, excepting when the volleys in the streets kill her young comrades of the schools. Then I have seen her almost faint, which proves she has a great heart under her tranquil beauty. Poor Natacha! I have seen her excited as I over the life of her father. My little friend, I have seen her searching in the middle of the night, with me, for infernal machines under the furniture, and then she has expressed the opinion that it is nervous, childish, unworthy of us to act like that, like timid beasts under the sofas, and she has left me to search by myself. True, she never quits the general. She is more reassured, and is reassuring to him, at his side. It has an excellent moral effect on him, while I walk about and search like a beast. And she has become as fatalistic as he, and now she sings verses to the guzla, like Boris, or talks in corners with Michael, which makes the two enraged each with the other. They are curious, the young women of St. Petersburg and Moscow, very curious. We were not like that in our time, at Orel. We did not try to enrage people. We would have received a box on the ears if we had."

Natacha came in upon this conversation, happy, in white voile, fresh and smiling like a girl who had passed an excellent night. She asked after the health of the young man very prettily and embraced Matrena, in truth as one embraces a much-beloved mother. She complained again of Matrena's night-watch.

"You have not stopped it, mamma; you have not stopped it, eh? You are not going to be a little reasonable at last? I beg of you! What has given me such a mother! Why don't you sleep? Night is made for sleep. Koupriane has upset you. All the terrible things are over in Moscow. There is no occasion to think of them any more. That Koupriane makes himself important with his police-agents and obsesses us all. I am convinced that the affair of the bouquet was the work of his police."

"Mademoiselle," said Rouletabille, "I have just had them all sent away, all of them—because I think very much the same as you do."

"Well, then, you will be my friend, Monsieur Rouletabille I promise you, since you have done that. Now that the police are gone we have nothing more to fear. Nothing. I tell you, mamma; you can believe me and not weep any more, mamma dear."

"Yes, yes; kiss me. Kiss me again!" repeated Matrena, drying her eyes. "When you kiss me I forget everything. You love me like your own mother, don't you?"

"Like my mother. Like my own mother."

"You have nothing to hide from me?—tell me, Natacha."

"Nothing to hide."

"Then why do you make Boris suffer so? Why don't you marry him?"

"Because I don't wish to leave you, mamma dear."

She escaped further parley by jumping up on the garden edge away from Khor, who had just been set free for the day.

"The dear child," said Matrena; "the dear little one, she little knows how much pain she has caused us without being aware of it, by her ideas, her extravagant ideas. Her father said to me one day at Moscow, 'Matrena Petrovna, I'll tell you what I think—Natacha is the victim of the wicked books that have turned the brains of all these poor rebellious students. Yes, yes; it would be better for her and for us if she did not know how to read, for there are moments—my word!—when she talks very wildly, and I have said to myself more than once that with such ideas her place is not in our salon hut behind a barricade. All the same,' he added after reflection, 'I prefer to find her in the salon where I can embrace her than behind a barricade where I would kill her like a mad dog.' But my husband, dear little monsieur, did not say what he really thinks, for he loves his daughter more than all the rest of the world put together, and there are things that even a general, yes, even a governor-general, would not be able to do without violating both divine and human laws. He suspects Boris also of setting Natacha's wits awry. We really have to consider that when they are married they will read everything they have a mind to. My husband has much more real respect for Michael Korsakoff because of his impregnable character and his granite conscience. More than once he has said, 'Here is the aide I should have had in the worst days of Moscow. He would have spared me much of the individual pain.' I can understand how that would please the general, but how such a tigerish nature succeeds in appealing to Natacha, how it succeeds in not actually revolting her, these young girls of the capital, one never can tell about them—they get away from all your notions of them."

Rouletabille inquired:

"Why did Boris say to Michael, 'We will return together'? Do they live together?"

"Yes, in the small villa on the Krestowsky Ostrov, the isle across from ours, that you can see from the window of the sitting-room. Boris chose it because of that. The orderlies wished to have camp-beds prepared for them right here in the general's house, by a natural devotion to him; but I opposed it, in order to keep them both from Natacha, in whom, of course, I have the most complete confidence, but one cannot be sure about the extravagance of men nowadays."

Ermolai came to announce the petit-dejeuner. They found Natacha already at table and she poured them coffee and milk, eating away all the time at a sandwich of anchovies and caviare.

"Tell me, mamma, do you know what gives me such an appetite? It is the thought of the way poor Koupriane must have taken this dismissal of his men. I should like to go to see him."

"If you see him," said Rouletabille, "it is unnecessary to tell him that the general will go for a long promenade among the isles this afternoon, because without fail he would send us an escort of gendarmes."

"Papa! A promenade among the islands? Truly? Oh, that is going to be lovely!"

Matrena Petrovna sprang to her feet.

"Are you mad, my dear little domovoi, actually mad?"

"Why? Why? It is fine. I must run and tell papa."

"Your father's room is locked," said Matrena brusquely.

"Yes, yes; he is locked in. You have the key. Locked away until death! You will kill him. It will be you who kills him."

She left the table without waiting for a reply and went and shut herself also in her chamber.

Matrena looked at Rouletabille, who continued his breakfast as though nothing had happened.

"Is it possible that you speak seriously?" she demanded, coming over and sitting down beside him. "A promenade! Without the police, when we have received again this morning a letter saying now that before forty-eight hours the general will be dead!"

"Forty-eight hours," said Rouletabille, soaking his bread in his chocolate, "forty-eight hours? It is possible. In any case, I know they will try something very soon."

"My God, how is it that you believe that? You speak with assurance."

"Madame, it is necessary to do everything I tell you, to the letter."

"But to have the general go out, unless he is guarded—how can you take such a responsibility? When I think about it, when I really think about it, I ask myself how you have dared send away the police. But here, at least, I know what to do in order to feel a little safe, I know that downstairs with Gniagnia and Ermolai we have nothing to fear. No stranger can approach even the basement. The provisions are brought from the lodge by our dvornicks whom we have had sent from my mother's home in the Orel country and who are as devoted to us as bull-dogs. Not a bottle of preserves is taken into the kitchens without having been previously opened outside. No package comes from any tradesman without being opened in the lodge. Here, within, we are able to feel a little safe, even without the police—but away from here— outside!"

"Madame, they are going to try to kill your husband within forty-eight hours. Do you desire me to save him perhaps for a long time—for good, perhaps?"

"Ah, listen to him! Listen to him, the dear little domovoi! But what will Koupriane say? He will not permit any venturing beyond the villa; none, at least for the moment. Ah, now, how he looks at me, the dear little domovoi! Oh, well, yes. There, I will do as you wish."

"Very well, come into the garden with me."

She accompanied him, leaning on his arm.

"Here's the idea," said Rouletabille. "This afternoon you will go with the general in his rolling-chair. Everybody will follow. Everyone, you understand, Madame—understand me thoroughly, I mean to say that everyone who wishes to come must be invited to. Only those who wish to remain behind will do so. And do not insist. Ah, now, I see, you understand me. Why do you tremble?"

"But who will guard the house?"

"No one. Simply tell the servant at the lodge to watch from the lodge those who enter the villa, but simply from the lodge, without interfering with them, and saying nothing to them, nothing."

"I will do as you wish. Do you want me to announce our promenade beforehand?"

"Why, certainly. Don't be uneasy; let everybody have the good news."

"Oh, I will tell only the general and his friends, you may be sure."

"Now, dear Madame, just one more word. Do not wait for me at luncheon."

"What! You are going to leave us?" she cried instantly, breathless. "No, no. I do not wish it. I am willing to do without the police, but I am not willing to do without you. Everything might happen in your absence. Everything! Everything!" she repeated with singular energy. "Because, for me, I cannot feel sure as I should, perhaps. Ah, you make me say these things. Such things! But do not go."

"Do not be afraid; I am not going to leave you, madame."

"Ah, you are good! You are kind, kind! Caracho! (Very well.)"

"I will not leave you. But I must not be at luncheon. If anyone asks where I am, say that I have my business to look after, and have gone to interview political personages in the city."

"There's only one political personage in Russia," replied Matrena Petrovna bluntly; "that is the Tsar."

"Very well; say I have gone to interview the Tsar."

"But no one will believe that. And where will you be?"

"I do not know myself. But I will be about the house."

"Very well, very well, dear little domovoi."

She left him, not knowing what she thought about it all, nor what she should think—her head was all in a muddle.

In the course of the morning Athanase Georgevitch and Thaddeus Tchnitchnikof arrived. The general was already in the veranda. Michael and Boris arrived shortly after, and inquired in their turn how he had passed the night without the police. When they were told that Feodor was going for a promenade that afternoon they applauded his decision. "Bravo! A promenade a la strielka (to the head of the island) at the hour when all St. Petersburg is driving there. That is fine. We will all be there." The general made them stay for luncheon. Natacha appeared for the meal, in rather melancholy mood. A little before luncheon she had held a double conversation in the garden with Michael and Boris. No one ever could have known what these three young people had said if some stenographic notes in Rouletabille's memorandum-book did not give us a notion; the reporter had overheard, by accident surely, since all self-respecting reporters are quite incapable of eavesdropping.

The memorandum notes:

Natacha went into the garden with a book, which she gave to Boris, who pressed her hand lingeringly to his lips. "Here is your book; I return it to you. I don't want any more of them, the ideas surge so in my brain. It makes my head ache. It is true, you are right, I don't love novelties. I can satisfy myself with Pouchkine perfectly. The rest are all one to me. Did you pass a good night?"

Boris (good-looking young man, about thirty years old, blonde, a little effeminate, wistful. A curious appurtenance in the military household of so vigorous a general). "Natacha, there is not an hour that I can call truly good if I spend it away from you, dear, dear Natacha."

"I ask you seriously if you have passed a good night?"

She touched his hand a moment and looked into his eyes, but he shook his head.

"What did you do last night after you reached home?" she demanded insistently. "Did you stay up?"

"I obeyed you; I only sat a half-hour by the window looking over here at the villa, and then I went to bed."

"Yes, it is necessary you should get your rest. I wish it for you as for everyone else. This feverish life is impossible. Matrena Petrovna is getting us all ill, and we shall be prostrated."

"Yesterday," said Boris, "I looked at the villa for a half-hour from my window. Dear, dear villa, dear night when I can feel you breathing, living near me. As if you had been against my heart. I could have wept because I could hear Michael snoring in his chamber. He seemed happy. At last, I heard nothing more, there was nothing more to hear but the double chorus of frogs in the pools of the island. Our pools, Natacha, are like the enchanted lakes of the Caucasus which are silent by day and sing at evening; there are innumerable throngs of frogs which sing on the same chord, some of them on a major and some on a minor. The chorus speaks from pool to pool, lamenting and moaning across the fields and gardens, and re-echoing like AEolian harps placed opposite one another."

"Do AEolian harps make so much noise, Boris?"

"You laugh? I don't find you yourself half the time. It is Michael who has changed you, and I am out of it. (Here they spoke in Russian.) I shall not be easy until I am your husband. I can't understand your manner with Michael at all."

(Here more Russian words which I do not understand.)

"Speak French; here is the gardener," said Natacha.

"I do not like the way you are managing our lives. Why do you delay our marriage? Why?"

(Russian words from Natacha. Gesture of desperation from Boris.)

"How long? You say a long time? But that says nothing—a long time. How long? A year? Two years? Ten years? Tell me, or I will kill myself at your feet. No, no; speak or I will kill Michael. On my word! Like a dog!"

"I swear to you, by the dear head of your mother, Boris, that the date of our marriage does not depend on Michael."

(Some words in Russian. Boris, a little consoled, holds her hand lingeringly to his lips.)

Conversation between Michael and Natacha in the garden:

"Well? Have you told him?"

"I ended at last by making him understand that there is not any hope. None. It is necessary to have patience. I have to have it myself."

"He is stupid and provoking."

"Stupid, no. Provoking, yes, if you wish. But you also, you are provoking."

"Natacha! Natacha!"

(Here more Russian.) As Natacha started to leave, Michael placed his hand on her shoulder, stopped her and said, looking her direct in the eyes:

"There will be a letter from Annouchka this evening, by a messenger at five o'clock." He made each syllable explicit. "Very important and requiring an immediate reply."

These notes of Rouletabille's are not followed by any commentary.

After luncheon the gentlemen played poker until half-past four, which is the "chic" hour for the promenade to the head of the island. Rouletabille had directed Matrena to start exactly at a quarter to five. He appeared in the meantime, announcing that he had just interviewed the mayor of St. Petersburg, which made Athanase laugh, who could not understand that anyone would come clear from Paris to talk with men like that. Natacha came from her chamber to join them for the promenade. Her father told her she looked too worried.

They left the villa. Rouletabille noted that the dvornicks were before the gate and that the schwitzar was at his post, from which he could detect everyone who might enter or leave the villa. Matrena pushed the rolling-chair herself. The general was radiant. He had Natacha at his right and at his left Athanase and Thaddeus. The two orderlies followed, talking with Rouletabille, who had monopolized them. The conversation turned on the devotion of Matrena Petrovna, which they placed above the finest heroic traits in the women of antiquity, and also on Natacha's love for her father. Rouletabille made them talk.

Boris Mourazoff explained that this exceptional love was accounted for by the fact that Natacha's own mother, the general's first wife, died in giving birth to their daughter, and accordingly Feodor Feodorovitch had been both father and mother to his daughter. He had raised her with the most touching care, not permitting anyone else, when she was sick, to have the care of passing the nights by her bedside.

Natacha was seven years old when Feodor Feodorovitch was appointed governor of Orel. In the country near Orel, during the summer, the general and his daughter lived on neighborly terms near the family of old Petroff, one of the richest fur merchants in Russia. Old Petroff had a daughter, Matrena, who was magnificent to see, like a beautiful field-flower. She was always in excellent humor, never spoke ill of anyone in the neighborhood, and not only had the fine manners of a city dame but a great, simple heart, which she lavished on the little Natacha.

The child returned the affection of the beautiful Matrena, and it was on seeing them always happy to find themselves together that Trebassof dreamed of reestablishing his fireside. The nuptials were quickly arranged, and the child, when she learned that her good Matrena was to wed her papa, danced with joy. Then misfortune came only a few weeks before the ceremony. Old Petroff, who speculated on the Exchange for a long time without anyone knowing anything about it, was ruined from top to bottom. Matrena came one evening to apprise Feodor Feodorovitch of this sad news and return his pledge to him. For all response Feodor placed Natacha in Matrena's arms. "Embrace your mother," he said to the child, and to Matrena, "From today I consider you my wife, Matrena Petrovna. You should obey me in all things. Take that reply to your father and tell him my purse is at his disposition."

The general was already, at that time, even before he had inherited the Cheremaieff, immensely rich. He had lands behind Nijni as vast as a province, and it would have been difficult to count the number of moujiks who worked for him on his property. Old Pretroff gave his daughter and did not wish to accept anything in exchange. Feodor wished to settle a large allowance on his wife; her father opposed that, and Matrena sided with him in the matter against her husband, because of Natacha. "It all belongs to the little one," she insisted. "I accept the position of her mother, but on the condition that she shall never lose a kopeck of her inheritance."

"So that," concluded Boris, "if the general died tomorrow she would be poorer than Job."

"Then the general is Matrena's sole resource," reflected Rouletabille aloud.

"I can understand her hanging onto him," said Michael Korsakoff, blowing the smoke of his yellow cigarette. "Look at her. She watches him like a treasure."

"What do you mean, Michael Nikolaievitch?" said Boris, curtly. "You believe, do you, that the devotion of Matrena Petrovna is not disinterested. You must know her very poorly to dare utter such a thought."

GASTON LEROUX

"I have never had that thought, Boris Alexandrovitch," replied the other in a tone curter still. "To be able to imagine that anyone who lives in the Trebassofs' home could have such a thought needs an ass's head, surely."

"We will speak of it again, Michael Nikolaievitch."

"At your pleasure, Boris Alexandrovitch."

They had exchanged these latter words tranquilly continuing their walk and negligently smoking their yellow tobacco. Rouletabille was between them. He did not regard them; he paid no attention even to their quarrel; he had eyes only for Natacha, who just now quit her place beside her father's wheel-chair and passed by them with a little nod of the head, seeming in haste to retrace the way back to the villa.

"Are you leaving us?" Boris demanded of her.

"Oh, I will rejoin you immediately. I have forgotten my umbrella."

"But I will go and get it for you," proposed Michael.

"No, no. I have to go to the villa; I will return right away."

She was already past them. Rouletabille, during this, looked at Matrena Petrovna, who looked at him also, turning toward the young man a visage pale as wax. But no one else noted the emotion of the good Matrena, who resumed pushing the general's wheel-chair.

Rouletabille asked the officers, "Was this arrangement because the first wife of the general, Natacha's mother, was rich?"

"No. The general, who always had his heart in his hand," said Boris, "married her for her great beauty. She was a beautiful girl of the Caucasus, of excellent family besides, that Feodor Feodorovitch had known when he was in garrison at Tiflis."

"In short," said Rouletabille, "the day that General Trebassof dies Madame Trebassof, who now possesses everything, will have nothing, and the daughter, who now has nothing, will have everything."

"Exactly that," said Michael.

"That doesn't keep Matrena Petrovna and Natacha Feodorovna from deeply loving each other," observed Boris.

The little party drew near the "Point." So far the promenade had been along pleasant open country, among the low meadows traversed by fresh streams, across which tiny bridges had been built, among bright gardens guarded by porcelain dwarfs, or in the shade of small weeds from the feet of whose trees the newly-cut grass gave a seasonal fragrance. All was reflected in the pools—which lay like glass whereon a scene-painter had cut the green hearts of the pond-lily leaves. An adorable country glimpse which seemed to have been created centuries back for the amusement of a queen and preserved, immaculately trimmed and cleaned, from generation to generation, for the eternal charm of such an hour as this on the banks of the Gulf of Finland.

Now they had reached the bank of the Gulf, and the waves rippled to the prows of the light ships, which dipped gracefully like huge and rapid sea-gulls, under the pressure of their great white sails.

Along the roadway, broader now, glided, silently and at walking pace, the double file of luxurious equipages with impatient horses, the open carriages in which the great personages of the court saw the view and let themselves be seen. Enormous coachmen held the reins high. Lively young women, negligently reclining against the cushions, displayed their new Paris toilettes, and kept young officers on horseback busy with salutes. There were all kinds of uniforms. No talking was heard. Everyone was kept busy looking. There rang in the pure, thin air only the noise of the champing bits and the tintinnabulation of the bells attached to the hairy Finnish ponies' collars. And all that, so beautiful, fresh, charming and clear, and silent, it all seemed more a dream than even that which hung in the pools, suspended between the crystal of the air and the crystal of the water. The transparence of the sky and the transparence of the gulf blended their two unrealities so that one could not note where the horizons met.

Rouletabille looked at the view and looked at the general, and in all his young vibrating soul there was a sense of infinite sadness, for he recalled those terrible words in the night: "They have gone into all the corners of the Russian land, and they have not found a single corner of that land where there are not moanings." "Well," thought he, "they have not come into this corner, apparently. I don't know anything lovelier or happier in the world." No, no, Rouletabille, they have not come here. In every country there is a corner of happy life, which the poor are ashamed to approach, which they know nothing of, and of which merely the sight would turn famished mothers enraged, with their thin bosoms, and, if it is not more beautiful than that, certainly no part of the earth is made so atrocious to live in for some, nor so happy for others as in this Scythian country, the boreal country of the world.

Meanwhile the little group about the general's rolling-chair had attracted attention. Some passers-by saluted, and the news spread quickly that General Trebassof had come for a promenade to "the Point." Heads turned as carriages passed; the general, noticing how much excitement his presence produced, begged Matrena Petrovna to push his chair into an adjacent by-path, behind a shield of trees where he would be able to enjoy the spectacle in peace.

He was found, nevertheless, by Koupriane, the Chief of Police, who was looking for him. He had gone to the datcha and been told there that the general, accompanied by his friends and the young Frenchman, had gone for a turn along the gulf. Koupriane had left his carriage at the datcha, and taken the shortest route after them.

He was a fine man, large, solid, clear-eyed. His uniform showed his fine build to advantage. He was generally liked in St. Petersburg, where his martial bearing and his well-known bravery had given him a sort of popularity in society, which, on the other hand, had great disdain for Gounsovski, the head of the Secret Police, who was known to be capable of anything underhanded and had been accused of sometimes playing into the hands of the Nihilists, whom he disguised as agents-provocateurs, without anybody really doubting it, and he had to fight against these widespread political suspicions.

Well-informed men declared that the death of the previous "prime minister," who had been blown up before Varsovie station when he was on his way to the Tsar at Peterhof, was Gounsovski's work and that in this he was the instrument of the party at court which had sworn the death of the minister which inconvenienced it.[1] On the other hand, everyone regarded Koupriane as incapable of participating in any such horrors and that he contented himself with honest performance of his obvious duties, confining himself to ridding the streets of its troublesome elements, and sending to Siberia as many as he could of the hot-heads, without lowering himself to the compromises which, more than once, had given grounds for the enemies of the empire to maintain that it was difficult to say whether the chiefs of the Russian police played the part of the law or that of the revolutionary party, even that the police had been at the end of a certain time of such mixed procedure hardly able to decide themselves which they did.

This afternoon Koupriane appeared very nervous. He paid his compliments to the general, grumbled at his imprudence, praised him for his bravery, and then at once picked out Rouletabille, whom he took aside to talk to.

---

1. Rumored cause of Plehve's assassination.

"You have sent my men back to me," said he to the young reporter. "You understand that I do not allow that. They are furious, and quite rightly. You have given publicly as explanation of their departure—a departure which has naturally astonished, stupefied the general's friends—the suspicion of their possible participation in the last attack. That is abominable, and I will not permit it. My men have not been trained in the methods of Gounsovski, and it does them a cruel injury, which I resent, for that matter, personally, to treat them this way. But let that go, as a matter of sentiment, and return to the simple fact itself, which proves your excessive imprudence, not to say more, and which involves you, you alone, in a responsibility of which you certainly have not measured the importance. All in all, I consider that you have strangely abused the complete authority that I gave you upon the Emperor's orders. When I learned what you had done I went to find the Tsar, as was my duty, and told him the whole thing. He was more astonished than can be expressed. He directed me to go myself to find out just how things were and to furnish the general the guard you had removed. I arrive at the isles and not only find the villa open like a mill where anyone may enter, but I am informed, and then I see, that the general is promenading in the midst of the crowd, at the mercy of the first miserable venturer. Monsieur Rouletabille, I am not satisfied. The Tsar is not satisfied. And, within an hour, my men will return to assume their guard at the datcha."

Rouletabille listened to the end. No one ever had spoken to him in that tone. He was red, and as ready to burst as a child's balloon blown too hard. He said:

"And I will take the train this evening."

"You will go?"

"Yes, and you can guard your general all alone. I have had enough of it. Ah, you are not satisfied! Ah, the Tsar is not satisfied! It is too bad. No more of it for me. Monsieur, I am not satisfied, and I say Good-evening to you. Only do not forget to send me from here every three or four days a letter which will keep me informed of the health of the general, whom I love dearly. I will offer up a little prayer for him."

Thereupon he was silent, for he caught the glance of Matrena Petrovna, a glance so desolated, so imploring, so desperate, that the poor woman inspired him anew with great pity. Natacha had not returned. What was the young girl doing at that moment? If Matrena really loved Natacha she must be suffering atrociously. Koupriane spoke; Rouletabille did not hear him, and he had already forgotten his own anger. His spirit was wrapped in the mystery.

"Monsieur," Koupriane finished by saying, tugging his sleeve, "do you hear me? I pray you at least reply to me. I offer all possible excuses for speaking to you in that tone. I reiterate them. I ask your pardon. I pray you to explain your conduct, which appeared imprudent to me but which, after all, should have some reason. I have to explain to the Emperor. Will you tell me? What ought I to say to the Emperor?"

"Nothing at all," said Rouletabille. "I have no explanation to give you or the Emperor, or to anyone. You can offer him my utmost homage and do me the kindness to vise my passport for this evening."

And he sighed:

"It is too bad, for we were just about to see something interesting."

Koupriane looked at him. Rouletabille had not quitted Matrena Petrovna's eyes, and her pallor struck Koupriane.

"Just a minute," continued the young man. "I'm sure there is someone who will miss me—that brave woman there. Ask her which she prefers, all your police, or her dear little domovoi. We are good friends already. And—don't forget to present my condolences to her when the terrible moment has come."

It was Koupriane's turn to be troubled.

He coughed and said:

"You believe, then, that the general runs a great immediate danger?"

"I do not only believe it, monsieur, I am sure of it. His death is a matter of hours for the poor dear man. Before I go I shall not fail to tell him, so that he can prepare himself comfortably for the great journey and ask pardon of the Lord for the rather heavy hand he has laid on these poor men of Presnia."

"Monsieur Rouletabille, have you discovered something?"

"Good Lord, yes, I have discovered something, Monsieur Koupriane. You don't suppose I have come so far to waste my time, do you?"

"Something no one else knows?"

"Yes, Monsieur Koupriane, otherwise I shouldn't have troubled to feel concerned. Something I have not confided to anyone, not even to my note-book, because a note-book, you know, a note-book can always be lost. I just mention that in case you had any idea of having me searched before my departure."

"Oh, Monsieur Rouletabille!"

"Eh, eh, like the way the police do in your country; in mine too, for that matter. Yes, that's often enough seen. The police, furious because they can't hit a clue in some case that interests them, arrest a reporter who knows more than they do, in order to make him talk. But—nothing of that sort with me, monsieur. You might have me taken to your famous 'Terrible Section,' I'd not open my mouth, not even in the famous rocking-chair, not even under the blows of clenched fists."

"Monsieur Rouletabille, what do you take us for? You are the guest of the Tsar."

"Ah, I have the word of an honest man. Very well, I will treat you as an honest man. I will tell you what I have discovered. I don't wish through any false pride to keep you in darkness about something which may perhaps—I say perhaps—permit you to save the general."

"Tell me. I am listening."

"But it is perfectly understood that once I have told you this you will give me my passport and allow me to depart?"

"You feel that you couldn't possibly," inquired Koupriane, more and more troubled, and after a moment of hesitation, "you couldn't possibly tell me that and yet remain?"

"No, monsieur. From the moment you place me under the necessity of explaining each of my movements and each of my acts, I prefer to go and leave to you that 'responsibility' of which you spoke just now, my dear Monsieur Koupriane."

Astonished and disquieted by this long conversation between Rouletabille and the Head of Police, Matrena Petrovna continually turned upon them her anguished glance, which always insensibly softened as it rested on Rouletabille. Koupriane read there all the hope that the brave woman had in the young reporter, and he read also in Rouletabille's eye all the extraordinary confidence that the mere boy had in himself. As a last consideration had he not already something in hand in circumstances where all the police of the world had admitted themselves vanquished? Koupriane pressed Rouletabille's hand and said just one word to him:

"Remain."

Having saluted the general and Matrena affectionately, and a group of friends in one courteous sweep, he departed, with thoughtful brow.

During all this time the general, enchanted with the promenade, told stories of the Caucasus to his friends, believing himself young again and re-living his nights as sub-lieutenant at Tills. As to Natacha, no one had seen her. They retraced the way to the villa along deserted by-paths. Koupriane's call made occasion for Athanase Georgevitch and Thaddeus, and the two officers also, to say that he was the only honest man in all the Russian police, and that Matrena Petrovna was a great woman to have dared rid herself of the entire clique of agents, who are often more revolutionary than the Nihilists themselves. Thus they arrived at the datcha.

The general inquired for Natacha, not understanding why she had left him thus during his first venture out. The schwitzar replied that the young mistress had returned to the house and had left again about a quarter of an hour later, taking the way that the party had gone on their promenade, and he had not seen her since.

Boris spoke up:

"She must have passed on the other side of the carriages while we were behind the trees, general, and not seeing us she has gone on her way, making the round of the island, over as far as the Barque."

The explanation seemed the most plausible one.

"Has anyone else been here?" demanded Matrena, forcing her voice to be calm. Rouletabille saw her hand tremble on the handle of the rolling-chair, which she had not quitted for a second during all the promenade, refusing aid from the officers, the friends, and even from Rouletabille.

"First there came the Head of Police, who told me he would go and find you, Barinia, and right after, His Excellency the Marshal of the Court. His Excellency will return, although he is very pressed for time, before he takes the train at seven o'clock for Krasnoie-Coelo."

All this had been said in Russian, naturally, but Matrena translated the words of the schwitzar into French in a low voice for Rouletabille, who was near her. The general during this time had taken Rouletabille's hand and pressed it affectionately, as if, in that mute way, to thank him for all the young man had done for them. Feodor himself also had confidence, and he was grateful for the freer air that he was being allowed to breathe. It seemed to him that he was emerging from prison. Nevertheless, as the promenade had been a little fatiguing, Matrena ordered him to go and rest immediately. Athanase and Thaddeus took their leave. The two officers were already at the end of the garden, talking coldly, and almost confronting one another, like wooden soldiers. Without doubt they were arranging the conditions of an encounter to settle their little difference at once.

The schwitzar gathered the general into his great arms and carried him into the veranda. Feodor demanded five minutes' respite before he was taken upstairs to his chamber. Matrena Petrovna had a light luncheon brought at his request. In truth, the good woman trembled with impatience and hardly dared move without consulting Rouletabille's face. While the general talked with Ermolai, who passed him his tea, Rouletabille made a sign to Matrena that she understood at once. She joined the young man in the drawing-room.

"Madame," he said rapidly, in a low voice, "you must go at once to see what has happened there."

He pointed to the dining-room.

"Very well."

It was pitiful to watch her.

"Go, madame, with courage."

"Why don't you come with me?"

"Because, madame, I have something to do elsewhere. Give me the keys of the next floor."

"No, no. What for?"

"Not a second's delay, for the love of Heaven. Do what I tell you on your side, and let me do mine. The keys! Come, the keys!"

He snatched them rather than took them, and pointed a last time to the dining-room with a gesture so commanding that she did not hesitate further. She entered the dining-room, shaking, while he bounded to the upper floor. He was not long. He took only time to open the doors, throw a glance into the general's chamber, a single glance, and to return, letting a cry of joy escape him, borrowed from his new and very limited accomplishment of Russian, "Caracho!"

How Rouletabille, who had not spent half a second examining the general's chamber, was able to be certain that all went well on that side, when it took Matrena—and that how many times a day!—at least a quarter of an hour of ferreting in all the corners each time she explored her house before she was even inadequately reassured, was a question. If that dear heroic woman had been with him during this "instant information" she would have received such a shock that, with all confidence gone, she would have sent for Koupriane immediately, and all his agents, reinforced by the personnel of the Okrana (Secret Police). Rouletabille at once rejoined the general, whistling. Feodor and Ermolai were deep in conversation about the Orel country. The young man did not disturb them. Then, soon, Matrena reappeared. He saw her come in quite radiant. He handed back her keys, and she took them mechanically. She was overjoyed and did not try to hide it. The general himself noticed it, and asked what had made her so.

"It is my happiness over our first promenade since we arrived at the datcha des Iles," she explained. "And now you must go upstairs to bed, Feodor. You will pass a good night, I am sure."

"I can sleep only if you sleep, Matrena."

"I promise you. It is quite possible now that we have our dear little domovoi. You know, Feodor, that he smokes his pipe just like the dear little porcelain domovoi."

"He does resemble him, he certainly does," said Feodor. "That makes us feel happy, but I wish him to sleep also."

"Yes, yes," smiled Rouletabille, "everybody will sleep here. That is the countersign. We have watched enough. Since the police are gone we can all sleep, believe me, general."

"Eh, eh, I believe you, on my word, easily enough. There were only they in the house capable of attempting that affair of the bouquet. I have thought that all out, and now I am at ease. And anyway, whatever happens, it is necessary to get sleep, isn't it? The chances of war! Nichevo!" He pressed Rouletabille's hand, and Matrena Petrovna took, as was her habit, Feodor Feodorovitch on her back and lugged him to his chamber. In that also she refused aid from anyone. The general clung to his wife's neck during the ascent and laughed like a child. Rouletabille remained in the hallway, watching the garden attentively. Ermolai walked out of the villa and crossed the garden, going to meet a personage in uniform whom the young man recognized immediately as the grand-marshal of the court, who had introduced him to the Tsar. Ermolai informed him that Madame Matrena was engaged in helping her husband retire, and the marshal remained at the end of the garden where he had found Michael and Boris talking in the kiosque. All three remained there for some time in conversation, standing by a table where General and Madame Trebassof sometimes dined when they had no guests. As they talked the marshal played with a box of white cardboard tied with a pink string. At this moment Matrena, who had not been able to resist the desire to talk for a moment with Rouletabille and tell him how happy she was, rejoined the young man.

"Little domovoi," said she, laying her hand on his shoulder, "you have not watched on this side?"

She pointed in her turn to the dining-room.

"No, no. You have seen it, madame, and I am sufficiently informed."

"Perfectly. There is nothing. No one has worked there! No one has touched the board. I knew it. I am sure of it. It is dreadful what we have thought about it! Oh, you do not know how relieved and happy I am. Ah, Natacha, Natacha, I have not loved you in vain. (She pronounced these words in accents of great beauty and tragic sincerity.) When I saw her leave us, my dear, ah, my legs sank under me. When she said, 'I have forgotten something; I must hurry back,' I felt I had not the strength to go a single step. But now I certainly am happy, that weight at least is off my heart, off my heart, dear little domovoi, because of you, because of you."

She embraced him, and then ran away, like one possessed, to resume her post near the general.

Notes in Rouletabille's memorandum-book: The affair of the little cavity under the floor not having been touched again proves nothing for or against Natacha (even though that excellent Matrena Petrovna thinks so). Natacha could very well have been warned by the too great care with which Madame Matrena watched the floor. My opinion, since I saw Matrena lift the carpet the first time without any real precaution, is that they have definitely abandoned the preparation of that attack and are trying to account for the secret becoming known. What Matrena feels so sure of is that the trap I laid by the promenade to the Point was against Natacha particularly. I knew beforehand that Natacha would absent herself during the promenade. I'm not looking for anything new from Natacha, but what I did need was to be sure that Matrena didn't detest Natacha, and that she had not faked the preparations for an attack under the floor in such a way as to throw almost certain suspicion on her step-daughter. I am sure about that now. Matrena is innocent of such a thing, the poor dear soul. If Matrena had been a monster the occasion was too good. Natacha's absence, her solitary presence for a quarter of an hour in the empty villa, all would have urged Matrena, whom I sent alone to search under the carpet in the dining-room, to draw the last nails from the board if she was really guilty of having drawn the others. Natacha would have been lost then! Matrena returned sincerely, tragically happy at not having found anything new, and now I have the material proof that I needed. Morally and physically Matrena is removed from it. So I am going to speak to her about the hat-pin. I believe that the matter is urgent on that side rather than on the side of the nails in the floor.

VI

THE MYSTERIOUS HAND

After the departure of Matrena, Rouletabille turned his attention to the garden. Neither the marshal of the court nor the officers were there any longer. The three men had disappeared. Rouletabille wished to know at once where they had gone. He went rapidly to the gate, named the officers and the marshal to Ermolai, and Ermolai made a sign that they had passed out. Even as he spoke he saw the marshal's carriage disappear around a corner of the road. As to the two officers, they were nowhere on the roadway. He was surprised that the marshal should have gone without seeing Matrena or the general or himself, and, above all, he was disquieted by the disappearance of the orderlies. He gathered from the gestures of Ermolai that they had passed before the lodge only a few minutes after the marshal's departure. They had gone together. Rouletabille set himself to follow them, traced their steps in the soft earth of the roadway and soon they crossed onto the grass. At this point the tracks through the massed ferns became very difficult to follow. He hurried along, bending close to the ground over such traces as he could see, which continually led him astray, but which conducted him finally to the thing that he sought. A noise of voices made him raise his head and then throw himself behind a tree. Not twenty steps from him Natacha and Boris were having an animated conversation. The young officer held himself erect directly in front of her, frowning and impatient. Under the uniform cloak that he had wrapped about him without having bothered to use the sleeves, which were tossed up over his chest, Boris had his arms crossed. His entire attitude indicated hauteur, coldness and disdain for what he was hearing. Natacha never appeared calmer or more mistress of herself. She talked to him rapidly and mostly in a low voice. Sometimes a word in Russian sounded, and then she resumed her care to speak low. Finally she ceased, and Boris, after a short silence, in which he had seemed to reflect deeply, pronounced distinctly these words in French, pronouncing them syllable by syllable, as though to give them additional force:

"You ask a frightful thing of me."

"It is necessary to grant it to me," said the young girl with singular energy. "You understand, Boris Alexandrovitch! It is necessary."

Her gaze, after she had glanced penetratingly all around her and discovered nothing suspicious, rested tenderly on the young officer, while she murmured, "My Boris!" The young man could not resist either the sweetness of that voice, nor the captivating charm of that glance. He took the hand she extended toward him and kissed it passionately. His eyes, fixed on Natacha, proclaimed that he granted everything that she wished and admitted himself vanquished. Then she said, always with that adorable gaze upon him, "This evening!" He replied, "Yes, yes. This evening! This evening!" upon which Natacha withdrew her hand and made a sign to the officer to leave, which he promptly obeyed. Natacha remained there still a long time, plunged in thought. Rouletabille had already taken the road back to the villa. Matrena Petrovna was watching for his return, seated on the first step of the landing on the great staircase which ran up from the veranda. When she saw him she ran to him. He had already reached the dining-room.

"Anyone in the house?" he asked.

"No one. Natacha has not returned, and. . ."

"Your step-daughter is coming in now. Ask her where she has been, if she has seen the orderlies, and if they said they would return this evening, in case she answers that she has seen them."

"Very well, little domovoi doukh. The orderlies left without my seeing when they went."

"Ah," interrupted Rouletabille, "before she arrives, give me all her hat-pins."

"What!"

"I say, all her hat-pins. Quickly!"

Matrena ran to Natacha's chamber and returned with three enormous hat-pins with beautifully-cut stones in them.

"These are all?"

"They are all I have found. I know she has two others. She has one on her head, or two, perhaps; I can't find them."

"Take these back where you found them," said the reporter, after glancing at them.

Matrena returned immediately, not understanding what he was doing.

"And now, your hat-pins. Yes, your hat-pins."

"Oh, I have only two, and here they are," said she, drawing them from the toque she had been wearing and had thrown on the sofa when she re-entered the house.

Rouletabille gave hers the same inspection.

"Thanks. Here is your step-daughter."

Natacha entered, flushed and smiling.

"Ah, well," said she, quite breathless, "you may boast that I had to search for you. I made the entire round, clear past the Barque. Has the promenade done papa good?"

"Yes, he is asleep," replied Matrena. "Have you met Boris and Michael?"

She appeared to hesitate a second, then replied:

"Yes, for an instant."

"Did they say whether they would return this evening?"

"No," she replied, slightly troubled. "Why all these questions?"

She flushed still more.

"Because I thought it strange," parried Matrena, "that they went away as they did, without saying goodby, without a word, without inquiring if the general needed them. There is something stranger yet. Did you see Kaltsof with them, the grand-marshal of the court?"

"No."

"Kaltsof came for a moment, entered the garden and went away again without seeing us, without saying even a word to the general."

"Ah," said Natacha.

With apparent indifference, she raised her arms and drew out her hat-pins. Rouletabille watched the pin without a word. The young girl hardly seemed aware of their presence. Entirely absorbed in strange thoughts, she replaced the pin in her hat and went to hang it in the veranda, which served also as vestibule. Rouletabille never quitted her eyes. Matrena watched the reporter with a stupid glance. Natacha crossed the drawing-room and entered her chamber by passing through her little sitting-room, through which all entrance to her chamber had to be made. That little room, though, had three doors. One opened into Natacha's chamber, one into the drawing-room, and the third into the little passage in a corner of the house where was the stairway by which the servants passed from the kitchens to the ground-floor and the upper floor. This passage had also a door giving directly upon the drawing-room. It was certainly a poor arrangement for serving the dining-room, which was on the other side of the drawing-room and behind the veranda, such a chance laying-out of a house as one often sees in the off-hand planning of many places in the country.

Alone again with Rouletabille, Matrena noticed that he had not lost sight of the corner of the veranda where Natacha had hung her hat. Beside this hat there was a toque that Ermolai had brought in. The old servant had found it in some corner of the garden or the conservatory where he had been. A hat-pin stuck out of that toque also.

"Whose toque is that?" asked Rouletabille. "I haven't seen it on the head of anyone here."

"It is Natacha's," replied Matrena.

She moved toward it, but the young man held her back, went into the veranda himself, and, without touching it, standing on tiptoe, he examined the pin. He sank back on his heels and turned toward Matrena. She caught a glimpse of fleeting emotion on the face of her little friend.

"Explain to me," she said.

But he gave her a glance that frightened her, and said low:

"Go and give orders right away that dinner be served in the veranda. All through dinner it is absolutely necessary that the door of Natacha's sitting-room, and that of the stairway passage, and that of the veranda giving on the drawing-room remain open all the time. Do you understand me? As soon as you have given your orders go to the general's chamber and do not quit the general's bedside, keep it in view. Come down to dinner when it is announced, and do not bother yourself about anything further."

So saying, he filled his pipe, lighted it with a sort of sigh of relief, and, after a final order to Matrena, "Go," he went into the garden, puffing great clouds. Anyone would have said he hadn't smoked in a week. He appeared not to be thinking but just idly enjoying himself. In fact, he played like a child with Milinki, Matrena's pet cat, which he pursued behind the shrubs, up into the little kiosque which, raised on piles, lifted its steep thatched roof above the panorama of the isles that Rouletabille settled down to contemplate like an artist with ample leisure.

The dinner, where Matrena, Natacha and Rouletabille were together again, was lively. The young man having declared that he was more and more convinced that the mystery of the bomb in the bouquet was simply a play of the police, Natacha reinforced his opinion, and following that they found themselves in agreement on about everything else. For himself, the reporter during that conversation hid a real horror which had seized him at the cynical and inappropriate tranquillity with which the young lady received all suggestions that accused the police or that assumed the general no longer ran any immediate danger. In short, he worked, or at least believed he worked, to clear Natacha as he had cleared Matrena, so that there would develop the absolute necessity of assuming a third person's intervention in the facts disclosed so clearly by Koupriane where Matrena or Natacha seemed alone to be possible agents. As he listened to Natacha Rouletabille commenced to doubt and quake just as he had seen Matrena do. The more he looked into the nature of Natacha the dizzier he grew. What abysmal obscurities were there in her nature!

Nothing interesting happened during dinner. Several times, in spite of Rouletabille's obvious impatience with her for doing it, Matrena went up to the general. She returned saying, "He is quiet. He doesn't sleep. He doesn't wish anything. He has asked me to prepare his narcotic. It is too bad. He has tried in vain, he cannot get along without it."

"You, too, mamma, ought to take something to make you sleep. They say morphine is very good."

"As for me," said Rouletabille, whose head for some few minutes had been dropping now toward one shoulder and now toward another, "I have no need of any narcotic to make me sleep. If you will permit me, I will get to bed at once."

"Eh, my little domovoi doukh, I am going to carry you there in my arms."

Matrena extended her large round arms ready to take Rouletabille as though he had been a baby.

"No, no. I will get up there all right alone," said Rouletabille, rising stupidly and appearing ashamed of his excessive sleepiness.

"Oh, well, let us both accompany him to his chamber," said Natacha, "and I will wish papa good-night. I'm eager for bed myself. We will all make a good night of it. Ermolai and Gniagnia will watch with the schwitzar in the lodge. Things are reasonably arranged now."

They all ascended the stairs. Rouletabille did not even go to see the general, but threw himself on his bed. Natacha got onto the bed beside her father, embraced him a dozen times, and went downstairs again. Matrena followed behind her, closed doors and windows, went upstairs again to close the door of the landing-place and found Rouletabille seated on his bed, his arms crossed, not appearing to have any desire for sleep at all. His face was so strangely pensive also that the anxiety of Matrena, who had been able to make nothing out of his acts and looks all day, came back upon her instantly in greater force than ever. She touched his arm in order to be sure that he knew she was there.

"My little friend," she said, "will you tell me now?"

"Yes, madame," he replied at once. "Sit in that chair and listen to me. There are things you must know at once, because we have reached a dangerous hour."

"The hat-pins first. The hat-pins!"

Rouletabille rose lightly from the bed and, facing her, but watching something besides her, said:

"It is necessary you should know that someone almost immediately is going to renew the attempt of the bouquet."

Matrena sprang to her feet as quickly as though she had been told there was a bomb in the seat of her chair. She made herself sit down again, however, in obedience to Rouletabille's urgent look commanding absolute quiet.

"Renew the attempt of the bouquet!" she murmured in a stifled voice. "But there is not a flower in the general's chamber."

"Be calm, madame. Understand me and answer me: You heard the tick-tack from the bouquet while you were in your own chamber?"

"Yes, with the doors open, naturally."

"You told me the persons who came to say good-night to the general. At that time there was no noise of tick-tack?"

"No, no."

"Do you think that if there had been any tick-tack then you would have heard it, with all those persons talking in the room?"

"I hear everything. I hear everything."

"Did you go downstairs at the same time those people did?"

"No, no; I remained near the general for some time, until he was sound asleep."

"And you heard nothing?"

"Nothing."

"You closed the doors behind those persons?"

"Yes, the door to the great staircase. The door of the servants' stairway was condemned a long time ago; it has been locked by me, I alone have the key and on the inside of the door opening into the general's chamber there is also a bolt which is always shot. All the other doors of the chambers have been condemned by me. In order to enter any of the four rooms on this floor it is necessary now to pass by the door of my chamber, which gives on the main staircase."

"Perfect. Then, no one has been able to enter the apartment. No one had been in the apartment for at least two hours excepting you and the general, when you heard the clockwork. From that the only conclusion is that only the general and you could have started it going."

"What are you trying to say?" Matrena demanded, astounded.

"I wish to prove to you by this absurd conclusion, madame, that it is necessary never—never, you understand? Never—to reason solely upon even the most evident external evidence when those seemingly-conclusive appearances are in conflict with certain moral truths that also are clear as the light of day. The light of day for me, madame, is that the general does not desire to commit suicide and, above all, that he would not choose the strange method of suicide by clockwork. The light of day for me is that you adore your husband and that you are ready to sacrifice your life for his."

"Now!" exclaimed Matrena, whose tears, always ready in emotional moments, flowed freely. "But, Holy Mary, why do you speak to me without looking at me? What is it? What is it?"

"Don't turn! Don't make a movement! You hear—not a move! And speak low, very low. And don't cry, for the love of God!"

"But you say at once. . . the bouquet! Come to the general's room!"

"Not a move. And continue listening to me without interrupting," said he, still inclining his ear, and still without looking at her. "It is because these things were as the light of day to me that I say to myself, 'It is impossible that it should be impossible for a third person not to have placed the bomb in the bouquet. Someone is able to enter the general's chamber even when the general is watching and all the doors are locked.'"

"Oh, no. No one could possibly enter. I swear it to you."

As she swore it a little too loudly, Rouletabille seized her arm so that she almost cried out, but she understood instantly that it was to keep her quiet.

"I tell you not to interrupt me, once for all."

"But, then, tell me what you are looking at like that."

"I am watching the corner where someone is going to enter the general's chamber when everything is locked, madame. Do not move!"

Matrena, her teeth chattering, recalled that when she entered Rouletabille's chamber she had found all the doors open that communicated with the chain of rooms: the young man's chamber with hers, the dressing-room and the general's chamber. She tried, under Rouletabille's look, to keep calm, but in spite of all the reporter's exhortations she could not hold her tongue.

"But which way? Where will they enter?"

"By the door."

"Which door?"

"That of the chamber giving on the servants' stair-way."

"Why, how? The key! The bolt!"

"They have made a key."

"But the bolt is drawn this side."

"They will draw it back from the other side."

"What! That is impossible."

Rouletabille laid his two hands on Matrena's strong shoulders and repeated, detaching each syllable, "They will draw it back from the other side."

"It is impossible. I repeat it."

"Madame, your Nihilists haven't invented anything. It is a trick much in vogue with sneak thieves in hotels. All it needs is a little hole the size of a pin bored in the panel of the door above the bolt."

"God!" quavered Matrena. "I don't understand what you mean by your little hole. Explain to me, little domovoi."

"Follow me carefully, then," continued Rouletabille, his eyes all the time fixed elsewhere. "The person who wishes to enter sticks through the hole a brass wire that he has already given the necessary curve to and which is fitted on its end with a light point of steel curved inward. With such an instrument it is child's play, if the hole has been made where it ought to be, to touch the bolt on the inside from the outside, pick the knob on it, withdraw it, and open the door if the bolt is like this one, a small door-bolt."

"Oh, oh, oh," moaned Matrena, who paled visibly. "And that hole?"

"It exists."

"You have discovered it?"

"Yes, the first hour I was here."

"Oh, domovoi! But how did you do that when you never entered the general's chamber until tonight?"

"Doubtless, but I went up that servants' staircase much earlier than that. And I will tell you why. When I was brought into the villa the first time, and you watched me, bidden behind the door, do you know what

I was watching myself, while I appeared to be solely occupied digging out the caviare? The fresh print of boot-nails which left the carpet near the table, where someone had spilled beer (the beer was still running down the cloth). Someone had stepped in the beer. The boot-print was not clearly visible excepting there. But from there it went to the door of the servants' stairway and mounted the stairs. That boot was too fine to be mounting a stairway reserved to servants and that Koupriane told me had been condemned, and it was that made me notice it in a moment; but just then you entered."

"You never told me anything about it. Of course if I had known there was a boot-print. . ."

"I didn't tell you anything about it because I had my reasons for that, and, anyway, the trace dried while I was telling you about my journey."

"Ah, why not have told me later?"

"Because I didn't know you yet."

"Subtle devil! You will kill me. I can no longer. . . Let us go into the general's chamber. We will wake him."

"Remain here. Remain here. I have not told you anything. That boot-print preoccupied me, and later, when I could get away from the dining-room, I was not easy until I had climbed that stairway myself and gone to see that door, where I discovered what I have just told you and what I am going to tell you now."

"What? What? In all you have said there has been nothing about the hat-pins."

"We have come to them now."

"And the bouquet attack, which is going to happen again? Why? Why?"

"This is it. When this evening you let me go to the general's chamber, I examined the bolt of the door without your suspecting it. My opinion was confirmed. It was that way that the bomb was brought, and it is by that way that someone has prepared to return."

"But how? You are sure the little hole is the way someone came? But what makes you think that is how they mean to return? You know well enough that, not having succeeded in the general's chamber, they are at work in the dining-room."

"Madame, it is probable, it is certain that they have given up the work in the dining-room since they have commenced this very day working again in the general's chamber. Yes, someone returned, returned that way, and I was so sure of that, of the forthcoming return, that I removed the police in order to be able to study everything more at my ease. Do you understand now my confidence and why I have been able to assume so heavy a responsibility? It is because I knew I had only one thing to watch: one little hat-pin. It is not difficult, madame, to watch a single little hat-pin."

"A mistake," said Matrena, in a low voice. "Miserable little domovoi who told me nothing, me whom you let go to sleep on my mattress, in front of that door that might open any moment."

"No, madame. For I was behind it!"

"Ah, dear little holy angel! But what were you thinking of! That door has not been watched this afternoon. In our absence it could have been opened. If someone has placed a bomb during our absence!"

"That is why I sent you at once in to the dining-room on that search that I thought would be fruitless, dear madame. And that is why I hurried upstairs to the bedroom. I went to the stairway door instantly. I had prepared for proof positive if anyone had pushed it open even half a millimeter. No, no one had touched the door in our absence.

"Ah, dear heroic little friend of Jesus! But listen to me. Listen to me, my angel. Ah, I don't know where I am or what I say. My brain is no more than a flabby balloon punctured with pins, with little holes of hat-pins. Tell me about the hat-pins. Right off! No, at first, what is it that makes you believe—good God!—that someone will return by that door? How can you see that, all that, in a poor little hat-pin?"

"Madame, it is not a single hat-pin hole; there are two of them.

"Two hat-pin holes?"

"Yes, two. An old one and a new one. One quite new. Why this second hole? Because the old one was judged a little too narrow and they wished to enlarge it, and in enlarging it they broke off the point of a hat-pin in it. Madame, the point is there yet, filling up the little old hole and the piece of metal is very sharp and very bright."

"Now I understand the examination of the hat-pins. Then it is so easy as that to get through a door with a hat-pin?"

"Nothing easier, especially if the panel is of pine. Sometimes one happens to break the point of a pin in the first hole. Then of necessity one makes a second. In order to commence the second hole, the point of the pin being broken, they have used the point of a pen-knife, then have finished the hole with the hat-pin. The second hole is still nearer the bolt than the first one. Don't move like that, madame."

"But they are going to come! They are going to come!"

"I believe so."

"But I can't understand how you can remain so quiet with such a certainty. Great heavens! what proof have you that they have not been there already?"

"Just an ordinary pin, madame, not a hat-pin this time. Don't confuse the pins. I will show you in a little while."

"He will drive me distracted with his pins, dear light of my eyes! Bounty of Heaven! God's envoy! Dear little happiness-bearer!"

In her transport she tried to take him in her trembling arms, but he waved her back. She caught her breath and resumed:

"Did the examination of all the hat-pins tell you anything?"

"Yes. The fifth hat-pin of Mademoiselle Natacha's, the one in the toque out in the veranda, has the tip newly broken off."

"O misery!" cried Matrena, crumpling in her chair.

Rouletabille raised her.

"What would you have? I have examined your own hat-pins. Do you think I would have suspected you if I had found one of them broken? I would simply have thought that someone had used your property for an abominable purpose, that is all."

"Oh, that is true, that is true. Pardon me. Mother of Christ, this boy crazes me! He consoles me and he horrifies me. He makes me think of such dreadful things, and then he reassures me. He does what he wishes with me. What should I become without him?"

And this time she succeeded in taking his head in her two hands and kissing him passionately. Rouletabille pushed her back roughly.

"You keep me from seeing," he said.

She was in tears over his rebuff. She understood now. Rouletabille during all this conversation had not ceased to watch through the open doors of Matrena's room and the dressing-room the farther fatal door whose brass bolt shone in the yellow light of the night-lamp.

At last he made her a sign and the reporter, followed by Matrena, advanced on tip-toe to the threshold of the general's chamber, keeping close to the wall. Feodor Feodorovitch slept. They heard his heavy breath, but he appeared to be enjoying peaceful sleep. The horrors of the night before had fled. Matrena was perhaps right in attributing the nightmares to the narcotic prepared for him each night, for the glass from which he drank it when he felt he could not sleep was still full and obviously had not been touched. The bed of the general was so placed that whoever occupied it, even if they were wide awake, could not see the door giving on the servants' stairway. The little table where the glass and various phials were placed and which had borne the dangerous bouquet, was placed near the bed, a little back of it, and nearer the door. Nothing would have been easier than for someone who could open the door to stretch an arm and place the infernal machine among the wild flowers, above all, as could easily be believed, if he had waited for that treachery until the heavy breathing of the general told them outside that he was fast asleep, and if, looking through the key-hole, he had made sure Matrena was occupied in her own chamber. Rouletabille, at the threshold, glided to one side, out of the line of view from the hole, and got down on all fours. He crawled toward the door. With his head to the floor he made sure that the little ordinary pin which he had placed on guard that evening, stuck in the floor against the door, was still erect, having thus additional proof that the door had not been moved. In any other case the pin would have lain flat on the floor. He crept back, rose to his feet, passed into the dressing-room and, in a corner, had a rapid conversation in a low voice with Matrena.

"You will go," said he, "and take your mattress into the corner of the dressing-room where you can still see the door but no one can see you by looking through the key-hole. Do that quite naturally, and then go to your rest. I will pass the night on the mattress, and I beg you to believe that I will be more comfortable there than on a bed of staircase wood where I spent the night last night, behind the door."

"Yes, but you will fall asleep. I don't wish that."

"What are you thinking, madame?"

"I don't wish it. I don't wish it. I don't wish to quit the door where the eye is. And since I'm not able to sleep, let me watch."

He did not insist, and they crouched together on the mattress. Rouletabille was squatted like a tailor at work; but Matrena remained on all-fours, her jaw out, her eyes fixed, like a bulldog ready to spring. The minutes passed by in profound silence, broken only by the irregular breathing and puffing of the general. His face stood out pallid and tragic on the pillow; his mouth was open and, at times, the lips moved. There was fear at any moment of nightmare or his awakening. Unconsciously he threw an arm over toward the table where the glass of narcotic stood. Then he lay still again and snored lightly. The night-lamp on the mantelpiece caught queer yellow reflections from the corners of the furniture, from the gilded frame of a picture on the wall and from the phials and glasses on the table. But in all the chamber Matrena Petrovna saw nothing, thought of nothing but the brass bolt which shone there on the door. Tired of being on her knees, she shifted, her chin in her hands, her gaze steadily fixed. As time passed and nothing happened she heaved a sigh. She could not have said whether she hoped for or dreaded the coming of that something new which Rouletabille had indicated. Rouletabille felt her shiver with anguish and impatience.

As for him, he had not hoped that anything would come to pass until toward dawn, the moment, as everyone knows, when deep sleep is most apt to vanquish all watchfulness and all insomnia. And as he waited for that moment he had not budged any more than a Chinese ape or the dear little porcelain domovoi doukh in the garden. Of course it might be that it was not to happen this night.

Suddenly Matrena's hand fell on Rouletabille's. His imprisoned hers so firmly that she understood she was forbidden to make the least movement. And both, with necks extended, ears erect, watched like beasts, like beasts on the scent.

Yes, yes, there had been a slight noise in the lock. A key turned, softly, softly, in the lock, and then—silence; and then another little noise, a grinding sound, a slight grating of wire, above, then on the bolt; upon the bolt which shone in the subdued glow of the night-lamp. The bolt softly, very softly, slipped slowly.

Then the door was pushed slowly, so slowly. It opened.

Through the opening the shadow of an arm stretched, an arm which held in its fingers something which shone. Rouletabille felt Matrena ready to bound. He encircled her, he pressed her in his arms, he restrained her in silence, and he had a horrible fear of hearing her suddenly shout, while the arm stretched out, almost touched the pillow on the bed where the general continued to sleep a sleep of peace such as he had not known for a long time.

VII

Arsenate of Soda

The mysterious hand held a phial and poured the entire contents into the potion. Then the hand withdrew as it had come, slowly, prudently, slyly, and the key turned in the lock and the bolt slipped back into place.

Like a wolf, Rouletabille, warning Matrena for a last time not to budge, gained the landing-place, bounded towards the stairs, slid down the banister right to the veranda, crossed the drawing-room like a flash, and reached the little sitting-room without having jostled a single piece of furniture. He noticed nothing, saw nothing. All around was undisturbed and silent.

The first light of dawn filtered through the blinds. He was able to make out that the only closed door was the one to Natacha's chamber. He stopped before that door, his heart beating, and listened. But no sound came to his ear. He had glided so lightly over the carpet that he was sure he had not been heard. Perhaps that door would open. He waited. In vain. It seemed to him there was nothing alive in that house except his heart. He was stifled with the horror that he glimpsed, that he almost touched, although that door remained closed. He felt along the wall in order to reach the window, and pulled aside the curtain. Window and blinds of the little room giving on the Neva were closed. The bar of iron inside was in its place. Then he went to the passage, mounted and descended the narrow servants' stairway, looked all about, in all the rooms, feeling everywhere with silent hands, assuring himself that no lock had been tampered with. On his return to the veranda, as he raised his head, he saw at the top of the main staircase a figure wan as death, a spectral apparition amid the shadows of the passing night, who leaned toward him. It was Matrena Petrovna. She came down, silent as a phantom and he no longer recognized her voice when she demanded of him, "Where? I require that you tell me. Where?"

"I have looked everywhere," he said, so low that Matrena had to come nearer to understand his whisper. "Everything is shut tight. And there is no one about."

Matrena looked at Rouletabille with all the power of her eyes, as though she would discover his inmost thoughts, but his clear glance did not waver, and she saw there was nothing he wished to hide. Then Matrena pointed her finger at Natacha's chamber.

"You have not gone in there?" she inquired.

He replied, "It is not necessary to enter there."

"I will enter there, myself, nevertheless," said she, and she set her teeth.

He barred her way with his arms spread out.

"If you hold the life of someone dear," said he, "don't go a step farther."

"But the person is in that chamber. The person is there! It is there you will find out!" And she waved him aside with a gesture as though she were sleepwalking.

To recall her to the reality of what he had said to her and to make her understand what he desired, he had to grip her wrist in the vice of his nervous hand.

"The person is not there, perhaps," he said, shaking his head. "Understand me now."

But she did not understand him. She said:

"Since the person is nowhere else, the person must be there."

But Rouletabille continued obstinately:

"No, no. Perhaps he is gone."

"Gone! And everything locked on the inside!"

"That is not a reason," he replied.

But she could not follow his thoughts any further. She wished absolutely to make her way into Natacha's chamber. The obsession of that was upon her.

"If you enter there," said he, "and if (as is most probable) you don't find what you seek there, all is lost! And as to me, I give up the whole thing."

She sank in a heap onto a chair.

"Don't despair," he murmured. "We don't know for sure yet."

She shook her poor old head dejectedly.

"We know that only she is here, since no one has been able to enter and since no one has been able to leave."

That, in truth, filled her brain, prevented her from discerning in any corner of her mind the thought of Rouletabille. Then the impossible dialogue resumed.

"I repeat that we do not know but that the person has gone," repeated the reporter, and demanded her keys.

"Foolish," she said. "What do you want them for?"

"To search outside as we have searched inside."

"Why, everything is locked on the inside!"

"Madame, once more, that is no reason that the person may not be outside."

He consumed five minutes opening the door of the veranda, so many were his precautions. She watched him impatiently.

He whispered to her:

"I am going out, but don't you lose sight of the little sitting-room. At the least movement call me; fire a revolver if you need to."

He slipped into the garden with the same precautions for silence. From the corner that she kept to, through the doors left open, Matrena could follow all the movements of the reporter and watch Natacha's chamber at the same time. The attitude of Rouletabille continued to confuse her beyond all expression. She watched what he did as if she thought him besotted. The dyernick on guard out in the roadway also watched the young man through the bars of the gate in consternation, as though he thought him a fool. Along the paths of beaten earth or cement which offered no chance for footprints Rouletabille hurried silently. Around him he noted that the grass of the lawn had not been trodden. And then he paid no more attention to his steps. He seemed to study attentively the rosy color in the east, breathing the delicacy of dawning morning in the Isles, amid the silence of the earth, which still slumbered.

Bare-headed, face thrown back, hands behind his back, eyes raised and fixed, he made a few steps, then suddenly stopped as if he had been given an electric shock. As soon as he seemed to have recovered from that shock he turned around and went a few steps back to another path, into which he advanced, straight ahead, his face high, with the same fixed look that he had had up to the time he so suddenly stopped, as if something or someone advised or warned him not to go further. He continually worked back toward the house, and thus he traversed all the paths that led from the villa, but in all these excursions he took pains not to place himself in the field of vision from Natacha's window, a restricted field because of its location just around an abutment of the building. To ascertain about this window he crept on all-fours up to the garden-edge that ran along the foot of the wall and had sufficient proof that no one had jumped out that way. Then he went to rejoin Matrena in the veranda.

"No one has come into the garden this morning," said he, "and no one has gone out of the villa into the garden. Now I am going to look outside the grounds. Wait here; I'll be back in five minutes."

He went away, knocked discreetly on the window of the lodge and waited some seconds. Ermolai came out and opened the gate for him. Matrena moved to the threshold of the little sitting-room and watched Natacha's door with horror. She felt her legs give under her, she could not stand up under the diabolic thought of such a crime. Ah, that arm, that arm! reaching out, making its way, with a little shining phial in its hand. Pains of Christ! What could there be in the damnable books over which Natacha and her companions pored that could make such abominable crimes possible? Ah, Natacha, Natacha! it was from her that she would have desired the answer, straining her almost to stifling on her rough bosom and strangling her with her own strong hand that she might not hear the response. Ah, Natacha, Natacha, whom she had loved so much! She sank to the floor, crept across the carpet to the door, and lay there, stretched like a beast, and buried her head in her arms while she wept over her daughter. Natacha, Natacha, whom she had cherished as her own child, and who did not hear her. Ah, what use that the little fellow had gone to search outside when the whole truth lay behind this door? Thinking of him, she was embarrassed lest he should find her in that animalistic posture, and she rose to her knees and worked her way over to the window that looked out upon the Neva. The angle of the slanting blinds let her see well enough what passed outside, and what she saw made her spring to her feet. Below her the reporter was going through the same incomprehensible maneuvers that she had seen him do in the garden. Three pathways led to the little road that ran along the wall of the villa by the bank of the Neva. The young man, still with his hands behind his back and with his face up, took them one after the other. In the first he stopped at the first step. He didn't take more than two steps in the second. In the third, which cut obliquely toward the right and seemed to run to the bank nearest Krestowsky Ostrow, she saw him advance slowly at first, then more quickly among the small trees and hedges. Once only he stopped and looked closely at the trunk of a tree against which he seemed to pick out something invisible, and then he continued to the bank. There he sat down on a stone and appeared to reflect, and then suddenly he cast off his jacket and trousers, picked out a certain place on the bank across from him, finished undressing and plunged into the stream. She saw at once that he swam like a porpoise, keeping beneath and showing his head from time to time, breathing, then diving below the surface again. He reached Krestowsky Ostrow in a clump of reeds. Then he disappeared. Below him, surrounded by trees, could be seen the red tiles of the villa which sheltered Boris and Michael. From that villa a person could see the window of the sitting-room in General Trebassof's residence, but not what might occur along the bank of the river just below its walls. An isvotchick drove along the distant route of Krestowsky, conveying in his carriage a company of young officers and young women who had been feasting and who sang as they rode; then deep silence ensued. Matrena's eyes searched for Rouletabille, but could not find him. How long was he going to stay hidden like that? She pressed her face against the chill window. What was she waiting for? She waited perhaps for someone to make a move on this side, for the door near her to open and the traitorous figure of The Other to appear.

A hand touched her carefully. She turned.

Rouletabille was there, his face all scarred by red scratches, without collar or neck-tie, having hastily resumed his clothes. He appeared furious as he surprised her in his disarray. She let him lead her as though she were a child. He drew her to his room and closed the door.

"Madame," he commenced, "it is impossible to work with you. Why in the world have you wept not two feet from your step-daughter's door? You and your Koupriane, you commence to make me regret the Faubourg Poissoniere, you know. Your step-daughter has certainly heard you. It is lucky that she attaches no importance at all to your nocturnal phantasmagorias, and that she has been used to them a long time. She has more sense than you, Mademoiselle Natacha has. She sleeps, or at least she pretends to sleep, which leaves everybody in peace. What reply will you give her if it happens that she asks you the reason today for your marching and counter-marching up and down the sitting-room and complains that you kept her from sleeping?"

Matrena only shook her old, old head.

"No, no, she has not heard me. I was there like a shadow, like a shadow of myself. She will never hear me. No one hears a shadow."

Rouletabille felt returning pity for her and spoke more gently.

"In any case, it is necessary, you must understand, that she should attach no more importance to what you have done tonight than to the things she knows of your doing other nights. It is not the first time, is it, that you have wandered in the sitting-room? You understand me? And tomorrow, madame, embrace her as you always have."

"No, not that," she moaned. "Never that. I could not."

"Why not?"

Matrena did not reply. She wept. He took her in his arms like a child consoling its mother.

"Don't cry. Don't cry. All is not lost. Someone did leave the villa this morning."

"Oh, little domovoi! How is that? How is that? How did you find that out?"

"Since we didn't find anything inside, it was certainly necessary to find something outside."

"And you have found it?"

"Certainly."

"The Virgin protect you!"

"She is with us. She will not desert us. I will even say that I believe she has a special guardianship over the Isles. She watches over them from evening to morning."

"What are you saying?"

"Certainly. You don't know what we call in France 'the watchers of the Virgin'?"

"Oh, yes, they are the webs that the dear little beasts of the good God spin between the trees and that. . ."

"Exactly. You understand me and you will understand further when you know that in the garden the first thing that struck me across the face as I went into it was these watchers of the Virgin spun by the dear little spiders of the good God. At first when I felt them on my face I said to myself, 'Hold on, no one has passed this way,' and so I went to search other places. The webs stopped me everywhere in the garden. But, outside the garden, they kept out of the way and let me pass undisturbed down a pathway which led to the Neva. So then I said to myself, 'Now, has the Virgin by accident overlooked her work in this pathway? Surely not. Someone has ruined it.' I found the shreds of them hanging to the bushes, and so I reached the river."

"And you threw yourself into the river, my dear angel. You swim like a little god."

"And I landed where the other landed. Yes, there were the reeds all freshly broken. And I slipped in among the bushes."

"Where to?"

"Up to the Villa Krestowsky, madame—where they both live."

"Ah, it was from there someone came?"

There was a silence between them.

She questioned:

"Boris?"

"Someone who came from the villa and who returned there. Boris or Michael, or another. They went and returned through the reeds. But in coming they used a boat; they returned by swimming."

Her customary agitation reasserted itself.

She demanded ardently:

"And you are sure that he came here and that he left here?"

"Yes, I am sure of it."

"How?"

"By the sitting-room window."

"It is impossible, for we found it locked."

"It is possible, if someone closed it behind him."

"Ah!"

She commenced to tremble again, and, falling back into her nightmarish horror, she no longer wasted fond expletives on her domovoi as on a dear little angel who had just rendered a service ten times more precious to her than life. While he listened patiently, she said brutally:

"Why did you keep me from throwing myself on him, from rushing upon him as he opened the door? Ah, I would have, I would have. . . we would know."

"No. At the least noise he would have closed the door. A turn of the key and he would have escaped forever. And he would have been warned."

"Careless boy! Why then, if you knew he was going to come, didn't you leave me in the bedroom and you watch below yourself?"

"Because so long as I was below he would not have come. He only comes when there is no one downstairs."

"Ah, Saints Peter and Paul pity a poor woman. Who do you think it is, then? Who do you think it is? I can't think any more. Tell me, tell me that. You ought to know—you know everything. Come—who? I demand the truth. Who? Still some agent of the Committee, of the Central Committee? Still the Nihilists?"

"If it was only that!" said Rouletabille quietly.

"You have sworn to drive me mad! What do you mean by your 'if it was only that'?"

Rouletabille, imperturbable, did not reply.

"What have you done with the potion?" said he.

"The potion? The glass of the crime! I have locked it in my room, in the cupboard—safe, safe!"

"Ah, but, madame, it is necessary to replace it where you took it from."

"What!"

"Yes, after having poured the poison into a phial, to wash the glass and fill it with another potion."

"You are right. You think of everything. If the general wakes and wants his potion, he must not be suspicious of anything, and he must be able to have his drink."

"It is not necessary that he should drink."

"Well, then, why have the drink there?"

"So that the person can be sure, madame, that if he has not drunk it is simply because he has not wished to. A pure chance, madame, that he is not poisoned. You understand me this time?"

"Yes, yes. O Christ! But how now, if the general wakes and wishes to drink his narcotic?"

"Tell him I forbid it. And here is another thing you must do. When— Someone—comes into the general's chamber, in the morning, you must quite openly and naturally throw out the potion, useless and vapid, you see, and so Someone will have no right to be astonished that the general continues to enjoy excellent health."

"Yes, yes, little one; you are wiser than King Solomon. And what will I do with the phial of poison?"

"Bring it to me."

"Right away."

She went for it and returned five minutes later.

"He is still asleep. I have put the glass on the table, out of his reach. He will have to call me."

"Very good. Then push the door to, close it; we have to talk things over."

"But if someone goes back up the servants' staircase?"

"Be easy about that. They think the general is poisoned already. It is the first care-free moment I have been able to enjoy in this house."

"When will you stop making me shake with horror, little demon! You keep your secret well, I must say. The general is sleeping better than if he really were poisoned. But what shall we do about Natacha? I dare ask you that—you and you alone."

"Nothing at all."

"How—nothing?"

"We will watch her. . ."

"Ah, yes, yes."

"Still, Matrena, you let me watch her by myself."

"Yes, yes, I promise you. I will not pay any attention to her. That is promised. That is promised. Do as you please. Why, just now, when I spoke of the Nihilists to you, did you say, 'If it were only that!'? You believe, then, that she is not a Nihilist? She reads such things—things like on the barricades. . ."

"Madame, madame, you think of nothing but Natacha. You have promised me not to watch her; promise me not to think about her."

"Why, why did you say, 'If it was only that!'?"

"Because, if there were only Nihilists in your affair, dear madame, it would be too simple, or, rather, it would have been more simple. Can you possibly believe, madame, that simply a Nihilist, a Nihilist who was only a Nihilist, would take pains that his bomb exploded from a vase of flowers?—that it would have mattered where, so long as it overwhelmed the general? Do you imagine that the bomb would have had less effect behind the door than in front of it? And the little cavity under the floor, do you believe that a genuine revolutionary, such as you have here in Russia, would amuse himself by penetrating to the villa only to draw out two nails from a board, when one happens to give him time between two visits to the dining-room? Do you suppose that a revolutionary who wished to avenge the dead of Moscow and who could succeed in getting so far as the door behind which General Trebassof slept would amuse himself by making a little hole with a pin in order to draw back the bolt and amuse himself by pouring poison into a glass? Why, in such a case, he would have thrown his bomb outright, whether it blew him up along with the villa, or he was arrested on the spot, or had to submit to the martyrdom of the dungeons in the Fortress of SS. Peter and Paul, or be hung at Schlusselburg. Isn't that what always happens? That is the way he would have done, and not have acted like a hotel-rat! Now, there is someone in your home (or who comes to your home) who acts like a hotel-rat because he does not wish to be seen, because he does not wish to be discovered, because he does not wish to be taken in the act. Now, the moment that he fears nothing so much as to be taken in the act, so that he plays all these tricks of legerdemain, it is certain that his object lies beyond the act itself, beyond the bomb, beyond the poison. Why all this necessity for bombs of deferred explosion, for clockwork placed where it will be confused with other things, and not on a bare staircase forbidden to everybody, though you visit it twenty times a day?"

"But this man comes in as he pleases by day and by night? You don't answer. You know who he is, perhaps?"

"I know him, perhaps, but I am not sure who it is yet."

"You are not curious, little domovoi doukh! A friend of the house, certainly, and who enters the house as he wishes, by night, because someone opens the window for him. And who comes from the Krestowsky Villa! Boris or Michael! Ah, poor miserable Matrena! Why don't they kill poor Matrena? Their general! Their general! And they are soldiers—soldiers who come at night to kill their general. Aided by—by whom? Do you believe that? You? Light of my eyes! you believe that! No, no, that is not possible! I want you to understand, monsieur le domovoi, that I am not able to believe anything so horrible. No, no, by Jesus Christ Who died on the Cross, and Who searches our hearts, I do not believe that Boris—who, however, has very advanced ideas, I admit—it is necessary not to forget that; very advanced; and who composes very advanced verses also, as I have always told him—I will not believe that Boris is capable of such a fearful crime. As to Michael, he is an honest man, and my daughter, my Natacha, is an honest girl. Everything looks very bad, truly, but I do not suspect either Michael or Boris or my pure and beloved Natacha (even though she has made a translation into French of very advanced verses, certainly most improper for the daughter of a general). That is what lies at the bottom of my mind, the bottom of my heart—you have understood me perfectly, little angel of paradise? Ah, it is you the general owes his life to, that Matrena owes her life. Without you this house would already be a coffin. How shall I ever reward you? You wish for nothing! I annoy you! You don't even listen to me! A coffin—we would all be in our coffins! Tell me what you desire. All that I have belongs to you!"

"I desire to smoke a pipe.

"Ah, a pipe! Do you want some yellow perfumed tobacco that I receive every month from Constantinople, a treat right from the harem? I will get enough for you, if you like it, to smoke ten thousand pipes full."

"I prefer caporal," replied Rouletabille. "But you are right. It is not wise to suspect anybody. See, watch, wait. There is always time, once the game is caught, to say whether it is a hare or a wild boar. Listen to me, then, my good mamma. We must know first what is in the phial. Where is it?"

"Here it is."

She drew it from her sleeve. He stowed it in his pocket.

"You wish the general a good appetite, for me. I am going out. I will be back in two hours at the latest. And, above all, don't let the general know anything. I am going to see one of my friends who lives in the Aptiekarski pereolek."[1]

"Depend on me, and get back quickly for love of me. My blood clogs in my heart when you are not here, dear servant of God."

She mounted to the general's room and came down at least ten times to see if Rouletabille had not returned. Two hours later he was around the villa, as he had promised. She could not keep herself from running to meet him, for which she was scolded.

"Be calm. Be calm. Do you know what was in the phial?"

"No."

"Arsenate of soda, enough to kill ten people."

"Holy Mary!"

"Be quiet. Go upstairs to the general."

Feodor Feodorovitch was in charming humor. It was his first good night since the death of the youth of Moscow. He attributed it to his not having touched the narcotic and resolved, once more, to give up the narcotic, a resolve Rouletabille and Matrena encouraged. During the conversation there was a knock at the door of Matrena's chamber. She ran to see who was there, and returned with Natacha, who wished to embrace her father. Her face showed traces of fatigue. Certainly she had not passed as good a night as her father, and the general reproached her for looking so downcast.

"It is true. I had dreadful dreams. But you, papa, did you sleep well? Did you take your narcotic?"

"No, no, I have not touched a drop of my potion."

"Yes, I see. Oh, well, that is all right; that is very good. Natural sleep must be coming back. . ."

Matrena, as though hypnotized by Rouletabille, had taken the glass from the table and ostentatiously carried it to the dressing-room to throw it out, and she delayed there to recover her self-possession.

Natacha continued:

---

1. The little street of the apothecaries.

"You will see, papa, that you will be able to live just like everyone else finally. The great thing was to clear away the police, the atrocious police; wasn't it, Monsieur Rouletabille?"

"I have always said, for myself, that I am entirely of Mademoiselle Natacha's mind. You can be entirely reassured now, and I shall leave you feeling reassured. Yes, I must think of getting my interviews done quickly, and departing. Ah well, I can only say what I think. Run things yourselves and you will not run any danger. Besides, the general gets much better, and soon I shall see you all in France, I hope. I must thank you now for your friendly hospitality."

"Ah, but you are not going? You are not going!" Matrena had already set herself to protest with all the strenuous torrent of words in her poor desolated heart, when a glance from the reporter cut short her despairing utterances.

"I shall have to remain a week still in the city. I have engaged a chamber at the Hotel de France. It is necessary. I have so many people to see and to receive. I will come to make you a little visit from time to time."

"You are then quite easy," demanded the general gravely, "at leaving me all alone?"

"Entirely easy. And, besides, I don't leave you all alone. I leave you with Madame Trebassof and Mademoiselle. I repeat: All three of you stay as I see you now. No more police, or, in any case, the fewest possible."

"He is right, he is right," repeated Natacha again.

At this moment there were fresh knocks at the door of Matrena's chamber. It was Ermolai, who announced that his Excellency the Marshal of the Court, Count Keltzof, wished to see the general, acting for His Majesty.

"Go and receive the Count, Natacha, and tell him that your father will be downstairs in a moment."

Natacha and Rouletabille went down and found the Count in the drawing-room. He was a magnificent specimen, handsome and big as one of the Swiss papal guard. He seemed watchful in all directions and all among the furniture, and was quite evidently disquieted. He advanced immediately to meet the young lady, inquiring the news.

"It is all good news," replied Natacha. "Everybody here is splendid. The general is quite gay. But what news have you, monsieur le marechal? You appear preoccupied."

The marshal had pressed Rouletabille's hand.

"And my grapes?" he demanded of Natacha.

"How, your grapes? What grapes?"

"If you have not touched them, so much the better. I arrived here very anxious. I brought you yesterday, from Krasnoie-Coelo, some of the Emperor's grapes that Feodor Feodorovitch enjoyed so much. Now this morning I learned that the eldest son of Doucet, the French head-gardener of the Imperial conservatories at Krasnoie, had died from eating those grapes, which he had taken from those gathered for me to bring here. Imagine my dismay. I knew, however, that at the general's table, grapes would not be eaten without having been washed, but I reproached myself for not having taken the precaution of leaving word that Doucet recommend that they be washed thoroughly. Still, I don't suppose it would matter. I couldn't see how my gift could be dangerous, but when I learned of little Doucet's death this morning, I jumped into the first train and came straight here."

"But, your Excellency," interrupted Natacha, "we have not seen your grapes."

"Ah, they have not been served yet? All the better. Thank goodness!"

"The Emperor's grapes are diseased, then?" interrogated Rouletabille. "Phylloxera pest has got into the conservatories?"

"Nothing can stop it, Doucet told me. So he didn't want me to leave last evening until he had washed the grapes. Unfortunately, I was pressed for time and I took them as they were, without any idea that the mixture they spray on the grapes to protect them was so deadly. It appears that in the vineyard country they have such accidents every year. They call it, I think, the. . . the mixture. . ."

"The Bordeaux mixture," was heard in Rouletabille's trembling voice "And do you know what it is, Your Excellency, this Bordeaux mixture?"

"Why, no."

At this moment the general came down the stairs, clinging to the banister and supported by Matrena Petrovna.

"Well," continued Rouletabille, watching Natacha, "the Bordeaux mixture which covered the grapes you brought the general yesterday was nothing more nor less than arsenate of soda."

"Ah, God!" cried Natacha.

As for Matrena Petrovna, she uttered a low exclamation and let go the general, who almost fell down the staircase. Everybody rushed. The general laughed. Matrena, under the stringent look of Rouletabille, stammered that she had suddenly felt faint. At last they were all together in the veranda. The general settled back on his sofa and inquired:

"Well, now, were you just saying something, my dear marshal, about some grapes you have brought me?"

"Yes, indeed," said Natacha, quite frightened, "and what he said isn't pleasant at all. The son of Doucet, the court gardener, has just been poisoned by the same grapes that monsieur le marschal, it appears, brought you."

"Where was this? Grapes? What grapes? I haven't seen any grapes!" exclaimed Matrena. "I noticed you, yesterday, marshal, out in the garden, but you went away almost immediately, and I certainly was surprised that you did not come in. What is this story?"

"Well, we must clear this matter up. It is absolutely necessary that we know what happened to those grapes."

"Certainly," said Rouletabille, "they could cause a catastrophe."

"If it has not happened already," fretted the marshal.

"But how? Where are they? Whom did you give them to?"

"I carried them in a white cardboard box, the first one that came to hand in Doucet's place. I came here the first time and didn't find you. I returned again with the box, and the general was just lying down. I was pressed for my train and Michael Nikolaievitch and Boris Alexandrovitch were in the garden, so I asked them to execute my commission, and I laid the box down near them on the little garden table, telling them not to forget to tell you it was necessary to wash the grapes as Doucet expressly recommended."

"But it is unbelievable! It is terrible!" quavered Matrena. "Where can the grapes be? We must know."

"Absolutely," approved Rouletabille.

"We must ask Boris and Michael," said Natacha. "Good God! surely they have not eaten them! Perhaps they are sick."

"Here they are," said the general. All turned. Michael and Boris were coming up the steps. Rouletabille, who was in a shadowed corner under the main staircase, did not lose a single play of muscle on the two faces which for him were two problems to solve. Both faces were smiling; too smiling, perhaps.

"Michael! Boris! Come here," cried Feodor Feodorovitch. "What have you done with the grapes from monsieur le marechal?"

They both looked at him upon this brusque interrogation, seemed not to understand, and then, suddenly recalling, they declared very naturally that they had left them on the garden table and had not thought about them.

"You forgot my caution, then?" said Count Kaltzof severely.

"What caution?" said Boris. "Oh, yes, the washing of the grapes. Doucet's caution."

"Do you know what has happened to Doucet with those grapes? His eldest son is dead, poisoned. Do you understand now why we are anxious to know what has become of my grapes?"

"But they ought to be out there on the table," said Michael.

"No one can find them anywhere," declared Matrena, who, no less than Rouletabille, watched every change in the countenances of the two officers. "How did it happen that you went away yesterday evening without saying good-bye, without seeing us, without troubling yourselves whether or not the general might need you?"

"Madame," said Michael, coldly, in military fashion, as though he replied to his superior officer himself, "we have ample excuse to offer you and the general. It is necessary that we make an admission, and the general will pardon us, I am sure. Boris and I, during the promenade, happened to quarrel. That quarrel was in full swing when we reached here and we were discussing the way to end it most promptly when monsieur le marechal entered the garden. We must make that our excuse for giving divided attention to what he had to say. As soon as he was gone we had only one thought, to get away from here to settle our difference with arms in our hands."

"Without speaking to me about it!" interrupted Trehassof. "I never will pardon that."

"You fight at such a time, when the general is threatened! It is as though you fought between yourselves in the face of the enemy. It is treason!" added Matrena.

"Madame," said Boris, "we did not fight. Someone pointed out our fault, and I offered my excuses to Michael Nikolaievitch, who generously accepted them. Is that not so, Michael Nikolaievitch?"

"And who is this that pointed out your fault?" demanded the marshal.

"Natacha."

"Bravo, Natacha. Come, embrace me, my daughter."

The general pressed his daughter effusively to his broad chest.

"And I hope you will not have further disputing," he cried, looking over Natacha's shoulder.

"We promise you that, General," declared Boris. "Our lives belong to you."

"You did well, my love. Let us all do as well. I have passed an excellent night, messieurs. Real sleep! I have had just one long sleep."

"That is so," said Matrena slowly. "The general had no need of narcotic. He slept like a child and did not touch his potion."

"And my leg is almost well."

"All the same, it is singular that those grapes should have disappeared," insisted the marshal, following his fixed idea.

"Ermolai," called Matrena.

The old servant appeared.

"Yesterday evening, after these gentlemen had left the house, did you notice a small white box on the garden table?"

"No, Barinia."

"And the servants? Have any of them been sick? The dvornicks? The schwitzar? In the kitchens? No one sick? No? Go and see; then come and tell me."

He returned, saying, "No one sick."

Like the marshal, Matrena Petrovna and Feodor Feodorovitch looked at one another, repeating in French, "No one sick! That is strange!"

Rouletabille came forward and gave the only explanation that was plausible—for the others.

"But, General, that is not strange at all. The grapes have been stolen and eaten by some domestic, and if the servant has not been sick it is simply that the grapes monsieur le marechal brought escaped the spraying of the Bordeaux mixture. That is the whole mystery."

"The little fellow must be right," cried the delighted marshal.

"He is always right, this little fellow," beamed Matrena, as proudly as though she had brought him into the world.

But "the little fellow," taking advantage of the greetings as Athanase Georgevitch and Ivan Petrovitch arrived, left the villa, gripping in his pocket the phial which held what is required to make grapes flourish or to kill a general who is in excellent health. When he had gone a few hundred steps toward the bridges one must cross to go into the city, he was overtaken by a panting dvornick, who brought him a letter that had just come by courier. The writing on the envelope was entirely unknown to him. He tore it open and read, in excellent French:

"Request to M. Joseph Rouletabille not to mix in matters that do not concern him. The second warning will be the last." It was signed: "The Central Revolutionary Committee."

"So, ho!" said Rouletabille, slipping the paper into his pocket, "that's the line it takes, is it! Happily I have nothing more to occupy myself with at all. It is Koupriane's turn now! Now to go to Koupriane's!"

On this date, Rouletabille's note-book: "Natacha to her father: 'But you, papa, have you had a good night? Did you take your narcotic?'

"Fearful, and (lest I confuse heaven and hell) I have no right to take any further notes."[2]

---

2. As a matter of fact, after this day no more notes are found in Rouletabille's memorandum-book. The last one is that above, bizarre and romantic, and necessary, as Sainclair, the Paris advocate and friend of Rouletabille, indicates opposite it in the papers from which we have taken all the details of this story.

VIII

The Little Chapel of the Guards

Rouletabille took a long walk which led him to the Troitsky Bridge, then, re-descending the Naberjnaia, he reached the Winter Palace. He seemed to have chased away all preoccupation, and took a child's pleasure in the different aspects of the life that characterizes the city of the Great Peter. He stopped before the Winter Palace, walked slowly across the square where the prodigious monolith of the Alexander Column rises from its bronze socket, strolled between the palace and the colonnades, passed under an immense arch: everything seemed Cyclopean to him, and he never had felt so tiny, so insignificant. None the less he was happy in his insignificance, he was satisfied with himself in the presence of these colossal things; everything pleased him this morning. The speed of the isvos, the bickering humor of the osvotchicks, the elegance of the women, the fine presences of the officers and their easy naturalness under their uniforms, so opposed to the wooden posturing of the Berlin military men whom he had noticed at the "Tilleuls" and in the Friederichstrasse between two trains. Everything enchanted him—the costume even of the moujiks, vivid blouses, the red shirts over the trousers, the full legs and the boots up to the knees, even the unfortunates who, in spite of the soft atmosphere, were muffled up in sheepskin coats, all impressed him favorably, everything appeared to him original and congenial.

Order reigned in the city. The guards were polite, decorative and superb in bearing. The passers-by in that quarter talked gayly among themselves, often in French, and had manners as civilized as anywhere in the world. Where, then, was the Bear of the North? He never had seen bears so well licked. Was it this very city that only yesterday was in revolution? This was certainly the Alexander Park where troops a few weeks before had fired on children who had sought refuge in the trees, like sparrows. Was this the very pavement where the Cossacks had left so many bodies? Finally he saw before him the Nevsky Prospect, where the bullets rained like hail not long since upon a people dressed for festivities and very joyous. Nichevo! Nichevo! All that was so soon forgotten. They forgot yesterday as they forget tomorrow.

The Nihilists? Poets, who imagined that a bomb could accomplish anything in that Babylon of the North more important than the noise of its explosion! Look at these people who pass. They have no more thought for the old attack than for those now preparing in the shadow of the "tracktirs." Happy men, full of serenity in this bright quarter, who move about their affairs and their pleasures in the purest air, the lightest, the most transparent on earth. No, no; no one knows the joy of mere breathing if he has not breathed the air there, the finest in the north of the world, which gives food and drink of beautiful white eau-de-vie and yellow pivo, and strikes the blood and makes one a beast vigorous and joyful and fatalistic, and mocks at the Nihilists and, as well, at the ten thousand eyes of the police staring from under the porches of houses, from under the skulls of dvornicks—all police, the dvornicks; all police, also the joyous concierges with extended hands. Ah, ah, one mocks at it all in such air, provided one has roubles in one's pockets, plenty of roubles, and that one is not besotted by reading those extraordinary books that preach the happiness of all humanity to students and to poor girl-students too. Ah, ah, seed of the Nihilists, all that! These poor little fellows and poor little girls who have their heads turned by lectures that they cannot digest! That is all the trouble, the digestion. The digestion is needed. Messieurs the commercial travelers for champagne, who talk together importantly in the lobbies of the Grand Morskaia Hotel and who have studied the Russian people even in the most distant cities where champagne is sold, will tell you that over any table of hors-d'oeuvres, and will regulate the whole question of the Revolution between two little glasses of vodka, swallowed properly, quickly, elbow up, at a single draught, in the Russian manner. Simply an affair of digestion, they tell you. Who is the fool that would dare compare a young gentleman who has well digested a bottle of champagne or two, and another young man who has poorly digested the lucubrations of, who shall we say?—the lucubrations of the economists? The economists? The economists! Fools who compete which can make the most violent statements! Those who read them and don't understand them go off like a bomb! Your health! Nichevo! The world goes round still, doesn't it?

Discussion political, economic, revolutionary, and other in the room where they munch hors-d'oeuvres! You will hear it all as you pass through the hotel to your chamber, young Rouletabille. Get quickly now to the home of Koupriane, if you don't wish to arrive there at luncheon-time; then you would have to put off these serious affairs until evening.

The Department of Police. Massive entrance, heavily guarded, a great lobby, halls with swinging doors, many obsequious schwitzars on the lookout for tips, many poor creatures sitting against the walls on dirty benches, desks and clerks, brilliant boots and epaulets of gay young officers who are telling tales of the Aquarium with great relish.

"Monsieur Rouletabille! Ah, yes. Please be seated. Delighted, M. Koupriane will be very happy to receive you, but just at this moment he is at inspection. Yes, the inspection of the police dormitories in the barracks. We will take you there. His own idea! He doesn't neglect anything, does he? A great Chief. Have you seen the police-guards' dormitory? Admirable! The first dormitories of the world. We say that without wishing to offend France. We love France. A great nation! I will take you immediately to M. Koupriane. I shall be delighted."

"I also," said Rouletabille, who put a rouble into the honorable functionary's hand.

"Permit me to precede you."

Bows and salutes. For two roubles he would have walked obsequiously before him to the end of the world.

"These functionaries are admirable," thought Rouletabille as he was led to the barracks. He felt he had not paid too much for the services of a personage whose uniform was completely covered with lace. They tramped, they climbed, they descended. Stairways, corridors. Ah, the barracks at last. He seemed to have entered a convent. Beds very white, very narrow, and images of the Virgin and saints everywhere, monastic neatness and the most absolute silence. Suddenly an order sounded in the corridor outside, and the police-guard, who sprang from no one could tell where, stood to attention at the head of their beds. Koupriane and his aide appeared. Koupriane looked at everything closely, spoke to each man in turn, called them by their names, inquired about their needs, and the men stammered replies, not knowing what to answer, reddening like children. Koupriane observed Rouletabille. He dismissed his aide with a gesture. The inspection was over. He drew the young man into a little room just off the dormitory. Rouletabille, frightened, looked about him. He found himself in a chapel. This little chapel completed the effect of the guards' dormitory. It was all gilded, decorated in marvelous colors, thronged with little ikons that bring happiness, and, naturally, with the portrait of the Tsar, the dear Little Father.

"You see," said Koupriane, smiling at Rouletabille's amazement, "we deny them nothing. We give them their saints right here in their quarters." Closing the door, he drew a chair toward Rouletabille and motioned him to sit down. They sat before the little altar loaded with flowers, with colored paper and winged saints.

"We can talk here without being disturbed," he said. "Yonder there is such a crowd of people waiting for me. I'm ready to listen."

"Monsieur," said Rouletabille, "I have come to give you the report of my mission here, and to terminate my connection with it. All that is left for clearing this obscure affair is to arrest the guilty person, with which I have nothing to do. That concerns you. I simply inform you that someone tried to poison the general last night by pouring arsenate of soda into his sleeping-potion, which I bring you in this phial, arsenate which was secured most probably by washing it from grapes brought to General Trebassof by the marshal of the court, and which disappeared without anyone being able to say how."

"Ah, ah, a family affair, a plot within the family. I told you so," murmured Koupriane.

"The affair at least has happened within the family, as you think, although the assassin came from outside. Contrary to what you may be able to believe, he does not live in the house."

"Then how does he get there?" demanded Koupriane.

"By the window of the room overlooking the Neva. He has often come that way. And that is the way he returns also, I am sure. It is there you can take him if you act with prudence."

"How do you know he often comes that way?"

"You know the height of the window above the little roadway. To reach it he uses a water-trough, whose iron rings are bent, and also the marks of a grappling-iron that he carries with him and uses to hoist himself to the window are distinctly visible on the ironwork of the little balcony outside. The marks are quite obviously of different dates."

"But that window is closed."

"Someone opens it for him."

"Who, if you please?"

"I have no desire to know."

"Eh, yes. It necessarily is Natacha. I was sure that the Villa des Iles had its viper. I tell you she doesn't dare leave her nest because she knows she is watched. Not one of her movements outside escapes us! She knows it. She has been warned. The last time she ventured outside alone was to go into the old quarters of Derewnia. What has she to do in such a rotten quarter? I ask you that. And she turned in her tracks without seeing anyone, without knocking at a single door, because she saw that she was followed. She isn't able to get to see them outside, therefore she has to see them inside."

"They are only one, and always the same one."

"Are you sure?"

"An examination of the marks on the wall and on the pipe doesn't leave any doubt of it, and it is always the same grappling-iron that is used for the window."

"The viper!"

"Monsieur Koupriane, Mademoiselle Natacha seems to preoccupy you exceedingly. I did not come here to talk about Mademoiselle Natacha. I came to point out to you the route used by the man who comes to do the murder."

"Eh, yes, it is she who opens the way."

"I can't deny that."

"The little demon! Why does she take him into her room at night? Do you think perhaps there is some love-affair. . . ?"

"I am sure of quite the opposite."

"I too. Natacha is not a wanton. Natacha has no heart. She has only a brain. And it doesn't take long for a brain touched by Nihilism to get so it won't hesitate at anything."

Koupriane reflected a minute, while Rouletabille watched him in silence.

"Have we solely to do with Nihilism?" resumed Koupriane. "Everything you tell me inclines me more and more to my idea: a family affair, purely in the family. You know, don't you, that upon the general's death Natacha will be immensely rich?"

"Yes, I know it," replied Rouletabille, in a voice that sounded singular to the ear of the Chief of Police and which made him raise his head.

"What do you know?"

"I? Nothing," replied the reporter, this time in a firmer tone. "I ought, however, to say this to you: I am sure that we are dealing with Nihilism. . ."

"What makes you believe it?"

"This."

And Rouletabille handed Koupriane the message he had received that same morning.

"Oh, oh," cried Koupriane. "You are under watch! Look out."

"I have nothing to fear; I'm not bothering myself about anything further. Yes, we have an affair of the revolutionaries, but not of the usual kind. The way they are going about it isn't like one of their young men that the Central Committee arms with a bomb and who is sacrificed in advance."

"Where are the tracks that you have traced?"

"Right up to the little Krestowsky Villa."

Koupriane bounded from his chair.

"Occupied by Boris. Parbleu! Now we have them. I see it all now. Boris, another cracked brain! And he is engaged. If he plays the part of the Revolutionaries, the affair would work out big for him."

"That villa," said Rouletabille quietly, "is also occupied by Michael Korosakoff."

"He is the most loyal, the most reliable soldier of the Tsar."

"No one is ever sure of anything, my dear Monsieur Koupriane."

"Oh, I am sure of a man like that."

"No man is ever sure of any man, my dear Monsieur Koupriane."

"I am, in every case, for those I employ."

"You are wrong."

"What do you say?"

"Something that can serve you in the enterprise you are going to undertake, because I trust you can catch the murderer right in his nest. To do that, I'll not conceal from you that I think your agents will have to be enormously clever. They will have to watch the datcha des Iles at night, without anyone possibly suspecting it. No more maroon coats with false astrakhan trimmings, eh? But Apaches, Apaches on the wartrail, who blend themselves with the ground, with the trees, with the stones in the roadway. But among those Apaches don't send that agent of your Secret Service who watched the window while the assassin climbed to it."

"What?"

"Why, these climbs that you can read the proofs of on the wall and on the iron forgings of the balcony went on while your agents, night and day, were watching the villa. Have you noticed, monsieur, that it was always the same agent who took the post at night, behind the villa, under the window? General Trebassof's book in which he kept a statement of the exact disposal of each of your men during the period of siege was most instructive on that point. The other posts changed in turn, but the same agent, when he was among the guard, demanded always that same post, which was not disputed by anybody, since it is no fun to pass the hours of the night behind a wall, in an empty field. The others much preferred to roll away the time watching in the villa or in front of the lodge, where vodka and Crimean wine, kwass and pivo, kirsch and tchi, never ran short. That agent's name is Touman."

"Touman! Impossible! He is one of the best agents from Kiew. He was recommended by Gounsovski."

Rouletabille chuckled.

"Yes, yes, yes," grumbled the Chief of Police. "Someone always laughs when his name is mentioned."

Koupriane had turned red. He rose, opened the door, gave a long direction in Russian, and returned to his chair.

"Now," said he, "go ahead and tell me all the details of the poison and the grapes the marshal of the court brought. I'm listening."

Rouletabille told him very briefly and without drawing any deductions all that we already know. He ended his account as a man dressed in a maroon coat with false astrakhan was introduced. It was the same man Rouletabille had met in General Trebassof's drawing-room and who spoke French. Two gendarmes were behind him. The door had been closed. Koupriane turned toward the man in the coat.

"Touman," he said, "I want to talk to you. You are a traitor, and I have proof. You can confess to me, and I will give you a thousand roubles and you can take yourself off to be hanged somewhere else."

The man's eyes shrank, but he recovered himself quickly. He replied in Russian.

"Speak French. I order it," commanded Koupriane.

"I answer, Your Excellency," said Touman firmly, "that I don't know what Your Excellency means."

"I mean that you have helped a man get into the Trebassof villa by night when you were on guard under the window of the little sitting-room. You see that there is no use deceiving us any longer. I play with you frankly, good play, good money. The name of that man, and you have a thousand roubles."

"I am ready to swear on the ikon of. . ."

"Don't perjure yourself."

"I have always loyally served. . ."

"The name of that man."

"I still don't know yet what Your Excellency means."

"Oh, you understand me," replied Koupriane, who visibly held in an anger that threatened to break forth any moment. "A man got into the house while you were watching. . ."

"I never saw anything. After all, it is possible. There were some very dark nights. I went back and forth."

"You are not a fool. The name of that man."

"I assure you, Excellency. . ."

"Strip him."

"What are you going to do?" cried Rouletabille.

But already the two guards had thrown themselves on Touman and had drawn off his coat and shirt. The man was bare to the waist.

"What are you going to do? What are you going to do?"

"Leave them alone," said Koupriane, roughly pushing Rouletabille back.

Seizing a whip which hung at the waist of the guards he struck Touman a blow across the shoulders that drew blood. Touman, mad with the outrage and the pain, shouted, "Yes, it is true! I brag of it!"

Koupriane did not restrain his rage. He showered the unhappy man with blows, having thrown Rouletabille to the end of the room when he tried to interfere. And while he proceeded with the punishment the Chief of Police hurled at the agent who had betrayed him an accompaniment of fearful threats, promising him that before he was hanged he should rot in the bottom-most dungeon of Peter and Paul, in the slimy pits lying under the Neva. Touman, between the two guards who held him, and who sometimes received blows on the rebound that were not intended for them, never uttered a complaint. Outside the invectives of Koupriane there was heard only the swish of the cords and the cries of Rouletabille, who continued to protest that it was abominable, and called the Chief of Police a savage. Finally the savage stopped. Gouts of blood had spattered all about.

"Monsieur," said Rouletabille, who supported himself against the wall. "I shall complain to the Tsar."

"You are right," Koupriane replied, "but I feel relieved now. You can't imagine the harm this man can have done to us in the weeks he has been here."

Touman, across whose shoulders they had thrown his coat and who lay now across a chair, found strength to look up and say:

"It is true. You can't do me as much harm as I have done you, whether you think so or not. All the harm that can be done me by you and yours is already accomplished. My name is not Touman, but Matiev. Listen. I had a son that was the light of my eyes. Neither my son nor I had ever been concerned with politics. I was employed in Moscow. My son was a student. During the Red Week we went out, my son and I, to see a little of what was happening over in the Presnia quarter. They said everybody had been killed over there! We passed before the Presnia gate. Soldiers called to us to stop because they wished to search us. We opened our coats. The soldiers saw my son's student waistcoat and set up a cry. They unbuttoned the vest, drew a note-book out of his pocket and they found a workman's song in it that had been published in the Signal. The soldiers didn't know how to read. They believed the paper was a proclamation, and they arrested my son. I demanded to be arrested with him. They pushed me away. I ran to the governor's house. Trebassof had me thrust away from his door with blows from the butt-ends of his Cossacks' guns. And, as I persisted, they kept me locked up all that night and the morning of the next day. At noon I was set free. I demanded my son and they replied they didn't know what I was talking about. But a soldier that I recognized as having arrested my son the evening before pointed out a van that was passing, covered with a tarpaulin and surrounded by Cossacks. 'Your son is there,' he said; 'they are taking him to the graves.' Mad with despair, I ran after the van. It went to the outskirts of Golountrine cemetery. There I saw in the white snow a huge grave, wide, deep. I shall see it to my last minute. Two vans had already stopped near the hole. Each van held thirteen corpses. The vans were dumped into the trench and the soldiers commenced to sort the bodies into rows of six. I watched for my son. At last I recognized him in a body that half hung over the edge of the trench. Horrors of suffering were stamped in the expression of his face. I threw myself beside him. I said that I was his father. They let me embrace him a last time and count his wounds. He had fourteen. Someone had stolen the gold chain that had hung about his neck and held the picture of his mother, who died the year before. I whispered into his ear, I swore to avenge him. Forty-eight hours later I had placed myself at the disposition of the Revolutionary Committee. A week had not passed before Touman, whom, it seems, I resemble and who was one of the Secret Service agents in Kiew, was assassinated in the train that was taking him to St. Petersburg. The assassination was kept a secret. I received all his papers and I took his place with you. I was doomed beforehand and I asked nothing better, so long as I might last until after the execution of Trebassof. Ah, how I longed to kill him with my own hands! But another had already been assigned the duty and my role was to help him. And do you suppose I am going to tell you the name of that other? Never! And if you discover that other, as you have discovered me, another will come, and another, and another, until Trebassof has paid for his crimes. That is all I have to say to you, Koupriane. As for you, my little fellow," added he, turning to Rouletabille, "I wouldn't give much for your bones. Neither of you will last long. That is my consolation."

Koupriane had not interrupted the man. He looked at him in silence, sadly.

"You know, my poor man, you will be hanged now?" he said.

"No," growled Rouletabille. "Monsieur Koupriane, I'll bet you my purse that he will not be hanged."

"And why not?" demanded the Chief of rolice, while, upon a sign from him, they took away the false Touman.

"Because it is I who denounced him."

"What a reason! And what would you like me to do?"

"Guard him for me; for me alone, do you understand?"

"In exchange for what?"

"In exchange for the life of General Trebassof, if I must put it that way."

"Eh? The life of General Trebassof! You speak as if it belonged to you, as if you could dispose of it."

Rouletabille laid his hand on Koupriane's arm.

"Perhaps that's so," said he.

"Would you like me to tell you one thing, Monsieur Rouletabille? It is that General Trebassof's life, after what has just escaped the lips of this Touman, who is not Touman, isn't worth any more than—than yours if you remain here. Since you are disposed not to do anything more in this affair, take the train, monsieur, take the train, and go."

Rouletabille walked back and forth, very much worked up; then suddenly he stopped short.

"Impossible," he said. "It is impossible. I cannot; I am not able to go yet."

"Why?"

"Good God, Monsieur Koupriane, because I have to interview the President of the Duma yet, and complete my little inquiry into the politics of the cadets."

"Oh, indeed!"

Koupriane looked at him with a sour grin.

"What are you going to do with that man?" demanded Rouletabille.

"Have him fixed up first."

"And then?"

"Then take him before the judges."

"That is to say, to the gallows?"

"Certainly."

"Monsieur Koupriane, I offer it to you again. Life for life. Give me the life of that poor devil and I promise you General Trebassof's."

"Explain yourself."

"Not at all. Do you promise me that you will maintain silence about the case of that man and that you will not touch a hair of his head?"

Koupriane looked at Rouletabille as he had looked at him during the altercation they had on the edge of the Gulf. He decided the same way this time.

"Very well," said he. "You have my word. The poor devil!"

"You are a brave man, Monsieur Koupriane, but a little quick with the whip. . ."

"What would you expect? One's work teaches that."

"Good morning. No, don't trouble to show me out. I am compromised enough already," said Rouletabille, laughing.

"Au revoir, and good luck! Get to work interviewing the President of the Duma," added Koupriane knowingly, with a great laugh.

But Rouletabille was already gone.

"That lad," said the Chief of Police aloud to himself, "hasn't told me a bit of what he knows."

IX

ANNOUCHKA

"And now it's between us two, Natacha," murmured Rouletabille as soon as he was outside. He hailed the first carriage that passed and gave the address of the datcha des Iles. When he got in he held his head between his hands; his face burned, his jaws were set. But by a prodigious effort of his will he resumed almost instantly his calm, his self-control. As he went back across the Neva, across the bridge where he had felt so elated a little while before, and saw the isles again he sighed heavily. "I thought I had got it all over with, so far as I was concerned, and now I don't know where it will stop." His eyes grew dark for a moment with somber thoughts and the vision of the Lady in Black rose before him; then he shook his head, filled his pipe, lighted it, dried a tear that had been caused doubtless by a little smoke in his eye, and stopped sentimentalizing. A quarter of an hour later he gave a true Russian nobleman's fist-blow in the back to the coachman as an intimation that they had reached the Trebassof villa. A charming picture was before him. They were all lunching gayly in the garden, around the table in the summer-house. He was astonished, however, at not seeing Natacha with them. Boris Mourazoff and Michael Korsakoff were there. Rouletabille did not wish to be seen. He made a sign to Ermolai, who was passing through the garden and who hurried to meet him at the gate.

"The Barinia," said the reporter, in a low voice and with his finger to his lips to warn the faithful attendant to caution.

In two minutes Matrena Petrovna joined Rouletabille in the lodge.

"Well, where is Natacha?" he demanded hurriedly as she kissed his hands quite as though she had made an idol of him.

"She has gone away. Yes, out. Oh, I did not keep her. I did not try to hold her back. Her expression frightened me, you can understand, my little angel. My, you are impatient! What is it about? How do we stand? What have you decided? I am your slave. Command me. Command me. The keys of the villa?"

"Yes, give me a key to the veranda; you must have several. I must be able to get into the house tonight if it becomes necessary."

She drew a key from her gown, gave it to the young man and said a few words in Russian to Ermolai, to enforce upon him that he must obey the little domovoi-doukh in anything, day or night.

"Now tell me where Natacha has gone."

"Boris's parents came to see us a little while ago, to inquire after the general. They have taken Natacha away with them, as they often have done. Natacha went with them readily enough. Little domovoi, listen to me, listen to Matrena Petrovna—Anyone would have said she was expecting it!"

"Then she has gone to lunch at their house?"

"Doubtless, unless they have gone to a cafe. I don't know. Boris's father likes to have the family lunch at the Barque when it is fine. Calm yourself, little domovoi. What ails you? Bad news, eh? Any bad news?"

"No, no; everything is all right. Quick, the address of Boris's family."

"The house at the corner of La Place St. Isaac and la rue de la Poste."

"Good. Thank you. Adieu."

He started for the Place St. Isaac, and picked up an interpreter at the Grand Morskaia Hotel on the way. It might be useful to have him. At the Place St. Isaac he learned the Morazoffs and Natacha Trebassof had gone by train for luncheon at Bergalowe, one of the nearby stations in Finland.

"That is all," said he, and added apart to himself, "And perhaps that is not true."

He paid the coachman and the interpreter, and lunched at the Brasserie de Vienne nearby. He left there a half-hour later, much calmer. He took his way to the Grand Morskaia Hotel, went inside and asked the schwitzar:

"Can you give me the address of Mademoiselle Annouchka?"

"The singer of the Krestowsky?"

"That is who I mean."

"She had luncheon here. She has just gone away with the prince."

Without any curiosity as to which prince, Rouletabille cursed his luck and again asked for her address.

"Why, she lives in an apartment just across the way."

Rouletabille, feeling better, crossed the street, followed by the interpreter that he had engaged. Across the way he learned on the landing of the first floor that Mademoiselle Annouchka was away for the day. He descended, still followed by his interpreter, and recalling how someone had told him that in Russia it was always profitable to be generous, he gave five roubles to the interpreter and asked him for some information about Mademoiselle Annouchka's life in St. Petersburg. The interpreter whispered:

"She arrived a week ago, but has not spent a single night in her apartment over there."

He pointed to the house they had just left, and added:

"Merely her address for the police."

"Yes, yes," said Rouletabille, "I understand. She sings this evening, doesn't she?"

"Monsieur, it will be a wonderful debut."

"Yes, yes, I know. Thanks."

All these frustrations in the things he had undertaken that day instead of disheartening him plunged him deep into hard thinking. He returned, his hands in his pockets, whistling softly, to the Place St. Isaac, walked around the church, keeping an eye on the house at the corner, investigated the monument, went inside, examined all its details, came out marveling, and finally went once again to the residence of the Mourazoffs, was told that they had not yet returned from the Finland town, then went and shut himself in his room at the hotel, where he smoked a dozen pipes of tobacco. He emerged from his cloud of smoke at dinner-time.

At ten that evening he stepped out of his carriage before the Krestowsky. The establishment of Krestowsky, which looms among the Isles much as the Aquarium does, is neither a theater, nor a music-hall, nor a cafe-concert, nor a restaurant, nor a public garden; it is all of these and some other things besides. Summer theater, winter theater, open-air theater, hall for spectacles, scenic mountain, exercise-ground, diversions of all sorts, garden promenades, cafes, restaurants, private dining-rooms, everything is combined here that can amuse, charm, lead to the wildest orgies, or provide those who never think of sleep till toward three or four o'clock of a morning the means to await the dawn with patience. The most celebrated companies of the old and the new world play there amid an enthusiasm that is steadily maintained by the foresight of the managers: Russian and foreign dancers, and above all the French chanteuses, the little dolls of the cafes-concerts, so long as they are young, bright, and elegantly dressed, may meet their fortune there. If there is no such luck, they are sure at least to find every evening some old beau, and often some officer, who willingly pays twenty-five roubles for the sole pleasure of having a demoiselle born on the banks of the Seine for his companion at the supper-table. After their turn at the singing, these women display their graces and their eager smiles in the promenades of the garden or among the tables where the champagne-drinkers sit. The head-liners, naturally, are not driven to this wearying perambulation, but can go away to their rest if they are so inclined. However, the management is appreciative if they accept the invitation of some dignitary of the army, of administration, or of finance, who seeks the honor of hearing from the chanteuse, in a private room and with a company of friends not disposed to melancholy, the Bohemian songs of the Vieux Derevnia. They sing, they loll, they talk of Paris, and above all they drink. If sometimes the little fete ends rather roughly, it is the friendly and affectionate champagne that is to blame, but usually the orgies remain quite innocent, of a character that certainly might trouble the temperance societies but need not make M. le Senateur Berenger feel involved.

A war whose powder fumes reeked still, a revolution whose last defeated growls had not died away at the period of these events, had not at all diminished the nightly gayeties of Kretowsky. Many of the young men who displayed their uniforms that evening and called their "Nichevo" along the brilliantly lighted paths of the public gardens, or filled the open-air tables, or drank vodka at the buffets, or admired the figures of the wandering soubrettes, had come here on the eve of their departure for the war and had returned with the same child-like, enchanted smile, the same ideal of futile joy, and kissed their passing comrades as gayly as ever. Some of them had a sleeve lying limp now, or walked with a crutch, or even on a wooden leg, but it was, all the same, "Nichevo!"

The crowd this evening was denser than ordinarily, because there was the chance to hear Annouchka again for the first time since the somber days of Moscow. The students were ready to give her an ovation, and no one opposed it, because, after all, if she sang now it was because the police were willing at last. If the Tsar's government had granted her her life, it was not in order to compel her to die of hunger. Each earned a livelihood as was possible. Annouchka only knew how to sing and dance, and so she must sing and dance!

When Rouletabille entered the Krestowsky Gardens, Annouchka had commenced her number, which ended with a tremendous "Roussalka." Surrounded by a chorus of male and female dancers in the national dress and with red boots, striking tambourines with their fingers, then suddenly taking a rigid pose to let the young woman's voice, which was of rather ordinary register, come out, Annouchka had centered the attention of the immense audience upon herself. All the other parts of the establishment were deserted, the tables had been removed, and a panting crowd pressed about the open-air theater. Rouletabille stood up on his chair at the moment tumultuous "Bravos" sounded from a group of students. Annouchka bowed toward them, seeming to ignore the rest of the audience, which had not dared declare itself yet. She sang the old peasant songs arranged to present-day taste, and interspersed them with dances. They had an enormous success, because she gave her whole soul to them and sang with her voice sometimes caressing, sometimes menacing, and sometimes magnificently desperate, giving much significance to words which on paper had not aroused the suspicions of the censor. The taste of the day was obviously still a taste for the revolution, which retained its influence on the banks of the Neva. What she was doing was certainly very bold, and apparently she realized how audacious she was, because, with great adroitness, she would bring out immediately after some dangerous phrase a patriotic couplet which everybody was anxious to applaud. She succeeded by such means in appealing to all the divergent groups of her audience and secured a complete triumph for herself. The students, the revolutionaries, the radicals and the cadets acclaimed the singer, glorifying not only her art but also and beyond everything else the sister of the engineer Volkousky, who had been doomed to perish with her brother by the bullets of the Semenovsky regiment. The friends of the Court on their side could not forget that it was she who, in front of the Kremlin, had struck aside the arm of Constantin Kochkarof, ordered by the Central Revolutionary Committee to assassinate the Grand Duke Peter Alexandrovitch as he drove up to the governor's house in his sleigh. The bomb burst ten feet away, killing Constantin Kochkarof himself. It may be that before death came he had time to hear Annouchka cry to him, "Wretch! You were told to kill the prince, not to assassinate his children." As it happened, Peter Alexandrovitch held on his knees the two little princesses, seven and eight years old. The Court had wished to recompense her for that heroic act. Annouchka had spit at the envoy of the Chief of Police who called to speak to her of money. At the Hermitage in Moscow, where she sang then, some of her admirers had warned her of possible reprisals on the part of the revolutionaries. But the revolutionaries gave her assurance at once that she had nothing to fear. They approved her act and let her know that they now counted on her to kill the Grand Duke some time when he was alone; which had made Annouchka laugh. She was an enfant terrible, whose friends no one knew, who passed for very wise, and whose lines of intrigue were inscrutable. She enjoyed making her hosts in the private supper-rooms quake over their meal. One day she had said bluntly to one of the most powerful tchinovnicks of Moscow: "You, my old friend, you are president of the Black Hundred. Your fate is sealed. Yesterday you were condemned to death by the delegates of the Central Committee at Presnia. Say your prayers." The man reached for champagne. He never finished his glass. The dvornicks carried him out stricken with apoplexy. Since the time she saved the little grand-duchesses the police had orders to allow her to act and talk as she pleased. She had been mixed up in the deepest plots against the government. Those who lent the slightest countenance to such plottings and were not of the police simply disappeared. Their friends dared not even ask for news of them. The only thing not in doubt about them was that they were at hard labor somewhere in the mines of the Ural Mountains. At the moment of the revolution Annouchka had a brother who was an engineer on the Kasan-Moscow line. This Volkousky was one of the leaders on the Strike Committee. The authorities had an eye on him. The revolution started. He, with the help of his sister, accomplished one of those formidable acts which will carry their memory as heroes to the farthest posterity. Their work accomplished, they were taken by Trebassof's soldiers. Both were condemned to death. Volkousky was executed first, and the sister was taking her turn when an officer of the government arrived on horseback to stop the firing. The Tsar, informed of her intended fate, had sent a pardon by telegraph. After that she disappeared. She was supposed to have gone on some tour across Europe, as was her habit, for she spoke all the languages, like a true Bohemian. Now she had reappeared in all her joyous glory at Krestowsky. It was certain, however, that she had not forgotten her brother. Gossips said that if the government and the police showed themselves so long-enduring they found it to their interest to do so. The open, apparent life Annouchka led was less troublesome to them than her hidden activities would be. The lesser police who surrounded the Chief of the St. Petersburg Secret Service, the famous Gounsovski, had meaning smiles when the matter was discussed. Among them Annouchka had the ignoble nickname, "Stool-pigeon."

Rouletabille must have been well aware of all these particulars concerning Annouchka, for he betrayed no astonishment at the great interest and the strong emotion she aroused. From the corner where he was he could see only a bit of the stage, and he was standing on tiptoes to see the singer when he felt his coat pulled. He turned. It was the jolly advocate, well known for his gastronomic feats, Athanase Georgevitch, along with the jolly Imperial councilor, Ivan Petrovitch, who motioned him to climb down.

"Come with us; we have a box."

Rouletabille did not need urging, and he was soon installed in the front of a box where he could see the stage and the public both. Just then the curtain fell on the first part of Annouchka's performance. The friends were soon rejoined by Thaddeus Tchitchnikoff, the great timber-merchant, who came from behind the scenes.

"I have been to see the beautiful Onoto," announced the Lithuanian with a great satisfied laugh. "Tell me the news. All the girls are sulking over Annouchka's success."

"Who dragged you into the Onoto's dressing-room then?" demanded Athanase.

"Oh, Gounsovski himself, my dear. He is very amateurish, you know."

"What! do you knock around with Gounsovski?"

"On my word, I tell you, dear friends, he isn't a bad acquaintance. He did me a little service at Bakou last year. A good acquaintance in these times of public trouble."

"You are in the oil business now, are you?"

"Oh, yes, a little of everything for a livelihood. I have a little well down Bakou way, nothing big; and a little house, a very small one for my small business."

"What a monopolist Thaddeus is," declared Athanase Georgevitch, hitting him a formidable slap on the thigh with his enormous hand. "Gounsovski has come himself to keep an eye on Annouchka's debut, eh? Only he goes into Onoto's dressing-room, the rogue."

"Oh, he doesn't trouble himself. Do you know who he is to have supper with? With Annouchka, my dears, and we are invited."

"How's that?" inquired the jovial councilor.

"It seems Gounsovski influenced the minister to permit Annouchka's performance by declaring he would be responsible for it all. He required from Annouchka solely that she have supper with him on the evening of her debut."

"And Annouchka consented?"

"That was the condition, it seems. For that matter, they say that Annouchka and Gounsovski don't get along so badly together. Gounsovski has done Annouchka many a good turn. They say he is in love with her."

"He has the air of an umbrella merchant," snorted Athanase Georgevitch.

"Have you seen him at close range?" inquired Ivan.

"I have dined at his house, though it is nothing to boast of, on my word."

"That is what he said," replied Thaddeus. "When he knew we were here together, he said to me: 'Bring him, he is a charming fellow who plies a great fork; and bring that dear man Ivan Petrovitch, and all your friends.'"

"Oh, I only dined at his house," grumbled Athanase, "because there was a favor he was going to do me."

"He does services for everybody, that man," observed Ivan Petrovitch.

"Of course, of course; he ought to," retorted Athanase. "What is a chief of Secret Service for if not to do things for everybody? For everybody, my dear friends, and a little for himself besides. A chief of Secret Service has to be in with everybody, with everybody and his father, as La Fontaine says (if you know that author), if he wants to hold his place. You know what I mean."

Athanase laughed loudly, glad of the chance to show how French he could be in his allusions, and looked at Rouletabille to see if he had been able to catch the tone of the conversation; but Rouletabille was too much occupied in watching a profile wrapped in a mantilla of black lace, in the Spanish fashion, to repay Athanase's performance with a knowing smile.

"You certainly have naive notions. You think a chief of Secret Police should be an ogre," replied the advocate as he nodded here and there to his friends.

"Why, certainly not. He needs to be a sheep in a place like that, a thorough sheep. Gounsovski is soft as a sheep. The time I dined with him he had mutton streaked with fat. He is just like that. I am sure he is mainly layers of fat. When you shake hands you feel as though you had grabbed a piece of fat. My word! And when he eats he wags his jaw fattishly. His head is like that, too; bald, you know, with a cranium like fresh lard. He speaks softly and looks at you like a kid looking to its mother for a juicy meal."

"But—why—it is Natacha!" murmured the lips of the young man.

"Certainly it is Natacha, Natacha herself," exclaimed Ivan Petrovitch, who had used his glasses the better to see whom the young French journalist was looking at. "Ah, the dear child! she has wanted to see Annouchka for a long time."

"What, Natacha! So it is. So it is. Natacha! Natacha!" said the others. "And with Boris Mourazoff's parents."

"But Boris is not there," sniggered Thaddeus Tehitchnikoff.

"Oh, he can't be far away. If he was there we would see Michael Korsakoff too. They keep close on each other's heels."

"How has she happened to leave the general? She said she couldn't bear to be away from him."

"Except to see Annouchka," replied Ivan. "She wanted to see her, and talked so about it when I was there that even Feodor Feodorovitch was rather scandalized at her and Matrena Petrovna reproved her downright rudely. But what a girl wishes the gods bring about. That's the way."

"That's so, I know," put in Athanase. "Ivan Petrovitch is right. Natacha hasn't been able to hold herself in since she read that Annouchka was going to make her debut at Krestowsky. She said she wasn't going to die without having seen the great artist."

"Her father had almost drawn her away from that crowd," affirmed Ivan, "and that was as it should be. She must have fixed up this affair with Boris and his parents."

"Yes, Feodor certainly isn't aware that his daughter's idea was to applaud the heroine of Kasan station. She is certainly made of stern stuff, my word," said Athanase.

"Natacha, you must remember, is a student," said Thaddeus, shaking his head; "a true student. They have misfortunes like that now in so many families. I recall, apropos of what Ivan said just now, how today she asked Michael Korsakoff, before me, to let her know where Annouchka would sing. More yet, she said she wished to speak to that artist if it were possible. Michael frowned on that idea, even before me. But Michael couldn't refuse her, any more than the others. He can reach Annouchka easier than anyone else. You remember it was he who rode hard and arrived in time with the pardon for that beautiful witch; she ought not to forget him if she cared for her life."

"Anyone who knows Michael Nikolaievitch knows that he did his duty promptly," announced Athanase Georgevitch crisply. "But he would not have gone a step further to save Annouchka. Even now he won't compromise his career by being seen at the home of a woman who is never from under the eyes of Gounsovski's agents and who hasn't been nicknamed 'Stool-pigeon' for nothing."

"Then why do we go to supper tonight with Annouchka?" asked Ivan.

"That's not the same thing. We are invited by Gounsovski himself. Don't forget that, if stories concerning it drift about some day, my friends," said Thaddeus.

"For that matter, Thaddeus, I accept the invitation of the honorable chief of our admirable Secret Service because I don't wish to slight him. I have dined at his house already. By sitting opposite him at a public table here I feel that I return that politeness. What do you say to that?"

"Since you have dined with him, tell us what kind of a man he is aside from his fattish qualities," said the curious councilor. "So many things are said about him. He certainly seems to be a man it is better to stand in with than to fall out with, so I accept his invitation. How could you manage to refuse it, anyway?"

"When he first offered me hospitality," explained the advocate, "I didn't even know him. I never had been near him. One day a police agent came and invited me to dinner by command—or, at least, I understood it wasn't wise to refuse the invitation, as you said, Ivan Petrovitch. When I went to his house I thought I was entering a fortress, and inside I thought it must be an umbrella shop. There were umbrellas everywhere, and goloshes. True, it was a day of pouring rain. I was struck by there being no guard with a big revolver in the antechamber. He had a little, timid schwitzar there, who took my umbrella, murmuring 'barine' and bowing over and over again. He conducted me through very ordinary rooms quite unguarded to an average sitting-room of a common kind. We dined with Madame Gounsovski, who appeared fattish like her husband, and three or four men whom I had never seen anywhere. One servant waited on us. My word!

"At dessert Gounsovski took me aside and told me I was unwise to 'argue that way.' I asked him what he meant by that. He took my hands between his fat hands and repeated, 'No, no, it is not wise to argue like that.' I couldn't draw anything else out of him. For that matter, I understood him, and, you know, since that day I have cut out certain side passages unnecessary in my general law pleadings that had been giving me a reputation for rather too free opinions in the papers. None of that at my age! Ah, the great Gounsovski! Over our coffee I asked him if he didn't find the country in pretty strenuous times. He replied that he looked forward with impatience to the month of May, when he could go for a rest to a little property with a small garden that he had bought at Asnieres, near Paris. When he spoke of their house in the country Madame Gounsovski heaved a sigh of longing for those simple country joys. The month of May brought tears to her eyes. Husband and wife looked at one another with real tenderness. They had not the air of thinking for one second: tomorrow or the day after, before our country happiness comes, we may find ourselves stripped of everything. No! They were sure of their happy vacation and nothing seemed able to disquiet them under their fat. Gounsovski has done everybody so many services that no one really wishes him ill, poor man. Besides, have you noticed, my dear old friends, that no one ever tries to work harm to chiefs of Secret Police? One goes after heads of police, prefects of police, ministers, grand-dukes, and even higher, but the chiefs of Secret Police are never, never attacked. They can promenade tranquilly in the streets or in the gardens of Krestowsky or breathe the pure air of the Finland country or even the country around Paris. They have done so many little favors for this one and that, here and there, that no one wishes to do them the least injury. Each person always thinks, too, that others have been less well served than he. That is the secret of the thing, my friends, that is the secret. What do you say?"

The others said: "Ah, ah, the good Gounsovski. He knows. He knows. Certainly, accept his supper. With Annouchka it will be fun."

"Messieurs," asked Rouletabille, who continued to make discoveries in the audience, "do you know that officer who is seated at the end of a row down there in the orchestra seats? See, he is getting up."

"He? Why, that is Prince Galitch, who was one of the richest lords of the North Country. Now he is practically ruined."

"Thanks, gentlemen; certainly it is he. I know him," said Rouletabille, seating himself and mastering his emotion.

"They say he is a great admirer of Annouchka," hazarded Thaddeus. Then he walked away from the box.

"The prince has been ruined by women," said Athanase Georgevitch, who pretended to know the entire chronicle of gallantries in the empire.

"He also has been on good terms with Gounsovski," continued Thaddeus.

"He passes at court, though, for an unreliable. He once made a long visit to Tolstoi."

"Bah! Gounsovski must have rendered some signal service to that imprudent prince," concluded Athanase. "But for yourself, Thaddeus, you haven't said what you did with Gounsovski at Bakou."

(Rouletabille did not lose a word of what was being said around him, although he never lost sight of the profile hidden in the black mantle nor of Prince Galitch, his personal enemy,[1] who reappeared, it seemed to him, at a very critical moment.)

"I was returning from Balakani in a drojki," said Thaddeus Tchitchnikoff, "and I was drawing near Bakou after having seen the debris of my oil shafts that had been burned by the Tartars, when I met Gounsovski in the road, who, with two of his friends, found themselves badly off with one of the wheels of their carriage broken. I stopped. He explained to me that he had a Tartar coachman, and that this coachman having seen an Armenian on the road before him, could find nothing better to do than run full tilt into the Armenian's equipage. He had reached over and taken the reins from him, but a wheel of the carriage was broken." (Rouletabille quivered, because he caught a glance of communication between Prince Galitch and Natacha, who was leaning over the edge of her box.) "So I offered to take Gounsovski and his friends into my carriage, and we rode all together to Bakou after Gounsovski, who always wishes to do a service, as Athanase Georgevitch says, had warned his Tartar coachman not to finish the Armenian." (Prince Galitch, at the moment the orchestra commenced the introductory music for Annouchka's new number, took advantage of all eyes being turned toward the rising curtain to pass near Natacha's seat. This time he did not look at Natacha, but Rouletabille was sure that his lips had moved as he went by her.)

Thaddeus continued: "It is necessary to explain that at Bakou my little house is one of the first before you reach the quay. I had some Armenian employees there. When arrived, what do you suppose I saw? A file of soldiers with cannon, yes, with a cannon, on my word, turned against my house and an officer saying quietly, 'there it is. Fire!'" (Rouletabille made yet another discovery—two, three discoveries. Near by, standing back of Natacha's seat, was a figure not unknown to the young reporter, and there, in one of the orchestra chairs, were two other men whose faces he had seen that same morning in Koupriane's barracks. Here was where a memory for faces stood him in good stead. He saw that he was not the

---

1. as told in "The Lady In Black."

only person keeping close watch on Natacha.) "When I heard what the officer said," Thaddeus went on, "I nearly dropped out of the drojki. I hurried to the police commissioner. He explained the affair promptly, and I was quick to understand. During my absence one of my Armenian employees had fired at a Tartar who was passing. For that matter, he had killed him. The governor was informed and had ordered the house to be bombarded, for an example, as had been done with several others. I found Gounsovski and told him the trouble in two words. He said it wasn't necessary for him to interfere in the affair, that I had only to talk to the officer. 'Give him a good present, a hundred roubles, and he will leave your house. I went back to the officer and took him aside; he said he wanted to do anything that he could for me, but that the order was positive to bombard the house. I reported his answer to Gounsovski, who told me: 'Tell him then to turn the muzzle of the cannon the other way and bombard the building of the chemist across the way, then he can always say that he mistook which house was intended.' I did that, and he had them turn the cannon. They bombarded the chemist's place, and I got out of the whole thing for the hundred roubles. Gounsovski, the good fellow, may be a great lump of fat and be like an umbrella merchant, but I have always been grateful to him from the bottom of my heart, you can understand, Athanase Georgevitch."

"What reputation has Prince Galitch at the court?" inquired Rouletabille all at once.

"Oh, oh!" laughed the others. "Since he went so openly to visit Tolstoi he doesn't go to the court any more."

"And—his opinions? What are his opinions?"

"Oh, the opinions of everybody are so mixed nowadays, nobody knows."

Ivan Petrovitch said, "He passes among some people as very advanced and very much compromised."

"Yet they don't bother him?" inquired Rouletabille.

"Pooh, pooh," replied the gay Councilor of Empire, "it is rather he who tries to mix with them."

Thaddeus stooped down and said, "They say that he can't be reached because of the hold he has over a certain great personage in the court, and it would be a scandal—a great scandal."

"Be quiet, Thaddeus," interrupted Athanase Georgevitch, roughly. "It is easy to see that you are lately from the provinces to speak so recklessly, but if you go on this way I shall leave."

"Athanase Georgevitch is right; hang onto your mouth, Thaddeus," counseled Ivan Petrovitch.

The talkers all grew silent, for the curtain was rising. In the audience there were mysterious allusions being made to this second number of Annouchka, but no one seemed able to say what it was to be, and it was, as a matter of fact, very simple. After the whirl-wind of dances and choruses and all the splendor with which she had been accompanied the first time, Annouchka appeared as a poor Russian peasant in a scene representing the barren steppes, and very simply she sank to her knees and recited her evening prayers. Annouchka was singularly beautiful. Her aquiline nose with sensitive nostrils, the clean-cut outline of her eyebrows, her look that now was almost tender, now menacing, always unusual, her pale rounded cheeks and the entire expression of her face showed clearly the strength of new ideas, spontaneity, deep resolution and, above all, passion. The prayer was passionate. She had an admirable contralto voice which affected the audience strangely from its very first notes. She asked God for daily bread for everyone in the immense Russian land, daily bread for the flesh and for the spirit, and she stirred the tears of everyone there, to which-ever party they belonged. And when, as her last note sped across the desolate steppe and she rose and walked toward the miserable hut, frantic bravos from a delirious audience told her the prodigious emotions she had aroused. Little Rouletabille, who, not understanding the words, nevertheless caught the spirit of that prayer, wept. Everybody wept. Ivan Petrovitch, Athanase Georgevitch, Thaddeus Tchitchnikoff were standing up, stamping their feet and clapping their hands like enthusiastic boys. The students, who could be easily distinguished by the uniform green edging they wore on their coats, uttered insensate cries. And suddenly there rose the first strains of the national hymn. There was hesitation at first, a wavering. But not for long. Those who had been dreading some counter-demonstration realized that no objection could possibly be raised to a prayer for the Tsar. All heads uncovered and the Bodje Taara Krari mounted, unanimously, toward the stars.

Through his tears the young reporter never gave up his close watch on Natacha. She had half risen, and, sinking back, leaned on the edge of the box. She called, time and time again, a name that Rouletabille could not hear in the uproar, but that he felt sure was "Annouchka! Annouchka!" "The reckless girl," murmured Rouletabille, and, profiting by the general excitement, he left the box without being noticed. He made his way through the crowd toward Natacha, whom he had sought futilely since morning. The audience, after clamoring in vain for a repetition of the prayer by Annouchka, commenced to disperse, and the reporter was swept along with them for a few moments. When he reached the range of boxes he saw that Natacha and the family she had been with were gone. He looked on all sides without seeing the object of his search and like a madman commenced to run through the passages, when a sudden idea struck his blood cold. He inquired where the exit for the artists was and as soon as it was pointed out, he hurried there. He was not mistaken. In the front line of the crowd that waited to see Annouchka come out he recognized Natacha, with her head enveloped in the black mantle so that none should see her face. Besides, this corner of the garden was in a half-gloom. The police barred the way; he could not approach as near Natacha as he wished. He set himself to slip like a serpent through the crowd. He was not separated from Natacha by more than four or five persons when a great jostling commenced. Annouchka was coming out. Cries rose: "Annouchka! Annouchka!" Rouletabille threw himself on his knees and on all-fours succeeded in sticking his head through into the way kept by the police for Annouchka's passage. There, wrapped in a great red mantle, his hat on his arm, was a man Rouletabille immediately recognized. It was Prince Galitch. They were hurrying to escape the impending pressure of the crowd. But Annouchka as she passed near Natacha stopped just a second—a movement that did not escape Rouletabille—and, turning toward her said just the one word, "Caracho." Then she passed on. Rouletabille got up and forced his way back, having once more lost Natacha. He searched for her. He ran to the carriage-way and arrived just in time to see her seated in a carriage with the Mourazoff family. The carriage started at once in the direction of the datcha des Iles. The young man remained standing there, thinking. He made a gesture as though he were ready now to let luck take its course. "In the end," said he, "it will be better so, perhaps," and then, to himself, "Now to supper, my boy."

He turned in his tracks and soon was established in the glaring light of the restaurant. Officers standing, glass in hand, were saluting from table to table and waving a thousand compliments with grace that was almost feminine.

He heard his name called joyously, and recognized the voice of Ivan Petrovitch. The three boon companions were seated over a bottle of champagne resting in its ice-bath and were being served with tiny pates while they waited for the supper-hour, which was now near.

Rouletabille yielded to their invitation readily enough, and accompanied them when the head-waiter informed Thaddeus that the gentlemen were desired in a private room. They went to the first floor and were ushered into a large apartment whose balcony opened on the hall of the winter-theater, empty now. But the apartment was already occupied. Before a table covered with a shining service Gounsovski did the honors.

He received them like a servant, with his head down, an obsequious smile, and his back bent, bowing several times as each of the guests were presented to him. Athanase had described him accurately enough, a mannikin in fat. Under the vast bent brow one could hardly see his eyes, behind the blue glasses that seemed always ready to fall as he inclined too far his fat head with its timid and yet all-powerful glance. When he spoke in his falsetto voice, his chin dropped in a fold over his collar, and he had a steady gesture with the thumb and index finger of his right hand to retain the glasses from sliding down his short, thick nose.

Behind him there was the fine, haughty silhouette of Prince Galitch. He had been invited by Annouchka, for she had consented to risk this supper only in company with three or four of her friends, officers who could not be further compromised by this affair, as they were already under the eye of the Okrana (Secret Police) despite their high birth. Gounsovski had seen them come with a sinister chuckle and had lavished upon them his marks of devotion.

He loved Annouchka. It would have sufficed to have surprised just once the jealous glance he sent from beneath his great blue glasses when he gazed at the singer to have understood the sentiments that actuated him in the presence of the beautiful daughter of the Black Land.

Annouchka was seated, or, rather, she lounged, Oriental fashion, on the sofa which ran along the wall behind the table. She paid attention to no one. Her attitude was forbidding, even hostile. She indifferently allowed her marvelous black hair that fell in two tresses over her shoulder to be caressed by the perfumed hands of the beautiful Onoto, who had heard her this evening for the first time and had thrown herself with enthusiasm into her arms after the last number. Onoto was an artist too, and the pique she felt at first over Annouchka's success could not last after the emotion aroused by the evening prayer before the hut. "Come to supper," Annouchka had said to her.

"With whom?" inquired the Spanish artist.

"With Gounsovski."

"Never."

"Do come. You will help me pay my debt and perhaps he will be useful to you as well. He is useful to everybody."

Decidedly Onoto did not understand this country, where the worst enemies supped together.

Rouletabille had been monopolized at once by Prince Galitch, who took him into a corner and said:

"What are you doing here?"

"Do I inconvenience you?" asked the boy.

The other assumed the amused smile of the great lord.

"While there is still time," he said, "believe me, you ought to start, to quit this country. Haven't you had sufficient notice?"

"Yes," replied the reporter. "And you can dispense with any further notice from this time on."

He turned his back.

"Why, it is the little Frenchman from the Trebassof villa," commenced the falsetto voice of Gounsovski as he pushed a seat towards the young man and begged him to sit between him and Athanase Georgevitch, who was already busy with the hors-d'oeuvres.

"How do you do, monsieur?" said the beautiful, grave voice of Annouchka.

Rouletabille saluted.

"I see that I am in a country of acquaintances," he said, without appearing disturbed.

He addressed a lively compliment to Annouchka, who threw him a kiss.

"Rouletabille!" cried la belle Onoto. "Why, then, he is the little fellow who solved the mystery of the Yellow Room."

"Himself."

"What are you doing here?"

"He came to save the life of General Trebassof," sniggered Gounsovski. "He is certainly a brave little young man."

"The police know everything," said Rouletabille coldly. And he asked for champagne, which he never drank.

The champagne commenced its work. While Thaddeus and the officers told each other stories of Bakou or paid compliments to the women, Gounsovski, who was through with raillery, leaned toward

Rouletabille and gave that young man fatherly counsel with great unction.

"You have undertaken, young man, a noble task and one all the more difficult because General Trebassof is condemned not only by his enemies but still more by the ignorance of Koupriane. Understand me thoroughly: Koupriane is my friend and a man whom I esteem very highly. He is good, brave as a warrior, but I wouldn't give a kopeck for his police. He has mixed in our affairs lately by creating his own secret police, but I don't wish to meddle with that. It amuses us. It's the new style, anyway; everybody wants his secret police nowadays. And yourself, young man, what, after all, are you doing here? Reporting? No. Police work? That is our business and your business. I wish you good luck, but I don't expect it. Remember that if you need any help I will give it you willingly. I love to be of service. And I don't wish any harm to befall you."

"You are very kind, monsieur," was all Rouletabille replied, and he called again for champagne.

Several times Gounsovski addressed remarks to Annouchka, who concerned herself with her meal and had little answer for him.

"Do you know who applauded you the most this evening?"

"No," said Annouchka indifferently.

"The daughter of General Trebassof."

"Yes, that is true, on my word," cried Ivan Petrovitch.

"Yes, yes, Natacha was there," joined in the other friends from the datcha des Iles.

"For me, I saw her weep," said Rouletabille, looking at Annouchka fixedly.

But Annouchka replied in an icy tone:

"I do not know her."

"She is unlucky in having a father. . ." Prince Galitch commenced.

"Prince, no politics, or let me take my leave," clucked Gounsovski. "Your health, dear Annouchka."

"Your health, Gounsovski. But you have no worry about that."

"Why?" demanded Thaddeus Tchitchnikoff in equivocal fashion.

"Because he is too useful to the government," cried Ivan Petrovitch.

"No," replied Annouchka; "to the revolutionaries."

All broke out laughing. Gounsovski recovered his slipping glasses by his usual quick movement and sniggered softly, insinuatingly, like fat boiling in the pot:

"So they say. And it is my strength."

"His system is excellent," said the prince. "As he is in with everybody, everybody is in with the police, without knowing it."

"They say. . . ah, ah. . . they say. . ." (Athanase was choking over a little piece of toast that he had soaked in his soup) "they say that he has driven away all the hooligans and even all the beggars of the church of Kasan."

Thereupon they commenced to tell stories of the hooligans, street-thieves who since the recent political troubles had infested St. Petersburg and whom nobody, could get rid of without paying for it.

Athanase Georgevitch said:

"There are hooligans that ought to have existed even if they never have. One of them stopped a young girl before Varsovie station. The girl, frightened, immediately held out her purse to him, with two roubles and fifty kopecks in it. The hooligan took it all. 'Goodness,' cried she, 'I have nothing now to take my train with.' 'How much is it?' asked the hooligan. 'Sixty kopecks.' 'Sixty kopecks! Why didn't you say so?' And the bandit, hanging onto the two roubles, returned the fifty-kopeck piece to the trembling child and added a ten-kopeck piece out of his own pocket."

"Something quite as funny happened to me two winters ago, at Moscow," said la belle Onoto. "I had just stepped out of the door when I was stopped by a hooligan. 'Give me twenty kopecks,' said the hooligan. I was so frightened that I couldn't get my purse open. 'Quicker,' said he. Finally I gave him twenty kopecks. 'Now,' said he then, 'kiss my hand.' And I had to kiss it, because he held his knife in the other."

"Oh, they are quick with their knives," said Thaddeus. "As I was leaving Gastinidvor once I was stopped by a hooligan who stuck a huge carving-knife under my nose. 'You can have it for a rouble and a half,' he said. You can believe that I bought it without any haggling. And it was a very good bargain. It was worth at least three roubles. Your health, belle Onoto."

"I always take my revolver when I go out," said Athanase. "It is more prudent. I say this before the police. But I would rather be arrested by the police than stabbed by the hooligans."

"There's no place any more to buy revolvers," declared Ivan Petrovitch. "All such places are closed."

Gounsovski settled his glasses, rubbed his fat hands and said:

"There are some still at my locksmith's place. The proof is that today in the little Kaniouche my locksmith, whose name is Smith, went into the house of the grocer at the corner and wished to sell him a revolver. It was a Browning. 'An arm of the greatest reliability,' he said to him, 'which never misses fire and which works very easily.' Having pronounced these words, the locksmith tried his revolver and lodged a ball in the grocer's lung. The grocer is dead, but before he died he bought the revolver. 'You are right,' he said to the locksmith; 'it is a terrible weapon.' And then he died."

The others laughed heartily. They thought it very funny. Decidedly this great Gounsovski always had a funny story. Who would not like to be his friend? Annouchka had deigned to smile. Gounsovski, in recognition, extended his hand to her like a mendicant. The young woman touched it with the end of her fingers, as if she were placing a twenty-kopeck piece in the hand of a hooligan, and withdrew from it with disgust. Then the doors opened for the Bohemians. Their swarthy troupe soon filled the room. Every evening men and women in their native costumes came from old Derevnia, where they lived all together in a sort of ancient patriarchal community, with customs that had not changed for centuries; they scattered about in the places of pleasure, in the fashionable restaurants, where they gathered large sums, for it was a fashionable luxury to have them sing at the end of suppers, and everyone showered money on them in order not to be behind the others. They accompanied on guzlas, on castanets, on tambourines, and sang the old airs, doleful and languorous, or excitable and breathless as the flight of the earliest nomads in the beginnings of the world.

When they had entered, those present made place for them, and Rouletabille, who for some moments had been showing marks of fatigue and of a giddiness natural enough in a young man who isn't in the habit of drinking the finest champagnes, profited by the diversion to get a corner of the sofa not far from Prince Galitch, who occupied the place at Annouchka's right.

"Look, Rouletabille is asleep," remarked la belle Onoto.

"Poor boy!" said Annouchka.

And, turning toward Gounsovski:

"Aren't you soon going to get him out of our way? I heard some of our brethren the other day speaking in a way that would cause pain to those who care about his health."

"Oh, that," said Gounsovski, shaking his head, "is an affair I have nothing to do with. Apply to Koupriane. Your health, belle Annouchka."

But the Bohemians swept some opening chords for their songs, and the singers took everybody's attention, everybody excepting Prince Galitch and Annouchka, who, half turned toward one another, exchanged some words on the edge of all this musical uproar. As for Rouletabille, he certainly must have been sleeping soundly not to have been waked by all that noise, melodious as it was. It is true that he had—apparently—drunk a good deal and, as everyone knows, in Russia drink lays out those who can't stand it. When the Bohemians had sung three times Gounsovski made a sign that they might go to charm other ears, and slipped into the hands of the chief of the band a twenty-five rouble note. But Onoto wished to give her mite, and a regular collection commenced. Each one threw roubles into the plate held out by a little swarthy Bohemian girl with crow-black hair, carelessly combed, falling over her forehead, her eyes and her face, in so droll a fashion that one would have said the little thing was a weeping-willow soaked in ink. The plate reached Prince Galitch, who futilely searched his pockets.

"Bah!" said he, with a lordly air, "I have no money. But here is my pocket-book; I will give it to you for a souvenir of me, Katharina."

Thaddeus and Athanase exclaimed at the generosity of the prince, but Annouchka said:

"The prince does as he should, for my friends can never sufficiently repay the hospitality that that little thing gave me in her dirty hut when I was in hiding, while your famous department was deciding what to do about me, my dear Gounsovski."

"Eh," replied Gounsovski, "I let you know that all you had to do was to take a fine apartment in the city."

Annouchka spat on the ground like a teamster, and Gounsovski from yellow turned green.

"But why did you hide yourself that way, Annouchka?" asked Onoto as she caressed the beautiful tresses of the singer.

"You know I had been condemned to death, and then pardoned. I had been able to leave Moscow, and I hadn't any desire to be re-taken here and sent to taste the joys of Siberia."

"But why were you condemned to death?"

"Why, she doesn't know anything!" exclaimed the others.

"Good Lord, I'm just back from London and Paris—how should I know anything! But to have been condemned to death! That must have been amusing."

"Very amusing," said Annouchka icily. "And if you have a brother whom you love, Onoto, think how much more amusing it must be to have him shot before you."

"Oh, my love, forgive me!"

"So you may know and not give any pain to your Annouchka in the future, I will tell you, madame, what happened to our dear friend," said Prince Galitch.

"We would do better to drive away such terrible memories," ventured Gounsovski, lifting his eyelashes behind his glasses, but he bent his head as Annouchka sent him a blazing glance.

"Speak, Galitch."

The Prince did as she said.

"Annouchka had a brother, Vlassof, an engineer on the Kasan line, whom the Strike Committee had ordered to take out a train as the only means of escape for the leaders of the revolutionary troops when Trebassof's soldiers, aided by the Semenowsky regiment, had become masters of the city. The last resistance took place at the station. It was necessary to get started. All the ways were guarded by the military. There were soldiers everywhere! Vlassof said to his comrades, 'I will save you;' and his comrades saw him mount the engine with a woman. That woman was—well, there she sits. Vlassof's fireman had been killed the evening before, on a barricade; it was Annouchka who took his place. They busied themselves and the train started like a shot. On that curved line, discovered at once, easy to attack, under a shower of bullets, Vlassof developed a speed of ninety versts an hour. He ran the indicator up to the explosion point. The lady over there continued to pile coal into the furnace. The danger came to be less from the military and more from an explosion at any moment. In the midst of the balls Vlassof kept his usual coolness. He sped not only with the firebox open but with the forced draught. It was a miracle that the engine was not smashed against the curve of the embankment. But they got past. Not a man was hurt. Only a woman was wounded. She got a ball in the chest."

"There!" cried Annouchka.

With a magnificent gesture she flung open her white and heaving chest, and put her finger on a scar that Gounsovski, whose fat began to melt in heavy drops of sweat about his temples, dared not look at.

"Fifteen days later," continued the prince, "Vlassof entered an inn at Lubetszy. He didn't know it was full of soldiers. His face never altered. They searched him. They found a revolver and papers on him. They knew whom they had to do with. He was a good prize. Vlassof was taken to Moscow and condemned to be shot. His sister, wounded as she was, learned of his arrest and joined him. 'I do not wish,' she said to him, 'to leave you to die alone.' She also was condemned. Before the execution the soldiers offered to bandage their eyes, but both refused, saying they preferred to meet death face to face. The orders were to shoot all the other condemned revolutionaries first, then Vlassof, then his sister. It was in vain that Vlassof asked to die last. Their comrades in execution sank to their knees, bleeding from their death wounds. Vlassof embraced his sister and walked to the place of death. There he addressed the soldiers: 'Now you have to carry out your duty according to the oath you have taken. Fulfill it honestly as I have fulfilled mine. Captain, give the order.' The volley sounded. Vlassof remained erect, his arms crossed on his breast, safe and sound. Not a ball had touched him. The soldiers did not wish to fire at him. He had to summon them again to fulfill their duty, and obey their chief. Then they fired again, and he fell. He looked at his sister with his eyes full of horrible suffering. Seeing that he lived, and wishing to appear charitable, the captain, upon Annouchka's prayers, approached and cut short his sufferings by firing a revolver into his ear. Now it was Annouchka's turn. She knelt by the body of her brother, kissed his bloody lips, rose and said, 'I am ready.' As the guns were raised, an officer came running, bearing the pardon of the Tsar. She did not wish it, and she whom they had not bound when she was to die had to be restrained when she learned she was to live."

Prince Galitch, amid the anguished silence of all there, started to add some words of comment to his sinister recital, but Annouchka interrupted:

"The story is ended," said she. "Not a word, Prince. If I asked you to tell it in all its horror, if I wished you to bring back to us the atrocious moment of my brother's death, it is so that monsieur" (her fingers pointed to Gounsovski) "shall know well, once for all, that if I have submitted for some hours now to this promiscuous company that has been imposed upon me, now that I have paid the debt by accepting this abominable supper, I have nothing more to do with this purveyor of bagnios and of hangman's ropes who is here."

"She is mad," he muttered. "She is mad. What has come over her? What has happened? Only today she was so, so amiable."

And he stuttered, desolately, with an embarrassed laugh:

"Ah, the women, the women! Now what have I done to her?"

"What have you done to me, wretch? Where are Belachof, Bartowsky and Strassof? And Pierre Slutch? All the comrades who swore with me to revenge my brother? Where are they? On what gallows did you have them hung? What mine have you buried them in? And still you follow your slavish task. And my friends, my other friends, the poor comrades of my artist life, the inoffensive young men who have not committed any other crime than to come to see me too often when I was lively, and who believed they could talk freely in my dressing-room—where are they? Why have they left me, one by one? Why have they disappeared? It is you, wretch, who watched them, who spied on them, making me, I haven't any doubt, your horrible accomplice, mixing me up in your beastly work, you dog! You knew what they call me. You have known it for a long time, and you may well laugh over it. But I, I never knew until this evening; I never learned until this evening all I owe to you. 'Stool pigeon! Stool pigeon!' I! Horror! Ah, you dog, you dog! Your mother, when you were brought into the world, your mother. . ." Here she hurled at him the most offensive insult that a Russian can offer a man of that race.

She trembled and sobbed with rage, spat in fury, and stood up ready to go, wrapped in her mantle like a great red flag. She was the statue of hate and vengeance. She was horrible and terrible. She was beautiful. At the final supreme insult, Gounsovski started and rose to his feet as though he had received an actual blow in the face. He did not look at Annouchka, but fixed his eyes on Prince Galitch. His finger pointed him out:

"There is the man," he hissed, "who has told you all these fine things."

"Yes, it is I," said the Prince, tranquilly.

"Caracho!" barked Gounsovski, instantaneously regaining his coolness.

"Ah, yes, but you'll not touch him," clamored the spirited girl of the Black Land; "you are not strong enough for that."

"I know that monsieur has many friends at court," agreed the chief of the Secret Service with an ominous calm. "I don't wish ill to monsieur. You speak, madame, of the way some of your friends have had to be sacrificed. I hope that some day you will be better informed, and that you will understand I saved all of them I could."

"Let us go," muttered Annouchka. "I shall spit in his face."

"Yes, all I could," replied the other, with his habitual gesture of hanging on to his glasses. "And I shall continue to do so. I promise you not to say anything more disagreeable to the prince than as regards his little friend the Bohemian Katharina, whom he has treated so generously just now, doubtless because Boris Mourazoff pays her too little for the errands she runs each morning to the villa of Krestowsky Ostrow."

At these words the Prince and Annouchka both changed countenance. Their anger rose. Annouchka turned her head as though to arrange the folds of her cloak. Galitch contented himself with shrugging his shoulders impatiently and murmuring:

"Still some other abomination that you are concocting, monsieur, and that we don't know how to reply to."

After which he bowed to the supper-party, took Annouchka's arm and had her move before him. Gounsovski bowed, almost bent in two. When he rose he saw before him the three astounded and horrified figures of Thaddeus Tchitchnikoff, Ivan Petrovitch and Athanase Georgevitch.

"Messieurs," he said to them, in a colorless voice which seemed not to belong to him, "the time has come for us to part. I need not say that we have supped as friends and that, if you wish it to be so, we can forget everything that has been said here."

The three others, frightened, at once protested their discretion. He added, roughly this time, "Service of the Tsar," and the three stammered, "God save the Tsar!" After which he saw them to the door. When the door had closed after them, he said, "My little Annouchka, you mustn't reckon without me." He hurried toward the sofa, where Rouletabille was lying forgotten, and gave him a tap on the shoulder.

"Come, get up. Don't act as though you were asleep. Not an instant to lose. They are going to carry through the Trebassof affair this evening."

Rouletabille was already on his legs.

"Oh, monsieur," said he, "I didn't want you to tell me that. Thanks all the same, and good evening."

He went out.

Gounsovski rang. A servant appeared.

"Tell them they may now open all the rooms on this corridor; I'll not hold them any longer." Thus had Gounsovski kept himself protected.

Left alone, the head of the Secret Service wiped his brow and drank a great glass of iced water which he emptied at a draught. Then he said:

"Koupriane will have his work cut out for him this evening; I wish him good luck. As to them, whatever happens, I wash my hands of them."

And he rubbed his hands.

X

A Drama in the Night

At the door of the Krestowsky Rouletabille, who was in a hurry for a conveyance, jumped into an open carriage where la belle Onoto was already seated. The dancer caught him on her knees.

"To Eliaguine, fast as you can," cried the reporter for all explanation.

"Scan! Scan! (Quickly, quickly)" repeated Onoto.

She was accompanied by a vague sort of person to whom neither of them paid the least attention.

"What a supper! You waked up at last, did you?" quizzed the actress. But Rouletabille, standing up behind the enormous coachman, urged the horses and directed the route of the carriage. They bolted along through the night at a dizzy pace. At the corner of a bridge he ordered the horses stopped, thanked his companions and disappeared.

"What a country! What a country! Caramba!" said the Spanish artist.

The carriage waited a few minutes, then turned back toward the city.

Rouletabille got down the embankment and slowly, taking infinite precautions not to reveal his presence by making the least noise, made his way to where the river is widest. Seen through the blackness of the night the blacker mass of the Trebassof villa loomed like an enormous blot, he stopped. Then he glided like a snake through the reeds, the grass, the ferns. He was at the back of the villa, near the river, not far from the little path where he had discovered the passage of the assassin, thanks to the broken cobwebs. At that moment the moon rose and the birch-trees, which just before had been like great black staffs, now became white tapers which seemed to brighten that sinister solitude.

The reporter wished to profit at once by the sudden luminance to learn if his movements had been noticed and if the approaches to the villa on that side were guarded. He picked up a small pebble and threw it some distance from him along the path. At the unexpected noise three or four shadowy heads were outlined suddenly in the white light of the moon, but disappeared at once, lost again in the dark tufts of grass.

He had gained his information.

The reporter's acute ear caught a gliding in his direction, a slight swish of twigs; then all at once a shadow grew by his side and he felt the cold of a revolver barrel on his temple. He said "Koupriane," and at once a hand seized his and pressed it.

The night had become black again. He murmured: "How is it you are here in person?"

The Prefect of Police whispered in his ear:

"I have been informed that something will happen tonight. Natacha went to Krestowsky and exchanged some words with Annouchka there. Prince Galitch is involved, and it is an affair of State."

"Natacha has returned?" inquired Rouletabille.

"Yes, a long time ago. She ought to be in bed. In any case she is pretending to be abed. The light from her chamber, in the window over the garden, has been put out."

"Have you warned Matrena Petrovna?"

"Yes, I have let her know that she must keep on the sharp look-out tonight."

"That's a mistake. I shouldn't have told her anything. She will take such extra precautions that the others will be instantly warned."

"I have told her she should not go to the ground-floor at all this night, and that she must not leave the general's chamber."

"That is perfect, if she will obey you."

"You see I have profited by all your information. I have followed your instructions. The road from the Krestowsky is under surveillance."

"Perhaps too much. How are you planning?"

"We will let them enter. I don't know whom I have to deal with. I want to strike a sure blow. I shall take him in the act. No more doubt after this, you trust me."

"Adieu."

"Where are you going?"

"To bed. I have paid my debt to my host. I have the right to some repose now. Good luck!"

But Koupriane had seized his hand.

"Listen."

With a little attention they detected a light stroke on the water. If a boat was moving at this time for this bank of the Neva and wished to remain hidden, the right moment had certainly been chosen. A great black cloud covered the moon; the wind was light. The boat would have time to get from one bank to the other without being discovered.

Rouletabille waited no longer. On all-fours he ran like a beast, rapidly and silently, and rose behind the wall of the villa, where he made a turn, reached the gate, aroused the dvornicks and demanded Ermolai, who opened the gate for him.

"The Barinia?" he said.

Ermolai pointed his finger to the bedroom floor.

"Caracho!"

Rouletabille was already across the garden and had hoisted himself by his fingers to the window of Natacha's chamber, where he listened. He plainly heard Natacha walking about in the dark chamber. He fell back lightly onto his feet, mounted the veranda steps and opened the door, then closed it so lightly that Ermolai, who watched him from outside not two feet away, did not hear the slightest grinding of the hinges. Inside the villa Rouletabille advanced on tiptoe. He found the door of the drawing-room open. The door of the sitting-room had not been closed, or else had been reopened. He turned in his tracks, felt in the dark for a chair and sat down, with his hand on his revolver in his pocket, waiting for the events that would not delay long now. Above he heard distinctly from time to time the movements of Matrena Petrovna. And this would evidently give a sense of security to those who needed to have the ground-floor free this night. Rouletabille imagined that the doors of the rooms on the ground-floor had been left open so that it would be easier for those who would be below to hear what was happening upstairs. And perhaps he was not wrong.

Suddenly there was a vertical bar of pale light from the sitting-room that overlooked the Neva. He deduced two things: first, that the window was already slightly open, then that the moon was out from the clouds again. The bar of light died almost instantly, but Rouletabille's eyes, now used to the obscurity, still distinguished the open line of the window. There the shade was less deep. Suddenly he felt the blood pound at his temples, for the line of the open window grew larger, increased, and the shadow of a man gradually rose on the balcony. Rouletabille drew his revolver.

The man stood up immediately behind one of the shutters and struck a light blow on the glass. Placed as he was now he could be seen no more. His shadow mixed with the shadow of the shutter. At the noise on the glass Natacha's door had opened cautiously, and she entered the sitting-room. On tiptoe she went quickly to the window and opened it. The man entered. The little light that by now was commencing to dawn was enough to show Rouletabille that Natacha still wore the toilette in which he had seen her that same evening at Krestowsky. As for the man, he tried in vain to identify him; he was only a dark mass wrapped in a mantle. He leaned over and kissed Natacha's hand. She said only one word: "Scan!" (Quickly).

But she had no more than said it before, under a vigorous attack, the shutters and the two halves of the window were thrown wide, and silent shadows jumped rapidly onto the balcony and sprang into the villa. Natacha uttered a shrill cry in which Rouletabille believed still he heard more of despair than terror, and the shadows threw themselves on the man; but he, at the first alarm, had thrown himself upon the carpet and had slipped from them between their legs. He regained the balcony and jumped from it as the others turned toward him. At least, it was so that Rouletabille believed he saw the mysterious struggle go in the half-light, amid most impressive silence, after that frightened cry of Natacha's. The whole affair had lasted only a few seconds, and the man was still hanging over the balcony, when from the bottom of the hall a new person sprang. It was Matrena Petrovna.

Warned by Koupriane that something would happen that night, and foreseeing that it would happen on the ground-floor where she was forbidden to be, she had found nothing better to do than to make her faithful maid go secretly to the bedroom floor, with orders to walk about there all night, to make all think she herself was near the general, while she remained below, hidden in the dining-room.

Matrena Petrovna now threw herself out onto the balcony, crying in Russian, "Shoot! Shoot!" In just that moment the man was hesitating whether to risk the jump and perhaps break his neck, or descend less rapidly by the gutter-pipe. A policeman fired and missed him, and the man, after firing back and wounding the policeman, disappeared. It was still too far from dawn for them to see clearly what happened below, where the barking of Brownings alone was heard. And there could be nothing more sinister than the revolver-shots unaccompanied by cries in the mists of the morning. The man, before he disappeared, had had only time by a quick kick to throw down one of the two ladders which had been used by the police in climbing; down the other one all the police in a bunch, even to the wounded one, went sliding, falling, rising, running after the shadow which fled still, discharging the Browning steadily; other shadows rose from the river-bank, hovering in the mist. Suddenly Koupriane's voice was heard shouting orders, calling upon his agents to take the quarry alive or dead. From the balcony Matrena Petrovna cried out also, like a savage, and Rouletabille tried in vain to keep her quiet. She was delirious at the thought "The Other" might escape yet. She fired a revolver, she also, into the group, not knowing whom she might wound. Rouletabille grabbed her arm and as she turned on him angrily she observed Natacha, who, leaning until she almost fell over the balcony, her lips trembling with delirious utterance, followed as well as she could the progress of the struggle, trying to understand what happened below, under the trees, near the Neva, where the tumult by now extended. Matrena Petrovna pulled her back by the arms. Then she took her by the neck and threw her into the drawing-room in a heap. When she had almost strangled her step-daughter, Matrena Petrovna saw that the general was there. He appeared in the pale glimmerings of dawn like a specter. By what miracle had Feodor Feodorovitch been able to descend the stairs and reach there? How had it been brought about? She saw him tremble with anger or with wretchedness under the folds of the soldier's cape that floated about him. He demanded in a hoarse voice, "What is it?"

Matrena Petrovna threw herself at his feet, made the orthodox sign of the Cross, as if she wished to summon God to witness, and then, pointing to Natacha, she denounced his daughter to her husband as she would have pointed her out to a judge.

"The one, Feodor Feodorovitch, who has wished more than once to assassinate you, and who this night has opened the datcha to your assassin is your daughter."

The general held himself up by his two hands against the wall, and, looking at Matrena and Natacha, who now were both upon the floor before him like suppliants, he said to Matrena:

"It is you who assassinate me."

"Me! By the living God!" babbled Matrena Petrovna desperately. "If I had been able to keep this from you, Jesus would have been good! But I say no more to crucify you. Feodor Feodorovitch, question your daughter, and if what I have said is not true, kill me, kill me as a lying, evil beast. I will say thank you, thank you, and I will die happier than if what I have said was true. Ah, I long to be dead! Kill me!"

Feodor Feodorovitch pushed her back with his stick as one would push a worm in his path. Without saying anything further, she rose from her knees and looked with her haggard eyes, with her crazed face, at Rouletabille, who grasped her arm. If she had had her hands still free she would not have hesitated a second in wreaking justice upon herself under this bitter fate of alienating Feodor. And it seemed frightful to Rouletabille that he should be present at one of those horrible family dramas the issue of which in the wild times of Peter the Great would have sent the general to the hangman either as a father or as a husband.

The general did not deign even to consider for any length of time Matrena's delirium. He said to his daughter, who shook with sobs on the floor, "Rise, Natacha Feodorovna." And Feodor's daughter understood that her father never would believe in her guilt. She drew herself up towards him and kissed his hands like a happy slave.

At this moment repeated blows shook the veranda door. Matrena, the watch-dog, anxious to die after Feodor's reproach, but still at her post, ran toward what she believed to be a new danger. But she recognized Koupriane's voice, which called on her to open. She let him in herself.

"What is it?" she implored.

"Well, he is dead."

A cry answered him. Natacha had heard.

"But who—who—who?" questioned Matrena breathlessly.

Koupriane went over to Feodor and grasped his hands.

"General," he said, "there was a man who had sworn your ruin and who was made an instrument by your enemies. We have just killed that man."

"Do I know him?" demanded Feodor.

"He is one of your friends, you have treated him like a son."

"His name?"

"Ask your daughter, General."

Feodor turned toward Natacha, who burned Koupriane with her gaze, trying to learn what this news was he brought—the truth or a ruse.

"You know the man who wished to kill me, Natacha?"

"No," she replied to her father, in accents of perfect fury. "No, I don't know any such man."

"Mademoiselle," said Koupriane, in a firm, terribly hostile voice, "you have yourself, with your own hands, opened that window tonight; and you have opened it to him many other times besides. While everyone else here does his duty and watches that no person shall be able to enter at night the house where sleeps General Trebassof, governor of Moscow, condemned to death by the Central Revolutionary Committee now reunited at Presnia, this is what you do; it is you who introduce the enemy into this place."

"Answer, Natacha; tell me, yes or no, whether you have let anybody into this house by night."

"Father, it is true."

Feodor roared like a lion:

"His name!"

"Monsieur will tell you himself," said Natacha, in a voice thick with terror, and she pointed to Koupriane. "Why does he not tell you himself the name of that person? He must know it, if the man is dead."

"And if the man is not dead," replied Feodor, who visibly held onto himself, "if that man, whom you helped to enter my house this night, has succeeded in escaping, as you seem to hope, will you tell us his name?"

"I could not tell it, Father."

"And if I prayed you to do so?"

Natacha desperately shook her head.

"And if I order you?"

"You can kill me, Father, but I will not pronounce that name."

"Wretch!"

He raised his stick toward her. Thus Ivan the Terrible had killed his son with a blow of his boar-spear.

But Natacha, instead of bowing her head beneath the blow that menaced her, turned toward Koupriane and threw at him in accents of triumph:

"He is not dead. If you had succeeded in taking him, dead or alive, you would already have his name."

Koupriane took two steps toward her, put his hand on her shoulder and said:

"Michael Nikolaievitch."

"Michael Korsakoff!" cried the general.

Matrena Petrovna, as if revolted by that suggestion, stood upright to repeat:

"Michael Korsakoff!"

The general could not believe his ears, and was about to protest when he noticed that his daughter had turned away and was trying to flee to her room. He stopped her with a terrible gesture.

"Natacha, you are going to tell us what Michael Korsakoff came here to do tonight."

"Feodor Feodorovitch, he came to poison you."

It was Matrena who spoke now and whom nothing could have kept silent, for she saw in Natacha's attempt at flight the most sinister confession. Like a vengeful fury she told over with cries and terrible gestures what she had experienced, as if once more stretched before her the hand armed with the poison, the mysterious hand above the pillow of her poor invalid, her dear, rigorous tyrant; she told them about the preceding night and all her terrors, and from her lips, by her voluble staccato utterance that ominous recital had grotesque emphasis. Finally she told all that she had done, she and the little Frenchman, in order not to betray their suspicions to The Other, in order to take finally in their own trap all those who for so many days and nights schemed for the death of Feodor Feodorovitch. As she ended she pointed out Rouletabille to Feodor and cried, "There is the one who has saved you."

Natacha, as she listened to this tragic recital, restrained herself several times in order not to interrupt, and Rouletabille, who was watching her closely, saw that she had to use almost superhuman efforts in order to achieve that. All the horror of what seemed to be to her as well as to Feodor a revelation of Michael's crime did not subdue her, but seemed, on the contrary, to restore to her in full force all the life that a few seconds earlier had fled from her. Matrena had hardly finished her cry, "There is the one who has saved you," before Natacha cried in her turn, facing the reporter with a look full of the most frightful hate, "There is the one who has been the death of an innocent man!" She turned to her father. "Ah, papa, let me, let me say that Michael Nikolaievitch, who came here this evening, I admit, and whom, it is true, I let into the house, that Michael Nikolaievitch did not come here yesterday, and that the man who has tried to poison you is certainly someone else."

At these words Rouletabille turned pale, but he did not let himself lose self-control. He replied simply:

"No, mademoiselle, it was the same man."

And Koupriane felt compelled to add:

"Anyway, we have found the proof of Michael Nikolaievitch's relations with the revolutionaries."

"Where have you found that?" questioned the young girl, turning toward the Chief of Police a face ravished with anguish.

"At Krestowsky, mademoiselle."

She looked a long time at him as though she would penetrate to the bottom of his thoughts.

"What proofs?" she implored.

"A correspondence which we have placed under seal."

"Was it addressed to him? What kind of correspondence?"

"If it interests you, we will open it before you."

"My God! My God!" she gasped. "Where have you found this correspondence? Where? Tell me where!"

"I will tell you. At the villa, in his chamber. We forced the lock of his bureau."

She seemed to breathe again, but her father took her brutally by the arm.

"Come, Natacha, you are going to tell us what that man was doing here tonight."

"In her chamber!" cried Matrena Petrovna.

Natacha turned toward Matrena:

"What do you believe, then? Tell me now."

"And I, what ought I to believe?" muttered Feodor. "You have not told me yet. You did not know that man had relations with my enemies. You are innocent of that, perhaps. I wish to think so. I wish it, in the name of Heaven I wish it. But why did you receive him? Why? Why did you bring him in here, as a robber or as a. . ."

"Oh, papa, you know that I love Boris, that I love him with all my heart, and that I would never belong to anyone but him."

"Then, then, then.—speak!"

The young girl had reached the crisis.

"Ah, Father, Father, do not question me! You, you above all, do not question me now. I can say nothing! There is nothing I can tell you. Excepting that I am sure—sure, you understand—that Michael Nikolaievitch did not come here last night."

"He did come," insisted Rouletabille in a slightly troubled voice.

"He came here with poison. He came here to poison your father, Natacha," moaned Matrena Petrovna, who twined her hands in gestures of sincere and naive tragedy.

"And I," replied the daughter of Feodor ardently, with an accent of conviction which made everyone there vibrate, and particularly Rouletabille, "and I, I tell you it was not he, that it was not he, that it could not possibly be he. I swear to you it was another, another."

"But then, this other, did you let him in as well?" said Koupriane.

"Ah, yes, yes. It was I. It was I. It was I who left the window and blinds open. Yes, it is I who did that. But I did not wait for the other, the other who came to assassinate. As to Michael Nikolaievitch, I swear to you, my father, by all that is most sacred in heaven and on earth, that he could not have committed the crime that you say. And now—kill me, for there is nothing more I can say."

"The poison," replied Koupriane coldly, "the poison that he poured into the general's potion was that arsenate of soda which was on the grapes the Marshal of the Court brought here. Those grapes were left by the Marshal, who warned Michael Nikolaievitch and Boris Alexandrovitch to wash them. The grapes disappeared. If Michael is innocent, do you accuse Boris?"

Natacha, who seemed to have suddenly lost all power for defending herself, moaned, begged, railed, seemed dying.

"No, no. Don't accuse Boris. He has nothing to do with it. Don't accuse Michael. Don't accuse anyone so long as you don't know. But these two are innocent. Believe me. Believe me. Ah, how shall I say it, how shall I persuade you! I am not able to say anything to you. And you have killed Michael. Ah, what have you done, what have you done!"

"We have suppressed a man," said the icy voice of Koupriane, "who was merely the agent for the base deeds of Nihilism."

She succeeded in recovering a new energy that in her depths of despair they would have supposed impossible. She shook her fists at Koupriane:

"It is not true, it is not true. These are slanders, infamies! The inventions of the police! Papers devised to incriminate him. There is nothing at all of what you said you found at his house. It is not possible. It is not true."

"Where are those papers?" demanded the curt voice of Feodor. "Bring them here at once, Koupriane; I wish to see them."

Koupriane was slightly troubled, and this did not escape Natacha, who cried:

"Yes, yes, let him give us them, let him bring them if he has them. But he hasn't," she clamored with a savage joy. "He has nothing. You can see, papa, that he has nothing. He would already have brought them out. He has nothing. I tell you he has nothing. Ah, he has nothing! He has nothing!"

And she threw herself on the floor, weeping, sobbing, "He has nothing, he has nothing!" She seemed to weep for joy.

"Is that true?" demanded Feodor Feodorovitch, with his most somber manner. "Is it true, Koupriane, that you have nothing?"

"It is true, General, that we have found nothing. Everything had already been carried away."

But Natacha uttered a veritable torrent of glee:

"He has found nothing! Yet he accuses him of being allied with the revolutionaries. Why? Why? Because I let him in? But I, am I a revolutionary? Tell me. Have I sworn to kill papa? I? I? Ah, he doesn't know what to say. You see for yourself, papa, he is silent. He has lied. He has lied."

"Why have you made this false statement, Koupriane?"

"Oh, we have suspected Michael for some time, and truly, after what has just happened, we cannot have any doubt."

"Yes, but you declared you had papers, and you have not. That is abominable procedure, Koupriane," replied Feodor sternly. "I have heard you condemn such expedients many times."

"General! We are sure, you hear, we are absolutely sure that the man who tried to poison you yesterday and the man today who is dead are one and the same."

"And what reason have you for being so sure? It is necessary to tell it," insisted the general, who trembled with distress and impatience.

"Yes, let him tell now."

"Ask monsieur," said Koupriane.

They all turned to Rouletabille.

The reporter replied, affecting a coolness that perhaps he did not entirely feel:

"I am able to state to you, as I already have before Monsieur the Prefect of Police, that one, and only one, person has left the traces of his various climbings on the wall and on the balcony."

"Idiot!" interrupted Natacha, with a passionate disdain for the young man. "And that satisfies you?"

The general roughly seized the reporter's wrist:

"Listen to me, monsieur. A man came here this night. That concerns only me. No one has any right to be astonished excepting myself. I make it my own affair, an affair between my daughter and me. But you, you have just told us that you are sure that man is an assassin. Then, you see, that calls for something else. Proofs are necessary, and I want the proofs at once. You speak of traces; very well, we will go and examine those traces together. And I wish for your sake, monsieur, that I shall be as convinced by them as you are."

Rouletabille quietly disengaged his wrist and replied with perfect calm:

"Now, monsieur, I am no longer able to prove anything to you."

"Why?"

"Because the ladders of the police agents have wiped out all my proofs, monsieur.

"So now there remains for us only your word, only your belief in yourself. And if you are mistaken?"

"He would never admit it, papa," cried Natacha. "Ah, it is he who deserves the fate Michael Nikolaievitch has met just now. Isn't it so? Don't you know it? And that will be your eternal remorse! Isn't there something that always keeps you from admitting that you are mistaken? You have had an innocent man killed. Now, you know well enough, you know well that I would not have admitted Michael Nikolaievitch here if I had believed he was capable of wishing to poison my father."

"Mademoiselle," replied Rouletabille, not lowering his eyes under Natacha's thunderous regard, "I am sure of that."

He said it in such a tone that Natacha continued to look at him with incomprehensible anguish in her eyes. Ah, the baffling of those two regards, the mute scene between those two young people, one of whom wished to make himself understood and the other afraid beyond all other things of being thoroughly understood. Natacha murmured:

"How he looks at me! See, he is the demon; yes, yes, the little domovoi, the little domovoi. But look out, poor wretch; you don't know what you have done."

She turned brusquely toward Koupriane:

"Where is the body of Michael Nikolaievitch?" said she. "I wish to see it. I must see it."

Feodor Feodorovitch had fallen, as though asleep, upon a chair. Matrena Petrovna dared not approach him. The giant appeared hurt to the death, disheartened forever. What neither bombs, nor bullets, nor poison had been able to do, the single idea of his daughter's co-operation in the work of horror plotted about him—or rather the impossibility he faced of understanding Natacha's attitude, her mysterious conduct, the chaos of her explanations, her insensate cries, her protestations of innocence, her accusations, her menaces, her prayers and all her disorder, the avowed fact of her share in that tragic nocturnal adventure where Michael Nikolaievitch found his death, had knocked over Feodor Feodorovitch like a straw. One instant he sought refuge in some vague hope that Koupriane was less assured than he pretended of the orderly's guilt. But that, after all, was only a detail of no importance in his eyes. What alone mattered was the significance of Natacha's act, and the unhappy girl seemed not to be concerned over what he would think of it. She was there to fight against Koupriane, Rouletabille and Matrena Petrovna, defending her Michael Nikolaievitch, while he, the father, after having failed to overawe her just now, was there in a corner suffering agonizedly.

Koupriane walked over to him and said:

"Listen to me carefully, Feodor Feodorovitch. He who speaks to you is Head of the Police by the will of the Tsar, and your friend by the grace of God. If you do not demand before us, who are acquainted with all that has happened and who know how to keep any necessary secret, if you do not demand of your daughter the reason for her conduct with Michael Nikolaievitch, and if she does not tell you in all sincerity, there is nothing more for me to do here. My men have already been ordered away from this house as unworthy to guard the most loyal subject of His Majesty; I have not protested, but now I in my turn ask you to prove to me that the most dangerous enemy you have had in your house is not your daughter."

These words, which summed up the horrible situation, came as a relief for Feodor. Yes, they must know. Koupriane was right. She must speak. He ordered his daughter to tell everything, everything.

Natacha fixed Koupriane again with her look of hatred to the death, turned from him and repeated in a firm voice:

"I have nothing to say."

"There is the accomplice of your assassins," growled Koupriane then, his arm extended.

Natacha uttered a cry like a wounded beast and fell at her father's feet. She gathered them within her supplicating arms. She pressed them to her breasts. She sobbed from the bottom of her heart. And he, not comprehending, let her lie there, distant, hostile, somber. Then she moaned, distractedly, and wept bitterly, and the dramatic atmosphere in which she thus suddenly enveloped Feodor made it all sound like those cries of an earlier time when the all-powerful, punishing father appeared in the women's apartments to punish the culpable ones.

"My father! Dear Father! Look at me! Look at me! Have pity on me, and do not require me to speak when I must be silent forever. And believe me! Do not believe these men! Do not believe Matrena Petrovna. And am I not your daughter? Your very own daughter! Your Natacha Feodorovna! I cannot make things dear to you. No, no, by the

Holy Virgin Mother of Jesus I cannot explain. By the holy ikons, it is because I must not. By my mother, whom I have not known and whose place you have taken, oh, my father, ask me nothing more! Ask me nothing more! But take me in your arms as you did when I was little; embrace me, dear father; love me. I never have had such need to be loved. Love me! I am miserable. Unfortunate me, who cannot even kill myself before your eyes to prove my innocence and my love. Papa, Papa! What will your arms be for in the days left you to live, if you no longer wish to press me to your heart? Papa! Papa!"

She laid her head on Feodor's knees. Her hair had come down and hung about her in a magnificent disorderly mass of black.

"Look in my eyes! Look in my eyes! See how they love you, Batouchka! Batouchka! My dear Batouchka!"

Then Feodor wept. His great tears fell upon Natacha's tears. He raised her head and demanded simply in a broken voice:

"You can tell me nothing now? But when will you tell me?"

Natacha lifted her eyes to his, then her look went past him toward heaven, and from her lips came just one word, in a sob:

"Never."

Matrena Petrovna, Koupriane and the reporter shuddered before the high and terrible thing that happened then. Feodor had taken his daughter's face between his hands. He looked long at those eyes raised toward heaven, the mouth which had just uttered the word "Never," then, slowly, his rude lips went to the tortured, quivering lips of the girl. He held her close. She raised her head wildly, triumphantly, and cried, with arm extended toward Matrena Petrovna:

"He believes me! He believes me! And you would have believed me also if you had been my real mother."

Her head fell back and she dropped unconscious to the floor. Feodor fell to his knees, tending her, deploring her, motioning the others out of the room.

"Go away! All of you, go! All! You, too, Matrena Petrovna. Go away!"

They disappeared, terrified by his savage gesture.

In the little datcha across the river at Krestowsky there was a body. Secret Service agents guarded it while they waited for their chief. Michael Nikolaievitch had come there to die, and the police had reached him just at his last breath. They were behind him as, with the death-rattle in his throat, he pulled himself into his chamber and fell in a heap. Katharina the Bohemian was there. She bent her quick-witted, puzzled head over his death agony. The police swarmed everywhere, ransacking, forcing locks, pulling drawers from the bureau and tables, emptying the cupboards. Their search took in everything, even to ripping the mattresses, and not respecting the rooms of Boris Mourazoff, who was away this night. They searched thoroughly, but they found absolutely nothing they were looking for in Michael's rooms. But they accumulated a multitude of publications that belonged to Boris: Western books, essays on political economy, a history of the French Revolution, and verses that a man ought to hang for. They put them all under seal. During the search Michael died in Katharina's arms. She had held him close, after opening his clothes over the chest, doubtless to make his last breaths easier. The unfortunate officer had received a bullet at the back of the head just after he had plunged into the Neva from the rear of the Trebassof datcha and started to swim across. It was a miracle that he had managed to keep going. Doubtless he hoped to die in peace if only he could reach his own house. He apparently had believed he could manage that once he had broken through his human bloodhounds. He did not know he was recognized and his place of retreat therefore known.

Now the police had gone from cellar to garret. Koupriane came from the Trebassof villa and joined them, Rouletabille followed him. The reporter could not stand the sight of that body, that still had a lingering warmth, of the great open eyes that seemed to stare at him, reproaching him for this violent death. He turned away in distaste, and perhaps a little in fright. Koupriane caught the movement.

"Regrets?" he queried.

"Yes," said Rouletabille. "A death always must be regretted. None the less, he was a criminal. But I'm sincerely sorry he died before he had been driven to confess, even though we are sure of it."

"Being in the pay of the Nihilists, you mean? That is still your opinion?" asked Koupriane.

"Yes."

"You know that nothing has been found here in his rooms. The only compromising papers that have been found belong to Boris Mourazoff."

"Why do you say that?"

"Oh—nothing."

Koupriane questioned his men further. They replied categorically. No, nothing had been found that directly incriminated anybody; and suddenly Rouletabille noted that the conversation of the police and their chief had grown more animated. Koupriane had become angry and was violently reproaching them. They excused themselves with vivid gesture and rapid speech.

Koupriane started away. Rouletabille followed him. What had happened?

As he came up behind Koupriane, he asked the question. In a few curt words, still hurrying on, Koupriane told the reporter he had just learned that the police had left the little Bohemian Katharina alone for a moment with the expiring officer. Katharina acted as housekeeper for Michael and Boris. She knew the secrets of them both. The first thing any novice should have known was to keep a constant eye upon her, and now no one knew where she was. She must be searched for and found at once, for she had opened Michael's shirt, and therein probably lay the reason that no papers were found on the corpse when the police searched it. The absence of papers, of a portfolio, was not natural.

The chase commenced in the rosy dawn of the isles. Already blood-like tints were on the horizon. Some of the police cried that they had the trail. They ran under the trees, because it was almost certain she had taken the narrow path leading to the bridge that joins Krestowsky to Kameny-Ostrow. Some indications discovered by the police who swarmed to right and left of the path confirmed this hypothesis. And no carriage in sight! They all ran on, Koupriane among the first. Rouletabille kept at his heels, but he did not pass him. Suddenly there were cries and calls among the police. One pointed out something below gliding upon the sloping descent. It was little Katharina. She flew like the wind, but in a distracted course. She had reached Kameny-Ostrow on the west bank. "Oh, for a carriage, a horse!" clamored Koupriane, who had left his turn-out at Eliaguine. "The proof is there. It is the final proof of everything that is escaping us!"

Dawn was enough advanced now to show the ground clearly. Katharina was easily discernible as she reached the Eliaguine bridge. There she was in Eliaguine-Ostrow. What was she doing there? Was she going to the Trebassof villa? What would she have to say to them? No, she swerved to the right. The police raced behind her. She was still far ahead, and seemed untiring. Then she disappeared among the trees, in the thicket, keeping still to the right. Koupriane gave a cry of joy. Going that way she must be taken. He gave some breathless orders for the island to be barred. She could not escape now! She could not escape! But where was she going? Koupriane knew that island better than anybody.

He took a short cut to reach the other side, toward which Katharina seemed to be heading, and all at once he nearly fell over the girl, who gave a squawk of surprise and rushed away, seeming all arms and legs.

"Stop, or I fire!" cried Koupriane, and he drew his revolver. But a hand grabbed it from him.

"Not that!" said Rouletabille, as he threw the revolver far from them. Koupriane swore at him and resumed the chase. His fury multiplied his strength, his agility; he almost reached Katharina, who was almost out of breath, but Rouletabille threw himself into the Chief's arms and they rolled together upon the grass. When Koupriane rose, it was to see Katharina mounting in mad haste the stairs that led to the Barque, the floating restaurant of the Strielka. Cursing Rouletabille, but believing his prey easily captured now, the Chief in his turn hurried to the Barque, into which Katharina had disappeared. He reached the bottom of the stairs. On the top step, about to descend from the festive place, the form of Prince Galitch appeared. Koupriane received the sight like a blow stopping him short in his ascent. Galitch had an exultant air which Koupriane did not mistake. Evidently he had arrived too late. He felt the certainty of it in profound discouragement. And this appearance of the prince on the Barque explained convincingly enough the reason for Katharina's flight here.

If the Bohemian had filched the papers or the portfolio from the dead, it was the prince now who had them in his pocket.

Koupriane, as he saw the prince about to pass him, trembled. The prince saluted him and ironically amused himself by inquiring:

"Well, well, how do you do, my dear Monsieur Koupriane. Your Excellency has risen in good time this morning, it seems to me. Or else it is I who start for bed too late."

"Prince," said Koupriane, "my men are in pursuit of a little Bohemian named Katharina, well known in the restaurants where she sings. We have seen her go into the Barque. Have you met her by any chance?"

"Good Lord, Monsieur Koupriane, I am not the concierge of the Barque, and I have not noticed anything at all, and nobody. Besides, I am naturally a little sleepy. Pardon me."

"Prince, it is not possible that you have not seen Katharina."

"Oh, Monsieur the Prefect of Police, if I had seen her I would not tell you about it, since you are pursuing her. Do you take me for one of your bloodhounds? They say you have them in all classes, but I insist that I haven't enlisted yet. You have made a mistake, Monsieur Koupriane."

The prince saluted again. But Koupriane still stood in his way.

"Prince, consider that this matter is very serious. Michael Nikolaievitch, General Trebassof's orderly, is dead, and this little girl has stolen his papers from his body. All persons who have spoken with Katharina will be under suspicion. This is an affair of State, monsieur, which may reach very far. Can you swear to me that you have not seen, that you have not spoken to Katharina?"

The prince looked at Koupriane so insolently that the Prefect turned pale with rage. Ah, if he were able—if he only dared!—but such men as this were beyond him. Galitch walked past him without a word of answer, and ordered the schwitzar to call him a carriage.

"Very well," said Koupriane, "I will make my report to the Tsar."

Galitch turned. He was as pale as Koupriane.

"In that case, monsieur," said he, "don't forget to add that I am His Majesty's most humble servant."

The carriage drew up. The prince stepped in. Koupriane watched him roll away, raging at heart and with his fists doubled. Just then his men came up.

"Go. Search," he said roughly, pointing into the Barque.

They scattered through the establishment, entering all the rooms. Cries of irritation and of protest arose. Those lingering after the latest of late suppers were not pleased at this invasion of the police. Everybody had to rise while the police looked under the tables, the benches, the long table-cloths. They went into the pantries and down into the hold. No sign of Katharina. Suddenly Koupriane, who leaned against a netting and looked vaguely out upon the horizon, waiting for the outcome of the search, got a start. Yonder, far away on the other side of the river, between a little wood and the Staria Derevnia, a light boat drew to the shore, and a little black spot jumped from it like a flea. Koupriane recognized the little black spot as Katharina. She was safe. Now he could not reach her. It would be useless to search the maze of the Bohemian quarter, where her country-people lived in full control, with customs and privileges that had never been infringed. The entire Bohemian population of the capital would have risen against him. It was Prince Galitch who had made him fail. One of his men came to him:

"No luck," said he. "We have not found Katharina, but she has been here nevertheless. She met Prince Galitch for just a minute, and gave him something, then went over the other side into a canoe."

"Very well," and the Prefect shrugged his shoulders. "I was sure of it."

He felt more and more, exasperated. He went down along the river edge and the first person he saw was Rouletabille, who waited for him without any impatience, seated philosophically on a bench.

"I was looking for you," cried the Prefect. "We have failed. By your fault! If you had not thrown yourself into my arms—"

"I did it on purpose," declared the reporter.

"What! What is that you say? You did it on purpose?"

Koupriane choked with rage.

"Your Excellency," said Rouletabille, taking him by the arm, "calm yourself. They are watching us. Come along and have a cup of tea at Cubat's place. Easy now, as though we were out for a walk."

"Will you explain to me?"

"No, no, Your Excellency. Remember that I have promised you General Trebassof's life in exchange for your prisoner's. Very well; by throwing myself in your arms and keeping you from reaching Katharina, I saved the general's life. It is very simple."

"Are you laughing at me? Do you think you can mock me?"

But the prefect saw quickly that Rouletabille was not fooling and had no mockery in his manner.

"Monsieur," he insisted, "since you speak seriously, I certainly wish to understand—"

"It is useless," said Rouletabille. "It is very necessary that you should not understand."

"But at least. . ."

"No, no, I can't tell you anything."

"When, then, will you tell me something to explain your unbelievable conduct?"

Rouletabille stopped in his tracks and declared solemnly:

"Monsieur Koupriane, recall what Natacha Feodorovna as she raised her lovely eyes to heaven, replied to her father, when he, also, wished to understand: 'Never.'"

XI

The Poison Continues

At ten o'clock that morning Rouletabille went to the Trebassof villa, which had its guard of secret agents again, a double guard, because Koupriane was sure the Nihilists would not delay in avenging Michael's death. Rouletabille was met by Ermolai, who would not allow him to enter. The faithful servant uttered some explanation in Russian, which the young man did not understand, or, rather, Rouletabille understood perfectly from his manner that henceforth the door of the villa was closed to him. In vain he insisted on seeing the general, Matrena Petrovna and Mademoiselle Natacha. Ermolai made no reply but "Niet, niet, niet." The reporter turned away without having seen anyone, and walked away deeply depressed. He went afoot clear into the city, a long promenade, during which his brain surged with the darkest forebodings. As he passed by the Department of Police he resolved to see Koupriane again. He went in, gave his name, and was ushered at once to the Chief of Police, whom he found bent over a long report that he was reading through with noticeable agitation.

"Gounsovski has sent me this," he said in a rough voice, pointing to the report. "Gounsovski, 'to do me a service,' desires me to know that he is fully aware of all that happened at the Trebassof datcha last night. He warns me that the revolutionaries have decided to get through with the general at once, and that two of them have been given the mission to enter the datcha in any way possible. They will have bombs upon their bodies and will blow the bombs and themselves up together as soon as they are beside the general. Who are the two victims designated for this horrible vengeance, and who have light-heartedly accepted such a death for themselves as well as for the general? That is what we don't know. That is what we would have known, perhaps, if you had not prevented me from seizing the papers that Prince Galitch has now," Koupriane finished, turning hostilely toward Rouletabille.

Rouletabille had turned pale.

"Don't regret what happened to the papers," he said. "It is I who tell you not to. But what you say doesn't surprise me. They must believe that Natacha has betrayed them."

"Ah, then you admit at last that she really is their accomplice?"

"I haven't said that and I don't admit it. But I know what I mean, and you, you can't. Only, know this one thing, that at the present moment I am the only person able to save you in this horrible situation. To do that I must see Natacha at once. Make her understand this, while I wait at my hotel for word. I'll not leave it."

Rouletabille saluted Koupriane and went out.

Two days passed, during which Rouletabille did not receive any word from either Natacha or Koupriane, and tried in vain to see them. He made a trip for a few hours to Finland, going as far as Pergalovo, an isolated town said to be frequented by the revolutionaries, then returned, much disturbed, to his hotel, after having written a last letter to Natacha imploring an interview. The minutes passed very slowly for him in the hotel's vestibule, where he had seemed to have taken up a definite residence.

Installed on a bench, he seemed to have become part of the hotel staff, and more than one traveler took him for an interpreter. Others thought he was an agent of the Secret Police appointed to study the faces of those arriving and departing. What was he waiting for, then? Was it for Annouchka to return for a luncheon or dinner in that place that she sometimes frequented? And did he at the same time keep watch upon Annouchka's apartments just across the way? If that was so, he could only bewail his luck, for Annouchka did not appear either at her apartments or the hotel, or at the Krestowsky establishment, which had been obliged to suppress her performance. Rouletabille naturally thought, in the latter connection, that some vengeance by Gounsovski lay back of this, since the head of the Secret Service could hardly forget the way he had been treated. The reporter could see already the poor singer, in spite of all her safeguards and the favor of the Imperial family, on the road to the Siberian steppes or the dungeons of Schlusselbourg.

"My, what a country!" he murmured.

But his thoughts soon quit Annouchka and returned to the object of his main preoccupation. He waited for only one thing, and for that as soon as possible—to have a private interview with Natacha. He had written her ten letters in two days, but they all remained unanswered. It was an answer that he waited for so patiently in the vestibule of the hotel—so patiently, but so nervously, so feverishly.

When the postman entered, poor Rouletabille's heart beat rapidly. On that answer he waited for depended the formidable part he meant

GASTON LEROUX

to play before quitting Russia. He had accomplished nothing up to now, unless he could play his part in this later development.

But the letter did not come. The postman left, and the schwitzar, after examining all the mail, made him a negative sign. Ah, the servants who entered, and the errand-boys, how he looked at them! But they never came for him. Finally, at six o'clock in the evening of the second day, a man in a frock-coat, with a false astrakhan collar, came in and handed the concierge a letter for Joseph Rouletabille. The reporter jumped up. Before the man was out the door he had torn open the letter and read it. The letter was not from Natacha. It was from Gounsovski. This is what it said:

"My dear Monsieur Joseph Rouletabille, if it will not inconvenience you, I wish you would come and dine with me today. I will look for you within two hours. Madame Gounsovski will be pleased to make your acquaintance. Believe me your devoted Gounsovski."

Rouletabille considered, and decided:

"I will go. He ought to have wind of what is being plotted, and as for me, I don't know where Annouchka has gone. I have more to learn from him than he has from me. Besides, as Athanase Georgevitch said, one may regret not accepting the Head of the Okrana's pleasant invitation."

From six o'clock to seven he still waited vainly for Natacha's response. At seven o'clock, he decided to dress for the dinner. Just as he rose, a messenger arrived. There was still another letter for Joseph Rouletabille. This time it was from Natacha, who wrote him:

"General Trebassof and my step-mother will be very happy to have you come to dinner today. As for myself, monsieur, you will pardon me the order which has closed to you for a number of days a dwelling where you have rendered services which I shall not forget all my life."

The letter ended with a vague polite formula. With the letter in his hand the reporter sat in thought. He seemed to be asking himself, "Is it fish or flesh?" Was it a letter of thanks or of menace? That was what he could not decide. Well, he would soon know, for he had decided to accept that invitation. Anything that brought him and Natacha into communication at the moment was a thing of capital importance to him. Half-an-hour later he gave the address of the villa to an isvotchick, and soon he stepped out before the gate where Ermolai seemed to be waiting for him.

Rouletabille was so occupied by thought of the conversation he was going to have with Natacha that he had completely forgotten the excellent Monsieur Gounsovski and his invitation.

The reporter found Koupriane's agents making a close-linked chain around the grounds and each watching the other. Matrena had not wished any agent to be in house. He showed Koupriane's pass and entered.

Ermolai ushered Rouletabille in with shining face. He seemed glad to have him there again. He bowed low before him and uttered many compliments, of which the reporter did not understand a word. Rouletabille passed on, entered the garden and saw Matrena Petrovna there walking with her step-daughter. They seemed on the best of terms with each other. The grounds wore an air of tranquillity and the residents seemed to have totally forgotten the somber tragedy of the other night. Matrena and Natacha came smilingly up to the young man, who inquired after the general. They both turned and pointed out Feodor Feodorovitch, who waved to him from the height of the kiosk, where it seemed the table had been spread. They were going to dine out of doors this fine night.

"Everything goes very well, very well indeed, dear little domovoi," said Matrena. "How glad it is to see you and thank you. If you only knew how I suffered in your absence, I who know how unjust my daughter was to you. But dear Natacha knows now what she owes you. She doesn't doubt your word now, nor your clear intelligence, little angel. Michael Nikolaievitch was a monster and he was punished as he deserved. You know the police have proof now that he was one of the Central Revolutionary Committee's most dangerous agents. And he an officer! Whom can we trust now!"

"And Monsieur Boris Mourazoff, have you seen him since?" inquired Rouletabille.

"Boris called to see us today, to say good-by, but we did not receive him, under the orders of the police. Natacha has written to tell him of Koupriane's orders. We have received letters from him; he is quitting St. Petersburg.

"What for?"

"Well, after the frightful bloody scene in his little house, when he learned how Michael Nikolaievitch had found his death, and after he himself had undergone a severe grilling from the police, and when he learned the police had sacked his library and gone through his papers, he resigned, and has resolved to live from now on out in the country, without seeing anyone, like the philosopher and poet he is. So far as I am concerned, I think he is doing absolutely right. When a young man is a poet, it is useless to live like a soldier. Someone has said that, I don't know the name now, and when one has ideas that may upset other people, surely they ought to live in solitude."

Rouletabille looked at Natacha, who was as pale as her white gown, and who added no word to her mother's outburst. They had drawn near the kiosk. Rouletabille saluted the general, who called to him to come up and, when the young man extended his hand, he drew him abruptly nearer and embraced him. To show Rouletabille how active he was getting again, Feodor Feodorovitch marched up and down the kiosk with only the aid of a stick. He went and came with a sort of wild, furious gayety.

"They haven't got me yet, the dogs. They haven't got me! And one (he was thinking of Michael) who saw me every day was here just for that. Very well. I ask you where he is now. And yet here I am! An attack! I'm always here! But with a good eye; and I begin to have a good leg. We shall see. Why, I recollect how, when I was at Tiflis, there was an insurrection in the Caucasus. We fought. Several times I could feel the swish of bullets past my hair. My comrades fell around me like flies. But nothing happened to me, not a thing. And here now! They will not get me, they will not get me. You know how they plan now to come to me, as living bombs. Yes, they have decided on that. I can't press a friend's hand any more without the fear of seeing him explode. What do you think of that? But they won't get me. Come, drink my health. A small glass of vodka for an appetizer. You see, young man, we are going to have zakouskis here. What a marvelous panorama! You can see everything from here. If the enemy comes," he added with a singular loud laugh, "we can't fail to detect him."

Certainly the kiosk did rise high above the garden and was completely detached, no wall being near. They had a clear view. No branches of trees hung over the roof and no tree hid the view. The rustic table of rough wood was covered with a short cloth and was spread with zakouskis. It was a meal under the open sky, a seat and a glass in the clear azure. The evening could not have been softer and clearer. And, as the general felt so gay, the repast would have promised to be most agreeable, if Rouletabille had not noticed that Matrena Petrovna and Natacha were uneasy and downcast. The reporter soon saw, too, that all the general's joviality was a little excessive. Anyone would have said that Feodor Feodorovitch spoke to distract himself, to keep himself from thinking. There was sufficient excuse for him after the outrageous drama of the other night. Rouletabille noticed further that the general never looked at his daughter, even when he spoke to her. There was too formidable a mystery lying between them for restraint not to increase day by day. Rouletabille involuntarily shook his head, saddened by all he saw. His movement was surprised by Matrena Petrovna, who pressed his hand in silence.

"Well, now," said the general, "well, now my children, where is the vodka?"

Among all the bottles which graced the table the general looked in vain for his flask of vodka. How in the world could he dine if he did not prepare for that important act by the rapid absorption of two or three little glasses of white wine, between two or three sandwiches of caviare!

"Ermolai must have left it in the wine-chest," said Matrena.

The wine-closet was in the dining-room. She rose to go there, but Natacha hurried before her down the little flight of steps, crying, "Stay there, mamma. I will go."

"Don't you bother, either. I know where it is," cried Rouletabille, and hurried after Natacha.

She did not stop. The two young people arrived in the dining-room at the same time. They were there alone, as Rouletabille had foreseen. He stopped Natacha and planted himself in front of her.

"Why, mademoiselle, did you not answer me earlier?"

"Because I don't wish to have any conversation with you."

"If that was so, you would not have come here, where you were sure I would follow."

She hesitated, with an emotion that would have been incomprehensible to all others perhaps, but was not to Rouletabille.

"Well, yes, I wished to say this to you: Don't write to me any more. Don't speak to me. Don't see me. Go away from here, monsieur; go away. They will have your life. And if you have found out anything, forget it. Ah, on the head of your mother, forget it, or you are lost. That is what I wished to tell you. And now, you go."

She grasped his hand in a quick sympathetic movement that she seemed instantly to regret.

"You go away," she repeated.

Rouletabille still held his place before her. She turned from him; she did not wish to hear anything further.

"Mademoiselle," said he, "you are watched closer than ever. Who will take Michael Nikolaievitch's place?"

"Madman, be silent! Hush!"

"I am here."

He said this with such simple bravery that tears sprang to her eyes.

"Dear man! Poor man! Dear brave man!" She did not know what to say. Her emotion checked all utterance. But it was necessary for her to enable him to understand that there was nothing he could do to help her in her sad straits.

"No. If they knew what you have just said, what you have proposed now, you would be dead tomorrow. Don't let them suspect. And above all, don't try to see me anywhere. Go back to papa at once. We have been here too long. What if they learn of it?—and they learn everything! They are everywhere, and have ears everywhere."

"Mademoiselle, just one word more, a single word. Do you doubt now that Michael tried to poison your father?"

"Ah, I wish to believe it. I wish to. I wish to believe it for your sake, my poor boy."

Rouletabille desired something besides "I wish to believe it for your sake, my poor boy." He was far from being satisfied. She saw him turn pale. She tried to reassure him while her trembling hands raised the lid of the wine-chest.

"What makes me think you are right is that I have decided myself that only one and the same person, as you said, climbed to the window of the little balcony. Yes, no one can doubt that, and you have reasoned well."

But he persisted still.

"And yet, in spite of that, you are not entirely sure, since you say, 'I wish to believe it, my poor boy.'"

"Monsieur Rouletabille, someone might have tried to poison my father, and not have come by way of the window."

"No, that is impossible."

"Nothing is impossible to them."

And she turned her head away again.

"Why, why," she said, with her voice entirely changed and quite indifferent, as if she wished to be merely 'the daughter of the house' in conversation with the young man, "the vodka is not in the wine chest, after all. What has Ermolai done with it, then?"

She ran over to the buffet and found the flask.

"Oh, here it is. Papa shan't be without it, after all."

Rouletabille was already into the garden again.

"If that is the only doubt she has," he said to himself, "I can reassure her. No one could come, excepting by the window. And only one came that way."

The young girl had rejoined him, bringing the flask. They crossed the garden together to the general, who was whiling away the time as he waited for his vodka explaining to Matrena Petrovna the nature of "the constitution." He had spilt a box of matches on the table and arranged them carefully.

"Here," he cried to Natacha and Rouletabille. "Come here and I will explain to you as well what this Constitution amounts to."

The young people leaned over his demonstration curiously and all eyes in the kiosk were intent on the matches.

"You see that match," said Feodor Feodorovitch. "It is the Emperor. And this other match is the Empress; this one is the Tsarevitch; and that one is the Grand-duke Alexander; and these are the other granddukes. Now, here are the ministers and there the principal governors, and then the generals; these here are the bishops."

The whole box of matches was used up, and each match was in its place, as is the way in an empire where proper etiquette prevails in government and the social order.

"Well," continued the general, "do you want to know, Matrena Petrovna, what a constitution is? There! That is the Constitution."

The general, with a swoop of his hand, mixed all the matches. Rouletabille laughed, but the good Matrena said:

"I don't understand, Feodor."

"Find the Emperor now."

Then Matrena understood. She laughed heartily, she laughed violently, and Natacha laughed also. Delighted with his success, Feodor Feodorovitch took up one of the little glasses that Natacha had filled with the vodka she brought.

"Listen, my children," said he. "We are going to commence the zakouskis. Koupriane ought to have been here before this."

Saying this, holding still the little glass in his hand, he felt in his pocket with the other for his watch, and drew out a magnificent large watch whose ticking was easily heard.

"Ah, the watch has come back from the repairer," Rouletabille remarked smilingly to Matrena Petrovna. "It looks like a splendid one."

"It has very fine works," said the general. "It was bequeathed to me by my grandfather. It marks the seconds, and the phases of the moon, and sounds the hours and half-hours."

Rouletabille bent over the watch, admiring it.

"You expect M. Koupriane for dinner?" inquired the young man, still examining the watch.

"Yes, but since he is so late, we'll not delay any longer. Your healths, my children," said the general as Rouletabille handed him back the watch and he put it in his pocket.

"Your health, Feodor Feodorovitch," replied Matrena Petrovna, with her usual tenderness.

Rouletabille and Natacha only touched their lips to the vodka, but Feodor Feodorovitch and Matrena drank theirs in the Russian fashion, head back and all at a draught, draining it to the bottom and flinging the contents to the back of the throat. They had no more than performed this gesture when the general uttered an oath and tried to expel what he had drained so heartily. Matrena Petrovna spat violently also, looking with horror at her husband.

"What is it? What has someone put in the vodka?" cried Feodor.

"What has someone put in the vodka?" repeated Matrena Petrovna in a thick voice, her eyes almost starting from her head.

The two young people threw themselves upon the unfortunates. Feodor's face had an expression of atrocious suffering.

"We are poisoned," cried the general, in the midst of his chokings. "I am burning inside."

Almost mad, Natacha took her father's head in her hands. She cried to him:

"Vomit, papa; vomit!"

"We must find an emetic," cried Rouletabille, holding on to the general, who had almost slipped from his arms.

Matrena Petrovna, whose gagging noises were violent, hurried down the steps of the kiosk, crossed the garden as though wild-fire were behind her, and bounded into the veranda. During this time the general succeeded in easing himself, thanks to Rouletabille, who had thrust a spoon to the root of his tongue. Natacha could do nothing but cry, "My God, my God, my God!" Feodor held onto his stomach, still crying, "I'm burning, I'm burning!" The scene was frightfully tragic and funny at the same time. To add to the burlesque, the general's watch in his pocket struck eight o'clock. Feodor Feodorovitch stood up in a final supreme effort. "Oh, it is horrible!" Matrena Petrovna showed a red, almost violet face as she came back; she distorted it, she choked, her mouth twitched, but she brought something, a little packet that she waved, and from which, trembling frightenedly, she shook a powder into the first two empty glasses, which were on her side of the table and were those she and the general had drained. She still had strength to fill them with water, while Rouletabille was almost overcome by the general, whom he still had in his arms, and Natacha concerned herself with nothing but her father, leaning over him as though to follow the progress of the terrible poison, to read in his eyes if it was to be life or death. "Ipecac," cried Matrena Petrovna, and she made the general drink it. She did not drink until after him. The heroic woman must have exerted superhuman force to go herself to find the saving antidote in her medicine-chest, even while the agony pervaded her vitals.

Some minutes later both could be considered saved. The servants, Ermolai at their head, were clustered about. Most of them had been at the lodge and they had not, it appeared, heard the beginning of the affair, the cries of Natacha and Rouletabille. Koupriane arrived just then. It was he who worked with Natacha in getting the two to bed. Then he directed one of his agents to go for the nearest doctors they could find.

This done, the Prefect of Police went toward the kiosk where he had left Rouletabille. But Rouletabille was not to be found, and the flask of vodka and the glasses from which they had drunk were gone also. Ermolai was near-by, and he inquired of the servant for the young Frenchman. Ermolai replied that he had just gone away, carrying the flask and the glasses. Koupriane swore. He shook Ermolai and even started to give him a blow with the fist for permitting such a thing to happen before his eyes without making a protest.

Ermolai, who had his own haughtiness, dodged Koupriane's fist and replied that he had wished to prevent the young Frenchman, but the reporter had shown him a police-paper on which Koupriane himself had declared in advance that the young Frenchman was to do anything he pleased.

XII

Pere Alexis

Koupriane jumped into his carriage and hurried toward St. Petersburg. On the way he spoke to three agents who only he knew were posted in the neighborhood of Eliaguine. They told him the route Rouletabille had taken. The reporter had certainly returned into the city. He hurried toward Troitski Bridge. There, at the corner of the Naberjnaia, Koupriane saw the reporter in a hired conveyance. Rouletabille was pounding his coachman in the back, Russian fashion, to make him go faster, and was calling with all his strength one of the few words he had had time to learn, "Naleva, naleva" (to the left). The driver was forced to understand at last, for there was no other way to turn than to the left. If he had turned to the right (naprava) he would have driven into the river. The conveyance clattered over the pointed flints of a neighborhood that led to a little street, Aptiekarski-Pereoulok, at the corner of the Katharine canal. This "alley of the pharmacists" as a matter of fact contained no pharmacists, but there was a curious sign of a herbarium, where Rouletabille made the driver stop. As the carriage rolled under the arch Rouletabille recognized Koupriane. He did not wait, but cried to him, "Ah, here you are. All right; follow me." He still had the flask and the glasses in his hands. Koupriane couldn't help noticing how strange he looked. He passed through a court with him, and into a squalid shop.

"What," said Koupriane, "do you know Pere Alexis?"

They were in the midst of a curious litter. Clusters of dried herbs hung from the ceiling, and all among them were clumps of old boots, shriveled skins, battered pans, scrap-iron, sheep-skins, useless touloupes, and on the floor musty old clothes, moth-eaten furs, and sheep-skin coats that even a moujik of the swamps would not have deigned to wear. Here and there were old teeth, ragged finery, dilapidated hats, and jars of strange herbs ranged upon some rickety shelving. Between the set of scales on the counter and a heap of little blocks of wood used for figuring the accounts of this singular business were ungilded ikons, oxidized silver crosses, and Byzantine pictures representing scenes from the Old and New Testaments. Jars of alcohol with what seemed to be the skeletons of frogs swimming in them filled what space was left. In a corner of this large, murky room, under the vault of mossed stone, a small altar stood and the light burned in a hanging glass of oil before the holy images. A man was praying before the altar. He wore the costume of old Russia, the caftan of green cloth, buttoned at the shoulder and tucked in at the waist by a narrow belt. He had a bushy beard and his hair fell to his shoulders. When he had finished his prayer he rose, perceived Rouletabille and came over to take his hand. He spoke French to the reporter:

"Well, here you are again, lad. Do you bring poison again today? This will end by being found out, and the police. . ."

Just then he discerned Koupriane's form in the shadow, drew close to make out who it was, and fell to his knees as he saw who it was. Rouletabille tried to raise him, but he insisted on prostrating himself. He was sure the Prefect of Police had come to his house to hang him. Finally he was reassured by Rouletabille's positive assertions and the great chief's robust laugh. The Prefect wished to know how the young man came to be acquainted with the "alchemist" of the police. Rouletabille told him in a few words.

Maitre Alexis, in his youth, went to France afoot, to study pharmacy, because of his enthusiasm for chemistry. But he always remained countrified, very much a Russian peasant, a semi-Oriental bear, and did not achieve his degree. He took some certificates, but the examinations were too much for him. For fifty years he lived miserably as a pharmacist's assistant in the back of a disreputable shop in the Notre Dame quarter. The proprietor of the place was implicated in the famous affair of the gold ingots, which started Rouletabille's reputation, and was arrested along with his assistant, Alexis. It was Rouletabille who proved, clear as day, that poor Alexis was innocent, and that he had never been cognizant of his master's evil ways, being absorbed in the depths of his laboratory in trying to work out a naive alchemy which fascinated him, though the world of chemistry had passed it by centuries ago. At the trial Alexis was acquitted, but found himself in the street. He shed what tears remained in his body upon the neck of the reporter, assuring him of paradise if he got him back to his own country, because he desired only the one thing more of life, that he might see his birth-land before he died. Rouletabille advanced the necessary means and sent him to St. Petersburg. There he was picked up at the end of two days by the police, in a petty gambling-game, and thrown into prison, where he promptly had a chance to show his talents. He cured some of his companions in misery, and even some of the guards. A guard who had an injured leg, whose healing he had despaired of, was cured by Alexis. Then there was found to be no actual charge against him. They set him free and, moreover, they interested themselves in him. They found meager employment for him in the Stchoukine-dvor, an immense popular bazaar. He accumulated a few roubles and installed himself on his own account at the back of a court in the Aptiekarski-Pereoulok, where he gradually piled up a heap of old odds and ends that no one wanted even in the Stchoukine-dvor. But he was happy, because behind his shop he had installed a little laboratory where he continued for his pleasure his experiments in alchemy and his study of plants. He still proposed to write a book that he had already spoken of in France to Rouletabille, to prove the truth of "Empiric Treatment of Medicinal Herbs, the Science of Alchemy, and the Ancient Experiments in Sorcery." Between times he continued to cure anyone who applied to him, and the police in particular. The police guards protected him and used him. He had splendid plasters for them after "the scandal," as they called the October riots. So when the doctors of the quarter tried to prosecute him for illegal practice, a deputation of police-guards went to Koupriane, who took the responsibility and discontinued proceedings against him. They regarded him as under protection of the saints, and Alexis soon came to be regarded himself as something of a holy man. He never failed every Christmas and Easter to send his finest images to Rouletabille, wishing him all prosperity and saying that if ever he came to St. Petersburg he should be happy to receive him at Aptiekarski-Pereoulok, where he was established in honest labor. Pere Alexis, like all the true saints, was a modest man.

When Alexis had recovered a little from his emotion Rouletabille said to him:

"Pere Alexis, I do bring you poison again, but you have nothing to fear, for His Excellency the Chief of Police is with me. Here is what we want you to do. You must tell us what poison these four glasses have held, and what poison is still in this flask and this little phial."

"What is that little phial?" demanded Koupriane, as he saw Rouletabille pull a small, stoppered bottle out of his pocket.

The reporter replied, "I have put into this bottle the vodka that was poured into Natacha's glass and mine and that we barely touched."

"Someone has tried to poison you!" exclaimed Pere Alexis.

"No, not me," replied Rouletabille, in bored fashion. "Don't think about that. Simply do what I tell you. Then analyze these two napkins, as well."

And he drew from his coat two soiled napkins.

"Well," said Koupriane, "you have thought of everything."

"They are the napkins the general and his wife used."

"Yes, yes, I understand that," said the Chief of Police.

"And you, Alexis, do you understand?" asked the reporter. "When can we have the result of your analysis?

"In an hour, at the latest."

"Very well," said Koupriane. "Now I need not tell you to hold your tongue. I am going to leave one of my men here. You will write us a note that you will seal, and he will bring it to head-quarters. Sure you understand? In an hour?"

"In an hour, Excellency."

They went out, and Alexis followed them, bowing to the floor. Koupriane had Rouletabille get into his carriage. The young man did as he was told. One would have said he did not know where he was or what he did. He made no reply to the chief's questions.

"This Pere Alexander," resumed Koupriane, "is a character, really quite a figure. And a bit of a schemer, I should say. He has seen how Father John of Cronstadt succeeded, and he says to himself, 'Since the sailors had their Father John of Cronstadt, why shouldn't the police-guard have their Father Alexis of Aptiekarski-Pereoulok?'"

But Rouletabille did not reply at all, and Koupriane wound up by demanding what was the matter with him.

"The matter is," replied Rouletabille, unable longer to conceal his anguish, "that the poison continues."

"Does that astonish you?" returned Koupriane. "It doesn't me."

Rouletabille looked at him and shook his head. His lips trembled as he said, "I know what you think. It is abominable. But the thing I have done certainly is more abominable still."

"What have you done, then, Monsieur Rouletabille?"

"Perhaps I have caused the death of an innocent man."

"So long as you aren't sure of it, you would better not fret about it, my dear friend."

"It is enough that the doubt has arisen," said the reporter, "almost to kill me;" and he heaved so gloomy a sigh that the excellent Monsieur Koupriane felt pity for the lad. He tapped him on the knee.

"Come, come, young man, you ought to know one thing by this time—'you can't make omelettes without breaking eggs,' as they say, I think, in Paris."

Rouletabille turned away from him with horror in his heart. If there should be another, someone besides Michael! If it was another hand than his that appeared to Matrena and him in the mysterious night! If Michael Nikolaievitch had been innocent! Well, he would kill himself, that was all. And those horrible words that he had exchanged with Natacha rose in his memory, singing in his ears as though they would deafen him.

"Do you doubt still?" he had asked her, "that Michael tried to poison your father?"

And Natacha had replied, "I wish to believe it! I wish to believe it, for your sake, my poor boy." And then he recalled her other words, still more frightful now! "Couldn't someone have tried to poison my father and not have come by the window?" He had faced such a hypothesis with assurance then—but now, now that the poison continued, continued within the house, where he believed himself so fully aware of all people and things—continued now that Michael Nikolaievitch was dead—ah, where did it come from, this poison?—and what was it? Pere Alexis would hurry his analysis if he had any regard for poor Rouletabille.

For Rouletabille to doubt, and in an affair where already there was one man dead through his agency, was torment worse than death.

When they arrived at police-headquarters, Rouletabille jumped from Koupriane's carriage and without saying a word hailed an empty isvotchick that was passing. He had himself driven back to Pere Alexis. His doubt mastered his will; he could not bear to wait away. Under the arch of Aptiekarski-Pereoulok he saw once more the man Koupriane had placed there with the order to bring him Alexis's message. The man looked at him in astonishment. Rouletabille crossed the court and entered the dingy old room once more. Pere Alexis was not there, naturally, engaged as he was in his laboratory. But a person whom he did not recognize at first sight attracted the reporter's attention. In the half-light of the shop a melancholy shadow leaned over the ikons on the counter. It was only when he straightened up, with a deep sigh, and a little light, deflected and yellow from passing through window-panes that had known no touch of cleaning since they were placed there, fell faintly on the face, that Rouletabille ascertained he was face to face with Boris Mourazoff. It was indeed he, the erstwhile brilliant officer whose elegance and charm the reporter had admired as he saw him at beautiful Natacha's feet in the datcha at Eliaguine. Now, no more in uniform, he had thrown over his bowed shoulders a wretched coat, whose sleeves swayed listlessly at his sides, in accord with his mood of languid desperation, a felt hat with the rim turned down hid a little the misery in his face in these few days, these not-many hours, how he was changed! But, even as he was, he still concerned Rouletabille. What was he doing there? Was he not going to go away, perhaps? He had picked up an ikon from the counter and carried it over to the window to examine its oxidized silver, giving such close attention to it that the reporter hoped he might reach the door of the laboratory without being noticed. He already had his hand on the knob of that door, which was behind the counter, when he heard his name called.

"It is you, Monsieur Rouletabille," said the low, sad voice of Boris. "What has brought you here, then?"

"Well, well, Monsieur Boris Mourazoff, unless I'm mistaken? I certainly didn't expect to find you here in Pere Alexis's place."

"Why not, Monsieur Rouletabille? One can find anything here in Pere Alexis's stock. See; here are two old ikons in wood, carved with sculptures, which came direct from Athos, and can't be equaled, I assure you, either at Gastini-Dvor nor even at Stchoukine-Dvor."

"Yes, yes, that is possible," said Rouletabille, impatiently. "Are you an amateur of such things?" he added, in order to say something.

"Oh, like anybody else. But I was going to tell you, Monsieur Rouletabille, I have resigned my commission. I have resolved to retire from the world; I am going on a long voyage." (Rouletabille thought: 'Why not have gone at once?') "And before going, I have come here to supply myself with some little gifts to send those of my friends I particularly care for, although now, my dear Monsieur Rouletabille, I don't care much for anything."

"You look desolate enough, monsieur."

Boris sighed like a child.

"How could it be otherwise?" he said. "I loved and believed myself beloved. But it proved to be—nothing, alas!"

"Sometimes one only imagines things," said Rouletabille, keeping his hand on the door.

"Oh, yes," said the other, growing more and more melancholy. "So a man suffers. He is his own tormentor; he himself makes the wheel on which, like his own executioner, he binds himself."

"It is not necessary, monsieur; it is not necessary," counseled the reporter.

"Listen," implored Boris in a voice that showed tears were not far away. "You are still a child, but still you can see things. Do you believe Natacha loves me?"

"I am sure of it, Monsieur Boris; I am sure of it."

"I am sure of it, too. But I don't know what to think now. She has let me go, without trying to detain me, without a word of hope."

"And where are you going like that?"

"I am returning to the Orel country, where I first saw her."

"That is good, very good, Monsieur Boris. At least there you are sure to see her again. She goes there every year with her parents for a few weeks. It is a detail you haven't overlooked, doubtless."

"Certainly I haven't. I will tell you that that prospect decided my place of retreat."

"See!"

"God gives me nothing, but He opens His treasures, and each takes what he can."

"Yes, yes; and Mademoiselle Natacha, does she know it is to Orel you have decided to retire?"

"I have no reason for concealing it from her, Monsieur Rouletabille."

"So far so good. You needn't feel so desolate, my dear Monsieur Boris. All is not lost. I will say even that I see a future for you full of hope."

"Ah, if you are able to say that truthfully, I am happy indeed to have met you. I will never forget this rope you have flung me when all the waters seemed closing over my head. 'What do you advise, then?"

"I advise you to go to Orel, monsieur, and as quickly as possible."

"Very well. You must have reasons for saying that. I obey you, monsieur, and go."

As Boris started towards the entrance-arch, Rouletabille slipped into the laboratory. Old Alexis was bent over his retorts. A wretched lamp barely lighted his obscure work. He turned at the noise the reporter made.

"Ah!—you, lad!"

"'Well?"

"Oh, nothing so quick. Still, I have already analyzed the two napkins, you know."

"Yes? The stains? Tell me, for the love of God!"

"Well, my boy, it is arsenate of soda again."

Rouletabille, stricken to the heart, uttered a low cry and everything seemed to dance around him. Pere Alexis in the midst of all the strange laboratory instruments seemed Satan himself, and he repulsed the kindly arms stretched forth to sustain him; in the gloom, where danced here and there the little blue flames from the crucibles, lively as flickering tongues, he believed he saw Michael Nikolaievitch's ghost come to cry, "The arsenate of soda continues, and I am dead." He fell against the door, which swung open, and he rolled as far as the counter, and struck his face against it. The shock, that might well have been fatal, brought him out of his intense nightmare and made him instantly himself again. He rose, jumped over the heap of boots and fol-de-rols, and leaped to the court. There Boris grabbed him by his coat. Rouletabille turned, furious:

"What do you want? You haven't started for the Orel yet?"

"Monsieur, I am going, but I will be very grateful if you will take these things yourself to—to Natacha." He showed him, still with despairing mien, the two ikons from Mount Athos, and Rouletabille took them from him, thrust them in his pocket, and hurried on, crying, "I understand."

Outside, Rouletabille tried to get hold of himself, to recover his coolness a little. Was it possible that he had made a mortal error? Alas, alas, how could he doubt it now! The arsenate of soda continued. He made a superhuman effort to ward off the horror of that, even momentarily—the death of innocent Michael Nikolaievitch—and to think of nothing except the immediate consequences, which must be carefully considered if he wished to avoid some new catastrophe. Ah, the assassin was not discouraged. And that time, what a piece of work he had tried! What a hecatomb if he had succeeded! The general, Matrena Petrovna, Natacha and Rouletabille himself (who almost regretted, so far as he was concerned, that it had not succeeded)—and Koupriane! Koupriane, who should have been there for luncheon. What a bag for the Nihilists! That was it, that was it. Rouletabille understood now why they had not hesitated to poison everybody at once: Koupriane was among them.

Michael Nikolaievitch would have been avenged!

The attempt had failed this time, but what might they not expect now! From the moment he believed Michael Nikolaievitch no longer guilty, as he had imagined, Rouletabille fell into a bottomless abyss.

Where should he go? After a few moments he made the circuit of the Rotunda, which serves as the market for this quarter and is the finest ornament of Aptiekarski-Pereoulok. He made the circuit without knowing it, without stopping for anything, without seeing or understanding anything. As a broken-winded horse makes its way in the treadmill, so he walked around with the thought that he also was lost in a treadmill that led him nowhere. Rouletabille was no longer Rouletabille.

XIII

The Living Bombs

At random—because now he could only act at random—he returned to the datcha. Great disorder reigned there. The guard had been doubled. The general's friends, summoned by Trebassof, surrounded the two poisoned sufferers and filled the house with their bustling devotion and their protestations of affection. However, an insignificant doctor from the common quarter of the Vasili-Ostrow, brought by the police, reassured everybody. The police had not found the general's household physician at home, but promised the immediate arrival of two specialists, whom they had found instead. In the meantime they had picked up on the way this little doctor, who was gay and talkative as a magpie. He had enough to do looking after Matrena Petrovna, who had been so sick that her husband, Feodor Feodorovitch, still trembled, "for the first time in his life," as the excellent Ivan Petrovitch said.

The reporter was astonished at not finding Natacha either in Matrena's apartment or Feodor's. He asked Matrena where her step-daughter was. Matrena turned a frightened face toward him. When they were alone, she said:

"We do not know where she is. Almost as soon as you left she disappeared, and no one has seen her since. The general has asked for her several times. I have had to tell him Koupriane took her with him to learn the details from her of what happened."

"She is not with Koupriane," said Rouletabille.

"Where is she? This disappearance is more than strange at the moment we were dying, when her father—O God! Leave me, my child; I am stifling; I am stifling."

Rouletabille called the temporary doctor and withdrew from the chamber. He had come with the idea of inspecting the house room by room, corner by corner, to make sure whether or not any possibility of entrance existed that he had not noticed before, an entrance would-be poisoners were continuing to use. But now a new fact confronted him and overshadowed everything: the disappearance of Natacha. How he lamented his ignorance of the Russian language—and not one of Koupriane's men knew French. He might draw something out of Ermolai.

Ermolai said he had seen Natacha just outside the gate for a moment, looking up and down the road. Then he had been called to the general, and so knew nothing further.

That was all the reporter could gather from the gestures rather than the words of the old servant.

An additional difficulty now was that twilight drew on, and it was impossible for the reporter to discern Natacha's foot-prints. Was it true that the young girl had fled at such a moment, immediately after the poisoning, before she knew whether her father and mother were entirely out of danger? If Natacha were innocent, as Rouletabille still wished to believe, such an attitude was simply incomprehensible. And the girl could not but be aware she would increase Koupriane's suspicions. The reporter had a vital reason for seeing her immediately, a vital reason for all concerned, above all in this moment when the Nihilists were culminating their plans, a vital reason for her and for him, equally menaced with death, to talk with her and to renew the propositions he had made a few minutes before the poisoning and which she had not wished to hear him talk about, in fearful pity for him or in defiance of him. Where was Natacha? He thought maybe she was trying to rejoin Annouchka, and there were reasons for that, both if she were innocent and if she were guilty. But where was Annouchka? Who could say! Gounsovski perhaps. Rouletabille jumped into an isvo, returning from the Point empty, and gave Gounsovski's address. He deigned then to recall that he had been invited that same day to dine with the Gounsovskis. They would no longer be expecting him. He blamed himself.

They received him, but they had long since finished dinner.

Monsieur and Madame Gounsovski were playing a game of draughts under the lamp. Rouletabille as he entered the drawing-room recognized the shining, fattish bald head of the terrible man. Gounsovski came to him, bowing, obsequious, his fat hands held out. He was presented to Madame Gounsovski, who was besprinkled with jewels over her black silk gown. She had a muddy skin and magnificent eyes. She also was tentatively effusive. "We waited for you, monsieur," she said, smirking timidly, with the careful charm of a woman a little along in years who relies still on infantine graces. As the recreant young man offered his apologies, "Oh, we know you are much occupied,

Monsieur Rouletabille. My husband said that to me only a moment ago. But he knew you would come finally. In the end one always accepts my husband's invitation." She said this with a fat smile of importance.

Rouletabille turned cold at this last phrase. He felt actual fear in the presence of these two figures, so atrociously commonplace, in their horrible, decent little drawing-room.

Madame continued:

"But you have had rather a bad dinner already, through that dreadful affair at General Trebassof's. Come into the dining-room." "Ah, so someone has told you?" said Rouletabille. "No, no, thanks; I don't need anything more. You know what has happened?"

"If you had come to dinner, perhaps nothing would have happened at all, you know," said Gounsovski tranquilly, seating himself again on the cushions and considering his game of draughts through his glasses. "Anyway, congratulations to Koupriane for being away from there through his fear."

For Gounsovski there was only Koupriane! The life or death of Trebassof did not occupy his mind. Only the acts and movements of the Prefect of Police had power to move him. He ordered a waiting-maid who glided into the apartment without making more noise than a shadow to bring a small stand loaded with zakouskis and bottles of champagne close to the game-table, and he moved one of his pawns, saying, "You will permit me? This move is mine. I don't wish to lose it."

Rouletabille ventured to lay his hand on the oily, hairy fist which extended from a dubious cuff.

"What is this you tell me? How could you have foreseen it?"

"It was easy to foresee everything," replied Gounsovski, offering cigars, "to foresee everything from the moment Matiew's place was filled by Priemkof."

"Well?" questioned Rouletabille, recalling with some inquietude the sight of the whipping in the guards' chapel.

"Well, this Priemkof, between ourselves," (and he bent close to the reporter's ear) "is no better, as a police-guard for Koupriane than Matiew himself. Very dangerous. So when I learned that he took Matiew's place at the datcha des Iles, I thought there was sure to be some unfortunate happening. But it was no affair of mine, was it? Koupriane would have been able to say to me, 'Mind your own business.' I had gone far enough in warning him of the 'living bombs.' They had been denounced to us by the same agency that enabled us to seize the two living bombs (women, if you please!) who were going to the military tribunal at Cronstadt after the rebellion in the fleet. Let him recall that. That ought to make him reflect. I am a brave man. I know he speaks ill of me; but I don't wish him any harm. The interests of the Empire before all else between us! I wouldn't talk to you as I do if I didn't know the Tsar honors you with his favor. Then I invited you to dinner. As one dines one talks. But you did not come. And, while you were dining down there and while Priemkof was on guard at the datcha, that annoying affair Madame Gounsovski has spoken about happened."

Rouletabille had not sat down, in spite of Madame Gounsovski's insistences. He took the box of cigars brusquely out of the hand of the Chief of the Secret Service, who had continued tendering them, for this detail of hospitality only annoyed his mood, which had been dark enough for hours and was now deepened by what the other had just said. He comprehended only one thing, that a man named Priemkof, whom he had never heard spoken of, as determined as Matiew to destroy the general, had been entrusted by Koupriane with the guard of the datcha des Iles. It was necessary to warn Koupriane instantly.

"How is it that you have not done so already, yourself, Monsieur Gounsovski? Why wait to speak about it to me? It is unimaginable."

"Pardon, pardon," said Gounsovski, smiling softly behind his goggles; "it is not the same thing."

"No, no, it is not the same thing," seconded the lady with the black silk, brilliant jewels and flabby chin. "We speak here to a friend in the course of dinner-talk, to a friend who is not of the police. We never denounce anybody."

"We must tell you. But sit down now," Gounsovski still insisted, lighting his cigar. "Be reasonable. They have just tried to poison him, so they will take time to breathe before they try something else. Then, too, this poison makes me think they may have given up the idea of living bombs. Then, after all, what is to be will be."

"Yes, yes," approved the ample dame. "The police never have been able to prevent what was bound to happen. But, speaking of this Priemkof, it remains between us, eh? Between just us?"

"Yes, we must tell you now," Gounsovski slipped in softly, "that it will be much better not to let Koupriane know that you got the information from me. Because then, you understand, he would not believe you; or, rather, he would not believe me. That is why we take these precautions of dining and smoking a cigar. We speak of one thing and another and you do as you please with what we say. But, to make them useful, it is absolutely necessary, I repeat, to be silent about their source." (As he said that, Gounsovski gave Rouletabille a piercing glance through his goggles, the first time Rouletabille had seen such a look in his eyes. He never would have suspected him capable of such fire.) "Priemkof," continued Gounsovski in a low voice, using his handkerchief vigorously, "was employed here in my home and we separated on bad terms, through his fault, it is necessary to say. Then he got into Koupriane's confidence by saying the worst he could of us, my dear little monsieur."

"But what could he say?—servants' stories! my dear little monsieur," repeated the fat dame, and rolled her great magnificent black eyes furiously. "Stories that have been treated as they deserved at Court, certainly. Madame Daquin, the wife of His Majesty's head-cook, whom you certainly know, and the nephew of the second Maid of Honor to the Empress, who stands very well with his aunt, have told us so; servants' stories that might have ruined us but have not produced any effect on His Majesty, for whom we would give our lives, Christ knows. Well, you understand now that if you were to say to Koupriane, 'Gaspadine Gounsovski has spoken ill to me of Priemkof,' he would not care to hear a word further. Still, Priemkof is in the scheme for the living bombs, that is all I can tell you; at least, he was before the affair of the poisoning. That poisoning is certainly very astonishing, between us. It does not appear to have come from without, whereas the living bombs will have to come from without. And Priemkof is mixed up in it."

"Yes, yes," approved Madame Gounsovski again, "he is committed to it. There have been stories about him, too. Other people as well as he can tell tales; it isn't hard to do. He has got to make some showing now if he is to keep in with Annouchka's clique."

"Koupriane, our dear Koupriane," interrupted Gounsovski, slightly troubled at hearing his wife pronounce Annouchka's name, "Koupriane ought to be able to understand that this time Priemkof must bring things off, or he is definitely ruined."

"Priemkof knows it well enough," replied Madame as she re-filled the glasses, "but Koupriane doesn't know it; that is all we can tell you. Is it enough? All the rest is mere gossip."

It certainly was enough for Rouletabille; he had had enough of it! This idle gossip and these living bombs! These pinchbecks, these whispering tale-tellers in their bourgeois, countrified setting; these politico-police combinations whose grotesque side was always uppermost; while the terrible side, the Siberian aspect, prisons, black holes, hangings, disappearances, exiles and deaths and martyrdoms remained so jealously hidden that no one ever spoke of them! All that weight of horror, between a good cigar and "a little glass of anisette, monsieur, if you won't take champagne." Still, he had to drink before he left, touch glasses in a health, promise to come again, whenever he wished—the house was open to him. Rouletabille knew it was open to anybody—anybody who had a tale to tell, something that would send some other person to prison or to death and oblivion. No guard at the entrance to check a visitor—men entered Gounsovski's house as the house of a friend, and he was always ready to do you a service, certainly!

He accompanied the reporter to the stairs. Rouletabille was just about to risk speaking of Annouchka to him, in order to approach the subject of Natacha, when Gounsovski said suddenly, with a singular smile:

"By the way, do you still believe in Natacha Trebassof?"

"I shall believe in her until my death," Rouletabille thrust back; "but I admit to you that at this moment I don't know where she has gone."

"Watch the Bay of Lachtka, and come to tell me tomorrow if you will believe in her always," replied Gounsovski, confidentially, with a horrid sort of laugh that made the reporter hurry down the stairs.

And now here was Priemkof to look after! Priemkof after Matiew! It seemed to the young man that he had to contend against all the revolutionaries not only, but all the Russian police as well—and Gounsovski himself, and Koupriane! Everybody, everybody! But most urgent was Priemkof and his living bombs. What a strange and almost incomprehensible and harassing adventure this was between Nihilism and the Russian police. Koupriane and Gounsovski both employed a man they knew to be a revolutionary and the friend of revolutionaries. Nihilism, on its side, considered this man of the police force as one of its own agents. In his turn, this man, in order to maintain his perilous equilibrium, had to do work for both the police and the revolutionaries, and accept whatever either gave him to do as it came, because it was necessary he should give them assurances of his fidelity. Only imbeciles, like Gapone, let themselves be hanged or ended by being executed, like Azef, because of their awkward slips. But a Priemkof, playing both branches of the police, had a good chance of living a long time, and a Gounsovski would die tranquilly in his bed with all the solaces of religion.

However, the young hearts hot with sincerity, sheathed with dynamite, are mysteriously moved in the atrocious darkness of Holy Russia, and they do not know where they will be sent, and it is all one to them, because all they ask is to die in a mad spiritual delirium of hate and love—living bombs![1]

At the corner of Aptiekarski-Pereoulok Rouletabille came in the way of Koupriane, who was leaving for Pere Alexis's place and, seeing the reporter, stopped his carriage and called that he was going immediately to the datcha.

"You have seen Pere Alexis?"

"Yes," said Koupriane. "And this time I have it on you. What I told you, what I foresaw, has happened. But have you any news of the sufferers? Apropos, rather a curious thing has happened. I met Kister on the Nevsky just now."

"The physician?"

"Yes, one of Trebassof's physicians whom I had sent an inspector to his house to fetch to the datcha, as well as his usual associate, Doctor Litchkof. Well, neither Litchkof nor he had been summoned. They didn't know anything had happened at the datcha. They had not seen my inspector. I hope he has met some other doctor on the way and, in view of the urgency, has taken him to the datcha."

"That is what has happened," replied Rouletabille, who had turned very pale. "Still, it is strange these gentlemen had not been notified, because at the datcha the Trebassofs were told that the general's usual doctors were not at home and so the police had summoned two others who would arrive at once."

Koupriane jumped up in the carriage.

"But Kister and Litchkof had not left their houses. Kister, who had just met Litchkof, said so. What does this mean?"

"Can you tell me," asked Rouletabille, ready now for the thunder-clap that his question invited, "the name of the inspector you ordered to bring them?"

"Priemkof, a man with my entire confidence."

Koupriane's carriage rushed toward the Isles. Late evening had come. Alone on the deserted route the horses seemed headed for the stars; the carriage behind seemed no drag upon them. The coachman bent above

---

1. In the trial after the revolt at Cronstadt two young women were charged with wearing bombs as false bosoms.

them, arms out, as though he would spring into the ether. Ah, the beautiful night, the lovely, peaceful night beside the Neva, marred by the wild gallop of these maddened horses!

"Priemkof! Priemkof! One of Gounsovski's men! I should have suspected him," railed Koupriane after Rouletabille's explanations. "But now, shall we arrive in time?"

They stood up in the carriage, urging the coachman, exciting the horses: "Scan! Scan! Faster, douriak!" Could they arrive before the "living bombs"? Could they hear them before they arrived? Ah, there was Eliaguine!

They rushed from the one bank to the other as though there were no bridges in their insensate course. And their ears were strained for the explosion, for the abomination now to come, preparing slyly in the night so hypocritically soft under the cold glance of the stars. Suddenly, "Stop, stop!" Rouletabille cried to the coachman.

"Are you mad!" shouted Koupriane.

"We are mad if we arrive like madmen. That would make the catastrophe sure. There is still a chance. If we wish not to lose it, then we must arrive easily and calmly, like friends who know the general is out of danger."

"Our only chance is to arrive before the bogus doctors. Either they aren't there, or it already is all over. Priemkof must have been surprised at the affair of the poisoning, but he has seized the opportunity; fortunately he couldn't find his accomplices immediately."

"Here is the datcha, anyway. In the name of heaven, tell your driver to stop the horses here. If the 'doctors' are already there it is we who shall have killed the general."

"You are right."

Koupriane moderated his excitement and that of his driver and horses, and the carriage stopped noiselessly, not far from the datcha. Ermolai came toward them.

"Priemkof?" faltered Koupriane.

"He has gone again, Excellency."

"How—gone again?"

"Yes, but he has brought the doctors."

Koupriane crushed Rouletabille's wrist. The doctors were there!

"Madame Trebassof is better," continued Ermolai, who understood nothing of their emotion. "The general is going to meet them and take them to his wife himself."

"Where are they?"

"They are waiting in the drawing-room."

"Oh, Excellency, keep cool, keep cool, and all is not lost," implored the reporter.

Rouletabille and Koupriane slipped carefully into the garden. Ermolai followed them.

"There?" inquired Koupriane.

"There," Ermolai replied.

From the corner where they were, and looking through the veranda, they could see the "doctors" as they waited.

They were seated in chairs side by side, in a corner of the drawing-room from where they could see every-thing in the room and a part of the garden, which they faced, and could hear everything. A window of the first-floor was open above their heads, so that they could hear any noise from there. They could not be surprised from any side, and they held every door in view. They were talking softly and tranquilly, looking straight before them. They appeared young. One had a pleasant face, pale but smiling, with rather long, curly hair; the other was more angular, with haughty bearing and grave face, an eagle nose and glasses. Both wore long black coats buttoned over their calm chests.

Koupriane and the reporter, followed by Ermolai, advanced with the greatest precaution across the lawn. Screened by the wooden steps leading to the veranda and by the vine-clad balustrade, they got near enough to hear them. Koupriane gave eager ear to the words of these two young men, who might have been so rich in the many years of life that naturally belonged to them, and who were about to die so horrible a death in destroying all about them. They spoke of what time it was, of the softness of the night and the beauty of the sky; they spoke of the shadows under the birch-trees, of the gulf shining in the late evening's fading golden light, of the river's freshness and the sweetness of springtime in the North. That is what they talked about. Koupriane murmured, "The assassins!"

Now it was necessary to decide on action, and that necessity was horrible. A false movement, an awkwardness, and the "doctors" would be warned, and everything lost. They must have the bombs under their coats; there were certainly at least two "living bombs." Their chests, as they breathed, must heave to and fro and their hearts beat against an impending explosion.

Above on the bedroom floor, they heard the rapid arranging of the room, steps on the floor and a confusion of voices; shadows passed across the window-space. Koupriane rapidly interrogated Ermolai and learned that all the general's friends were there. The two doctors had arrived only a couple of minutes before the Prefect of Police and the reporter. The little doctor of Vassili-Ostrow had already gone, saying there was nothing more for him to do when two such celebrated specialists had arrived. However, in spite of their celebrity, no one had ever heard the names they gave. Koupriane believed the little doctor was an accomplice. The most necessary thing was to warn those in the room above. There was immediate danger that someone would come downstairs to find the doctors and take them to the general, or that the general would come down himself to meet them. Evidently that was what they were waiting for. They wished to die in his arms, to make sure that this time he did not escape them! Koupriane directed Ermolai to go into the veranda and speak in a commonplace way to them at the threshold of the drawing-room door, saying that he would go upstairs and see if he might now escort them to Madame Trebassof's room. Once in the room above, he could warn the others not to do anything but wait for Koupriane; then Ermolai was to come down and say to the men, "In just a moment, if you please."

Ermolai crept back as far as the lodge, and then came quite normally up the path, letting the gravel crunch under his countrified footsteps. He was an intelligent man, and grasped with extraordinary coolness the importance of the plan of campaign. Easily and naturally he mounted the veranda steps, paused at the threshold of the drawing-room, made the remark he had been told to make, and went upstairs. Koupriane and Rouletabille now watched the bedroom windows. The flitting shadows there suddenly became motionless. All moving about ceased; no more steps were heard, nothing. And that sudden silence made the two "doctors" raise their faces toward the ceiling. Then they exchanged an aroused glance. This change in the manner of things above was dangerous. Koupriane muttered, "The idiots!" It was such a blow for those upstairs to learn they walked over a mine ready to explode that it evidently had paralyzed their limbs. Happily Ermolai came down almost immediately and said to the "doctors" in his very best domestic manner:

"Just a second, messieurs, if you please."

He did it still with utter naturalness. And he returned to the ledge before he rejoined Koupriane and Rouletabille by way of the lawn. Rouletabille, entirely cool, quite master of himself, as calm now as Koupriane was nervous, said to the Prefect of Police:

"We must act now, and quickly. They are commencing to be suspicious. Have you a plan?"

"Here is all I can see," said Koupriane. "Have the general come down by the narrow servants' stairway, and slip out of the house from the window of Natacha's sitting-room, with the aid of a twisted sheet. Matrena Petrovna will come to speak to them during this time; that will keep them patient until the general is out of danger. As soon as Matrena has withdrawn into the garden, I will call my men, who will shoot them from a distance."

"And the house itself? And the general's friends?"

"Let them try to get away, too, by the servants' stairway and jump from the window after the general. We must try something. Say that I have them at the muzzle of my revolver."

"Your plan won't work," said Rouletabille, "unless the door of Natacha's sitting-room that opens on the drawing-room is closed."

"It is. I can see from here."

"And unless the door of the little passage-way before that staircase that opens into the drawing-room is closed also, and you cannot see it from here."

"That door is open," said Ermolai.

Koupriane swore. But he recovered himself promptly.

"Madame Trebassof will close the door when she speaks to them."

"It's impracticable," said the reporter. "That will arouse their suspicions more than ever. Leave it to me; I have a plan."

"What?"

"I have time to execute it, but not to tell you about it. They have already waited too long. I shall have to go upstairs, though. Ermolai will need to go with me, as with a friend of the family."

"I'll go too."

"That would give the whole show away, if they saw you, the Prefect of Police."

"Why, no. If they see me—and they know I ought to be there—as soon as I show myself to them they will conclude I don't know anything about it."

"You are wrong."

"It is my duty. I should be near the general to defend him until the last."

Rouletabille shrugged his shoulders before this dangerous heroism, but he did not stop to argue. He knew that his plan must succeed at once, or in five minutes at the latest there would be only ruins, the dead and the dying in the datcha des Iles.

Still he remained astonishingly calm. In principle he had admitted that he was going to die. The only hope of being saved which remained to them rested entirely upon their keeping perfectly cool and upon the patience of the living bombs. Would they still have three minutes' patience?

Ermolai went ahead of Koupriane and Rouletabille. At the moment they reached the foot of the veranda steps the servant said loudly, repeating his lesson:

"Oh, the general is waiting for you, Excellency. He told me to have you come to him at once. He is entirely well and Madame Trebassof also."

When they were in the veranda, he added:

"She is to see also, at once, these gentlemen, who will be able to tell her there is no more danger."

And all three passed while Koupriane and Rouletabille vaguely saluted the two conspirators in the drawing-room. It was a decisive moment. Recognizing Koupriane, the two Nihilists might well believe themselves discovered, as the reporter had said, and precipitate the catastrophe. However, Ermolai, Koupriane and Rouletabille climbed the stairs to the bedroom like automatons, not daring to look behind them, and expecting the end each instant. But neither stirred. Ermolai went down again, by Rouletabille's order, normally, naturally, tranquilly. They went into Matrena Petrovna's chamber. Everybody was there. It was a gathering of ghosts.

Here was what had happened above. That the "doctors" still remained below, that they had not been received instantly, in brief, that the catastrophe had been delayed up to now was due to Matrena Petrovna, whose watchful love, like a watch-dog, was always ready to scent danger. These two "doctors" whose names she did not know, who arrived so late, and the precipitate departure of the little doctor of Vassili-Ostrow aroused her watchfulness. Before allowing them to come upstairs to the general she resolved to have a look at them herself downstairs. She arose from her bed for that; and now her presentiment was justified. When she saw Ermolai, sober and mysterious, enter with Koupriane's message, she knew instinctively, before he spoke, that there were bombs in the house. When Ermolai did speak it was a blow for everybody. At first she, Matrena Perovna, had been a frightened, foolish figure in the big flowered dressing-gown belonging to Feodor that she had wrapped about her in her haste. When Ermolai left, the general, who knew she only trembled for him, tried to reassure her, and, in the midst of the frightened silence of all of them, said a few words recalling the failure of all the previous attempts. But she shook her head and trembled, shaking with fear for him, in agony at the thought that she could do nothing there above those living bombs but wait for them to burst. As to the friends, already their limbs were ruined, absolutely ruined, in very truth. For a moment they were quite incapable of moving. The jolly Councilor of Empire, Ivan Petrovitch, had no longer a lively tale to tell, and the abominable prospect of "this horrible mix-up" right at hand rendered him much less gay than in his best hours at Cubat's place. And poor Thaddeus Tchitchnikoff was whiter than the snow that covers old Lithuania's fields when the winter's chase is on. Athanase Georgevitch himself was not brilliant, and his sanguine face had quite changed, as though he had difficulty in digesting his last masterpiece with knife and fork. But, in justice to them, that was the first instantaneous effect. No one could learn like that, all of a sudden, that they were about to die in an indiscriminate slaughter without the heart being stopped for a little. Ermolai's words had turned these amiable loafers into waxen statues, but, little by little, their hearts commenced to beat again and each suggested some way of preventing the disaster—all of them sufficiently incoherent—while Matrena Petrovna invoked the Virgin and at the same time helped Feodor Feodorovitch adjust his sword and buckle his belt; for the general wished to die in uniform.

Athanase Georgevitch, his eyes sticking out of his head and his body bent as though he feared the Nihlists just below him might perceive his tall form—through the floor, no doubt—proposed that they should throw themselves out of the window, even at the cost of broken legs. The saddened Councilor of Empire declared that project simply idiotic, for as they fell they would be absolutely at the disposal of the Nihilists, who would be attracted by the noise and would make a handful of dust of them with a single gesture through the window. Thaddeus Tchitchnikoff, who couldn't think of anything at all, blamed Koupriane and the rest of the police for not having devised something. Why hadn't they already got rid of these Nihilists? After the frightened silence they had kept at first, now they all spoke at once, in low voices, hoarse and rapid, with shortened breath, making wild movements of the arms and head, and walked here and there in the chamber quite without motive, but very softly on tiptoe, going to the windows, returning, listening at the doors, peering through the key-holes, exchanging absurd suggestions, full of the wildest imaginings. "If we should. . . if. . . if,"—everybody speaking and everybody making signs for the others to be quiet. "Lower! If they hear us, we are lost." And Koupriane, who did not come, and his police, who themselves had brought two assassins into the house, and were not able now to make them leave without having everybody jump! They were certainly lost. There was nothing left but to say their prayers. They turned to the general and Matrena Petrovna, who were wrapped in a close embrace. Feodor had taken the poor disheveled head of the good Matrena between his hands and pressed it upon his shoulders as he embraced her. He said, "Rest quietly against my heart, Matrena Petrovna. Nothing can happen to us except what God wills."

At that sight and that remark the others grew ashamed of their confusion. The harmony of that couple embracing in the presence of death restored them to themselves, to their courage, and their "Nitchevo." Athanase Georgevitch, Ivan Petrovitch and Thaddeus Tchitchnikoff repeated after Matrena Petrovna, "As God wills." And then they said "Nitchevo! Nitchevo![2] We will all die with you, Feodor Feodorovitch." And they all kissed one another and clasped one another in their arms, their eyes dim with love one for another, as at the end of a great banquet when they had eaten and drunk heavily in honor of one another.

"Listen. Someone is coming up the stairs," whispered Matrena, with her keen ear, and she slipped from the restraint of her husband.

Breathless, they all hurried to the door opening on the landing, but with steps as light "as though they walked on eggs." All four of them were leaning over there close by the door, hardly daring to breathe. They heard two men on the stairs. Were they Koupriane and Rouletabille, or were they the others? They had revolvers in their hands and drew back a little when the footsteps sounded near the door. Behind them Trebassof was quietly seated in his chair. The door was opened and Koupriane and Rouletabille perceived these death-like figures, motionless and mute. No one dared to speak or make a movement until the door had been closed. But then:

"Well? Well? Save us! Where are they? Ah, my dear little domovoi-doukh, save the general, for the love of the Virgin!"

"Tsst! tsst! Silence."

---

2. "What does it matter!"

Rouletabille, very pale, but calm, spoke:

"The plan is simple. They are between the two staircases, watching the one and the other. I will go and find them and make them mount the one while you descend by the other."

"Caracho! That is simple enough. Why didn't we think of it sooner? Because everybody lost his head except the dear little domovoi-doukh!"

But here something happened Rouletabille had not counted on. The general rose and said, "You have forgotten one thing, my young friend; that is that General Trebassof will not descend by the servants' stairway."

His friends looked at him in stupefaction, and asked if he had gone mad.

"What is this you say, Feodor?" implored Matrena.

"I say," insisted the general, "that I have had enough of this comedy, and that since Monsieur Koupriane has not been able to arrest these men, and since, on their side, they don't seem to decide to do their duty, I shall go myself and put them out of my house."

He started a few steps, but had not his cane and suddenly he tottered. Matrena Petrovna jumped to him and lifted him in her arms as though he were a feather.

"Not by the servants' stairway, not by the servants' stairway," growled the obstinate general.

"You will go," Matrena replied to him, "by the way I take you."

And she carried him back into the apartment while she said quickly to Rouletabille:

"Go, little domovoi! And God protect us!"

Rouletabille disappeared at once through the door to the main staircase, and the group attended by Koupriane, passed through the dressing-room and the general's chamber, Matrena Petrovna in the lead with her precious burden. Ivan Petrovitch had his hand already on the famous bolt which locked the door to the servants' staircase when they all turned at the sound of a quick step behind them. Rouletabille had returned.

"They are no longer in the drawing-room."

"Not in the drawing-room! Where are they, then?"

Rouletabille pointed to the door they were about to open.

"Perhaps behind that door. Take care!"

All drew back.

"But Ermolai ought to know where they are," exclaimed Koupriane. "Perhaps they have gone, finding out they were discovered."

"They have assassinated Ermolai."

"Assassinated Ermolai!"

"I have seen his body lying in the middle of the drawing-room as I leaned over the top of the banister. But they were not in the room, and I was afraid you would run into them, for they may well be hidden in the servants' stairway."

"Then open the window, Koupriane, and call your men to deliver us."

"I am quite willing," replied Koupriane coldly, "but it is the signal for our deaths."

"Well, why do they wait so to make us die?" muttered Feodor Feodorovitch. "I find them very tedious about it, for myself. What are you doing, Ivan Petrovitch?"

The spectral figure of Ivan Petrovitch, bent beside the door of the stairway, seemed to be hearing things the others could not catch, but which frightened them so that they fled from the general's chamber in disorder. Ivan Petrovitch was close on them, his eyes almost sticking from his head, his mouth babbling:

"They are there! They are there!"

Athanase Georgevitch open a window wildly and said:

"I am going to jump."

But Thaddeus Tchitchnikofl' stopped him with a word. "For me, I shall not leave Feodor Feodorovitch."

Athanase and Ivan both felt ashamed, and trembling, but brave, they gathered round the general and said, "We will die together, we will die together. We have lived with Feodor Feodorovitch, and we will die with him."

"What are they waiting for? What are they waiting for?" grumbled the general.

Matrena Petrovna's teeth chattered. "They are waiting for us to go down," said Koupraine.

"Very well, let us do it. This thing must end," said Feodor.

"Yes, yes," they all said, for the situation was becoming intolerable; "enough of this. Go on down. Go on down. God, the Virgin and Saints Peter and Paul protect us. Let us go."

The whole group, therefore, went to the main staircase, with the movements of drunken men, fantastic waving of the arms, mouths speaking all together, saying things no one but themselves understood. Rouletabille had already hurriedly preceded them, was down the staircase, had time to throw a glance into the drawing-room, stepped over Ermolai's huge corpse, entered Natacha's sitting-room and her chamber, found all these places deserted and bounded back into the veranda at the moment the others commenced to descend the steps around Feodor Feodorovitch. The reporter's eyes searched all the dark corners and had perceived nothing suspicious when, in the veranda, he moved a chair. A shadow detached itself from it and glided under the staircase. Rouletabille cried to the group on the stairs.

"They are under the staircase!"

Then Rouletabille confronted a sight that he could never forget all his life.

At this cry, they all stopped, after an instinctive move to go back. Feodor Feodorovitch, who was still in Matrena Petrovna's arms, cried:

"Vive le Tsar!"

And then, those whom the reporter half expected to see flee, distracted, one way and another, or to throw themselves madly from the height of the steps, abandoning Feodor and Matrena, gathered themselves instead by a spontaneous movement around the general, like a guard of honor, in battle, around the flag. Koupriane marched ahead. And they insisted also upon descending the terrible steps slowly, and sang the Bodje tsara Krani, the national anthem!

With an overwhelming roar, which shocked earth and sky and the ears of Rouletabille, the entire house seemed lifted in the air; the staircase rose amid flame and smoke, and the group which sang the Bodje tsara Krani disappeared in a horrible apotheosis.

XIV

The Marshes

They ascertained the next day that there had been two explosions, almost simultaneous, one under each staircase. The two Nihilists, when they felt themselves discovered, and watched by Ermolai, had thrown themselves silently on him as he turned his back in passing them, and strangled him with a piece of twine. Then they separated each to watch one of the staircases, reasoning that Koupriane and General Trebassof would have to decide to descend.

The datcha des Iles was nothing now but a smoking ruin. But from the fact that the living bombs had exploded separately the destructive effect was diffused, and although there were numerous wounded, as in the case of the attack on the Stolypine datcha, at least no one was killed outright; that is, excepting the two Nihilists, of whom no trace could be found save a few rags.

Rouletabille had been hurled into the garden and he was glad enough to escape so, a little shaken, but without a scratch. The group composed of Feodor and his friends were strangely protected by the lightness of the datcha's construction. The iron staircase, which, so to speak, almost hung to the two floors, being barely attached at top and bottom, raised under them and then threw them off as it broke into a thousand pieces, but only after, by its very yielding, it had protected them from the first force of the bomb. They had risen from the ruins without mortal wounds. Koupriane had a hand badly burned, Athanase Georgevitch had his nose and cheeks seriously hurt, Ivan Petrovitch lost an ear; the most seriously injured was Thaddeus Tchitchnikoff, both of whose legs were broken. Extraordinarily enough, the first person who appeared, rising from the midst of the wreckage, was Matrena Petrovna, still holding Feodor in her arms. She had escaped with a few burns and the general, saved again by the luck of the soldier whom Death does not want, was absolutely uninjured. Feodor gave shouts of joy. They strove to quiet him, because, after all, around him some poor wretches had been badly hurt, as well as poor Ermolai, who lay there dead. The domestics in the basement had been more seriously wounded and burned because the main force of the explosion had gone downwards; which had probably saved the personages above.

Rouletabille had been taken with the other victims to a neighboring datcha; but as soon as he had shaken himself free of that terrible nightmare he escaped from the place. He really regretted that he was not dead. These successive waves of events had swamped him; and he accused himself alone of all this disaster. With acutest anxiety he had inquired about the condition of each of "his victims." Feodor had not been wounded, but now he was almost delirious, asking every other minute as the hours crept on for Natacha, who had not reappeared. That unhappy girl Rouletabille had steadily believed innocent. Was she a culprit? "Ah, if she had only chosen to! If she had had confidence," he cried, raising anguished hands towards heaven, "none of all this need have happened. No one would have attacked and no one would ever again attack the life of Trebassof. For I was not wrong in claiming before Koupriane that the general's life was in my hand, and I had the right to say to him, 'Life for life! Give me Matiew's and I will give you the general's.' And now there has been one more fruitless attempt to kill Feodor Feodorovitch and it is Natacha's fault—that I swear, because she would not listen to me. And is Natacha implicated in it? O my God" Rouletabille asked this vain question of the Divinity, for he expected no more help in answering it on earth.

Natacha! Innocent or guilty, where was she? What was she doing? to know that! To know if one were right or wrong—and if one were wrong, to disappear, to die!

Thus the unhappy Rouletabille muttered as he walked along the bank of the Neva, not far from the ruins of the poor datcha, where the joyous friends of Feodor Feodorovitch would have no more good dinners, never; so he soliloquized, his head on fire.

And, all at once, he recovered trace of the young girl, that trace lost earlier, a trace left at her moment of flight, after the poisoning and before the explosion. And had he not in that a terrible coincidence? Because the poison might well have been only in preparation for the final attack, the pretext for the tragic arrival of the two false doctors. Natacha, Natacha, the living mystery surrounded already by so many dead!

Not far from the ruins of the datcha Rouletabille soon made sure that a group of people had been there the night before, coming from the woods near-by, and returning to them. He was able to be sure of this because the boundaries of the datcha had been guarded by troops and police as soon as the explosion took place, under orders to keep back the crowd that hurried to Eliaguine. He looked attentively at the grass, the ferns, the broken and trampled twigs. Certainly a struggle had occurred there. He could distinguish clearly in the soft earth of a narrow glade the prints of Natacha's two little boots among all the large footprints.

He continued his search with his heart heavier and heavier, he had a presentiment that he was on the point of discovering a new misfortune. The footprints passed steadily under the branches along the side of the Neva. From a bush he picked a shred of white cloth, and it seemed to him a veritable battle had taken place there. Torn branches strewed the grass. He went on. Very close to the bank he saw by examination of the soil, where there was no more trace of tiny heels and little soles, that the woman who had been found there was carried, and carried, into a boat, of which the place of fastening to the bank was still visible.

"They have carried off Natacha," he cried in a surge of anguish. "bungler that I am, that is my fault too—all my fault—all my fault! They wished to avenge Michael Nikolaievitch's death, for which they hold Natacha responsible, and they have kidnapped her."

His eyes searched the great arm of the river for a boat. The river was deserted. Not a sail, nothing visible on the dead waters! "What shall I do? What shall I do? I must save her."

He resumed his course along the river. Who could give him any useful information? He drew near a little shelter occupied by a guard. The guard was speaking to an officer. Perhaps he had noticed something during his watch that evening along the river. That branch of the river was almost always deserted after the day was over. A boat plying between these shores in the twilight would certainly attract attention. Rouletabille showed the guard the paper Koupriane had given him in the beginning, and with the officer (who turned out to be a police officer) as interpreter, he asked his questions. As a matter of fact the guard had been sufficiently puzzled by the doings and comings of a light boat which, after disappearing for an instant, around the bend of the river, had suddenly rowed swiftly out again and accosted a sailing-yacht which appeared at the opening of the gulf. It was one of those small but rapid and elegant sailing craft such as are seen in the Lachtka regattas.

Lachtka! "The Bay of Lachtka!"

The word was a ray of light for the reporter, who recalled now the counsel Gounsovski had given him. "Watch the Bay of Lachtka, and tell me then if you still believe Natacha is innocent!" Gounsovski must have known when he said this that Natacha had embarked in company with the Nihilists, but evidently he was ignorant that she had gone with them under compulsion, as their prisoner.

Was it too late to save Natacha? In any case, before he died, he would try in every way possible, so as at least to have kept her as much as he could from the disaster for which he held himself responsible. He ran to the Barque, near the Point.

His voice was firm as he hailed the canoe of the floating restaurant where, thanks to him, Koupriane had been thwarted in impotent anger. He had himself taken to just below Staria-Derevnia and jumped out at the spot where he saw little Katharina disappear a few days before. He landed in the mud and climbed on hands and knees up the slope of a roadway which followed the bank. This bank led to the Bay of Lachtka, not far from the frontier of Finland.

On Rouletabille's left lay the sea, the immense gulf with slight waves; to his right was the decaying stretch of the marsh. Stagnant water stretching to the horizon, coarse grass and reeds, an extraordinary tangle of water-plants, small ponds whose greenish scum did not stir under the stiff breeze, water that was heavy and dirty. Along this narrow strip of land thrust thus between the marsh, the sky and the sea, he hurried, with many tumbling, his eyes fixed on the deserted gulf. Suddenly he turned his head at a singular noise. At first he didn't see anything, but heard in the distance a vague clamoring while a sort of vapor commenced to rise from the marsh. And then he noticed, nearer him, the high marsh grasses undulating. Finally he saw a countless flock rising from the bed of the marshes. Beasts, groups of beasts, whose horns one saw like bayonets, jostled each other trying to keep to the firm land. Many of them swam and on the backs of some were naked men, stark naked, with hair falling to their shoulders and streaming behind them like manes. They shouted war-cries and waved their clubs. Rouletabille stopped short before this prehistoric invasion. He would never have imagined that a few miles from the Nevsky Prospect he could have found himself in the midst of such a spectacle. These savages had not even a loin-cloth. Where did they come from with their herd? From what remote place in the world or in old and gone history had they emerged? What was this new invasion? What prodigious slaughter-house awaited these unruly herds? They made a noise like thunder in the marsh. Here were a thousand unkempt haunches undulating in the marsh like the ocean as a storm approaches. The stark-naked men jumped along the route, waving their clubs, crying gutturally in a way the beasts seemed to understand. They worked their way out from the marsh and turned toward the city, leaving behind, to swathe the view of them a while and then fade away, a pestilential haze that hung like an aura about the naked, long-haired men. It was terrible and magnificent. In order not to be shoved into the water, Rouletabille had climbed a small rock that stood beside the route, and had waited there as though petrified himself. When the barbarians had finally passed by he climbed down again, but the route had become a bog of trampled filth.

Happily, he heard the noise of a primitive conveyance behind him. It was a telega. Curiously primitive, the telega is four-wheeled, with two planks thrown crudely across the axle-trees. Rouletabille gave the man who was seated in it three roubles, and jumped into the planks beside him, and the two little Finnish horses, whose manes hung clear to the mud, went like the wind. Such crude conveyances are necessary on such crude roads, but it requires a strong constitution to make a journey on them. Still, the reporter felt none of the jolting, he was so intent on the sea and the coast of Lachtka Bay. The vehicle finally reached a wooden bridge, across a murky creek. As the day commenced to fade colorlessly, Rouletabille jumped off onto the shore and his rustic equipage crossed to the Sestroriesk side. It was a corner of land black and somber as his thoughts that he surveyed now. "Watch the Bay of Lachtka!" The reporter knew that this desolate plain, this impenetrable marsh, this sea which offered the fugitive refuge in innumerable fords, had always been a useful retreat for Nihilistic adventurers. A hundred legends circulated in St. Petersburg about the mysteries of Lachtka marshes. And that gave him his last hope. Maybe he would be able to run across some revolutionaries to whom he could explain about Natacha, as prudently as possible; he might even see Natacha herself. Gounsovski could not have spoken vain words to him.

Between the Lachtkrinsky marsh and the strand he perceived on the edge of the forests which run as far as Sestroriesk a little wooden house whose walls were painted a reddish-brown, and its roof green. It was not the Russian isba, but the Finnish touba. However, a Russian sign announced it to be a restaurant. The young man had to take only a few steps to enter it. He was the only customer there. An old man, with glasses and a long gray beard, evidently the proprietor of the establishment, stood behind the counter, presiding over the zakouskis. Rouletabille chose some little sandwiches which he placed on a plate. He took a bottle of pivo and made the man understand that later, if it were possible, he would like a good hot supper. The other made a sign that he understood and showed him into an adjoining room which was used for diners. Rouletabille was quite ready enough to die in the face of his failures, but he did not wish to perish from hunger.

A table was placed beside a window looking out over the sea and over the entrance to the bay. It could not have been better and, with his eye now on the horizon, now on the estuary near-by, he commenced to eat with gloomy avidity. He was inclined to feel sorry for himself, to indulge in self-pity. "Just the same, two and two always make four," he said to himself; "but in my calculations perhaps I have forgotten the surd. Ah, there was a time when I would not have overlooked anything. And even now I haven't overlooked anything, if Natacha is innocent!" Having literally scoured the plate, he struck the table a great blow with his fist and said: "She is!"

Just then the door opened. Rouletabille supposed the proprietor of the place was entering.

It was Koupriane.

He rose, startled. He could not imagine by what mystery the Prefect of Police had made his way there, but he rejoiced from the bottom of his heart, for if he was trying to rescue Natacha from the hands of the revolutionaries Koupriane would be a valuable ally. He clapped the Prefect on the shoulder.

"Well, well!" he said, almost joyfully. "I certainly did not expect you here. How is your wound?"

"Nitchevo! Not worth speaking about; it's nothing."

"And the general and—! Ah, that frightful night! And those two unfortunates who—?"

"Nitchevo! Nitchevo!"

"And poor Ermolai!"

"Nitchevo! Nitchevo! It is nothing."

Rouletabille looked him over. The Prefect of Police had an arm in a sling, but he was bright and shining as a new ten-rouble piece, while he, poor Rouletabille, was so abominably soiled and depressed. Where did he come from? Koupriane understood his look and smiled.

"Well, I have just come from the Finland train; it is the best way."

"But what can you have come here to do, Excellency?"

"The same thing as you."

"Bah!" exclaimed Rouletabille, "do you mean to say that you have come here to save Natacha?"

"How—to save her! I come to capture her."

"To capture her?"

"Monsieur Rouletabille, I have a very fine little dungeon in Saints Peter and Paul fortress that is all ready for her."

"You are going to throw Natacha into a dungeon!"

"The Emperor's order, Monsieur Rouletabille. And if you see me here in person it is simply because His Majesty requires that the thing be done as respectfully and discreetly as possible."

"Natacha in prison!" cried the reporter, who saw in horror all obstacles rising before him at one and the same time. "For what reasons, pray?"

"The reason is simple enough. Natacha Feodorovna is the last word in wickedness and doesn't deserve anybody's pity. She is the accomplice of the revolutionaries and the instigator of all the crimes against her father."

"I am sure that you are mistaken, Excellency. But how have you been guided to her?"

"Simply by you."

"By me?"

"Yes, we lost all trace of Natacha. But, as you had disappeared also, I made up my mind that you could only be occupied in searching for her, and that by finding you I might have the chance to lay my hands on her."

"But I haven't seen any of your men?"

"Why, one of them brought you here."

"Me?"

"Yes, you. Didn't you climb onto a telega?"

"Ah, the driver."

"Exactly. I had arranged to have him meet me at the Sestroriesk station. He pointed out the place where you dropped off, and here I am."

The reporter bent his head, red with chagrin. Decidedly the sinister idea that he was responsible for the death of an innocent man and all the ills which had followed out of it had paralyzed his detective talents. He recognized it now. What was the use of struggling! If anyone had told him that he would be played with that way sometime, he, Rouletabille! he would have laughed heartily enough—then. But now, well, he wasn't capable of anything further. He was his own most cruel enemy. Not only was Natacha in the hands of the revolutionaries through his fault, by his abominable error, but worse yet, in the very moment when he wished to save her, he foolishly, naively, had conducted the police to the very spot where they should have been kept away. It was the depth of his humiliation; Koupriane really pitied the reporter.

"Come, don't blame yourself too much," said he. "We would have found Natacha without you; Gounsovski notified us that she was going to embark in the Bay of Lachtka this evening with Priemkof."

"Natacha with Priemkof!" exclaimed Rouletabille. "Natacha with the man who introduced the two living bombs into her father's house! If she is with him, Excellency, it is because she is his prisoner, and that alone will be sufficient to prove her innocence. I thank the Heaven that has sent you here."

Koupriane swallowed a glass of vodka, poured another after it, and finally deigned to translate his thought:

"Natacha is the friend of these precious men and we will see them disembark hand in hand."

"Your men, then, haven't studied the traces of the struggle that 'these precious men' have had on the banks of the Neva before they carried away Natacha?"

"Oh, they haven't been hoodwinked. As a matter of fact, the struggle was quite too visible not to have been done for appearances' sake. What a child you are! Can't you see that Natacha's presence in the datcha had become quite too dangerous for that charming young girl after the poisoning of her father and step-mother failed and at the moment when her comrades were preparing to send General Trebassof a pleasant little gift of dynamite? She arranged to get away and yet to appear kidnapped. It is too simple."

Rouletabille raised his head.

"There is something simpler still to imagine than the culpability of Natacha. It is that Priemkof schemed to pour the poison into the flask of vodka, saying to himself that if the poison didn't succeed at least it would make the occasion for introducing his dynamite into the house in the pockets of the 'doctors' that they would go to find."

Koupriane seized Rouletabille's wrist and threw some terrible words at him, looking into the depths of his eyes:

"It was not Priemkof who poured the poison, because there was no poison in the flask."

Rouletabille, as he heard this extraordinary declaration, rose, more startled than he had ever been in the course of this startling campaign.

If there was no poison in the flask, the poison must have been poured directly into the glasses by a person who was in the kiosk! Now, there were only four persons in the kiosk: the two who were poisoned and Natacha and himself, Rouletabille. And that kiosk was so perfectly isolated that it was impossible for any other persons than the four who were there to pour poison upon the table.

"But it is not possible!" he cried.

"It is so possible that it is so. Pere Alexis declared that there is no poison in the flask, and I ought to tell you that an analysis I had made after his bears him out. There was no poison, either, in the small bottle you took to Pere Alexis and into which you yourself had poured the contents of Natacha's glass and yours; no trace of poison excepting in two of the four glasses, arsenate of soda was found only on the soiled napkins of Trebassof and his wife and in the two glasses they drank from."

"Oh, that is horrible," muttered the stupefied reporter; "that is horrible, for then the poisoner must be either Natacha or me."

"I have every confidence in you," declared Koupriane with a great laugh of satisfaction, striking him on the shoulder. "And I arrest Natacha, and you who love logic ought to be satisfied now."

Rouletabille hadn't a word more to say. He sat down again and let his head fall into his hands, like one sleep has seized.

"Ah, our young girls; you don't know them. They are terrible, terrible!" said Koupriane, lighting a big cigar. "Much more terrible than the boys. In good families the boys still enjoy themselves; but the girls—they read! It goes to their heads. They are ready for anything; they know neither father nor mother. Ah, you are a child, you cannot comprehend. Two lovely eyes, a melancholy air, a soft, low voice, and you are captured—you believe you have before you simply an inoffensive, good little girl. Well, Rouletabille, here is what I will tell you for your instruction. There was the time of the Tchipoff attack; the revolutionaries who were assigned to kill Tchipoff were disguised as coachmen and footmen. Everything had been carefully prepared and it would seem that no one could have discovered the bombs in the place they had been stored. Well, do you know the place where those bombs were found? In the rooms of the governor, of Wladmir's daughter! Exactly, my little friend, just there! The rooms of the governor's daughter, Mademoiselle Alexeieiv.

Ah, these young girls! Besides, it was this same Mademoiselle Alexeieiv who, so prettily, pierced the brain of an honest Swiss merchant who had the misfortune to resemble one of our ministers. If we had hanged that charming young girl earlier, my dear Monsieur Rouletabille, that last catastrophe might have been avoided. A good rope around the neck of all these little females—it is the only way, the only way!"

A man entered. Rouletabille recognized the driver of the telega. There were some rapid words between the Chief and the agent. The man closed the shutters of the room, but through the interstices they would be able to see what went on outside. Then the agent left; Koupriane, as he pushed aside the table that was near the window, said to the reporter:

"You had better come to the window; my man has just told me the boat is drawing near. You can watch an interesting sight. We are sure that Natacha is still aboard. The yacht, after the explosion at the datcha, took up two men who put off to it in a canoe, and since then it has simply sailed back and forth in the gulf. We have taken our precautions in Finland the same as here and it is here they are going to try to disembark. Keep an eye on them."

Koupriane was at his post of observation. Evening slowly fell. The sky was growing grayish-black, a tint that blended with the slate-colored sea. To those on the bank, the sound of the men about to die came softly across the water. There was a sail far out. Between the strand and the touba where Koupriane watched, was a ridge, a window, which, however, did not hide the shore or the bay from the prefect of police, because at the height where he was his glance passed at an angle above it. But from the sea this ridge entirely hid anyone who lay in ambush behind it. The reporter watched fifty moujiks flat on their stomachs crawling up the ridge, behind two of their number whose heads alone topped the ridge. In the line of gaze taken by those two heads was the white sail, looming much larger now. The yacht was heeled in the water and glided with real elegance, heading straight on. Suddenly, just when they supposed she was coming straight to shore, the sails fell and a canoe was dropped over the side. Four men got into it; then a woman jumped lightly down a little gangway into the canoe. It was Natacha. Koupriane had no difficulty in recognizing her through the gathering darkness.

"Ah, my dear Monsieur Rouletabille," said he, "see your prisoner of the Nihilists. Notice how she is bound. Her thongs certainly are causing her great pain. These revolutionaries surely are brutes!"

The truth was that Natacha had gone quite readily to the rudder and while the others rowed she steered the light boat to the place on the beach that had been pointed out to her. Soon the prow of the canoe touched the sands. There did not seem to be a soul about, and that was the conclusion the men in the canoe who stood up looking around, seemed to reach. They jumped out, and then it was Natacha's turn. She accepted the hand held out to her, talking pleasantly with the men all the time. She even turned to press the hand of one of them. The group came up across the beach. All this time the watchers in the little eating-house could see the false moujiks, who had wriggled on their stomachs to the very edge of the ridge, holding themselves ready to spring.

Behind his shutter, Koupriane could not restrain an exclamation of triumph; he gradually identified some of the figures in the group, and muttered:

"Eh! eh! There is Priemkof himself and the others. Gounsovski is right and he certainly is well-informed; his system is decidedly a good one. What a net-full!"

He hardly breathed as he watched the outcome. He could discern elsewhere, beside the bay, flat on the ground, concealed by the slightest elevation of the soil, other false moujiks. The wood of Sestroriesk was watched in the same way. The group of revolutionaries who strolled behind Natacha stopped to confer. In three—maybe two—minutes, they would be surrounded—cut off, taken in the trap. Suddenly a gunshot sounded in the night, and the group, with startled speed, turned in their tracks and made silently for the sea, while from all directions poured the concealed agents and threw themselves into the pursuit, jostling each other and crying after the fugitives. But the cries became cries of rage, for the group of revolutionaries gained the beach. They saw Natacha, who was held up by Priemkof himself, reject the aid of the Nihilist, who did not wish to abandon her, in order that he might save himself. She made him go and seeing that she was going to be taken, stopped short and waited for the enemy stoically, with folded arms. Meanwhile, her three companions succeeded in throwing themselves into the canoe and plied the oars hard while Koupriane's men, in the water up to their chests, discharged their revolvers at the fugitives. The men in the canoe, fearing to wound Natacha, made no reply to the firing. The yacht had sails up by the time they drew alongside, and made off like a bird toward the mysterious fords of Finland, audaciously hoisting the black flag of the Revolution.

Meantime, Koupriane's agents, trembling before his anger, gathered at the eating-house. The Prefect of Police let his fury loose on them and treated them like the most infamous of animals. The capture of Natacha was little comfort. He had planned for the whole bag, and his men's stupidity took away all his self-control. If he had had a whip at hand he would have found prompt solace for his mined hopes. Natacha, standing in a corner, with her face singularly calm, watched this extraordinary scene that was like a menagerie in which the tamer himself had become a wild beast. From another corner, Rouletabille kept his eyes fixed on Natacha who ignored him. Ah, that girl, sphinx to them all! Even to him who thought a while ago that he could read things invisible to other vulgar men in her features, in her eyes! The impassive face of that girl whose father they had tried to assassinate only a few hours before and who had just pressed the hand of Priemkof, the assassin! Once she turned her head slightly toward Rouletabille. The reporter then looked towards her with increased eagerness, his eyes burning, as though he would say: "Surely, Natacha, you are not the accomplice of your father's assassins; surely it was not you who poured the poison!"

But Natacha's glance passed the reporter coldly over. Ah, that mysterious, cold mask, the mouth with its bitter, impudent smile, an atrocious smile which seemed to say to the reporter: "If it is not I who poured the poison, then it is you!"

It was the visage common enough to the daughters whom Koupriane had spoken of a little while before, "the young girls who read" and, their reading done, set themselves to accomplish some terrible thing, some thing because of which, from time to time, they place stiff ropes around the necks of these young females.

Finally, Koupriane's frenzy wore itself out and he made a sign. The men filed out in dismal silence. Two of them remained to guard Natacha. From outside came the sounds of a carriage from Sestroriesk ready to convey the girl to the Dungeons of Sts. Peter and Paul. A final gesture from the Prefect of Police and the rough bands of the two guards seized the prisoner's frail wrists. They hustled her along, thrust her outside, jamming her against the doorway, venting thus their anger at the reproaches of their chief. A few seconds later the carriage departed, not to stop until the fortress was reached with the trickling tombs under the bed of the river where young girls about to die are confined—who have read too much, without entirely understanding, as Monsieur Kropotkine says.

Koupriane prepared to leave in turn. Rouletabille stopped him.

"Excellency, I wish you to tell me why you have shown such anger to your men just now."

"They are brute beasts," cried the Chief of Police, quite beside himself again. "They have made me miss the biggest catch of my life. They threw themselves on the group two minutes too early. Some of them fired a gun that they took for the signal and that served to warn the Nihilists. But I will let them all rot in prison until I learn which one fired that shot."

"You needn't look far for that," said Rouletabille. "I did it."

"You! Then you must have gone outside the touba?"

"Yes, in order to warn them. But still I was a little late, since you did take Natacha."

Koupriane's eyes blazed.

"You are their accomplice in all this," he hurled at the reporter, "and I am going to the Tsar for permission to arrest you."

"Hurry, then, Excellency," replied the reporter coldly, "because the Nihilists, who also think they have a little account to settle with me, may reach me before you."

And he saluted.

XV

"I Have Been Waiting for You"

At the hotel a note from Gounsovski: "Don't forget this time to come tomorrow to have luncheon with me. Warmest regards from Madame Gounsovski." Then a horrible, sleepless night, shaken with echoes of explosions and the clamor of the wounded; and the solemn shade of Pere Alexis, stretching out toward Rouletabille a phial of poison and saying, "Either Natacha or you!" Then, rising among the shades the bloody form of Michael Nikolaievitch the Innocent!

In the morning a note from the Marshal of the Court.

Monsieur le Marechal had no particular good news, evidently, for in terms quite without enthusiasm he invited the young man to luncheon for that same day, rather early, at midday, as he wished to see him once more before he left for France. "I see," said Rouletabille to himself; "Monsieur le Marechal pronounces my expulsion from the country"— and he forgot once more the Gounsovski luncheon. The meeting-place named was the great restaurant called the Bear. Rouletabille entered it promptly at noon. He asked the schwitzar if the Grand Marshal of the Court had arrived, and was told no one had seen him yet. They conducted him to the huge main hall, where, however, there was only one person. This man, standing before the table spread with zakouskis, was stuffing himself. At the sound of Rouletabille's step on the floor this sole famished patron turned and lifted his hands to heaven as he recognized the reporter. The latter would have given all the roubles in his pocket to have avoided the recognition. But he was already face to face with the advocate so celebrated for his table-feats, the amiable Athanase Georgevitch, his head swathed in bandages and dressings from the midst of which one could perceive distinctly only the eyes and, above all, the mouth.

"How goes it, little friend?"

"How are you?"

"Oh, I! There is nothing the matter. In a week we shall have forgotten it."

"What a terrible affair," said the reporter, "I certainly believed we were all dead men."

"No, no. It was nothing. Nitchevo!"

"And poor Thaddeus Tchitchnikoff with his two poor legs broken!"

"Eh! Nitchevo! He has plenty of good solid splints that will make him two good legs again. Nitchevo! Don't you think anything more about that! It is nothing. You have come here to dine? A very celebrated house this. Caracho!" He busied himself to do the honors. One would have said the restaurant belonged to him. He boasted of its architecture and the cuisine "a la Francaise."

"Do you know," he inquired confidently, "a finer restaurant room anywhere in the world?"

In fact, it seemed to Rouletabille as he looked up into the high glass arch that he was in a railway station decorated for some illustrious traveler, for there were flowers and plants everywhere. But the visitor whom the ball awaited was the Russian eater, the ogre who never failed to come to eat at The Bear. Pointing out the lines of tables shining with their white cloths and bright silver, Athanase Georgevitch, with his mouth full, said:

"Ah, my dear little French monsieur, you should see it at supper-time, with the women, and the jewels, and the music. There is nothing in France that can give you any idea of it, nothing! The gayety—the champagne—and the jewels, monsieur, worth millions and millions of roubles! Our women wear them all—everything they have. They are decked like sacred shrines! All the family jewels—from the very bottom of the caskets! it is magnificent, thoroughly Russian—Muscovite! What am I saying? It is Asiatic. Monsieur, in the evening, at a fete, we are Asiatic. Let me tell you something on the quiet. You notice that this enormous dining hall is surrounded by those windowed balconies. Each of those windows belongs to a separate private room. Well, you see that window there?—yes, there—that is the room of a grand duke—yes, he's the one I mean—a very gay grand duke. Do you know, one evening when there was a great crowd here—families, monsieur, family parties, high-born families—the window of that particular balcony was thrown open, and a woman stark naked, as naked as my hand, monsieur, was dropped into the dining-hall and ran across it full-speed. It was a wager, monsieur, a wager of the jolly grand duke's, and the demoiselle won it. But what a scandal! Ah, don't speak of it; that would be very bad form. But—sufficiently Asiatic, eh? Truly Asiatic. And—something much more unfortunate—you see that table? It happened the Russian New Year Eve, at supper. All the beauty, the whole capital, was here. Just at midnight the orchestra struck up the Bodje tsara krani[1] to inaugurate the joyful Russian New Year, and everybody stood up, according to custom, and listened in silence, as loyal subjects should. Well, at that table, accompanying his family, there was a young student, a fine fellow, very correct, and in uniform. This unhappy young student, who had risen like everybody else, to listen to the Bodje tsara krani, inadvertently placed his knee on a chair. Truly that is not a correct attitude, monsieur, but really it was no reason for killing him, was it now? Certainly not. Well, a brute in uniform, an officer quite immaculately gotten-up, drew a revolver from his pocket and discharged it at the student point-blank. You can imagine the scandal, for the student was dead! There were Paris journalists there, besides, who had never been there before, you see! Monsieur Gaston Leroux was at that very table. What a scandal! They had a regular battle. They broke carafes over the head of the assassin— for he was neither more nor less than an assassin, a drinker of blood— an Asiatic. They picked up the assassin, who was bleeding all over, and carried him off to look after him. As to the dead man, he lay stretched out there under a table-cloth, waiting for the police—and those at the tables went on with their drinking. Isn't that Asiatic enough for you? Here, a naked woman; there, a corpse! And the jewels—and the champagne! What do you say to that?"

"His Excellency the Grand Marshal of the Court is waiting for you, Monsieur."

Rouletabille shook hands with Athanase Georgevitch, who returned to his zakouskis, and followed the interpreter to the door of one of the private rooms. The high dignitary was there. With a charm in his politeness of which the high-born Russian possesses the secret over almost everybody else in the world, the Marshal intimated to Rouletabille that he had incurred imperial displeasure.

"You have been denounced by Koupriane, who holds you responsible for the checks he has suffered in this affair."

"Monsieur Koupriane is right," replied Rouletabille, "and His Majesty should believe him, since it is the truth. But don't fear anything from me, Monsieur le Grand Marechal, for I shall not inconvenience Monsieur Koupriane any further, nor anybody else. I shall disappear."

"I believe Koupriane is already directed to vise your passport."

---

1. The Russian national anthem.

"He is very good, and he does himself much harm."

"All that is a little your fault, Monsieur Rouletabille. We believed we could consider you as a friend, and you have never failed, it appears, on each occasion to give your help to our enemies.

"Who says that?"

"Koupriane. Oh, it is necessary to be one with us. And you are not one with us. And if you are not for us you are against us. You understand that, I think. That is the way it has to be. The Terrorists have returned to the methods of the Nihilists, who succeeded altogether too well against Alexander II. When I tell you that they succeeded in placing their messages even in the imperial palace. . ."

"Yes, yes," said Rouletabille, vaguely, as though he were already far removed from the contingencies of this world. "I know that Czar Alexander II sometimes found under his napkin a letter announcing his condemnation to death."

"Monsieur, at the Chateau yesterday morning something happened that is perhaps more alarming than the letter found by Alexander II under his napkin."

"What can it be? Have bombs been discovered?"

"No. It is a bizarre occurrence and almost unbelievable. The eider downs, all the eider down coverings belonging to the imperial family disappeared yesterday morning."[2]

"Surely not!"

"It is just as I say. And it was impossible to learn what had become of them—until yesterday evening, when they were found again in their proper places in the chambers. That is the new mystery!"

"Certainly. But how were they taken out?"

"Shall we ever know? All we found was two feathers, this morning, in the boudoir of the Empress, which leads us to think that the eider downs were taken out that way. I am taking the two feathers to Koupriane."

"Let me see them," asked the reporter.

Rouletabille looked them over and handed them back.

"And what do you think the whole affair means?"

"We are inclined to regard it as a threat by the revolutionaries. If they can carry away the eider downs, it would be quite as easy for them to carry away. . ."

---

2. Historically authentic.

"The Imperial family? No, I don't think it is that."

"What do you mean, then?"

"I? Nothing any more. Not only do I not think any more, but I don't wish to. Tell me, Monsieur le Grand Marechal, it is useless, I suppose, to try to see His Majesty before I go?"

"What good would it do, monsieur? We know everything now. This Natacha that you defended against Koupriane is proved the culprit. The last affair does not leave that in any reasonable doubt. And she is taken care of from this time on. His Majesty wishes never to hear Natacha spoken of again under any pretext."

"And what are you going to do with that young girl?"

"The Tsar has decided that there shall not be any trial and that the daughter of General Trebassof shall be sent, by administrative order, to Siberia. The Tsar, monsieur, is very good, for he might have had her hanged. She deserved it."

"Yes, yes, the Tsar is very good."

"You are very absorbed, Monsieur Rouletabille, and you are not eating."

"I have no appetite, Monsieur le Marechal. Tell me,—the Emperor must be rather bored at Tsarskoie-Coelo?"

"Oh, he has plenty of work. He rises at seven o'clock and has a light English luncheon—tea and toast. At eight o'clock he starts and works till ten. From ten to eleven he promenades."

"In the jail-yard?" asked Rouletabille innocently.

"What's that you say? Ah, you are an enfant terrible! Certainly we do well to send you away. Until eleven he promenades in a pathway of the park. From eleven to one he holds audience; luncheon at one; then he spends the time until half-past two with his family."

"What does he eat?"

"Soup. His Majesty is wonderfully fond of soup. He takes it at every meal. After luncheon he smokes, but never a cigar—always cigarettes, gifts of the Sultan; and he only drinks one liqueur, Maraschino. At half-past two he goes out again for a little air—always in his park; then he sets himself to work until eight o'clock. It is simply frightful work, with heaps of useless papers and numberless signatures. No secretary can spare him that ungrateful bureaucratic duty. He must sign, sign, sign, and read, read, read the reports. And it is work without any beginning or end; as soon as some reports go, others arrive. At eight o'clock, dinner, and then more signatures, working right up to eleven o'clock. At eleven o'clock he goes to bed."

"And he sleeps to the rhythmical tramp of the guards on patrol," added Rouletabille, bluntly.

"O young man, young man!"

"Pardon me, Monsieur le Grand Marechal," said the reporter, rising; "I am, indeed, a disturbing spirit and I know that I have nothing more to do in this country. You will not see me any more, Monsieur le Grand Marechal; but before leaving I ought to tell you how much I have been touched by the hospitality of your great nation. That hospitality is sometimes a little dangerous, but it is always magnificent. No other nation in the world knows like the Russians how to receive a man, Your Excellency. I speak as I feel; and that isn't affected by my manner of quitting you, for you know also how to put a man to the door. Adieu, then; without any rancor. My most respectful homage to His Majesty. Ah, just one word more! You will recall that Natacha Feodorovna was engaged to poor Boris Mourazoff, still another young man who has disappeared and who, before disappearing, charged me to deliver to General Trebassof's daughter this last token—these two little ikons. I entrust you with this mission, Monsieur le Grand Marechal. Your servant, Excellency."

Rouletabille re-descended the great Kaniouche. "Now," said he to himself, "it is my turn to buy farewell presents." And he made his way slowly across la Place des Grandes-Ecuries and the bridge of the Katharine canal. He entered Aptiekarski-Pereoulok and pushed open Pere Alexis's door, under the arch, at the back of the obscure court.

"Health and prosperity, Alexis Hutch!"

"Ah, you again, little man! Well? Koupriane has let you know the result of my analyses?"

"Yes, yes. Tell me, Alexis Hutch, you are sure you are not mistaken? You don't think you might be mistaken? Think carefully before you answer. It is a question of life or death."

"For whom?"

"For me."

"For you, good little friend! You want to make your old Pere Alexis laugh—or weep!"

"Answer me."

"No, I couldn't be mistaken. The thing is as certain as that we two are here—arsenate of soda in the stains on the two napkins and traces of arsenate of soda in two of the four glasses; none in the carafe, none in the little bottle, none in the two glasses. I say it before you and before God."

"So it is really true. Thank you, Alexis Hutch. Koupriane has not tried to deceive me. There has been nothing of that sort. Well, do you know, Alexis Hutch, who has poured the poison? It is she or I. And as it is not I, it is she. And since it is she, well, I am going to die!"

"You love her, then?" inquired Pere Alexis.

"No," replied Rouletabille, with a self-mocking smile. "No, I don't love her. But if it is she who poured the poison, then it was not Michael Nikolaievitch, and it is I who had Michael Nikolaievitch killed. You can see now that therefore I must die. Show me your finest images.

"Ah, my little one, if you will permit your old Alexis to make you a gift, I would offer you these two poor ikons that are certainly from the convent of Troitza at its best period. See how beautiful they are, and old. Have you ever seen so beautiful a Mother of God? And this St. Luke, would you believe that the hand had been mended, eh? Two little masterpieces, little friend! If the old masters of Salonika returned to the world they would be satisfied with their pupils at Troitza. But you mustn't kill yourself at your age!"

"Come, bat ouclzka (little father), I accept your gift, and, if I meet the old Salonican masters on the road I am going to travel, I shan't fail to tell them there is no person here below who appreciates them like a certain pere of Aptiekarski-Pereoulok, Alexis Hutch."

So saying Rouletabille wrapped up the two little ikons and put them in his pocket. The Saint Luke would be sure to appeal to his friend Sainclair. As to the Mother of God, that would be his dying gift to the Dame en noir.

"Ah, you are sad, little son; and your voice, as it sounds now, hurts me."

Rouletabille turned his head at the sound of two moujiks who entered, carrying a long basket.

"What do you want?" demanded Pere Alexis in Russian, "and what is that you are bringing in? Do you intend to fill that huge basket with my goods? In that case you are very welcome and I am your humble servant."

But the two chuckled.

"Yes, yes, we have come to rid your shop of a wretched piece of goods that litters it."

"What is this you say?" inquired the old man, anxiously, and drawing near Rouletabille. "Little friend, watch these men; I don't recognize their faces and I can't understand why they have come here."

Rouletabille looked at the new-comers, who drew near the counter, after depositing their long basket close to the door. There was a sarcastic and malicious mocking way about them that struck him from the first. But while they kept up their jabbering with Pere Alexis he filled his pipe and proceeded to light it. Just then the door was pushed open again and three men entered, simply dressed, like respectable small merchants. They also acted curiously and looked all around the shop. Pere Alexis grew more and more alarmed and the others pulled rudely at his beard.

"I believe these men here have come to rob me," he cried in French. "What do you say, my son?—Shall I call the police?"

"Hold on," replied Rouletabille impassively. "They are all armed; they have revolvers in their pockets."

Pere Alexis's teeth commenced to chatter. As he tried to get near the door he was roughly pushed back and a final personage entered, apparently a gentleman, and dressed as such, save that he wore a visored leather cap.

"Ah," said he at once in French, "why, it is the young French journalist of the Grand-Morskaia Hotel. Salutations and your good health! I see with pleasure that you also appreciate the counsels of our dear Pere Alexis."

"Don't listen to him, little friend; I don't know him," cried Alexis Hutch.

But the gentleman of the Neva went on:

"He is a man close to the first principles of science, and therefore not far from divine; he is a holy man, whom it is good to consult at moments when the future appears difficult. He knows how to read as no one else can—Father John of Cronstadt excepted, to be strictly accurate—on the sheets of bull-hide where the dark angels have traced mysterious signs of destiny."

Here the gentleman picked up an old pair of boots, which he threw on the counter in the midst of the ikons.

"Pere Alexis, perhaps these are not bull-hide, but good enough cow-hide. Don't you want to read on this cow-hide the future of this young man?"

But here Rouletabille advanced to the gentleman, and blew an enormous cloud of smoke full in his face.

"It is useless, monsieur," said Rouletabille, "to waste your time and your breath. I have been waiting for you."

XVI

Before the Revolutionary Tribunal

Only, Rouletabille refused to be put into the basket. He would not let them disarm him until they promised to call a carriage. The Vehicle rolled into the court, and while Pere Alexis was kept back in his shop at the point of a revolver, Rouletabille quietly got in, smoking his pipe. The man who appeared to be the chief of the band (the gentleman of the Neva) got in too and sat down beside him. The carriage windows were shuttered, preventing all communication with the outside, and only a tiny lantern lighted the interior. They started. The carriage was driven by two men in brown coats trimmed with false astrakhan. The dvornicks saluted, believing it a police affair. The concierge made the sign of the cross.

The journey lasted several hours without other incidents than those brought about by the tremendous jolts, which threw the two passengers inside one on top of the other. This might have made an opening for conversation; and the "gentleman of the Neva" tried it; but in vain. Rouletabille would not respond. At one moment, indeed, the gentleman, who was growing bored, became so pressing that the reporter finally said in the curt tone he always used when he was irritated:

"I pray you, monsieur, let me smoke my pipe in peace."

Upon which the gentleman prudently occupied himself in lowering one of the windows, for it grew stifling.

Finally, after much jolting, there was a stop while the horses were changed and the gentleman asked Rouletabille to let himself be blindfolded. "The moment has come; they are going to hang me without any form of trial," thought the reporter, and when, blinded with the bandage, he felt himself lifted under the arms, there was revolt of his whole being, that being which, now that it was on the point of dying, did not wish to cease. Rouletabille would have believed himself stronger, more courageous, more stoical at least. But blind instinct swept all of this away, that instinct of conservation which had no concern with the minor bravadoes of the reporter, no concern with the fine heroic manner, of the determined pose to die finely, because the instinct of conservation, which is, as its rigid name indicates, essentially materialistic, demands only, thinks of nothing but, to live. And it was that instinct which made Rouletabille's last pipe die out unpuffed.

The young man was furious with himself, and he grew pale with the fear that he might not succeed in mastering this emotion, he took fierce hold of himself and his members, which had stiffened at the contact of seizure by rough hands, relaxed, and he allowed himself to be led. Truly, he was disgusted with his faintness and weakness. He had seen men die who knew they were going to die. His task as reporter had led him more than once to the foot of the guillotine. And the wretches he had seen there had died bravely. Extraordinarily enough, the most criminal had ordinarily met death most bravely. Of course, they had had leisure to prepare themselves, thinking a long time in advance of that supreme moment. But they affronted death, came to it almost negligently, found strength even to say banal or taunting things to those around them. He recalled above all a boy of eighteen years old who had cowardly murdered an old woman and two children in a back-country farm, and had walked to his death without a tremor, talking reassuringly to the priest and the police official, who walked almost sick with horror on either side of him. Could he, then, not be as brave as that child?

They made him mount some steps and he felt that he had entered the stuffy atmosphere of a closed room. Then someone removed the bandage. He was in a room of sinister aspect and in the midst of a rather large company.

Within these naked, neglected walls there were about thirty young men, some of them apparently quite as young as Rouletabille, with candid blue eyes and pale complexions. The others, older men, were of the physical type of Christs, not the animated Christs of Occidental painters, but those that are seen on the panels of the Byzantine school or fastened on the ikons, sculptures of silver or gold. Their long hair, deeply parted in the middle, fell upon their shoulders in curl-tipped golden masses. Some leant against the wall, erect, and motionless. Others were seated on the floor, their legs crossed. Most of them were in winter coats, bought in the bazaars. But there were also men from the country, with their skins of beasts, their sayons, their touloupes. One of them had his legs laced about with cords and was shod with twined willow twigs. The contrast afforded by various ones of these grave and attentive figures showed that representatives from the entire revolutionary party were present. At the back of the room, behind a table, three young men were seated, and the oldest of them was not more than twenty-five and had the benign beauty of Jesus on feast-days, canopied by consecrated palms.

In the center of the room a small table stood, quite bare and without any apparent purpose.

On the right was another table with paper, pens and ink-stands. It was there that Rouletabille was conducted and asked to be seated. Then he saw that another man was at his side, who was required to keep standing. His face was pale and desperate, very drawn. His eyes burned somberly, in spite of the panic that deformed his features Rouletabille recognized one of the unintroduced friends whom Gounsovski had brought with him to the supper at Krestowsky. Evidently since then the always-threatening misfortune had fallen upon him. They were proceeding with his trial. The one who seemed to preside over these strange sessions pronounced a name:

"Annouchka!"

A door opened, and Annouchka appeared.

Rouletabille hardly recognized her, she was so strangely dressed, like the Russian poor, with her under-jacket of red-flannel and the handkerchief which, knotted under her chin, covered all her beautiful hair.

She immediately testified in Russian against the man, who protested until they compelled him to be silent. She drew from her pocket papers which were read aloud, and which appeared to crush the accused. He fell back onto his seat. He shivered. He hid his head in his hands, and Rouletabille saw the hands tremble. The man kept that position while the other witnesses were heard, their testimony arousing murmurs of indignation that were quickly checked. Annouchka had gone to take her place with the others against the wall, in the shadows which more and more invaded the room, at this ending of a lugubrious day. Two windows reaching to the floor let a wan light creep with difficulty through their dirty panes, making a vague twilight in the room. Soon nothing could be seen of the motionless figures against the wall, much as the faces fade in the frescoes from which the centuries have effaced the colors in the depths of orthodox convents.

Now someone from the depths of the shadow and the appalling silence read something; the verdict, doubtless.

The voice ceased.

Then some of the figures detached themselves from the wall and advanced.

The man who crouched near Rouletabille rose in a savage bound and cried out rapidly, wild words, supplicating words, menacing words.

And then—nothing more but strangling gasps. The figures that had moved out from the wall had clutched his throat.

The reporter said, "It is cowardly."

Annouchka's voice, low, from the depths of shadow, replied, "It is just."

But Rouletabille was satisfied with having said that, for he had proved to himself that he could still speak. His emotion had been such, since they had pushed him into the center of this sinister and expeditious revolutionary assembly of justice, that he thought of nothing but the terror of not being able to speak to them, to say something to them, no matter what, which would prove to them that he had no fear. Well, that was over. He had not failed to say, "That is cowardly."

And he crossed his arms. But he soon had to turn away his head in order not to see the use the table was put to that stood in the center of the room, where it had seemed to serve no purpose.

They had lifted the man, still struggling, up onto the little table. They placed a rope about his neck. Then one of the "judges," one of the blond young men, who seemed no older than Rouletabille, climbed on the table and slipped the other end of the rope through a great ring-bolt that projected from a beam of the ceiling. During this time the man struggled futilely, and his death-rattle rose at last though the continued noise of his resistance and its overcoming. But his last breath came with so violent a shake of the body that the whole death-apparatus, rope and ring-bolt, separated from the ceiling, and rolled to the ground with the dead man.

Rouletabille uttered a cry of horror. "You are assassins!" he cried. But was the man surely dead? It was this that the pale figures with the yellow hair set themselves to make sure of. He was. Then they brought two sacks and the dead man was slipped into one of them.

Rouletabille said to them:

"You are braver when you kill by an explosion, you know."

He regretted bitterly that he had not died the night before in the explosion. He did not feel very brave. He talked to them bravely enough, but he trembled as his time approached. That death horrified him. He tried to keep from looking at the other sack. He took the two ikons, of

Saint Luke and of the Virgin, from his pocket and prayed to them. He thought of the Lady in Black and wept.

A voice in the shadows said:

"He is crying, the poor little fellow."

It was Annouchka's voice.

Rouletabille dried his tears and said:

"Messieurs, one of you must have a mother."

But all the voices cried:

"No, no, we have mothers no more!"

"They have killed them," cried some. "They have sent them to Siberia," cried others.

"Well, I have a mother still," said the poor lad. "I will not have the opportunity to embrace her. It is a mother that I lost the day of my birth and that I have found again, but—I suppose it is to be said—on the day of my death. I shall not see her again. I have a friend; I shall not see him again either. I have two little ikons here for them, and I am going to write a letter to each of them, if you will permit it. Swear to me that you will see these reach them."

"I swear it," said, in French, the voice of Annouchka.

"Thanks, madame, you are kind. And now, messieurs, that is all I ask of you. I know I am here to reply to very grave accusations. Permit me to say to you at once that I admit them all to be well founded. Consequently, there need be no discussion between us. I have deserved death and I accept it. So permit me not to concern myself with what will be going on here. I ask of you simply, as a last favor, not to hasten your preparations too much, so that I may be able to finish my letters."

Upon which, satisfied with himself this time, he sat down again and commenced to write rapidly. They left him in peace, as he desired. He did not raise his head once, even at the moment when a murmur louder than usual showed that the hearers regarded Rouletabille's crimes with especial detestation. He had the happiness of having entirely completed his correspondence when they asked him to rise to hear judgment pronounced upon him. The supreme communion that he had just had with his friend Sainclair and with the dear Lady in Black restored all his spirit to him. He listened respectfully to the sentence which condemned him to death, though he was busy sliding his tongue along the gummed edge of his envelope.

These were the counts on which he was to be hanged:

1. Because he had come to Russia and mixed in affairs that did not concern his nationality, and had done this in spite of warning to remain in France.
2. Because he had not kept the promises of neutrality he freely made to a representative of the Central Revolutionary Committee.
3. For trying to penetrate the mystery of the Trebassof datcha.
4. For having Comrade Matiew whipped and imprisoned by Koupriane.
5. For having denounced to Koupriane the identity of the two "doctors" who had been assigned to kill General Trebassof.
6. For having caused the arrest of Natacha Feodorovna.

It was a list longer than was needed for his doom. Rouletabille kissed his ikons and handed them to Annouchka along with the letters. Then he declared, with his lips trembling slightly, and a cold sweat on his forehead, that he was ready to submit to his fate.

XVII

The Last Cravat

The gentleman of the Neva said to him: "If you have nothing further to say, we will go into the courtyard."

Rouletabille understood at last that hanging him in the room where judgment had been pronounced was rendered impossible by the violence of the prisoner just executed. Not only the rope and the ring-bolt had been torn away, but part of the beam had splintered.

"There is nothing more," replied Rouletabille.

He was mistaken. Something occurred to him, an idea flashed so suddenly that he became white as his shirt, and had to lean on the arm of the gentleman of the Neva in order to accompany him.

The door was open. All the men who had voted his death filed out in gloomy silence. The gentleman of the Neva, who seemed charged with the last offices for the prisoner, pushed him gently out into the court.

It was vast, and surrounded by a high board wall; some small buildings, with closed doors, stood to right and left. A high chimney, partially demolished, rose from one corner. Rouletabille decided the whole place was part of some old abandoned mill. Above his head the sky was pale as a winding sheet. A thunderous, intermittent, rhythmical noise appraised him that he could not be far from the sea.

He had plenty of time to note all these things, for they had stopped the march to execution a moment and had made him sit down in the open courtyard on an old box. A few steps away from him under the shed where he certainly was going to be hanged, a man got upon a stool (the stool that would serve Rouletabille a few moments later) with his arm raised, and drove with a few blows of a mallet a great ring-bolt into a beam above his head.

The reporter's eyes, which had not lost their habit of taking everything in, rested again on a coarse canvas sack that lay on the ground. The young man felt a slight tremor, for he saw quickly that the sack swathed a human form. He turned his head away, but only to confront another empty sack that was intended for him. Then he closed his eyes. The sound of music came from somewhere outside, notes of the balalaika. He said to himself, "Well, we certainly are in Finland"; for he knew that, if the guzla is Russian the balalaika certainly is Finnish. It is a kind of ccordion that the peasants pick plaintively in the doorways of their toubas. He had seen and heard them the afternoon that he went to Pergalovo, and also a little further away, on the Viborg line. He pictured to himself the ruined structure where he now found himself shut in with the revolutionary tribunal, as it must appear from the outside to passers-by; unsinister, like many others near it, sheltering under its decaying roof a few homes of humble workers, resting now as they played the balalaika at their thresholds, with the day's labor over.

And suddenly from the ineffable peace of his last evening, while the balalaika mourned and the man overhead tested the solidity of his ring-bolt, a voice outside, the grave, deep voice of Annouchka, sang for the little Frenchman:

> *"For whom weave we now the crown*
> *Of lilac, rose and thyme?*
> *When my hand falls lingering down*
> *Who then will bring your crown*
> *Of lilac, rose and thyme?*
>
> *O that someone among you would hear,*
> *And come, and my lonely hand*
> *Would press, and shed the friendly tear—*
> *For alone at the end I stand.*
>
> *Who now will bring the crown*
> *Of lilac, rose and thyme?"*

Rouletabille listened to the voice dying away with the last sob of the balalaika. "It is too sad," he said, rising. "Let us go," and he wavered a little.

They came to search him. All was ready above. They pushed him gently towards the shed. When he was under the ring-bolt, near the stool, they made him turn round and they read him something in Russian, doubtless less for him than for those there who did not understand French. Rouletabille had hard work to hold himself erect.

The gentleman of the Neva said to him further:

"Monsieur, we now read you the final formula. It asks you to say whether, before you die, you have anything you wish to add to what we know concerning the sentence which has been passed upon you."

Rouletabille thought that his saliva, which at that moment he had the greatest difficulty in swallowing, would not permit him to utter a word. But disdain of such a weakness, when he recalled the coolness of so many illustrious condemned people in their last moments, brought him the last strength needed to maintain his reputation.

"Why," said he, "this sentence is not wrongly drawn up. I blame it only for being too short. Why has there been no mention of the crime I committed in contriving the tragic death of poor Michael Korsakoff?"

"Michael Korsakoff was a wretch," pronounced the vindictive voice of the young man who had presided at the trial and who, at this supreme moment, happened to be face to face with Rouletabille. "Koupriane's police, by killing that man, ridded us of a traitor."

Rouletabille uttered a cry, a cry of joy, and while he had some reason for believing that at the point he had reached now of his too-short career only misfortune could befall him, yet here Providence, in his infinite grace, sent him before he died this ineffable consolation: the certainty that he had not been mistaken.

"Pardon, pardon," he murmured, in an excess of joy which stifled him almost as much as the wretched rope would shortly do that they were getting ready behind him. "Pardon. One second yet, one little second. Then, messieurs, then, we are agreed in that, are we? This Michael, Michael Nikolaievitch was the the last of traitors."

"The first," said the heavy voice.

"It is the same thing, my dear monsieur. A traitor, a wretched traitor," continued Rouletabille.

"A poisoner," replied the voice.

"A vulgar poisoner! Is that not so? But, tell me how—a vulgar poisoner who, under cover of Nihilism, worked for his own petty ends, worked for himself and betrayed you all!"

Now Rouletabille's voice rose like a fanfare. Someone said:

"He did not deceive us long; our enemies themselves undertook his punishment."

"It was I," cried Rouletabille, radiant again. "It was I who wound up that career. I tell you that was managed right. It was I who rid you of him. Ah, I knew well enough, messieurs, in the bottom of my heart I knew that I could not be mistaken. Two and two make four always, don't they? And Rouletabille is always Rouletabille. Messieurs, it is all right, after all."

But it was probable that it was also all wrong, for the gentleman of the Neva came up to him hat in hand and said:

"Monsieur, you know now why the witnesses at your trial did not raise a fact against you that, on the contrary, was entirely in your favor. Now it only remains for us to execute the sentence which is entirely justified on other grounds."

"Ah, but—wait a little. What the devil! Now that I am sure I have not been mistaken and that I have been myself, Rouletabille, all the time I cling to life a little—oh, very much!"

A hostile murmur showed the condemned man that the patience of his judges was getting near its limit.

"Monsieur," interposed the president, "we know that you do not belong to the orthodox religion; nevertheless, we will bring a priest if you wish it."

"Yes, yes, that is it, go for the priest," cried Rouletabille.

And he said to himself, "It is so much time gained."

One of the revolutionaries started over to a little cabin that had been transformed into a chapel, while the rest of them looked at the reporter with a good deal less sympathy than they had been showing. If his bravado had impressed them agreeably in the trial room, they were beginning to be rather disgusted by his cries, his protestations and all the maneuvers by which he so apparently was trying to hold off the hour of his death.

But all at once Rouletabille jumped up onto the fatal stool. They believed he had decided finally to make an end of the comedy and die with dignity; but he had mounted there only to give them a discourse.

"Messieurs, understand me now. If it is true that you are not suppressing me in order to avenge Michael Nikolaievitch, then why do you hang me? Why do you inflict this odious punishment on me? Because you accuse me of causing Natacha Feodorovna's arrest? Truly I have been awkward. Of that, and that alone, I accuse myself."

"It was you, with your revolver, who gave the signal to Koupriane's agents! You have done the dirty work for the police."

Rouletabille tried vainly to protest, to explain, to say that his revolver shot, on the contrary, had saved the revolutionaries. But no one cared to listen and no one believed him.

"Here is the priest, monsieur," said the gentleman of the Neva.

"One second! These are my last words, and I swear to you that after this I will pass the rope about my neck myself! But listen to me! Listen to me closely! Natacha Feodorovna was the most precious recruit you had, was she not?"

"A veritable treasure," declared the president, his voice more and more impatient.

"It was a terrible blow, then," continued the reporter, "a terrible blow for you, this arrest?"

"Terrible," some of them exclaimed.

"Do not interrupt me! Very well, then, I am going to say this to you: 'If I ward off this blow—if, after having been the unintentional cause of Natacha's arrest, I have the daughter of General Trebassof set at liberty, and that within twenty-four hours,—what do you say? Would you still hang me?'"

The president, he who had the Christ-like countenance, said:

"Messieurs, Natacha Feodorovna has fallen the victim of terrible machinations whose mystery we so far have not been able to penetrate. She is accused of trying to poison her father and her step-mother, and under such conditions that it seems impossible for human reason to demonstrate the contrary. Natacha Feodorovna herself, crushed by the tragic occurrence, was not able to answer her accusers at all, and her silence has been taken for a confession of guilt. Messieurs, Natacha Feodorovna will be started for Siberia tomorrow. We can do nothing for her. Natacha Feodorovna is lost to us."

Then, with a gesture to those who surrounded Rouletabille:

"Do your duty, messieurs."

"Pardon, pardon. But if I do prove the innocence of Natacha? Just wait, messieurs. There is only I who can prove that innocence! You lose Natacha by killing me!"

"If you had been able to prove that innocence, monsieur, the thing would already be done. You would not have waited."

"Pardon, pardon. It is only at this moment that I have become able to do it."

"How is that?"

"It is because I was sick, you see—very seriously sick. That affair of Michael Nikolaievitch and the poison that still continued after he was dead simply robbed me of all my powers. Now that I am sure I have not been the means of killing an innocent man—I am Rouletabille again! It is not possible that I shall not find the way, that I shall not see through this mystery."

The terrible voice of the Christ-like figure said monotonously:

"Do your duty, messieurs."

"Pardon, pardon. This is of great importance to you—and the proof is that you have not yet hanged me. You were not so procrastinating with my predecessor, were you? You have listened to me because you have hoped! Very well, let me think, let me consider. Oh, the devil! I was there myself at the fatal luncheon, and I know better than anyone else all that happened there. Five minutes! I demand five minutes of you; it is not much. Five little minutes!"

These last words of the condemned man seemed to singularly influence the revolutionaries. They looked at one another in silence.

Then the president took out his watch and said:

"Five minutes. We grant them to you."

"Put your watch here. Here on this nail. It is five minutes to seven, eh? You will give me until the hour?"

"Yes, until the hour. The watch itself will strike when the hour has come."

"Ah, it strikes! Like the general's watch, then. Very well, here we are."

Then there was the curious spectacle of Rouletabille standing on the hangman's stool, the fatal rope hanging above his head, his legs crossed, his elbow on his knees in that eternal attitude which Art has always given to human thought, his fists under his jaws, his eyes fixed—all around him, all those young men intent on his silence, not moving a muscle, turned into statues themselves that they might not disturb the statue which thought and thought.

XVIII

A Singular Experience

The five minutes ticked away and the watch commenced to strike the hour's seven strokes. Did it sound the death of Rouletabille? Perhaps not! For at the first silver tinkle they saw Rouletabille shake himself, and raise his head, with his face alight and his eyes shining. They saw him stand up, spread out his arms and cry:

"I have found it!"

Such joy shone in his countenance that there seemed to be an aureole around him, and none of those there doubted that he had the solution of the impossible problem.

"I have found it! I have found it!"

They gathered around him. He waved them away as in a waking dream.

"Give me room. I have found it, if my experiment works out. One, two, three, four, five. . ."

What was he doing? He counted his steps now, in long paces, as in dueling preliminaries. And the others, all of them, followed him in silence, puzzled, but without protest, as if they, too, were caught in the same strange day-dream. Steadily counting his steps he crossed thus the court, which was vast. "Forty, forty-one, forty-two," he cried excitedly. "This is certainly strange, and very promising."

The others, although they did not understand, refrained from questioning him, for they saw there was nothing to do but let him go ahead without interruption, just as care is taken not to wake a somnambulist abruptly. They had no mistrust of his motives, for the idea was simply untenable that Rouletabille was fool enough to hope to save himself from them by an imbecile subterfuge. No, they yielded to the impression his inspired countenance gave them, and several were so affected that they unconsciously repeated his gestures. Thus Rouletabille reached the edge of the court where judgment had been pronounced against him. There he had to mount a rickety flight of stairs, whose steps he counted. He reached a corridor, but moving away from the side where the door was opening to the exterior he turned toward a staircase leading to the upper floor, and still counted the steps as he climbed them.

Some of the company followed him, others hurried ahead of him. But he did not seem aware of either the one or the other, as he walked along living only in his thoughts. He reached the landing-place, hesitated, pushed open a door, and found himself in a room furnished with a table, two chairs, a mattress and a huge cupboard. He went to the cupboard, turned the key and opened it. The cupboard was empty. He closed it again and put the key in his pocket. Then he went out onto the landing-place again. There he asked for the key of the chamber-door he had just left. They gave it to him and he locked that door and put that key also in his pocket. Now he returned into the court. He asked for a chair. It was brought him. Immediately he placed his head in his hands, thinking hard, took the chair and carried it over a little behind the shed. The Nihilists watched everything he did and they did not smile, because men do not smile when death waits at the end of things, however foolish.

Finally, Rouletabille spoke:

"Messieurs," said he, his voice low and shaken, because he knew that now he touched the decisive minute, after which there could only be an irrevocable fate. "Messieurs, in order to continue my experiment I am obliged to go through movements that might suggest to you the idea of an attempt at escape, or evasion. I hope you don't regard me as fool enough to have any such thought."

"Oh, monsieur," said the chief, "you are free to go through all the maneuvers you wish. No one escapes us. Outside we should have you within arm's reach quite as well as here. And, besides, it is entirely impossible to escape from here."

"Very well. Then that is understood. In such a case, I ask you now to remain just where you are and not to budge, whatever I do, if you don't wish to inconvenience me. Only please send someone now up to the next floor, where I am going to go again, and let him watch what happens from there, but without interfering. And don't speak a word to me during the experiment."

Two of the revolutionaries went to the upper floor, and opened a window in order to keep track of what went on in the court. All now showed their intense interest in the acts and gestures of Rouletabille.

The reporter placed himself in the shed, between his death-stool and his hanging-rope.

"Ready," said he; "I am going to begin"

And suddenly he jumped like a wild man, crossed the court in a straight line like a flash, disappeared in the touba, bounded up the staircase, felt in his pocket and drew out the keys, opened the door of the chamber he had locked, closed it and locked it again, turned right-about-face, came down again in the same haste, reached the court, and this time swerved to the chair, went round it, still running, and returned at the same speed to the shed. He no sooner reached there than he uttered a cry of triumph as he glanced at the watch banging from a post. "I have won," he said, and threw himself with a happy thrill upon the fatal scaffold. They surrounded him, and he read the liveliest curiosity in all their faces. Panting still from his mad rush, he asked for two words apart with the chief of the Secret committee.

The man who had pronounced judgment and who had the bearing of Jesus advanced, and there was a brief exchange of words between the two young men. The others drew back and waited at a distance, in impressive silence, the outcome of this mysterious colloquy, which certainly would settle Rouletabille's fate.

"Messieurs," said the chief, "the young Frenchman is going to be allowed to leave. We give him twenty-four hours to set Natacha Feodorovna free. In twenty-four hours, if he has not succeeded, he will return here to give himself up."

A happy murmur greeted these words. The moment their chief spoke thus, they felt sure of Natacha's fate.

The chief added:

"As the liberation of Natacha Feodorovna will be followed, the young Frenchman says, by that of our companion Matiew, we decide that, if these two conditions are fulfilled, M. Joseph Rouletabille is allowed to return in entire security to France, which he ought never to have left."

Two or three only of the group said, "That lad is playing with us; it is not possible."

But the chief declared:

"Let the lad try. He accomplishes miracles."

XIX

THE TSAR

"I have escaped by remarkable luck," cried Rouletabille, as he found himself, in the middle of the night, at the corner of the Katharine and the Aptiekarski Pereoulok Canals, while the mysterious carriage which had brought him there returned rapidly toward the Grande Ecurie. "What a country! What a country!"

He ran a little way to the Grand Morskaia, which was near, entered the hotel like a bomb, dragged the interpreter from his bed, demanded that his bill be made out and that he be told the time of the next train for Tsarskoie-Coelo. The interpreter told him that he could not have his bill at such an hour, that he could not leave town without his passport and that there was no train for Tsarskoie-Coelo, and Rouletabille made an outcry that woke the whole hotel. The guests, fearing always "une scandale," kept close to their rooms. But Monsieur le directeur came down, trembling. When he found all that it was about he was inclined to be peremptory, but Rouletabille, who had seen "Michael Strogoff" played, cried, "Service of the Tsar!" which turned him submissive as a sheep. He made out the young man's bill and gave him his passport, which had been brought back by the police during the afternoon. Rouletabille rapidly wrote a message to Koupriane's address, which the messenger was directed to have delivered without a moment's delay, under the pain of death! The manager humbly promised and the reporter did not explain that by "pain of death" he referred to his own. Then, having ascertained that as a matter of fact the last train had left for Tsarskoie-Coelo, he ordered a carriage and hurried to his room to pack.

And he, ordinarily so detailed, so particular in his affairs, threw things every which way, linen, garments, with kicks and shoves. It was a relief after the emotions he had gone through. "What a country!" he never ceased to exclaim. "What a country!"

Then the carriage was ready, with two little Finnish horses, whose gait he knew well, an evil-looking driver, who none the less would get him there; the trunk; roubles to the domestics. "Spacibo, barine. Spacibo." (Thank you, monsieur. Thank you.)

The interpreter asked what address he should give the driver.

"The home of the Tsar."

The interpreter hesitated, believing it to be an unbecoming pleasantry, then waved vaguely to the driver, and the horses started.

"What a curious trot! We have no idea of that in France," thought Rouletabille. "France! France! Paris! Is it possible that soon I shall be back! And that dear Lady in Black! Ah, at the first opportunity I must send her a dispatch of my return—before she receives those ikons, and the letters announcing my death. Scan! Scan! Scan! (Hurry!)"

The isvotchick pounded his horses, crowding past the dvornicks who watched at the corners of the houses during the St. Petersburg night. "Dirigi! dirigi! dirigi! (Look out!)"

The country, somber in the somber night. The vast open country. What monotonous desolation! Rapidly, through the vast silent spaces, the little car glided over the lonely route into the black arms of the pines.

Rouletabille, holding on to his seat, looked about him.

"God! this is as sad as a funeral display."

Little frozen huts, no larger than tombs, occasionally indicated the road, but there was no mark of life in that country except the noise of the journey and the two beasts with steaming coats.

Crack! One of the shafts broken. "What a country!" To hear Rouletabille one would suppose that only in Russia could the shaft of a carriage break.

The repair was difficult and crude, with bits of rope. And from then on the journey was slow and cautious after the frenzied speed. In vain Rouletabille reasoned with himself. "You will arrive anyway before morning. You cannot wake the Emperor in the dead of night." His impatience knew no reason. "What a country! What a country!"

After some other petty adventures (they ran into a ravine and had tremendous difficulty rescuing the trunk) they arrived at Tsarskoie-Coelo at a quarter of seven.

Even here the country was not pleasant. Rouletabille recalled the bright awakening of French country. Here it seemed there was something more dead than death: it was this little city with its streets where no one passed, not a soul, not a phantom, with its houses so impenetrable, the windows even of glazed glass and further blinded by the morning hoar-frost shutting out light more thoroughly than closed eyelids. Behind them he pictured to himself a world unknown, a world which neither spoke nor wept, nor laughed, a world in which no living chord resounded. "What a country! 'Where is the chateau? I do not know; I have been here only once, in the marshal's carriage. I do not know the way. Not the great palace! The idiot of a driver has brought me to this great palace in order to see it, I haven't a doubt. Does Rouletabille look like a tourist? Dourak! The home of the Tsar, I tell you. The Tsar's residence. The place where the Little Father lives. Chez Batouchka!"

The driver lashed his ponies. He drove past all the streets. "Stoi! (Stop!)" cried Rouletabille. A gate, a soldier, musket at shoulder, bayonet in play; another gate, another soldier, another bayonet; a park with walls around it, and around the walls more soldiers.

"No mistake; here is the place," thought Rouletabille. There was only one prisoner for whom such pains would be taken. He advanced towards the gate. Ah! They crossed bayonets under his nose. Halt! No fooling, Joseph Rouletabille, of "L'Epoque." A subaltern came from a guard-house and advanced toward him. Explanation evidently was going to be difficult. The young man saw that if he demanded to see the Tsar, they would think him crazed and that would further complicate matters. He asked for the Grand-Marshal of the Court. They replied that he could get the Marshal's address in Tsarskoie. But the subaltern turned his head. He saw someone advancing. It was the Grand-Marshal himself. Some exceptional service called him, without doubt, very early to the Court.

"Why, what are you doing here? You are not yet gone then, Monsieur Rouletabille?"

"Politeness before everything, Monsieur le Grand-Marechal! I would not go before saying 'Au revoir' to the Emperor. Be so good, since you are going to him and he has risen (you yourself have told me he rises at seven), be so good as to say to him that I wish to pay my respects before leaving."

"Your scheme, doubtless, is to speak to him once more regarding Natacha Feodorovna?"

"Not at all. Tell him, Excellency, that I am come to explain the mystery of the eider downs."

"Ah, ah, the eider downs! You know something?"

"I know all."

The Grand Marshal saw that the young man did not pretend. He asked him to wait a few minutes, and vanished into the park.

A quarter of an hour later, Joseph Rouletabille, of the journal "L'Epoque," was admitted into the cabinet that he knew well from the first interview he had had there with His Majesty. The simple work-room of a country-house: a few pictures on the walls, portraits of the Tsarina and the imperial children on the table; Oriental cigarettes in the tiny gold cups. Rouletabille was far from feeling any assurance, for the Grand-Marshal had said to him:

"Be cautious. The Emperor is in a terrible humor about you."

A door opened and closed. The Tsar made a sign to the Marshal, who disappeared. Rouletabille bowed low, then watched the Emperor closely.

Quite apparently His Majesty was displeased. The face of the Tsar, ordinarily so calm, so pleasant, and smiling, was severe, and his eyes had an angry light. He seated himself and lighted a cigarette.

"Monsieur," he commenced, "I am not otherwise sorry to see you before your departure in order to say to you myself that I am not at all pleased with you. If you were one of my subjects I would have already started you on the road to the Ural Mountains."

"I remove myself farther, Sire."

"Monsieur, I pray you not to interrupt me and not to speak unless I ask you a question."

"Oh, pardon, Sire, pardon."

"I am not duped by the pretext you have offered Monsieur le Grand-Marechal in order to penetrate here."

"It is not a pretext, Sire."

"Again!"

"Oh, pardon, Sire, pardon."

"I say to you that, called here to aid me against my enemies, they themselves have not found a stronger or more criminal support than in you."

"Of what am I accused, Sire?"

"Koupriane—"

"Ah! Ah! . . . Pardon!"

"My Chief of Police justly complains that you have traversed all his designs and that you have taken it upon yourself to ruin them. First, you removed his agents, who inconvenienced you, it seems; then, the moment that he had the proof in hand of the abominable alliance of Natacha Feodorovna with the Nihilists who attempt the assassination of her father your intervention has permitted that proof to escape him. And you have boasted of the feat, monsieur, so that we can only consider you responsible for the attempts that followed.

"Without you, Natacha would not have attempted to poison her father. Without you, they would not have sent to find physicians who could blow up the datcha des Iles. Finally, no later than yesterday, when this faithful servant of mine had set a trap they could not have escaped from, you have had the audacity, you, to warn them of it. They owe their escape to you. Monsieur, those are attempts against the security of the State which deserves the heaviest punishment. Why, you went out one day from here promising me to save General Trebassof from all the plotting assassins who lurked about him. And then you play the game of the assassins! Your conduct is as miserable as that of Natacha Feodorovna is monstrous!"

The Emperor ceased, and looked at Rouletabille, who had not lowered his eyes.

"What can you say for yourself? Speak—now."

"I can only say to Your Majesty that I come to take leave of you because my task here is finished. I have promised you the life of General Trebassof, and I bring it to you. He runs no danger any more! I say further to Your Majesty that there exists nowhere in the world a daughter more devoted to her father, even to the death, a daughter more sublime than Natacha Feodorovna, nor more innocent."

"Be careful, monsieur. I inform you that I have studied this affair personally and very closely. You have the proofs of these statements you advance?"

"Yes, Sire."

"And I, I have the proofs that Natacha Feodorovna is a renegade."

At this contradiction, uttered in a firm voice, the Emperor stirred, a flush of anger and of outraged majesty in his face. But, after this first movement, he succeeded in controlling himself, opened a drawer brusquely, took out some papers and threw them on the table.

"Here they are."

Rouletabille reached for the papers.

"You do not read Russian, monsieur. I will translate their purport for you. Know, then, that there has been a mysterious exchange of letters between Natacha Feodorovna and the Central Revolutionary Committee, and that these letters show the daughter of General Trebassof to be in perfect accord with the assassins of her father for the execution of their abominable project."

"The death of the general?"

"Exactly."

"I declare to Your Majesty that that is not possible."

"Obstinate man! I will read—"

"Useless, Sire. It is impossible. There may be in them the question of a project, but I am greatly surprised if these conspirators have been sufficiently imprudent to write in those letters that they count on Natacha to poison her father."

"That, as a matter of fact, is not written, and you yourself are responsible for it not being there. It does not follow any the less that Natacha Feodorovna had an understanding with the Nihilists."

"That is correct, Sire."

"Ah, you confess that?"

"I do not confess; I simply affirm that Natacha had an understanding with the Nihilists."

"Who plotted their abominable attacks against the ex-Governor of Moscow."

"Sire, since Natacha had an understanding with the Nihilists, it was not to kill her father, but to save him. And the project of which you hold here the proofs, but of whose character you are unaware, is to end the attacks of which you speak, instantly."

"You say that."

"I speak the truth, Sire."

"Where are the proofs? Show me your papers."

"I have none. I have only my word."

"That is not sufficient."

"It will be sufficient, once you have heard me."

"I listen."

"Sire, before revealing to you a secret on which depends the life of General Trebassof, you must permit me some questions. Your Majesty holds the life of the general very dear?"

"What has that to do with it?"

"Pardon. I desire that Your Majesty assure me on that point."

"The general has protected my throne. He has saved the Empire from one of the greatest dangers that it has ever run. If the servant who has done such a service should be rewarded by death, by the punishment that the enemies of my people prepare for him in the darkness, I should never forgive myself. There have been too many martyrs already!"

"You have replied to me, Sire, in such a way that you make me understand there is no sacrifice—even to the sacrifice of your amour-propre the greatest a ruler can suffer—no sacrifice too dear to ransom from death one of these martyrs."

"Ah, ah! These gentlemen lay down conditions to me! Money. Money. They need money. And at how much do they rate the head of the general?"

"Sire, that does not touch Your Majesty, and I never will come to offer you such a bargain. That matter concerns only Natacha Feodorovna, who has offered her fortune!"

"Her fortune! But she has nothing."

"She will have one at the death of the general. Now she engages to give it all to the Revolutionary Committee the day the general dies—if he dies a natural death!"

The Emperor rose, greatly agitated.

"To the Revolutionary Party! What do you tell me! The fortune of the general! Eh, but these are great riches."

"Sire, I have told you the secret. You alone should know it and guard it forever, and I have your sacred word that, when the hour comes, you will let the prize go where it is promised. If the general ever learns of such a thing, such a treaty, he would easily arrange that nothing should remain, and he would denounce his daughter who has saved him, and then he would promptly be the prey of his enemies and yours, from whom you wish to save him. I have told the secret not to the Emperor, but to the representative of God on the Russian earth. I have confessed it to the priest, who is bound to forget the words uttered only before God. Allow Natacha Feodorovna her own way, Sire! And her father, your servant, whose life is so dear to you, is saved. At the natural death of the general his fortune will go to his daughter, who has disposed of it."

Rouletabille stopped a moment to judge of the effect produced. It was not good. The face of his august listener was more and more in a frown.

The silence continued, and now the reporter did not dare to break it. He waited.

Finally, the Emperor rose and walked forward and backward across the room, deep in thought. For a moment he stopped at the window and waved paternally to the little Tsarevitch, who played in the park with the grand-duchesses.

Then he returned to Rouletabille and pinched his ear.

"But, tell me, how have you learned all this? And who then has poisoned the general and his wife, in the kiosk, if not Natacha?"

"Natacha is a saint. It is nothing, Sire, that she has been raised in luxury, and vows herself to misery; but it is sublime that she guards in her heart the secret of her sacrifice from everyone, and, in spite of all, because secrecy is necessary and has been required of her. See her guarding it before her father, who has been brought to believe in the dishonor of his daughter, and still to be silent when a word would have proved her innocent; guarding it face to face with her fiance, whom she loves, and repulses because marriage is forbidden to the girl who is supposed to be rich and who will be poor; guarding it, above all—and guarding it still—in the depths of the dungeon, and ready to take the road to Siberia under the accusation of assassination, because that ignominy is necessary for the safety of her father. That, Sire—oh, Sire, do you see!"

"But you, how have you been able to penetrate into this guarded secret?"

"By watching her eyes. By observing, when she believed herself alone, the look of terror and the gleams of love. And, beyond all, by looking at her when she was looking at her father. Ah, Sire, there were moments when on her mystic face one could read the wild joy and devotion of the martyr. Then, by listening and by piecing together scraps of phrases inconsistent with the idea of treachery, but which immediately acquired meaning if one thought of the opposite, of sacrifice. Ah, that is it, Sire! Consider always the alternative motive. What I finally could see myself, the others, who had a fixed opinion about Natacha, could not see. And why had they their fixed opinion? Simply because the idea of compromise with the Nihilists aroused at once the idea of complicity! For such people it is always the same thing—they never can see but the one side of the situation. But, nevertheless, the situation had two sides, as all situations have. The question was simple. The compromise was certain. But why had Natacha compromised herself with the Nihilists? Was it necessarily in order to lose her father? Might it not be, on the contrary, in order to save him? When one has rendezvous with an enemy it is not necessarily to enter into his game, sometimes it is to disarm him with an offer. Between these two hypotheses, which I alone took the trouble to examine, I did not hesitate long, because Natacha's every attitude proclaimed her innocence: and her eyes, Sire, in which one read purity and love, prevailed always with me against all the passing appearances of disgrace and crime.

"I saw that Natacha negotiated with them. But what had she to place in the scales against the life of her father? Nothing—except the fortune that she would have one day.

"Some words she spoke about the impossibility of immediate marriage, about poverty which could always knock at the door of any mansion, remarks that I was able to overhear between Natacha and Boris Mourazoff, which to him meant nothing, put me definitely on the right road. And I was not long in ascertaining that the negotiations in this formidable affair were taking place in the very house of Trebassof! Pursued without by the incessant spying of Koupriane, who sought to surprise her in company with the Nihilists, watched closely, too, by the jealous supervision of Boris, who was jealous of Michael Nikolaievitch, she had to seize the only opportunities possible for such negotiations, at night, in her own home, the sole place where, by the very audacity of it, she was able to play her part in any security.

"Michael Nikolaievitch knew Annouchka. There was certainly the point of departure for the negotiations which that felon-officer, traitor to all sides, worked at will toward the realization of his own infamous project. I do not think that Michael ever confided to Natacha that he was, from the very first, the instrument of the revolutionaries. Natacha, who sought to get in touch with the revolutionary party, had to entrust him with a correspondence for Annouchka, following which he assumed direction of the affair, deceiving the Nihilists, who, in their absolute penury, following the revolt, had been seduced by the proposition of General Trebassof's daughter, and deceiving Natacha, whom he pretended to love and by whom he believed himself loved. At this point in the affair Natacha came to understand that it was necessary to propitiate Michael Nikolaievitch, her indispensable intermediary, and she managed to do it so well that Boris Mourazoff felt the blackest jealousy. On his side, Michael came to believe that Natacha would have no other husband than himself, but he did not propose to marry a penniless girl! And, fatally, it followed that Natacha, in that infernal intrigue, negotiated for the life of her father through the agency of a man who, underhandedly, sought to strike at the general himself, because the immediate death of her father before the negotiation was completed would enrich Natacha, who had given Michael so much to hope. That frightful tragedy, Sire, in which we have lived our most painful hours, appeared to me, confident of Natacha's innocence, as absolutely simple as for the others it seemed complicated. Natacha believed she had in Michael Nikolaievitch a man who worked for her, but he worked only for himself. The day that I was convinced of it, Sire, by my examination of the approach to the balcony, I had a mind to warn Natacha, to go to her and say, 'Get rid of that man. He will betray you. If you need an agent, I am at your service.' But that day, at Krestowsky, destiny prevented my rejoining Natacha; and I must attribute it to destiny, which would not permit the loss of that man. Michael Nikolaievitch, who was a traitor, was too much in the 'combination,' and if he had been rejected he would have ruined everything. I caused him to disappear! The great misfortune then was that Natacha, holding me responsible for the death of a man she believed innocent, never wished to see me again, and, when she did see me, refused to have any conversation with me because I proposed that I take Michael's place for her with the revolutionaries. She would have nothing to do with me in order to protect her secret. Meantime, the Nihilists believed they were betrayed by Natacha when they learned of the death of Michael, and they undertook to avenge him. They seized Natacha, and bore her off by force. The unhappy girl learned then, that same evening, of the attack which destroyed the datcha and, happily, still spared her father. This time she reached a definite understanding with the revolutionary party. Her bargain was made. I offer you for proof of it only her attitude when she was arrested, and, even in that moment, her sublime silence."

While Rouletabille urged his view, the Emperor let him talk on and on, and now his eyes were dim.

"Is it possible that Natacha has not been the accomplice, in all, of Michael Nikolaievitch?" he demanded. "It was she who opened her father's house to him that night. If she was not his accomplice she would have mistrusted him, she would have watched him."

"Sire, Michael Nikolaievitch was a very clever man. He knew so well how to play upon Natacha, and Annouchka, in whom she placed all her hope. It was from Annouchka that she wished to hold the life of her father. It was the word, the signature of Annouchka that she demanded before giving her own. The evening Michael Nikolaievitch died, he was charged to bring her that signature. I know it, myself, because, pretending drunkenness, I was able to overhear enough of a conversation between Annouchka and a man whose name I must conceal. Yes, that last evening, Michael Nikolaievitch, when he entered the datcha, had the signature in his pocket, but also he carried the weapon or the poison with which he already had attempted and was resolved to reach the father of her whom he believed was assuredly to be his wife."

"You speak now of a paper, very precious, that I regret not to possess, monsieur," said the Tsar coldly, "because that paper alone would have proved to me the innocence of your protegee."

"If you have not it, Sire, you know well that it is because I have wished you to have it. The corpse had been searched by Katharina, the little Bohemian, and I, Sire, prevented Koupriane from finding that signature in Katharina's possession. In saving the secret I have saved General Trebassof's life, who would have preferred to die rather than accept such an arrangement."

The Tsar stopped Rouletabille in his enthusiastic outburst.

"All that would be very beautiful and perhaps admirable," said he, more and more coldly, because he had entirely recovered himself, "if Natacha had not, herself, with her own hand, poisoned her father and her step-mother!—always with arsenate of soda."

"Oh, some of that had been left in the house," replied Rouletabille. "They had not given me all of it for the analysis after the first attempt. But Natacha is innocent of that, Sire. I swear it to you. As true as that I have certainly escaped being hanged."

"How, hanged?"

"Oh, it has not amounted to much now, Your Majesty."

And Rouletabille recounted his sinister adventure, up to the moment of his death, or, rather, up to the moment when he had believed he was going to die.

The Emperor listened to the young reporter with complete stupefaction. He murmured, "Poor lad!" then, suddenly:

"But how have you managed to escape them?"

"Sire they have given me twenty-four hours for you to set Natacha at liberty, that is to say, that you restore her to her rights, all her rights, and she be always the recognized heiress of Trebassof. Do you understand me, Sire?

"I will understand you, perhaps, when you have explained to me how Natacha has not poisoned her father and step-mother."

"There are some things so simple, Sire, that one is able to think of them only with a rope around one's neck. But let us reason it out. We have here four persons, two of whom have been poisoned and the other two with them have not been. Now, it is certain that, of the four persons, the general has not wished to poison himself, that his wife has not wished to poison the general, and that, as for me, I have not wished to poison anybody. That, if we are absolutely sure of it, leaves as the poisoner only Natacha. That is so certain, so inevitable, that there is only one case, one alone, where, in such conditions, Natacha would not be regarded as the poisoner."

"I confess that, logically, I do not see," said the Tsar, "anything beyond that but more and more of a tangle. What is it?"

"Logically, the only case would be that where no one had been poisoned, that is to say, where no one had taken any poison."

"But the presence of the poison has been established!" cried the Emperor.

"Still, the presence of the poison proves only its presence, not the crime. Both poison and ipecac were found in the stomach expulsions. From which a crime has been concluded. What state of affairs was necessary for there to have been no crime? Simply that the poison should have appeared in the expulsions after the ipecac. Then there would have been no poisoning, but everyone would believe there had been. And, for that, someone would have poured the poison into the expulsions."

The Tsar never quitted Rouletabille's eyes.

"That is extraordinary," said he. "But of course it is possible. In any case, it is still only an hypothesis.

"And so long as it could be an hypothesis that no one thought of, it could be just that, Sire. But if I am here, it is because I have the proof that that hypothesis corresponds to the reality. That necessary proof of Natacha's innocence, Your Majesty, I have found with the rope around my neck. Ah, I tell you it was time! What has hindered us hitherto, I do not say to realize, but even to think, of that hypothesis? Simply that we thought the illness of the general had commenced before the absorption of the ipecac, since Matrena Petrovna had been obliged to go for it to her medicine-closet after his illness commenced, in order to counteract the poison of which she also appeared to be the victim.

"But, if I acquire proof that Matrena Petrovna had the ipecac at hand before the sickness, my hypothesis of pretense at poisoning has irresistible force. Because, if it was not to use it before, why did she have it with her before? And if it was not that she wished to hide the fact that she had used it before, why did she wish to make believe that she went to find it afterwards?

"Then, in order to show Natacha's innocence, here is what must be proved: that Matrena Petrovna had the ipecac on her, even when she went to look for it."

"Young Rouletabille, I hardly breathe," said the Tsar.

"Breathe, Sire. The proof is here. Matrena Petrovna necessarily had the ipecac on her, because after the sickness she had not the time for going to find it. Do you understand, Sire? Between the moment when she fled from the kiosk and when she returned there, she had not the actual time to go to her medicine-closet to find the ipecac."

"How have you been able to compute the time?" asked the Emperor.

"Sire, the Lord God directed, Who made me admire Feodor Feodorovitch's watch just when we went to read, and to read on the dial of that watch two minutes to the hour, and the Lord God directed yet, Who, after the scene of the poison, at the time Matrena returned carrying the ipecac publicly, made the hour strike from that watch in the general's pocket.

"Two minutes. It was impossible for Matrena to have covered that distance in two minutes. She could only have entered the deserted datcha and left it again instantly. She had not taken the trouble to mount to the floor above, where, she told us and repeated when she returned, the ipecac was in the medicine-closet. She lied! And if she lied, all is explained.

"It was the striking of a watch, Sire, with a striking apparatus and a sound like the general's, there in the quarters of the revolutionaries, that roused my memory and indicated to me in a second this argument of the time.

"I got down from my gallows-scaffold, Your Majesty, to experiment on that time-limit. Oh, nothing and nobody could have prevented my making that experiment before I died, to prove to myself that Rouletabille had all along been right. I had studied the grounds around the datcha enough to be perfectly exact about the distances. I found in the court where I was to be hanged the same number of steps that there were from the kiosk to the steps of the veranda, and, as the staircase of the revolutionaries had fewer steps, I lengthened my journey a few steps by walking around a chair. Finally, I attended to the opening and closing of the doors that Matrena would have had to do. I had looked at a watch when I started. When I returned, Sire, and looked at the watch again, I had taken three minutes to cover the distance—and it is not for me to boast, but I am a little livelier than the excellent Matrena.

"Matrena had lied. Matrena had simulated the poisoning of the general. Matrena had coolly poured ipecac in the general's glass while we were illustrating with matches a curious-enough theory of the nature of the constitution of the empire."

"But this is abominable!" cried the Emperor, this time definitely convinced by the intricate argument of Rouletabille. "And what end could this imitation serve?'"

"The end of preventing the real crime! The end that she believed herself to have attained, Sire, to have Natacha removed forever—Natacha whom she believed capable of any crime."

"Oh, it is monstrous! Feodor Feodorovitch has often told me that Matrena loved Natacha sincerely."

"She loved her sincerely up to the day that she believed her guilty. Matrena Petrovna was sure of Natacha's complicity in Michael Nikolaievitch's attempt to poison the general. I shared her stupor, her despair, when Feodor Feodorovitch took his daughter in his arms after that tragic night, and embraced her. He seemed to absolve her. It was then that Matrena resolved within herself to save the general in spite of himself, but I remain persuaded that, if she had dared such a plan against Natacha, it would only be because of what she believed definite proof of her step-daughter's infamy. These papers, Sire, that you have shown me, and which show, if nothing more, an understanding between Natacha and the revolutionaries, could only have been in the possession of Michael or of Natacha. Nothing was found in Michael's quarters. Tell me, then, that Matrena found them in Natacha's apartment. Then, she did not hesitate!"

"If one outlined her crime to her, do you believe she would confess it?" asked the Emperor.

"I am so sure of it that I have had her brought here. By now Koupriane should be here at the chateau, with Matrena Petrovna."

"You think of everything, monsieur."

The Tsar moved to ring a bell. Rouletabille raised his hand.

"Not yet, Sire. I ask that you permit me not to be present at the confusion of that brave, heroic, good woman who has loved me much. But before I go, Sire—do you promise me?"

The Emperor believed he had not heard correctly or did not grasp the meaning. He repeated what Rouletabille had said. The young reporter repeated it once more:

"Do you promise? No, Sire, I am not mad. I dare to ask you that. I have confided my honor to Your Majesty. I have told you Natacha's secret.

Well, now, before Matrena's confession, I dare to ask you: Promise me to forget that secret. It will not suffice merely to give Natacha back again to her father. It is necessary to leave her course open to her—if you really wish to save General Trebassof. What do you decide, Sire?"

"It is the first time anyone has questioned me, monsieur."

"Ah, well, it will be the last. But I humbly beg Your Majesty to reply."

"That would be many millions given to the Revolution."

"Oh, Sire, they are not given yet. The general is sixty-five, but he has many years ahead of him, if you wish it. By the time he dies—a natural death, if you wish it—your enemies will have disarmed."

"My enemies!" murmured the Tsar in a low voice. "No, no; my enemies never will disarm. Who, then, will be able to disarm them?" added he, melancholily, shaking his head.

"Progress, Sire! If you wish it."

The Tsar turned red and looked at the audacious young man, who met the gaze of His Majesty frankly.

"It is kind of you to say that, my young friend. But you speak as a child."

"As a child of France to the Father of the Russian people."

It was said in a voice so solemn and, at the same time, so naively touching, that the Tsar started. He gazed again for some time in silence at this boy who, this time, turned away his brimming eyes.

"Progress and pity, Sire."

"Well," said the Emperor, "it is promised."

Rouletabille was not able to restrain a joyous movement hardly in keeping.

"You can ring now, Sire."

And the Tsar rang.

The reporter passed into a little salon, where he found the Marshal, Koupriane and Matrena Petrovna, who was "in a state."

She threw a suspicious glance at Rouletabille, who was not treated this morning as the dear little domovoi-doukh. She permitted herself to be conducted, already trembling, before the Emperor.

"What happened?" asked Koupriane agitatedly.

"It so happened, my dear Monsieur Koupriane, that I have the pardon of the Emperor for all the crimes you have charged against me, and that I wish to shake hands before I go, without any rancor. Monsieur Koupriane, the Emperor will tell you himself that General Trebassof is saved, and that his life will never be in danger any more. Do you know what follows? It follows that you must at once set Matiew free, whom I have taken, if you remember, under my protection. Tell him that he is going to make his way in France. I will find him a place on condition that he forgets certain lashes."

"Such a promise! Such an attitude toward me!" cried Koupriane. "But I will wait for the Emperor to tell me all these fine things. And your Natacha, what do you do with her?"

"We release her also, monsieur. Natacha never has been the monster that you think."

"How can you say that? Someone at least is guilty."

"There are two guilty. The first, Monsieur le Marechal."

"What!" cried the Marshal.

"Monsieur le Marechal, who had the imprudence to bring such dangerous grapes to the datcha des Iles, and—and—"

"And the other?" asked Koupriane, more and more anxiously.

"Listen there," said Rouletabille, pointing toward the Emperor's cabinet.

The sound of tears and sobs reached them. The grief and the remorse of Matrena Petrovna passed the walls of the cabinet. Koupriane was completely disconcerted.

Suddenly the Emperor appeared. He was in a state of exaltation such as had never been known in him. Koupriane, dismayed, drew back.

"Monsieur," said the Tsar to him, "I require that Natacha Feodorovna be here within the next two hours, and that she be conducted with the honors due to her rank. Natacha is innocent, and we must make reparation to her."

Then, turning toward Rouletabille:

"I have learned what she knows and what she owes to you—we owe to you, my young friend."

The Tsar said "my young friend." Rouletabille, at this last moment before his departure, spoke Russian?

"Then she knows nothing, Sire. That is better, Sire, because Your Majesty and me, we must forget right from today that we know anything."

"You are right," said the Tsar thoughtfully. "But, my friend, what am I to do for you?"

"Sire, one favor. Do not let me miss the train at 10:55."

And he threw himself on his knees.

"Remain on your knees, my friend. You are ready, thus. Monsieur le Marechal will prepare at once a brevet, which I will immediately sign. Meantime, Monsieur le Marechal, find me, in my own closet, one of my St. Anne's collars."

And it was thus that Joseph Rouletabille, of "L'Epoque," was created officer of St. Anne of Russia by the Emperor himself, who gave him the accolade.

"They combine the whole course of time in this country," thought Rouletabille, pressing his hand to his eyes to hold back the tears.

For the train at 10:55 everybody had crowded at Tsarskoie-Coelo station. Among those who had come from St. Petersburg to press the young reporter's hand when they learned of his impending departure were Ivan Petrovitch, the jolly Councilor of the Emperor, and Athanase Georgevitch, the lively advocate so well known for his famous exploits with knife and fork. They had come naturally with all their bandages and dressings, which made them look like glorious ruins. They brought the greetings of Feodor Feodorovitch, who still had a little fever, and of Thaddeus Tchitchnikoff, the Lithuanian, who had both legs broken.

Even after he was in his compartment Rouletabille had to drink his last drink of champagne. When nothing remained in the bottle and everyone had embraced and re-embraced him, as the train did not start quite yet, Athanase Georgevitch opened a second "last" bottle. It was then that Monsieur le Grand Marechal arrived, out of breath. They invited him to drink, and he accepted. But he had need to speak to Rouletabille in private, and he drew the reporter, after excuses, out into the corridor.

"It is the Emperor himself who has sent me," said the high dignitary with emotion. "He has sent me about the eider downs. You forgot to explain the eider downs to him."

"Niet!" replied Rouletabille, laughing. "That is nothing. Nitchevo! His Majesty's eider downs are of the finest eider, as one of the feathers that you have shown me demonstrates. Well, open them now. They are a cheap imitation, as the second feather proves. The return of the false eider downs, before evening, proves then that they hoped the substitution would pass undetected. That is all. Caracho! Collapse of the hoax. Your health! Vive le Tsar!"

"Caracho! Caracho!"

The locomotive was puffing when a couple were seen running, a man and a woman. It was Monsieur and Madame Gounsovski.

Gounsovski stood on the running-board.

"Madame Gounsovski has insisted upon shaking hands. You are very congenial."

"Compliments, madame."

"Tell me, young man, you did wrong to fail for dinner at my house yesterday."

"I would have certainly escaped a disagreeable little journey into Finland. I do not regret it, monsieur."

The train trembled and moved. They cried, "Vive la France! Vive la Russe!" Athanase Georgevitch wept. Matrena Petrovna, at a window of the station, whither she had timidly retired, waved a handkerchief to the little domovoi-doukh, who had made her see everything in the right light, and whom she did not dare to embrace after the terrible affair of the false poison and the Tsar's anger.

The reporter threw her a respectful kiss.

As he said to Gounsovski, there was nothing to be regretted.

All the same, as the train took its way toward the frontier, Rouletabille threw himself back on the cushions, and said:

"Ouf!"

A Note About the Author

Gaston Leroux (1868–1927) was a French journalist and writer of detective fiction. Born in Paris, Leroux attended school in Normandy before returning to his home city to complete a degree in law. After squandering his inheritance, he began working as a court reporter and theater critic to avoid bankruptcy. As a journalist, Leroux earned a reputation as a leading international correspondent, particularly for his reporting on the 1905 Russian Revolution. In 1907, Leroux switched careers in order to become a professional fiction writer, focusing predominately on novels that could be turned into film scripts. With such novels as *The Mystery of the Yellow Room* (1908), Leroux established himself as a leading figure in detective fiction, eventually earning himself the title of Chevalier in the Legion of Honor, France's highest award for merit. *The Phantom of the Opera* (1910), his most famous work, has been adapted countless times for theater, television, and film, most notably by Andrew Lloyd Webber in his 1986 musical of the same name.

A Note from the Publisher

Spanning many genres, from non-fiction essays to literature classics to children's books and lyric poetry, Mint Edition books showcase the master works of our time in a modern new package. The text is freshly typeset, is clean and easy to read, and features a new note about the author in each volume. Many books also include exclusive new introductory material. Every book boasts a striking new cover, which makes it as appropriate for collecting as it is for gift giving. Mint Edition books are only printed when a reader orders them, so natural resources are not wasted. We're proud that our books are never manufactured in excess and exist only in the exact quantity they need to be read and enjoyed.

Discover more of your favorite classics with Bookfinity™.

- Track your reading with custom book lists.
- Get great book recommendations for your personalized Reader Type.
- Add reviews for your favorite books.
- AND MUCH MORE!

Visit **bookfinity.com** and take the fun Reader Type quiz to get started.

Enjoy our classic and modern companion pairings!